A
New York Times
Bestseller

An NPR Great
Read of the Year

The Praise for 5 Worlds Is Out of This World!

A Texas Library Association
Maverick Selection

A New York Public Library
Top Ten Best Books
for Kids Selection

A Junior Library
Guild Selection

"Cinematic beauty."
—*The New York Times Book Review*

"Make room on your shelf for the 5 Worlds series. A pinch of Kazu Kibuishi's Amulet, a pinch of Mœbius, and a heap of good ol' comic book adventure story. I fell in love immediately!"
—**Jeff Smith, creator of the *New York Times* bestselling Bone series**

"For kids who love fantasy and other-world adventures, and for any fans of graphic novels, this book is a must-read."
—**R. J. Palacio, #1 *New York Times* bestselling author of *Wonder***

"This stellar team has created a gorgeous and entrancing world like no other!"
—**Noelle Stevenson, *New York Times* bestselling author of *Nimona***

"Epic action, adventure, and mystery will draw you in, but the heartfelt characters and their seemingly impossible journey will keep you turning the pages."
—**Lisa Yee, author of the DC Super Hero Girls™ series**

★ "Gorgeous artwork, and riveting plot."
—*Booklist*, **Starred Review**

★ "A dazzling interplanetary fantasy."
—*Publishers Weekly,* **Starred Review**

"Give to fans of Judd Winick's Hilo or Kazu Kibuishi's Amulet series."
—*School Library Journal*

"Ends triumphantly and tantalizingly."
—*The Horn Book*

"Distinctly unique. . . . It oozes with imagination and creativity."
—*Bam! Smack! Pow!*

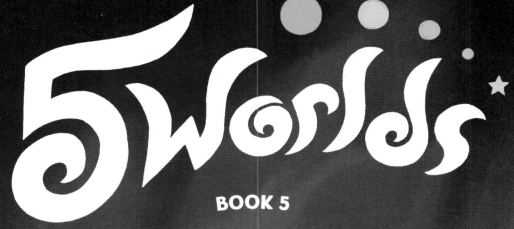

5 Worlds

BOOK 5

THE EMERALD GATE

Mark
SIEGEL

Alexis
SIEGEL

Xanthe
BOUMA

Boya
SUN

Matt
ROCKEFELLER

Random House New York

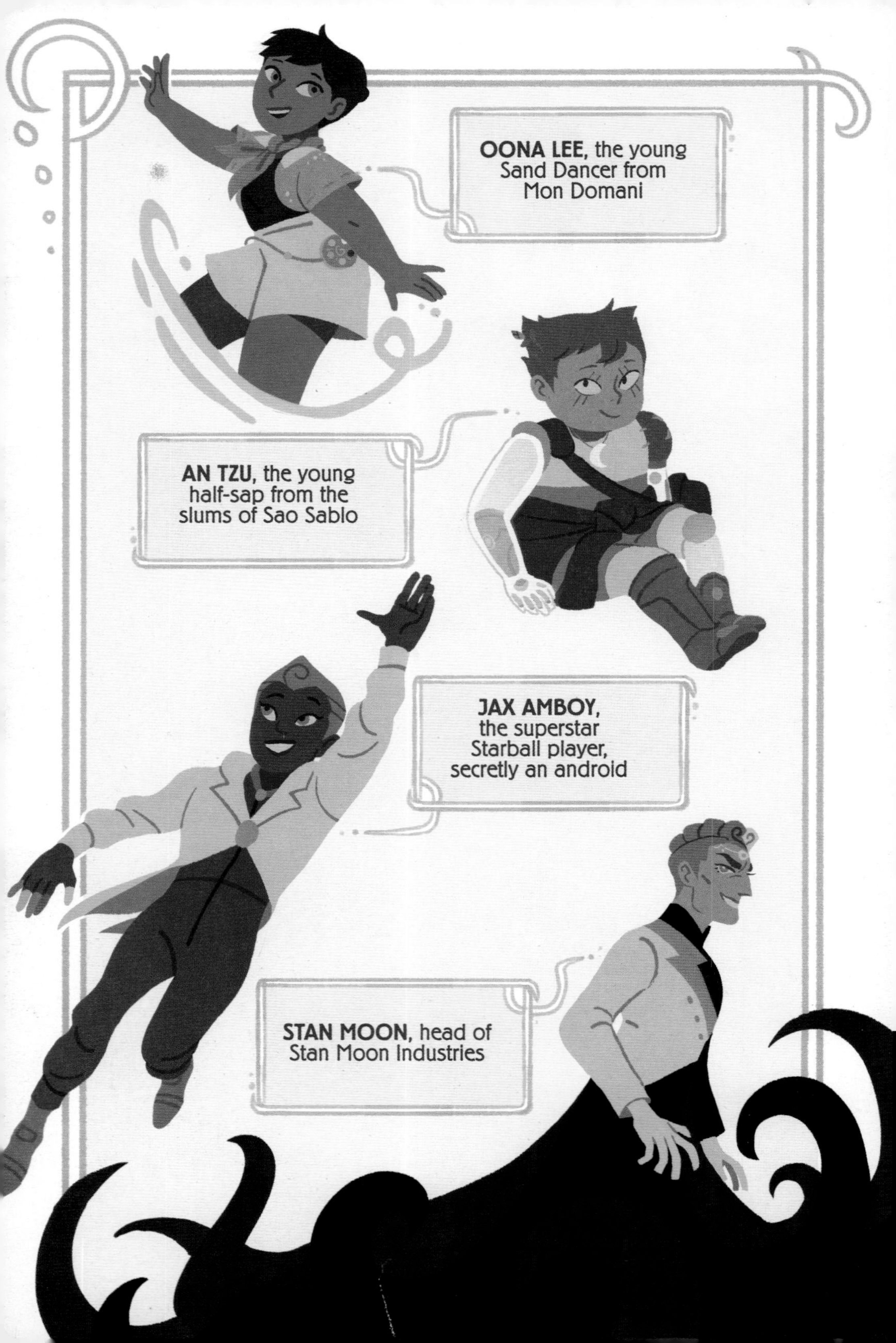
OONA LEE, the young Sand Dancer from Mon Domani
AN TZU, the young half-sap from the slums of Sao Sablo
JAX AMBOY, the superstar Starball player, secretly an android
STAN MOON, head of Stan Moon Industries

THE STORY SO FAR...

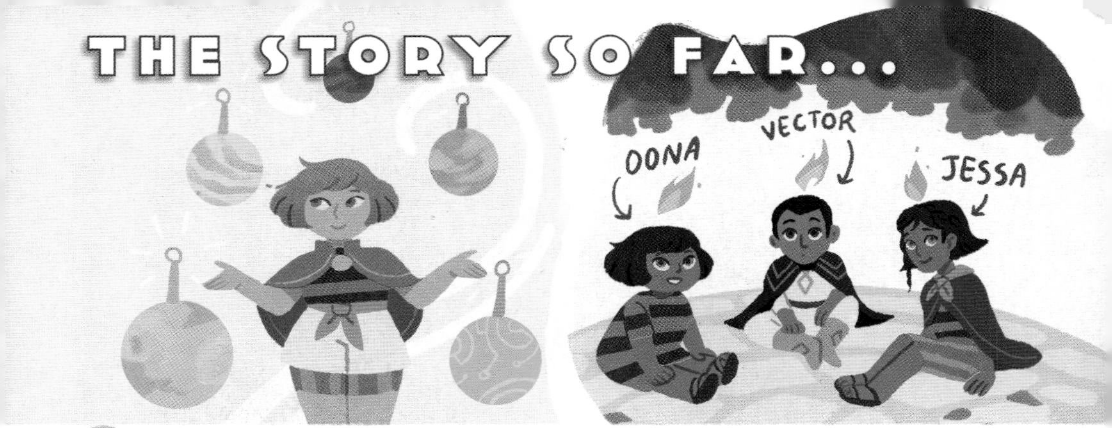

OONA
VECTOR
JESSA

To save the **FIVE WORLDS** from dying out, **OONA** and her friends must light all five ancient beacons: white, red, blue, yellow, and green.

For centuries, **the Living Fire** that lights beacons was the stuff of legend—until three children produced it on the blue world of **Toki.**

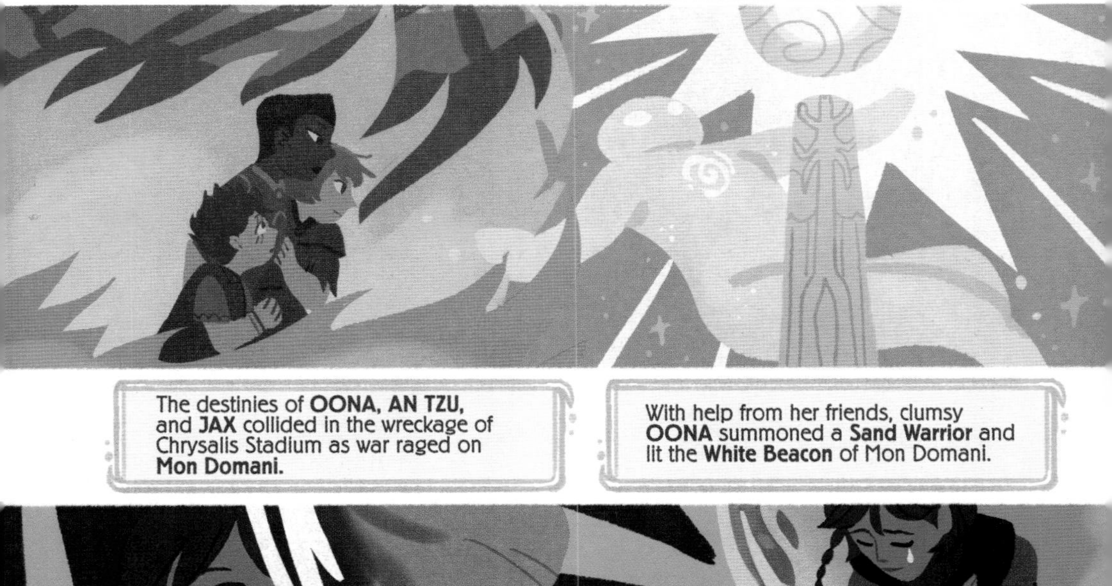

The destinies of **OONA, AN TZU,** and **JAX** collided in the wreckage of Chrysalis Stadium as war raged on **Mon Domani.**

With help from her friends, clumsy **OONA** summoned a **Sand Warrior** and lit the **White Beacon** of Mon Domani.

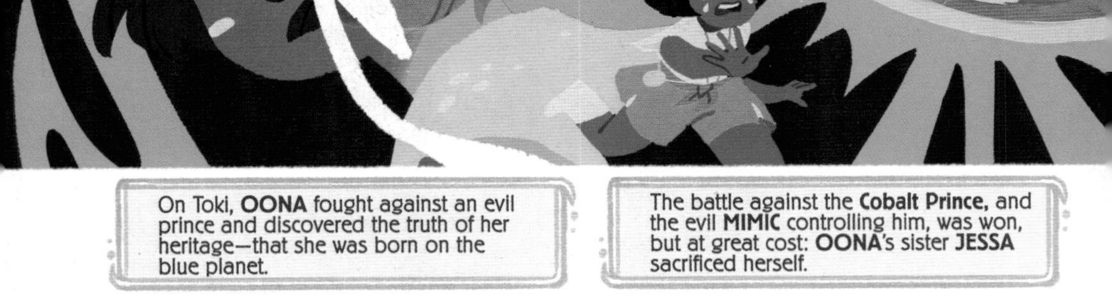

On Toki, **OONA** fought against an evil prince and discovered the truth of her heritage—that she was born on the blue planet.

The battle against the **Cobalt Prince,** and the evil **MIMIC** controlling him, was won, but at great cost: **OONA**'s sister **JESSA** sacrificed herself.

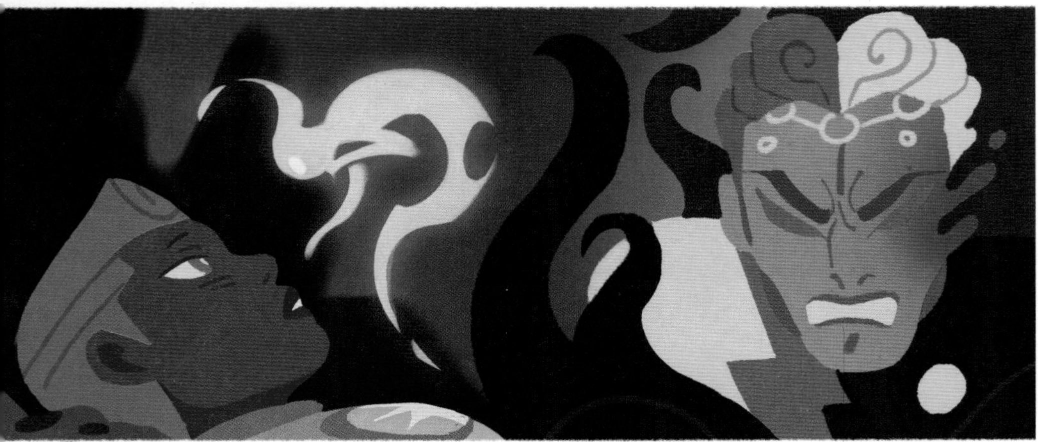

On **Salassandra, JAX** merged with a Salassi spirit known as a **DEVOTI** to become human.

STAN MOON, a tycoon possessed by the evil Mimic, is trying to seize power on all the worlds in order to stop **OONA.**

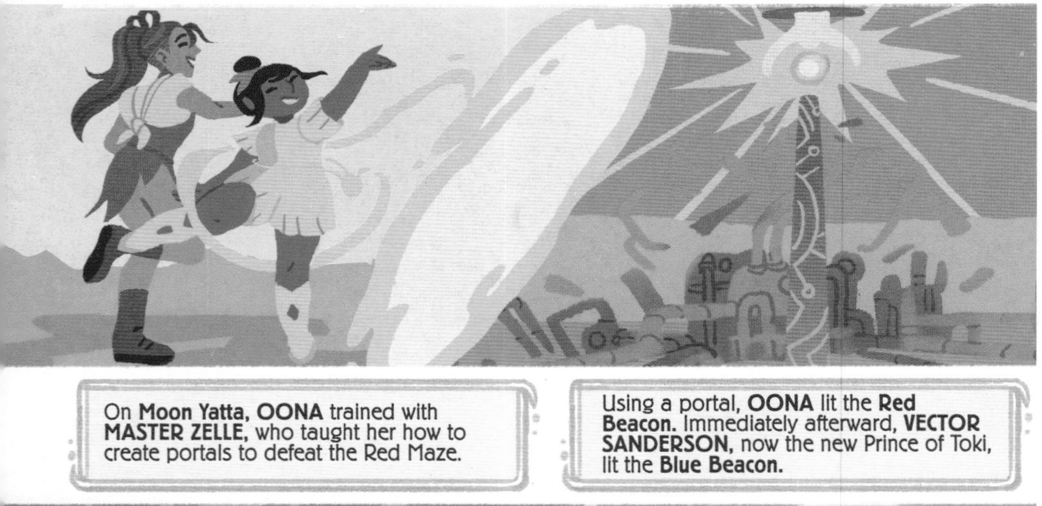

On **Moon Yatta, OONA** trained with **MASTER ZELLE,** who taught her how to create portals to defeat the Red Maze.

Using a portal, **OONA** lit the **Red Beacon.** Immediately afterward, **VECTOR SANDERSON,** now the new Prince of Toki, lit the **Blue Beacon.**

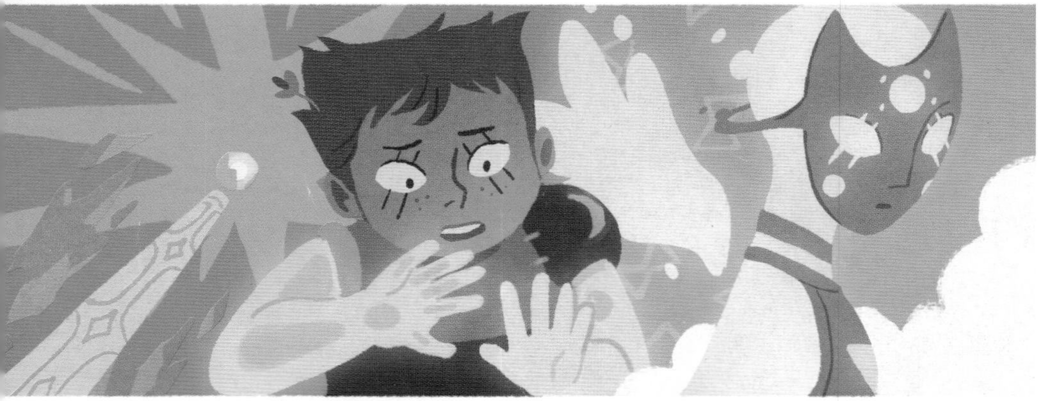

AN TZU suffers from a mysterious Vanishing Illness that causes his limbs to fade away. He uses prosthetics to help maintain his physical form.

As memories of his past life came back to him, **AN TZU** discovered he is the Felid **Prince NEKO**.

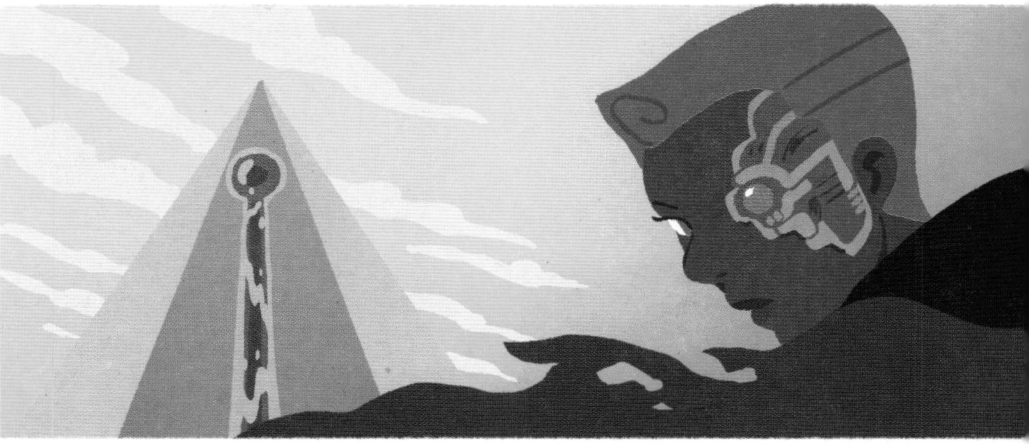

The Yellow Beacon of **Salassandra**, encased in amber, could not be lit unless ten thousand voices sang the unknown Amber Anthem.

Searching for the Anthem, **OONA** and her friends were pursued by **STAN MOON** and his allies. He sent a killer J.A.X. android after them.

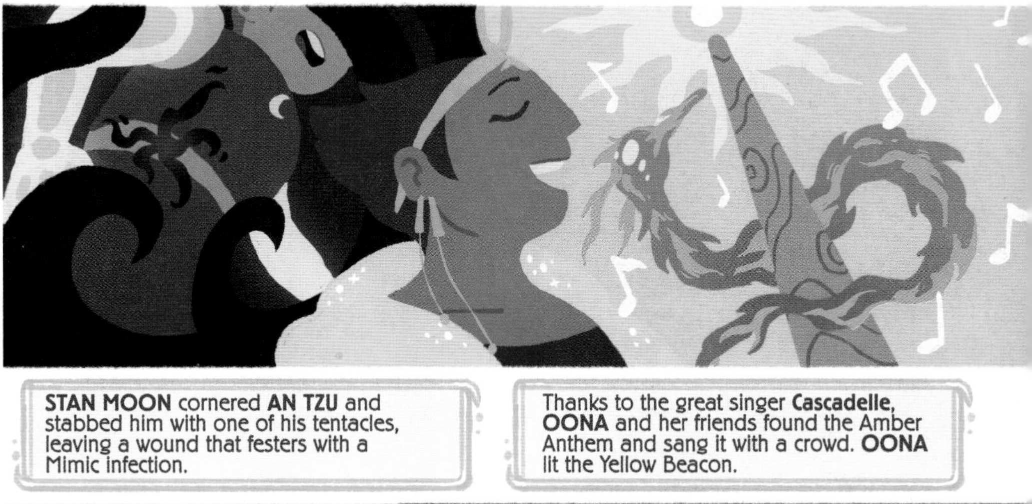

STAN MOON cornered **AN TZU** and stabbed him with one of his tentacles, leaving a wound that festers with a Mimic infection.

Thanks to the great singer **Cascadelle**, **OONA** and her friends found the Amber Anthem and sang it with a crowd. **OONA** lit the Yellow Beacon.

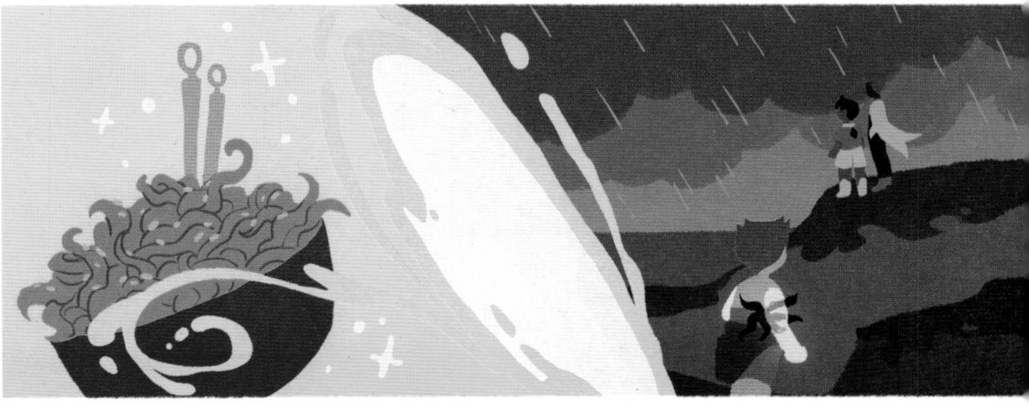

With one beacon left to light, **OONA** created a portal to **GRIMBO (E)** and crossed it with her friends.

There, **AN TZU** realized his Mimic infection means disaster if **OONA** lights the Green Beacon! How will he stop her?

"I serve the living universe."
—OONA LEE

PROLOGUE

MISTER MOON'S NEW PLAN

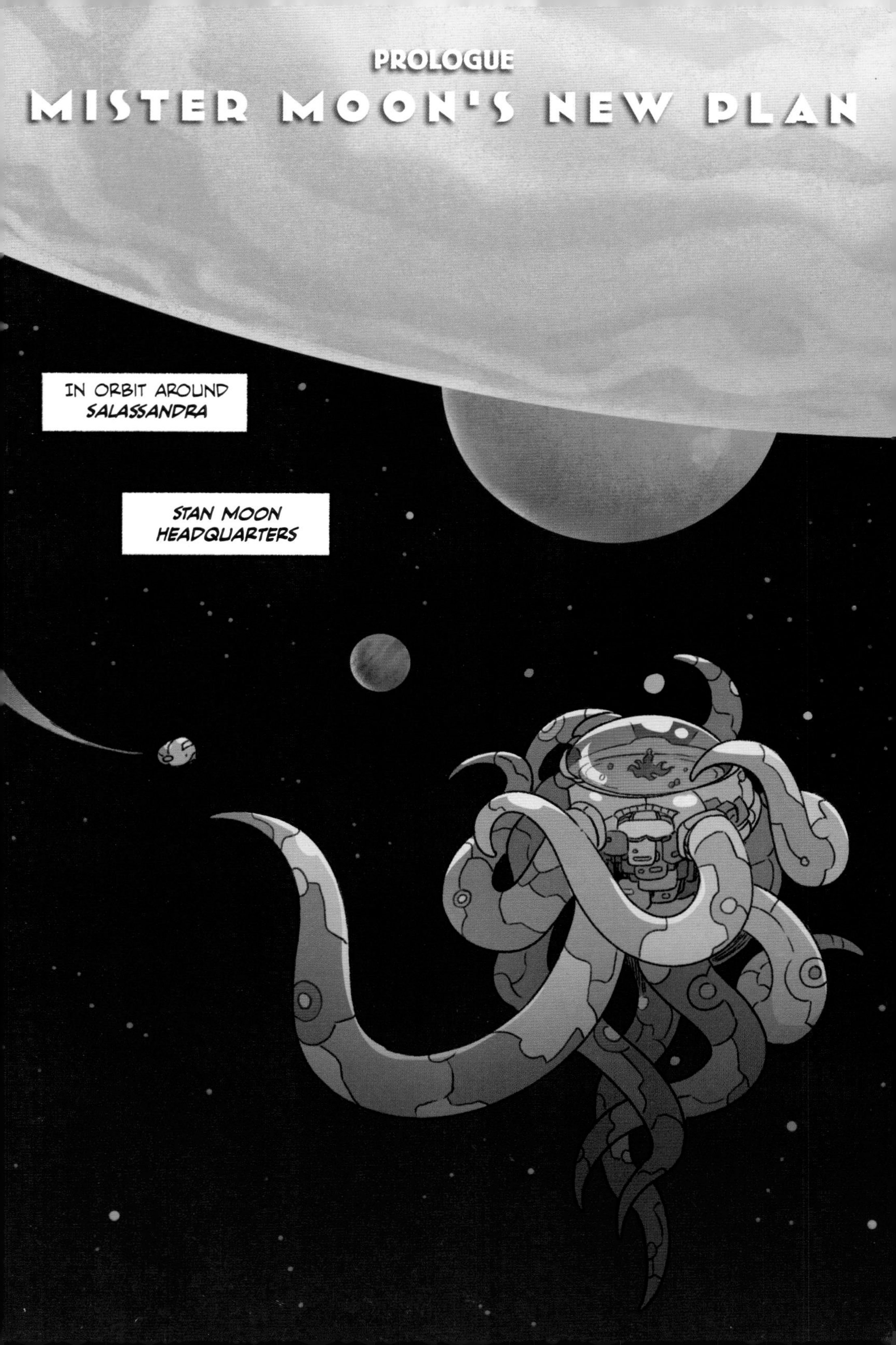
IN ORBIT AROUND SALASSANDRA
STAN MOON HEADQUARTERS

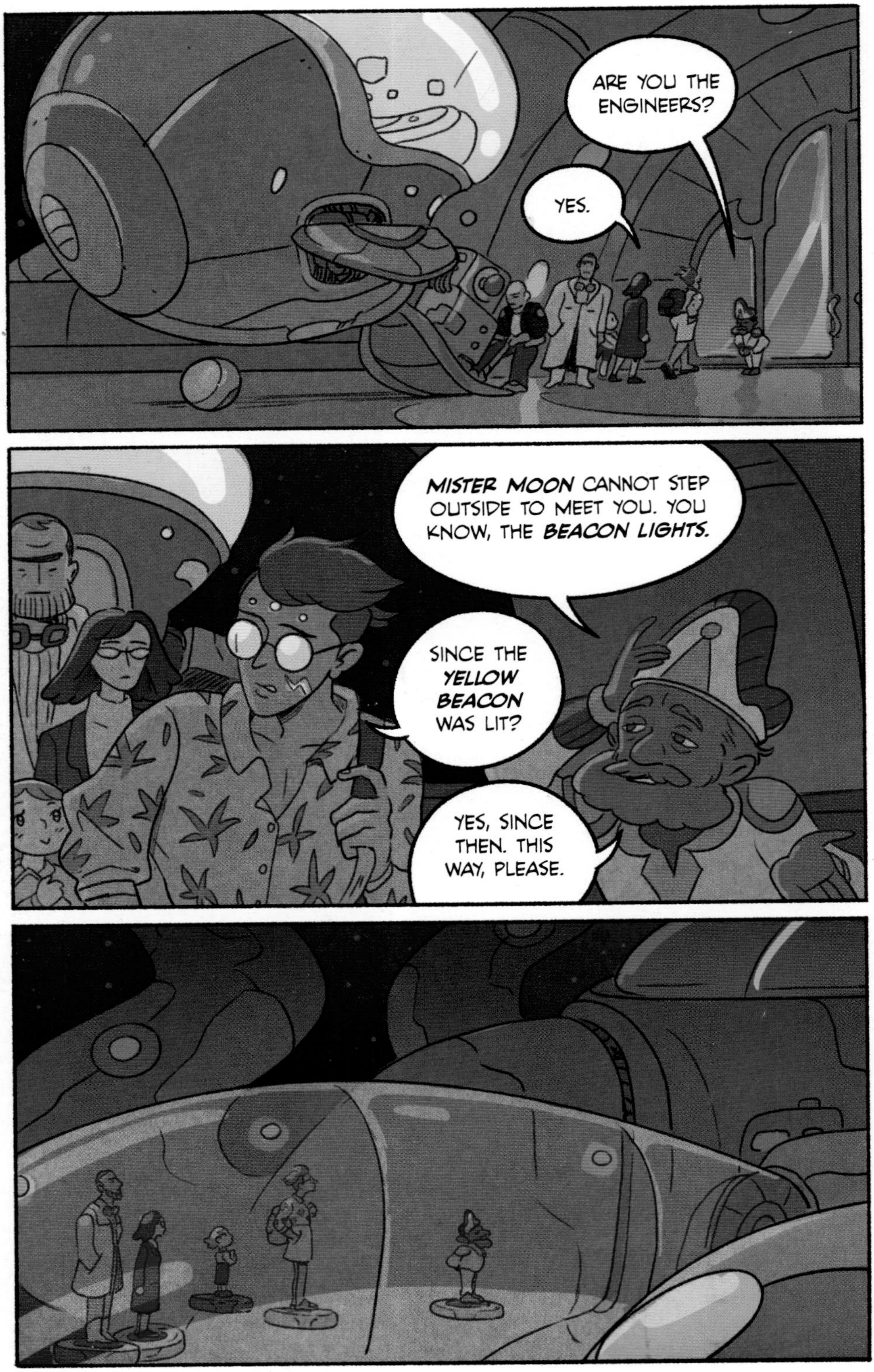
ARE YOU THE ENGINEERS?
YES.
MISTER MOON CANNOT STEP OUTSIDE TO MEET YOU. YOU KNOW, THE BEACON LIGHTS.
SINCE THE YELLOW BEACON WAS LIT?
YES, SINCE THEN. THIS WAY, PLEASE.

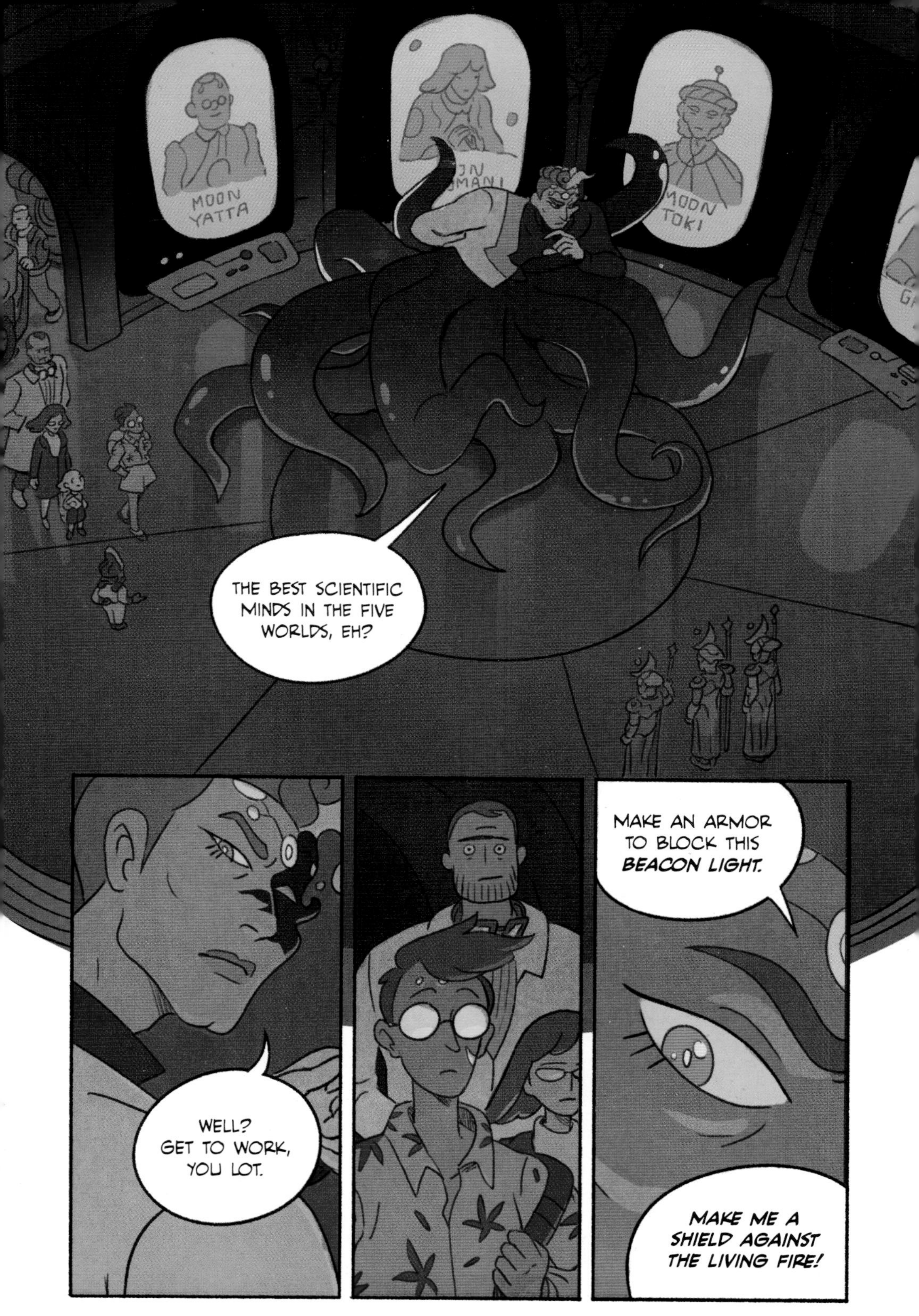
MOON YATTA
MOON TOKI
THE BEST SCIENTIFIC MINDS IN THE FIVE WORLDS, EH?
WELL? GET TO WORK, YOU LOT.
MAKE AN ARMOR TO BLOCK THIS *BEACON LIGHT.*
MAKE ME A SHIELD AGAINST THE LIVING FIRE!

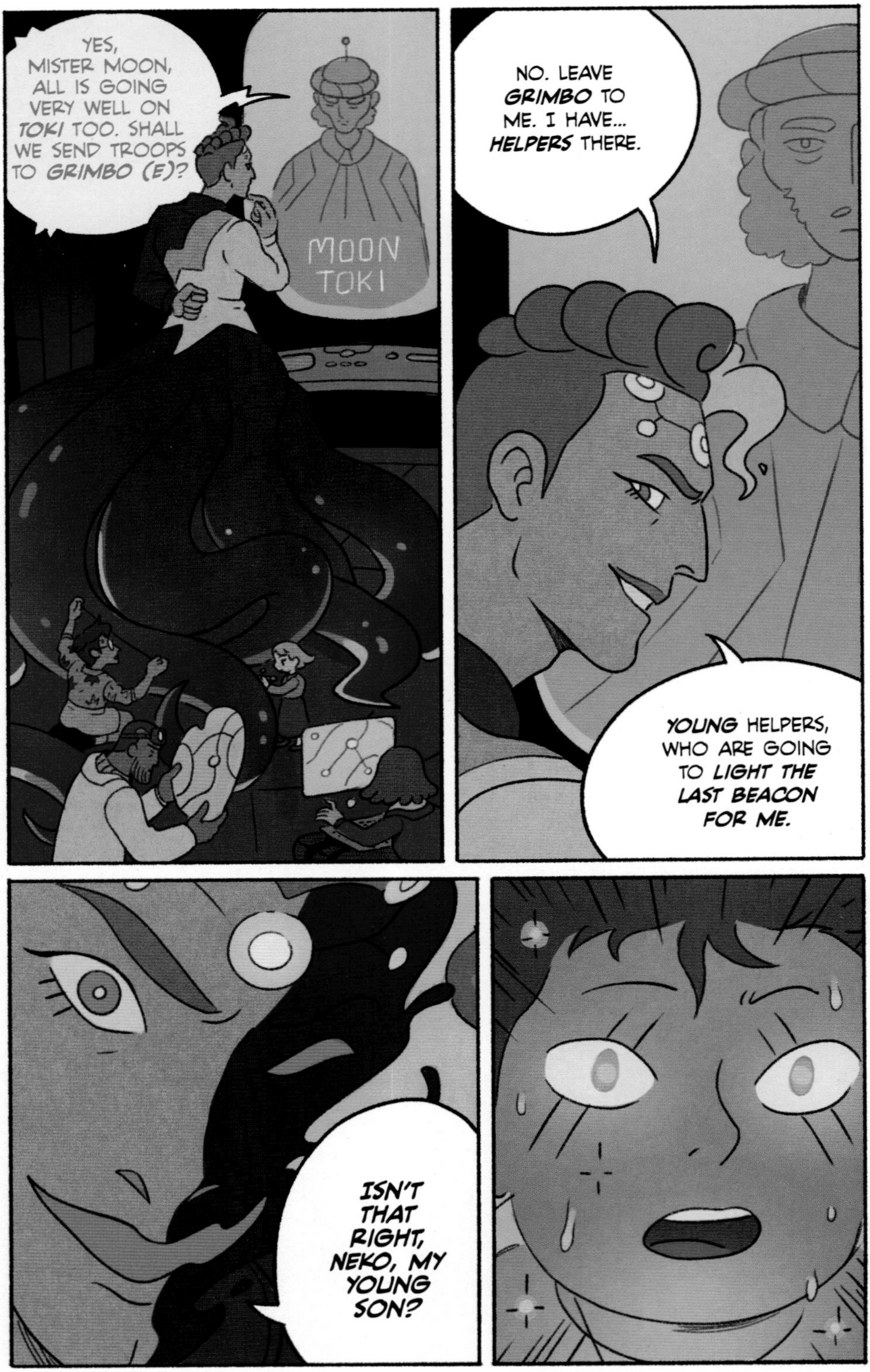
YES, MISTER MOON, ALL IS GOING VERY WELL ON TOKI TOO. SHALL WE SEND TROOPS TO GRIMBO (E)?
MOON TOKI
NO. LEAVE GRIMBO TO ME. I HAVE... HELPERS THERE.
YOUNG HELPERS, WHO ARE GOING TO LIGHT THE LAST BEACON FOR ME.
ISN'T THAT RIGHT, NEKO, MY YOUNG SON?

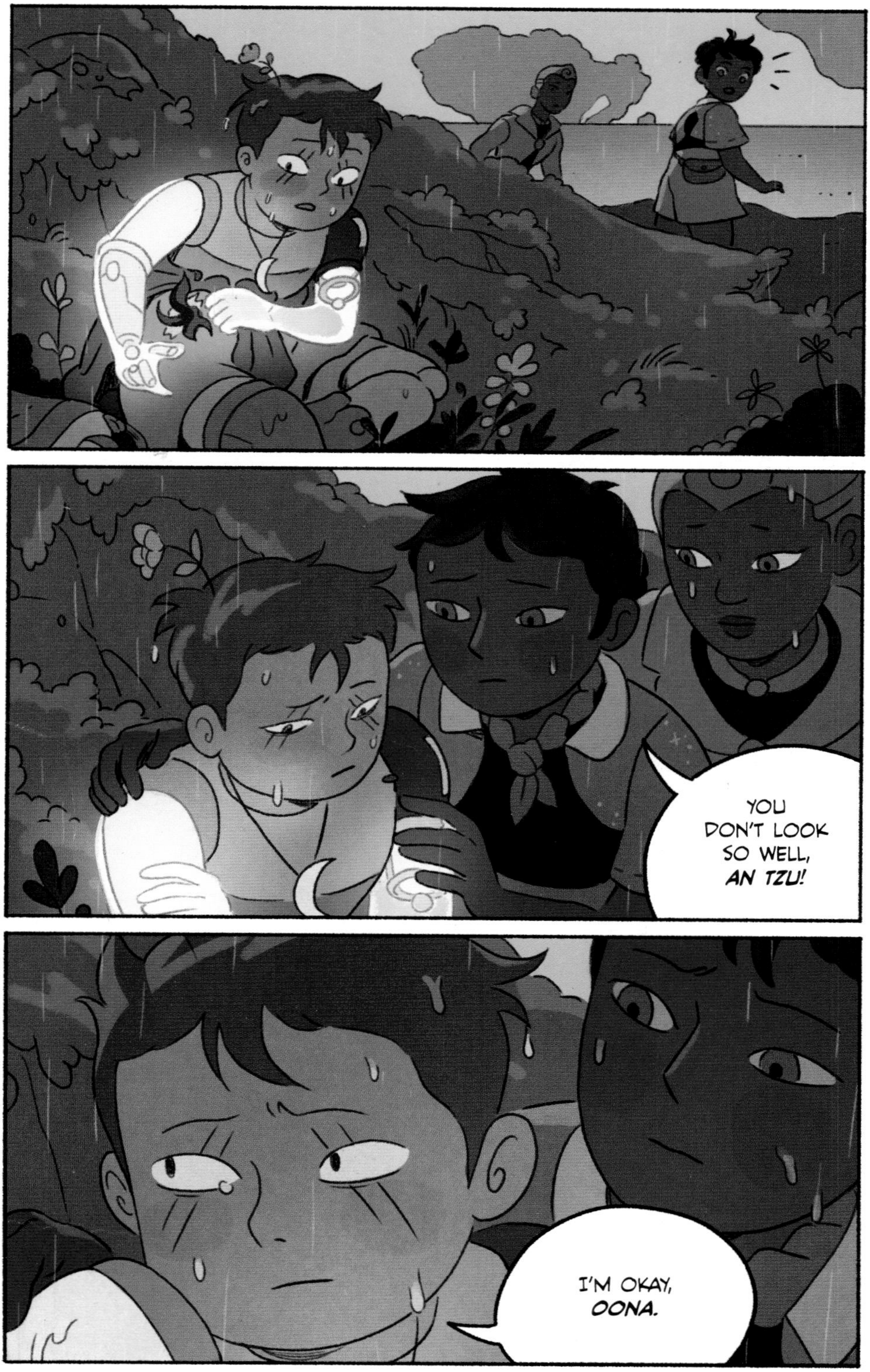
YOU DON'T LOOK SO WELL, AN TZU!
I'M OKAY, OONA.

CHAPTER 1
THE MISSING BEACON

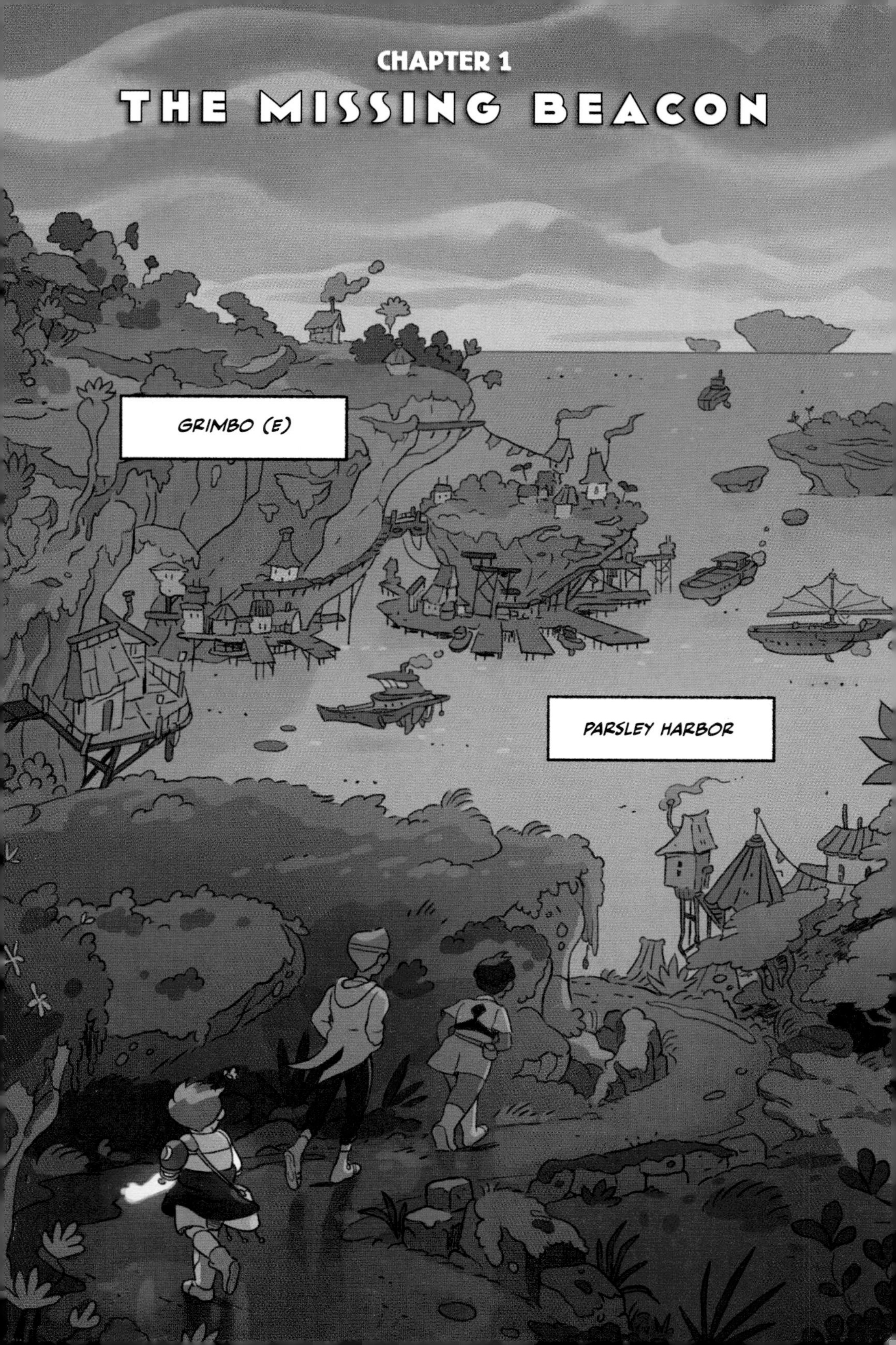
GRIMBO (E)
PARSLEY HARBOR

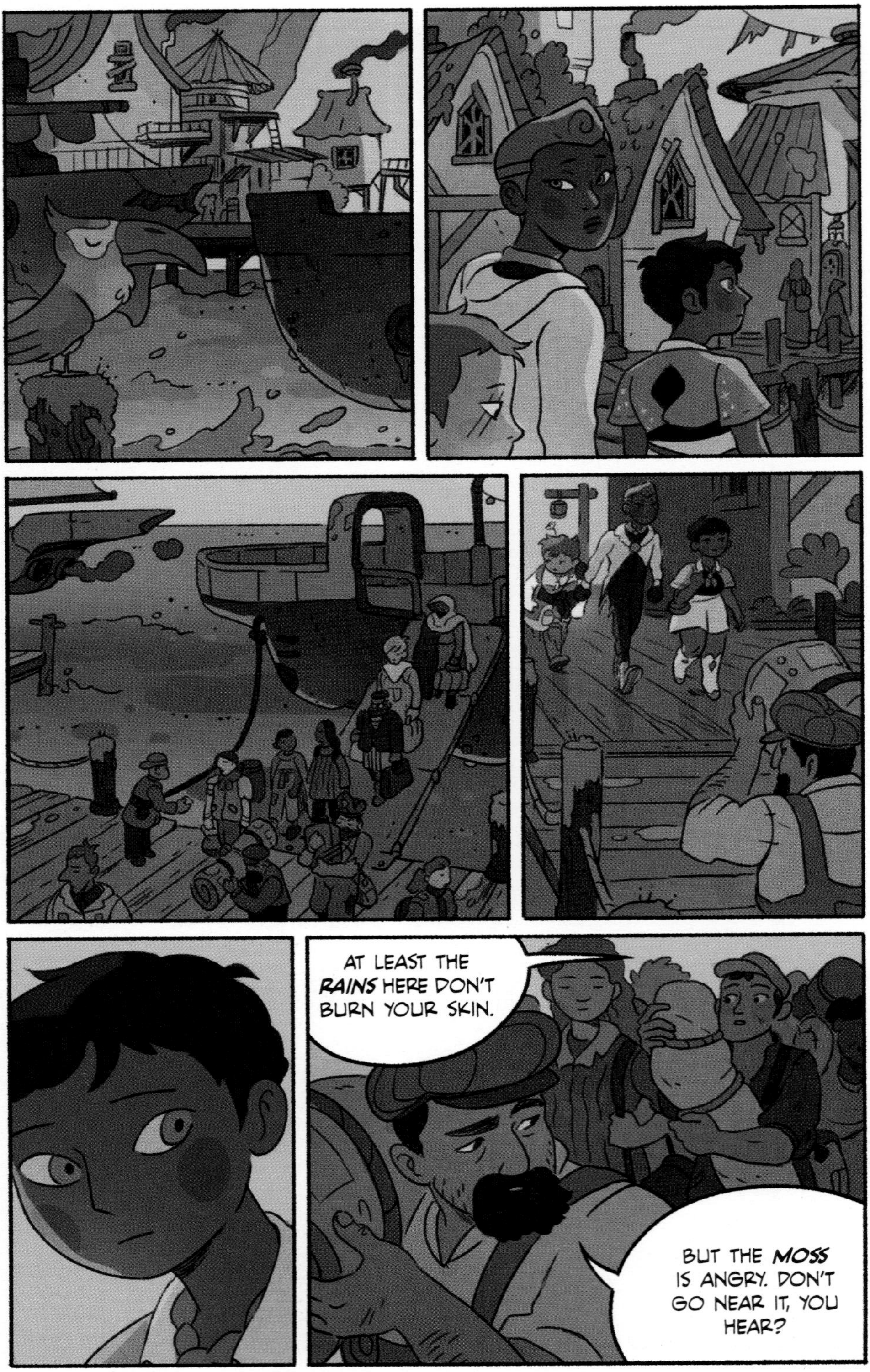
AT LEAST THE RAINS HERE DON'T BURN YOUR SKIN.
BUT THE MOSS IS ANGRY. DON'T GO NEAR IT, YOU HEAR?

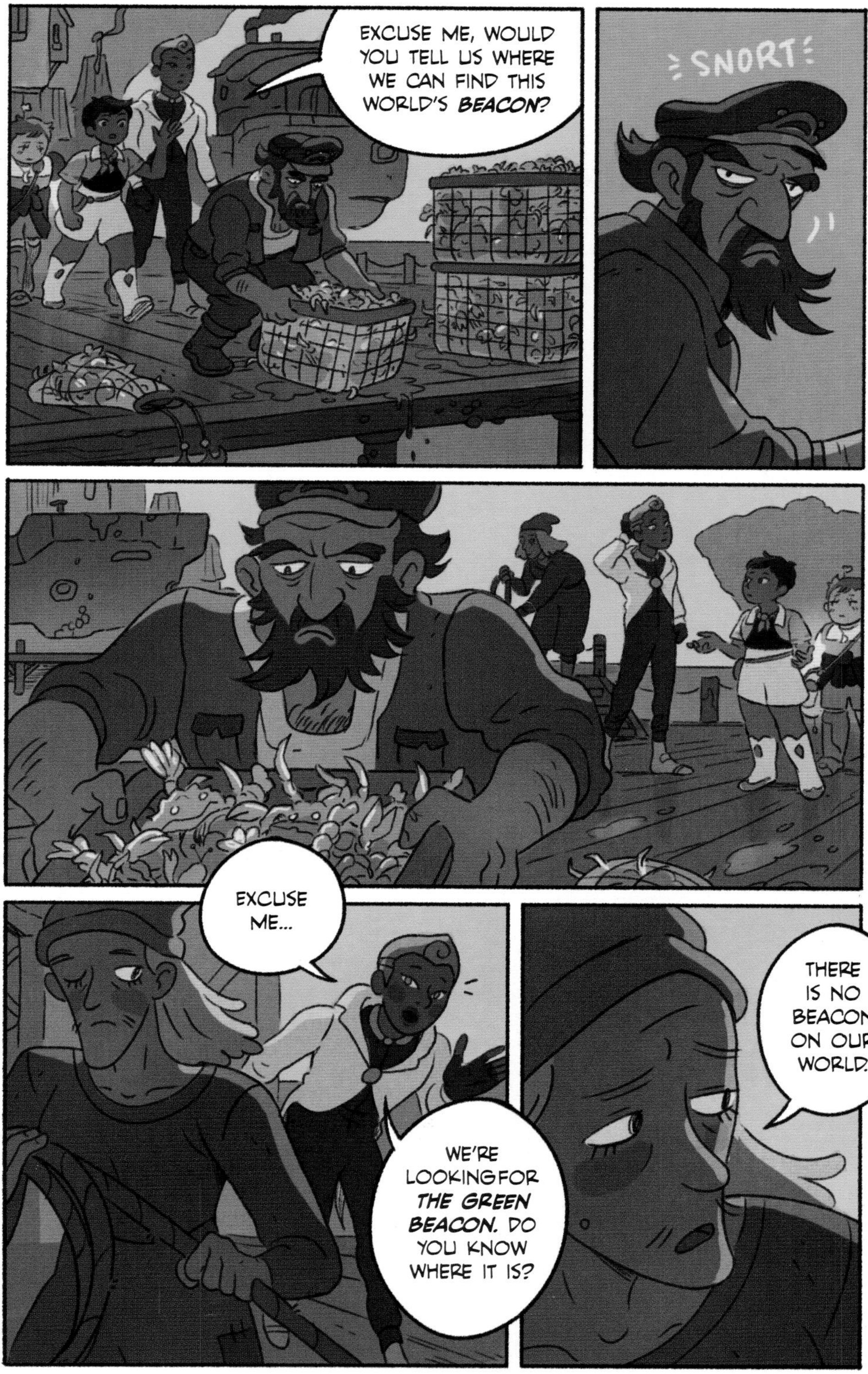
EXCUSE ME, WOULD YOU TELL US WHERE WE CAN FIND THIS WORLD'S ***BEACON***?
SNORT
EXCUSE ME...
WE'RE LOOKING FOR ***THE GREEN BEACON***. DO YOU KNOW WHERE IT IS?
THERE IS NO BEACON ON OUR WORLD.

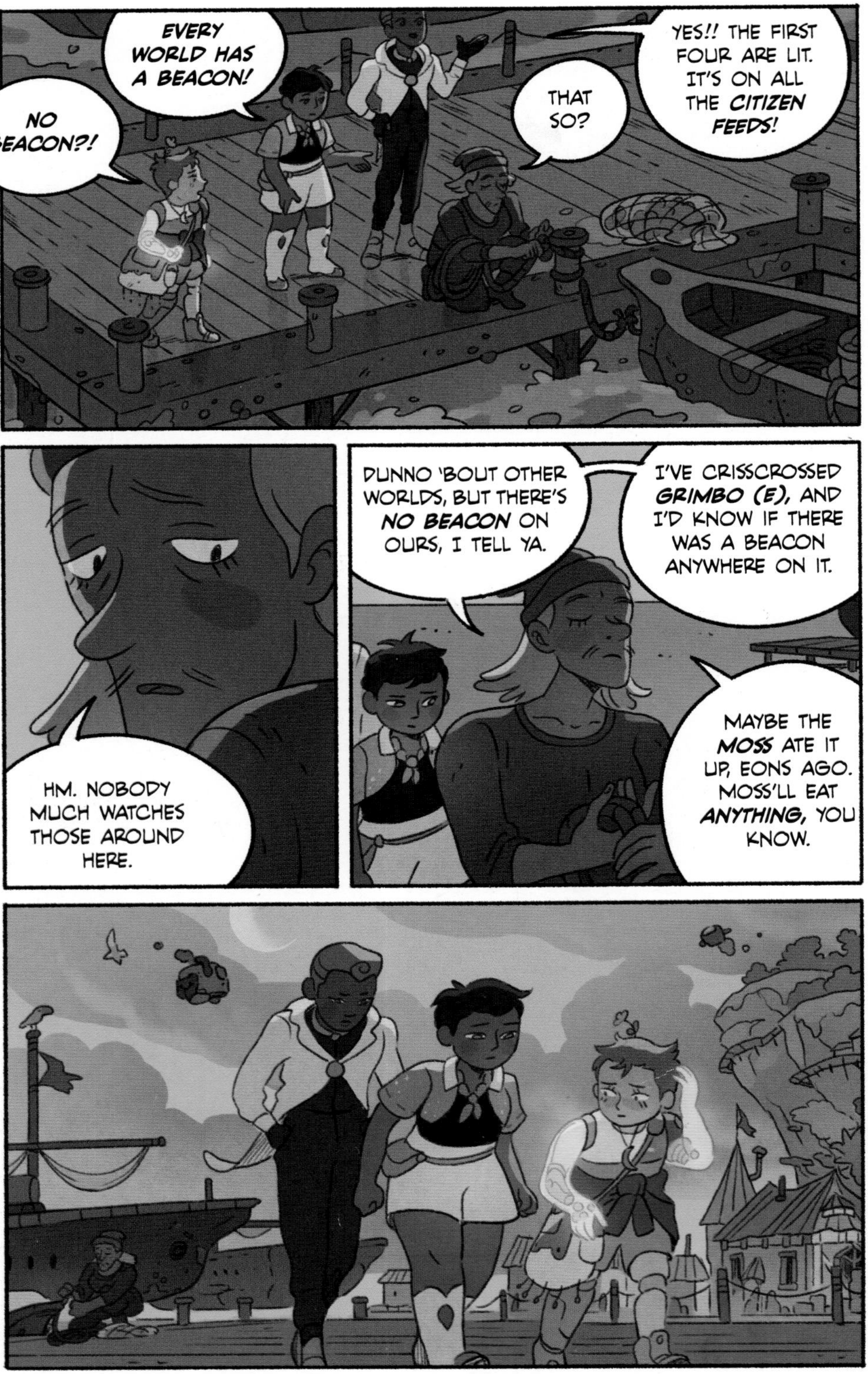
NO BEACON?!
EVERY WORLD HAS A BEACON!
THAT SO?
YES!! THE FIRST FOUR ARE LIT. IT'S ON ALL THE CITIZEN FEEDS!
HM. NOBODY MUCH WATCHES THOSE AROUND HERE.
DUNNO 'BOUT OTHER WORLDS, BUT THERE'S NO BEACON ON OURS, I TELL YA.
I'VE CRISSCROSSED GRIMBO (E), AND I'D KNOW IF THERE WAS A BEACON ANYWHERE ON IT.
MAYBE THE MOSS ATE IT UP, EONS AGO. MOSS'LL EAT ANYTHING, YOU KNOW.

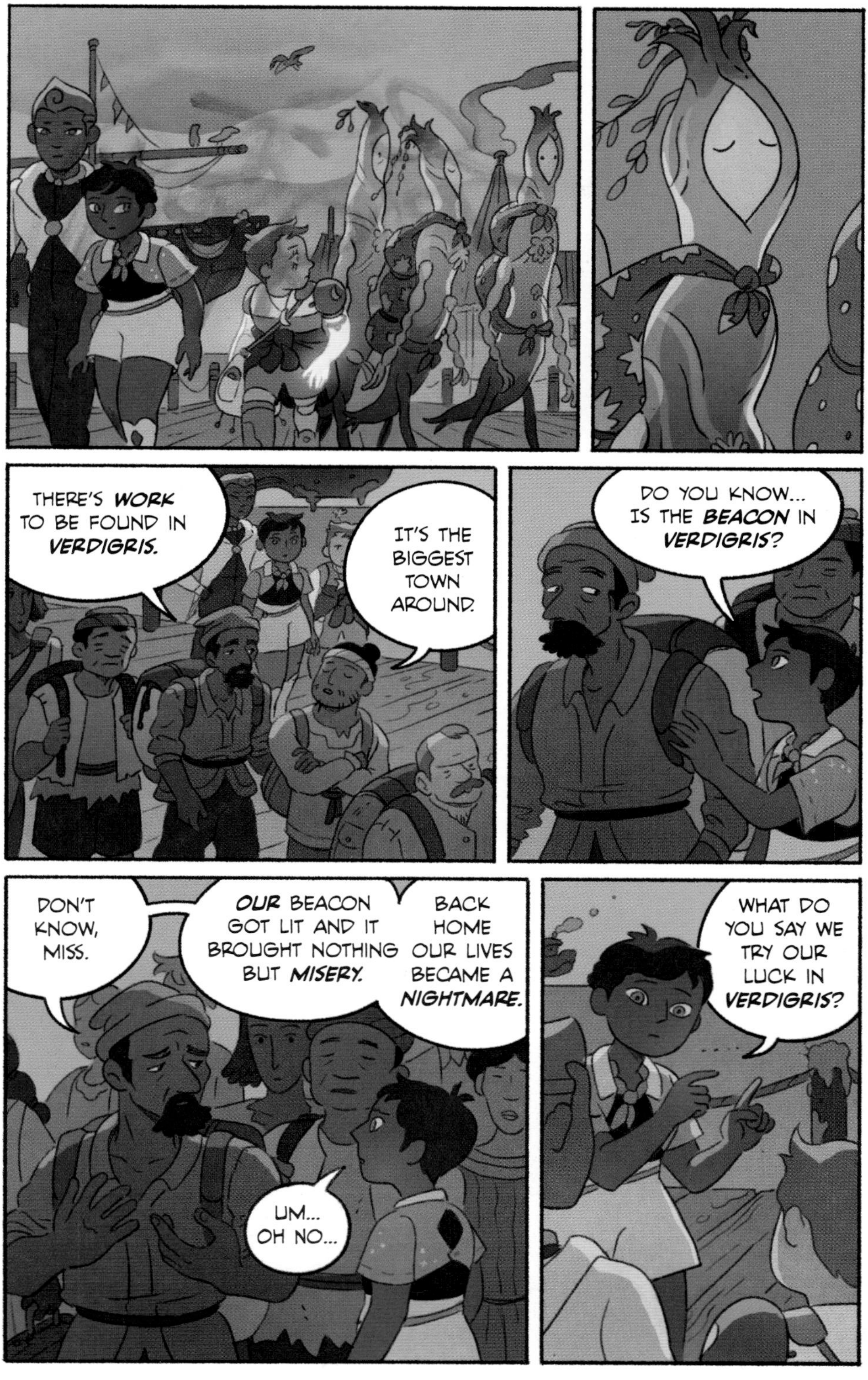
THERE'S WORK TO BE FOUND IN VERDIGRIS.
IT'S THE BIGGEST TOWN AROUND.
DO YOU KNOW... IS THE BEACON IN VERDIGRIS?
DON'T KNOW, MISS.
OUR BEACON GOT LIT AND IT BROUGHT NOTHING BUT MISERY.
BACK HOME OUR LIVES BECAME A NIGHTMARE.
UM... OH NO...
WHAT DO YOU SAY WE TRY OUR LUCK IN VERDIGRIS?

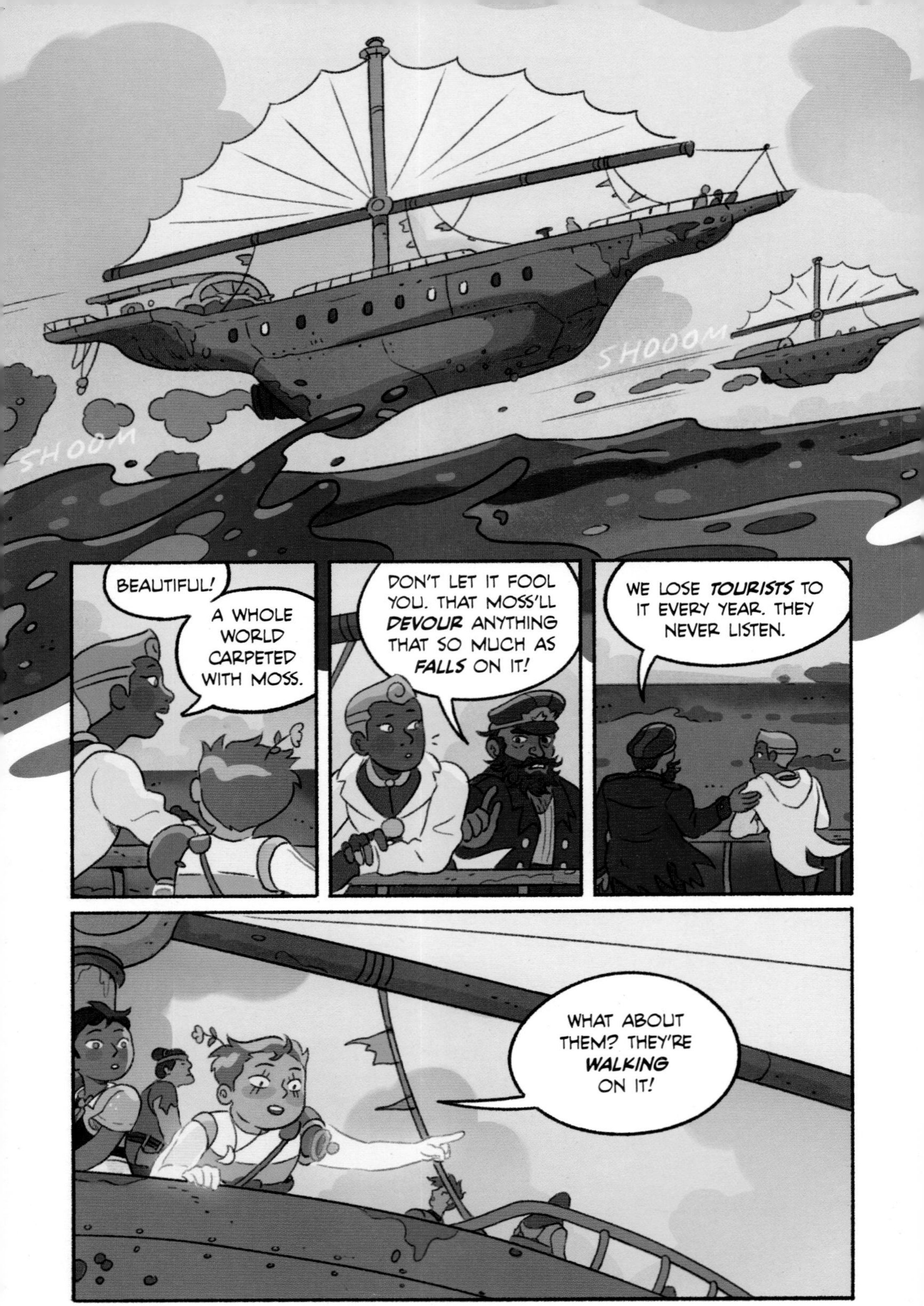
SHOOOM
SHOOM
BEAUTIFUL!
A WHOLE WORLD CARPETED WITH MOSS.
DON'T LET IT FOOL YOU. THAT MOSS'LL DEVOUR ANYTHING THAT SO MUCH AS FALLS ON IT!
WE LOSE TOURISTS TO IT EVERY YEAR. THEY NEVER LISTEN.
WHAT ABOUT THEM? THEY'RE WALKING ON IT!

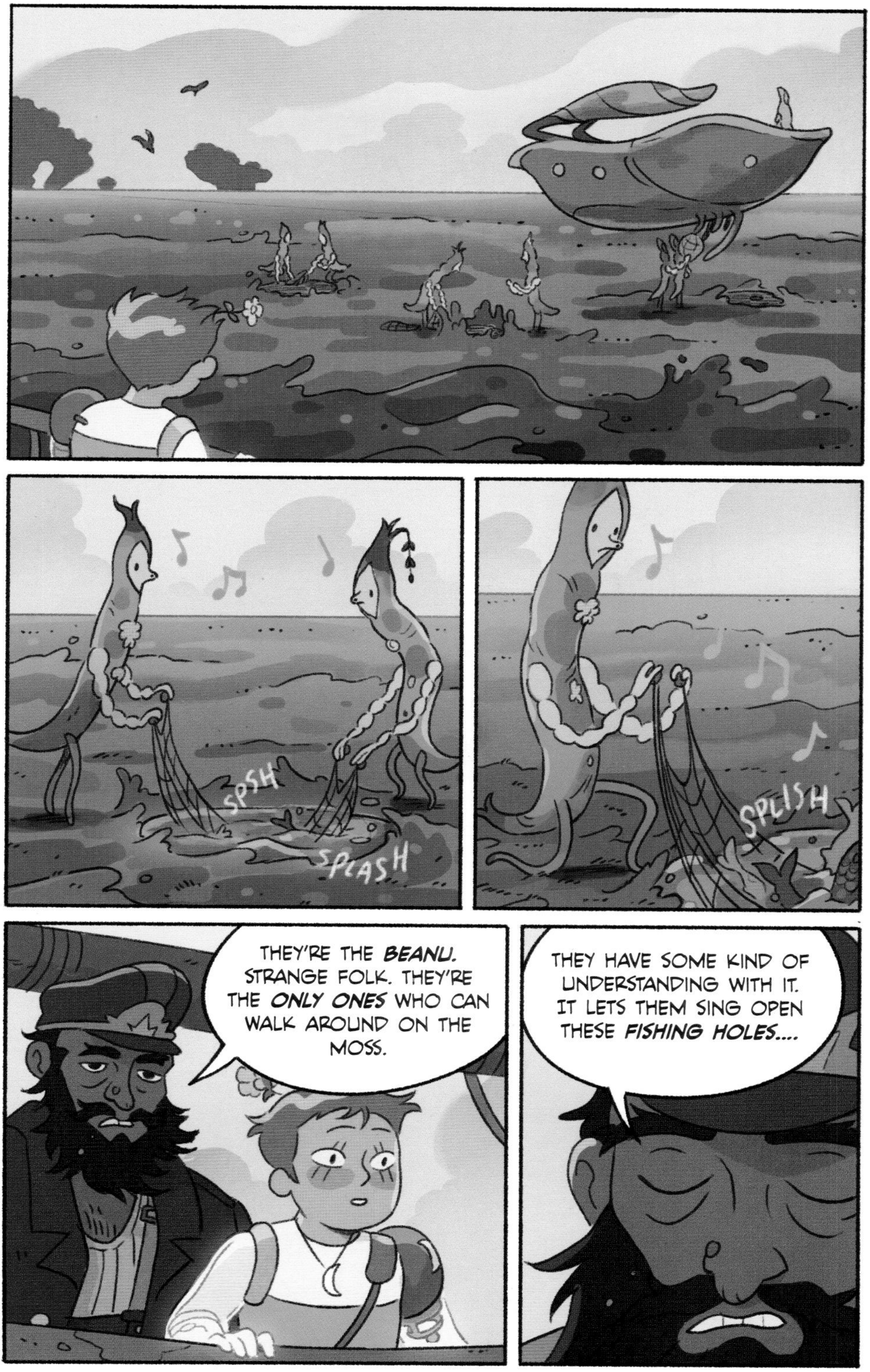
SPSH
SPLASH
SPLISH
THEY'RE THE BEANU. STRANGE FOLK. THEY'RE THE ONLY ONES WHO CAN WALK AROUND ON THE MOSS.
THEY HAVE SOME KIND OF UNDERSTANDING WITH IT. IT LETS THEM SING OPEN THESE FISHING HOLES....

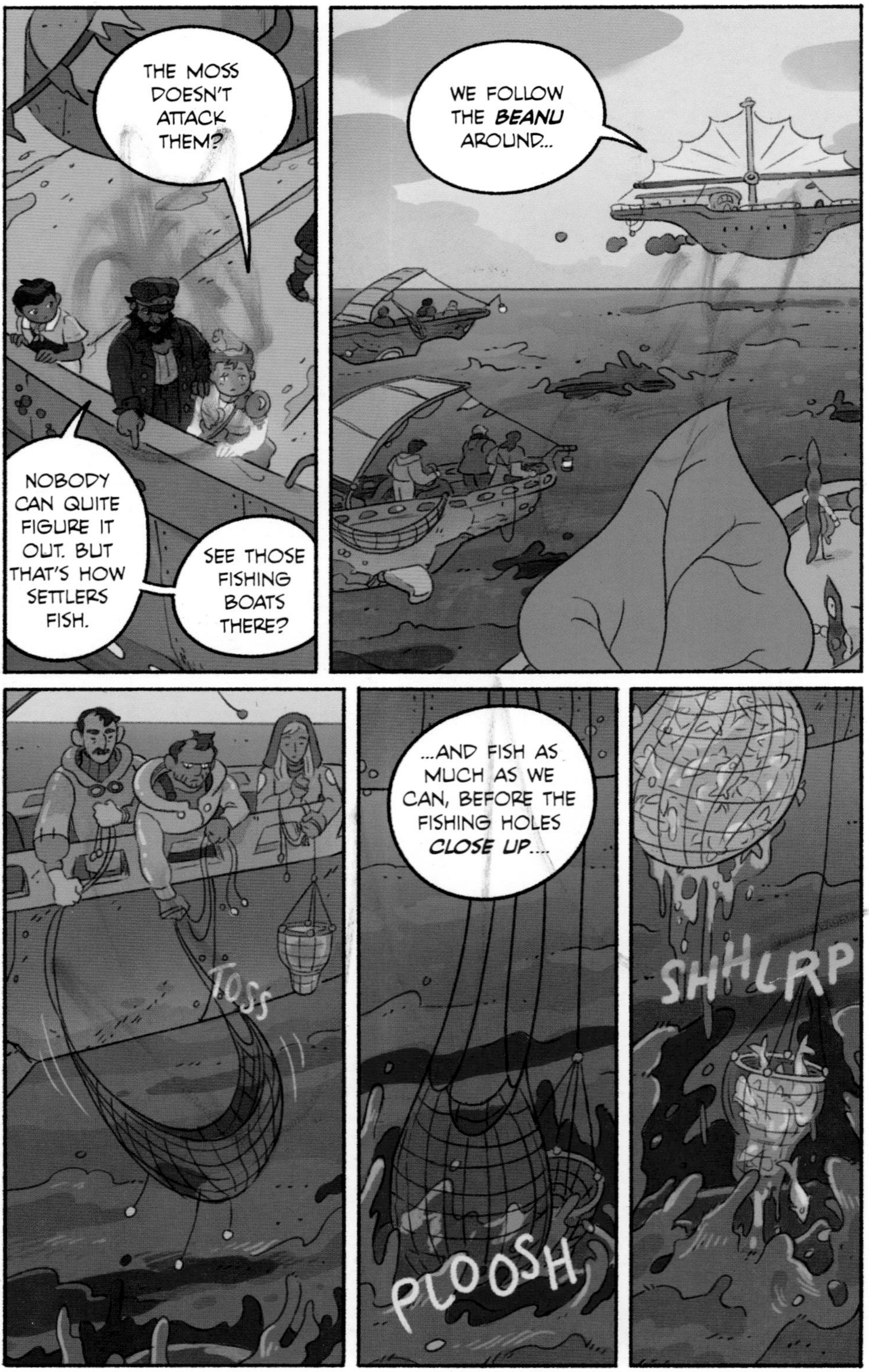
THE MOSS DOESN'T ATTACK THEM?
NOBODY CAN QUITE FIGURE IT OUT. BUT THAT'S HOW SETTLERS FISH.
SEE THOSE FISHING BOATS THERE?
WE FOLLOW THE *BEANU* AROUND...
TOSS
...AND FISH AS MUCH AS WE CAN, BEFORE THE FISHING HOLES *CLOSE UP*....
PLOOSH
SHHLRP

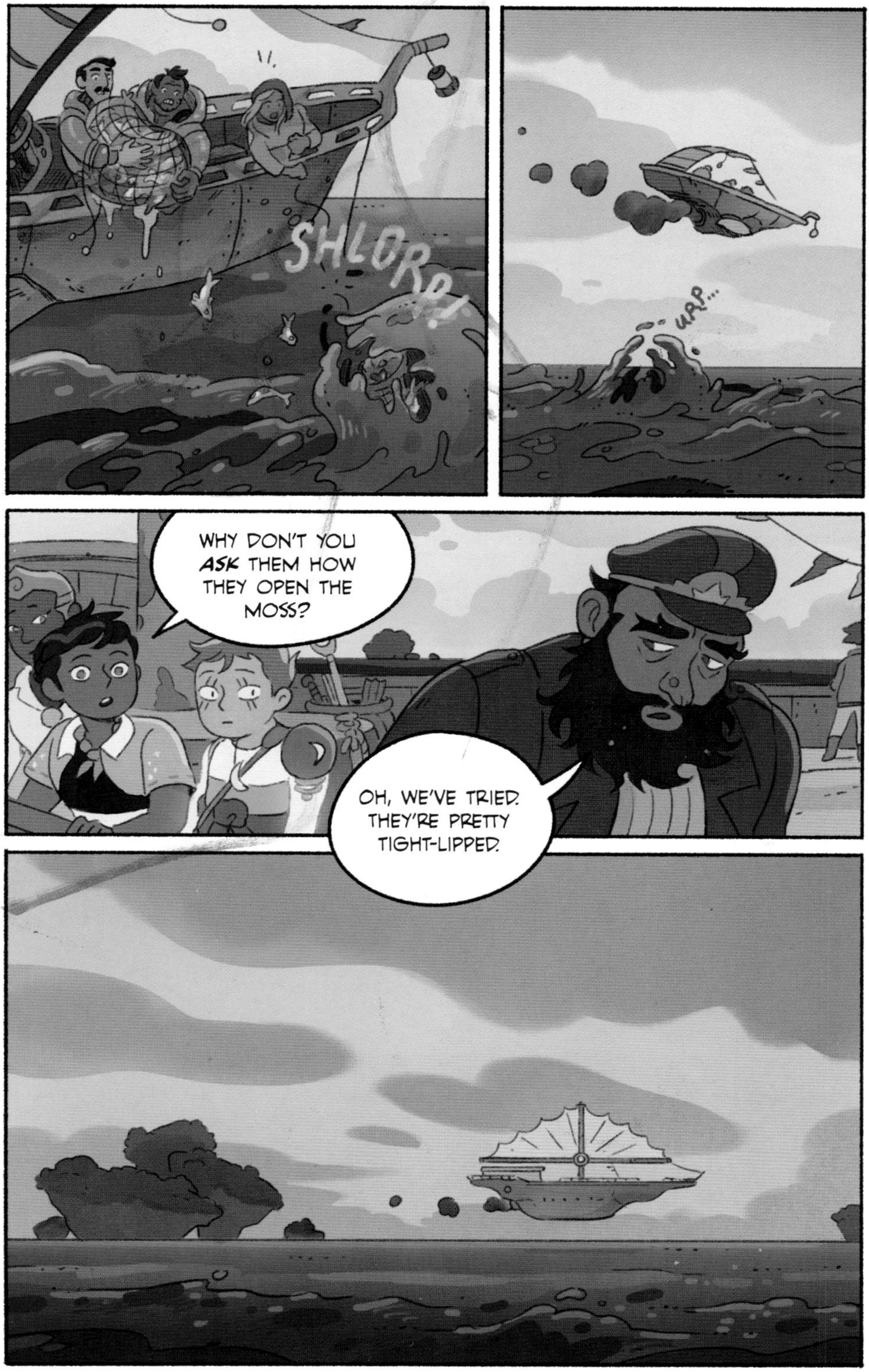
SHLORP!
ULP...
WHY DON'T YOU ***ASK*** THEM HOW THEY OPEN THE MOSS?
OH, WE'VE TRIED. THEY'RE PRETTY TIGHT-LIPPED.

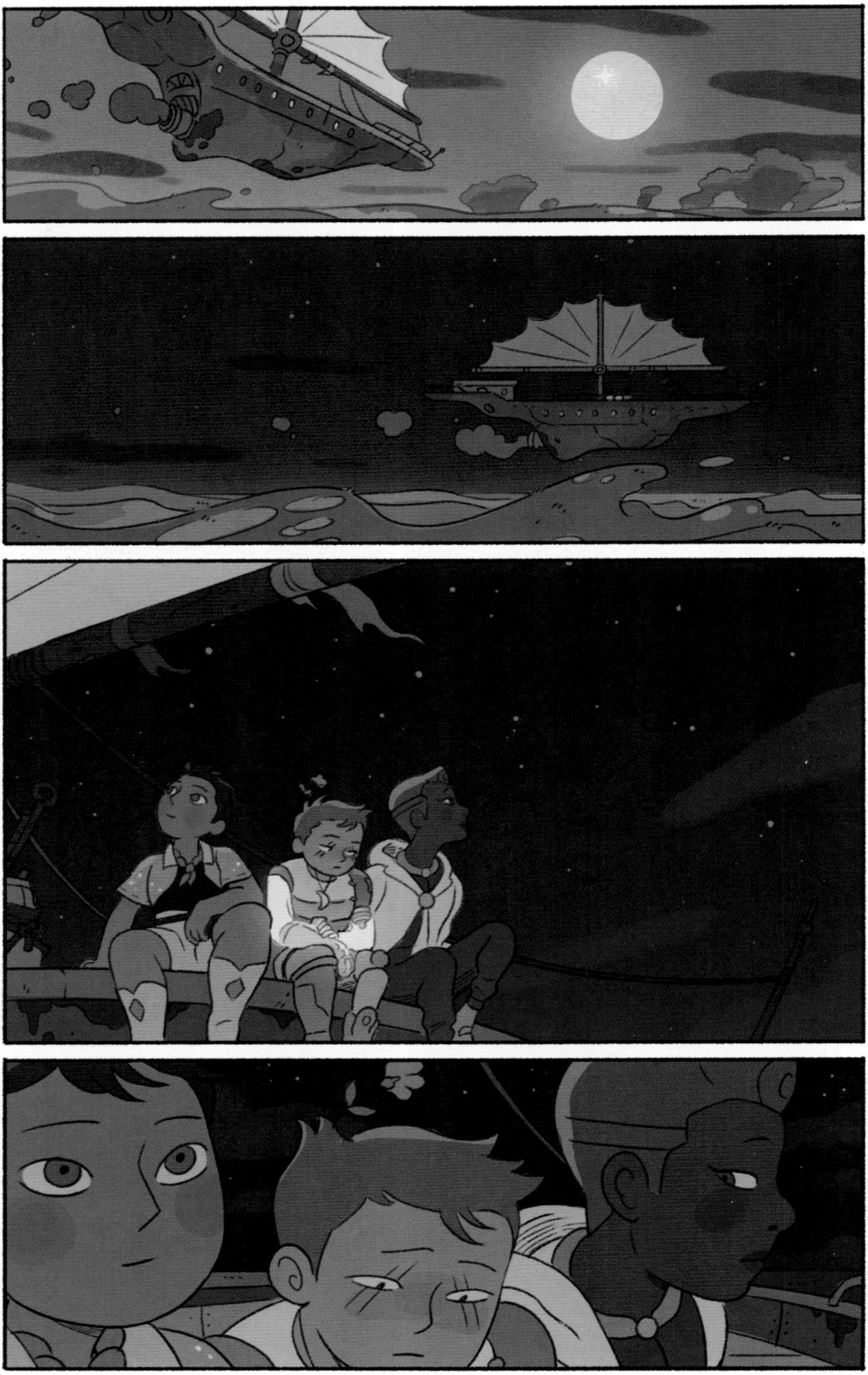

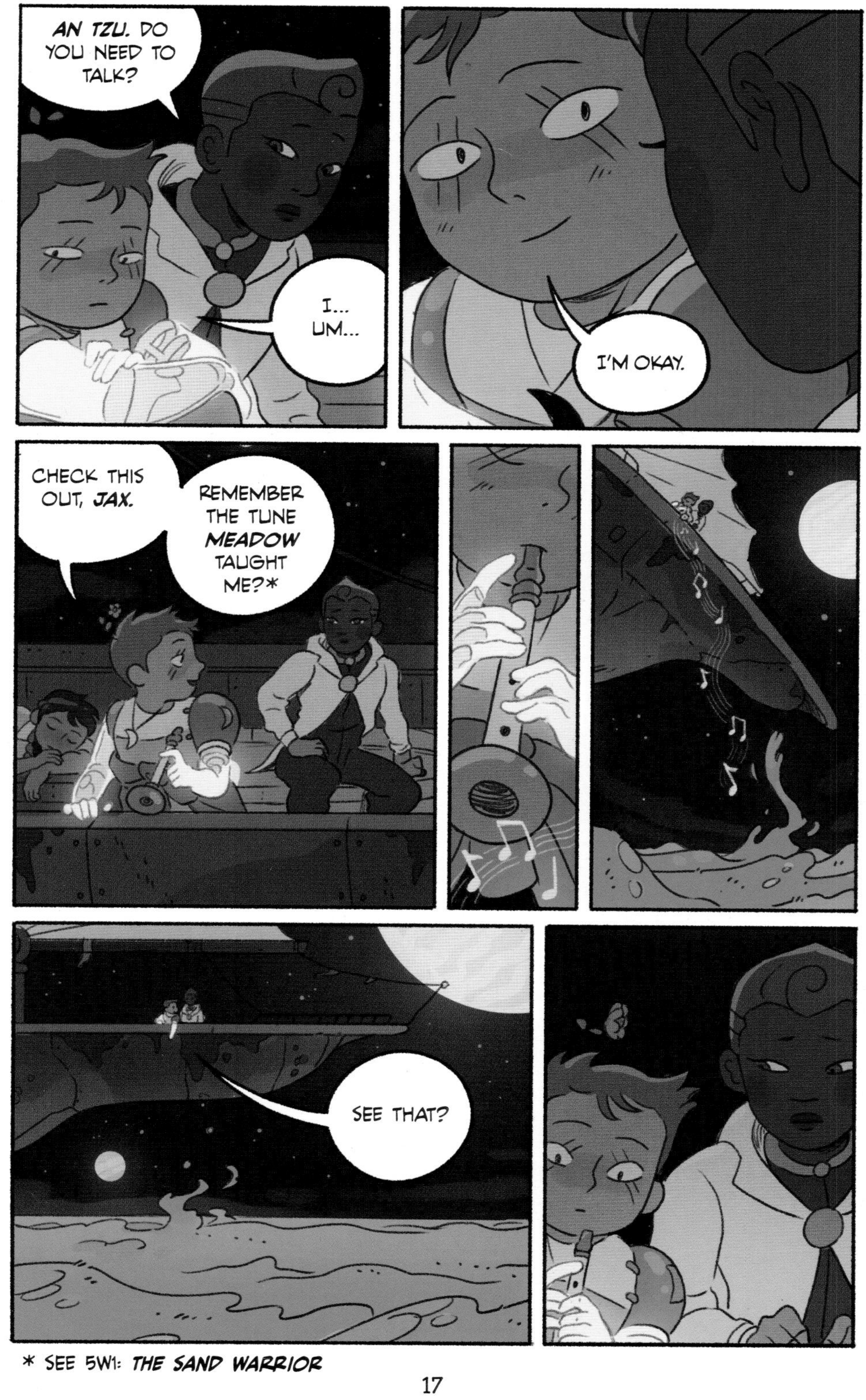
AN TZU. DO YOU NEED TO TALK?
I... UM...
I'M OKAY.
CHECK THIS OUT, JAX.
REMEMBER THE TUNE MEADOW TAUGHT ME?*
SEE THAT?

* SEE 5W1: ***THE SAND WARRIOR***

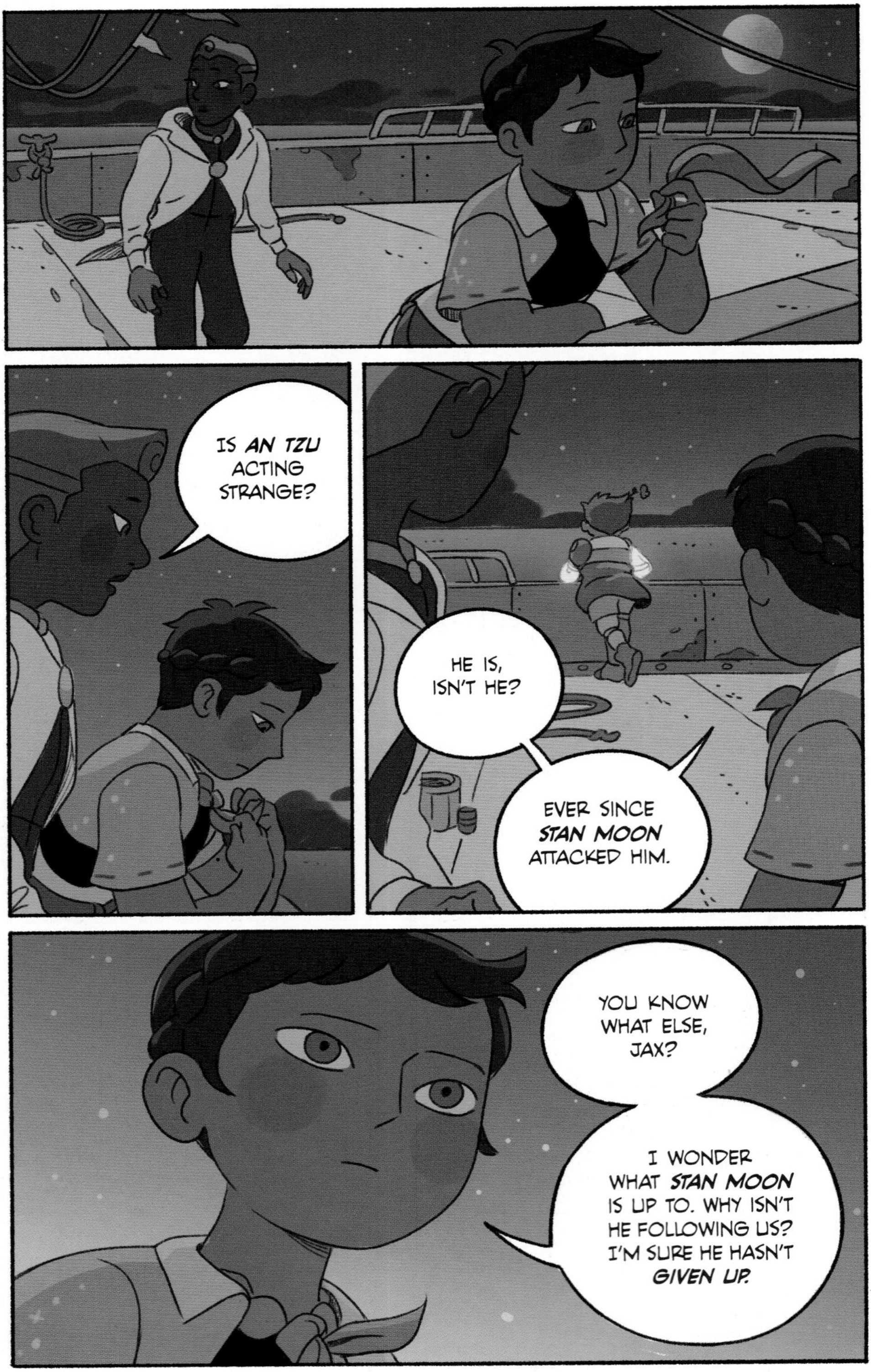
IS AN TZU ACTING STRANGE?
HE IS, ISN'T HE?
EVER SINCE STAN MOON ATTACKED HIM.
YOU KNOW WHAT ELSE, JAX?
I WONDER WHAT STAN MOON IS UP TO. WHY ISN'T HE FOLLOWING US? I'M SURE HE HASN'T GIVEN UP.

CHAPTER 2

ANOTHER LIFE

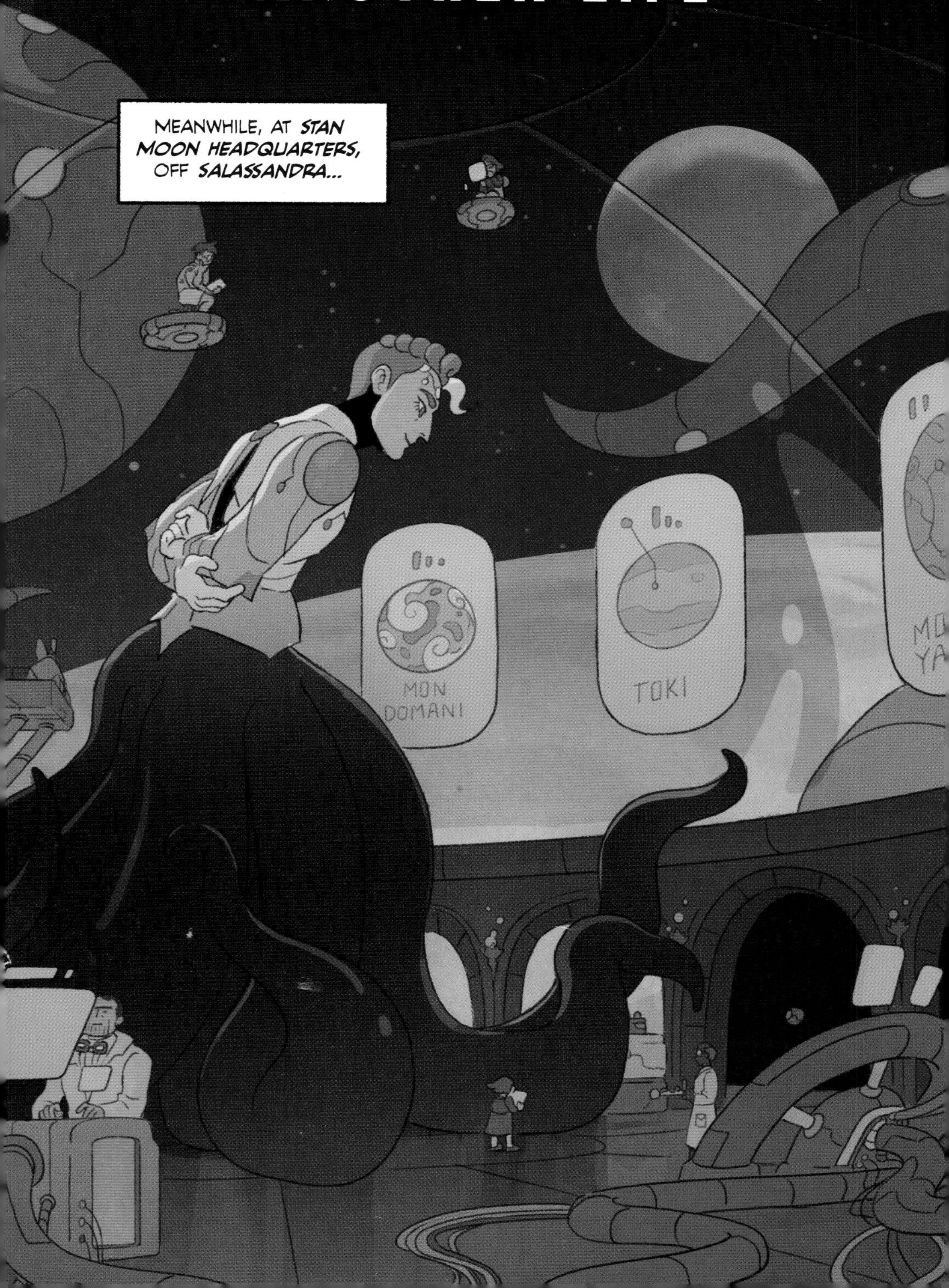
MEANWHILE, AT STAN MOON HEADQUARTERS, OFF SALASSANDRA...
MON DOMANI
TOKI

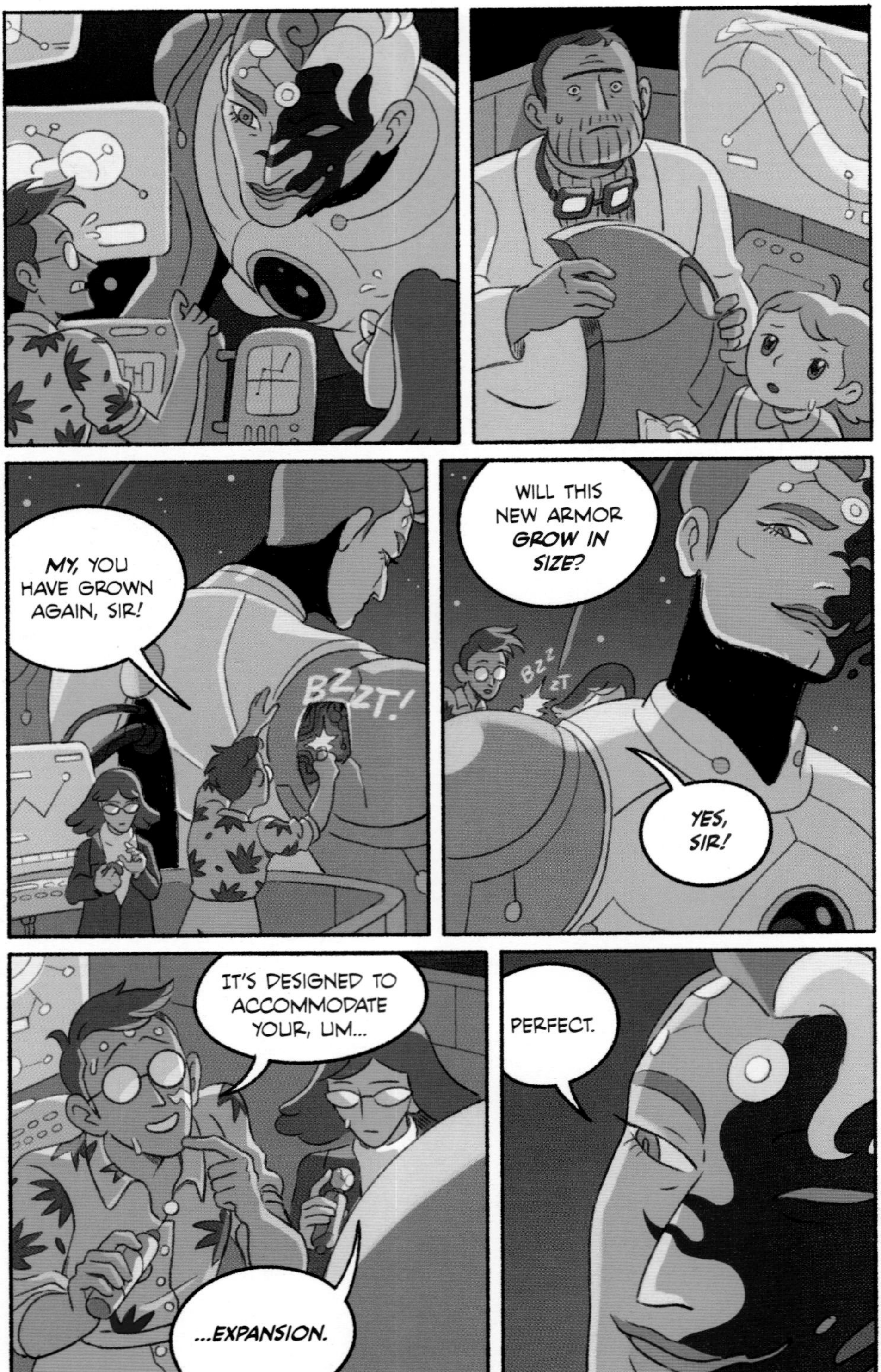
MY, YOU HAVE GROWN AGAIN, SIR!
BZZZT!
WILL THIS NEW ARMOR GROW IN SIZE?
BZZ ZT
YES, SIR!
IT'S DESIGNED TO ACCOMMODATE YOUR, UM...
...EXPANSION.
PERFECT.

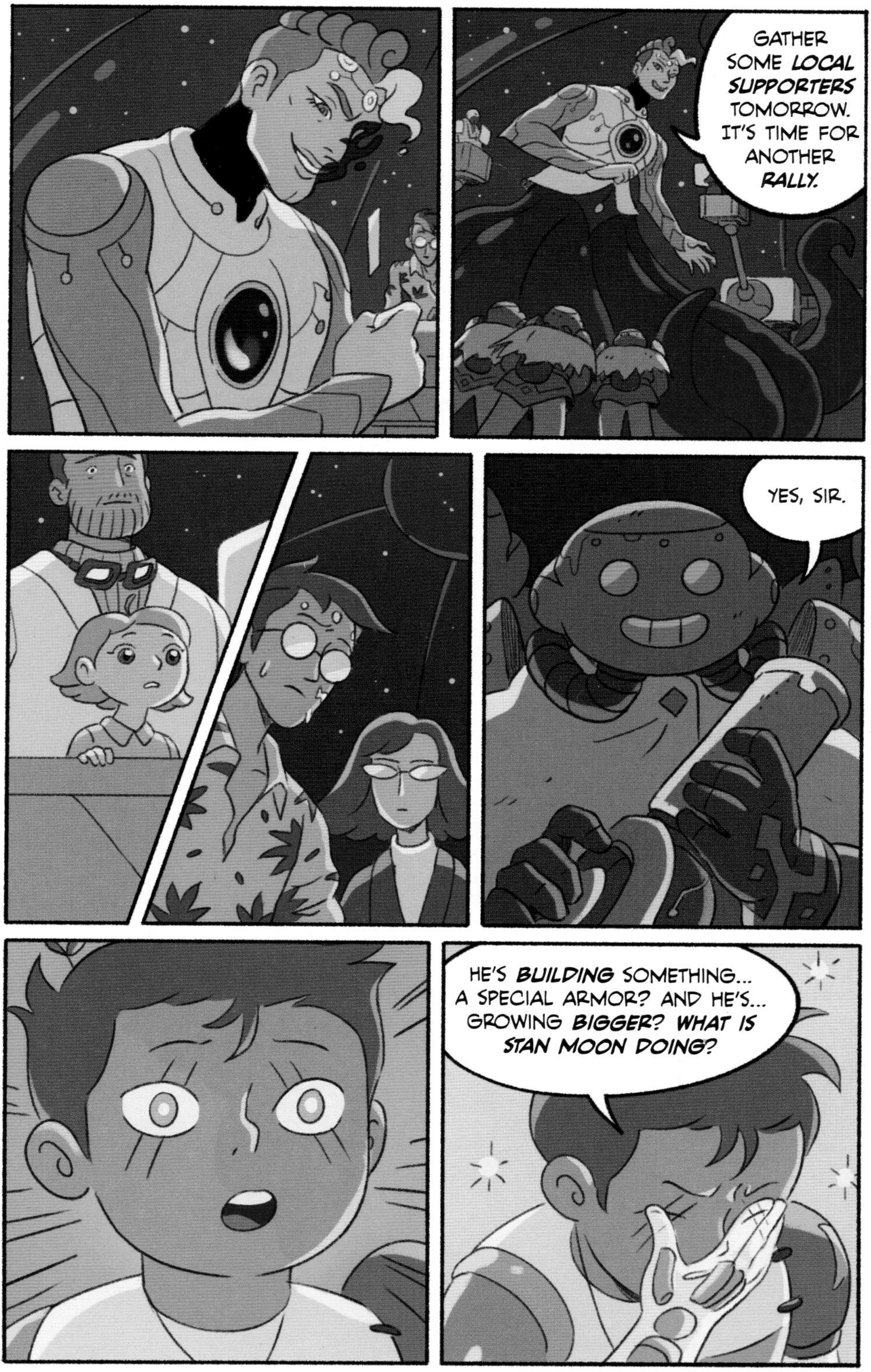
GATHER SOME *LOCAL SUPPORTERS* TOMORROW. IT'S TIME FOR ANOTHER *RALLY.*
YES, SIR.
HE'S *BUILDING* SOMETHING... A SPECIAL ARMOR? AND HE'S... GROWING *BIGGER? WHAT IS STAN MOON DOING?*

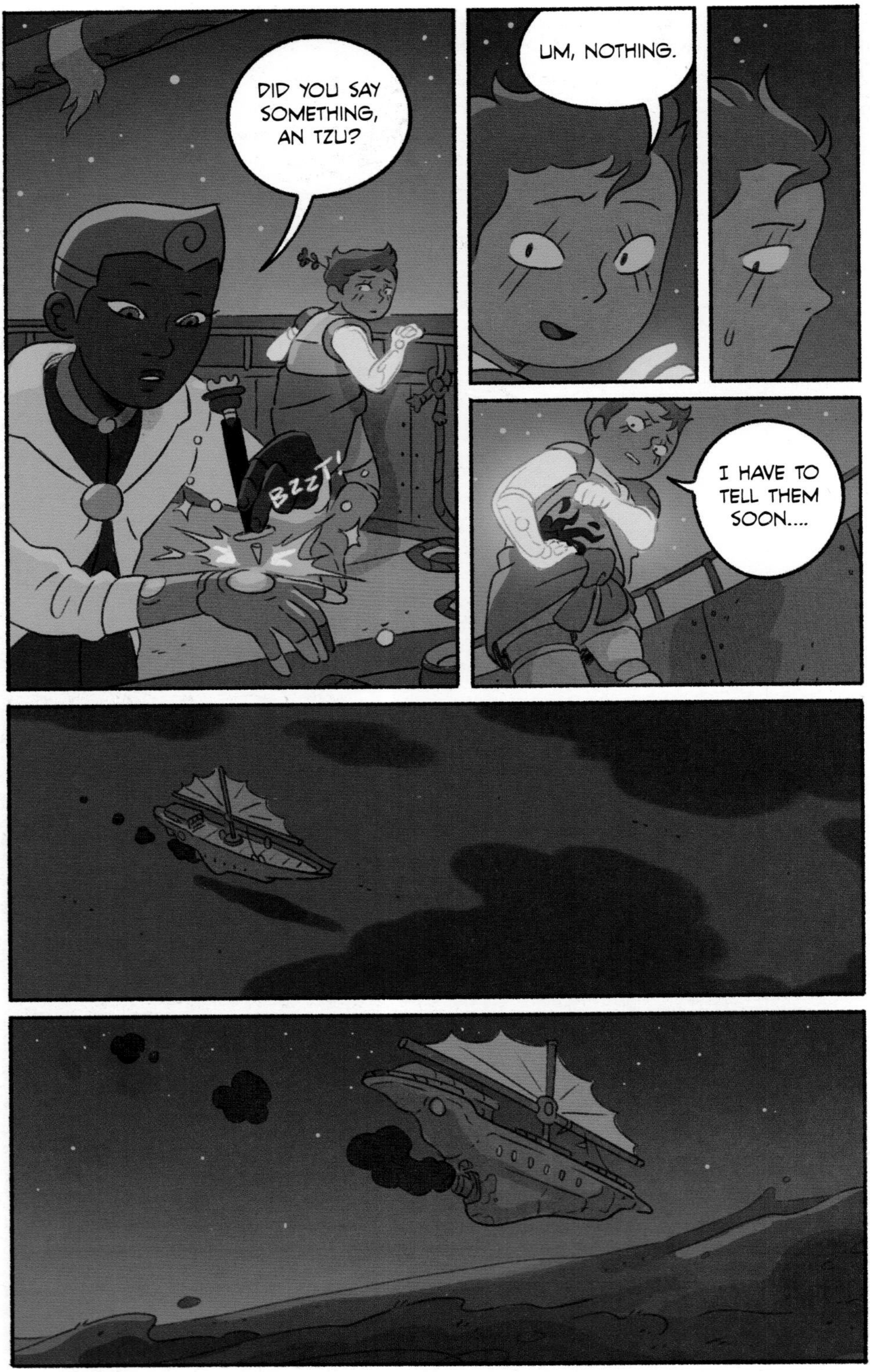
DID YOU SAY SOMETHING, AN TZU?
BZZT!
UM, NOTHING.
I HAVE TO TELL THEM SOON....

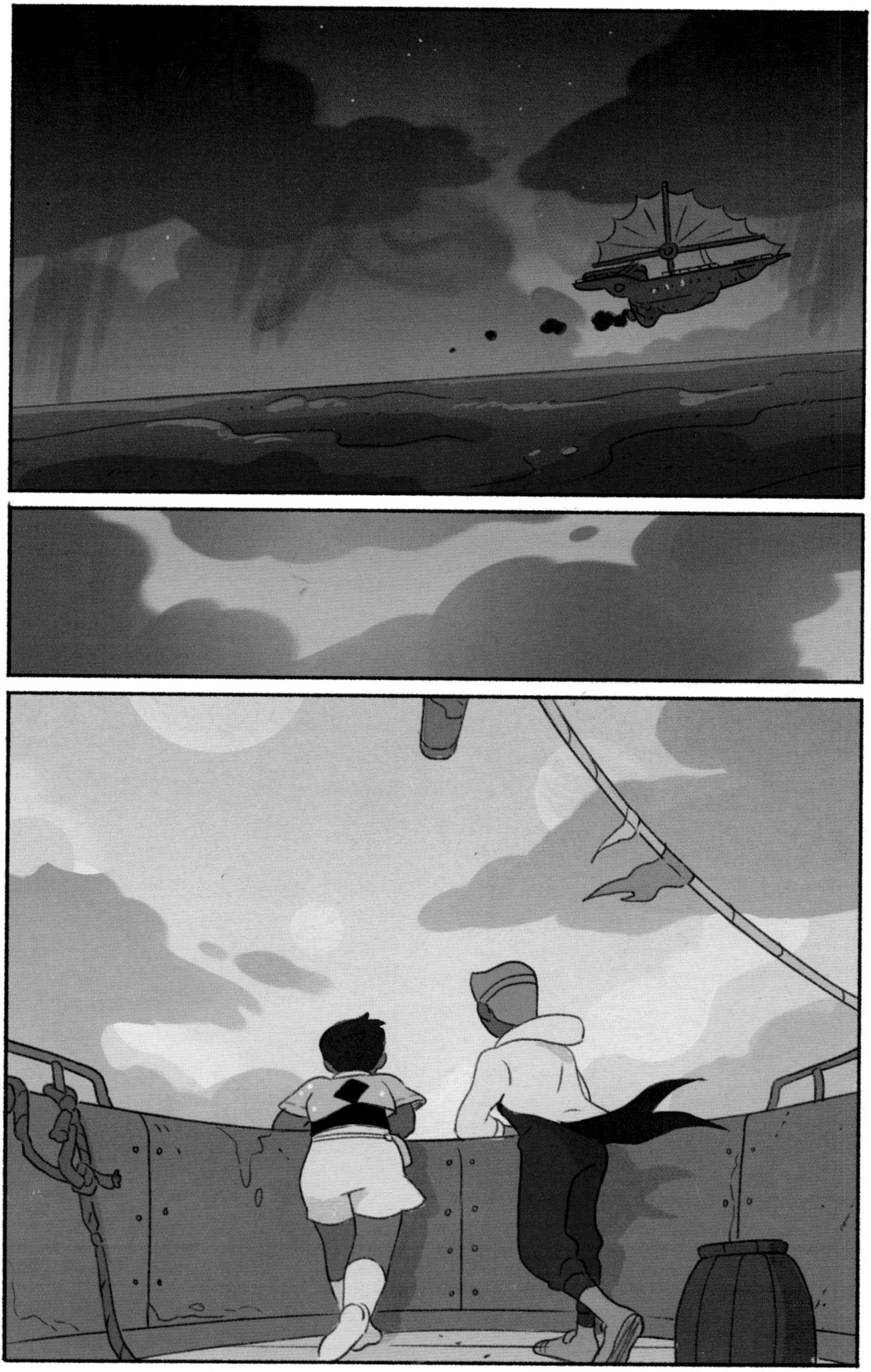

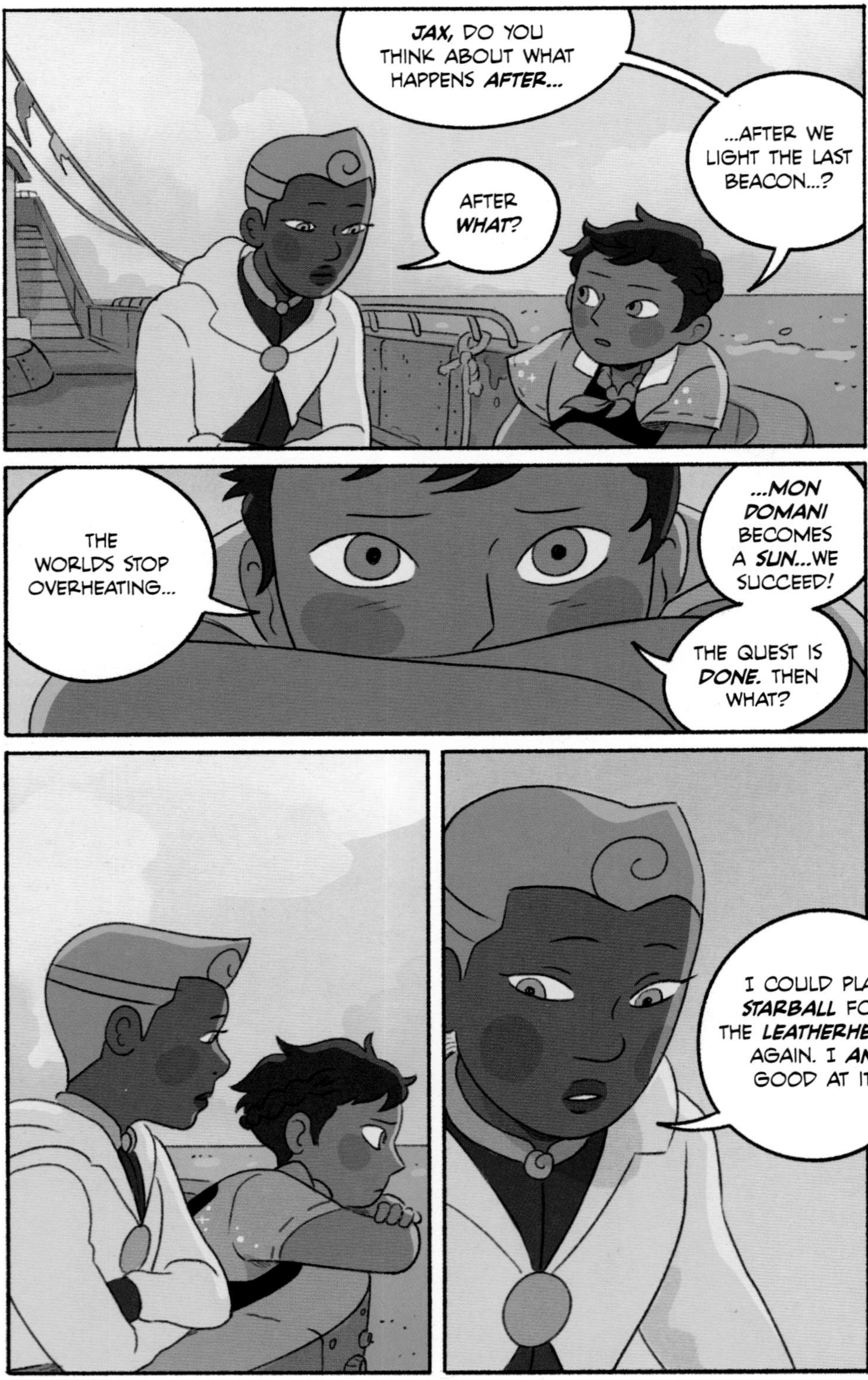
JAX, DO YOU THINK ABOUT WHAT HAPPENS AFTER...
AFTER WHAT?
...AFTER WE LIGHT THE LAST BEACON...?
THE WORLDS STOP OVERHEATING...
...MON DOMANI BECOMES A SUN...WE SUCCEED!
THE QUEST IS DONE. THEN WHAT?
I COULD PLAY STARBALL FOR THE LEATHERHEADS AGAIN. I AM GOOD AT IT.

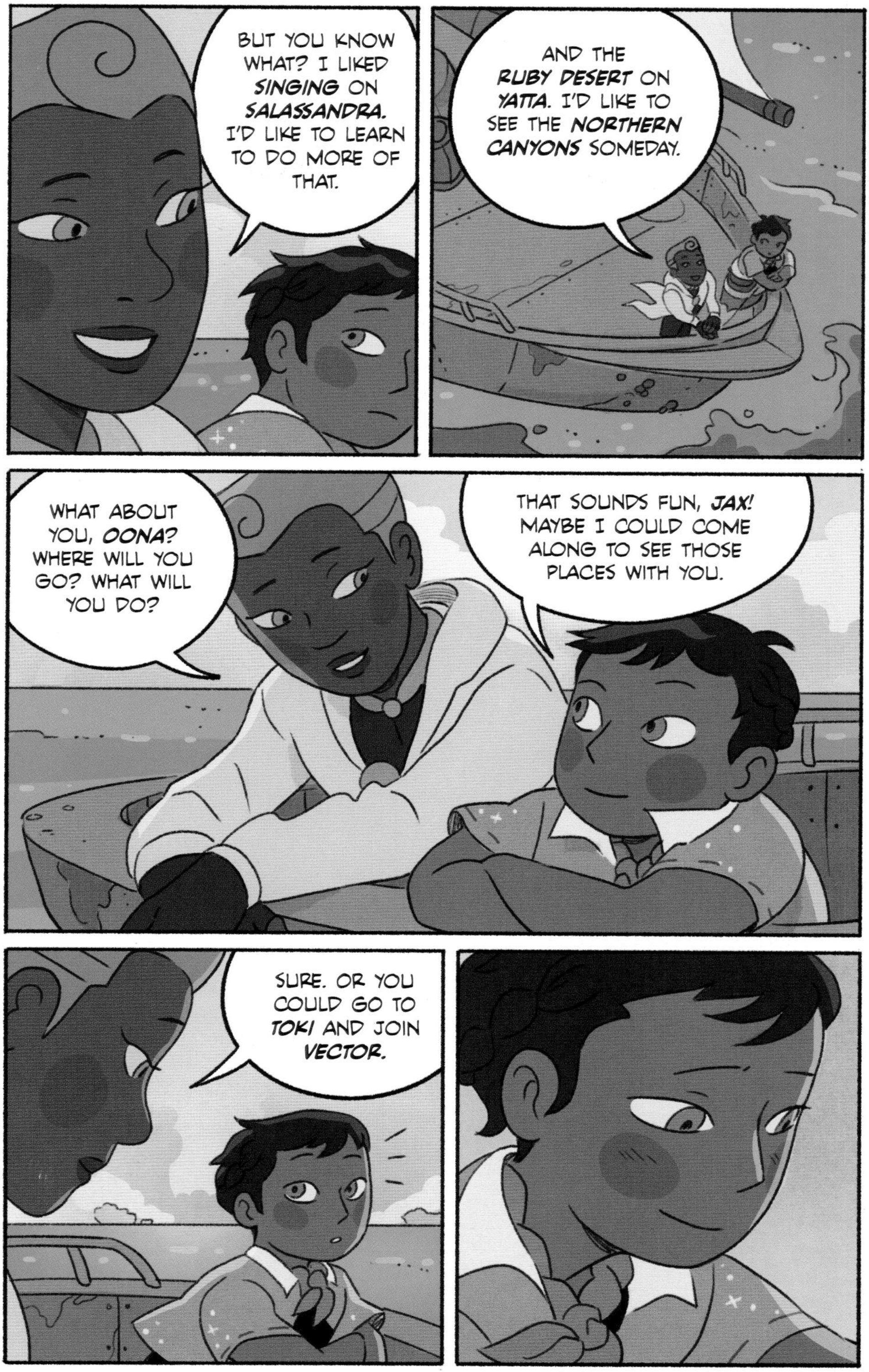
BUT YOU KNOW WHAT? I LIKED *SINGING* ON *SALASSANDRA.* I'D LIKE TO LEARN TO DO MORE OF THAT.
AND THE *RUBY DESERT* ON *YATTA.* I'D LIKE TO SEE THE *NORTHERN CANYONS* SOMEDAY.
WHAT ABOUT YOU, *OONA?* WHERE WILL YOU GO? WHAT WILL YOU DO?
THAT SOUNDS FUN, *JAX!* MAYBE I COULD COME ALONG TO SEE THOSE PLACES WITH YOU.
SURE. OR YOU COULD GO TO *TOKI* AND JOIN *VECTOR.*

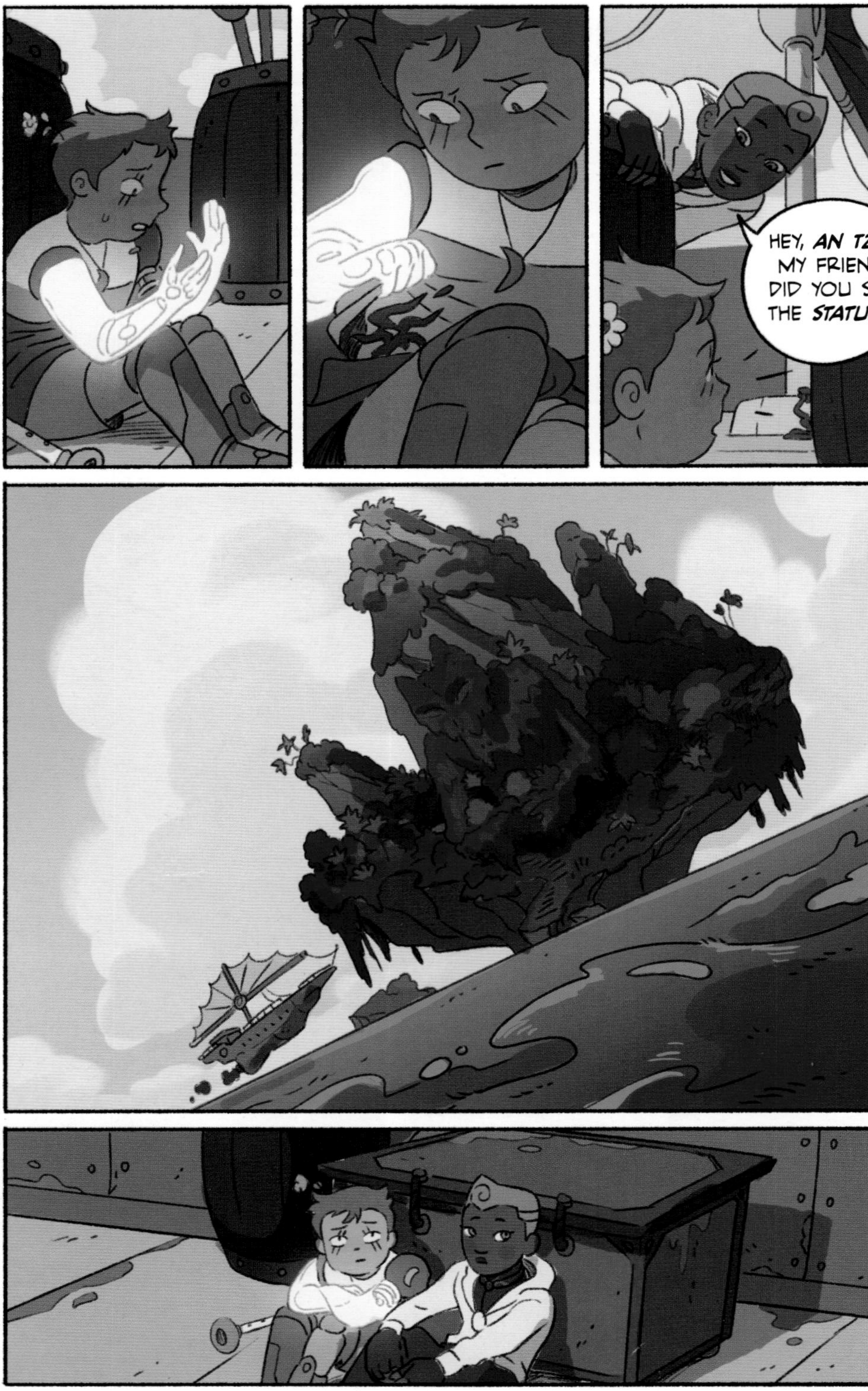
HEY, AN TZU, MY FRIEND. DID YOU SEE THE STATUE?

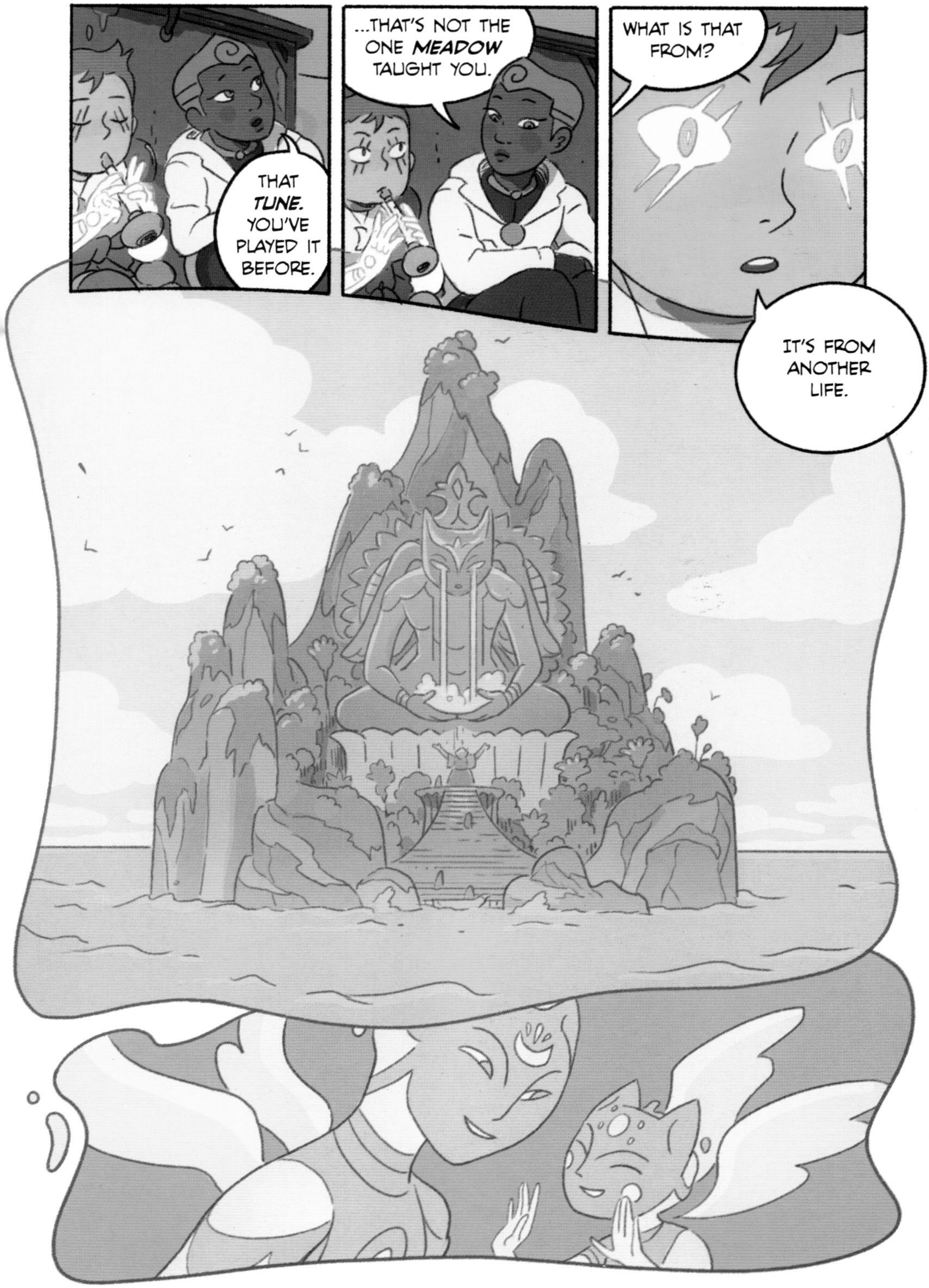
THAT TUNE. YOU'VE PLAYED IT BEFORE.
...THAT'S NOT THE ONE MEADOW TAUGHT YOU.
WHAT IS THAT FROM?
IT'S FROM ANOTHER LIFE.

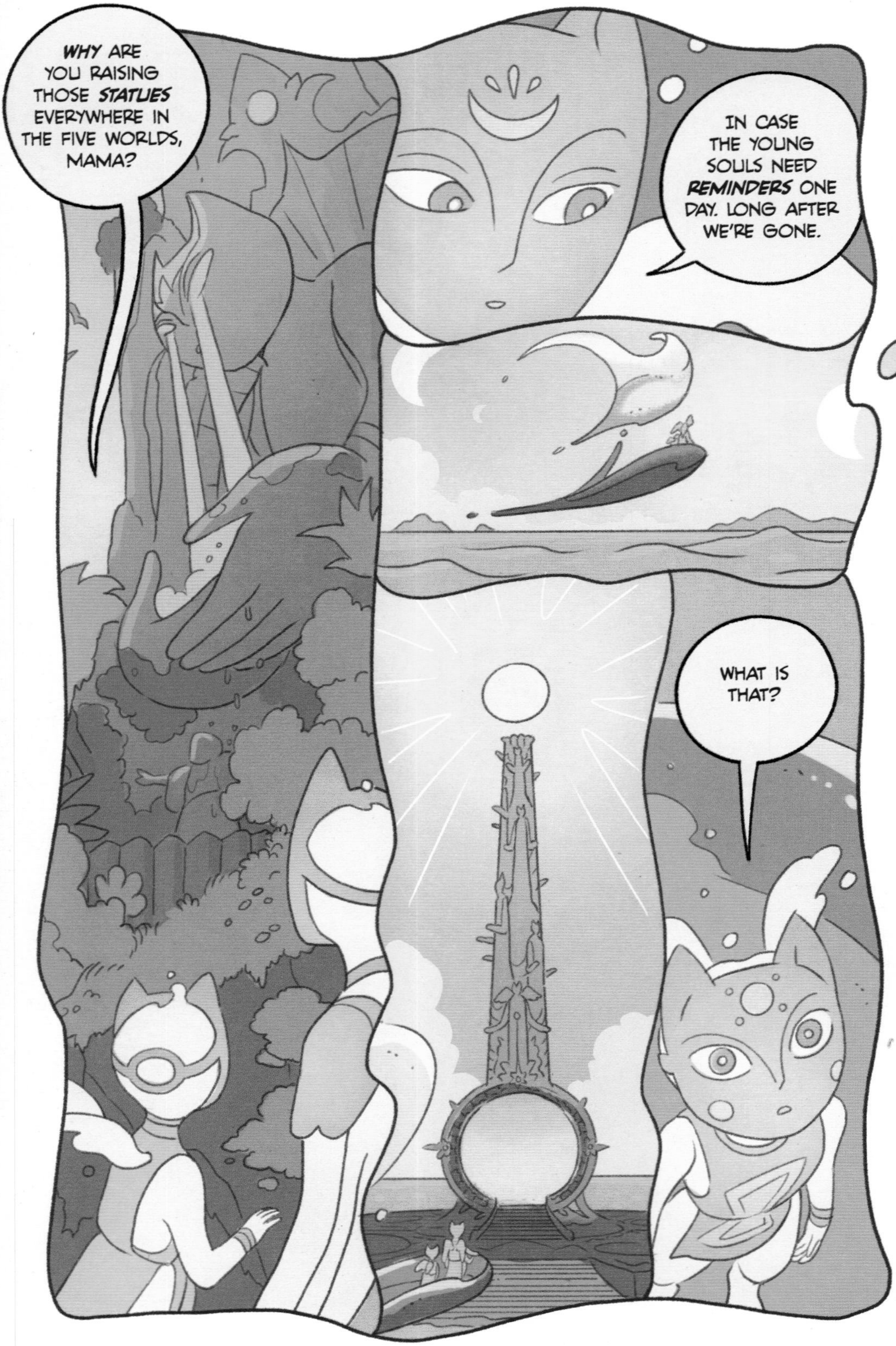
WHY ARE YOU RAISING THOSE STATUES EVERYWHERE IN THE FIVE WORLDS, MAMA?
IN CASE THE YOUNG SOULS NEED REMINDERS ONE DAY. LONG AFTER WE'RE GONE.
WHAT IS THAT?

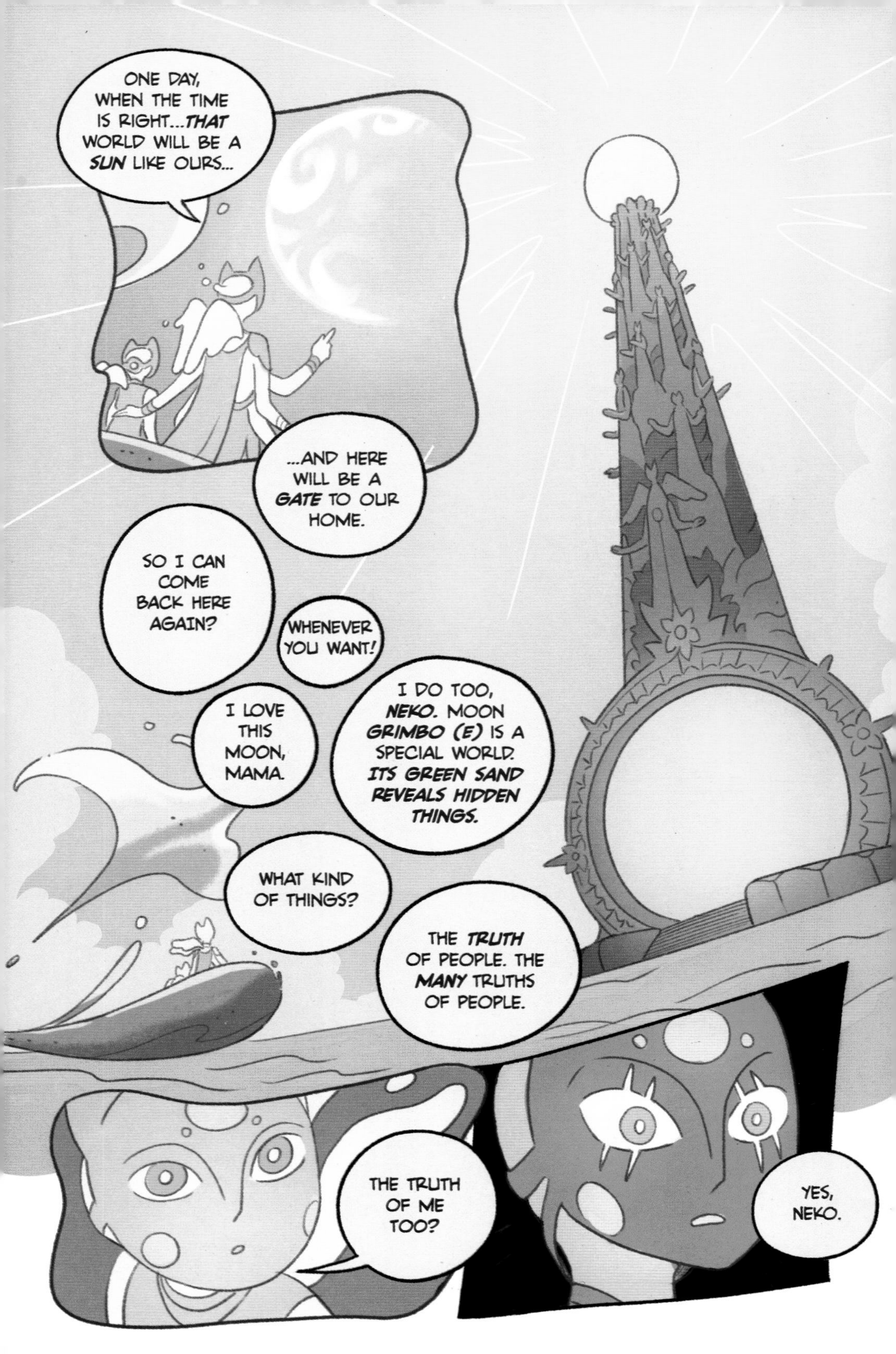
ONE DAY, WHEN THE TIME IS RIGHT...THAT WORLD WILL BE A SUN LIKE OURS...
...AND HERE WILL BE A GATE TO OUR HOME.
SO I CAN COME BACK HERE AGAIN?
WHENEVER YOU WANT!
I LOVE THIS MOON, MAMA.
I DO TOO, NEKO. MOON GRIMBO (E) IS A SPECIAL WORLD. ITS GREEN SAND REVEALS HIDDEN THINGS.
WHAT KIND OF THINGS?
THE TRUTH OF PEOPLE. THE MANY TRUTHS OF PEOPLE.
THE TRUTH OF ME TOO?
YES, NEKO.

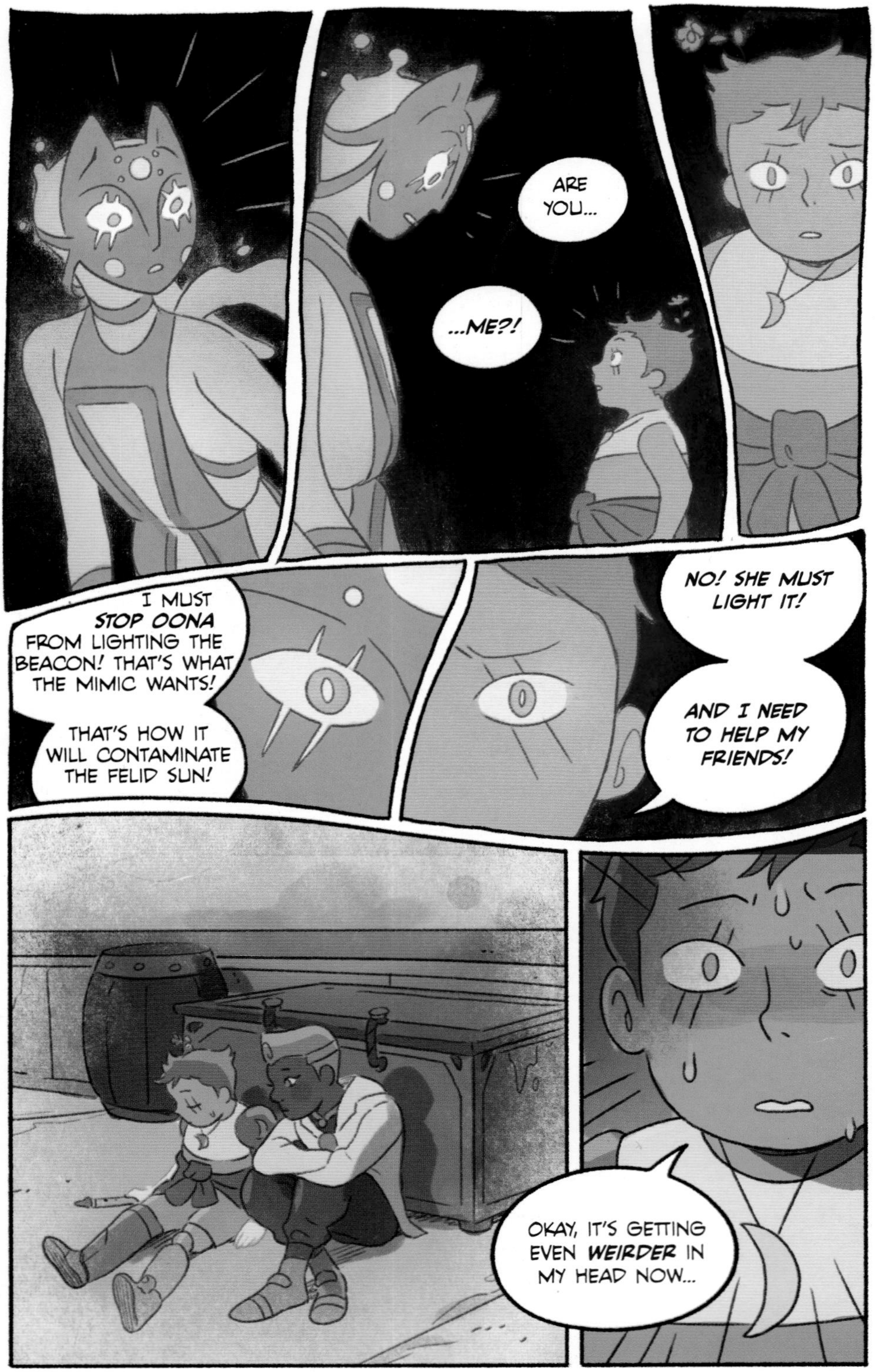
ARE YOU...
...ME?!
I MUST STOP OONA FROM LIGHTING THE BEACON! THAT'S WHAT THE MIMIC WANTS!
THAT'S HOW IT WILL CONTAMINATE THE FELID SUN!
NO! SHE MUST LIGHT IT!
AND I NEED TO HELP MY FRIENDS!
OKAY, IT'S GETTING EVEN WEIRDER IN MY HEAD NOW...

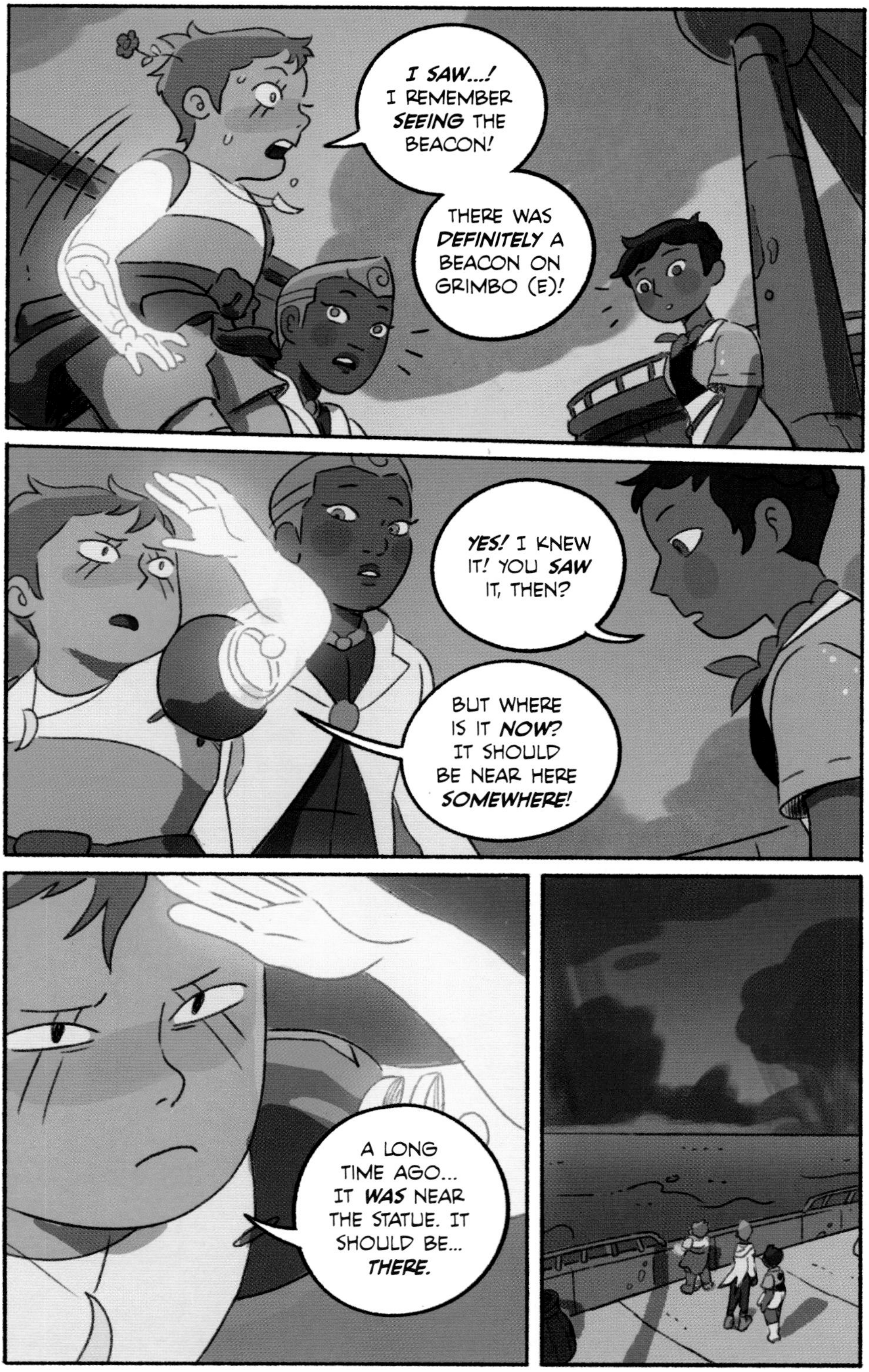
I SAW...! I REMEMBER SEEING THE BEACON!
THERE WAS DEFINITELY A BEACON ON GRIMBO (E)!
YES! I KNEW IT! YOU SAW IT, THEN?
BUT WHERE IS IT NOW? IT SHOULD BE NEAR HERE SOMEWHERE!
A LONG TIME AGO... IT WAS NEAR THE STATUE. IT SHOULD BE... THERE.

CHAPTER 3

DARK CLOUDS AND A DEAR FRIEND

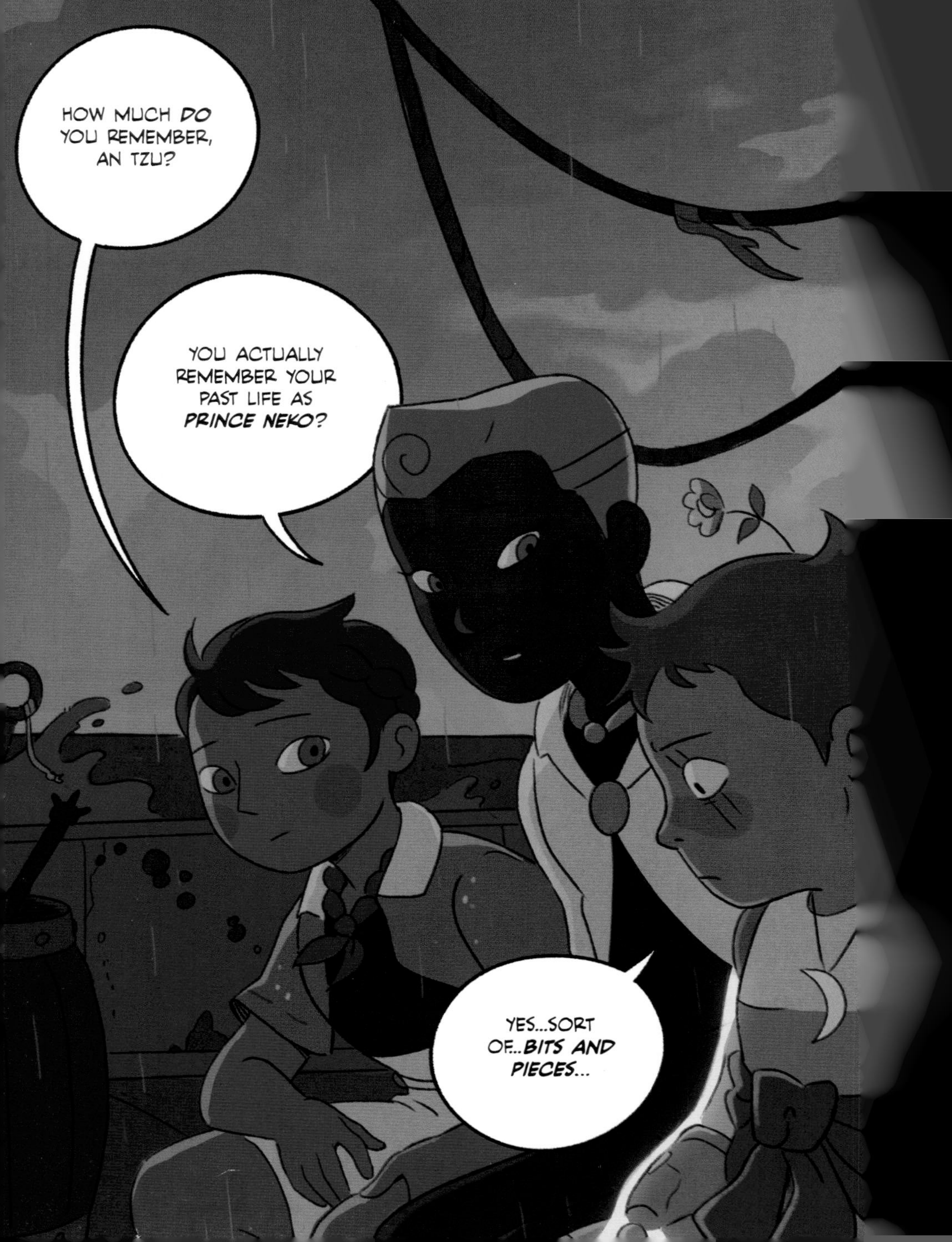
HOW MUCH *DO* YOU REMEMBER, AN TZU?
YOU ACTUALLY REMEMBER YOUR PAST LIFE AS *PRINCE NEKO*?
YES...SORT OF...*BITS AND PIECES*...

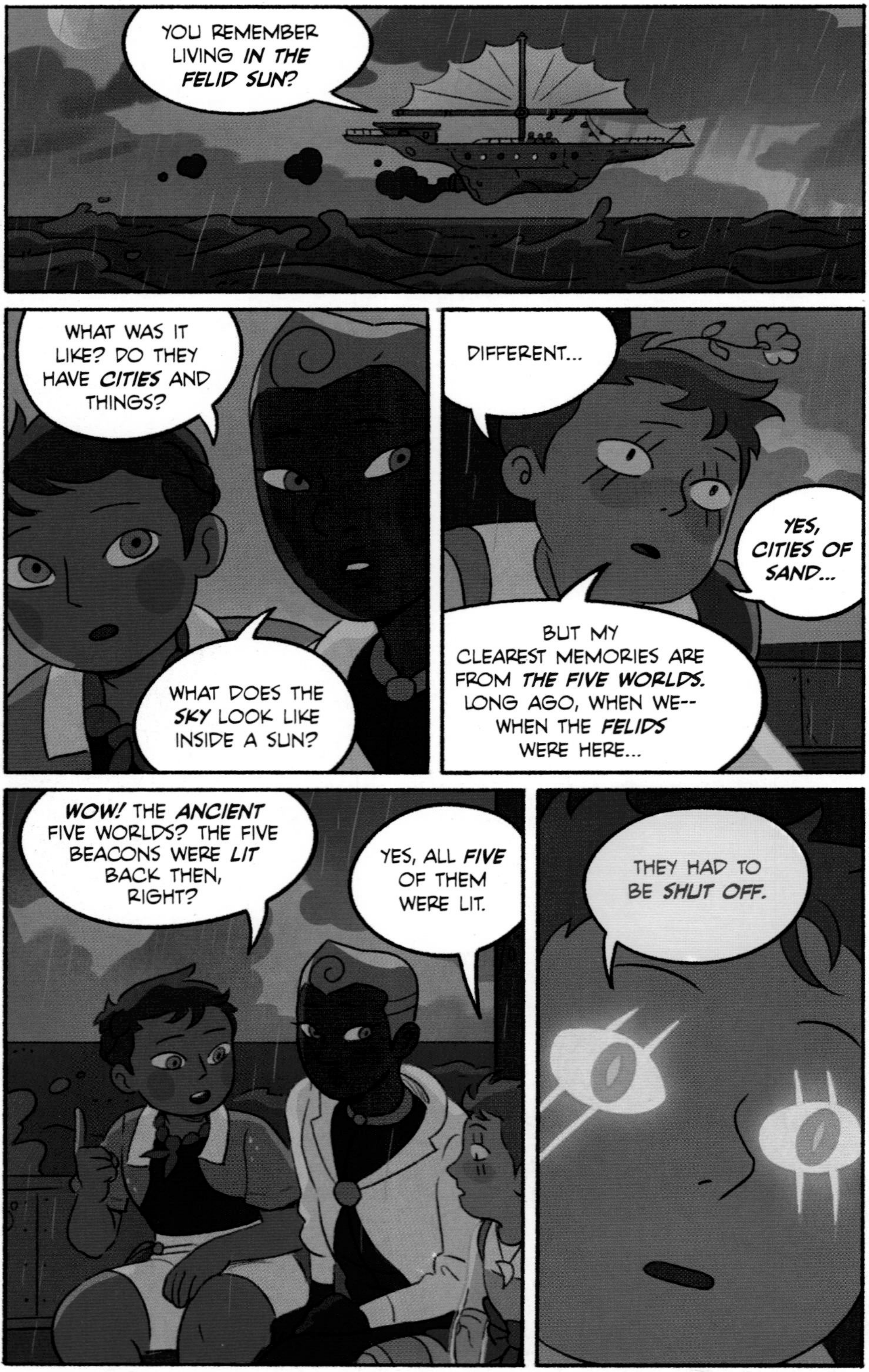
YOU REMEMBER LIVING IN THE FELID SUN?
WHAT WAS IT LIKE? DO THEY HAVE CITIES AND THINGS?
WHAT DOES THE SKY LOOK LIKE INSIDE A SUN?
DIFFERENT...
YES, CITIES OF SAND...
BUT MY CLEAREST MEMORIES ARE FROM THE FIVE WORLDS. LONG AGO, WHEN WE-- WHEN THE FELIDS WERE HERE...
WOW! THE ANCIENT FIVE WORLDS? THE FIVE BEACONS WERE LIT BACK THEN, RIGHT?
YES, ALL FIVE OF THEM WERE LIT.
THEY HAD TO BE SHUT OFF.

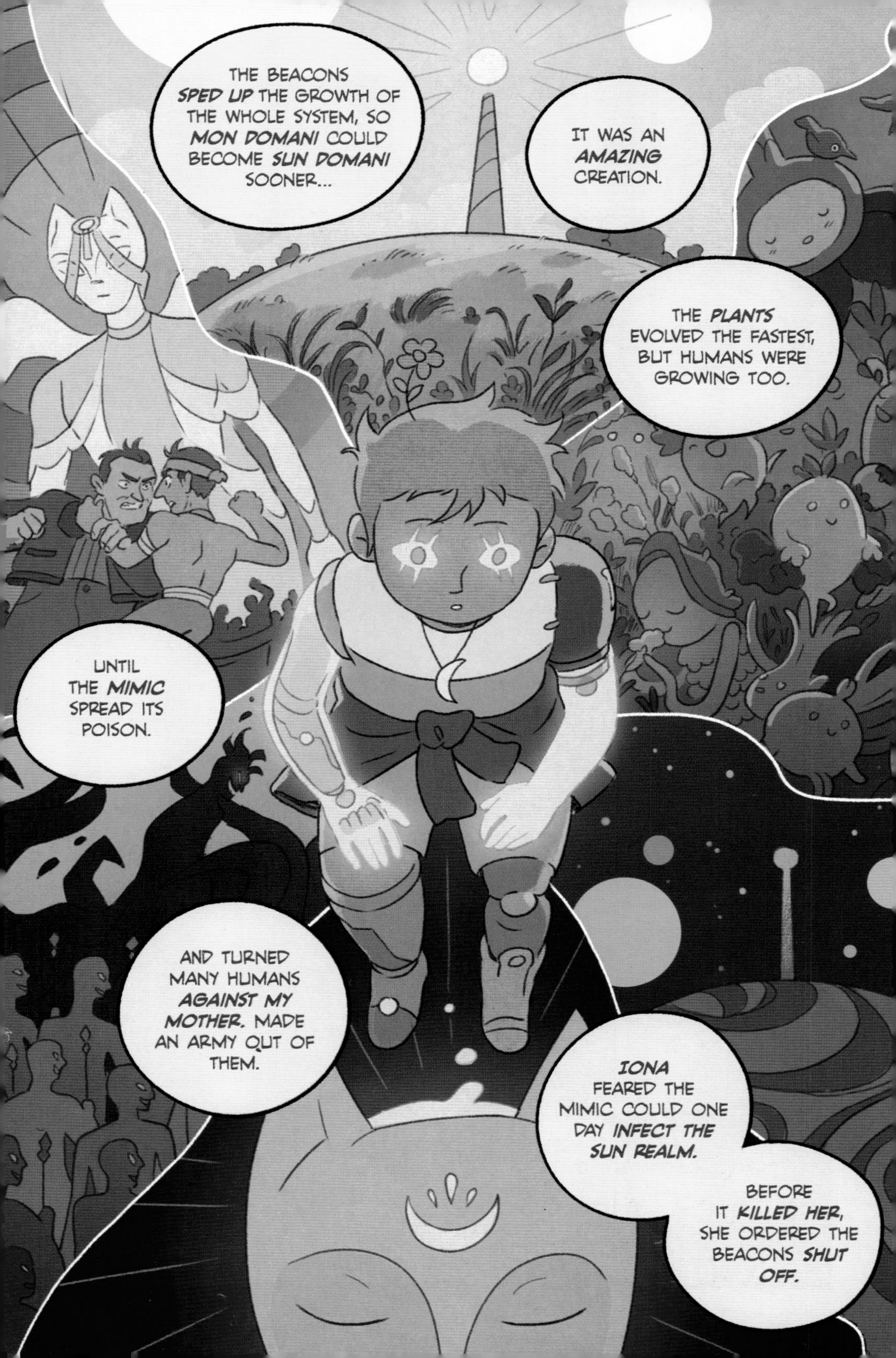
THE BEACONS SPED UP THE GROWTH OF THE WHOLE SYSTEM, SO MON DOMANI COULD BECOME SUN DOMANI SOONER...
IT WAS AN AMAZING CREATION.
THE PLANTS EVOLVED THE FASTEST, BUT HUMANS WERE GROWING TOO.
UNTIL THE MIMIC SPREAD ITS POISON.
AND TURNED MANY HUMANS AGAINST MY MOTHER. MADE AN ARMY OUT OF THEM.
IONA FEARED THE MIMIC COULD ONE DAY INFECT THE SUN REALM.
BEFORE IT KILLED HER, SHE ORDERED THE BEACONS SHUT OFF.

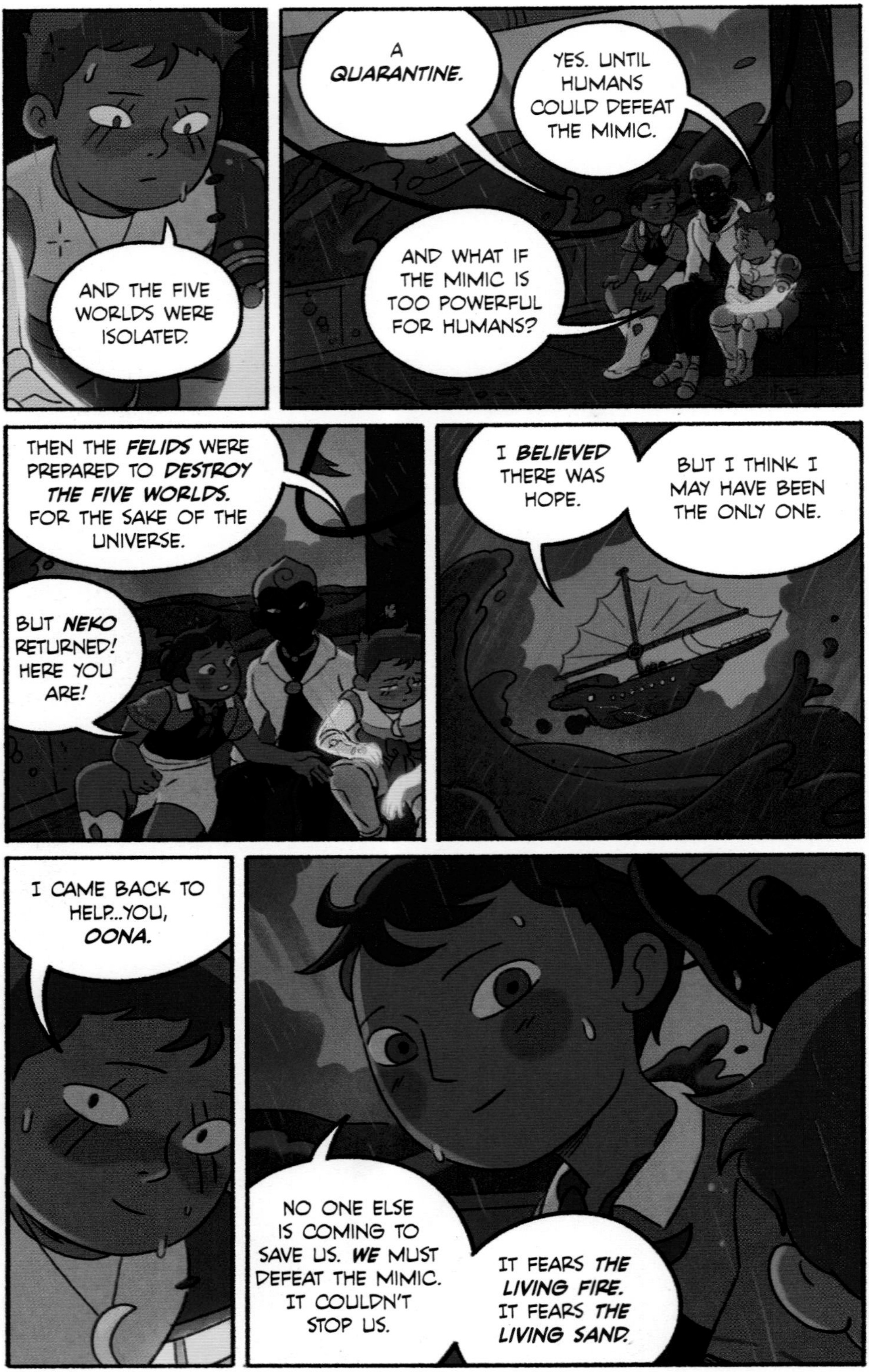
AND THE FIVE WORLDS WERE ISOLATED.
A QUARANTINE.
YES. UNTIL HUMANS COULD DEFEAT THE MIMIC.
AND WHAT IF THE MIMIC IS TOO POWERFUL FOR HUMANS?
THEN THE FELIDS WERE PREPARED TO DESTROY THE FIVE WORLDS. FOR THE SAKE OF THE UNIVERSE.
BUT NEKO RETURNED! HERE YOU ARE!
I BELIEVED THERE WAS HOPE.
BUT I THINK I MAY HAVE BEEN THE ONLY ONE.
I CAME BACK TO HELP...YOU, OONA.
NO ONE ELSE IS COMING TO SAVE US. WE MUST DEFEAT THE MIMIC. IT COULDN'T STOP US.
IT FEARS THE LIVING FIRE. IT FEARS THE LIVING SAND.

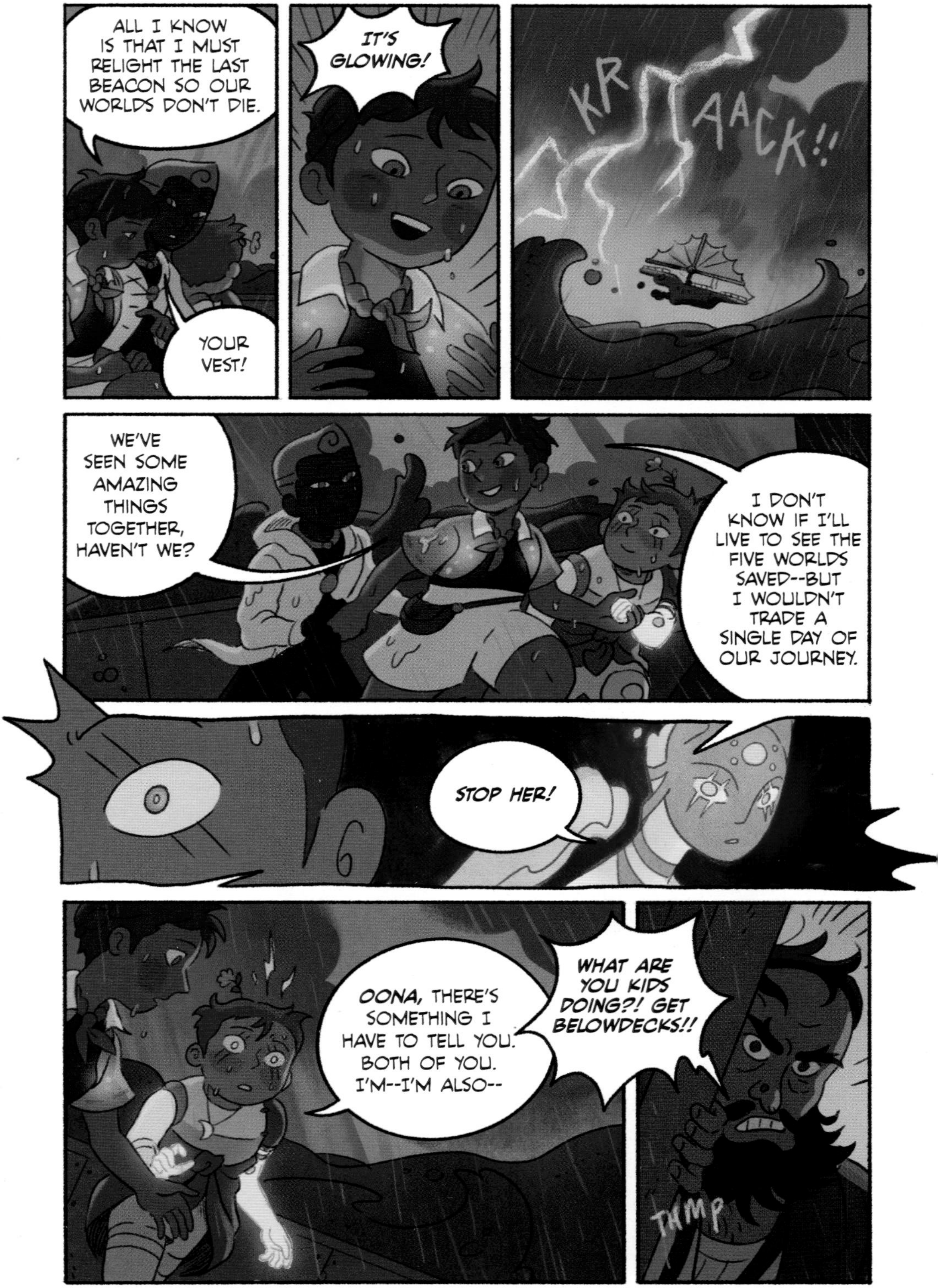
ALL I KNOW IS THAT I MUST RELIGHT THE LAST BEACON SO OUR WORLDS DON'T DIE.
YOUR VEST!
IT'S GLOWING!
KR AACK!!
WE'VE SEEN SOME AMAZING THINGS TOGETHER, HAVEN'T WE?
I DON'T KNOW IF I'LL LIVE TO SEE THE FIVE WORLDS SAVED--BUT I WOULDN'T TRADE A SINGLE DAY OF OUR JOURNEY.
STOP HER!
OONA, THERE'S SOMETHING I HAVE TO TELL YOU. BOTH OF YOU. I'M--I'M ALSO--
WHAT ARE YOU KIDS DOING?! GET BELOWDECKS!!
THMP

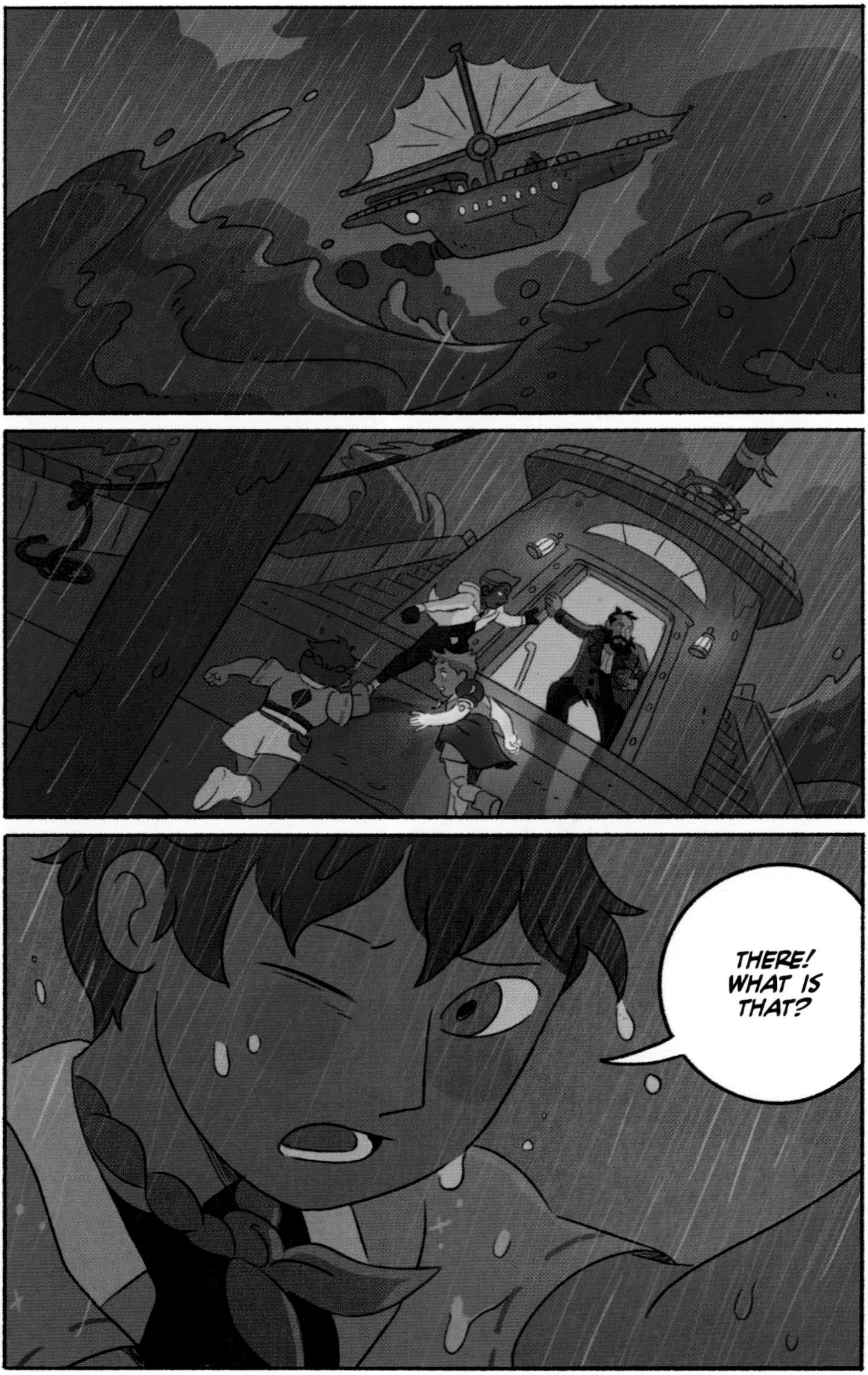
THERE! WHAT IS THAT?

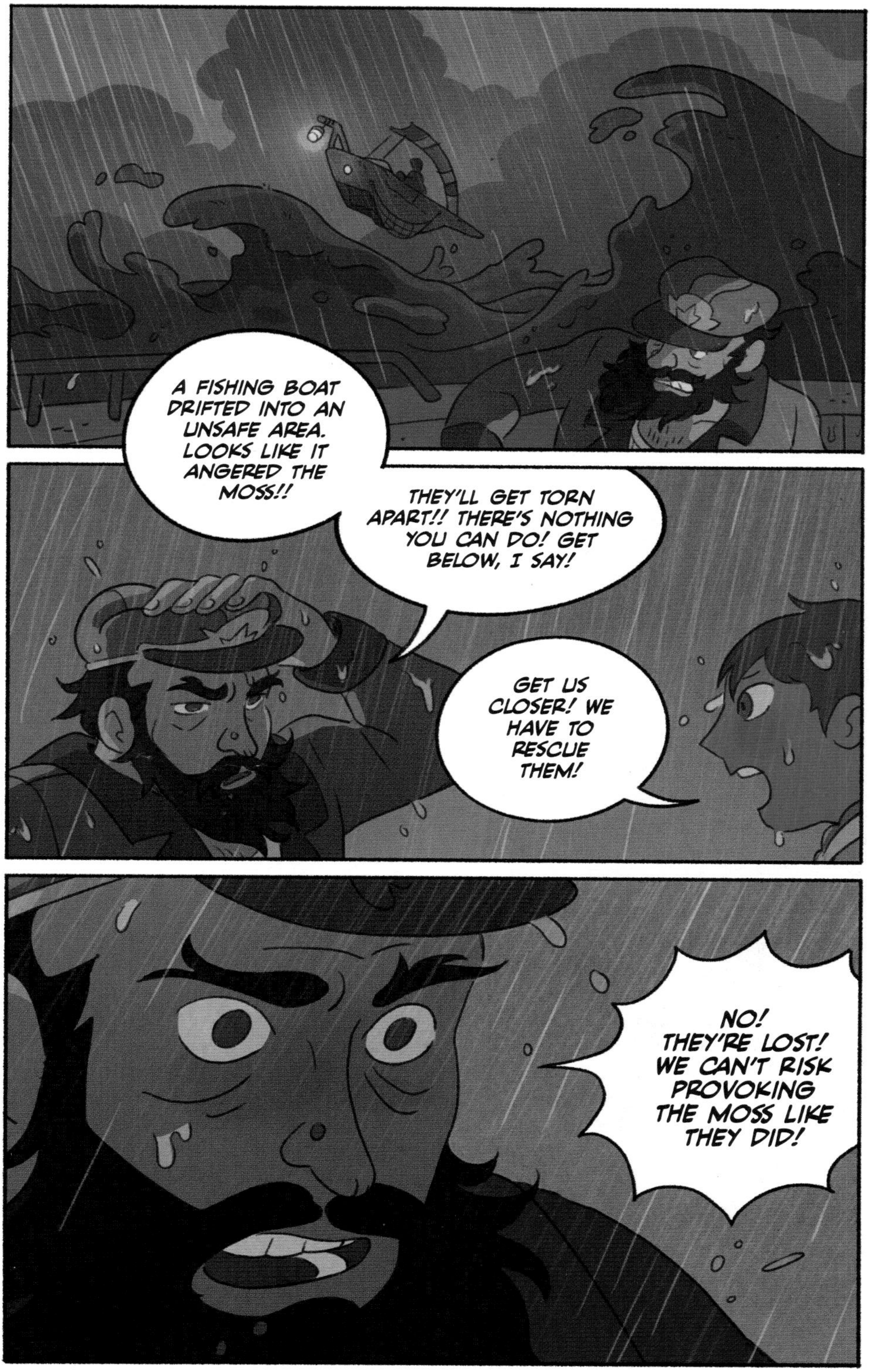
A FISHING BOAT DRIFTED INTO AN UNSAFE AREA. LOOKS LIKE IT ANGERED THE MOSS!!
THEY'LL GET TORN APART!! THERE'S NOTHING YOU CAN DO! GET BELOW, I SAY!
GET US CLOSER! WE HAVE TO RESCUE THEM!
NO! THEY'RE LOST! WE CAN'T RISK PROVOKING THE MOSS LIKE THEY DID!

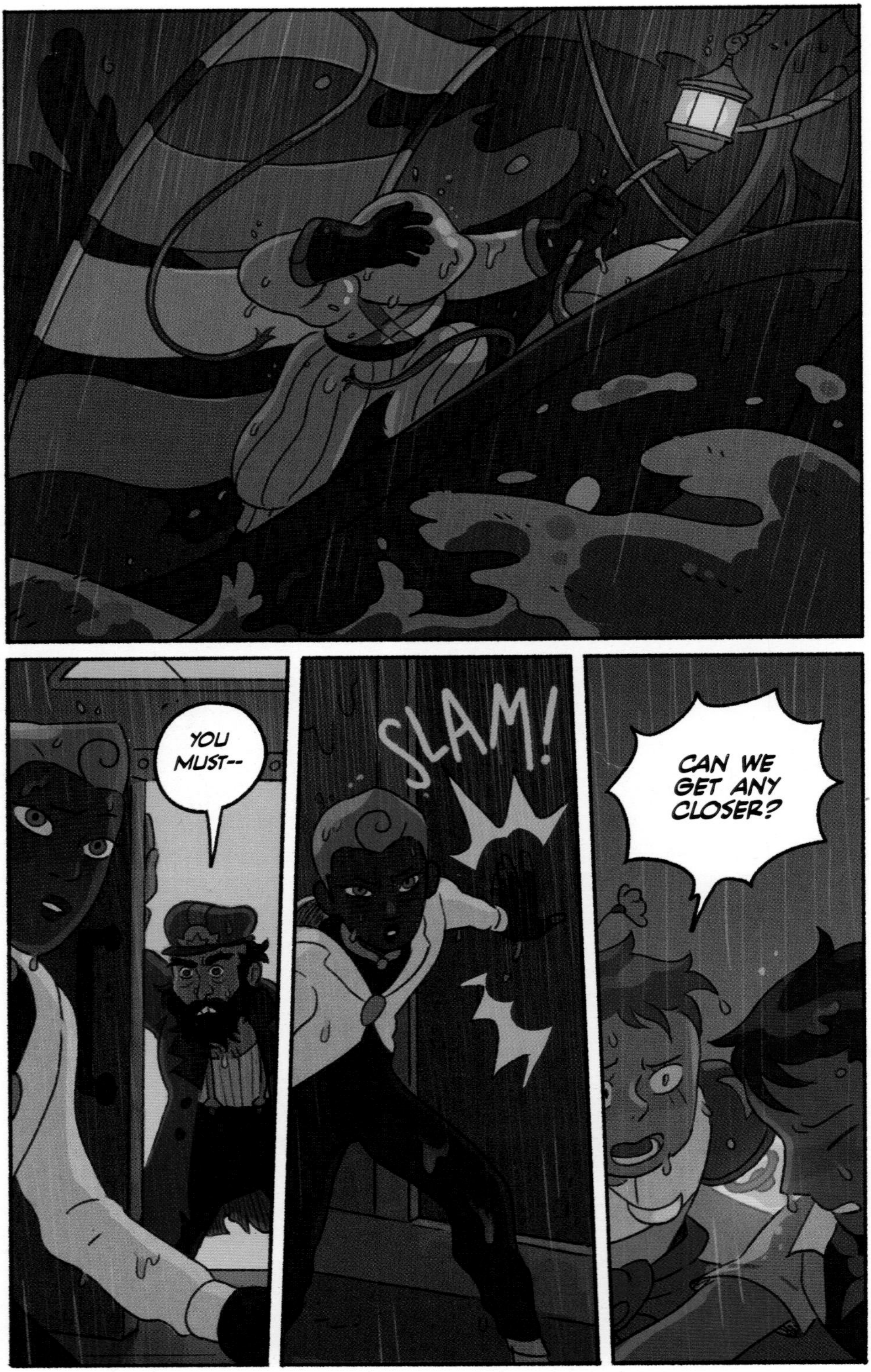
YOU MUST--
SLAM!
CAN WE GET ANY CLOSER?

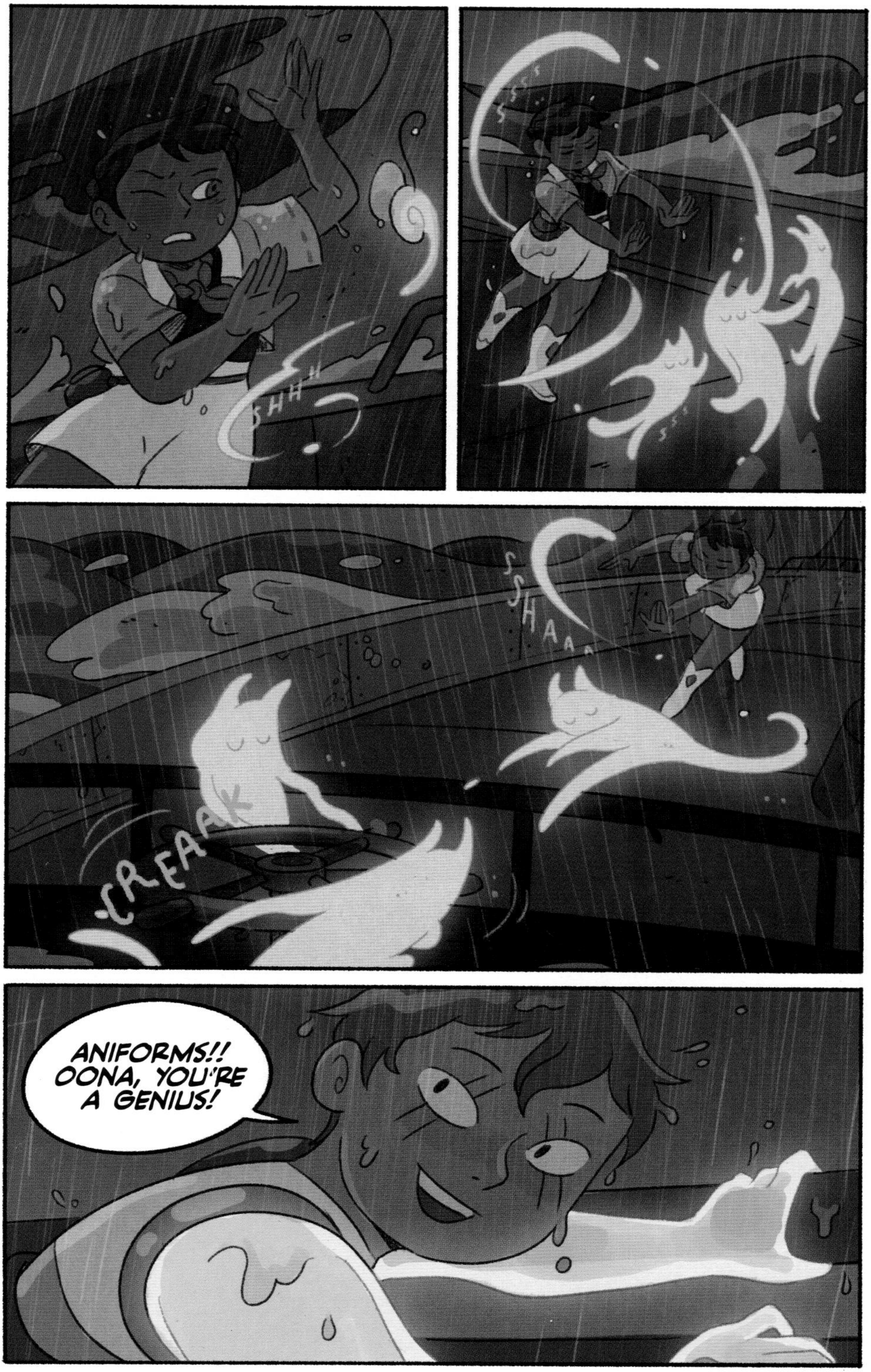
SHH
SSHAAA
CREAAK
ANIFORMS!! OONA, YOU'RE A GENIUS!

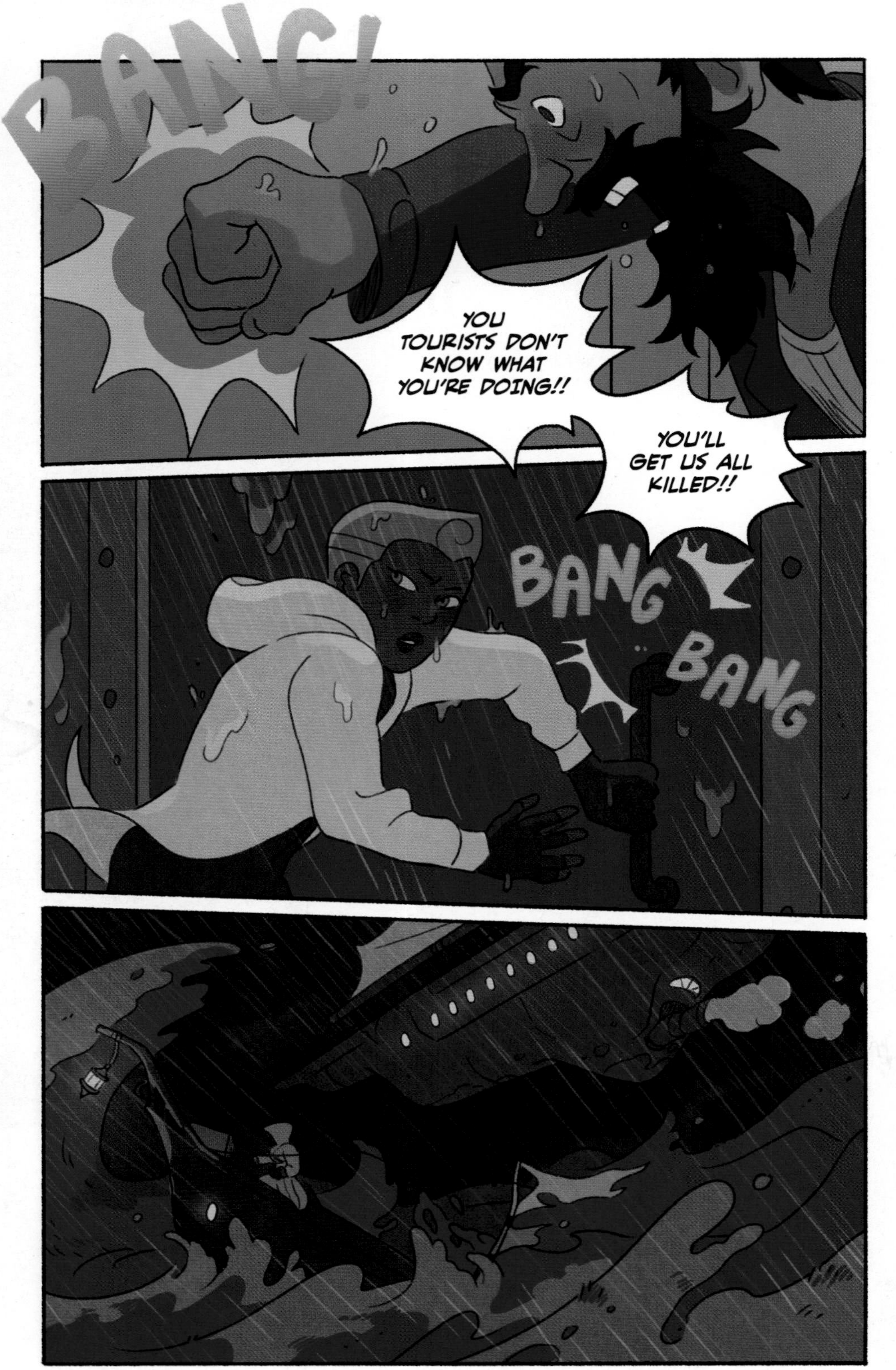
BANG!
YOU TOURISTS DON'T KNOW WHAT YOU'RE DOING!!
YOU'LL GET US ALL KILLED!!
BANG
BANG

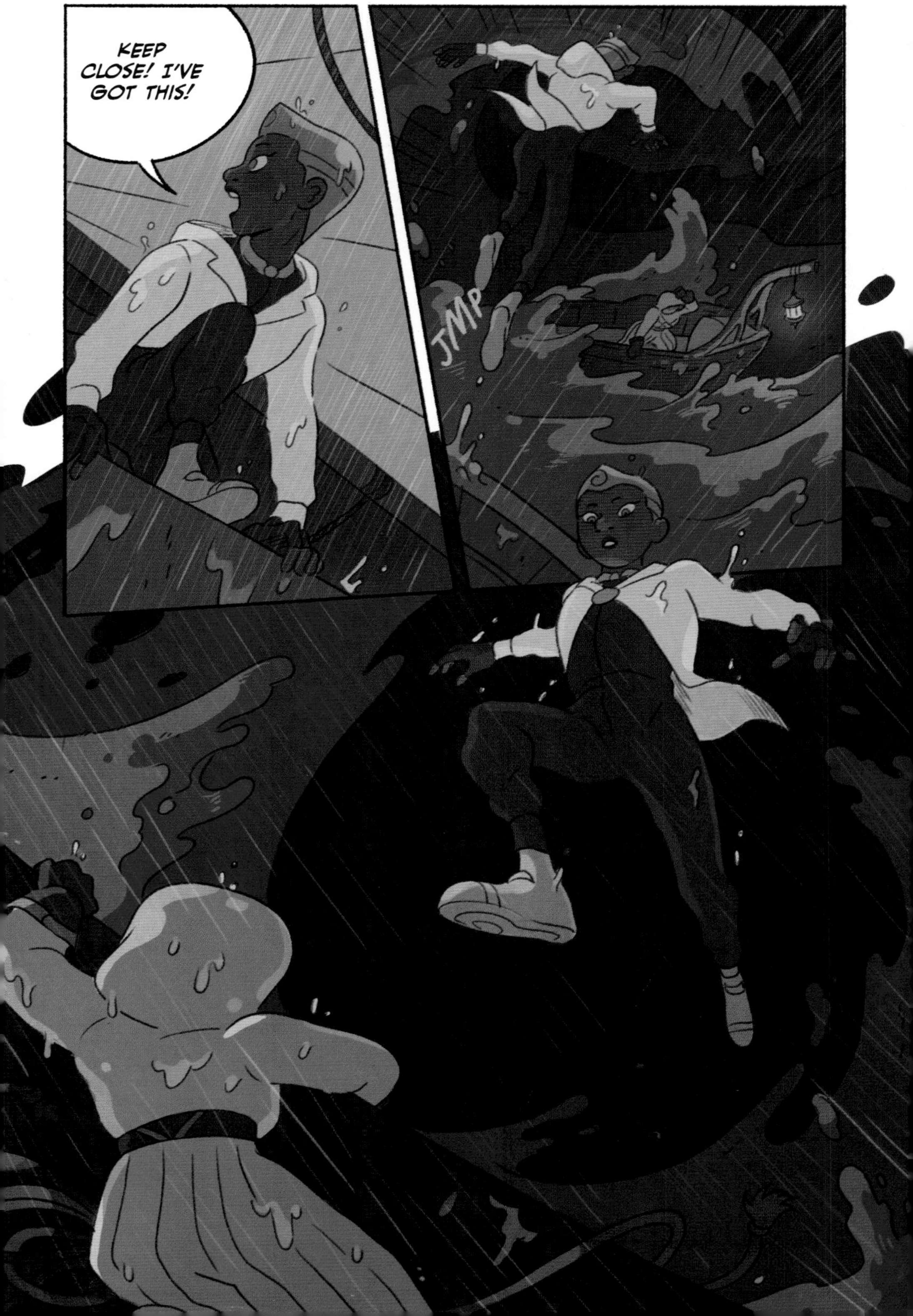
KEEP CLOSE! I'VE GOT THIS!
L
JMP

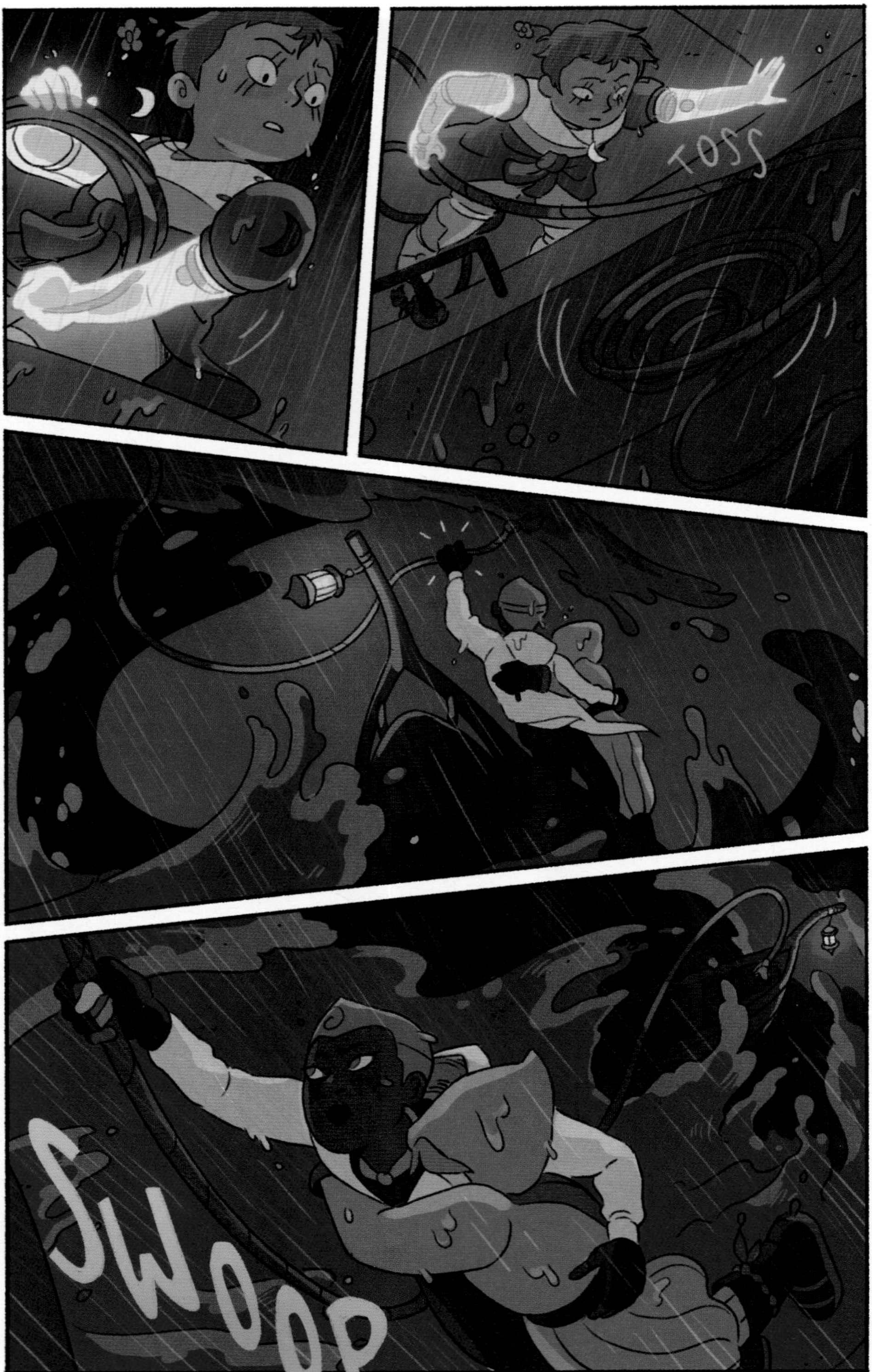
TOSS
SWOOP

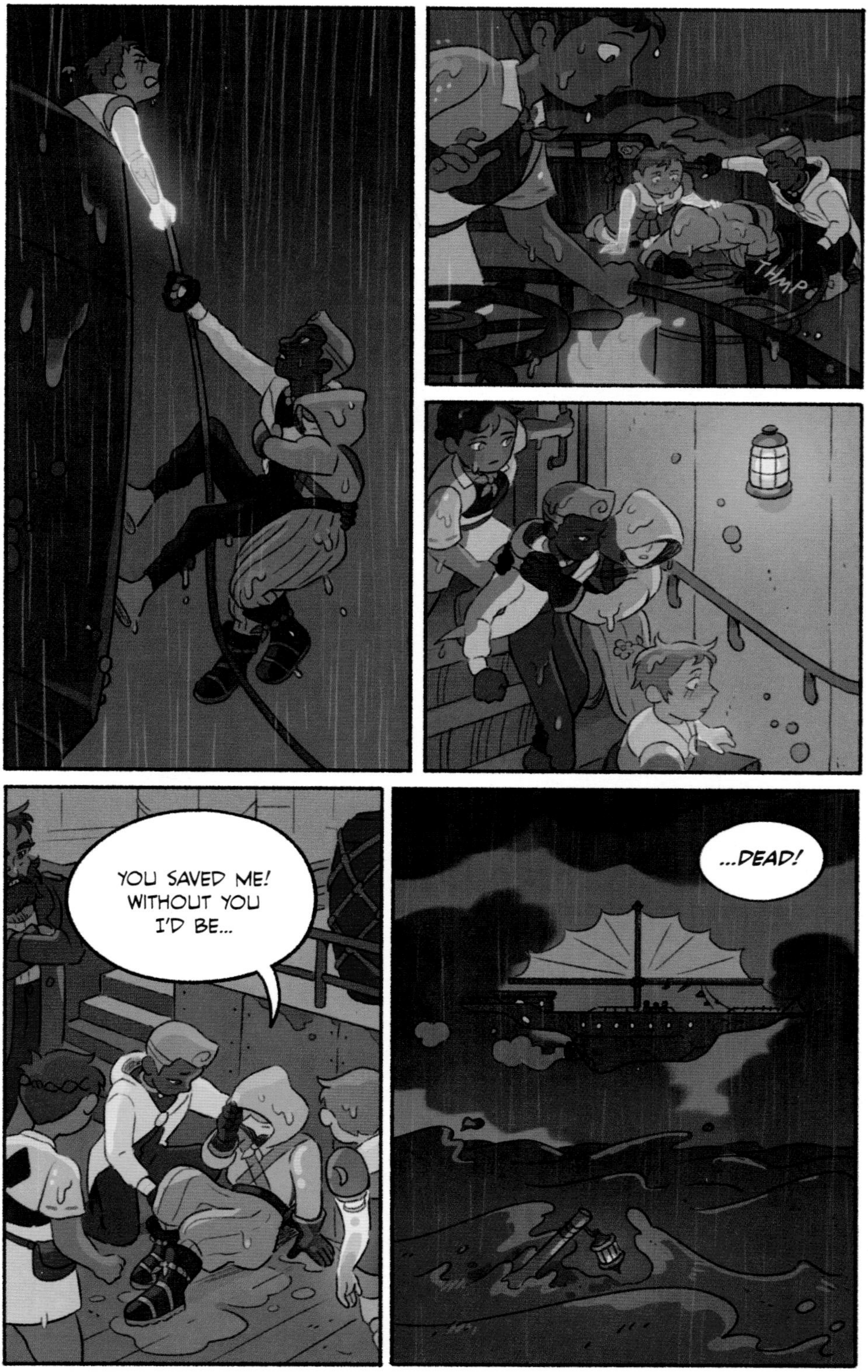
THMP
YOU SAVED ME! WITHOUT YOU I'D BE...
...DEAD!

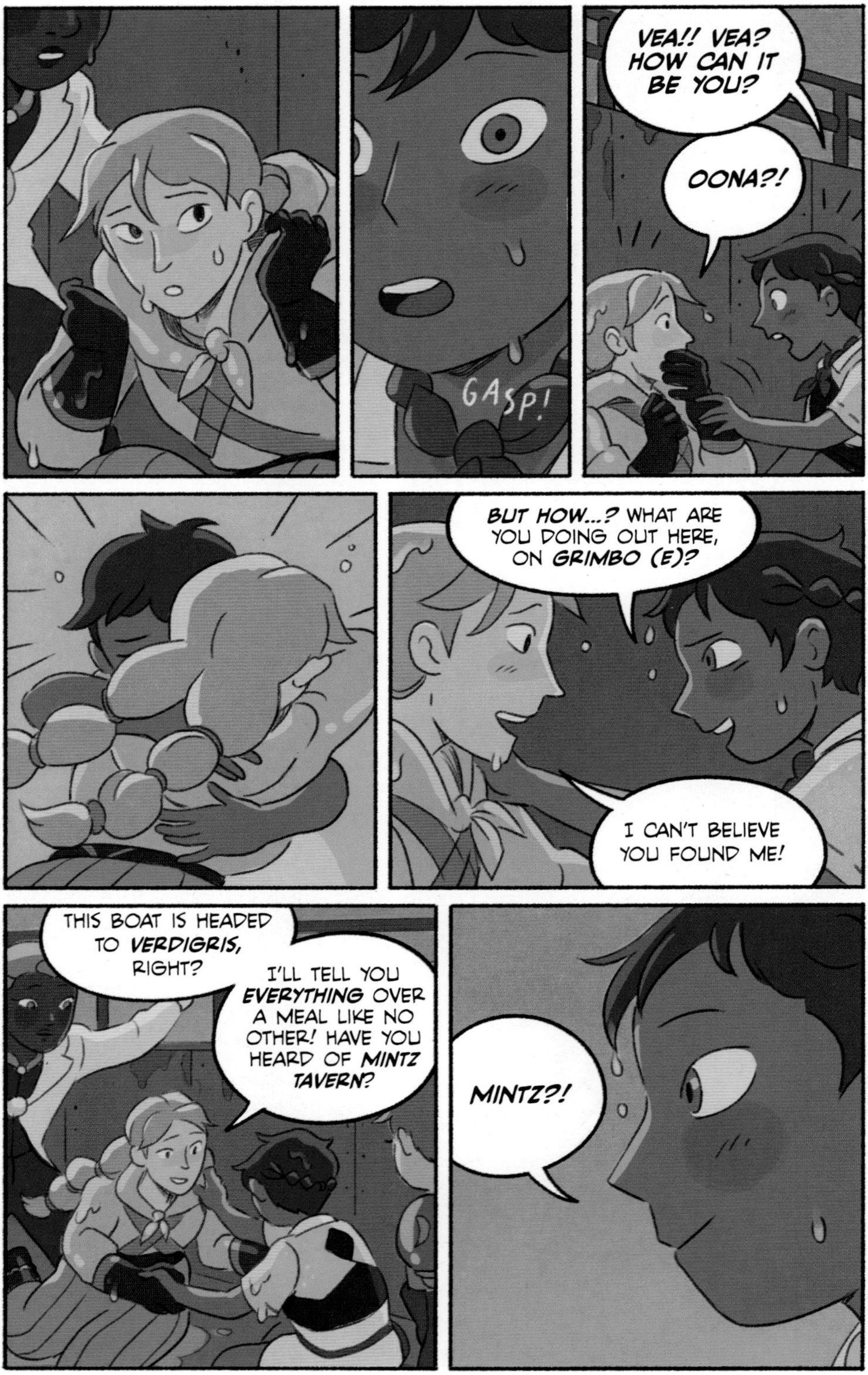
VEA!! VEA? HOW CAN IT BE YOU?
OONA?!
GASP!
BUT HOW...? WHAT ARE YOU DOING OUT HERE, ON GRIMBO (E)?
I CAN'T BELIEVE YOU FOUND ME!
THIS BOAT IS HEADED TO VERDIGRIS, RIGHT?
I'LL TELL YOU EVERYTHING OVER A MEAL LIKE NO OTHER! HAVE YOU HEARD OF MINTZ TAVERN?
MINTZ?!

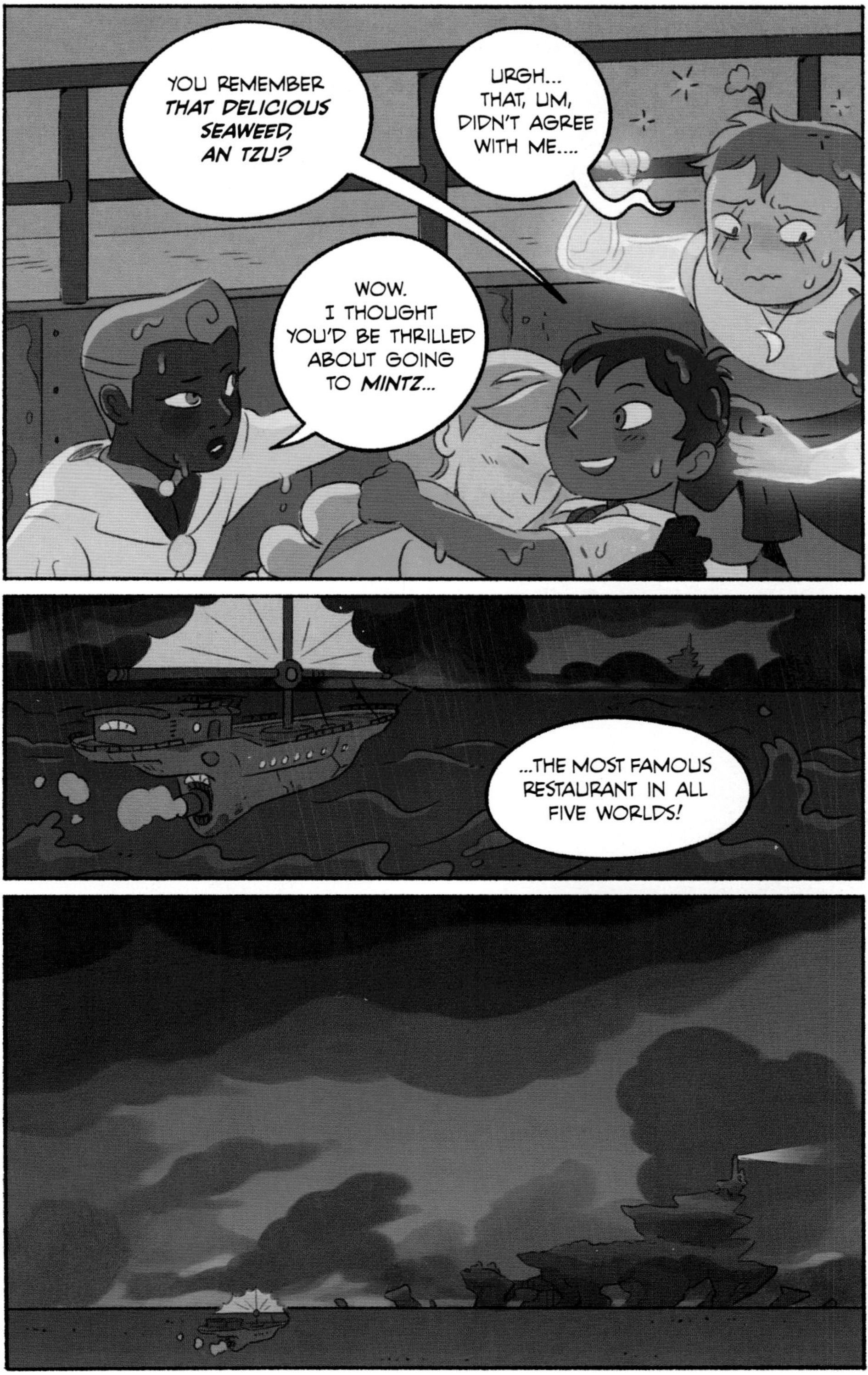
YOU REMEMBER *THAT DELICIOUS SEAWEED, AN TZU?*
URGH... THAT, UM, DIDN'T AGREE WITH ME....
WOW. I THOUGHT YOU'D BE THRILLED ABOUT GOING TO *MINTZ*...
...THE MOST FAMOUS RESTAURANT IN ALL FIVE WORLDS!

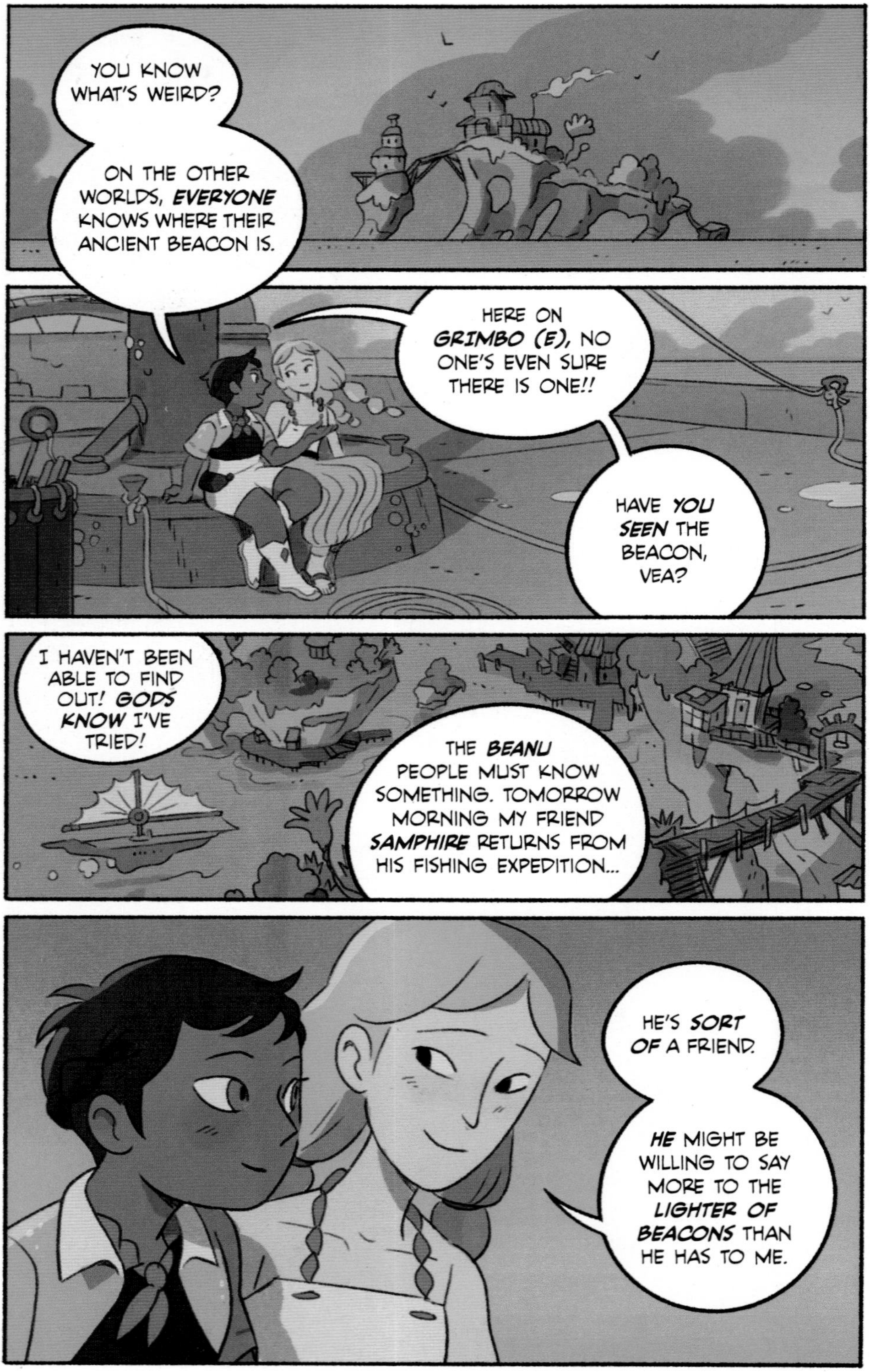
YOU KNOW WHAT'S WEIRD?
ON THE OTHER WORLDS, EVERYONE KNOWS WHERE THEIR ANCIENT BEACON IS.
HERE ON GRIMBO (E), NO ONE'S EVEN SURE THERE IS ONE!!
HAVE YOU SEEN THE BEACON, VEA?
I HAVEN'T BEEN ABLE TO FIND OUT! GODS KNOW I'VE TRIED!
THE BEANU PEOPLE MUST KNOW SOMETHING. TOMORROW MORNING MY FRIEND SAMPHIRE RETURNS FROM HIS FISHING EXPEDITION...
HE'S SORT OF A FRIEND.
HE MIGHT BE WILLING TO SAY MORE TO THE LIGHTER OF BEACONS THAN HE HAS TO ME.

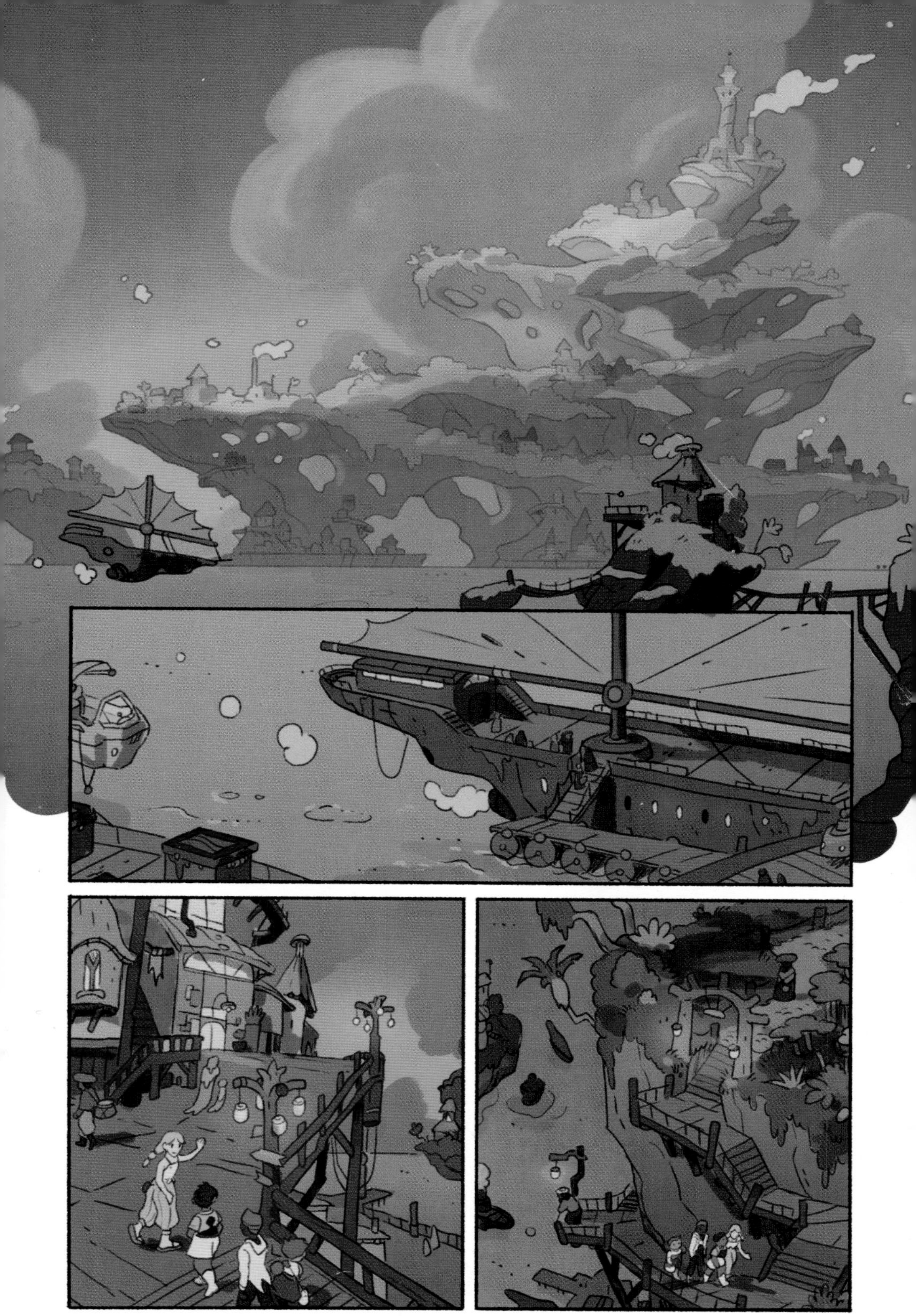

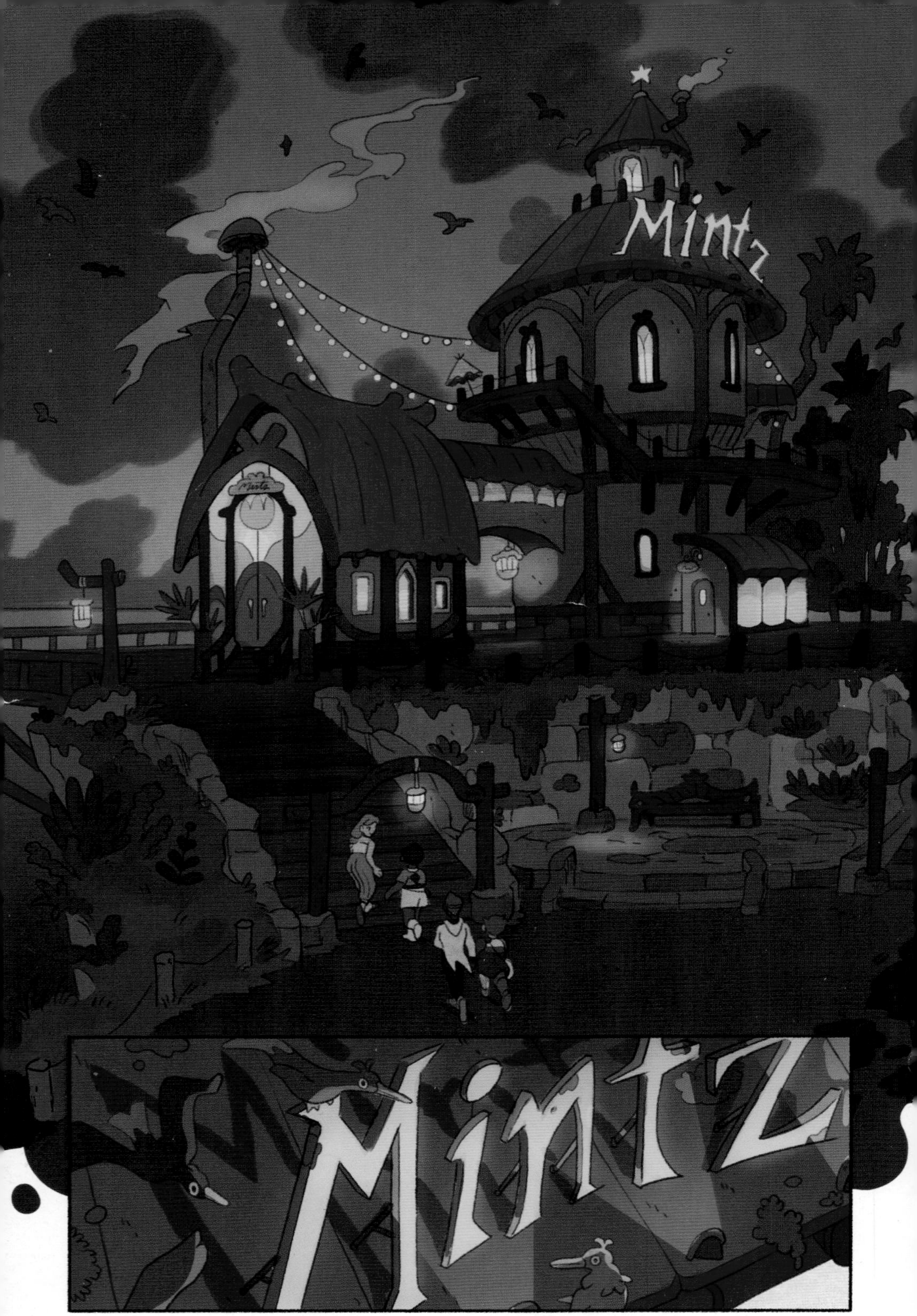
Mintz
Mintz
Mintz

CHAPTER 4

THE STRANGEST SAND

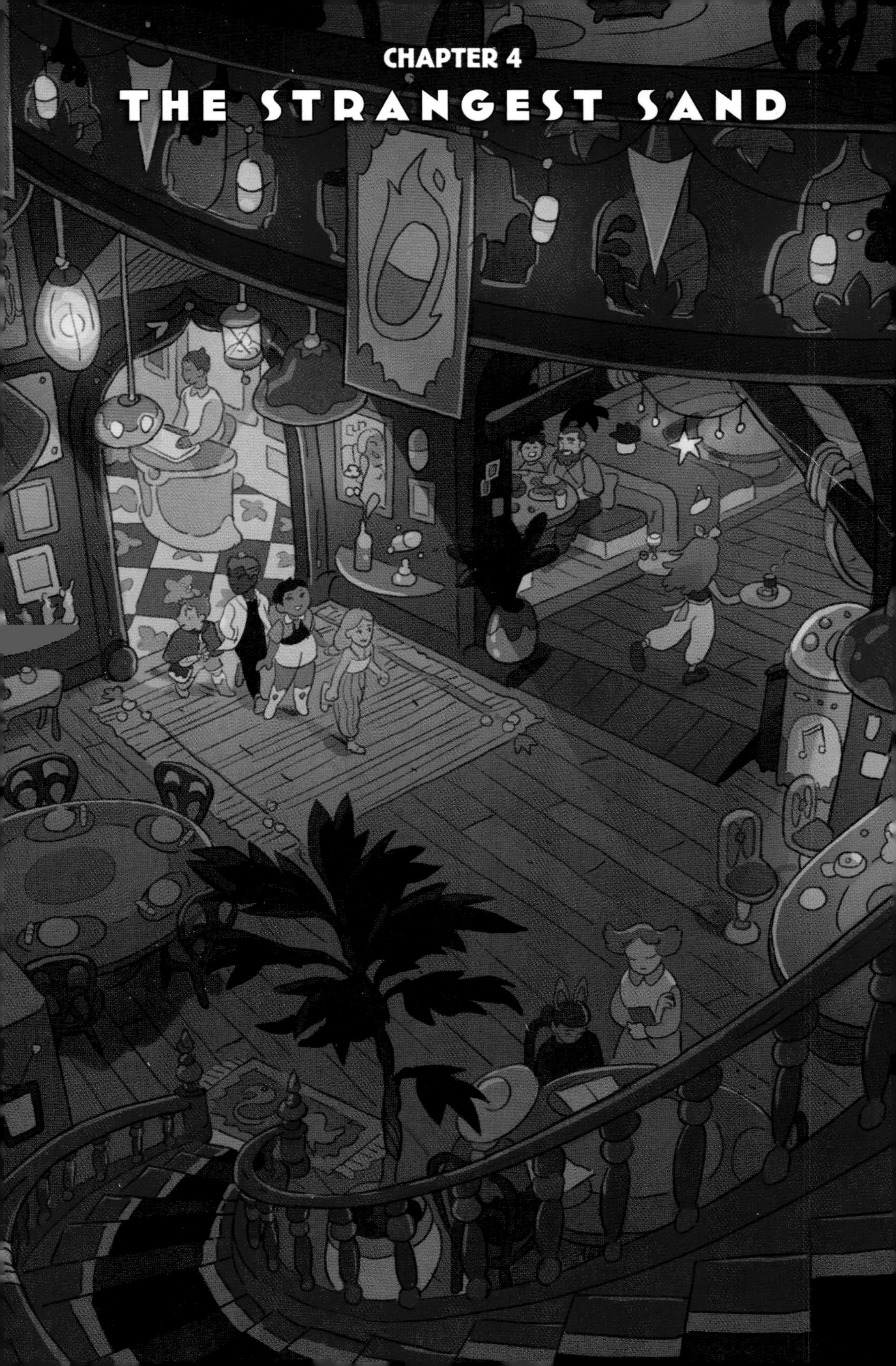

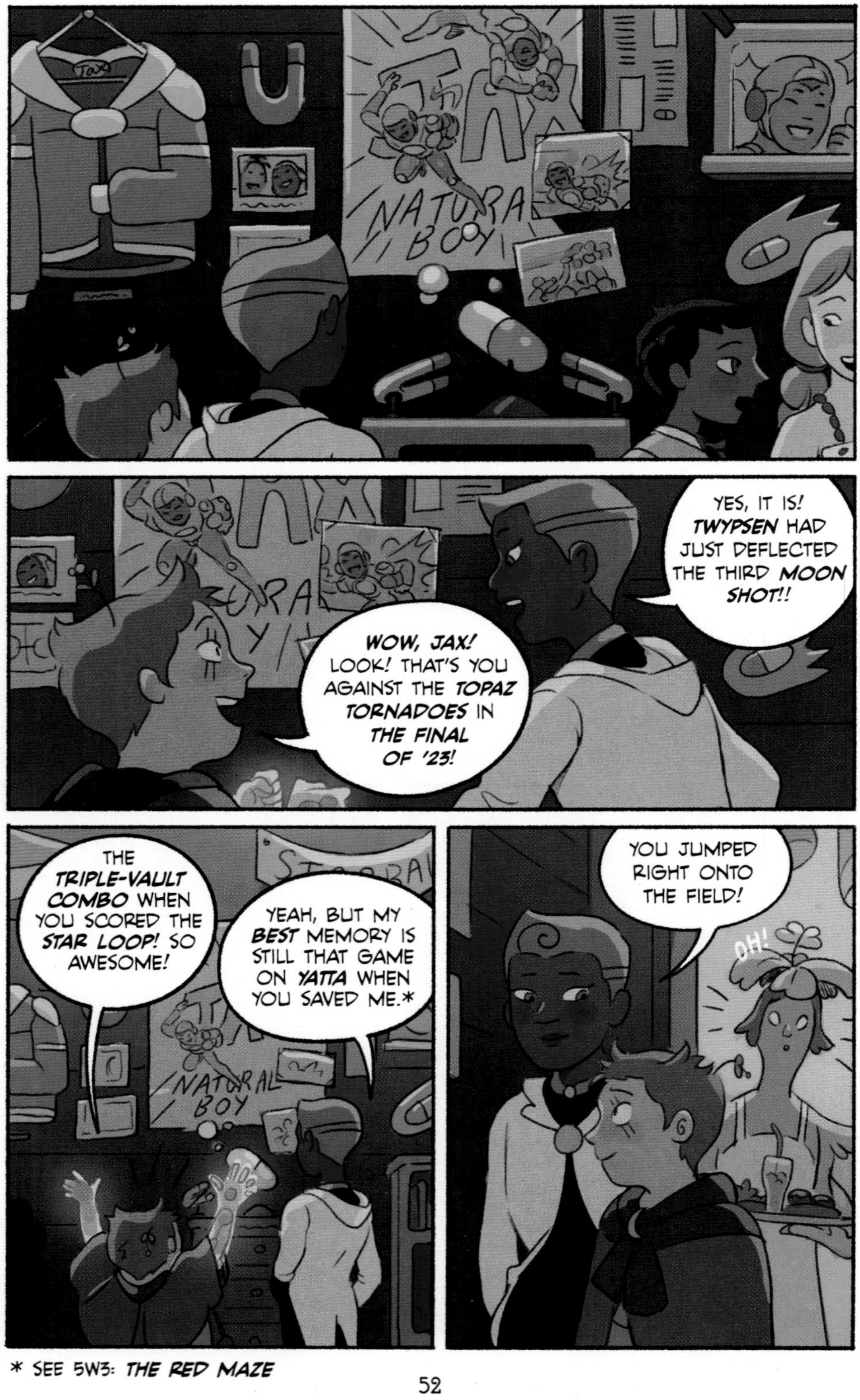
NATURAL BOY
YES, IT IS! TWYPSEN HAD JUST DEFLECTED THE THIRD MOON SHOT!!
WOW, JAX! LOOK! THAT'S YOU AGAINST THE TOPAZ TORNADOES IN THE FINAL OF '23!
THE TRIPLE-VAULT COMBO WHEN YOU SCORED THE STAR LOOP! SO AWESOME!
YEAH, BUT MY BEST MEMORY IS STILL THAT GAME ON YATTA WHEN YOU SAVED ME.*
YOU JUMPED RIGHT ONTO THE FIELD!
OH!

* SEE 5W3: *THE RED MAZE*

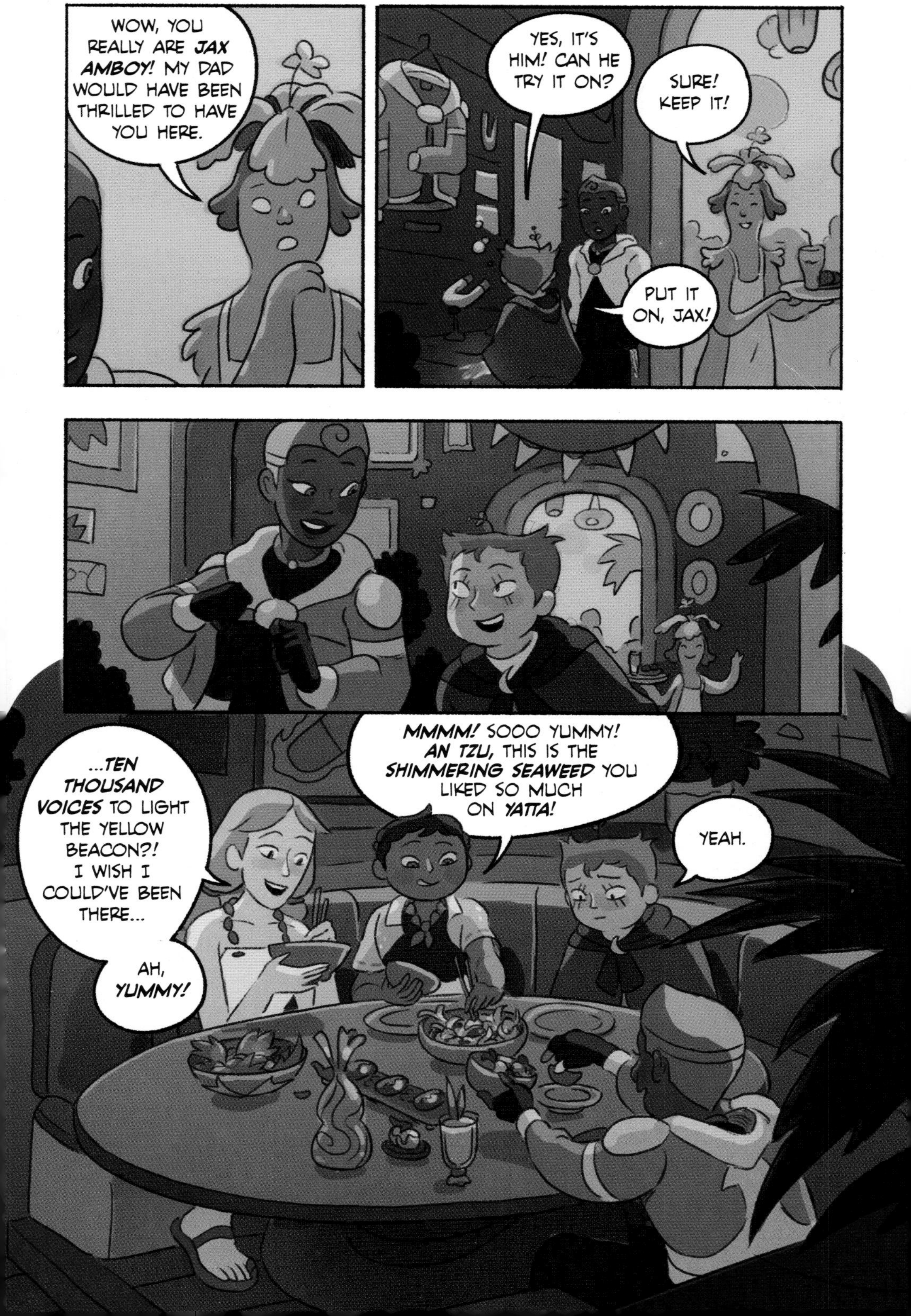
WOW, YOU REALLY ARE JAX AMBOY! MY DAD WOULD HAVE BEEN THRILLED TO HAVE YOU HERE.
YES, IT'S HIM! CAN HE TRY IT ON?
SURE! KEEP IT!
PUT IT ON, JAX!
...TEN THOUSAND VOICES TO LIGHT THE YELLOW BEACON?! I WISH I COULD'VE BEEN THERE...
MMMM! SOOO YUMMY! AN TZU, THIS IS THE SHIMMERING SEAWEED YOU LIKED SO MUCH ON YATTA!
YEAH.
AH, YUMMY!

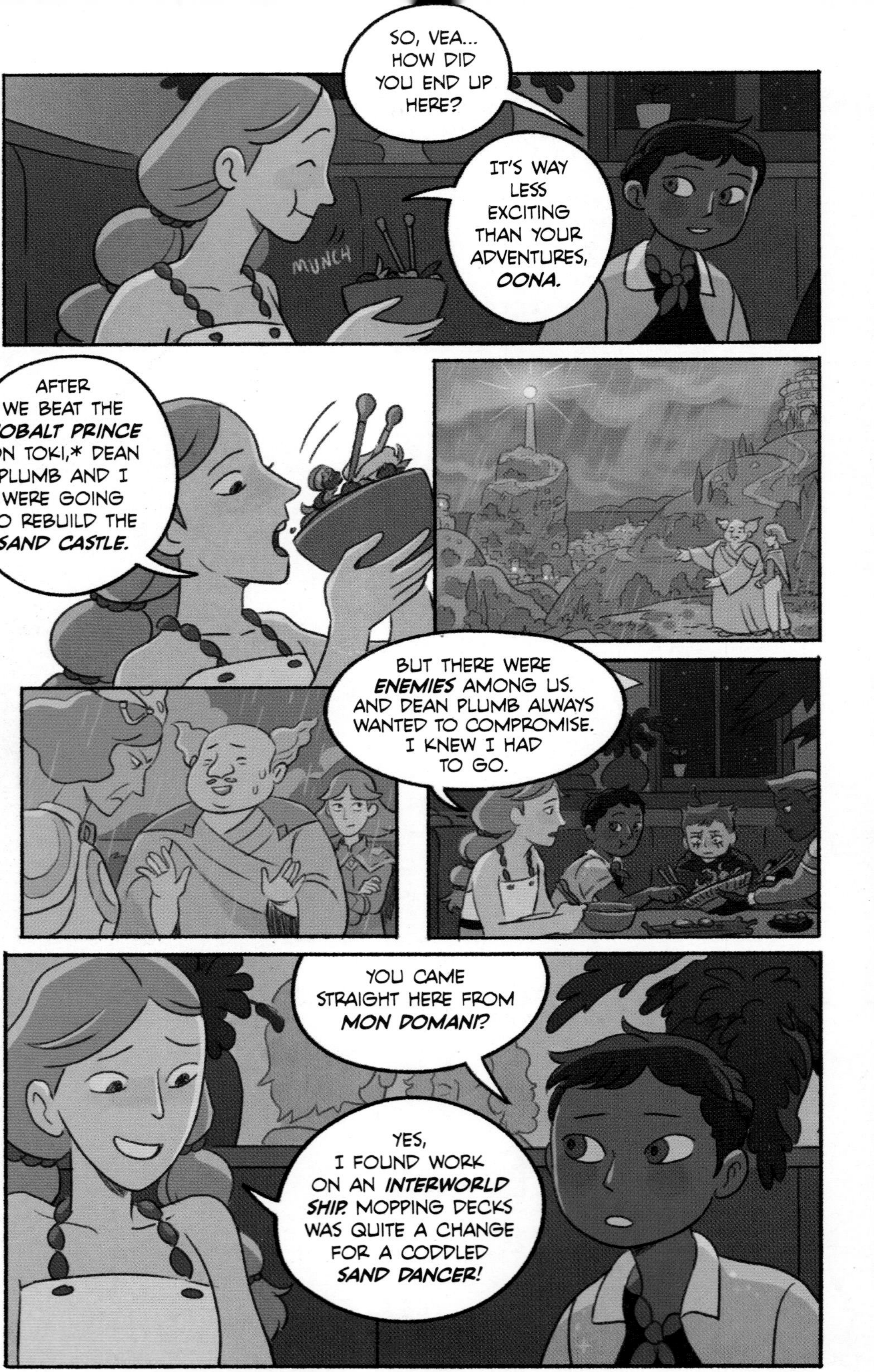
SO, VEA... HOW DID YOU END UP HERE?
IT'S WAY LESS EXCITING THAN YOUR ADVENTURES, OONA.
MUNCH
AFTER WE BEAT THE COBALT PRINCE ON TOKI,* DEAN PLUMB AND I WERE GOING TO REBUILD THE SAND CASTLE.
BUT THERE WERE ENEMIES AMONG US. AND DEAN PLUMB ALWAYS WANTED TO COMPROMISE. I KNEW I HAD TO GO.
YOU CAME STRAIGHT HERE FROM MON DOMANI?
YES, I FOUND WORK ON AN INTERWORLD SHIP. MOPPING DECKS WAS QUITE A CHANGE FOR A CODDLED SAND DANCER!

* SEE 5W2: *THE COBALT PRINCE*

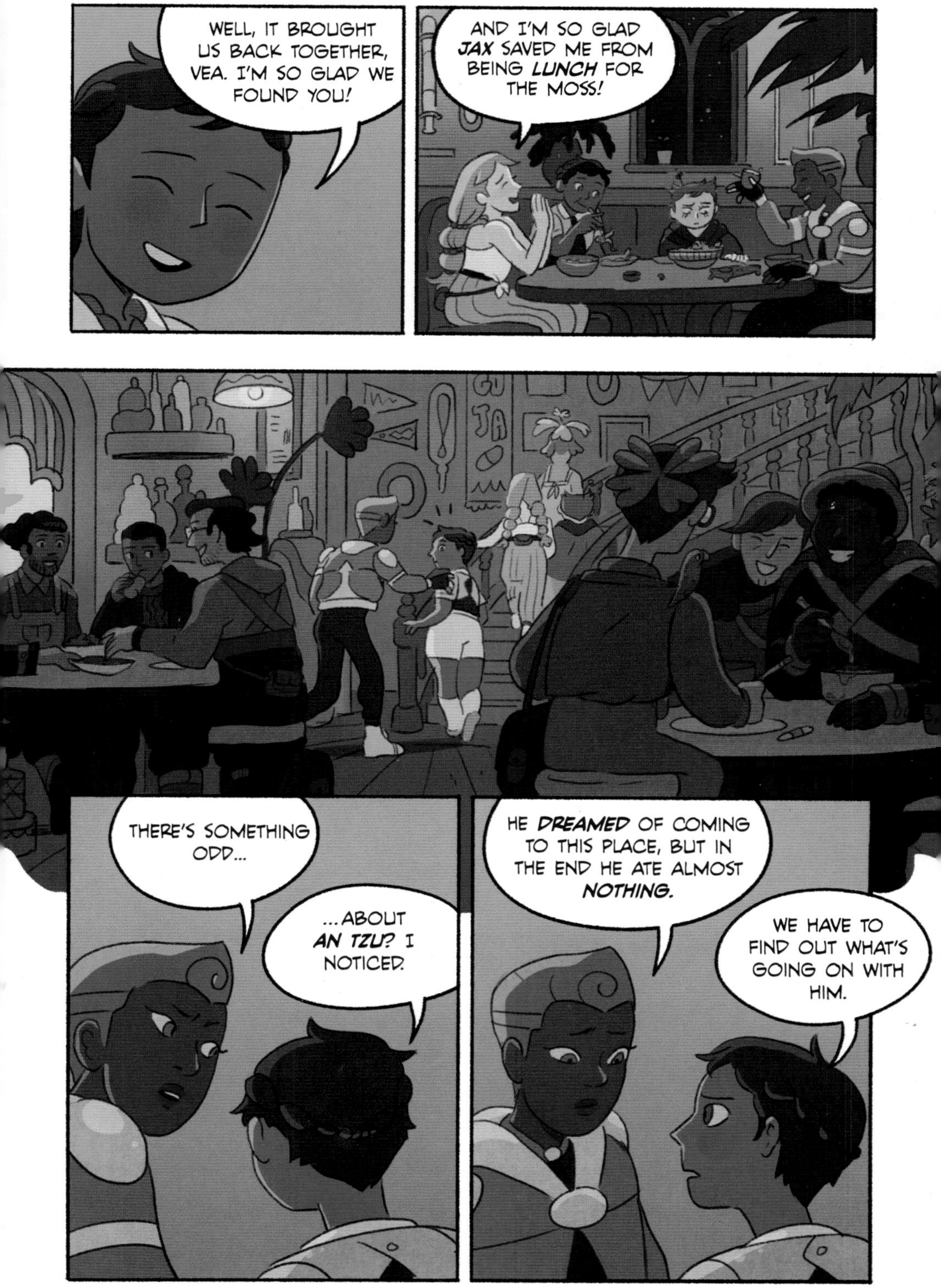
WELL, IT BROUGHT US BACK TOGETHER, VEA. I'M SO GLAD WE FOUND YOU!
AND I'M SO GLAD JAX SAVED ME FROM BEING LUNCH FOR THE MOSS!
THERE'S SOMETHING ODD...
...ABOUT AN TZU? I NOTICED.
HE DREAMED OF COMING TO THIS PLACE, BUT IN THE END HE ATE ALMOST NOTHING.
WE HAVE TO FIND OUT WHAT'S GOING ON WITH HIM.

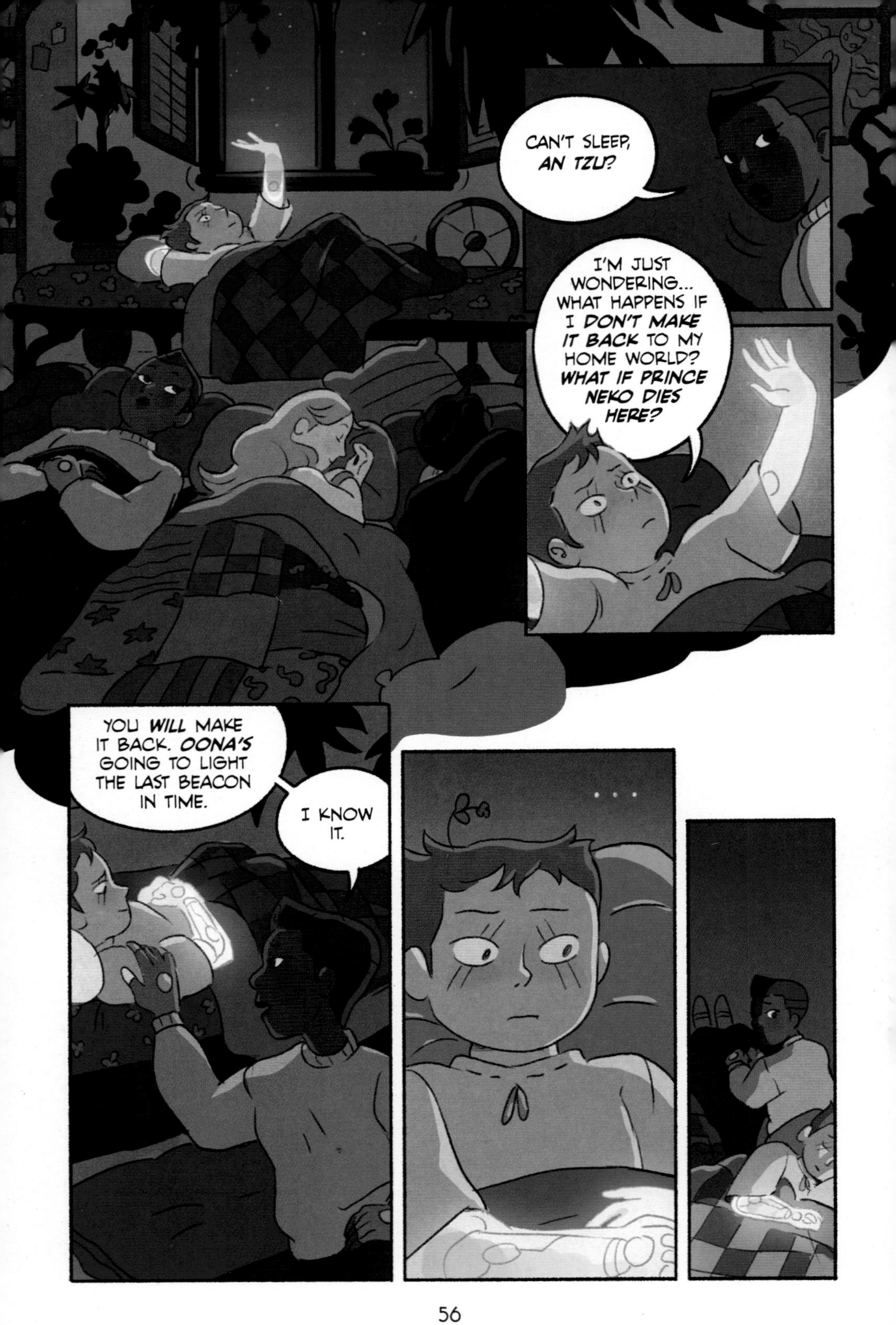
CAN'T SLEEP, AN TZU?
I'M JUST WONDERING... WHAT HAPPENS IF I DON'T MAKE IT BACK TO MY HOME WORLD? WHAT IF PRINCE NEKO DIES HERE?
YOU WILL MAKE IT BACK. OONA'S GOING TO LIGHT THE LAST BEACON IN TIME.
I KNOW IT.

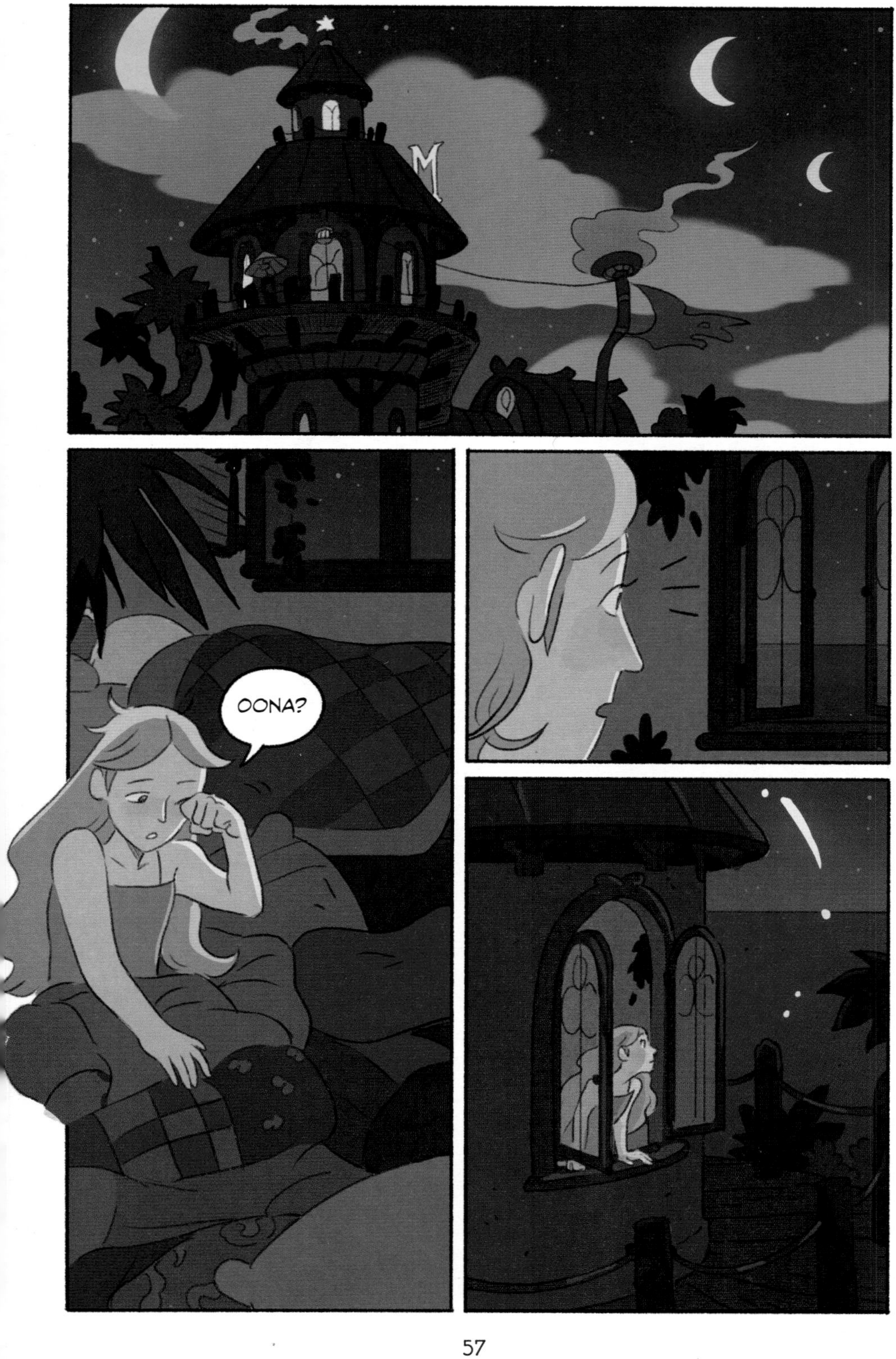
OONA?

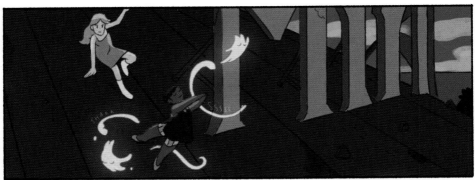

YOUR *ANIFORMS* DON'T RUN AWAY FROM YOU ANYMORE.

THEY HAD TO GET MY ATTENTION BACK THEN.

WOW, YOU'RE SO *FLUID* NOW, OONA.... I CAN'T TELL IF *YOU'RE* DANCING THE SAND OR IF *THE SAND IS DANCING YOU.*

I'VE ONLY WORKED WITH *MON DOMANI* AND *TOKI* SAND. WHAT ARE THE RED AND YELLOW SANDS LIKE?

THEY RESPOND TO DIFFERENT THINGS. TO UNLOCK *MOON YATTA'S* SAND, I HAD TO FILL UP WITH *JOY.*

AND THEN IT WAS INCREDIBLE! I COULD JUMP TO THE OTHER SIDE OF THE MOON!

I CAN OPEN *PORTALS* NOW!!

WOW, PORTALS!!

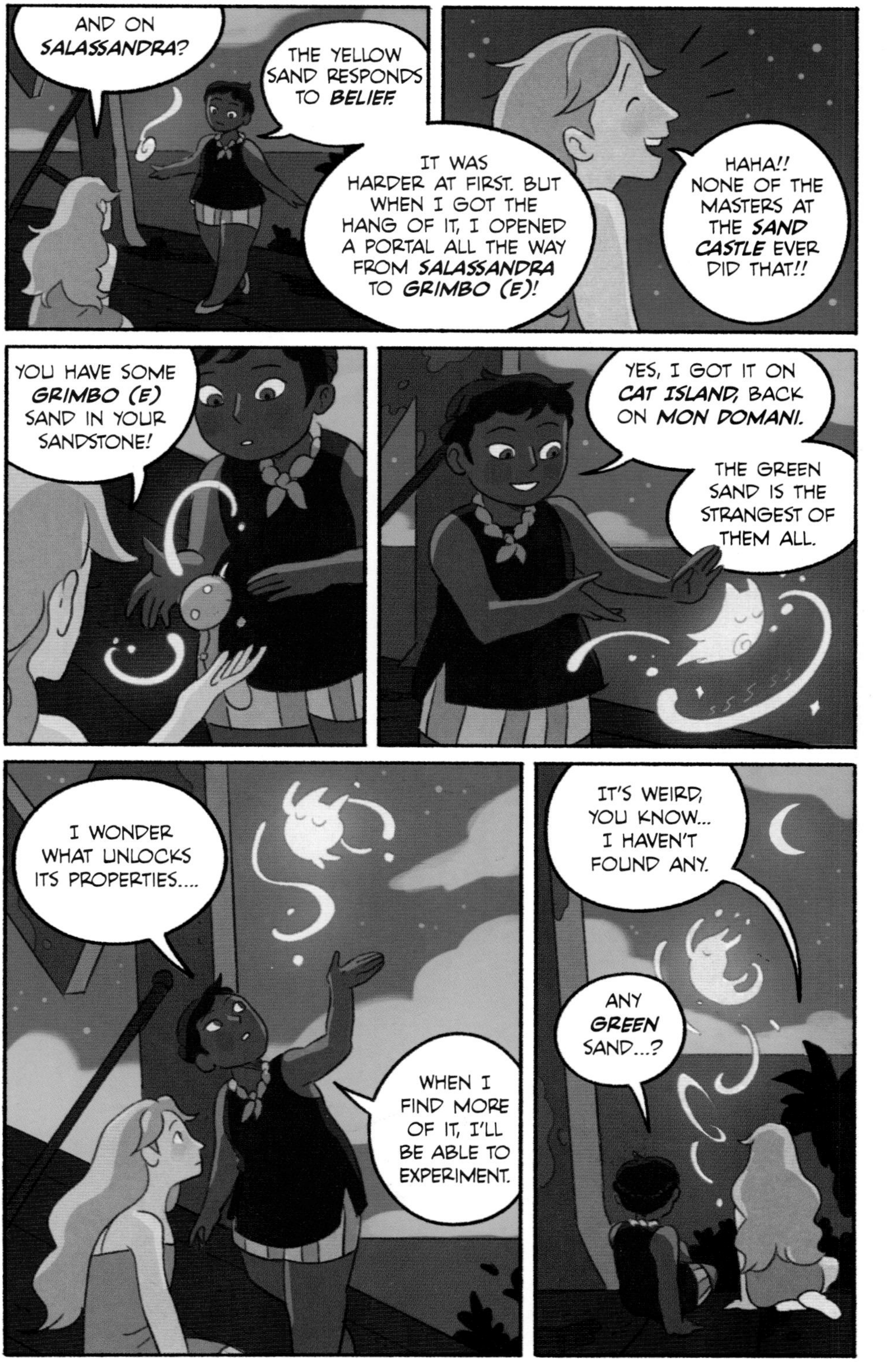
AND ON *SALASSANDRA?*
THE YELLOW SAND RESPONDS TO *BELIEF.*
IT WAS HARDER AT FIRST. BUT WHEN I GOT THE HANG OF IT, I OPENED A PORTAL ALL THE WAY FROM *SALASSANDRA* TO *GRIMBO (E)!*
HAHA!! NONE OF THE MASTERS AT THE *SAND CASTLE* EVER DID THAT!!
YOU HAVE SOME *GRIMBO (E)* SAND IN YOUR SANDSTONE!
YES, I GOT IT ON *CAT ISLAND,* BACK ON *MON DOMANI.*
THE GREEN SAND IS THE STRANGEST OF THEM ALL.
I WONDER WHAT UNLOCKS ITS PROPERTIES....
WHEN I FIND MORE OF IT, I'LL BE ABLE TO EXPERIMENT.
IT'S WEIRD, YOU KNOW... I HAVEN'T FOUND ANY.
ANY *GREEN* SAND...?

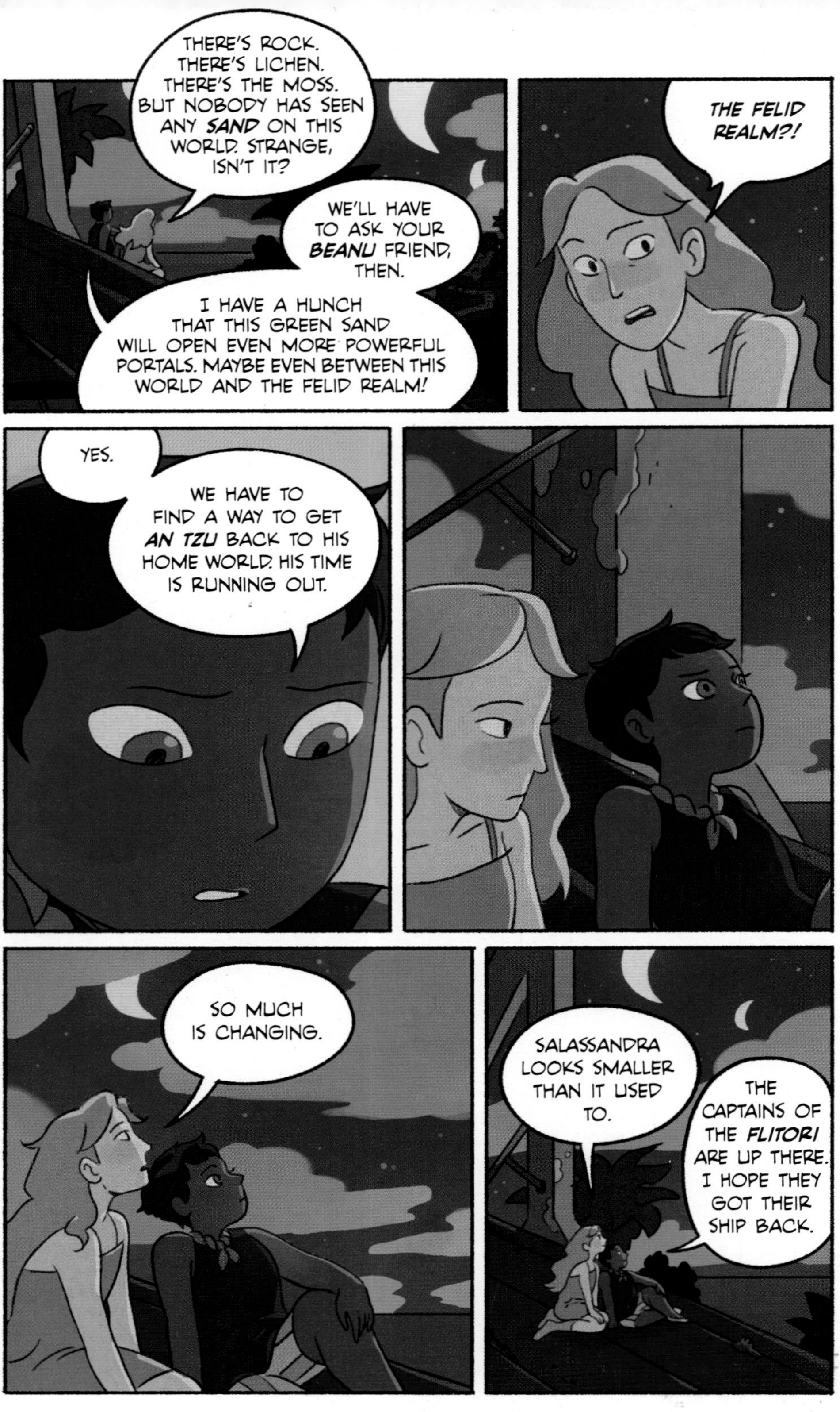
THERE'S ROCK. THERE'S LICHEN. THERE'S THE MOSS. BUT NOBODY HAS SEEN ANY *SAND* ON THIS WORLD. STRANGE, ISN'T IT?
WE'LL HAVE TO ASK YOUR *BEANU* FRIEND, THEN.
I HAVE A HUNCH THAT THIS GREEN SAND WILL OPEN EVEN MORE POWERFUL PORTALS. MAYBE EVEN BETWEEN THIS WORLD AND THE FELID REALM!
THE FELID REALM?!
YES.
WE HAVE TO FIND A WAY TO GET *AN TZU* BACK TO HIS HOME WORLD. HIS TIME IS RUNNING OUT.
SO MUCH IS CHANGING.
SALASSANDRA LOOKS SMALLER THAN IT USED TO.
THE CAPTAINS OF THE *FLITORI* ARE UP THERE. I HOPE THEY GOT THEIR SHIP BACK.

CHAPTER 5

SAMPHIRE DOES NOT TELL

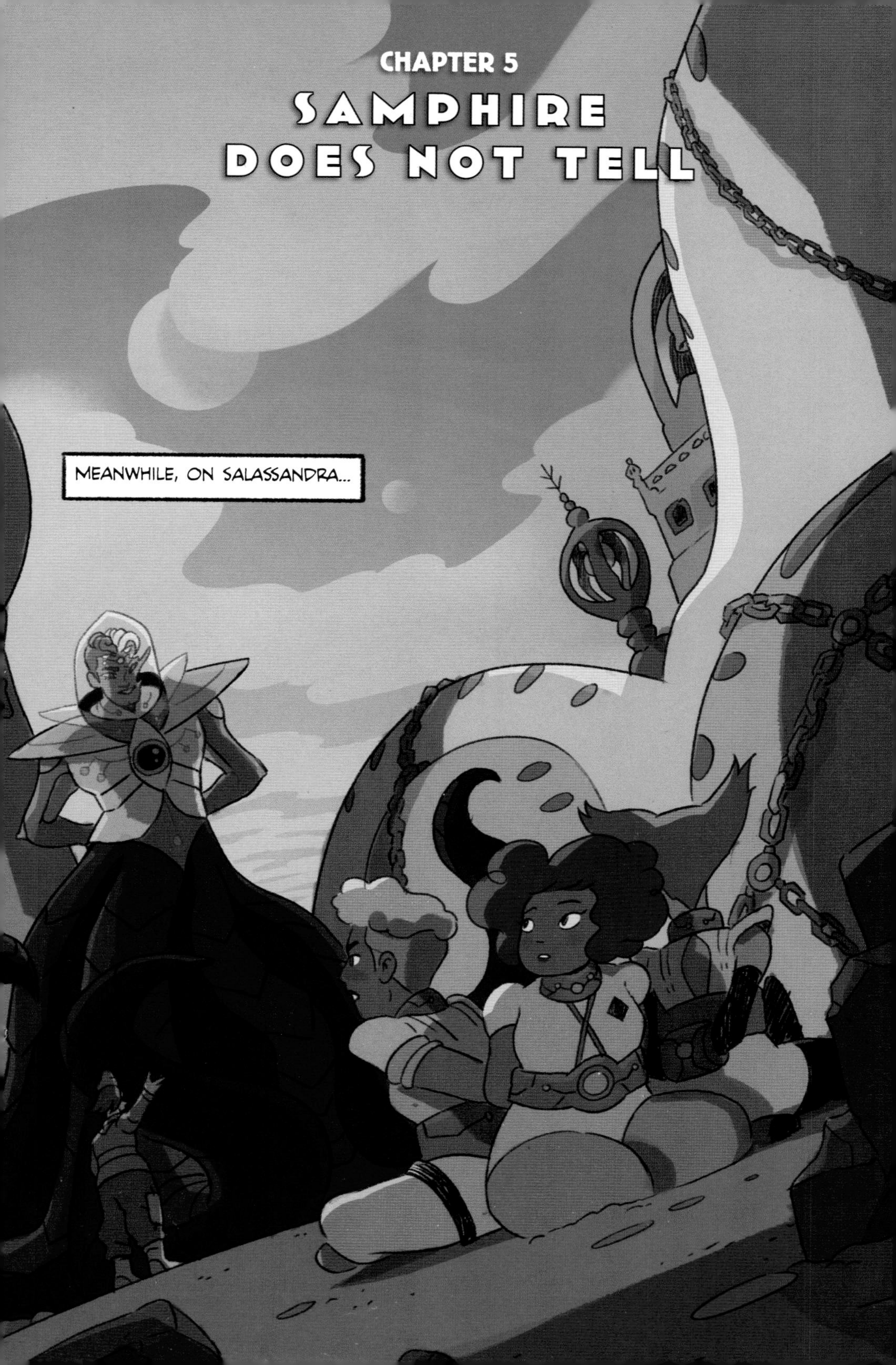
MEANWHILE, ON SALASSANDRA...

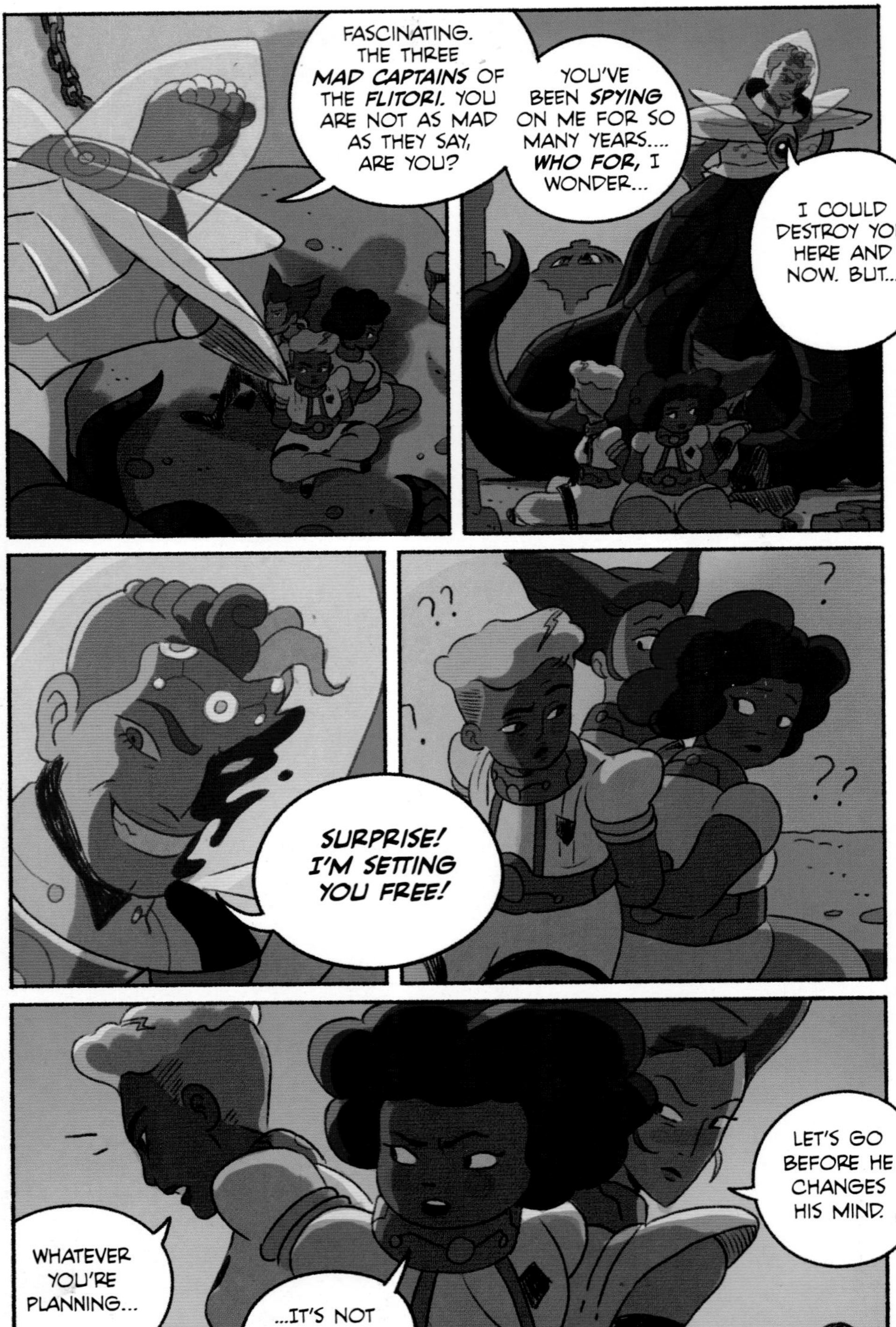
FASCINATING. THE THREE MAD CAPTAINS OF THE FLITORI. YOU ARE NOT AS MAD AS THEY SAY, ARE YOU?
YOU'VE BEEN SPYING ON ME FOR SO MANY YEARS.... WHO FOR, I WONDER...
I COULD DESTROY YOU HERE AND NOW. BUT...
SURPRISE! I'M SETTING YOU FREE!
??
?
??
LET'S GO BEFORE HE CHANGES HIS MIND.
WHATEVER YOU'RE PLANNING...
...IT'S NOT GOING TO WORK!

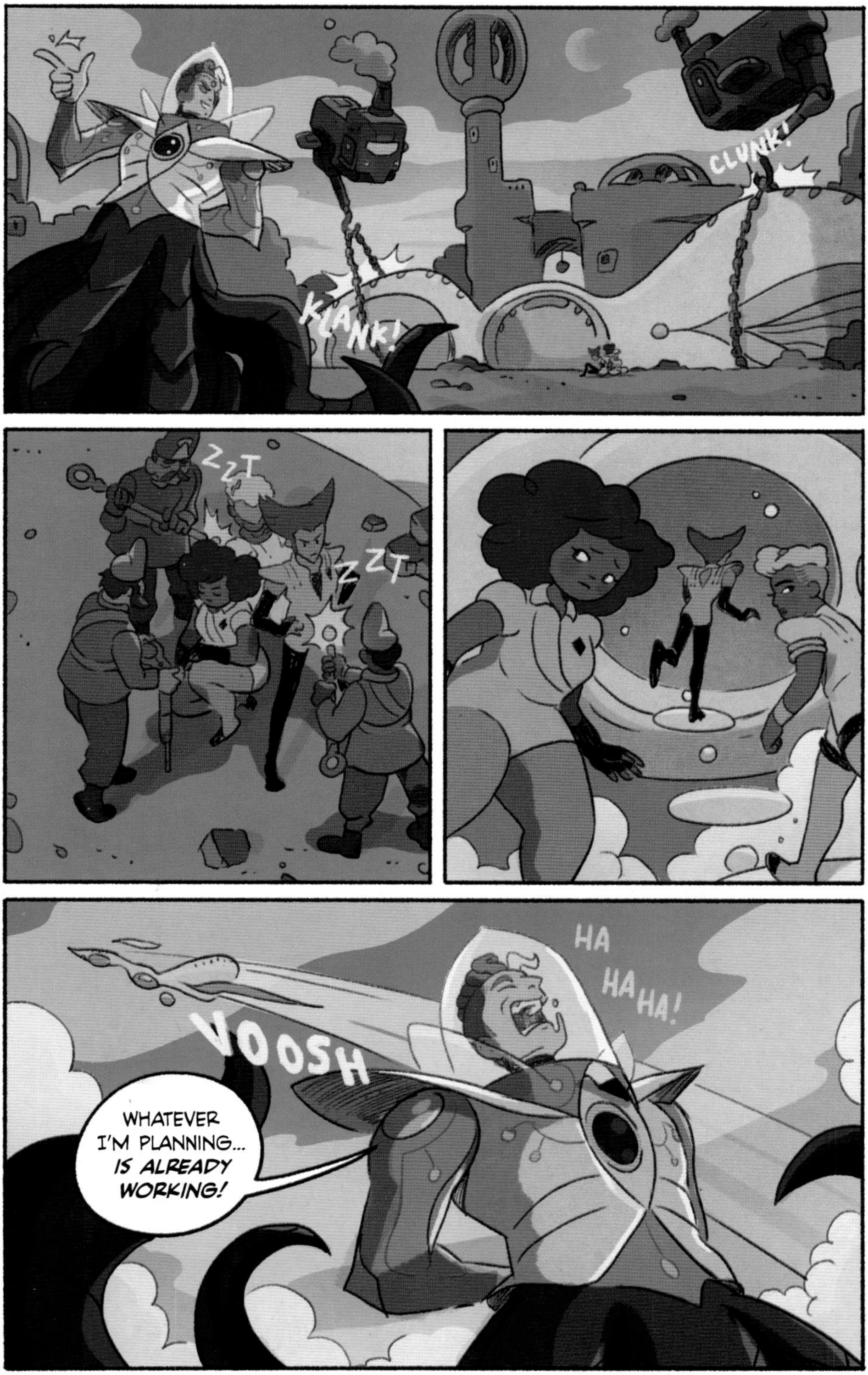
CLUNK!
KLANK!
ZZT
ZZT
VOOSH
HA
HA HA HA!
WHATEVER I'M PLANNING... *IS ALREADY WORKING!*

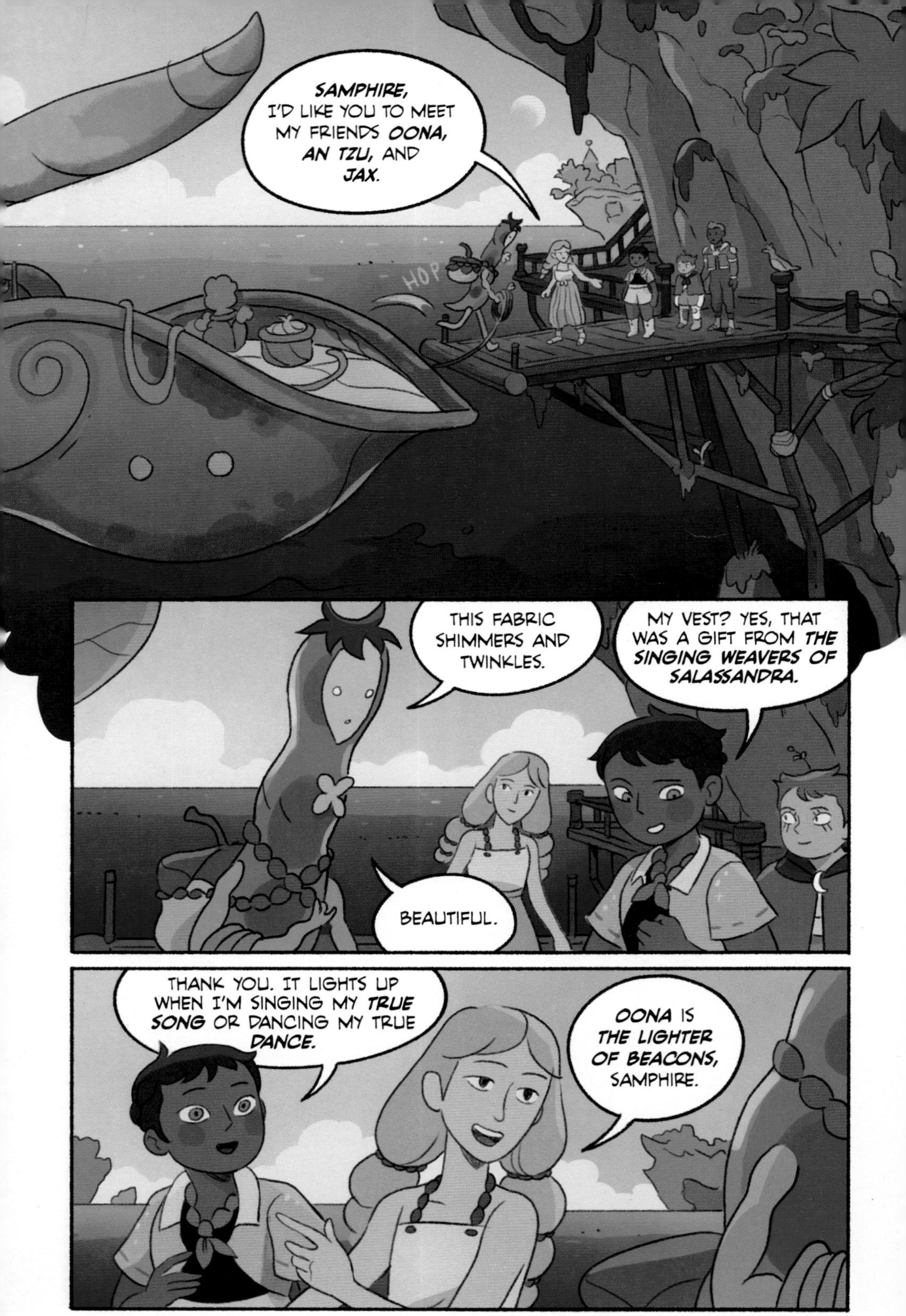
SAMPHIRE, I'D LIKE YOU TO MEET MY FRIENDS OONA, AN TZU, AND JAX.
HOP
THIS FABRIC SHIMMERS AND TWINKLES.
MY VEST? YES, THAT WAS A GIFT FROM THE SINGING WEAVERS OF SALASSANDRA.
BEAUTIFUL.
THANK YOU. IT LIGHTS UP WHEN I'M SINGING MY TRUE SONG OR DANCING MY TRUE DANCE.
OONA IS THE LIGHTER OF BEACONS, SAMPHIRE.

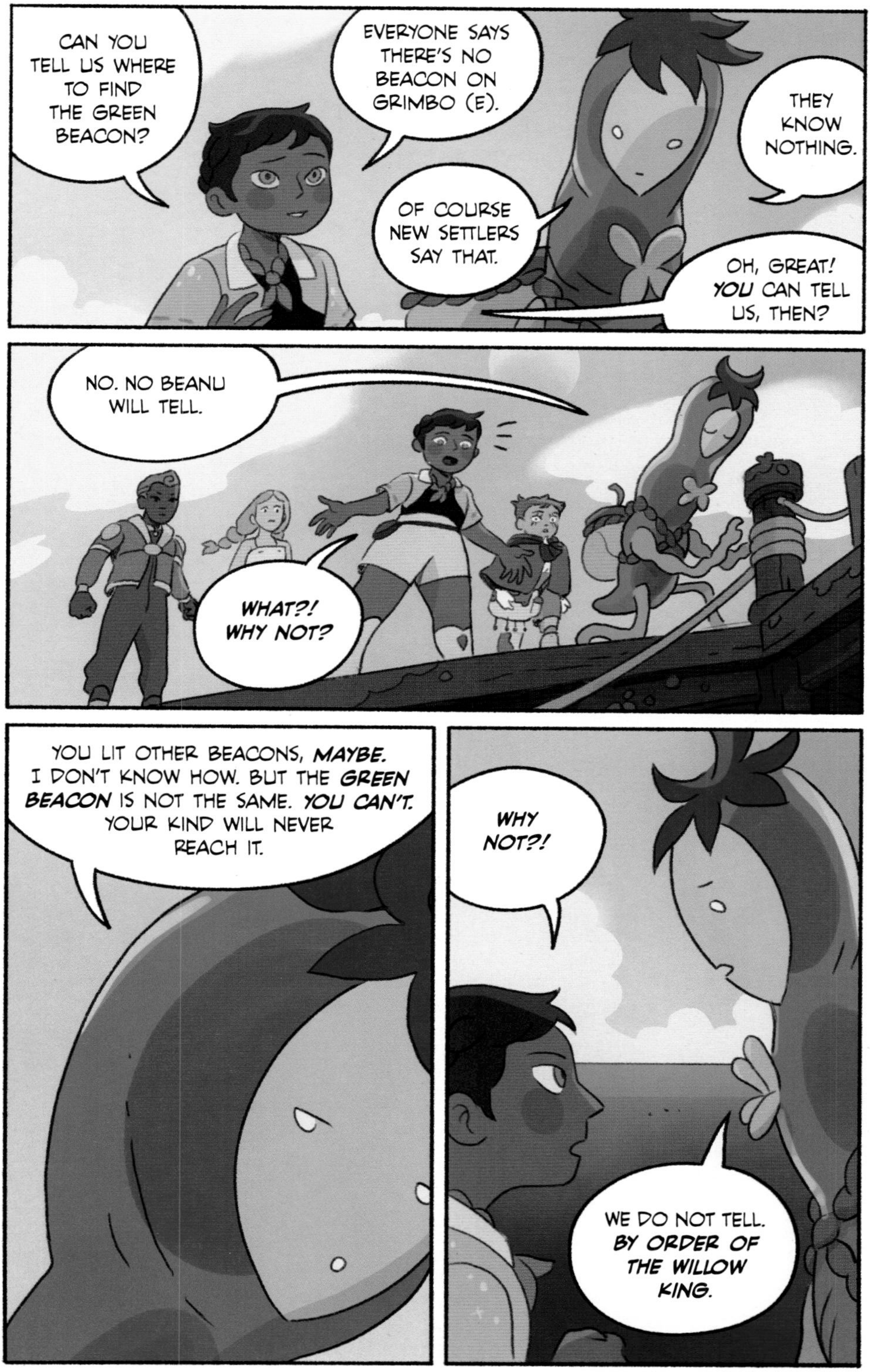
CAN YOU TELL US WHERE TO FIND THE GREEN BEACON?
EVERYONE SAYS THERE'S NO BEACON ON GRIMBO (E).
OF COURSE NEW SETTLERS SAY THAT.
THEY KNOW NOTHING.
OH, GREAT! *YOU* CAN TELL US, THEN?
NO. NO BEANU WILL TELL.
WHAT?! WHY NOT?
YOU LIT OTHER BEACONS, *MAYBE.* I DON'T KNOW HOW. BUT THE *GREEN BEACON* IS NOT THE SAME. *YOU CAN'T.* YOUR KIND WILL NEVER REACH IT.
WHY NOT?!
WE DO NOT TELL. *BY ORDER OF THE WILLOW KING.*

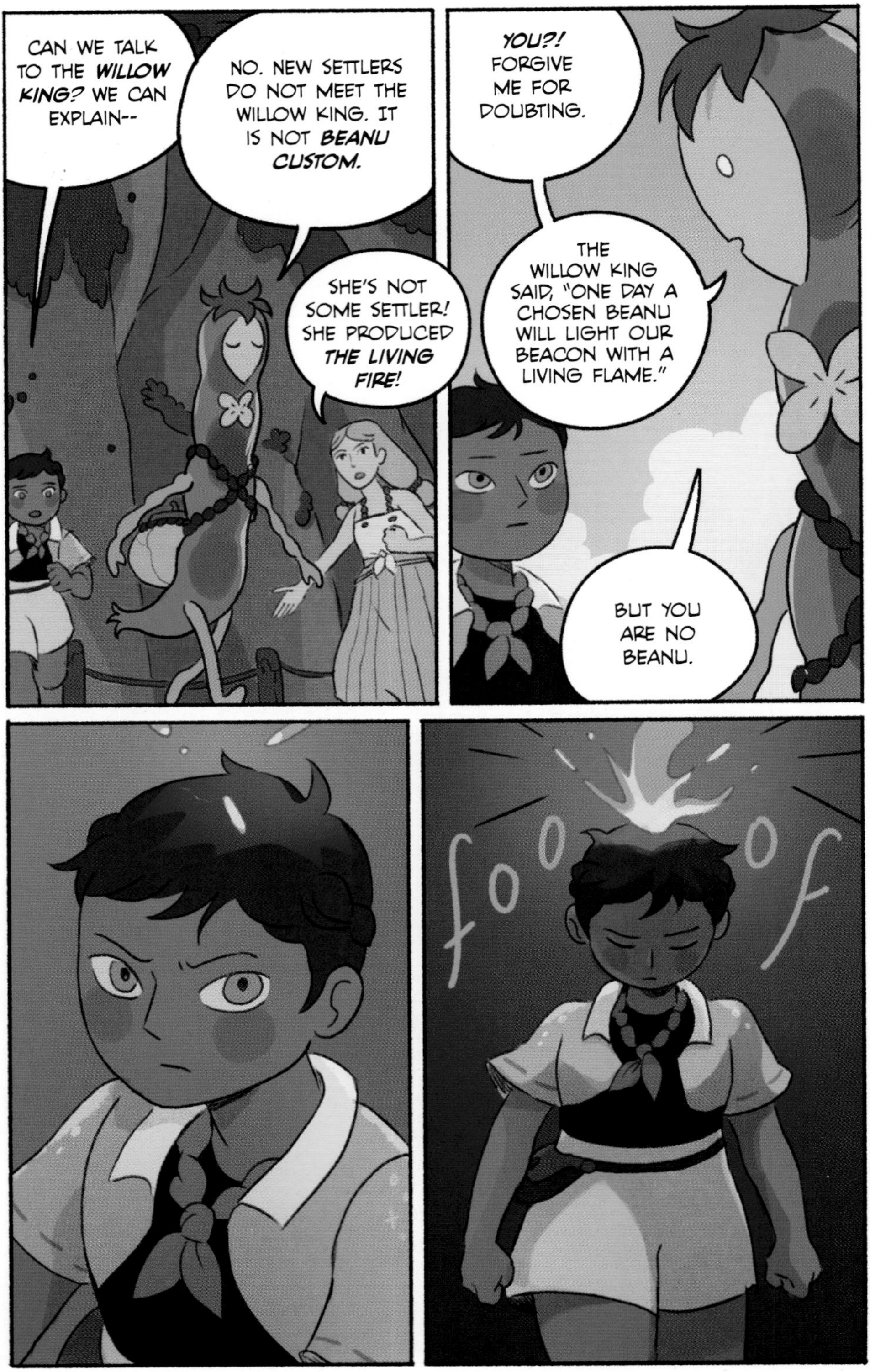
CAN WE TALK TO THE *WILLOW KING?* WE CAN EXPLAIN--
NO. NEW SETTLERS DO NOT MEET THE WILLOW KING. IT IS NOT ***BEANU CUSTOM.***
SHE'S NOT SOME SETTLER! SHE PRODUCED ***THE LIVING FIRE!***
YOU?! FORGIVE ME FOR DOUBTING.
THE WILLOW KING SAID, "ONE DAY A CHOSEN BEANU WILL LIGHT OUR BEACON WITH A LIVING FLAME."
BUT YOU ARE NO BEANU.
fooof

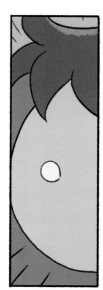

THE LIVING FIRE IS FOR EVERYONE.

THIS CHANGES... EVERYTHING.

THE GREAT WILLOW KING MUST KNOW.

I WILL BRING YOU TO HIM AT THE SACRED *FLOATING ROCK*.

CHAPTER 6
ENEMIES EVERYWHERE

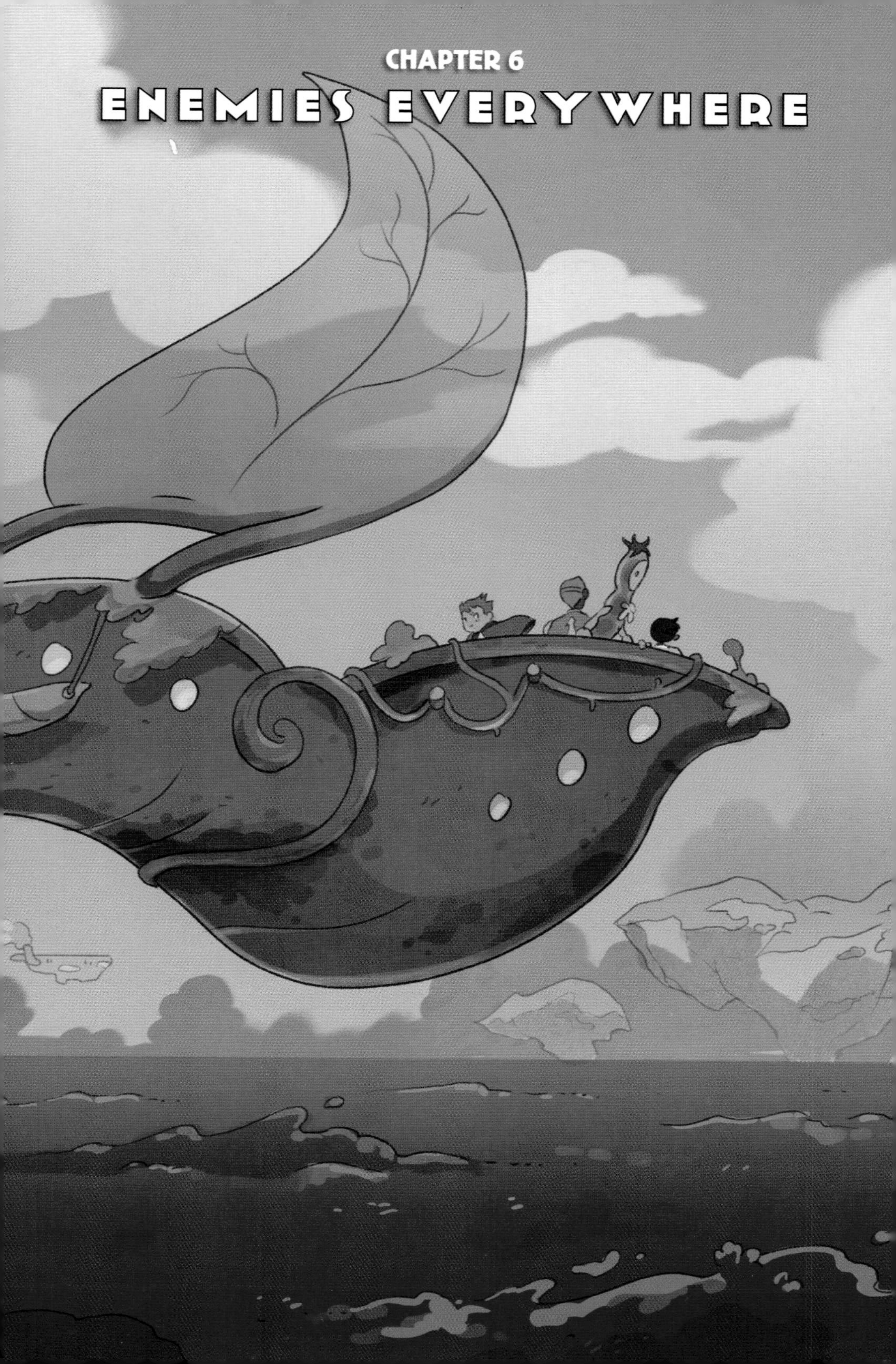

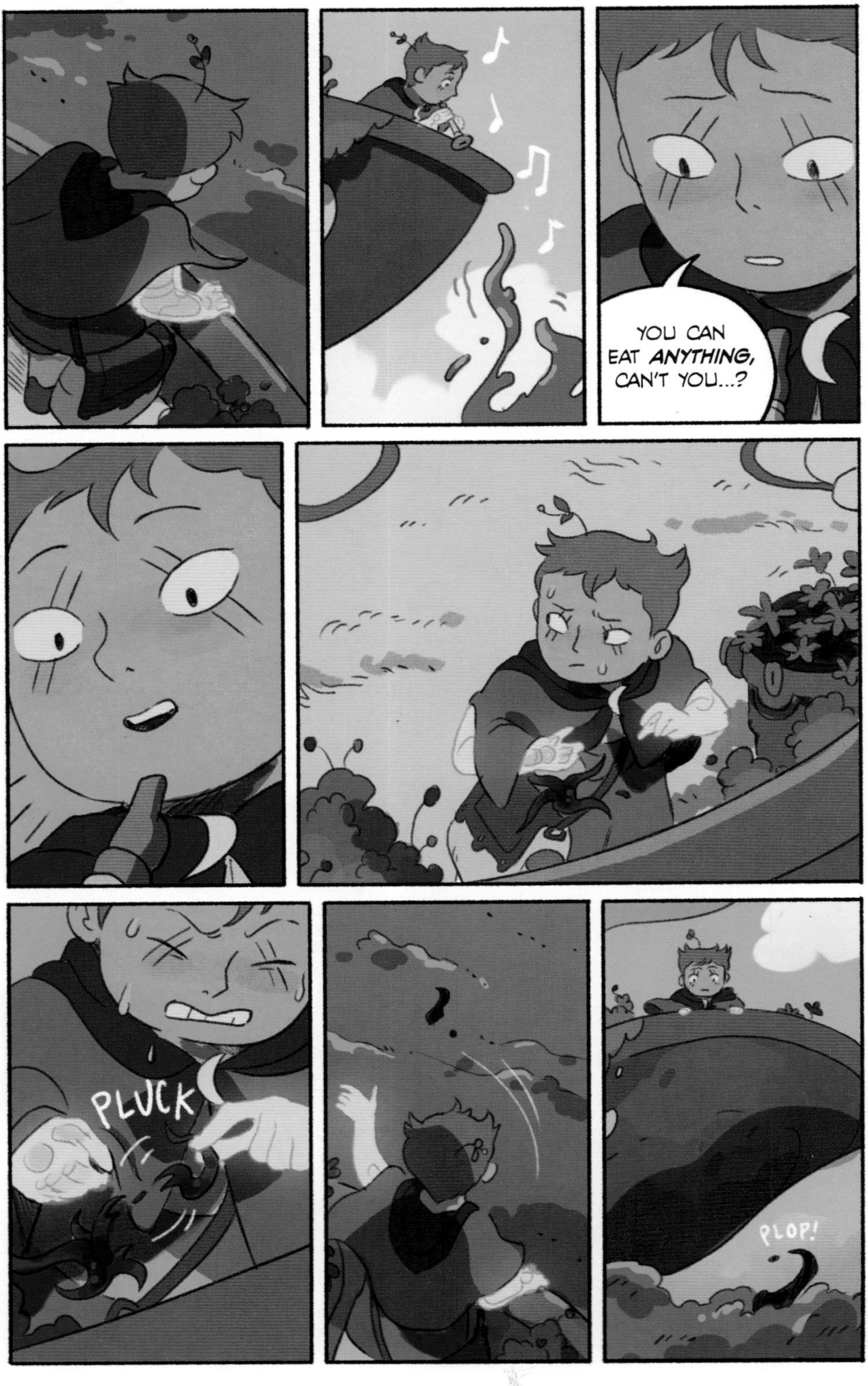
YOU CAN
EAT ANYTHING,
CAN'T YOU...?
PLUCK
PLOP!

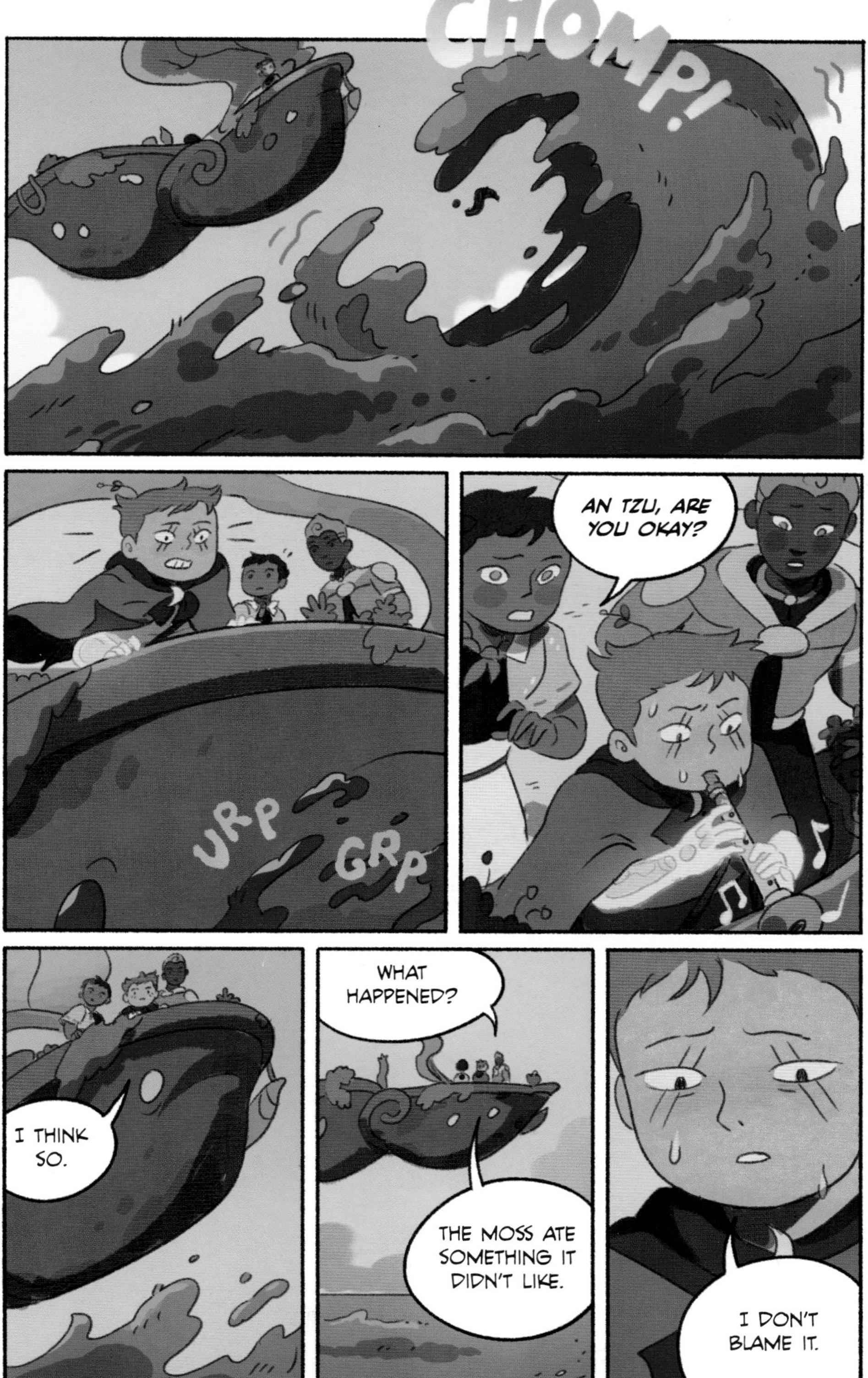
CHOMP!
URP
GRP
AN TZU, ARE YOU OKAY?
I THINK SO.
WHAT HAPPENED?
THE MOSS ATE SOMETHING IT DIDN'T LIKE.
I DON'T BLAME IT.

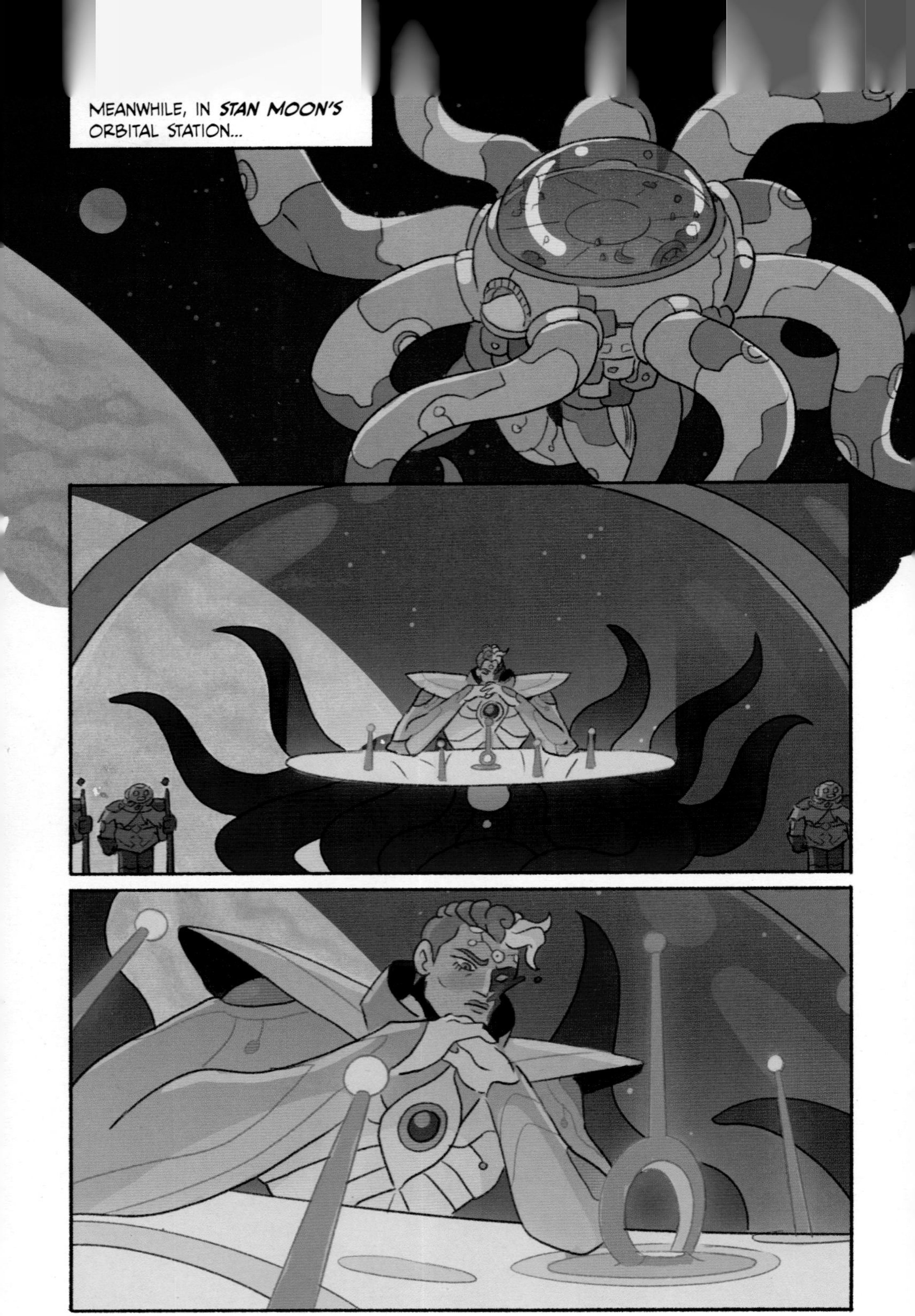
MEANWHILE, IN STAN MOON'S ORBITAL STATION...

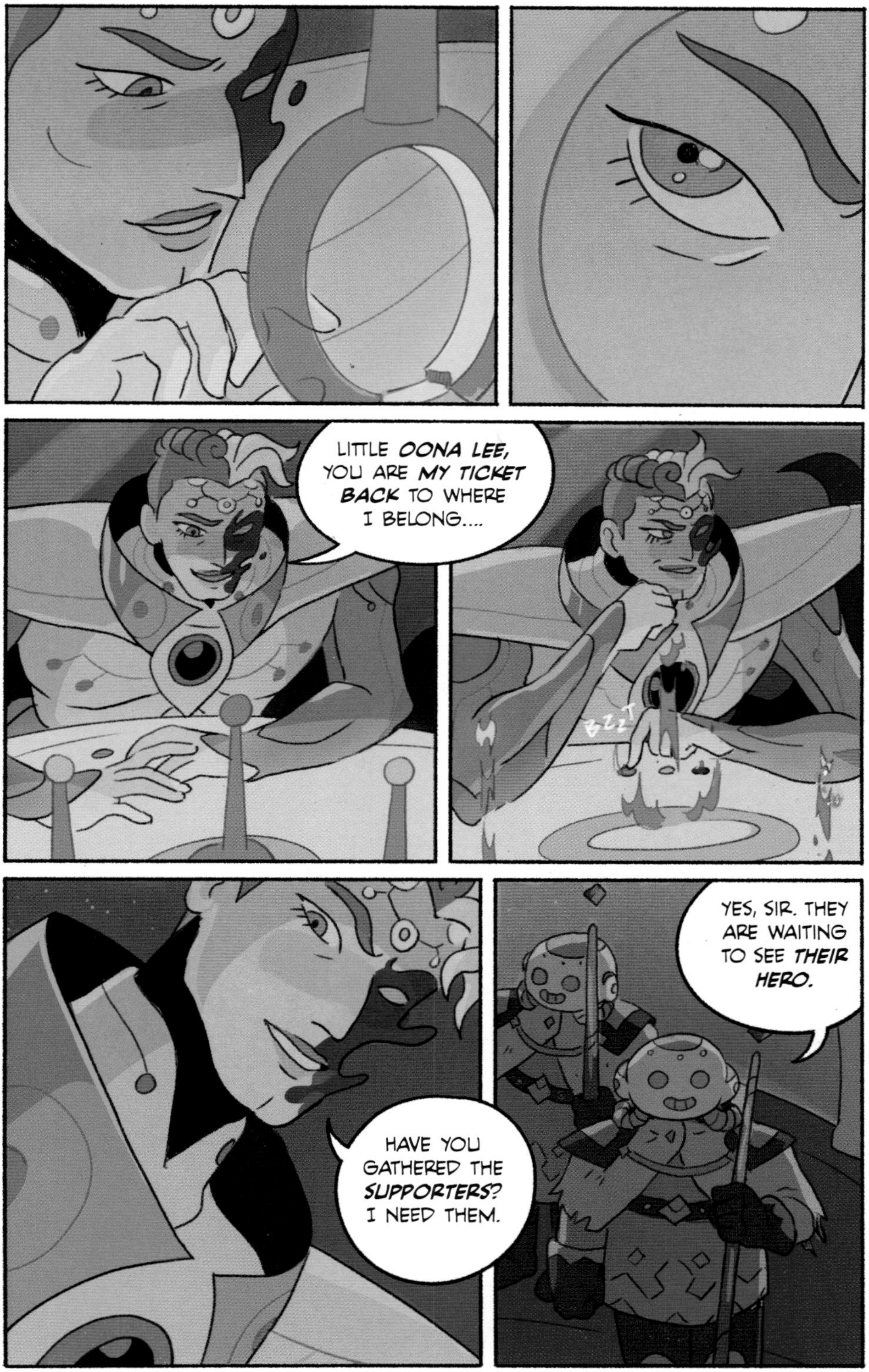
LITTLE **OONA LEE,** YOU ARE **MY TICKET BACK** TO WHERE I BELONG....
BZZT
HAVE YOU GATHERED THE ***SUPPORTERS?*** I NEED THEM.
YES, SIR. THEY ARE WAITING TO SEE ***THEIR HERO.***

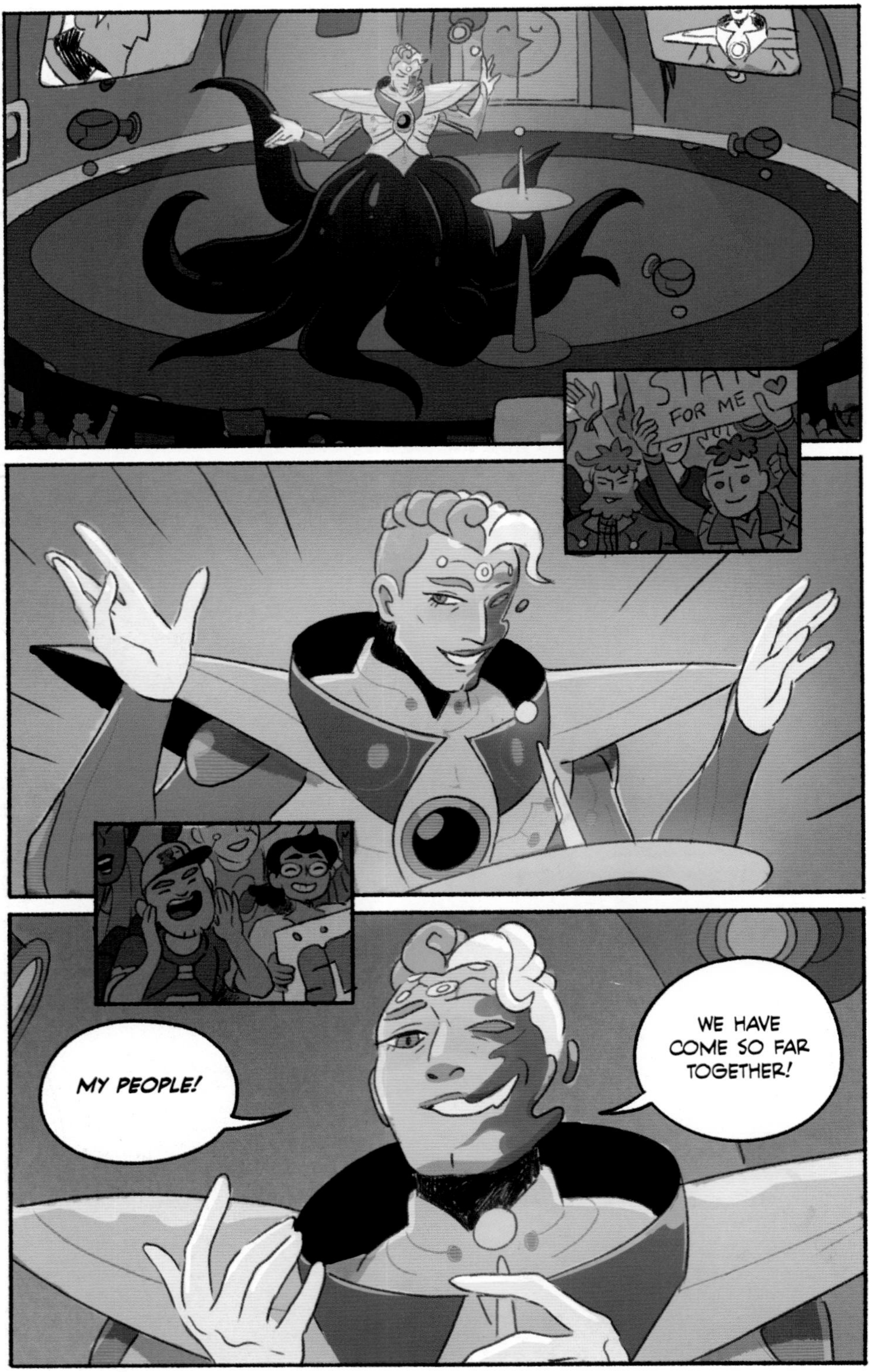
FOR ME
MY PEOPLE!
WE HAVE COME SO FAR TOGETHER!

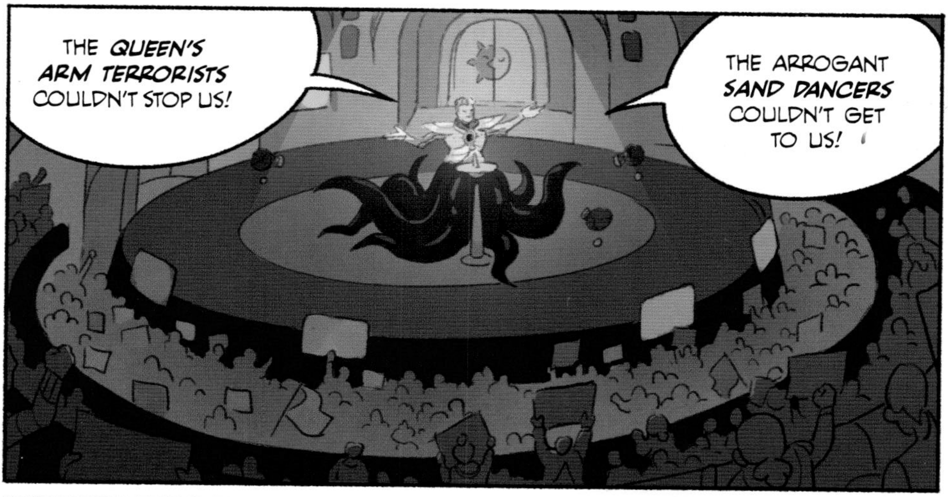
THE QUEEN'S ARM TERRORISTS COULDN'T STOP US!
THE ARROGANT SAND DANCERS COULDN'T GET TO US!
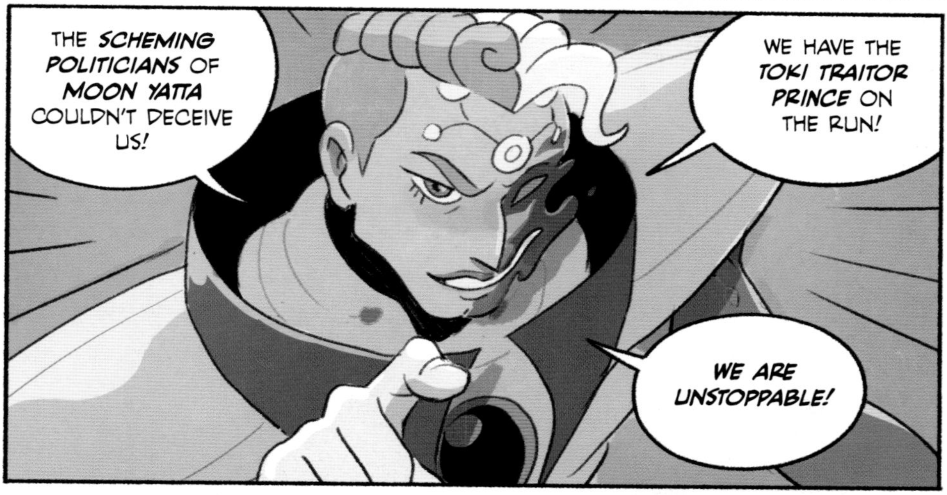
THE SCHEMING POLITICIANS OF MOON YATTA COULDN'T DECEIVE US!
WE HAVE THE TOKI TRAITOR PRINCE ON THE RUN!
WE ARE UNSTOPPABLE!
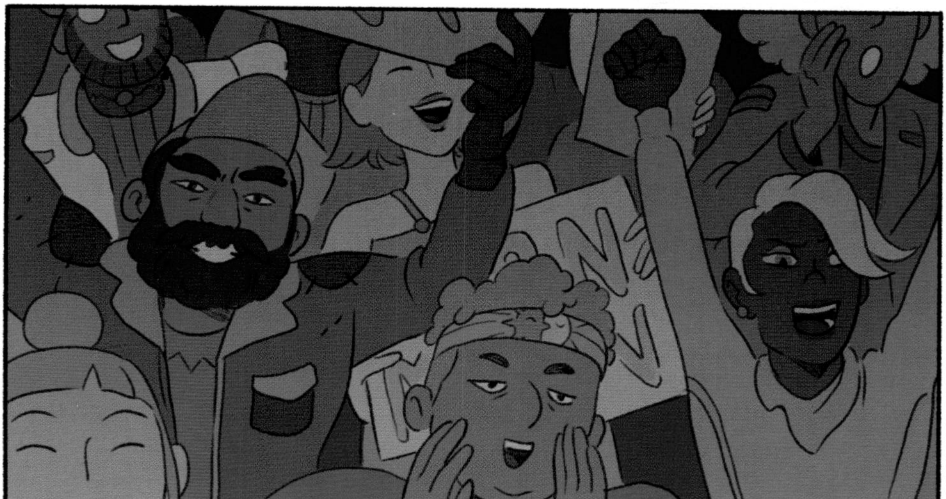

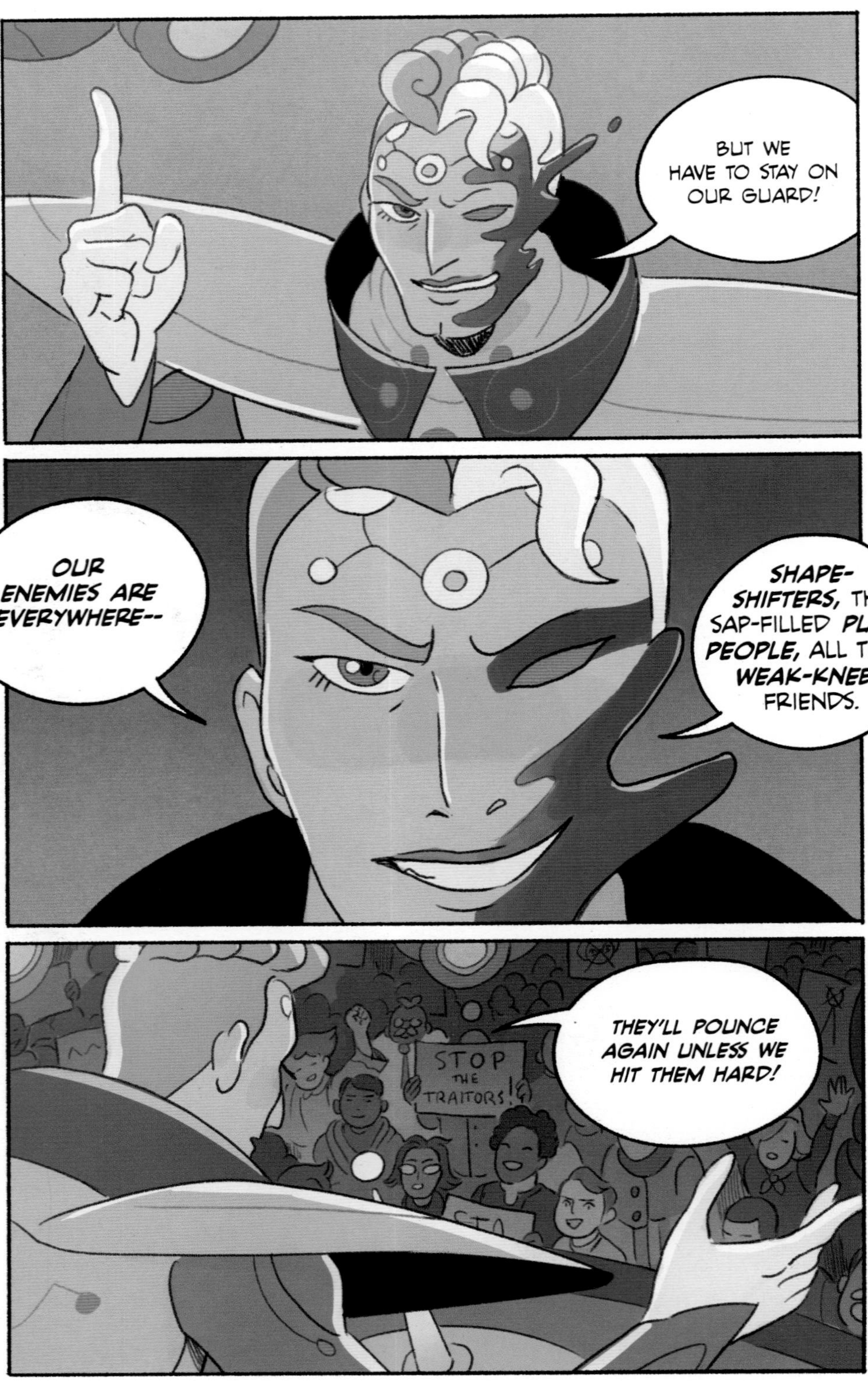
BUT WE HAVE TO STAY ON OUR GUARD!
OUR ENEMIES ARE EVERYWHERE--
SHAPE-SHIFTERS, THE SAP-FILLED PLANT PEOPLE, ALL THEIR WEAK-KNEED FRIENDS.
THEY'LL POUNCE AGAIN UNLESS WE HIT THEM HARD!
STOP THE TRAITORS!

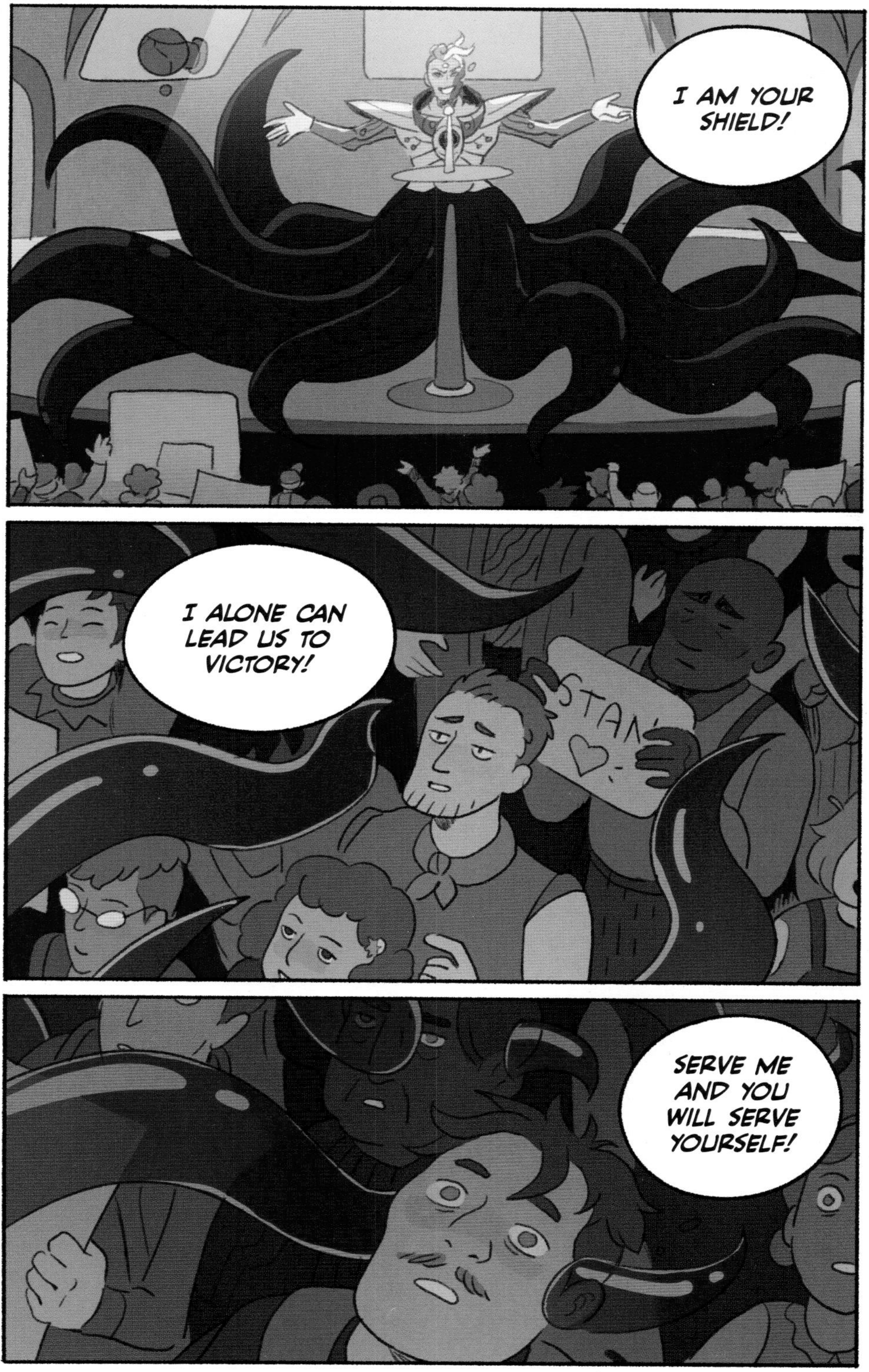
I AM YOUR SHIELD!
I ALONE CAN LEAD US TO VICTORY!
SERVE ME AND YOU WILL SERVE YOURSELF!

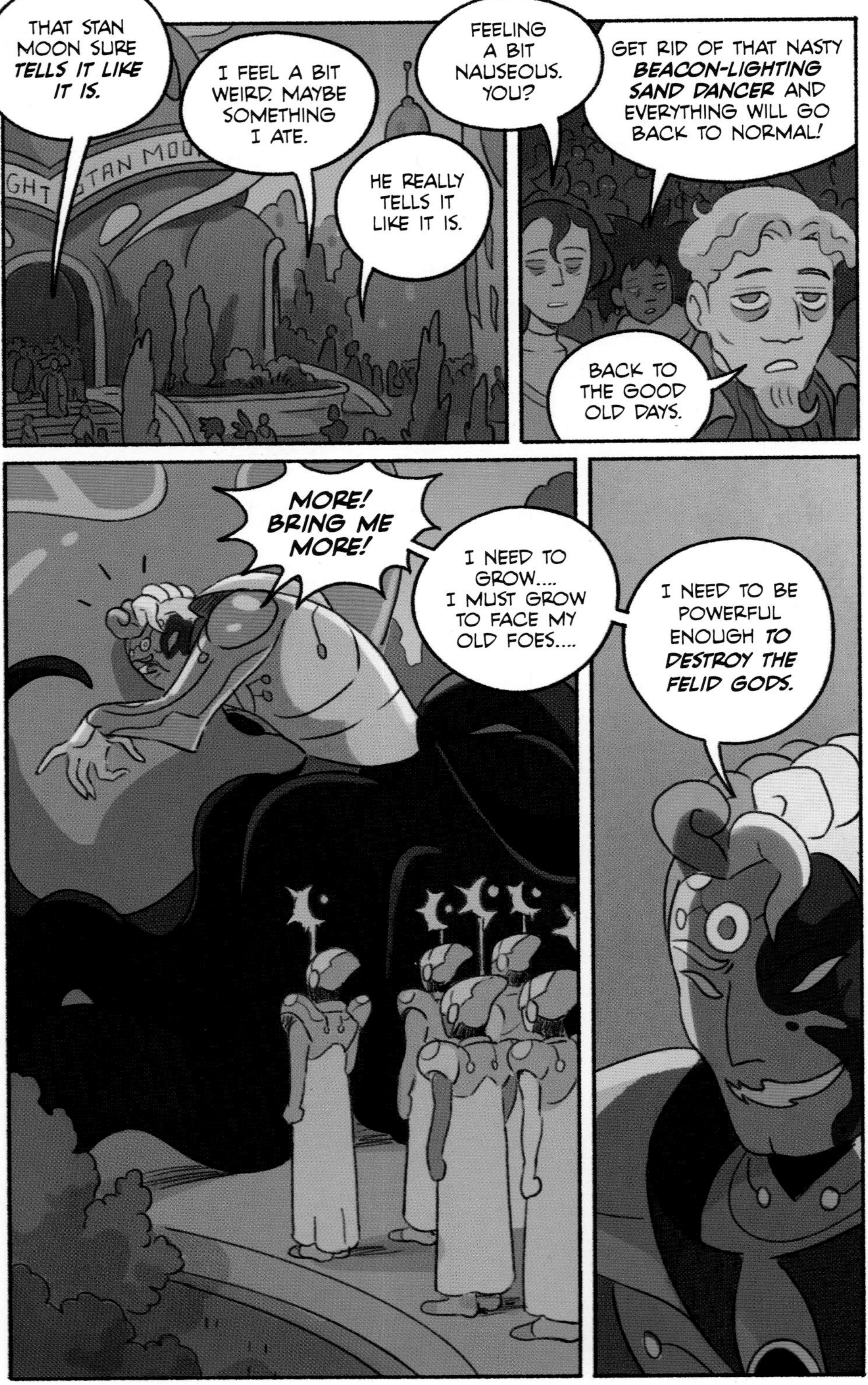

THAT STAN MOON SURE *TELLS IT LIKE IT IS.*
I FEEL A BIT WEIRD. MAYBE SOMETHING I ATE.
HE REALLY TELLS IT LIKE IT IS.
FEELING A BIT NAUSEOUS. YOU?
GET RID OF THAT NASTY ***BEACON-LIGHTING SAND DANCER*** AND EVERYTHING WILL GO BACK TO NORMAL!
BACK TO THE GOOD OLD DAYS.
MORE! BRING ME MORE!
I NEED TO GROW.... I MUST GROW TO FACE MY OLD FOES....
I NEED TO BE POWERFUL ENOUGH ***TO DESTROY THE FELID GODS.***

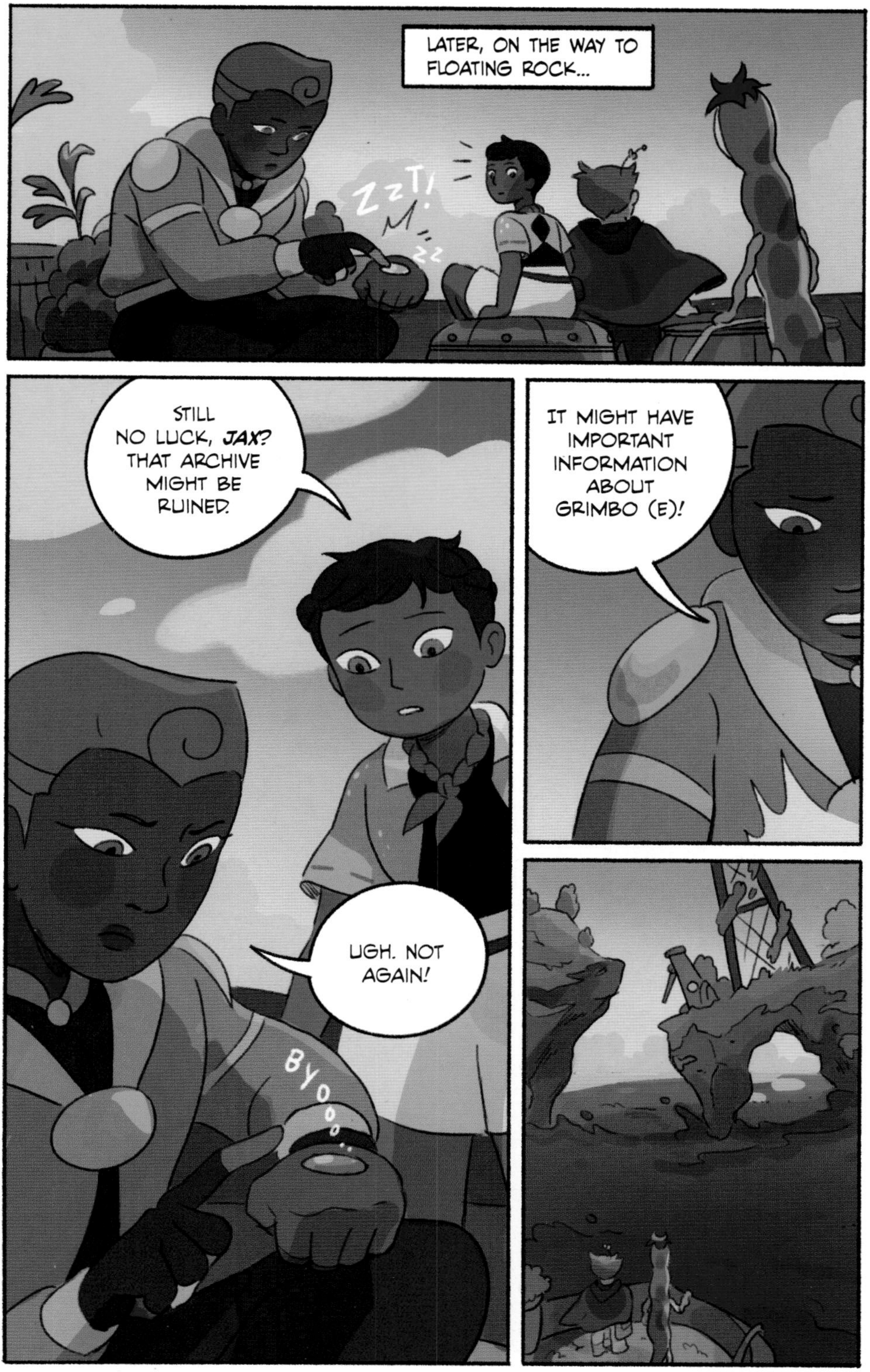
LATER, ON THE WAY TO FLOATING ROCK...
ZzT!
M
zz
STILL NO LUCK, JAX? THAT ARCHIVE MIGHT BE RUINED.
IT MIGHT HAVE IMPORTANT INFORMATION ABOUT GRIMBO (E)!
UGH. NOT AGAIN!
BYOOO..

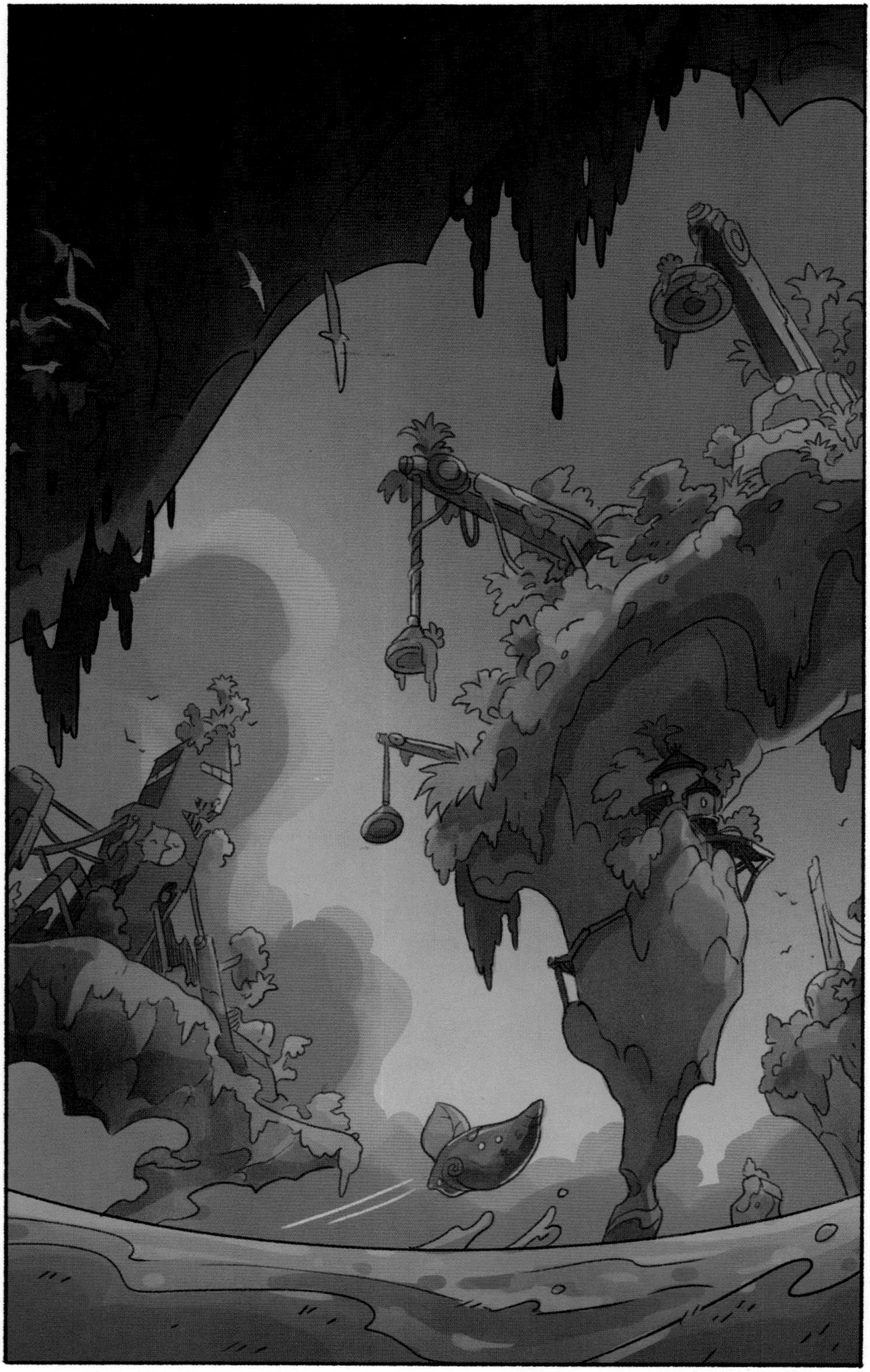

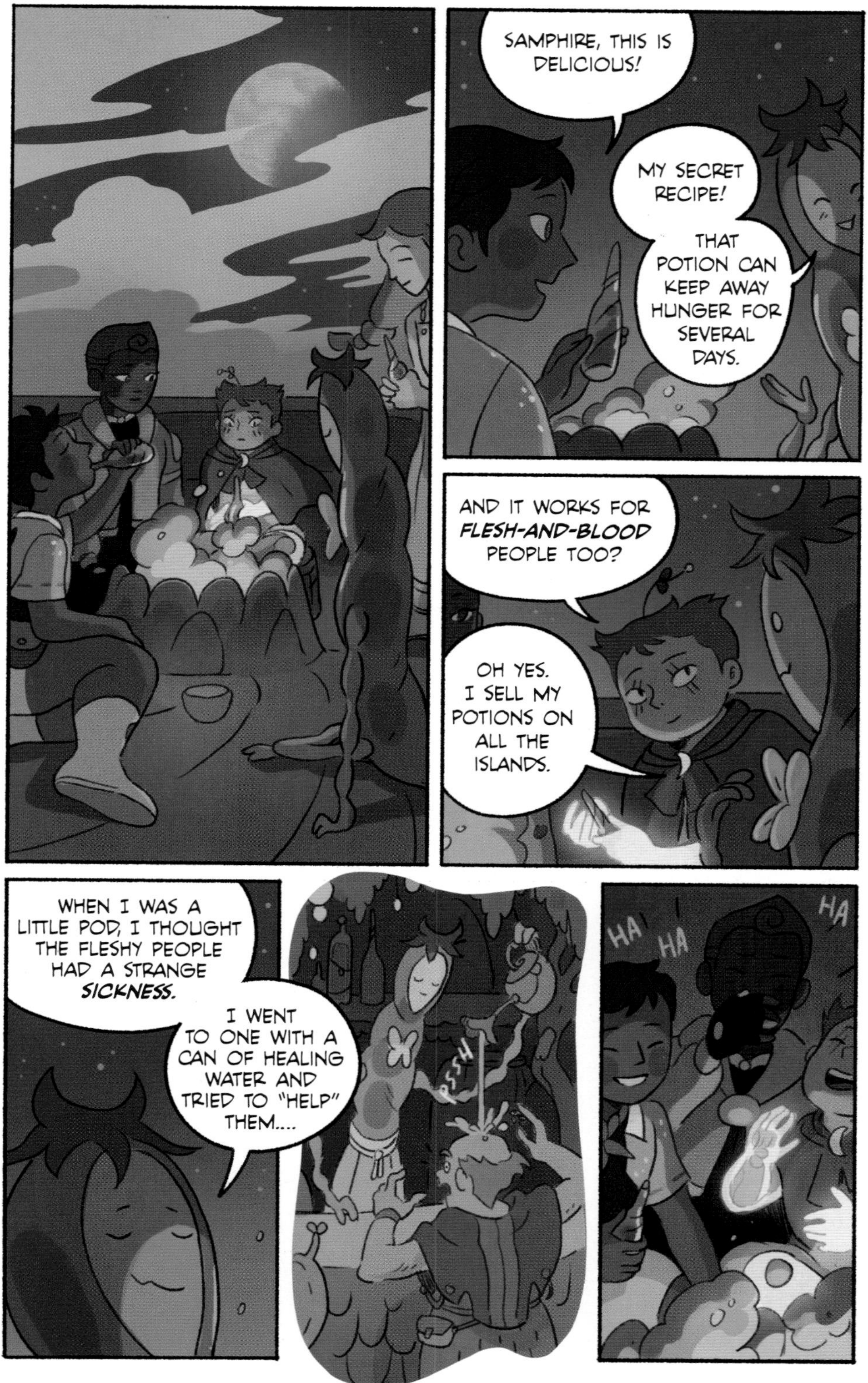
SAMPHIRE, THIS IS DELICIOUS!
MY SECRET RECIPE!
THAT POTION CAN KEEP AWAY HUNGER FOR SEVERAL DAYS.
AND IT WORKS FOR ***FLESH-AND-BLOOD*** PEOPLE TOO?
OH YES. I SELL MY POTIONS ON ALL THE ISLANDS.
WHEN I WAS A LITTLE POD, I THOUGHT THE FLESHY PEOPLE HAD A STRANGE ***SICKNESS.***
I WENT TO ONE WITH A CAN OF HEALING WATER AND TRIED TO "HELP" THEM....
PSSH
HA
HA
HA

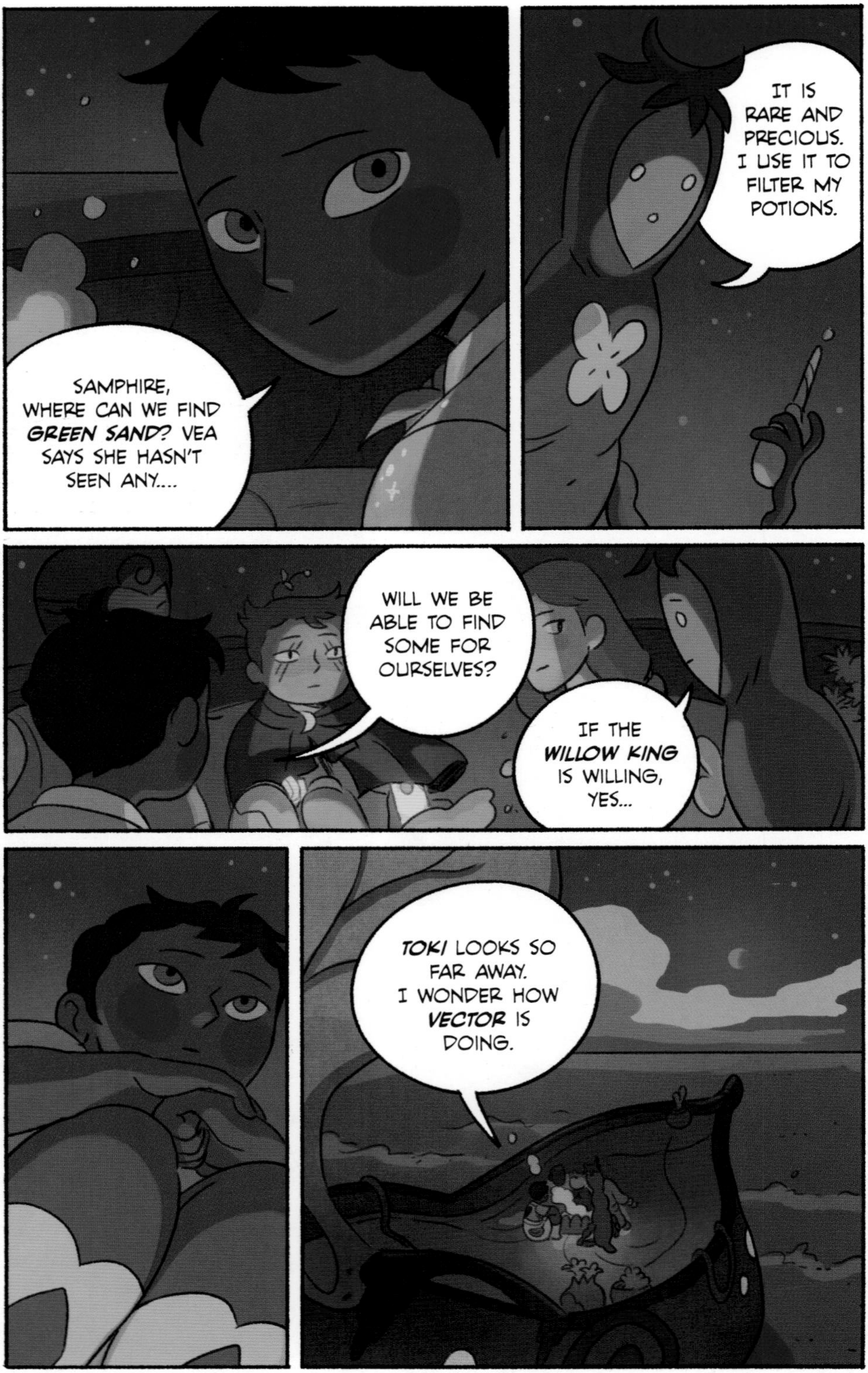
SAMPHIRE, WHERE CAN WE FIND GREEN SAND? VEA SAYS SHE HASN'T SEEN ANY....
IT IS RARE AND PRECIOUS. I USE IT TO FILTER MY POTIONS.
WILL WE BE ABLE TO FIND SOME FOR OURSELVES?
IF THE WILLOW KING IS WILLING, YES...
TOKI LOOKS SO FAR AWAY. I WONDER HOW VECTOR IS DOING.

CHAPTER 7
THE TOKI EXILE

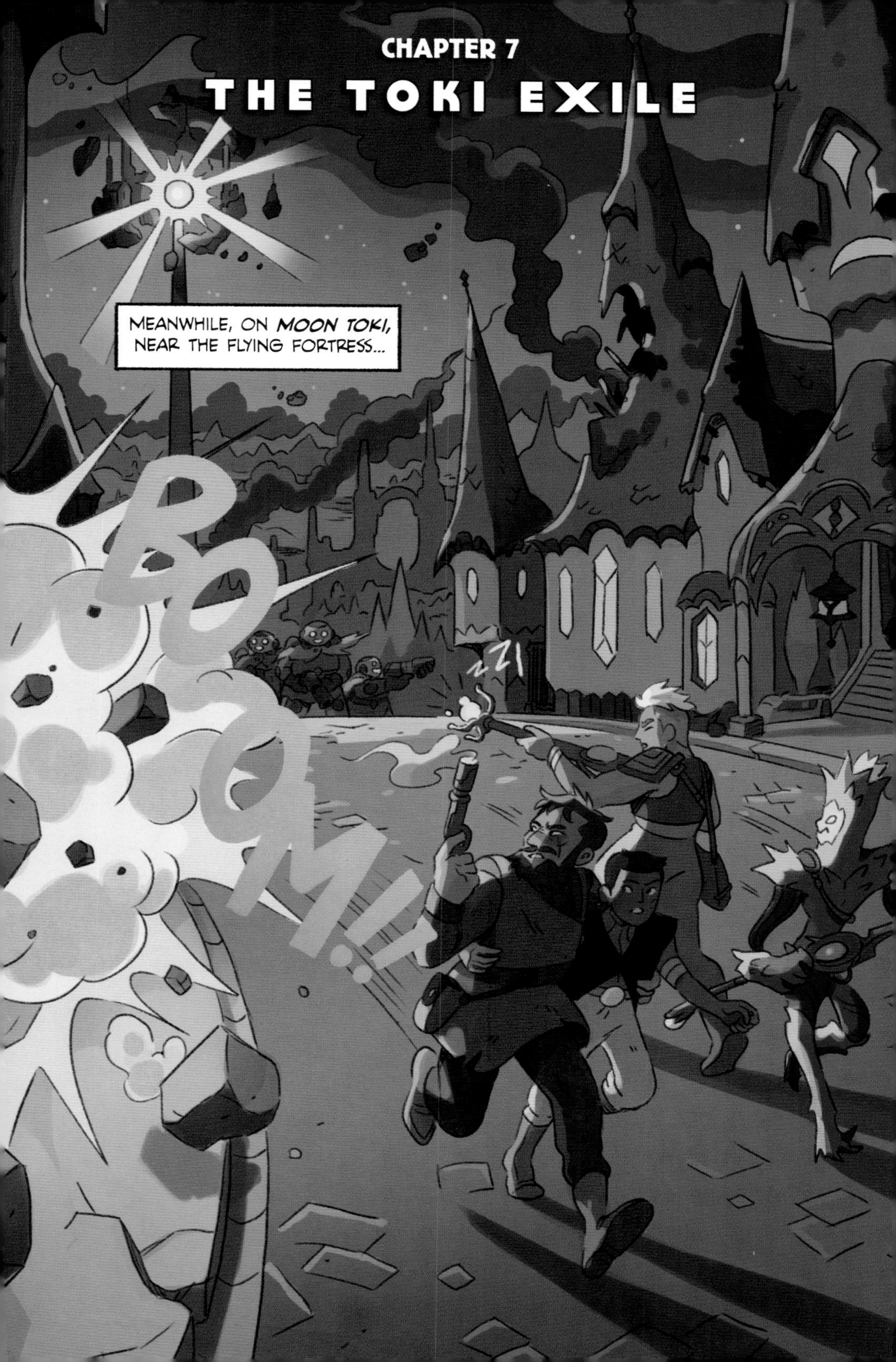
MEANWHILE, ON *MOON TOKI*, NEAR THE FLYING FORTRESS...
BOOM!!

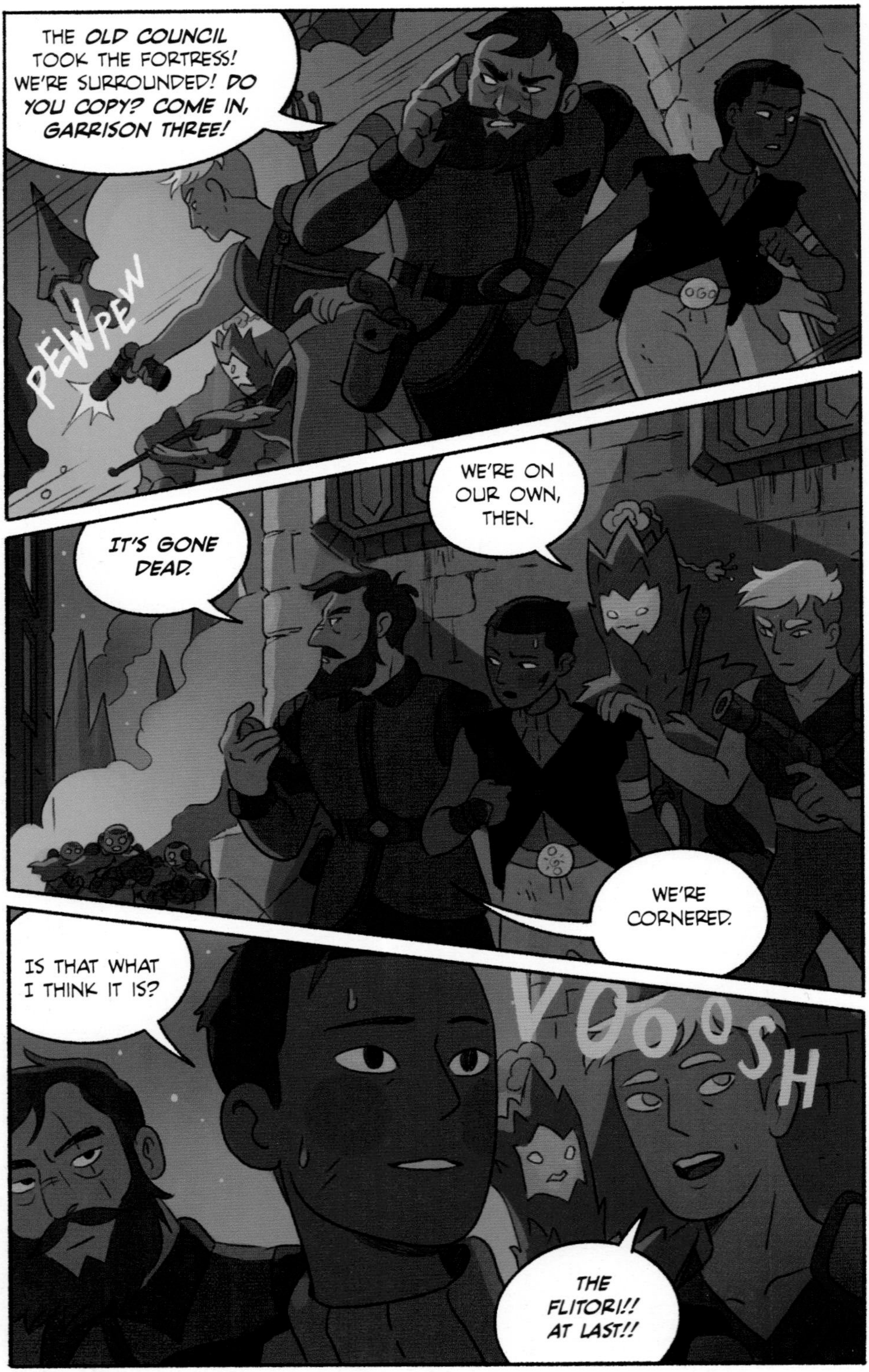
THE OLD COUNCIL TOOK THE FORTRESS! WE'RE SURROUNDED! DO YOU COPY? COME IN, GARRISON THREE!
PEWPEW
IT'S GONE DEAD.
WE'RE ON OUR OWN, THEN.
WE'RE CORNERED.
IS THAT WHAT I THINK IT IS?
VOOOSH
THE FLITORI!! AT LAST!!

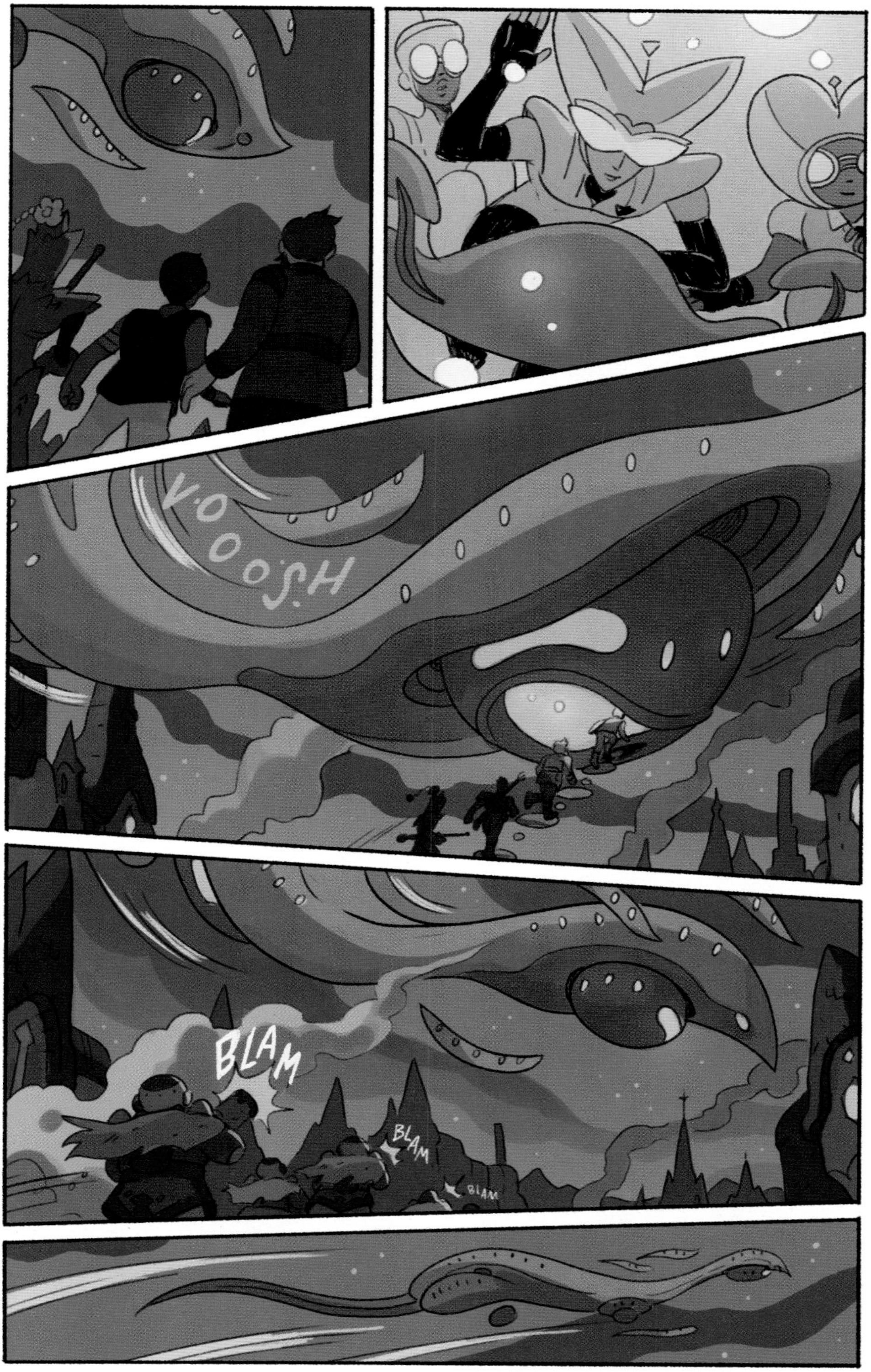
VOOOSH
BLAM
BLAM
BLAM

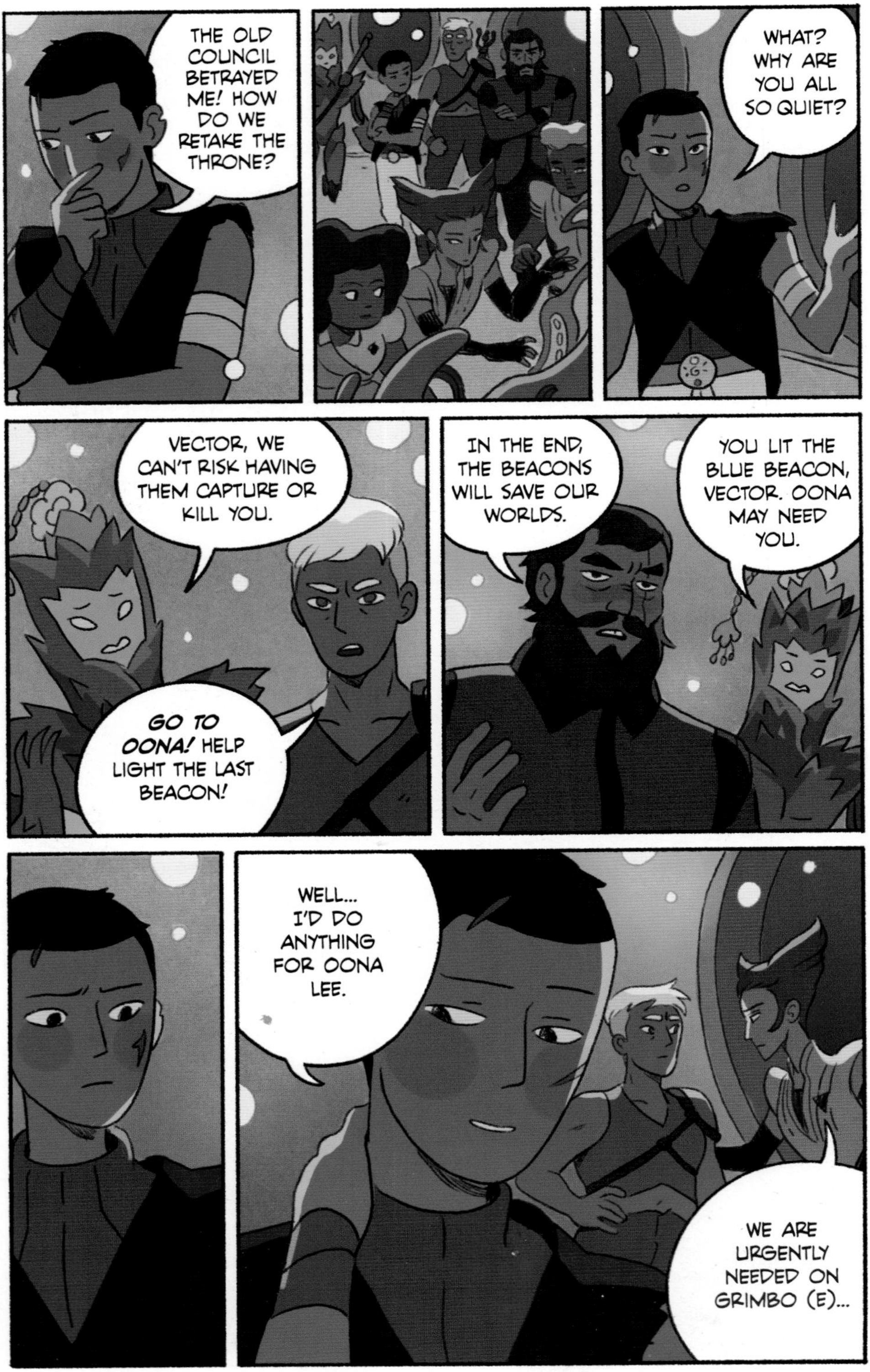
THE OLD COUNCIL BETRAYED ME! HOW DO WE RETAKE THE THRONE?
WHAT? WHY ARE YOU ALL SO QUIET?
VECTOR, WE CAN'T RISK HAVING THEM CAPTURE OR KILL YOU.
GO TO OONA! HELP LIGHT THE LAST BEACON!
IN THE END, THE BEACONS WILL SAVE OUR WORLDS.
YOU LIT THE BLUE BEACON, VECTOR. OONA MAY NEED YOU.
WELL... I'D DO ANYTHING FOR OONA LEE.
WE ARE URGENTLY NEEDED ON GRIMBO (E)...

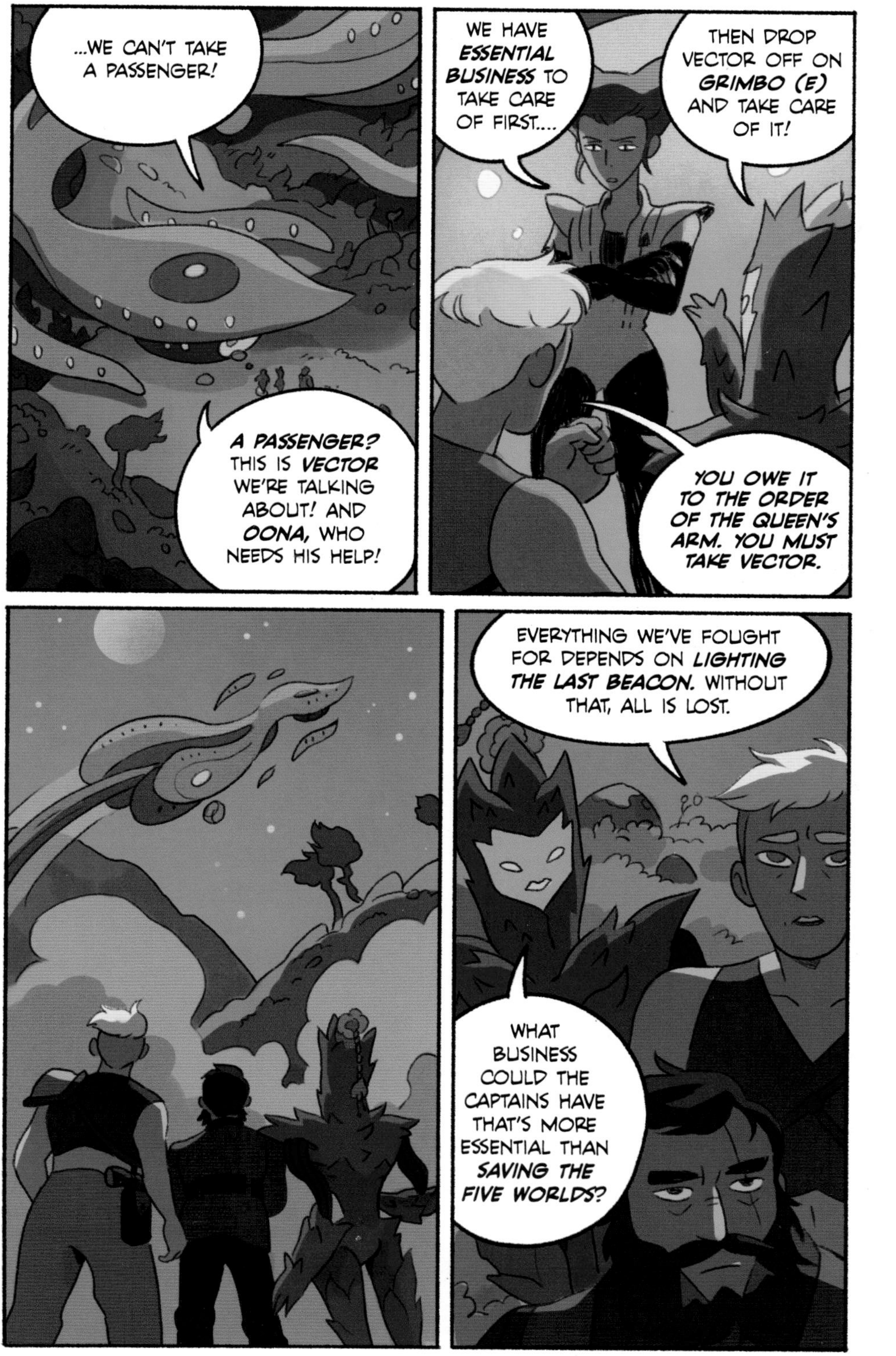
...WE CAN'T TAKE A PASSENGER!
A PASSENGER? THIS IS VECTOR WE'RE TALKING ABOUT! AND OONA, WHO NEEDS HIS HELP!
WE HAVE ESSENTIAL BUSINESS TO TAKE CARE OF FIRST....
THEN DROP VECTOR OFF ON GRIMBO (E) AND TAKE CARE OF IT!
YOU OWE IT TO THE ORDER OF THE QUEEN'S ARM. YOU MUST TAKE VECTOR.
EVERYTHING WE'VE FOUGHT FOR DEPENDS ON LIGHTING THE LAST BEACON. WITHOUT THAT, ALL IS LOST.
WHAT BUSINESS COULD THE CAPTAINS HAVE THAT'S MORE ESSENTIAL THAN SAVING THE FIVE WORLDS?

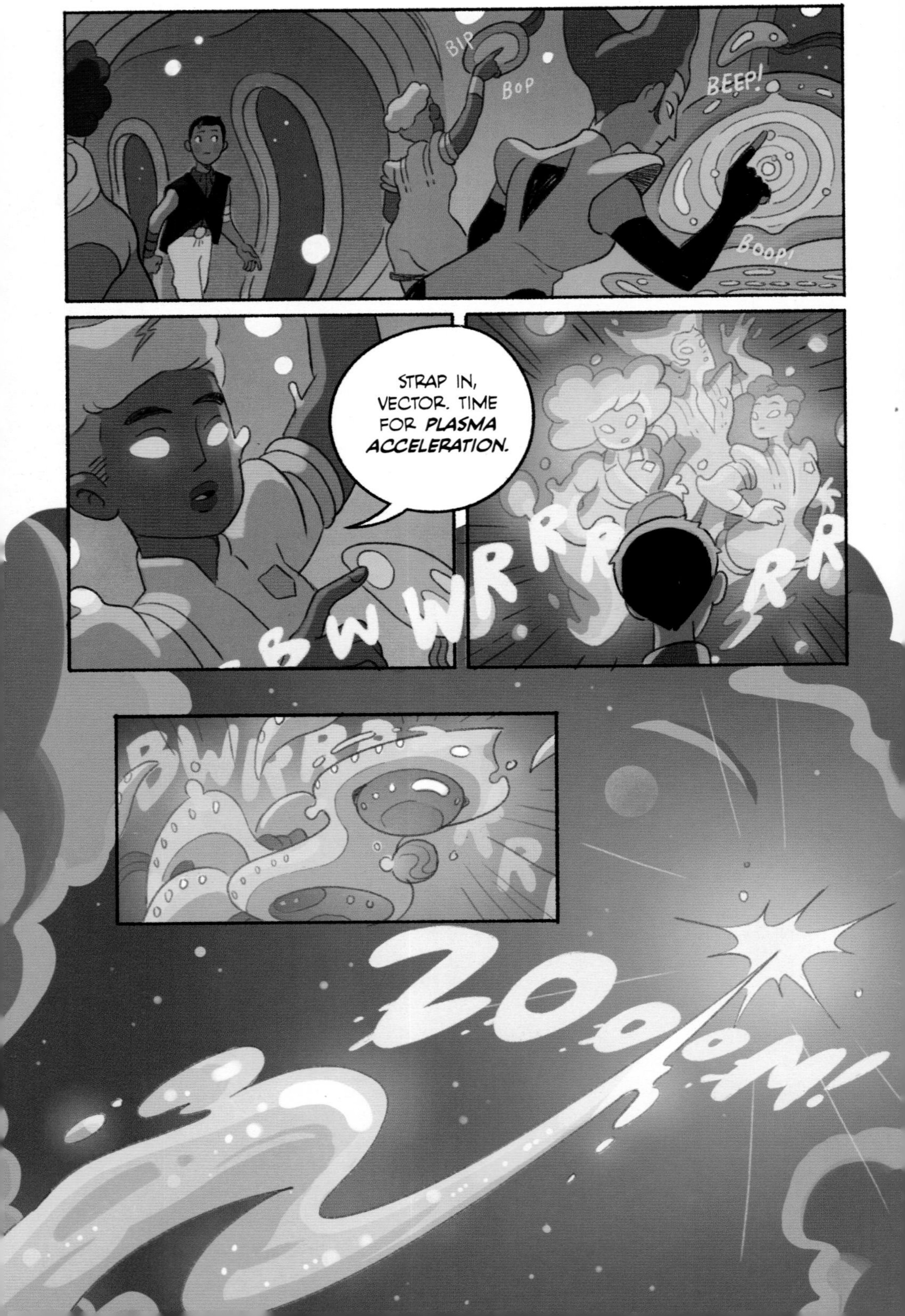
BIP
BOP
BEEP!
BOOP!
STRAP IN, VECTOR. TIME FOR *PLASMA ACCELERATION.*
BWWRRRRRR
ZOOOOM!

CHAPTER 8
THE WILLOW KING

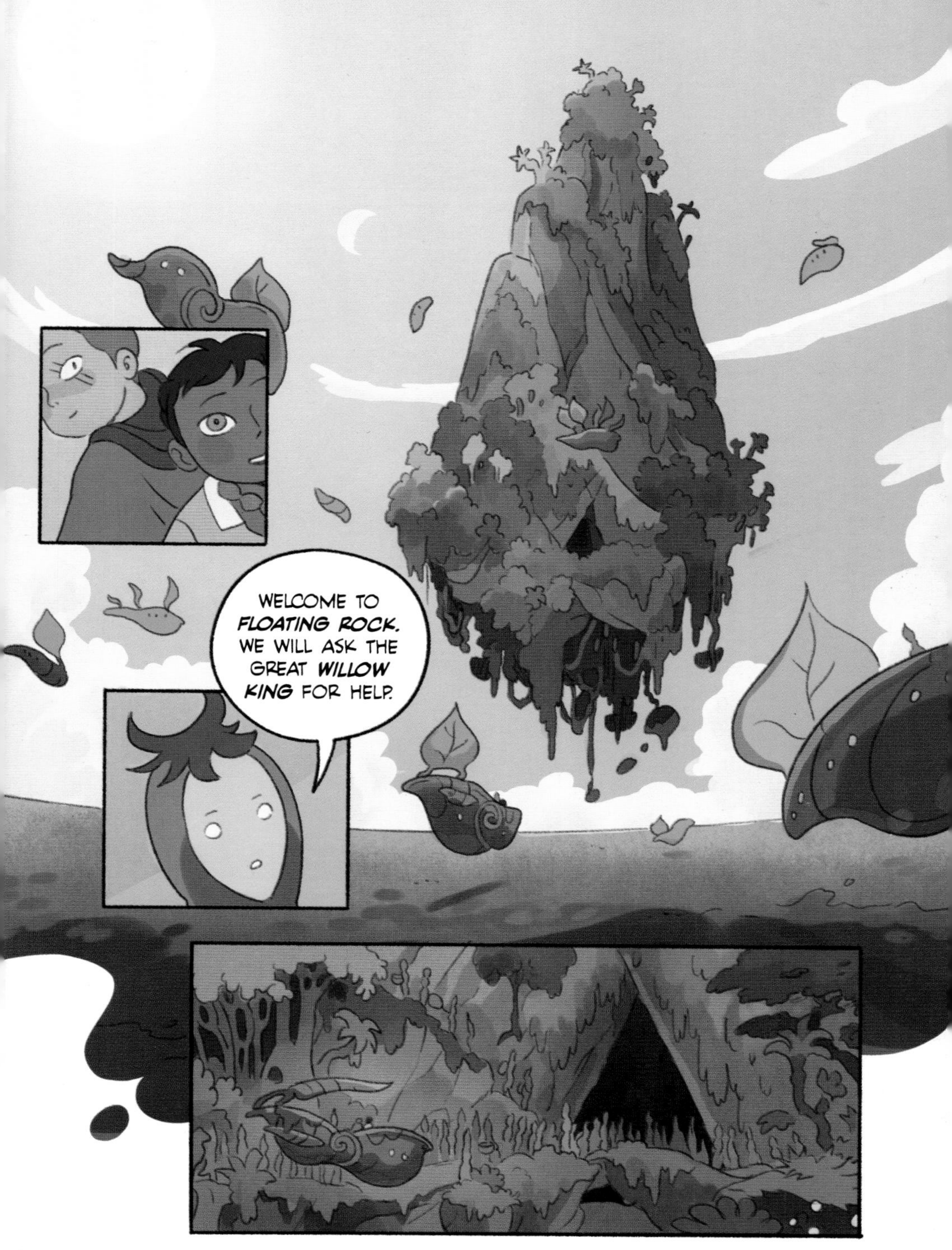
WELCOME TO FLOATING ROCK. WE WILL ASK THE GREAT WILLOW KING FOR HELP.

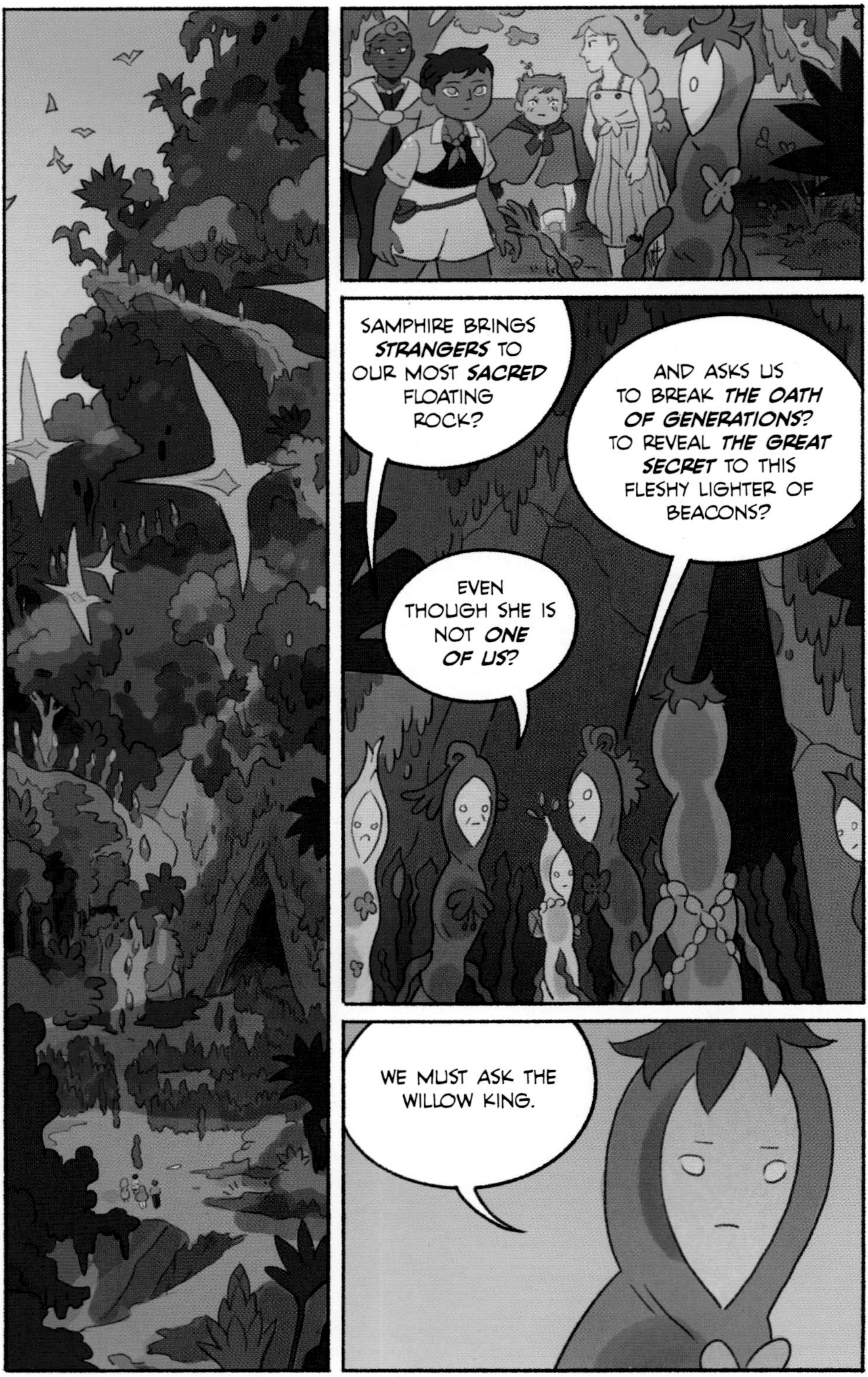
SAMPHIRE BRINGS *STRANGERS* TO OUR MOST *SACRED* FLOATING ROCK?
AND ASKS US TO BREAK *THE OATH OF GENERATIONS?* TO REVEAL *THE GREAT SECRET* TO THIS FLESHY LIGHTER OF BEACONS?
EVEN THOUGH SHE IS NOT *ONE OF US?*
WE MUST ASK THE WILLOW KING.

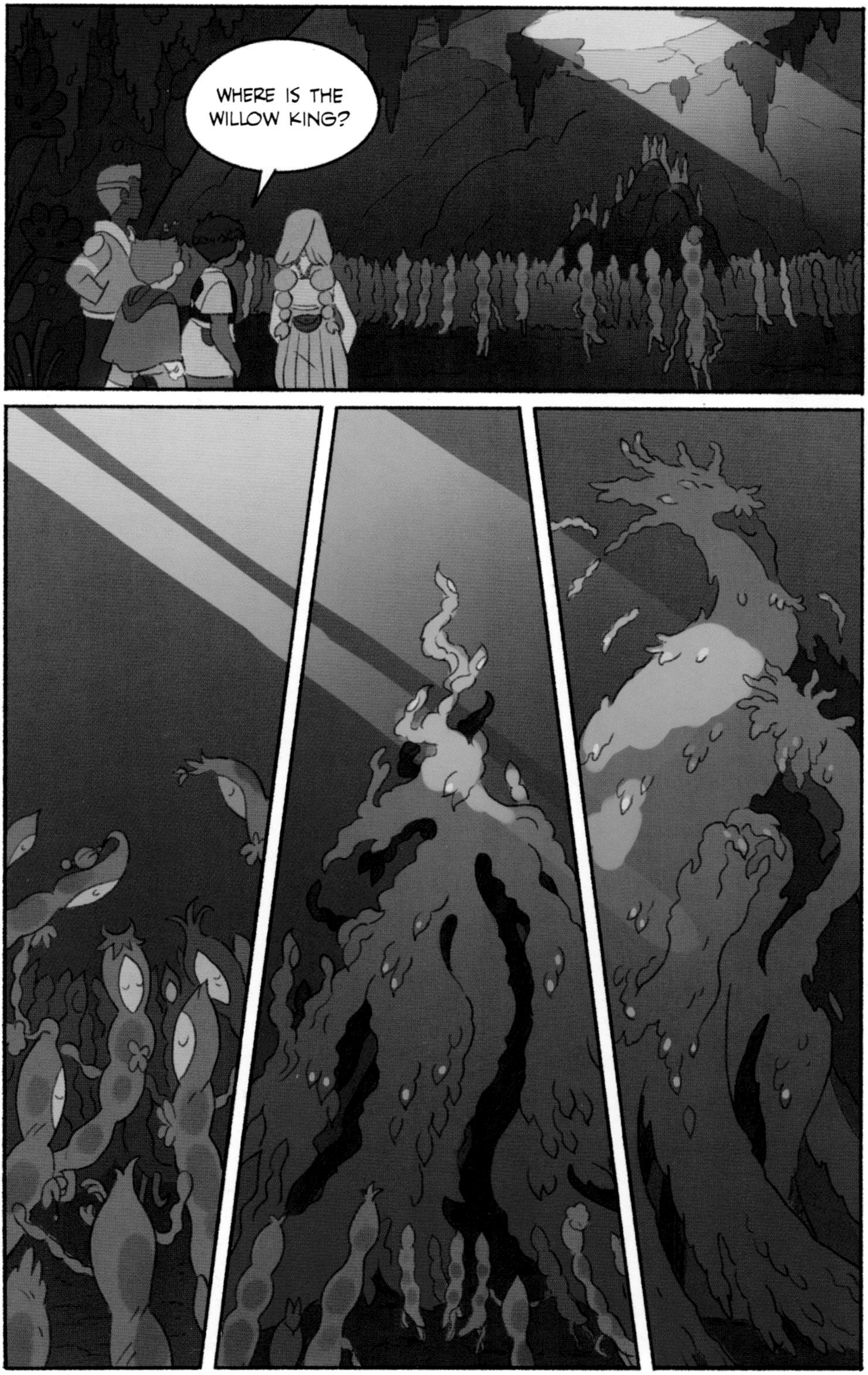
WHERE IS THE WILLOW KING?

WOW.

NOW WE *WAIT.*

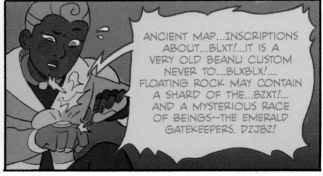

ANCIENT MAP...INSCRIPTIONS ABOUT...BLXT!...IT IS A VERY OLD BEANU CUSTOM NEVER TO....BLXBLX!.... FLOATING ROCK MAY CONTAIN A SHARD OF THE...BZXT!... AND A MYSTERIOUS RACE OF BEINGS--THE EMERALD GATEKEEPERS. DZJBZ!

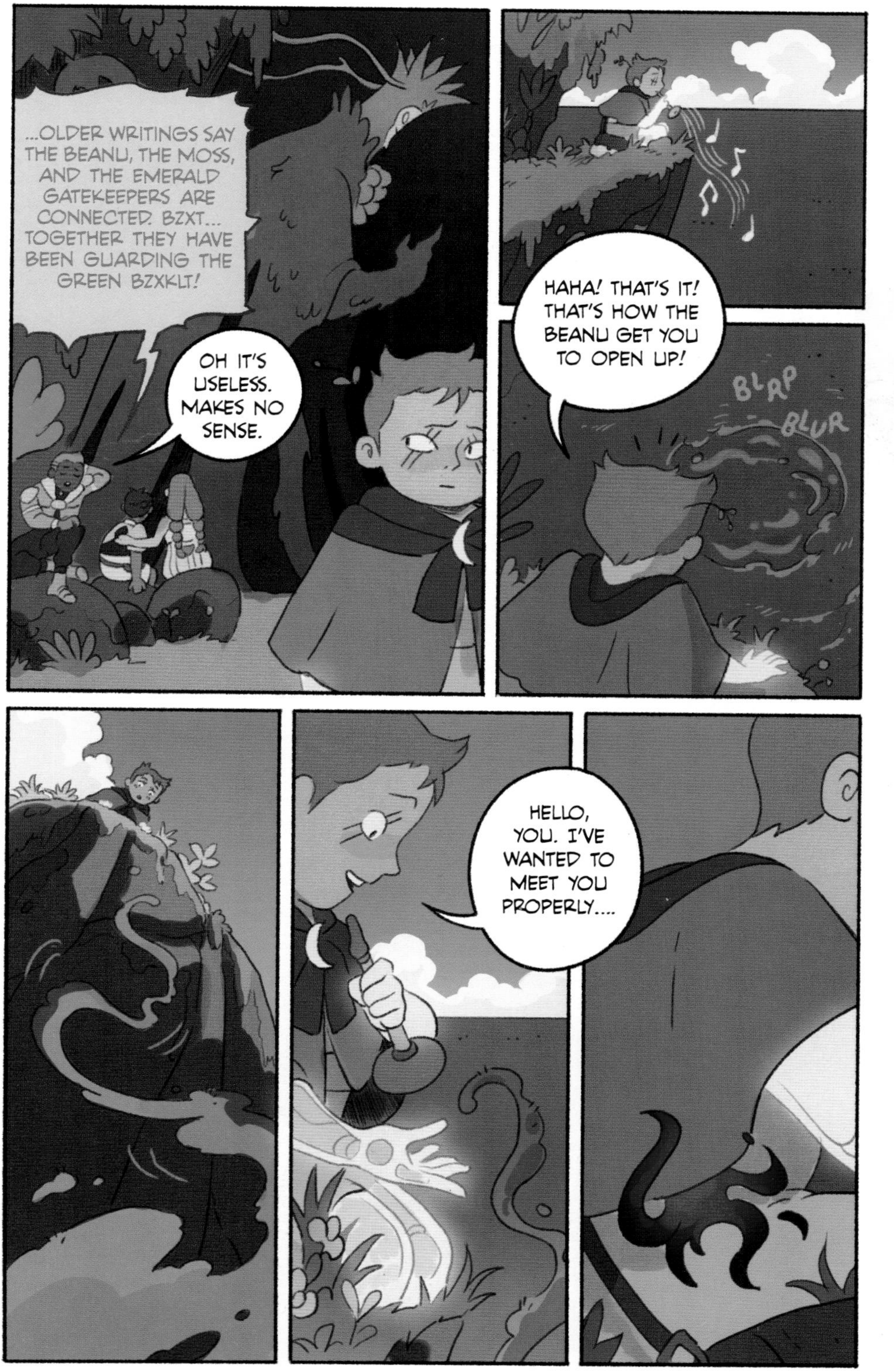
...OLDER WRITINGS SAY THE BEANU, THE MOSS, AND THE EMERALD GATEKEEPERS ARE CONNECTED. BZXT... TOGETHER THEY HAVE BEEN GUARDING THE GREEN BZXKLT!
OH IT'S USELESS. MAKES NO SENSE.
HAHA! THAT'S IT! THAT'S HOW THE BEANU GET YOU TO OPEN UP!
BLRP
BLUR
HELLO, YOU. I'VE WANTED TO MEET YOU PROPERLY....

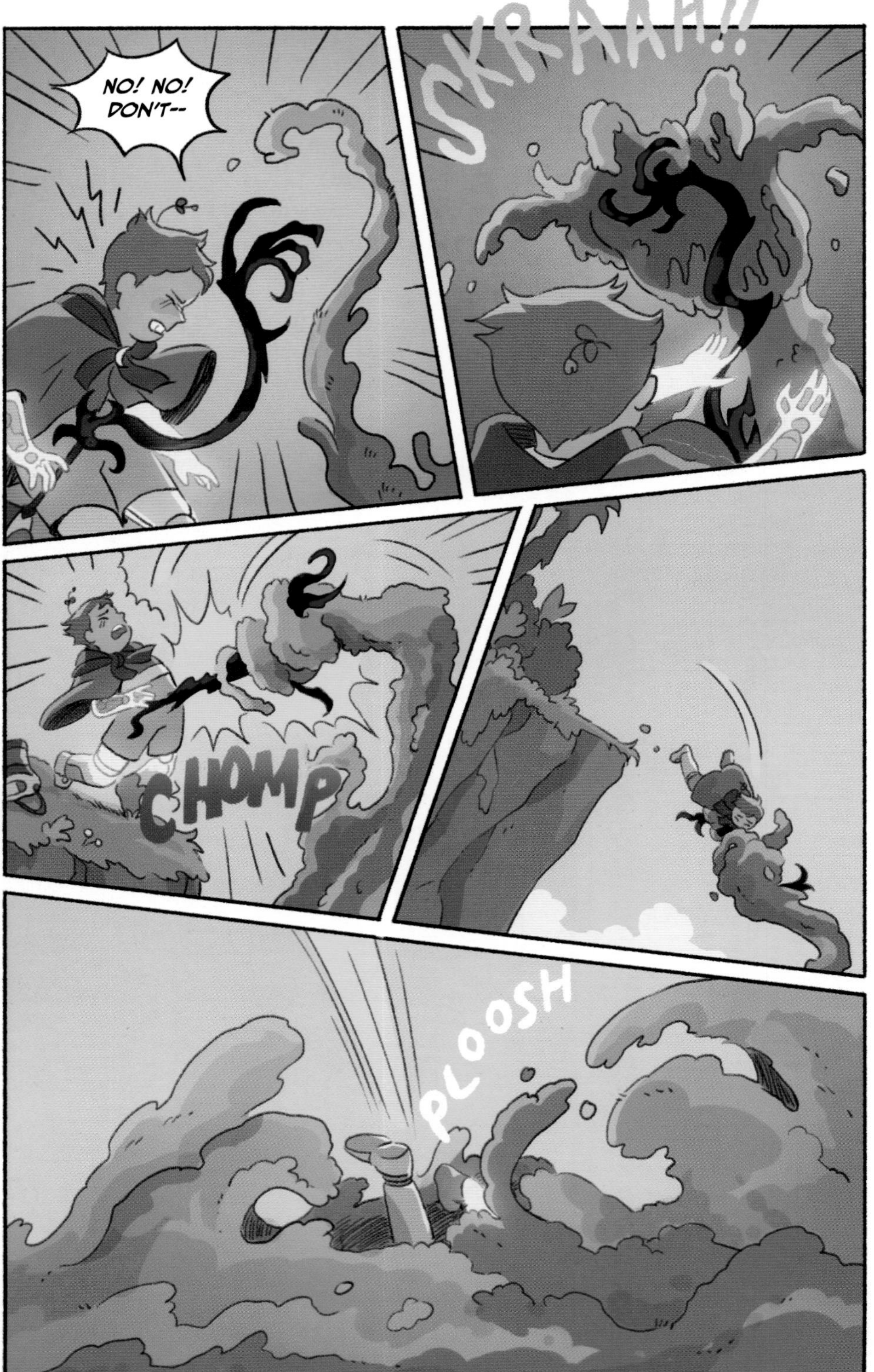
NO! NO! DON'T--
SKRAAH!!
CHOMP
PLOOSH

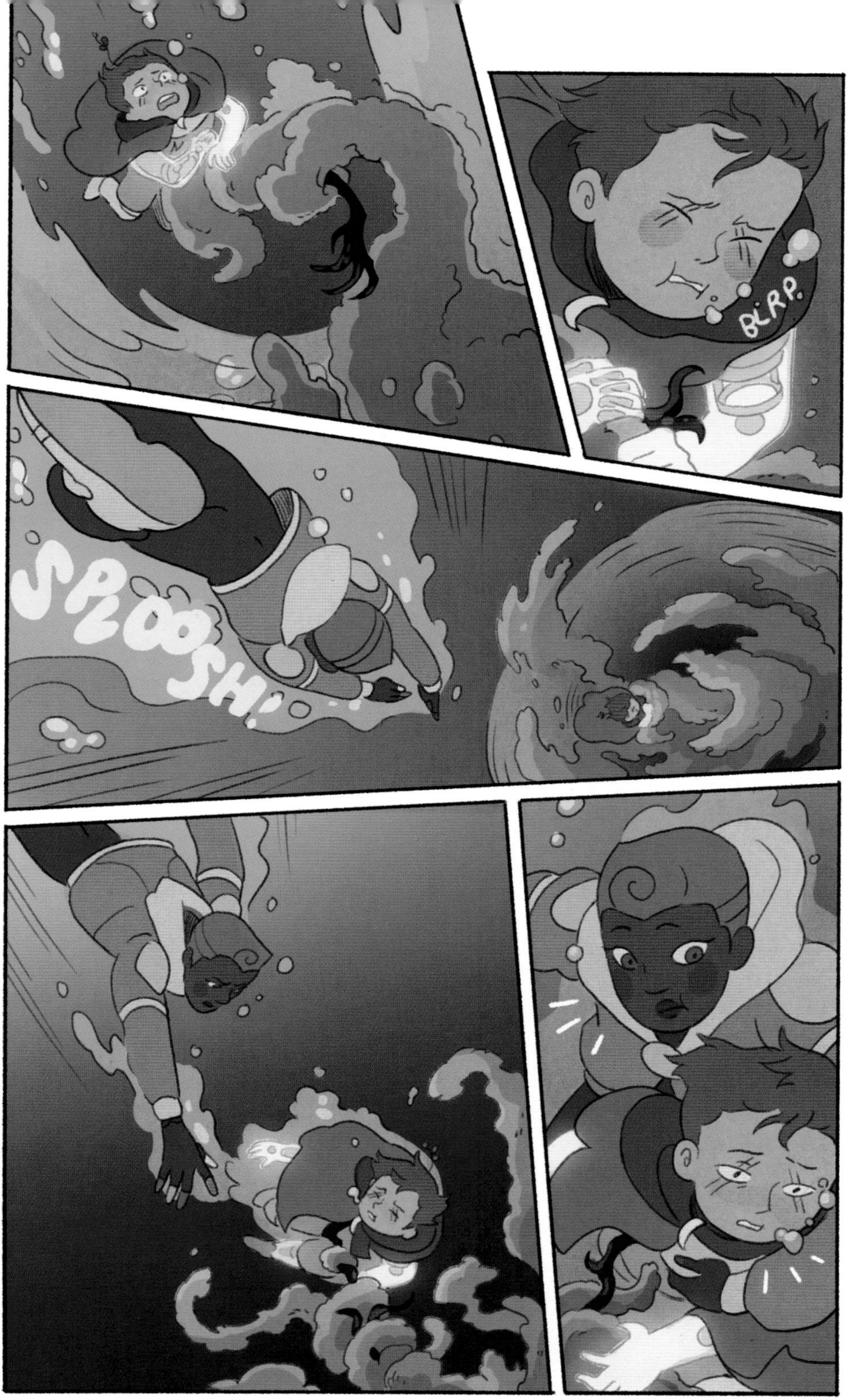
BLRP.
SPLOOSH!

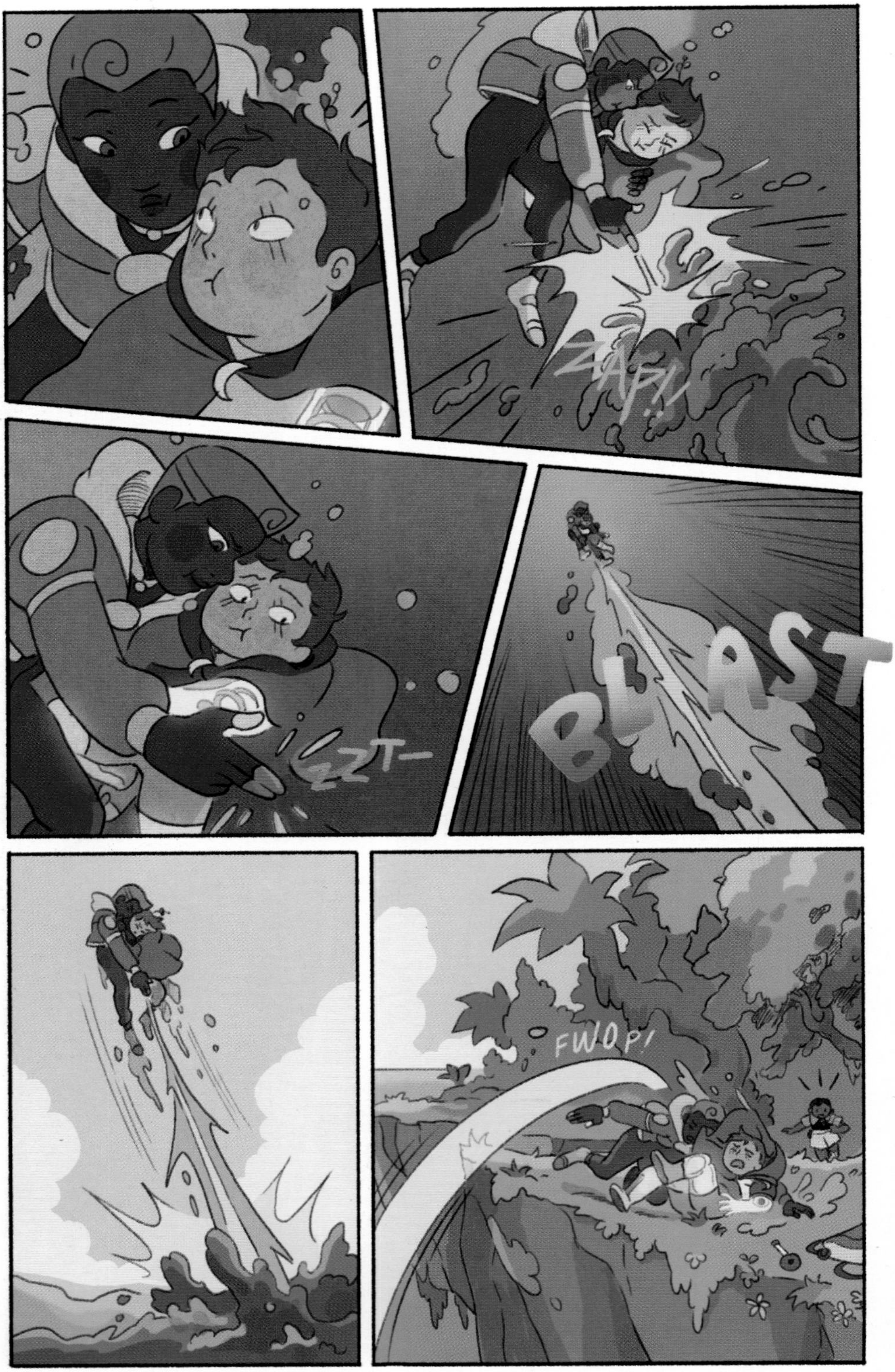
ZAP!!
ZZT—
BLAST
FWOP!

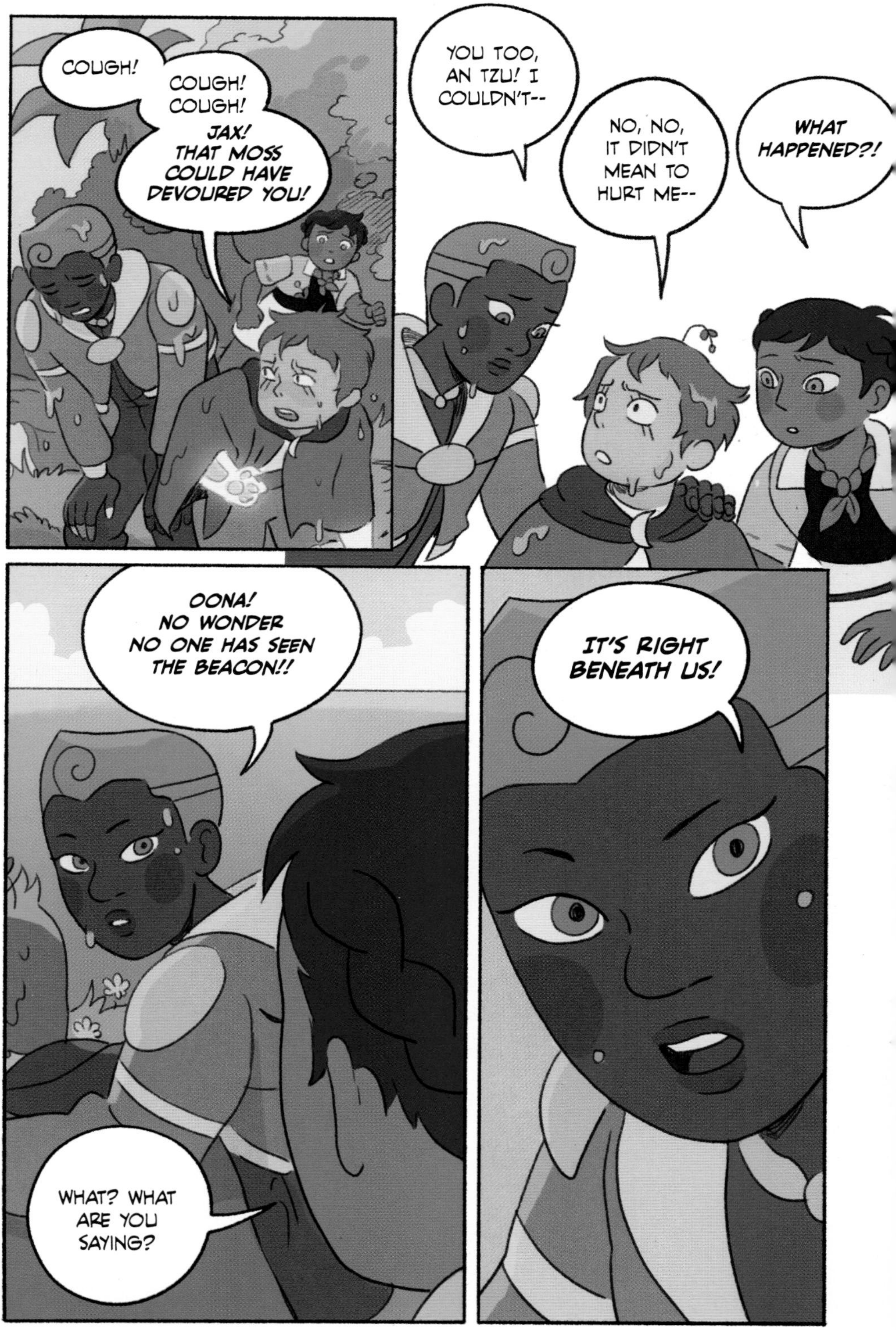
COUGH!
COUGH! COUGH!
JAX! THAT MOSS COULD HAVE DEVOURED YOU!
YOU TOO, AN TZU! I COULDN'T--
NO, NO, IT DIDN'T MEAN TO HURT ME--
WHAT HAPPENED?!
OONA! NO WONDER NO ONE HAS SEEN THE BEACON!!
WHAT? WHAT ARE YOU SAYING?
IT'S RIGHT BENEATH US!

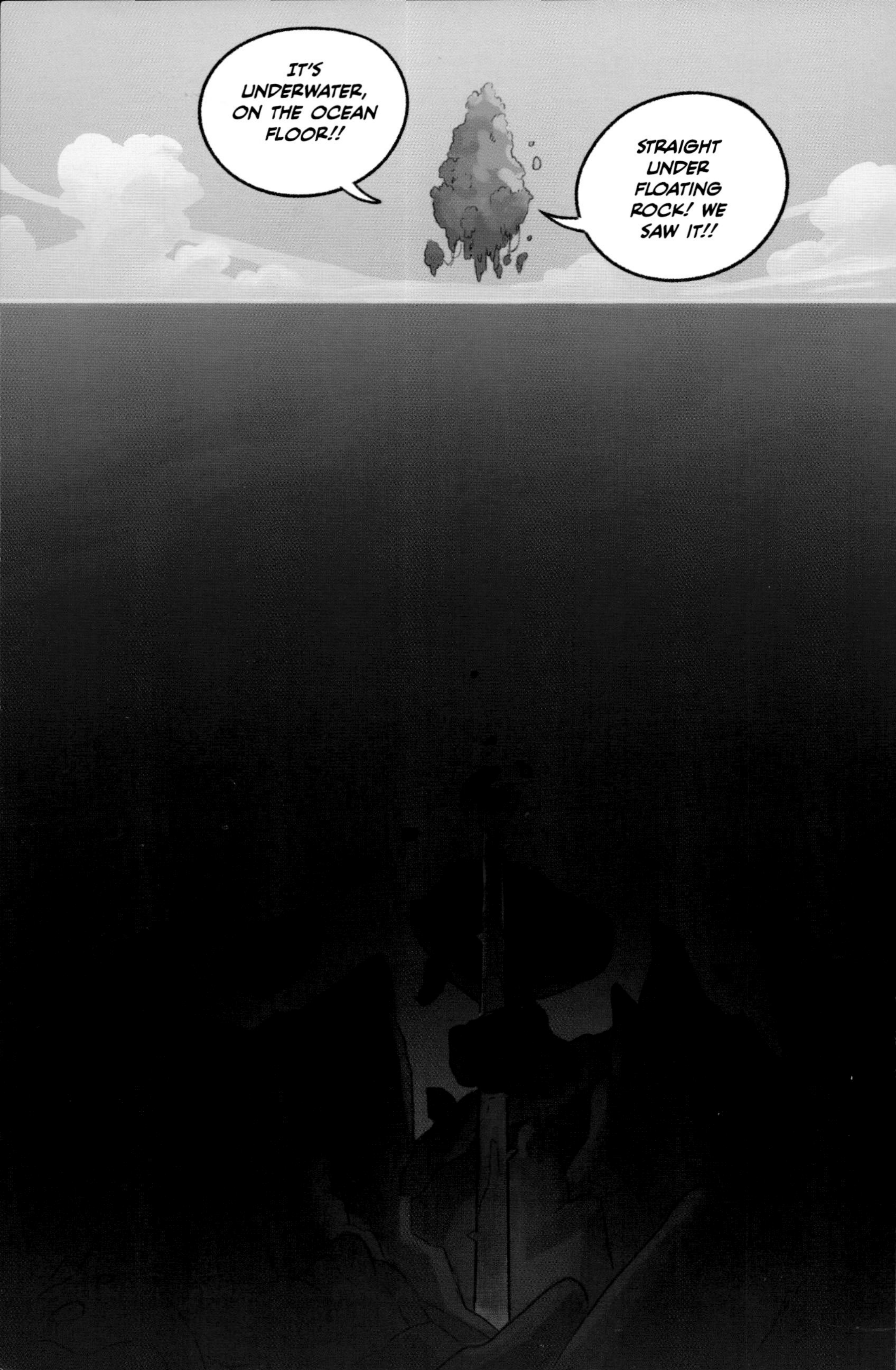
IT'S UNDERWATER, ON THE OCEAN FLOOR!!
STRAIGHT UNDER FLOATING ROCK! WE SAW IT!!

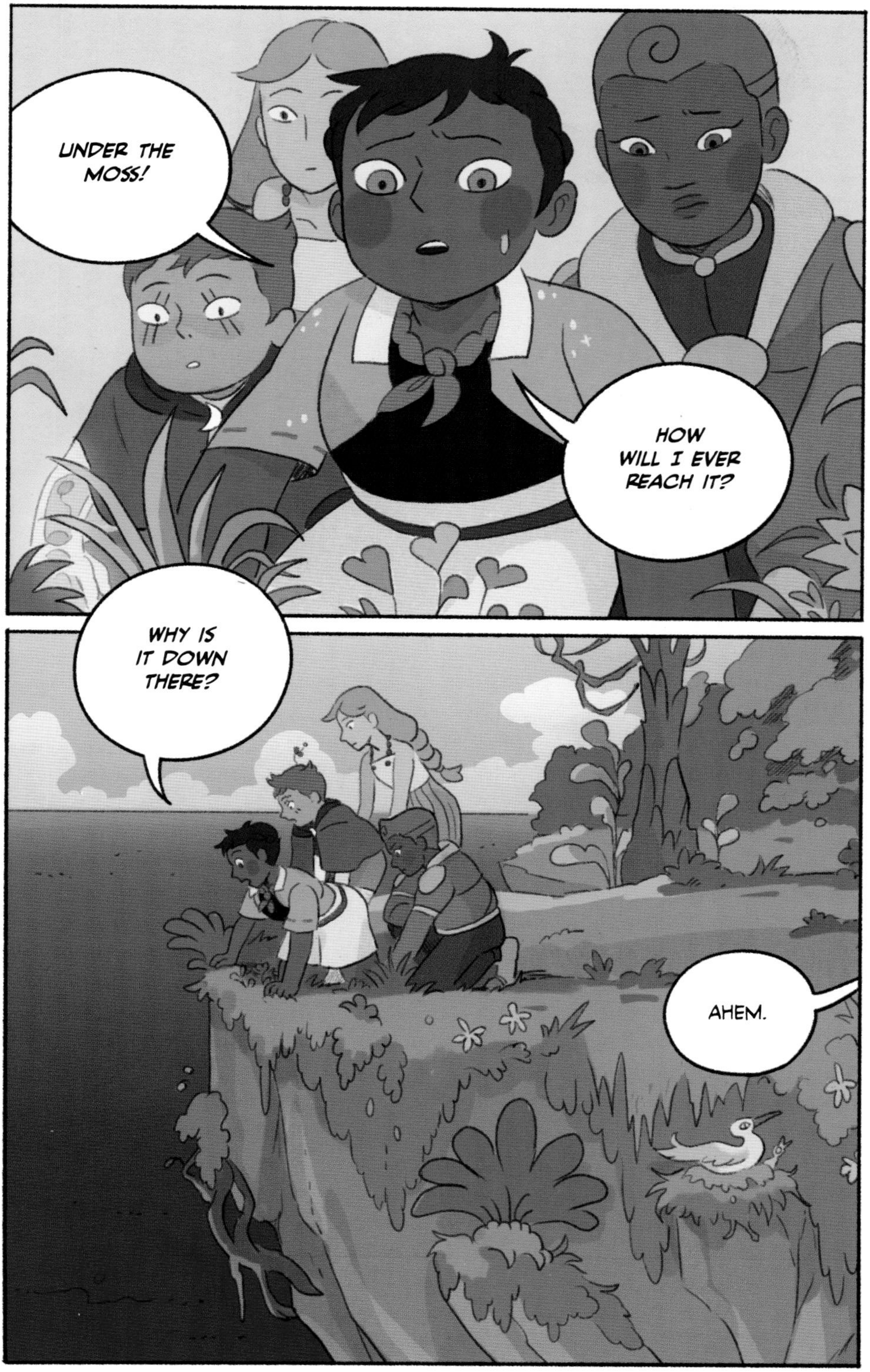
UNDER THE MOSS!
HOW WILL I EVER REACH IT?
WHY IS IT DOWN THERE?
AHEM.

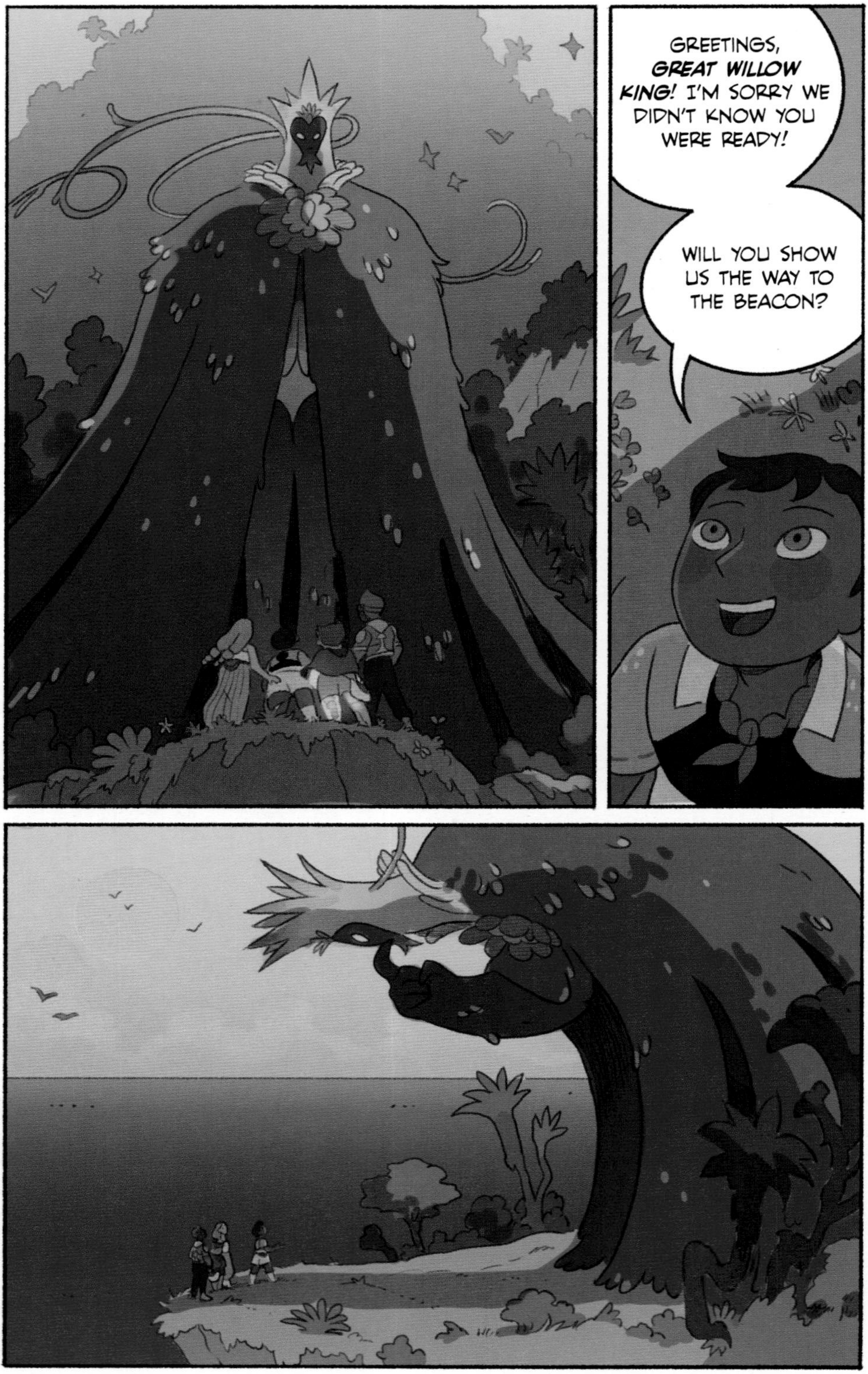
GREETINGS, **GREAT WILLOW KING!** I'M SORRY WE DIDN'T KNOW YOU WERE READY!
WILL YOU SHOW US THE WAY TO THE BEACON?

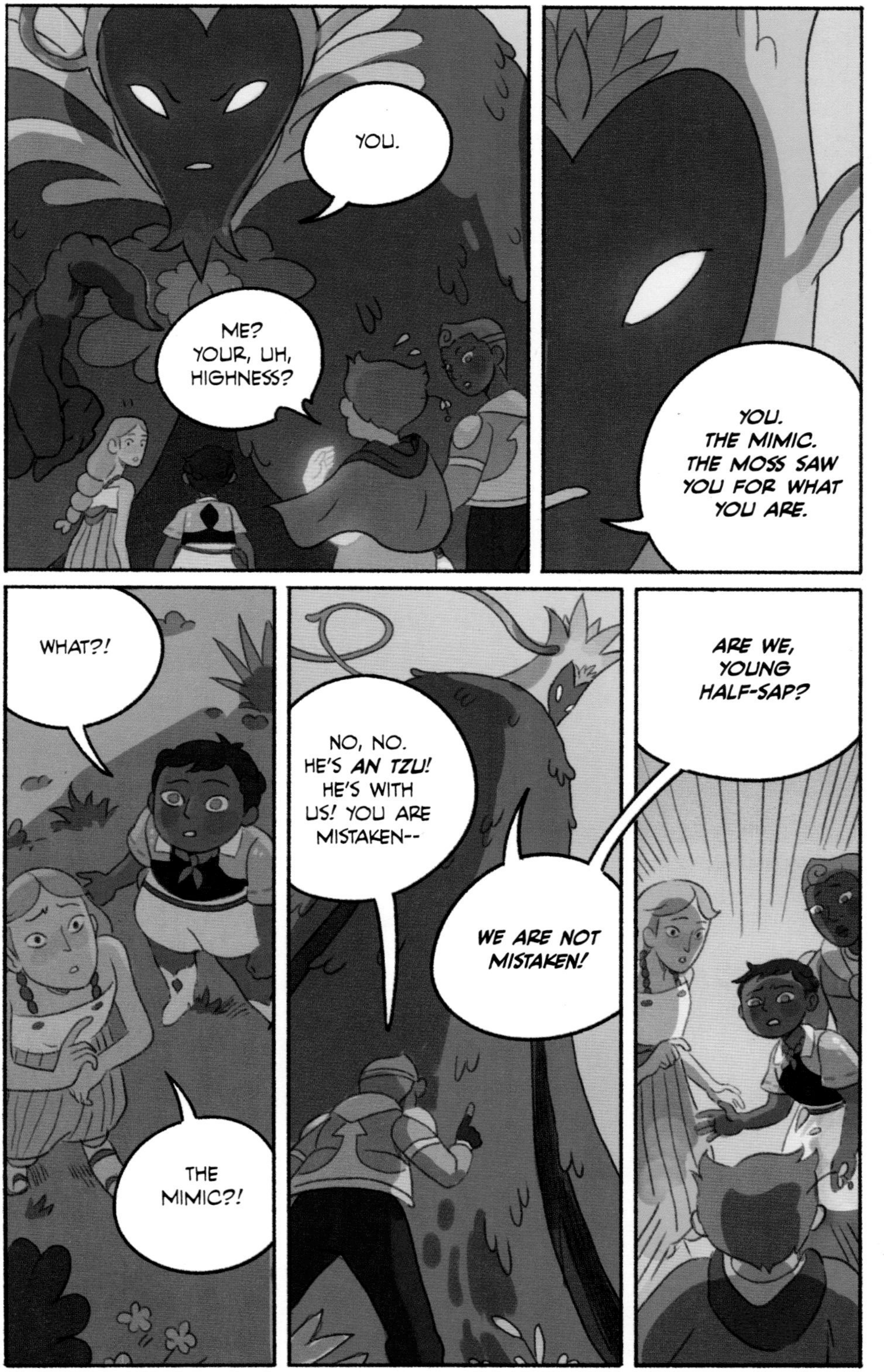
YOU.
ME? YOUR, UH, HIGHNESS?
YOU. THE MIMIC. THE MOSS SAW YOU FOR WHAT YOU ARE.
WHAT?!
THE MIMIC?!
NO, NO. HE'S *AN TZU!* HE'S WITH US! YOU ARE MISTAKEN--
WE ARE NOT MISTAKEN!
ARE WE, YOUNG HALF-SAP?

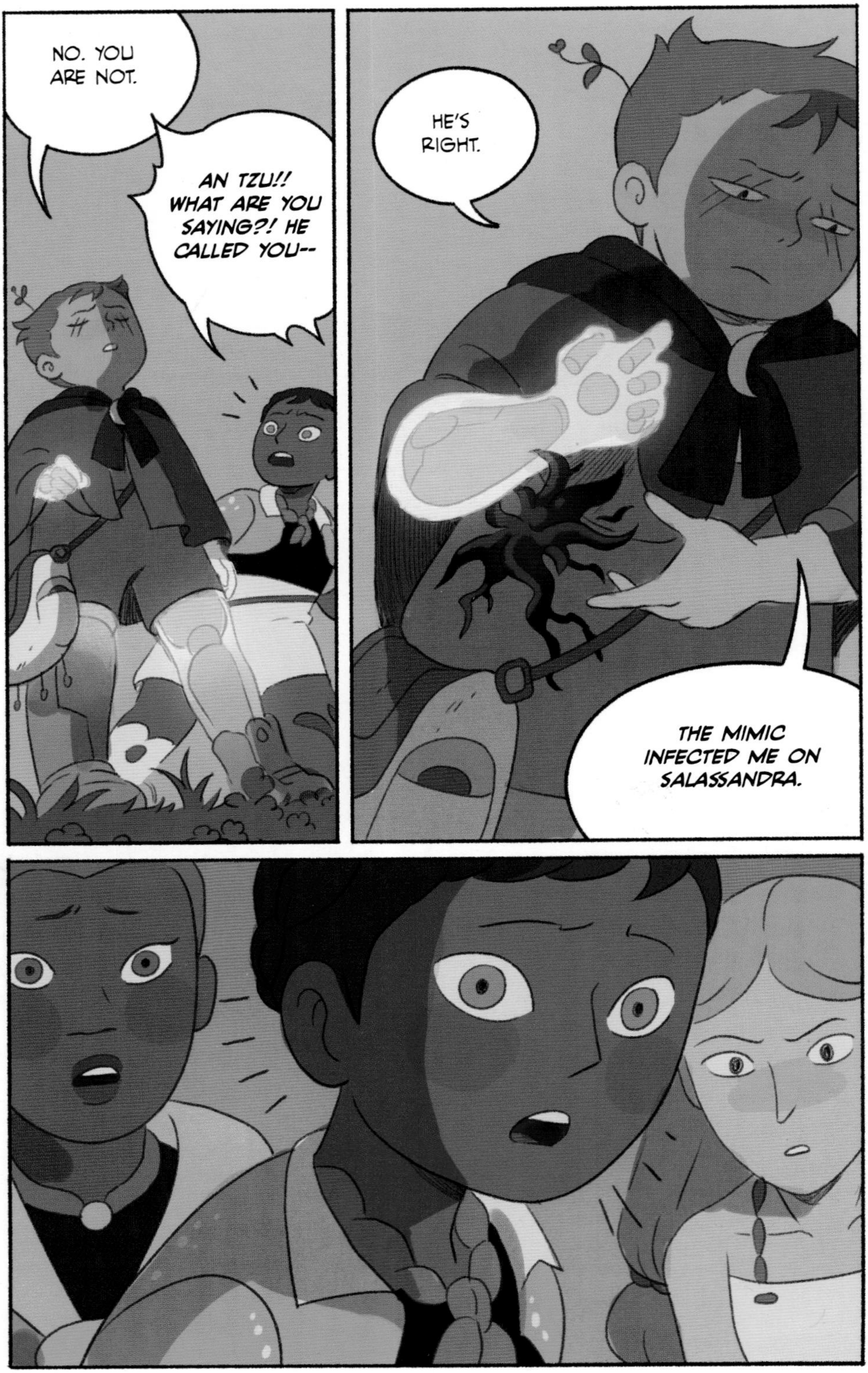
NO. YOU ARE NOT.
AN TZU!! WHAT ARE YOU SAYING?! HE CALLED YOU--
HE'S RIGHT.
THE MIMIC INFECTED ME ON SALASSANDRA.

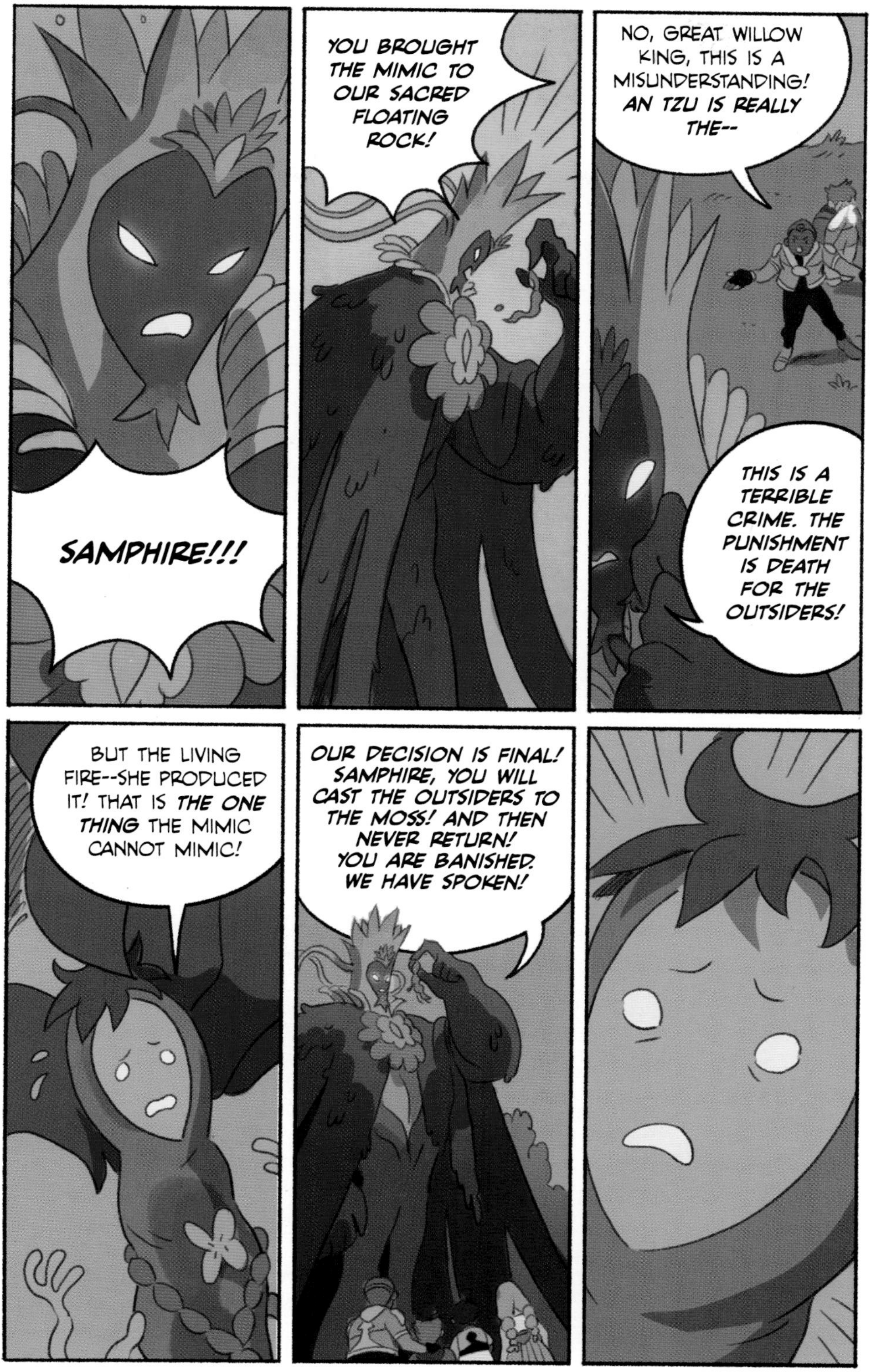
SAMPHIRE!!!
YOU BROUGHT THE MIMIC TO OUR SACRED FLOATING ROCK!
NO, GREAT WILLOW KING, THIS IS A MISUNDERSTANDING! AN TZU IS REALLY THE--
THIS IS A TERRIBLE CRIME. THE PUNISHMENT IS DEATH FOR THE OUTSIDERS!
BUT THE LIVING FIRE--SHE PRODUCED IT! THAT IS THE ONE THING THE MIMIC CANNOT MIMIC!
OUR DECISION IS FINAL! SAMPHIRE, YOU WILL CAST THE OUTSIDERS TO THE MOSS! AND THEN NEVER RETURN! YOU ARE BANISHED. WE HAVE SPOKEN!

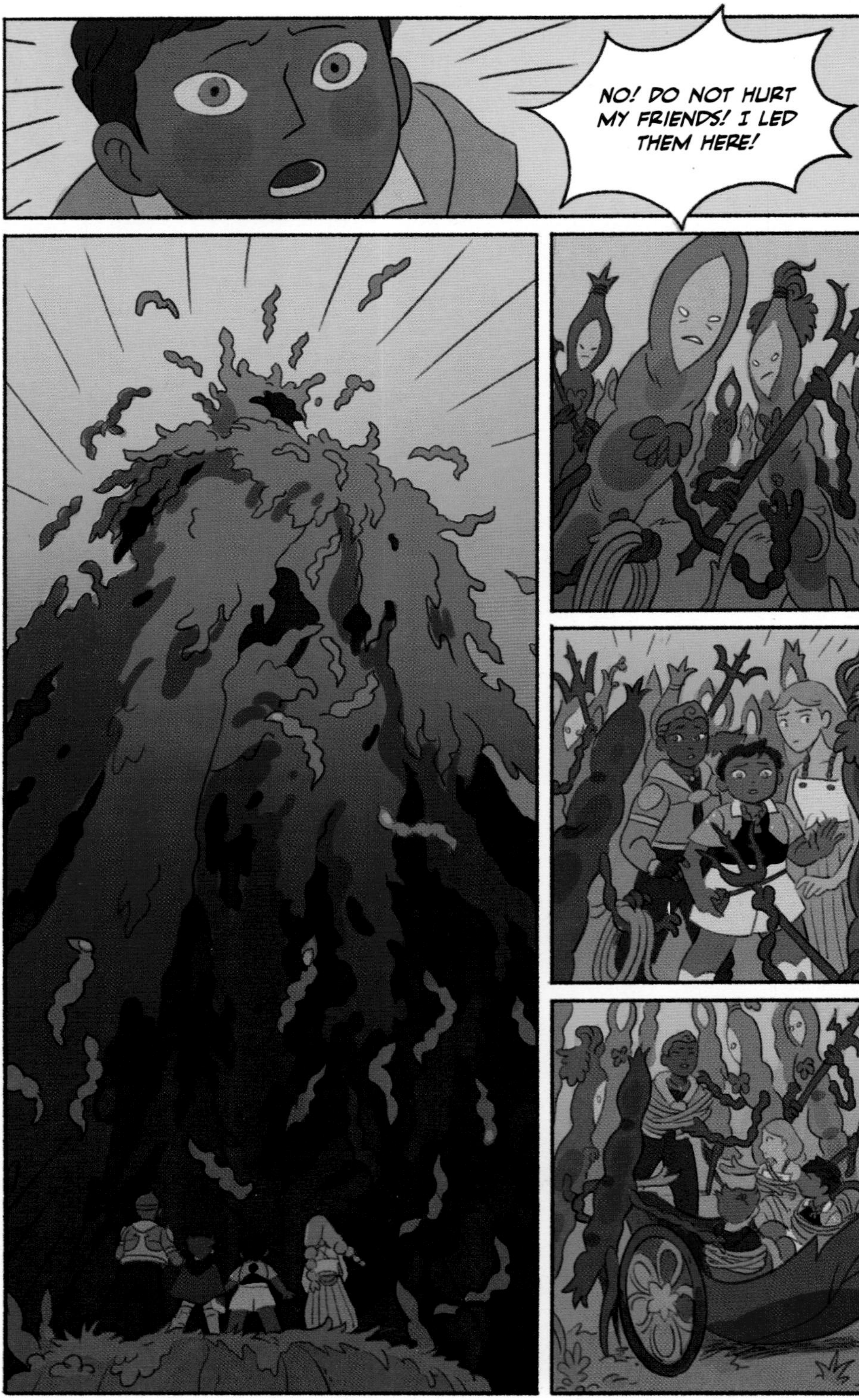
NO! DO NOT HURT
MY FRIENDS! I LED
THEM HERE!

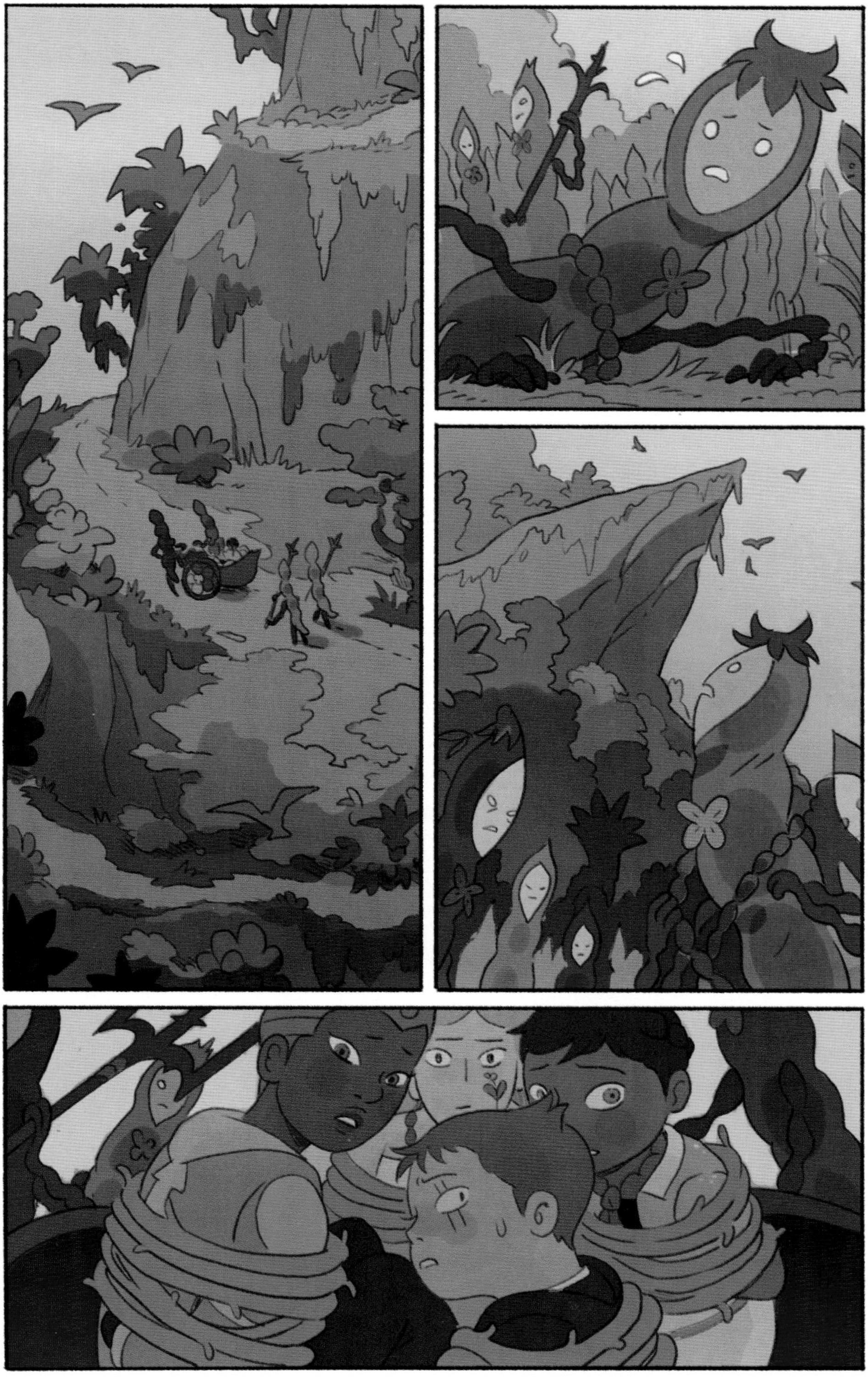

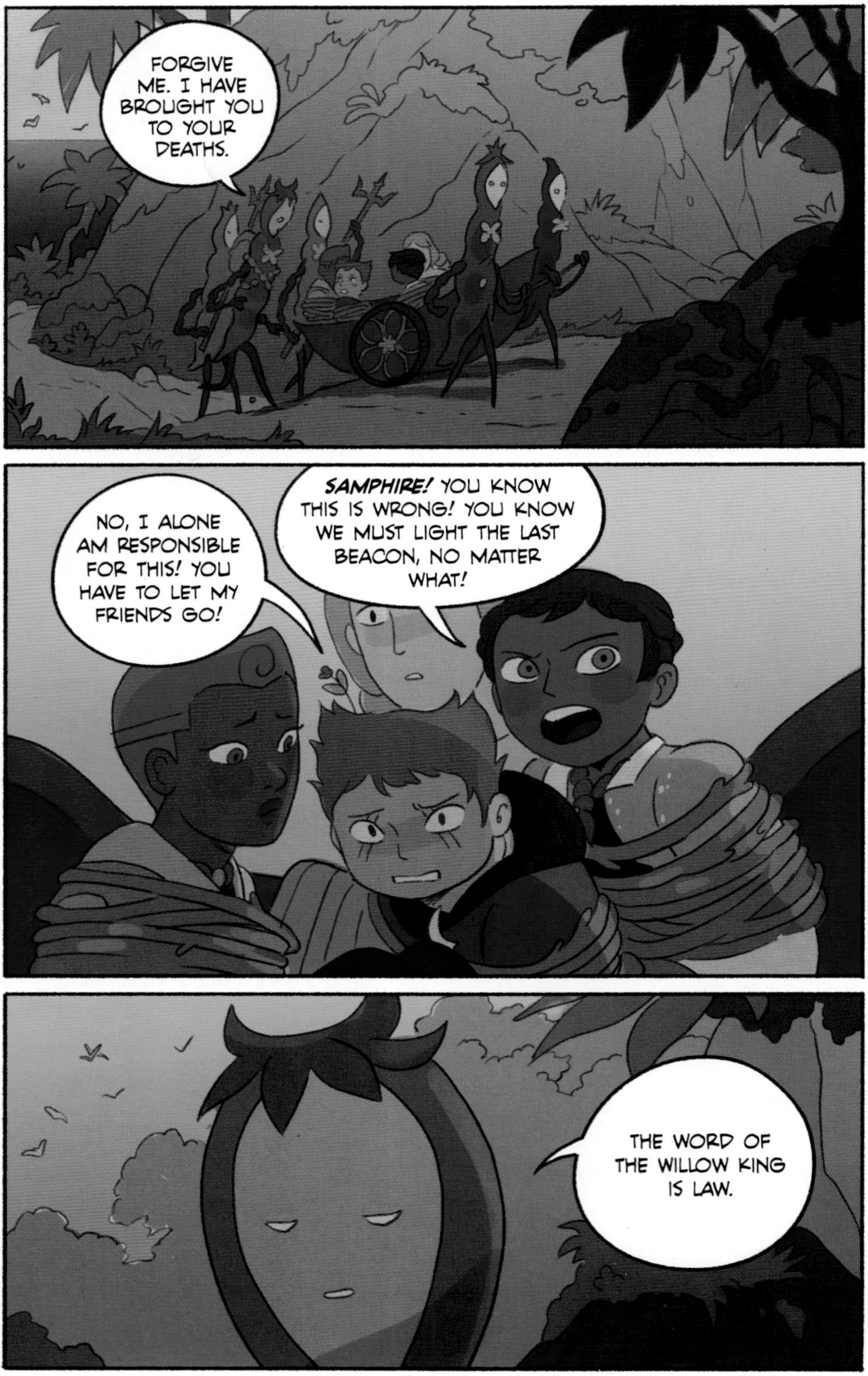
FORGIVE ME. I HAVE BROUGHT YOU TO YOUR DEATHS.
NO, I ALONE AM RESPONSIBLE FOR THIS! YOU HAVE TO LET MY FRIENDS GO!
SAMPHIRE! YOU KNOW THIS IS WRONG! YOU KNOW WE MUST LIGHT THE LAST BEACON, NO MATTER WHAT!
THE WORD OF THE WILLOW KING IS LAW.

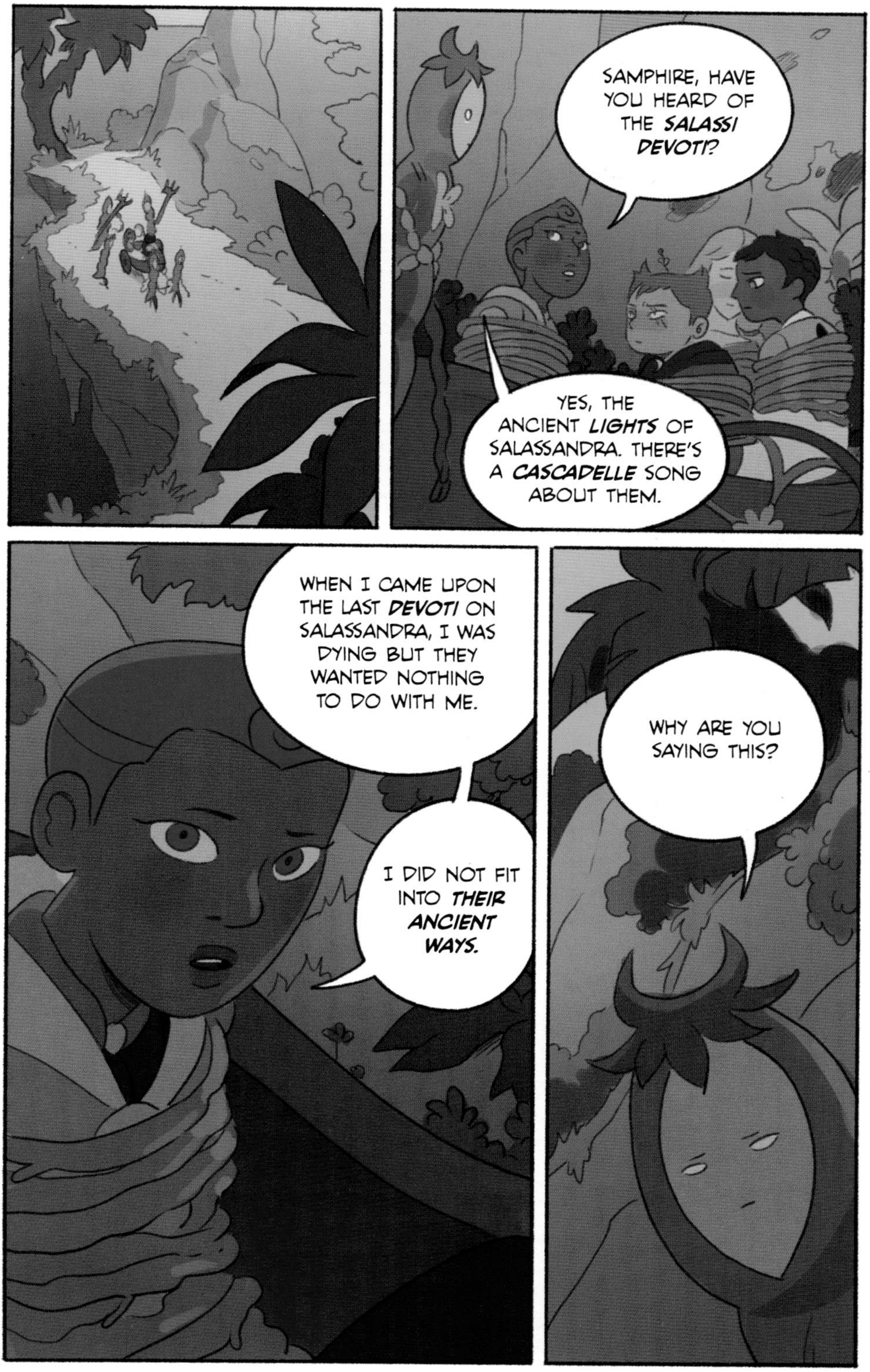
SAMPHIRE, HAVE YOU HEARD OF THE SALASSI DEVOTI?
YES, THE ANCIENT LIGHTS OF SALASSANDRA. THERE'S A CASCADELLE SONG ABOUT THEM.
WHEN I CAME UPON THE LAST DEVOTI ON SALASSANDRA, I WAS DYING BUT THEY WANTED NOTHING TO DO WITH ME.
I DID NOT FIT INTO THEIR ANCIENT WAYS.
WHY ARE YOU SAYING THIS?

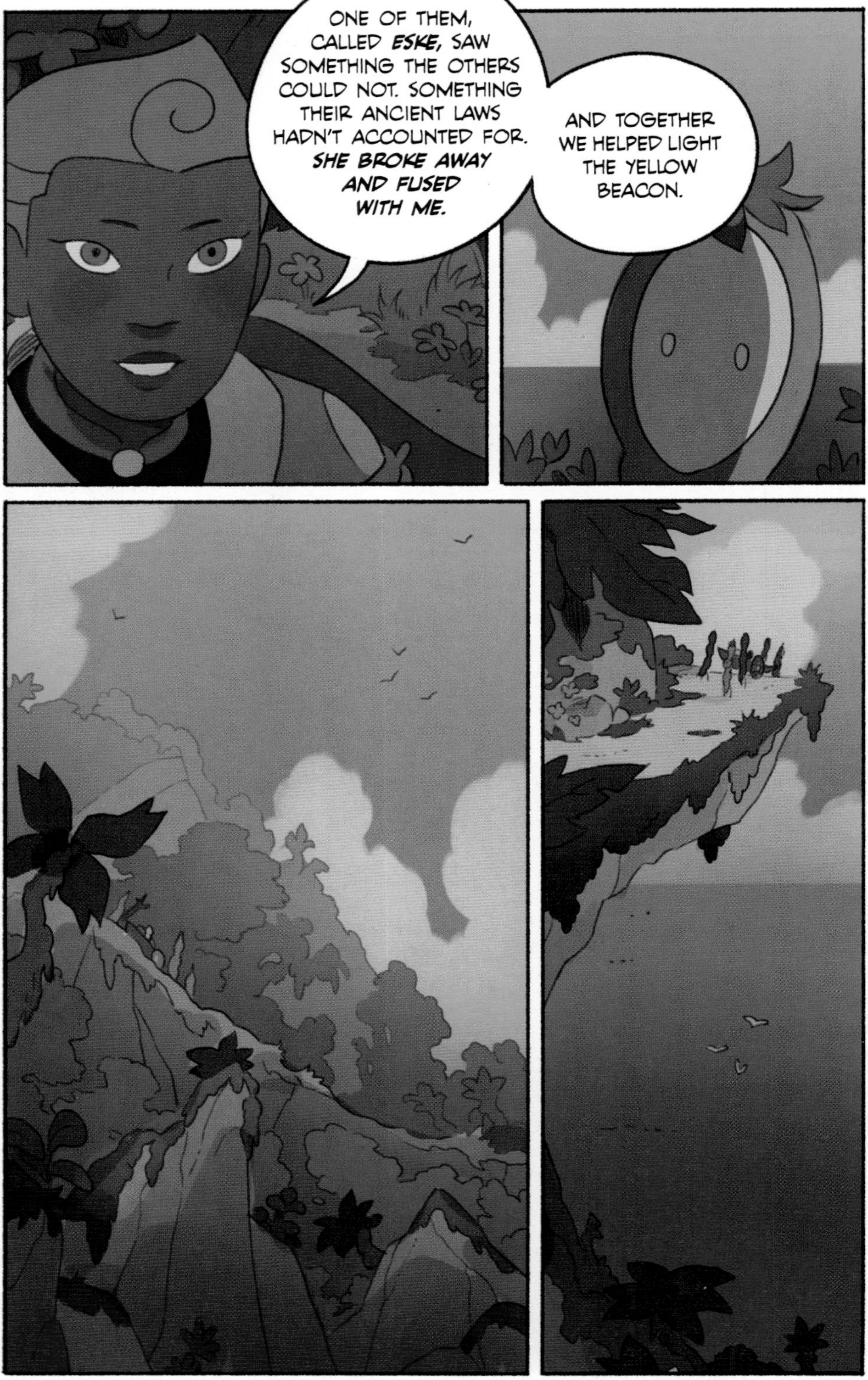

ONE OF THEM, CALLED ***ESKE,*** SAW SOMETHING THE OTHERS COULD NOT. SOMETHING THEIR ANCIENT LAWS HADN'T ACCOUNTED FOR. ***SHE BROKE AWAY AND FUSED WITH ME.***
AND TOGETHER WE HELPED LIGHT THE YELLOW BEACON.

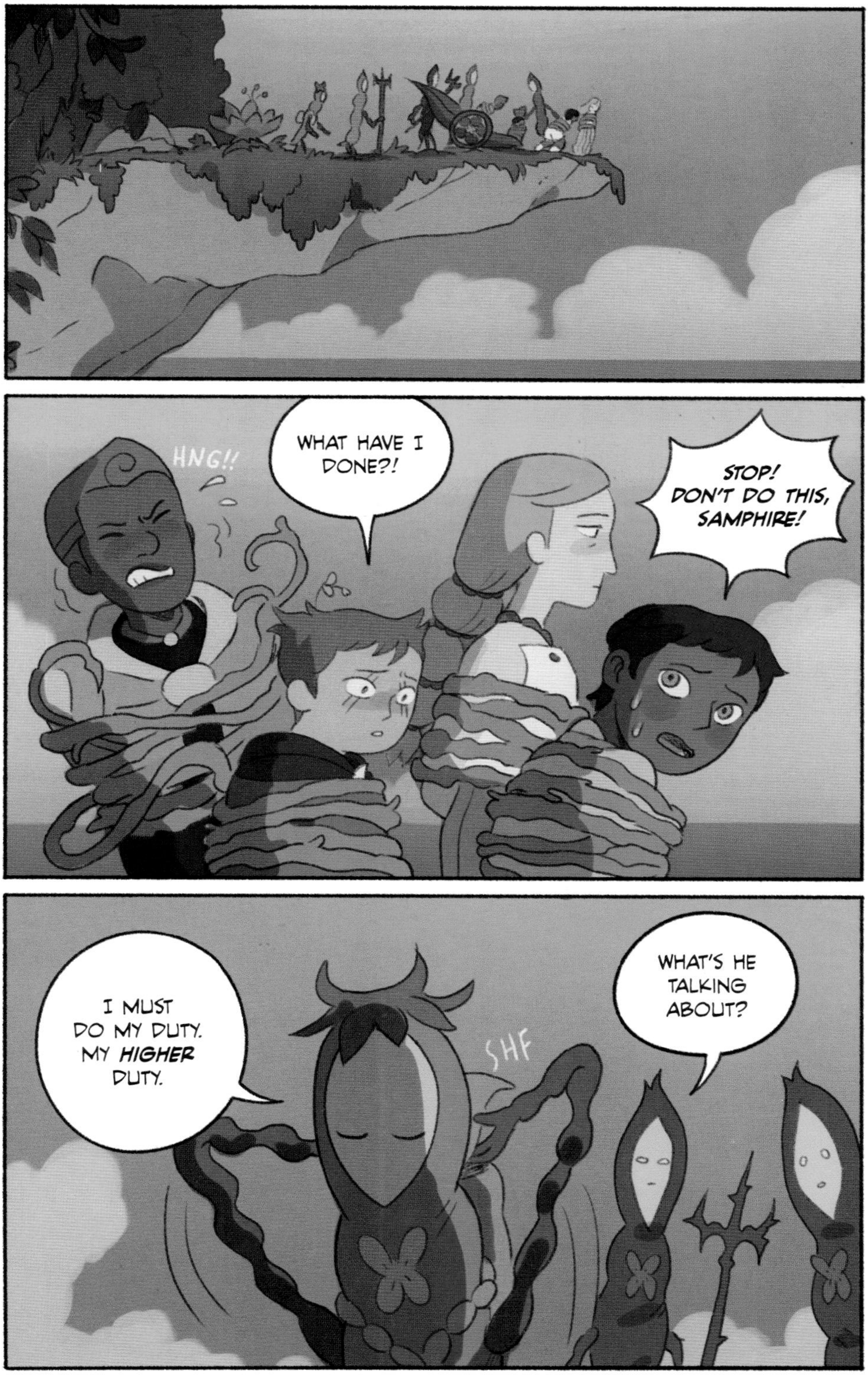
HNG!!
WHAT HAVE I DONE?!
STOP! DON'T DO THIS, SAMPHIRE!
I MUST DO MY DUTY. MY *HIGHER* DUTY.
SHF
WHAT'S HE TALKING ABOUT?

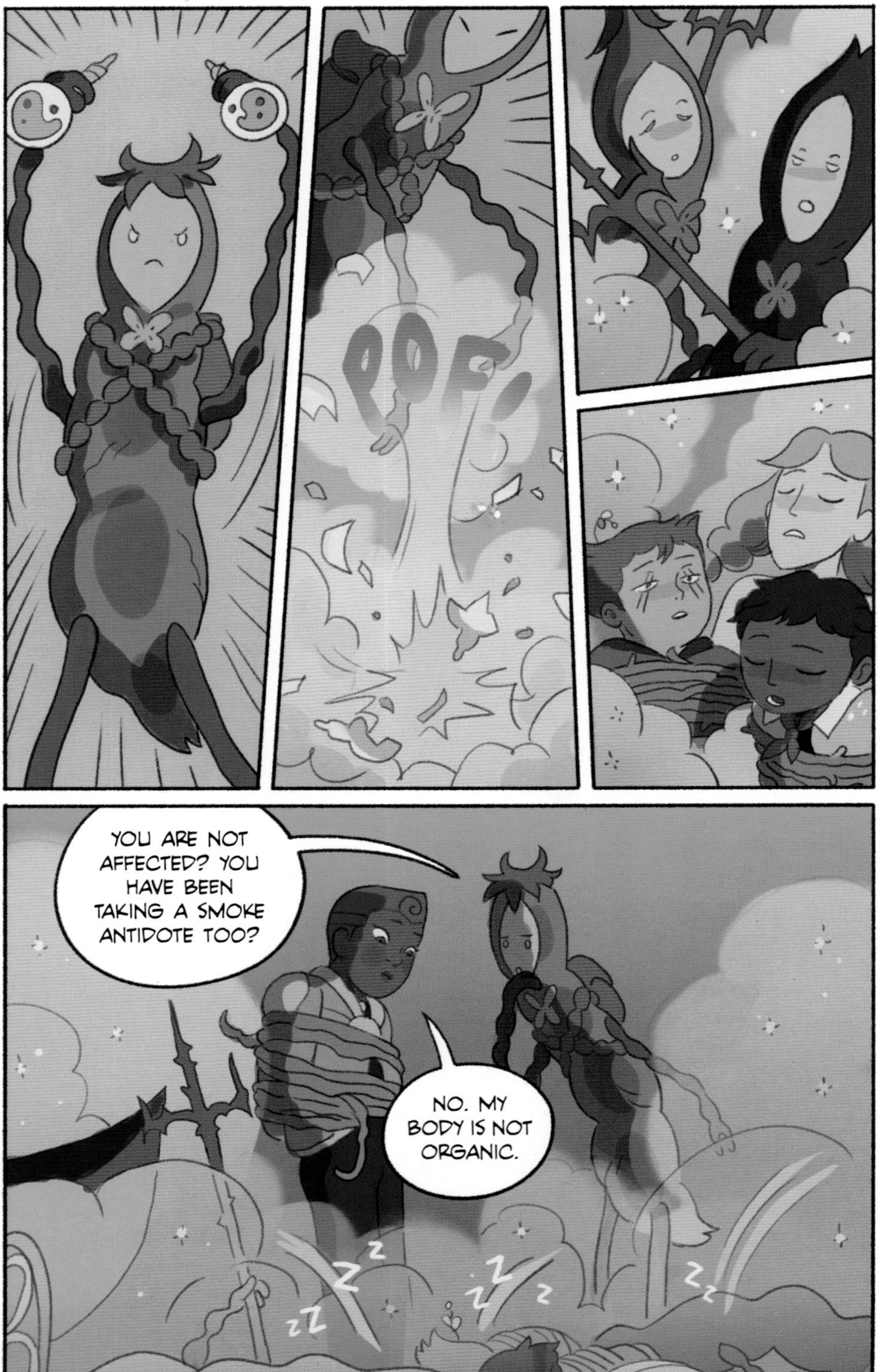
POF!
YOU ARE NOT AFFECTED? YOU HAVE BEEN TAKING A SMOKE ANTIDOTE TOO?
NO. MY BODY IS NOT ORGANIC.
ZZ
zZ
Z
Zz

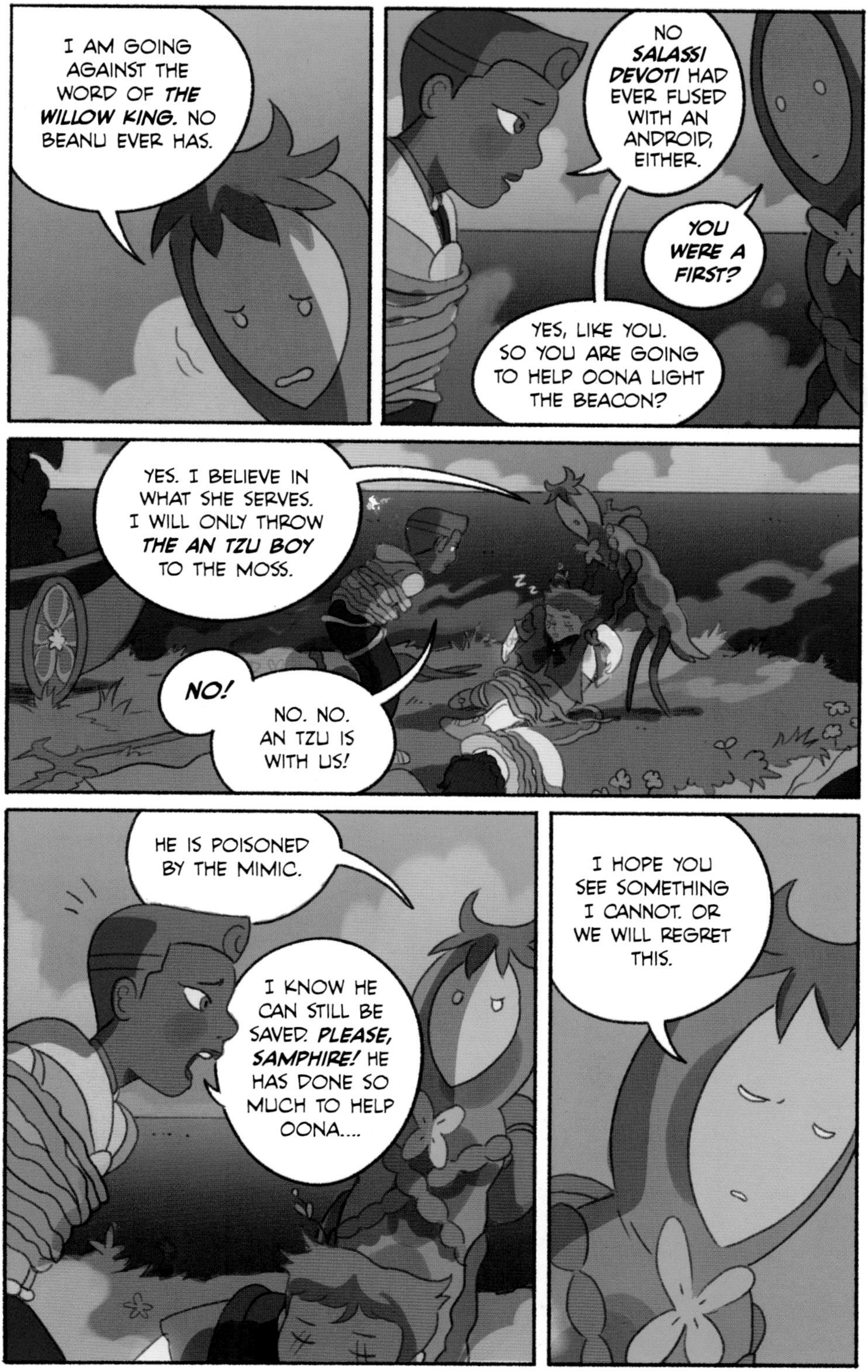
I AM GOING AGAINST THE WORD OF THE WILLOW KING. NO BEANU EVER HAS.
NO SALASSI DEVOTI HAD EVER FUSED WITH AN ANDROID, EITHER.
YOU WERE A FIRST?
YES, LIKE YOU. SO YOU ARE GOING TO HELP OONA LIGHT THE BEACON?
YES. I BELIEVE IN WHAT SHE SERVES. I WILL ONLY THROW THE AN TZU BOY TO THE MOSS.
Z Z
NO!
NO. NO. AN TZU IS WITH US!
HE IS POISONED BY THE MIMIC.
I KNOW HE CAN STILL BE SAVED. PLEASE, SAMPHIRE! HE HAS DONE SO MUCH TO HELP OONA....
I HOPE YOU SEE SOMETHING I CANNOT. OR WE WILL REGRET THIS.

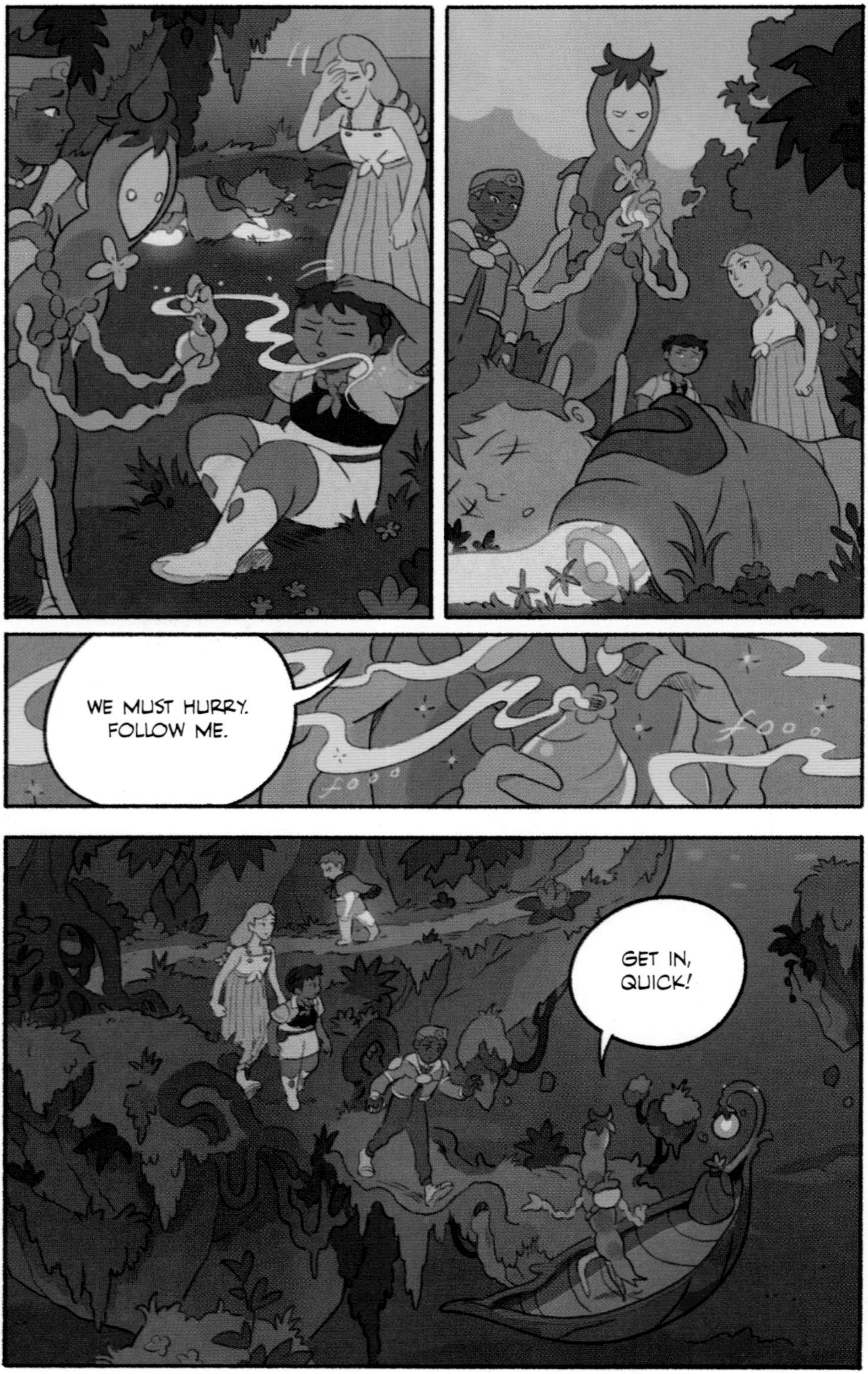
WE MUST HURRY. FOLLOW ME.
GET IN, QUICK!

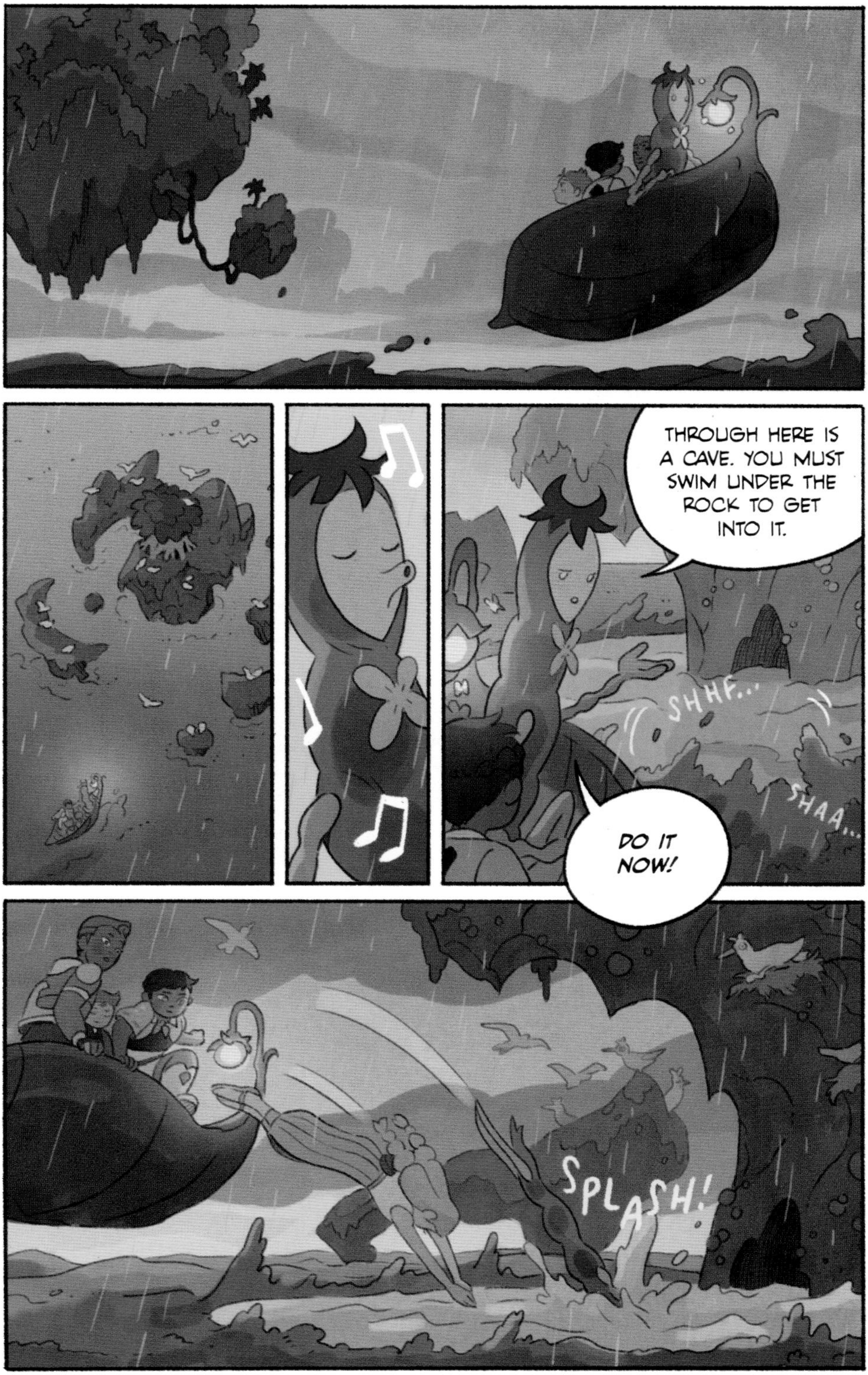
THROUGH HERE IS A CAVE. YOU MUST SWIM UNDER THE ROCK TO GET INTO IT.
SHHF...
SHAA...
DO IT NOW!
SPLASH!

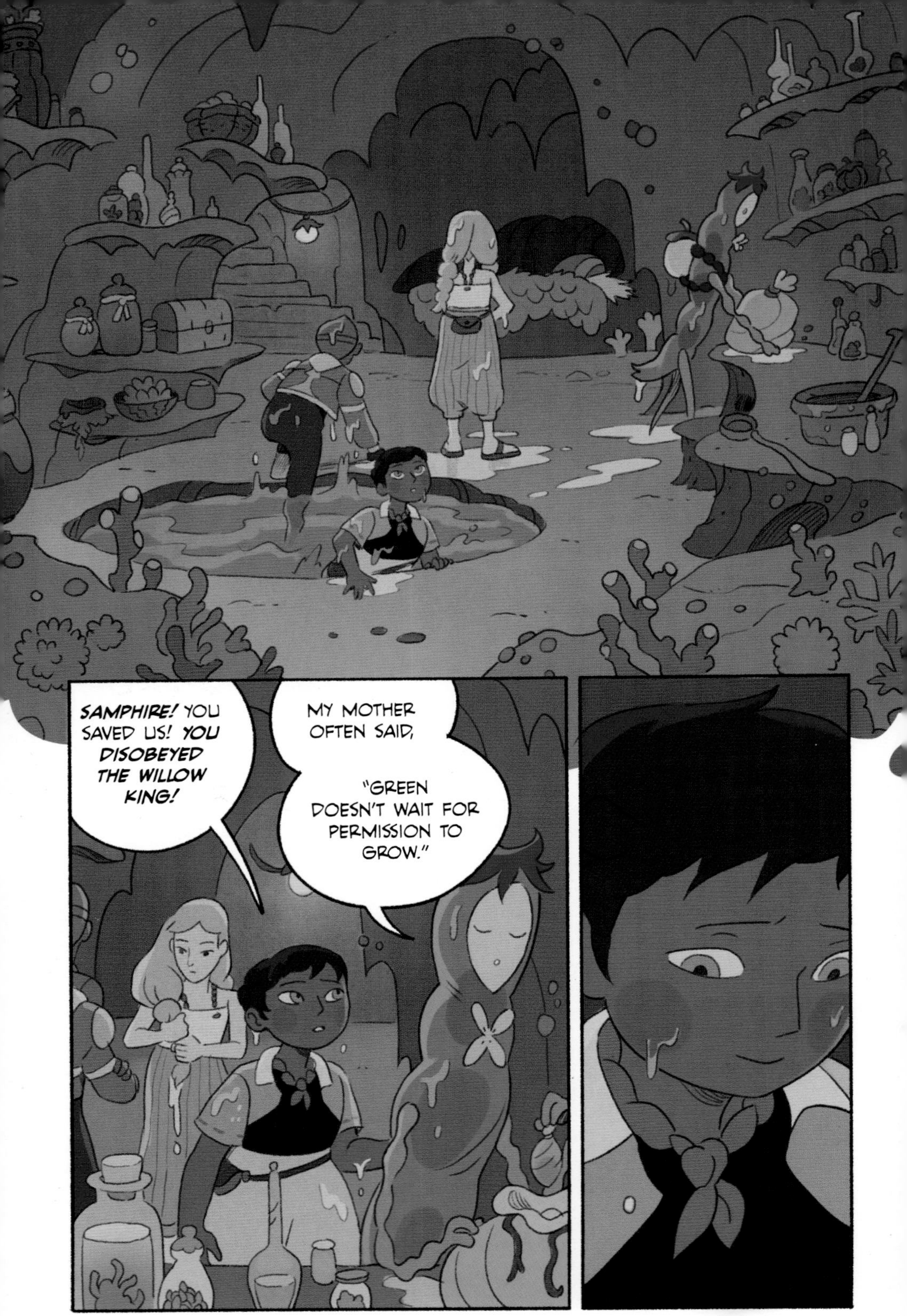

SAMPHIRE! YOU SAVED US! YOU DISOBEYED THE WILLOW KING!
MY MOTHER OFTEN SAID,
"GREEN DOESN'T WAIT FOR PERMISSION TO GROW."

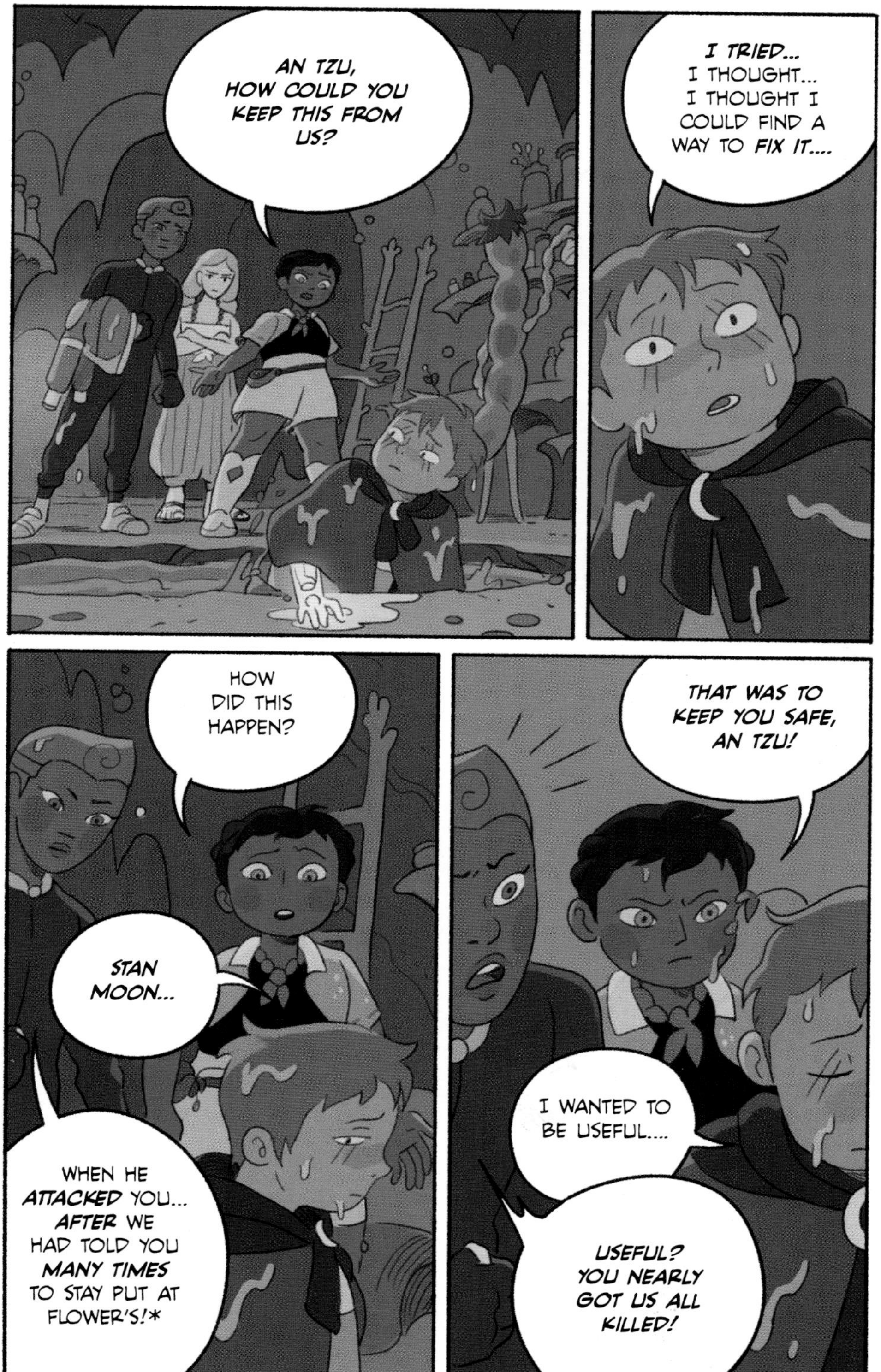
AN TZU, HOW COULD YOU KEEP THIS FROM US?
I TRIED... I THOUGHT... I THOUGHT I COULD FIND A WAY TO FIX IT....
HOW DID THIS HAPPEN?
STAN MOON...
WHEN HE ATTACKED YOU... AFTER WE HAD TOLD YOU MANY TIMES TO STAY PUT AT FLOWER'S!*
THAT WAS TO KEEP YOU SAFE, AN TZU!
I WANTED TO BE USEFUL....
USEFUL? YOU NEARLY GOT US ALL KILLED!

* SEE 5W4: *THE AMBER ANTHEM*

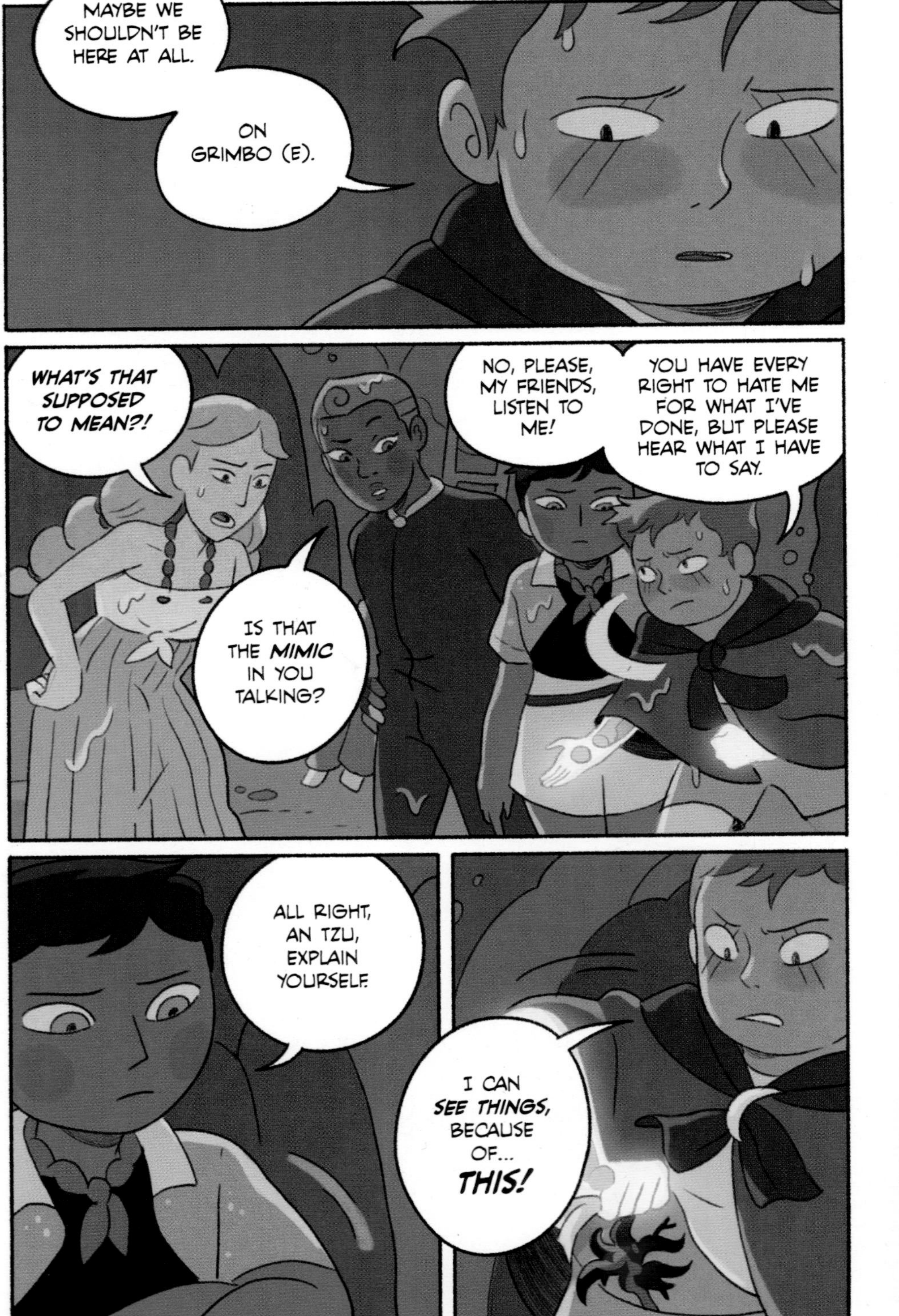
MAYBE WE SHOULDN'T BE HERE AT ALL.
ON GRIMBO (E).
WHAT'S THAT SUPPOSED TO MEAN?!
IS THAT THE MIMIC IN YOU TALKING?
NO, PLEASE, MY FRIENDS, LISTEN TO ME!
YOU HAVE EVERY RIGHT TO HATE ME FOR WHAT I'VE DONE, BUT PLEASE HEAR WHAT I HAVE TO SAY.
ALL RIGHT, AN TZU, EXPLAIN YOURSELF.
I CAN SEE THINGS, BECAUSE OF... THIS!

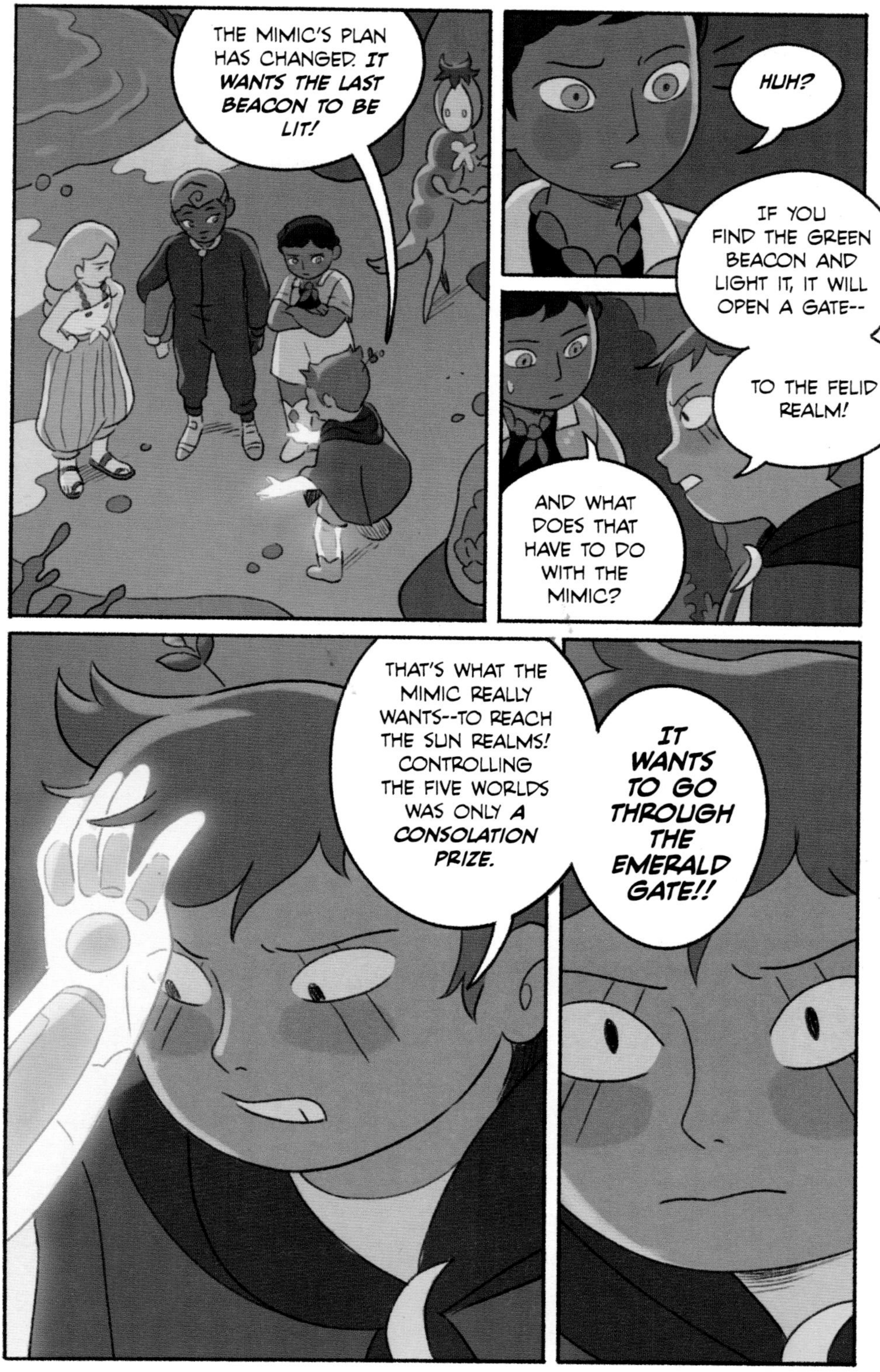
THE MIMIC'S PLAN HAS CHANGED. IT WANTS THE LAST BEACON TO BE LIT!
HUH?
IF YOU FIND THE GREEN BEACON AND LIGHT IT, IT WILL OPEN A GATE--
TO THE FELID REALM!
AND WHAT DOES THAT HAVE TO DO WITH THE MIMIC?
THAT'S WHAT THE MIMIC REALLY WANTS--TO REACH THE SUN REALMS! CONTROLLING THE FIVE WORLDS WAS ONLY A CONSOLATION PRIZE.
IT WANTS TO GO THROUGH THE EMERALD GATE!!

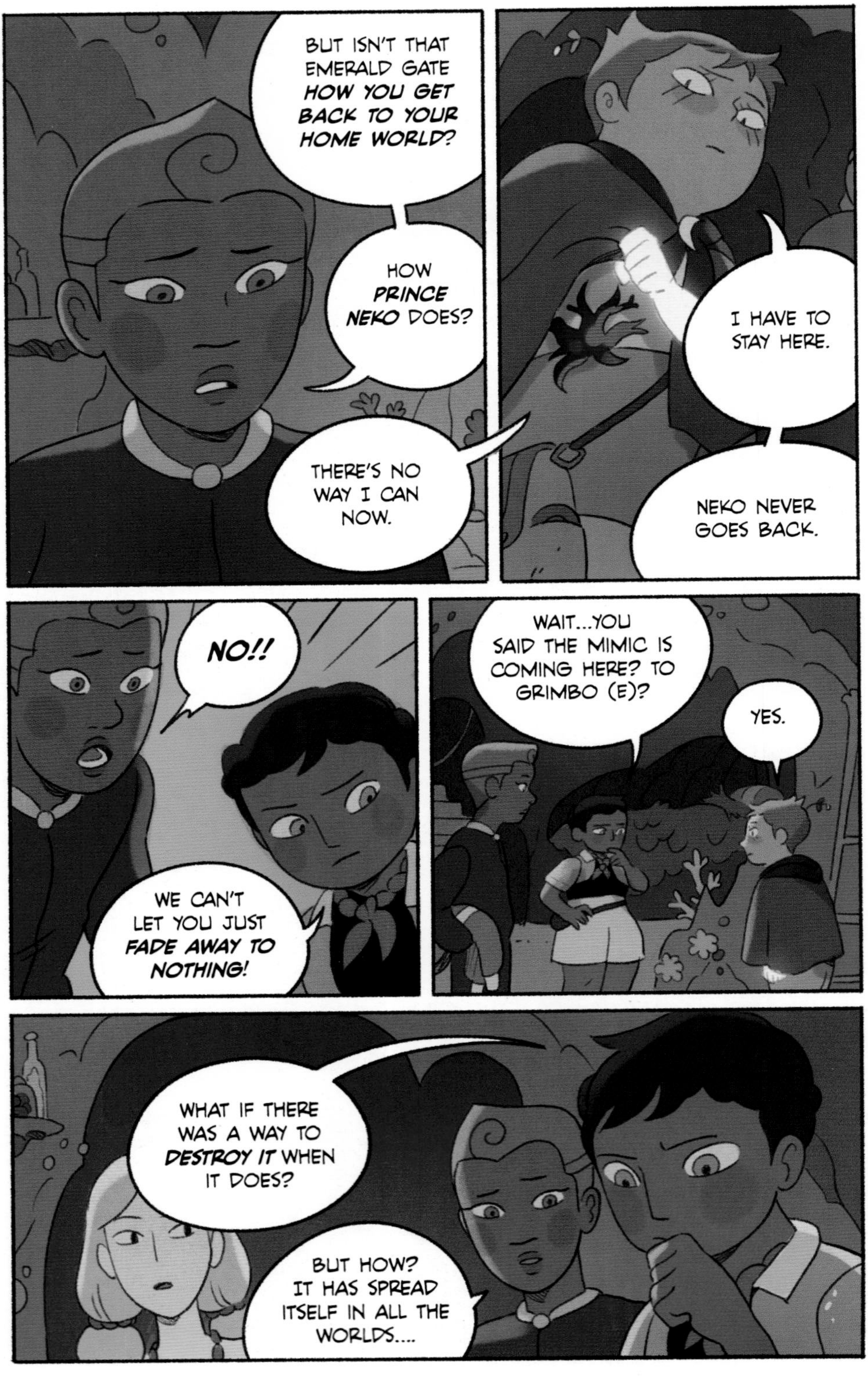
BUT ISN'T THAT EMERALD GATE *HOW YOU GET BACK TO YOUR HOME WORLD?*
HOW *PRINCE NEKO* DOES?
THERE'S NO WAY I CAN NOW.
I HAVE TO STAY HERE.
NEKO NEVER GOES BACK.
NO!!
WE CAN'T LET YOU JUST *FADE AWAY TO NOTHING!*
WAIT...YOU SAID THE MIMIC IS COMING HERE? TO GRIMBO (E)?
YES.
WHAT IF THERE WAS A WAY TO *DESTROY IT* WHEN IT DOES?
BUT HOW? IT HAS SPREAD ITSELF IN ALL THE WORLDS....

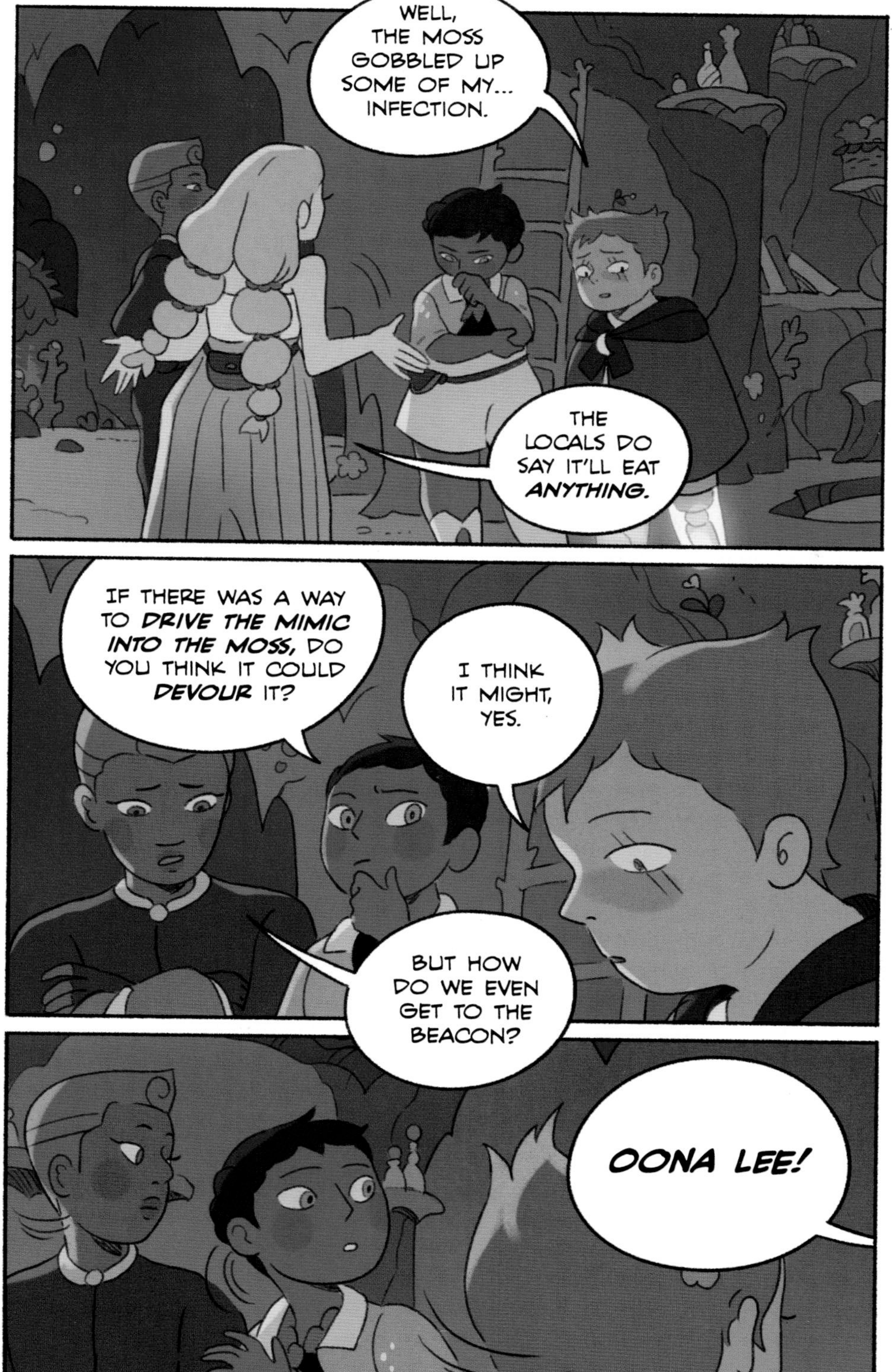
WELL, THE MOSS GOBBLED UP SOME OF MY... INFECTION.
THE LOCALS DO SAY IT'LL EAT *ANYTHING.*
IF THERE WAS A WAY TO *DRIVE THE MIMIC INTO THE MOSS,* DO YOU THINK IT COULD *DEVOUR* IT?
I THINK IT MIGHT, YES.
BUT HOW DO WE EVEN GET TO THE BEACON?
OONA LEE!

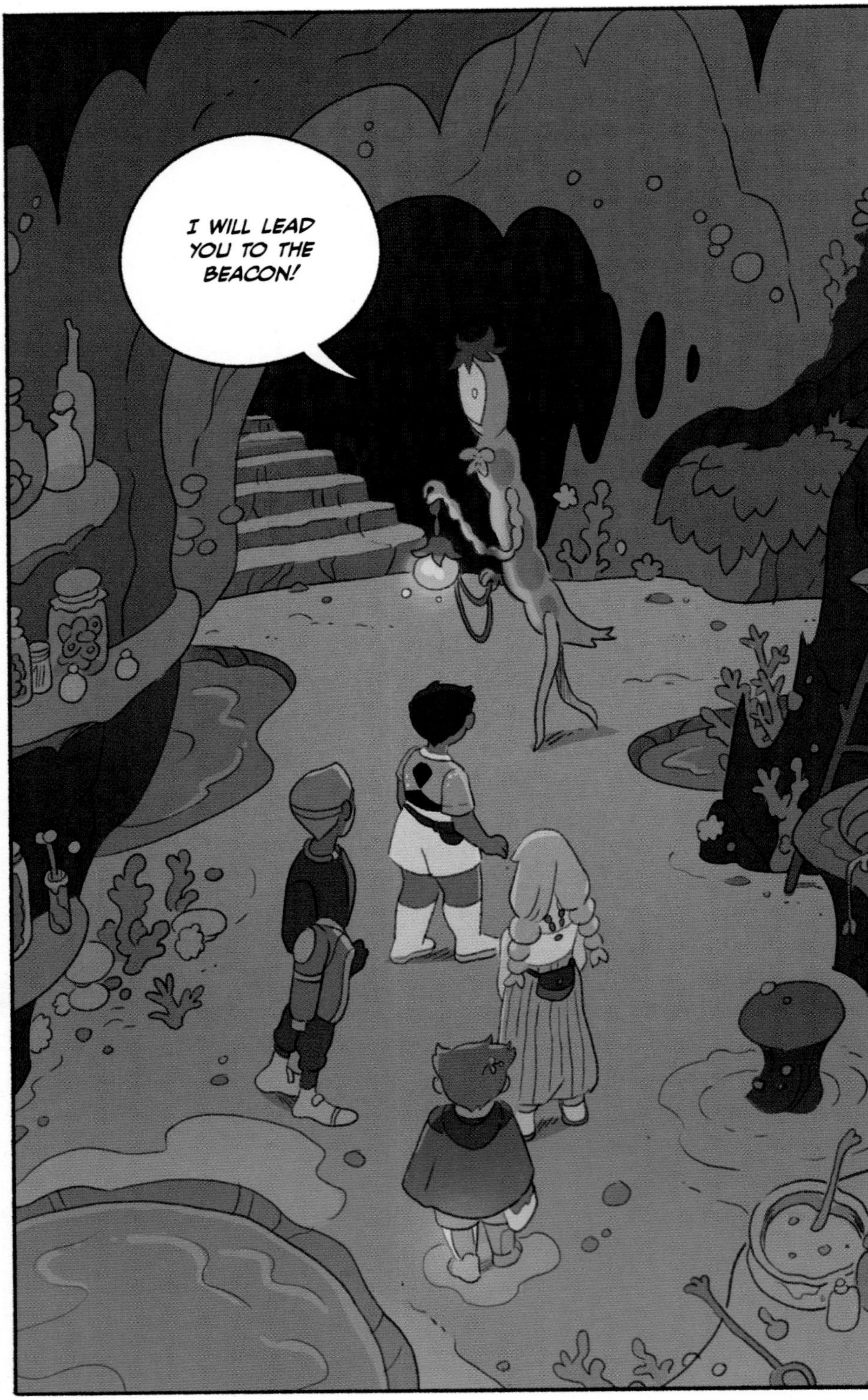
I WILL LEAD YOU TO THE BEACON!

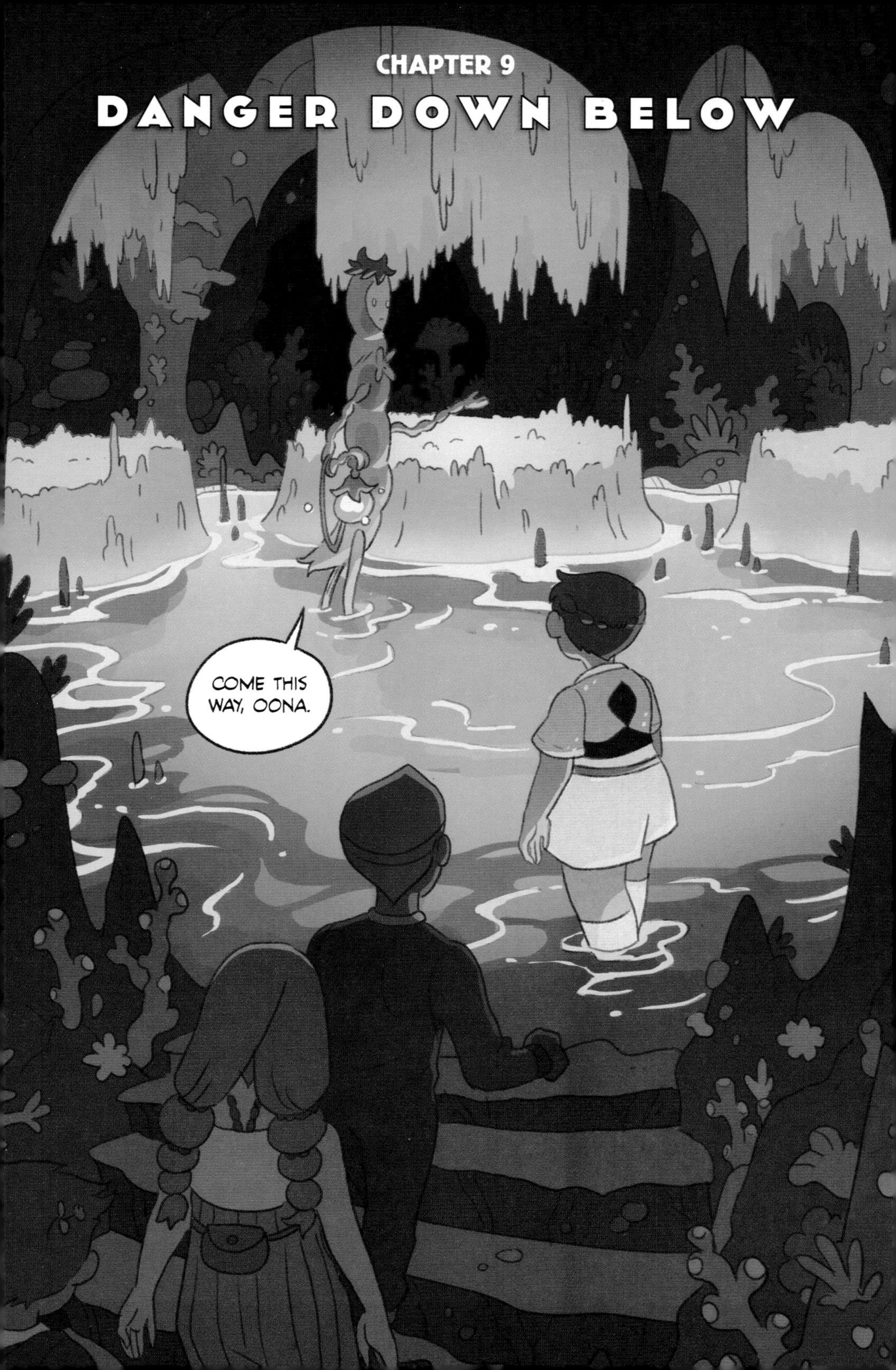
CHAPTER 9
DANGER DOWN BELOW
COME THIS WAY, OONA.

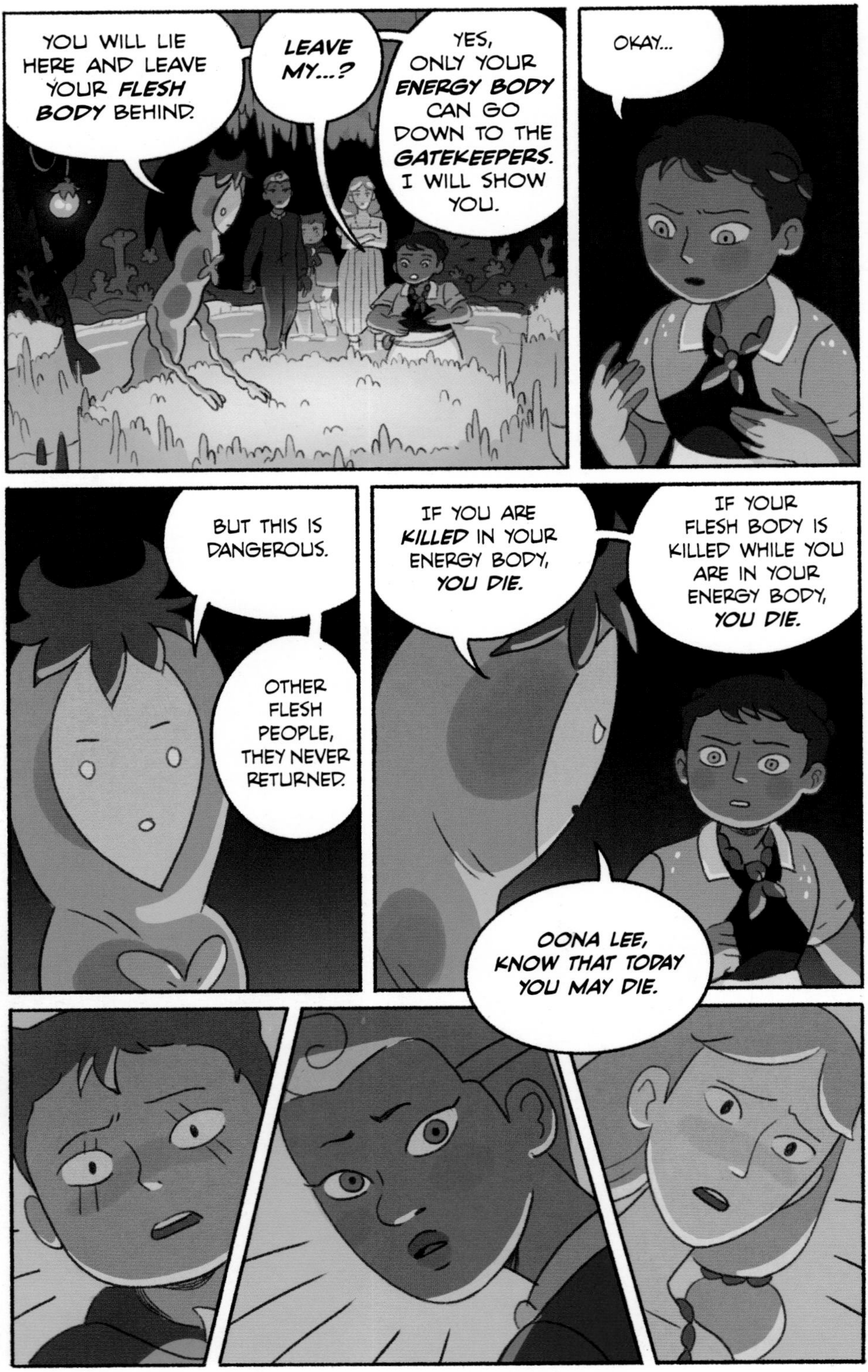
YOU WILL LIE HERE AND LEAVE YOUR FLESH BODY BEHIND.
LEAVE MY...?
YES, ONLY YOUR ENERGY BODY CAN GO DOWN TO THE GATEKEEPERS. I WILL SHOW YOU.
OKAY...
BUT THIS IS DANGEROUS.
OTHER FLESH PEOPLE, THEY NEVER RETURNED.
IF YOU ARE KILLED IN YOUR ENERGY BODY, YOU DIE.
IF YOUR FLESH BODY IS KILLED WHILE YOU ARE IN YOUR ENERGY BODY, YOU DIE.
OONA LEE, KNOW THAT TODAY YOU MAY DIE.

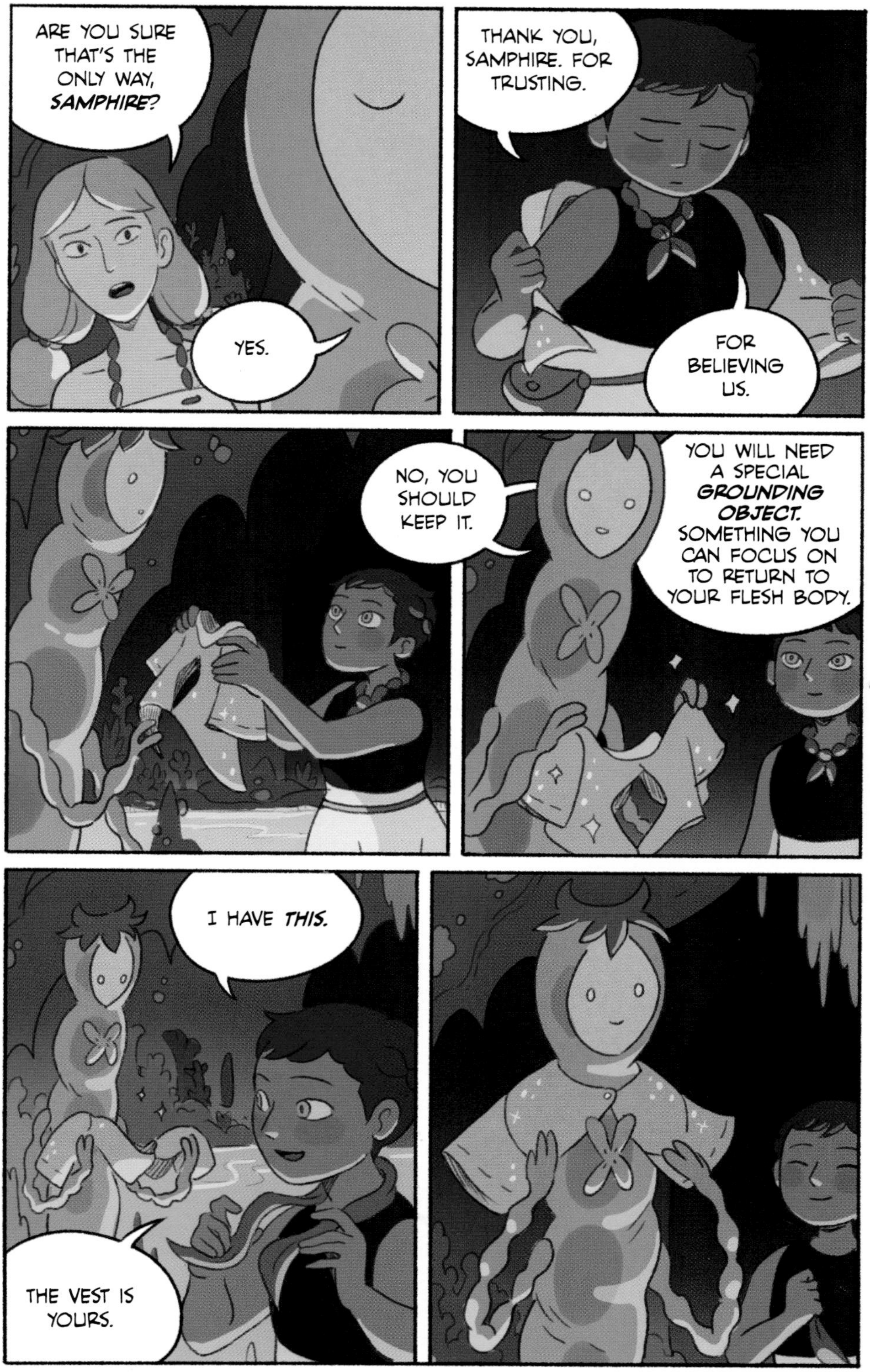
ARE YOU SURE THAT'S THE ONLY WAY, ***SAMPHIRE?***
YES.
THANK YOU, SAMPHIRE. FOR TRUSTING.
FOR BELIEVING US.
NO, YOU SHOULD KEEP IT.
YOU WILL NEED A SPECIAL ***GROUNDING OBJECT.*** SOMETHING YOU CAN FOCUS ON TO RETURN TO YOUR FLESH BODY.
I HAVE ***THIS.***
THE VEST IS YOURS.

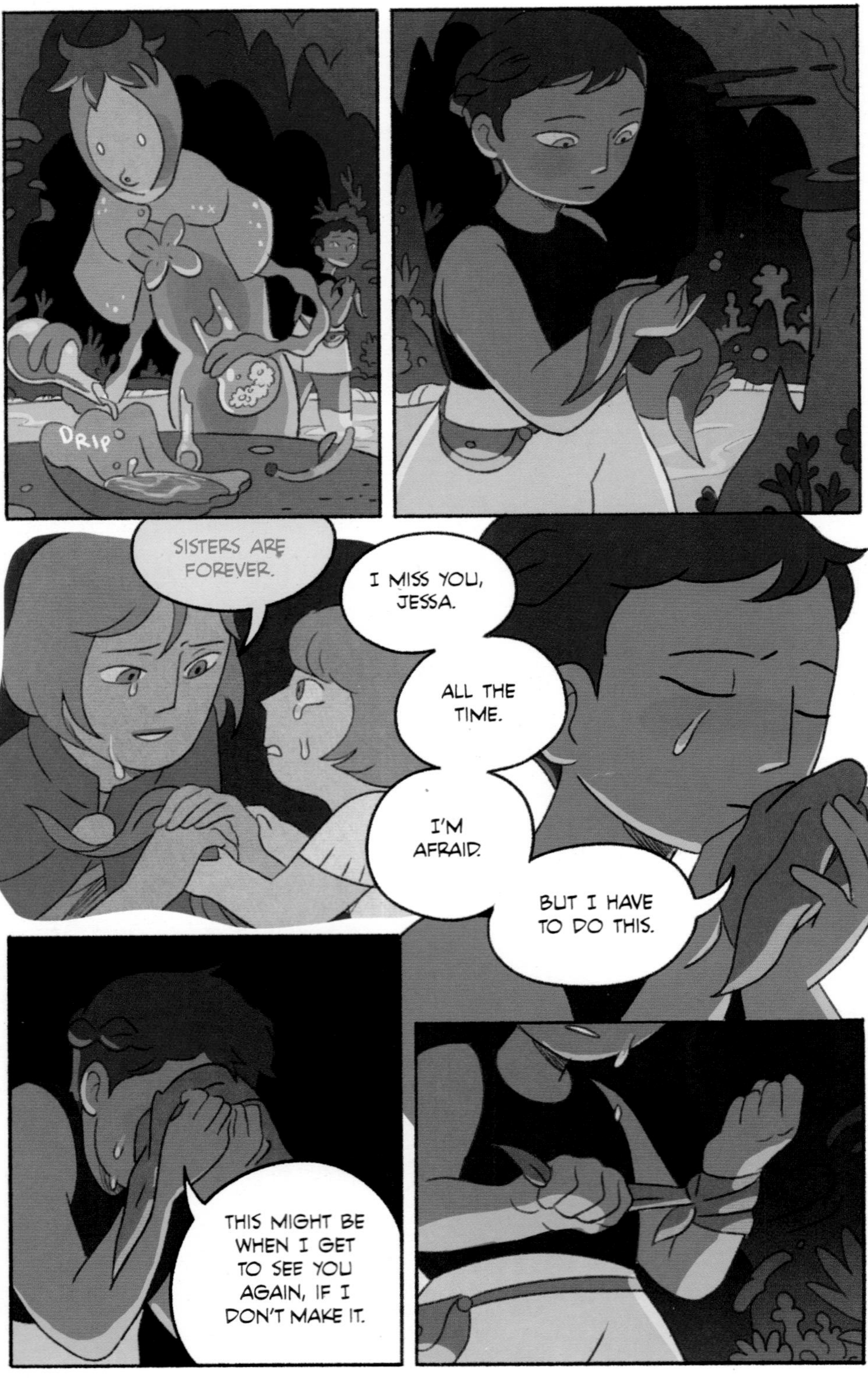
DRIP
SISTERS ARE FOREVER.
I MISS YOU, JESSA.
ALL THE TIME.
I'M AFRAID.
BUT I HAVE TO DO THIS.
THIS MIGHT BE WHEN I GET TO SEE YOU AGAIN, IF I DON'T MAKE IT.

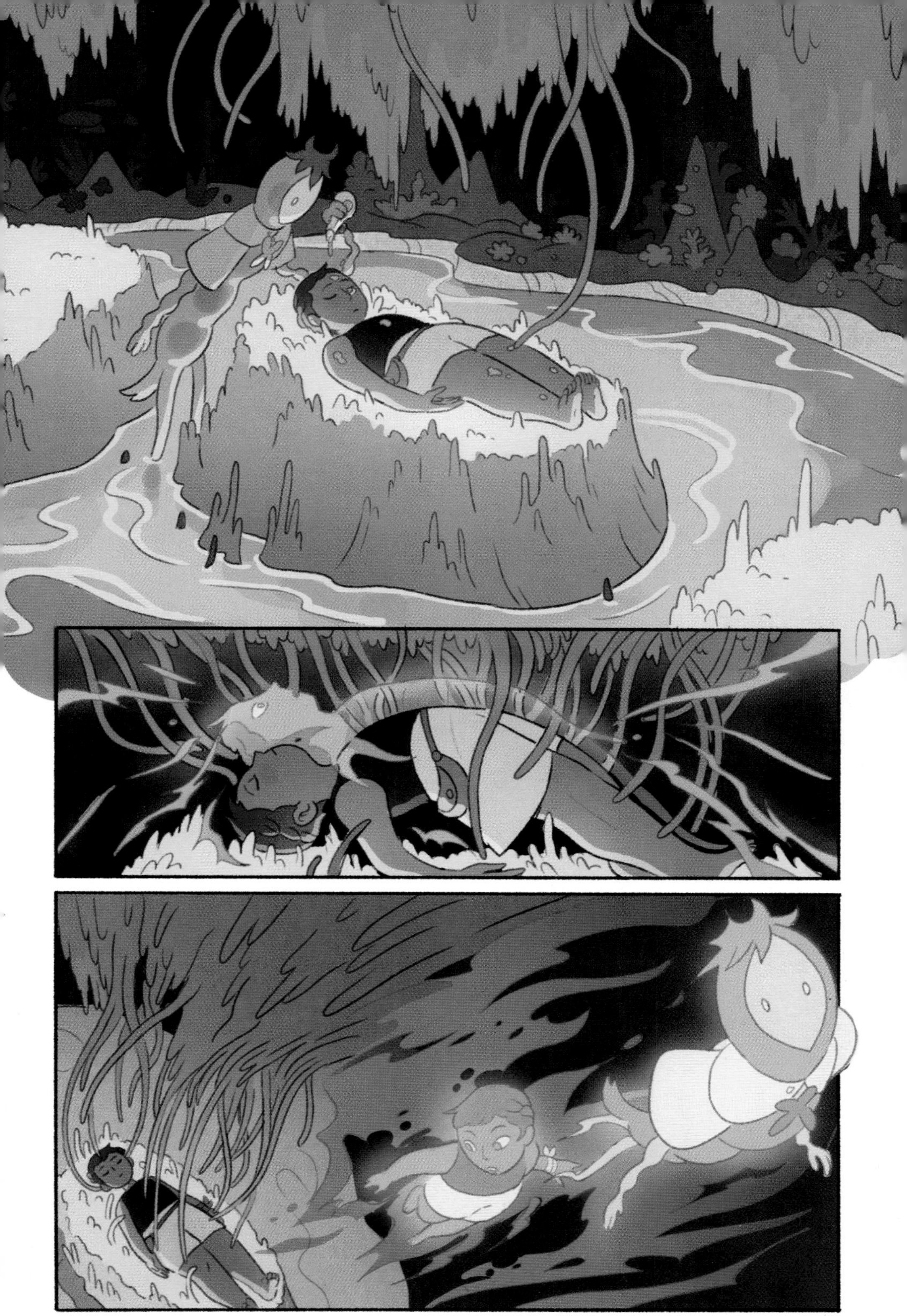

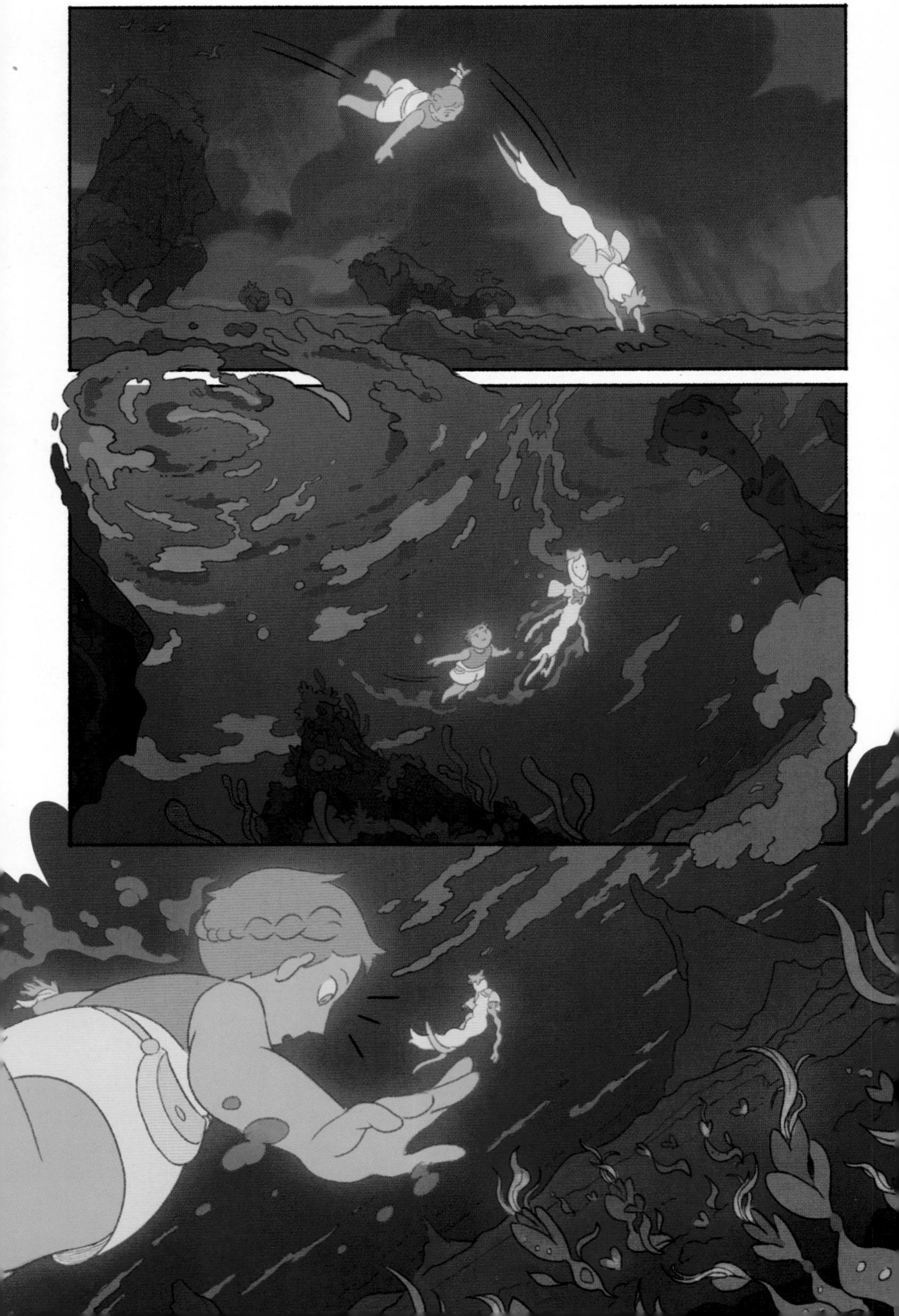

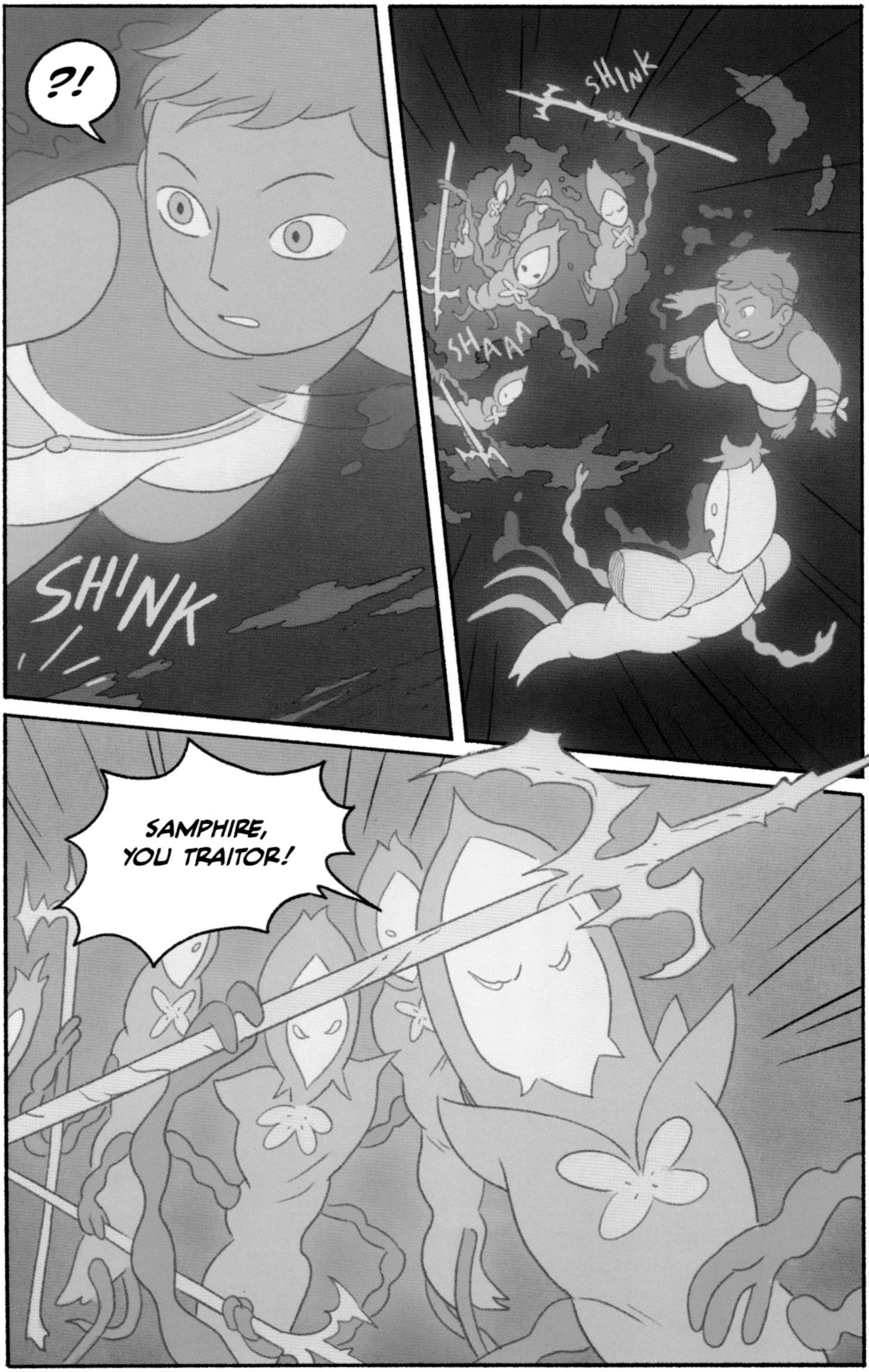
?!
SHINK
SHINK
SHAAA
SAMPHIRE, YOU TRAITOR!

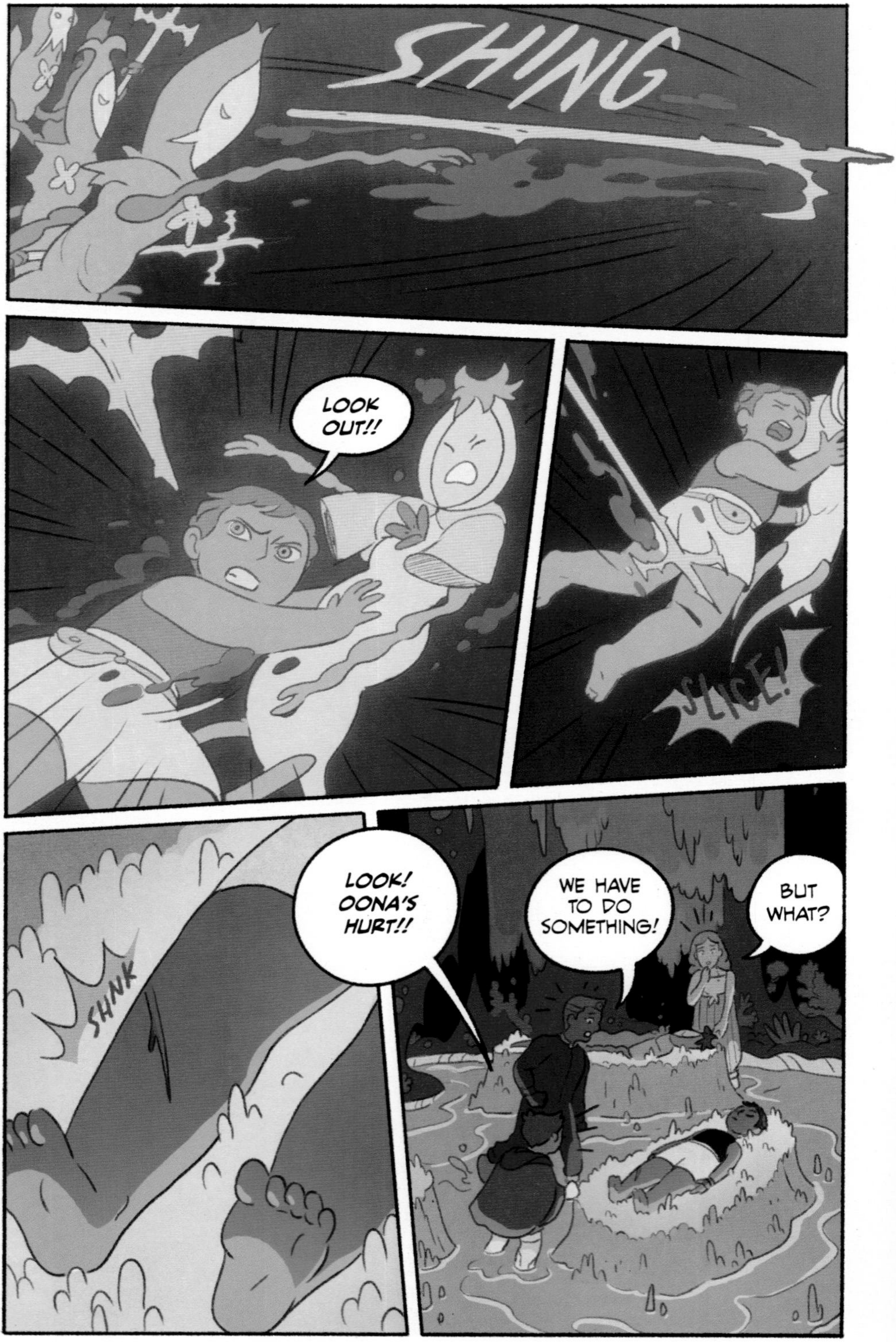
SHING
LOOK OUT!!
SLICE!
SHNK
LOOK! OONA'S HURT!!
WE HAVE TO DO SOMETHING!
BUT WHAT?

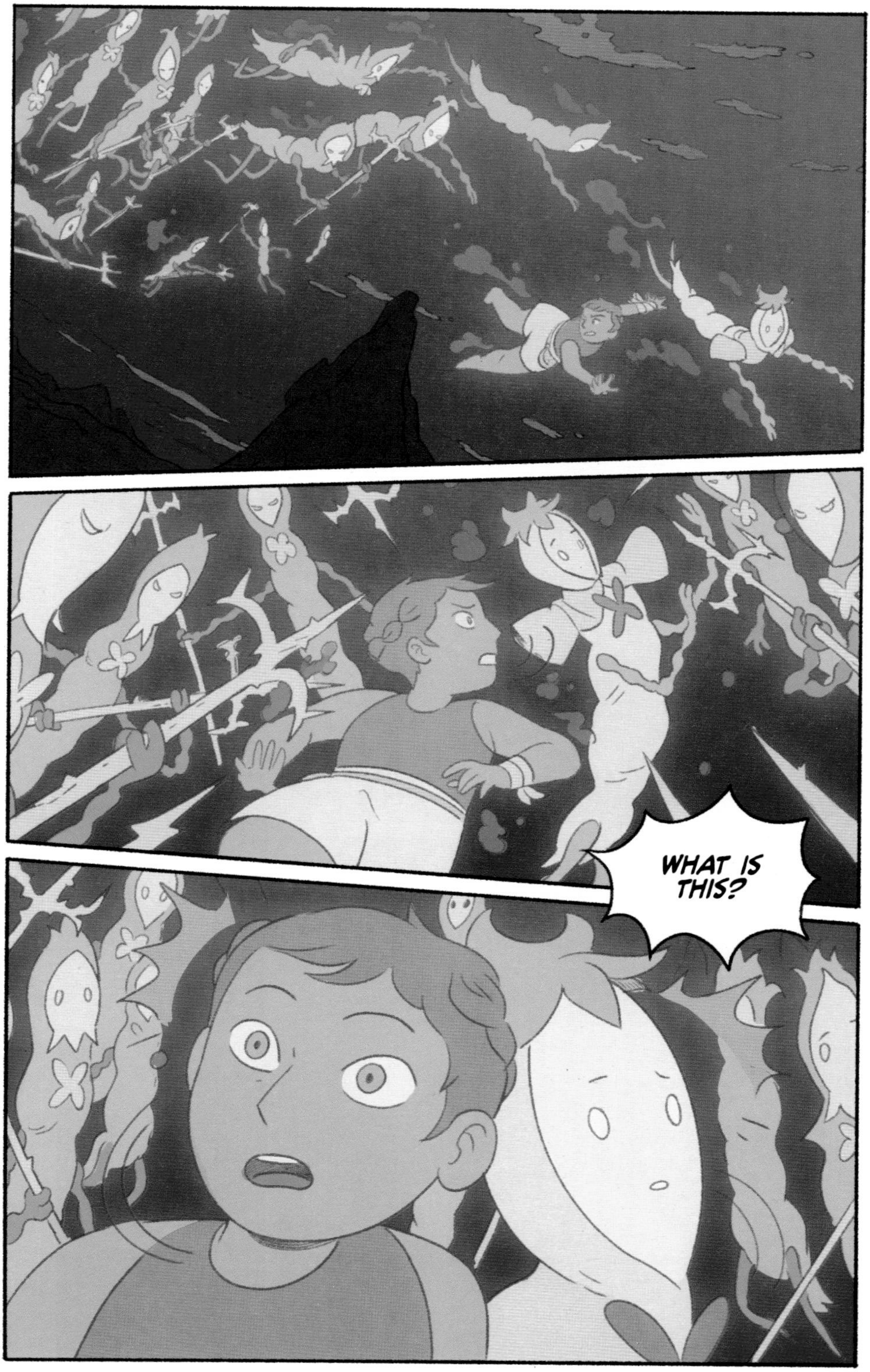
WHAT IS
THIS?

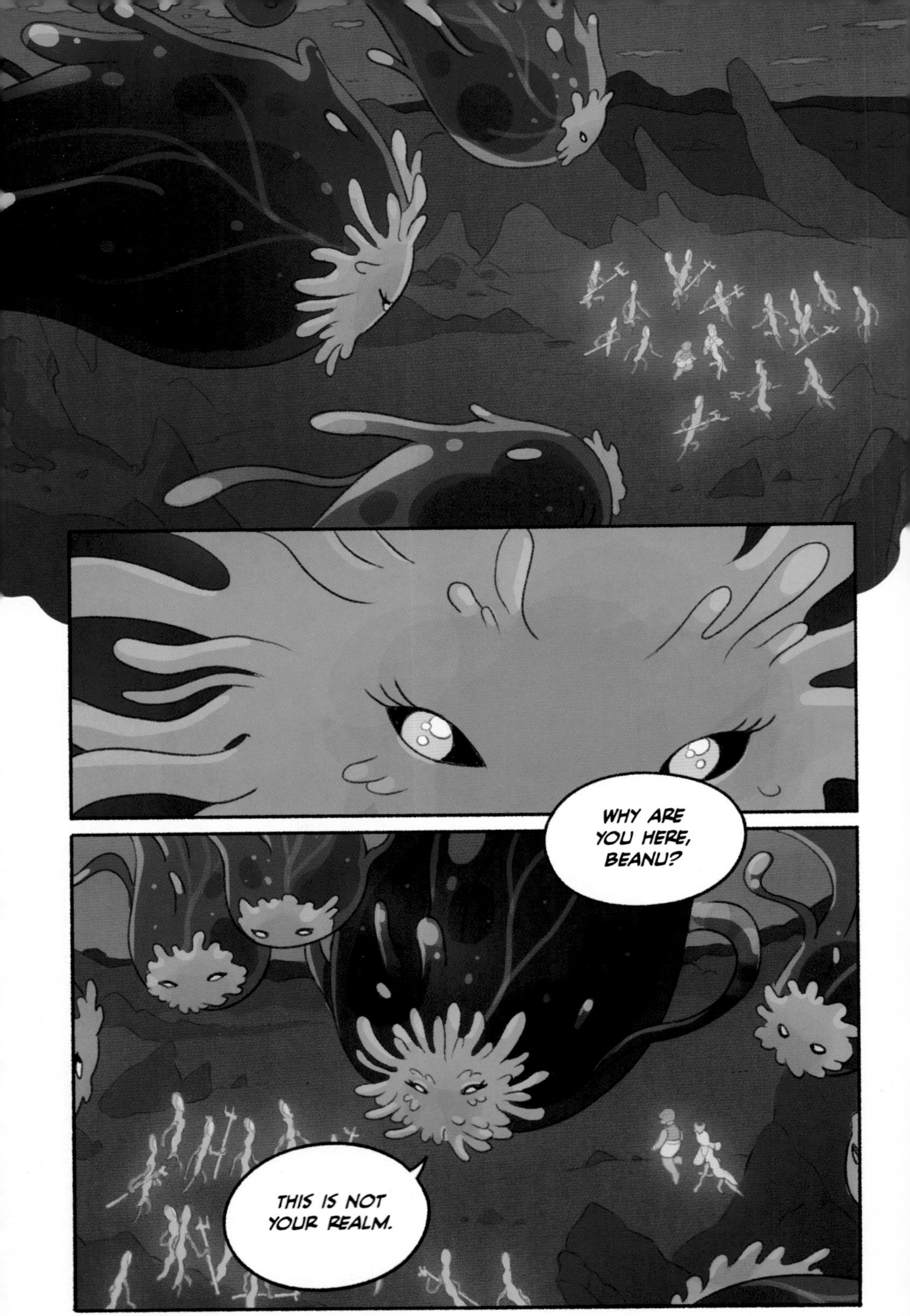
WHY ARE YOU HERE, BEANU?
THIS IS NOT YOUR REALM.

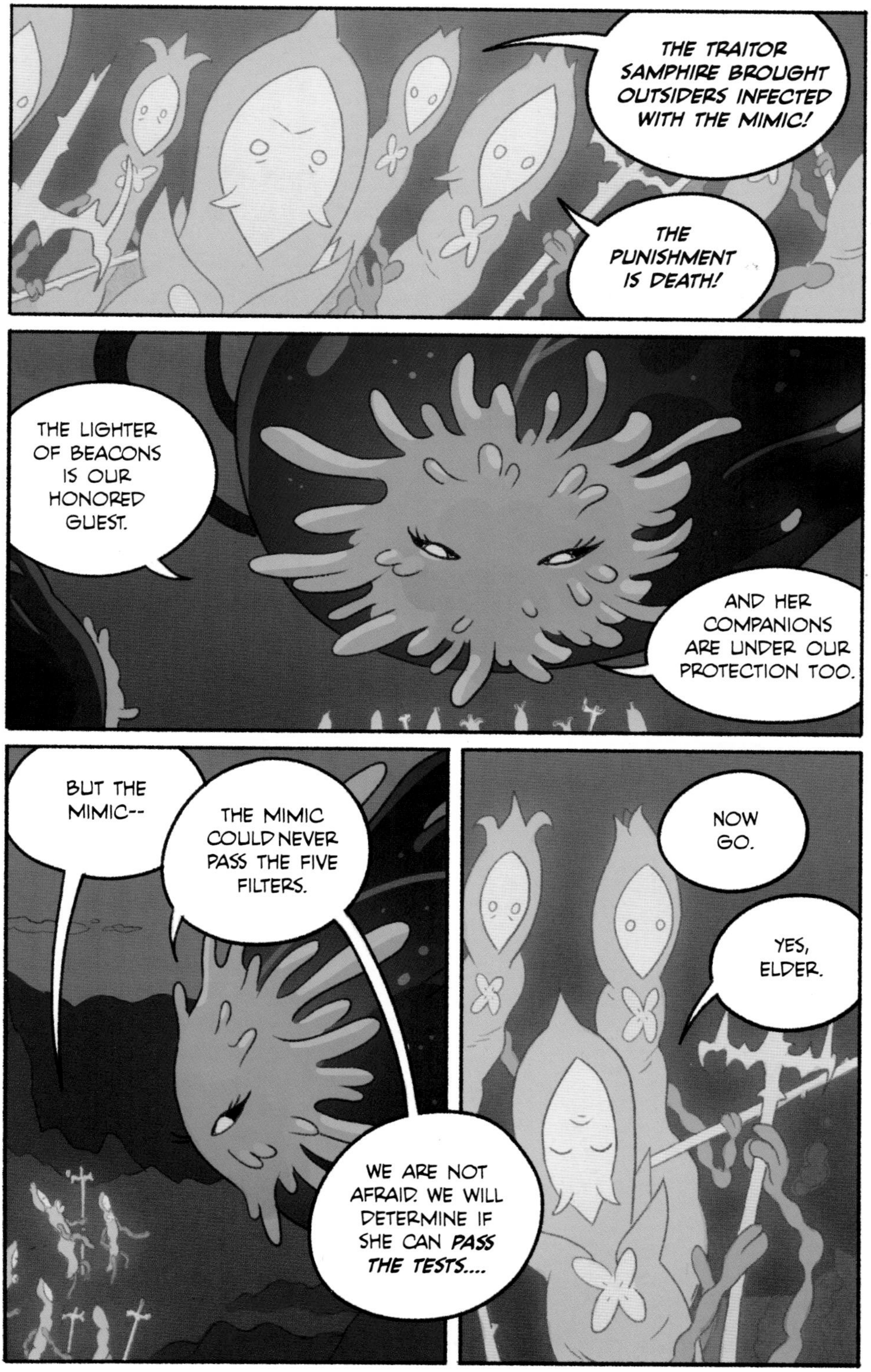
THE TRAITOR SAMPHIRE BROUGHT OUTSIDERS INFECTED WITH THE MIMIC!
THE PUNISHMENT IS DEATH!
THE LIGHTER OF BEACONS IS OUR HONORED GUEST.
AND HER COMPANIONS ARE UNDER OUR PROTECTION TOO.
BUT THE MIMIC--
THE MIMIC COULD NEVER PASS THE FIVE FILTERS.
WE ARE NOT AFRAID. WE WILL DETERMINE IF SHE CAN PASS THE TESTS....
NOW GO.
YES, ELDER.

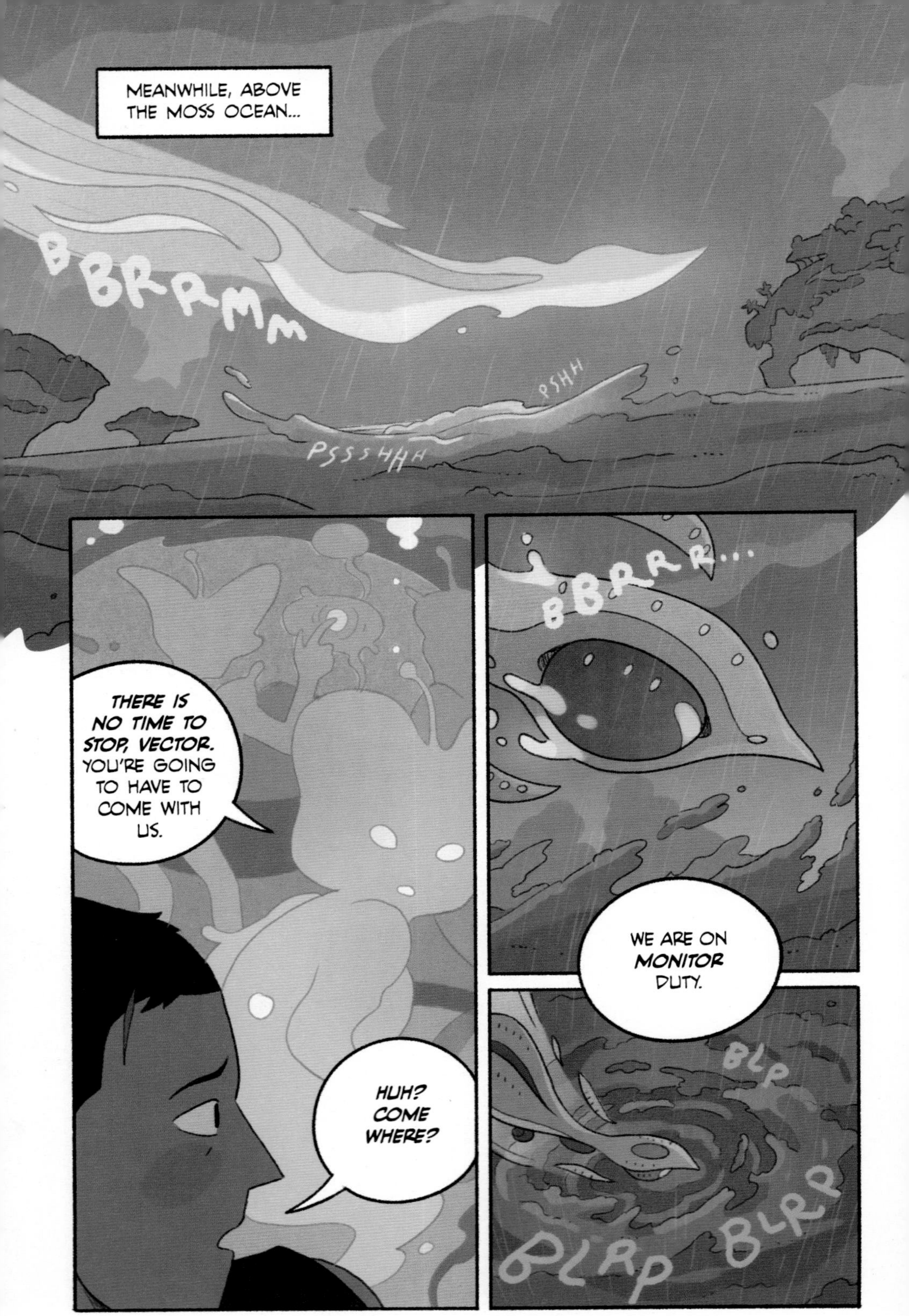
MEANWHILE, ABOVE THE MOSS OCEAN...
BBRRMM
PSHH
PSSSHHH
BBRRR...
THERE IS NO TIME TO STOP, VECTOR. YOU'RE GOING TO HAVE TO COME WITH US.
WE ARE ON MONITOR DUTY.
HUH? COME WHERE?
BLP
BLRP
BLRP
BLRP

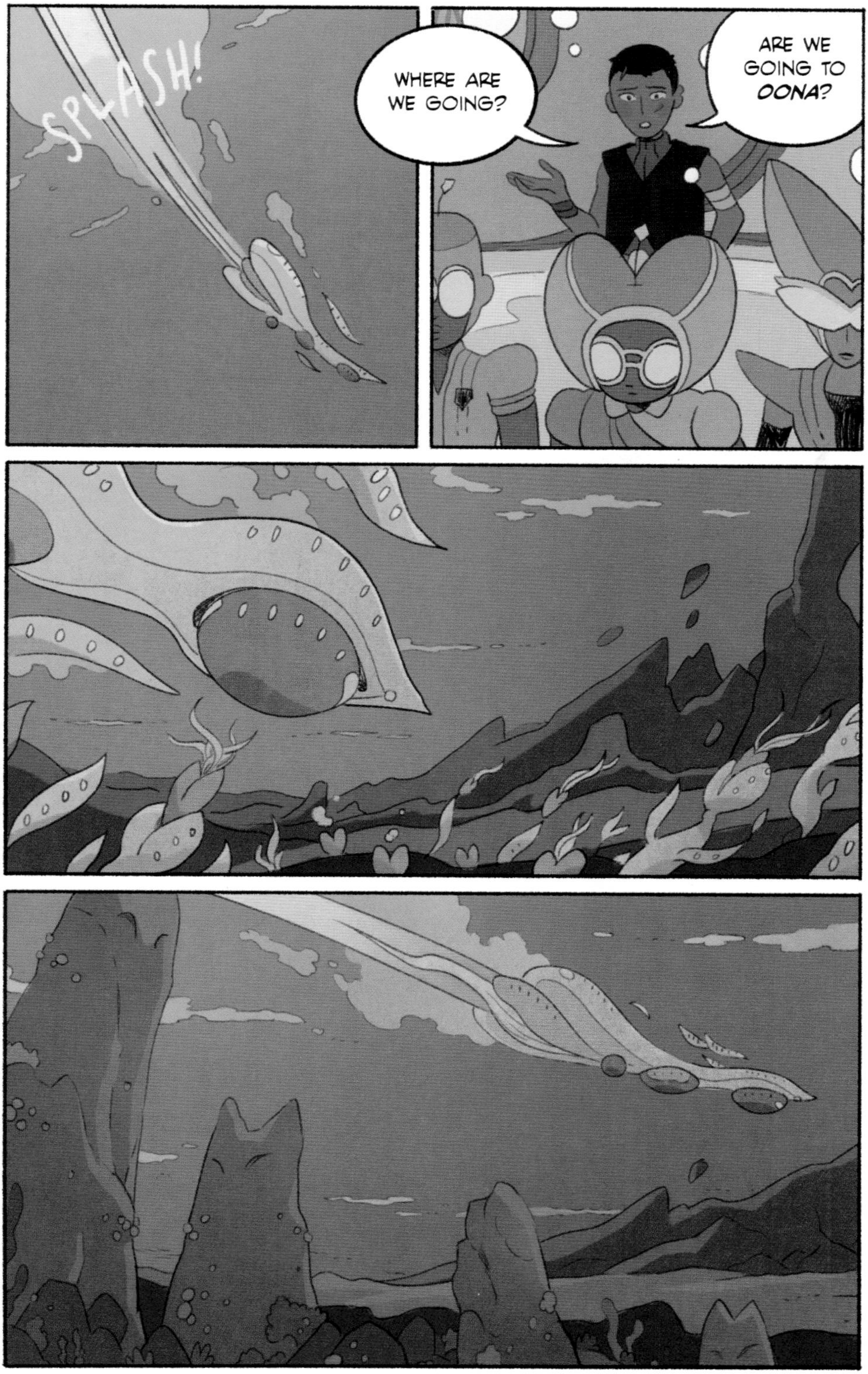
SPLASH!
WHERE ARE WE GOING?
ARE WE GOING TO *OONA*?

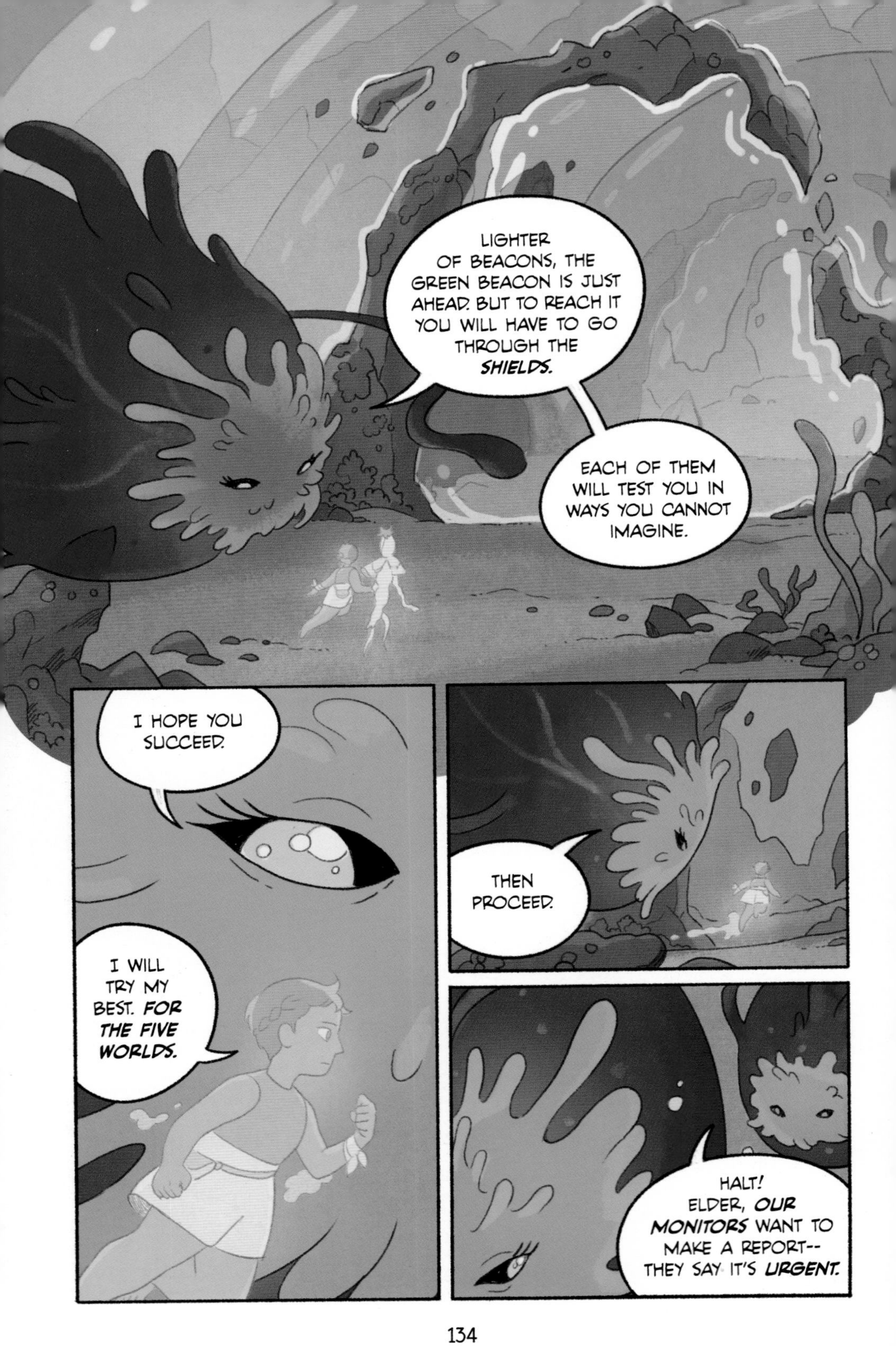
LIGHTER OF BEACONS, THE GREEN BEACON IS JUST AHEAD. BUT TO REACH IT YOU WILL HAVE TO GO THROUGH THE *SHIELDS.*
EACH OF THEM WILL TEST YOU IN WAYS YOU CANNOT IMAGINE.
I HOPE YOU SUCCEED.
THEN PROCEED.
I WILL TRY MY BEST. *FOR THE FIVE WORLDS.*
HALT! ELDER, *OUR MONITORS* WANT TO MAKE A REPORT-- THEY SAY IT'S *URGENT.*

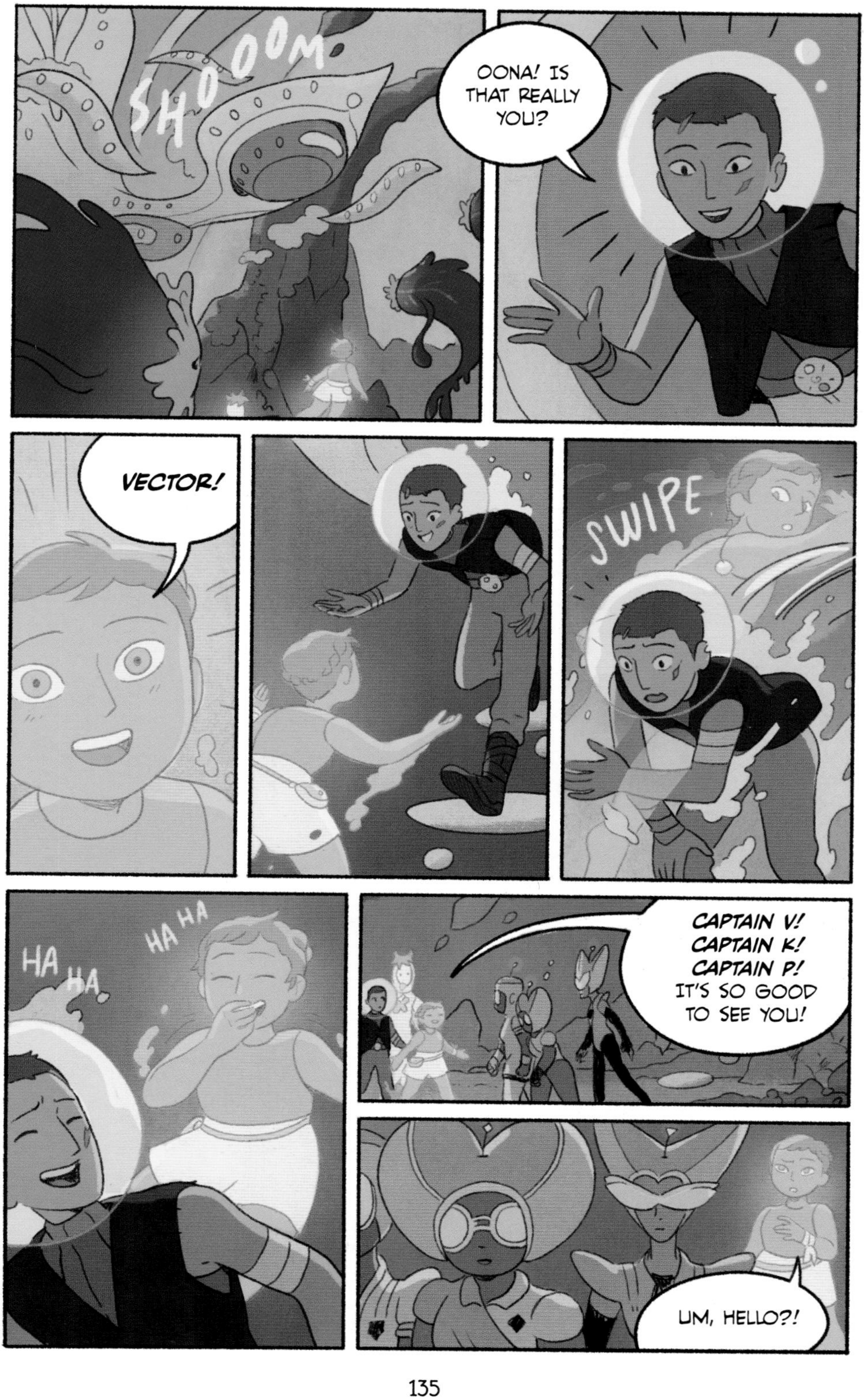
SHOOOM
OONA! IS THAT REALLY YOU?
VECTOR!
SWIPE
HA HA
HA HA
CAPTAIN V! CAPTAIN K! CAPTAIN P! IT'S SO GOOD TO SEE YOU!
UM, HELLO?!

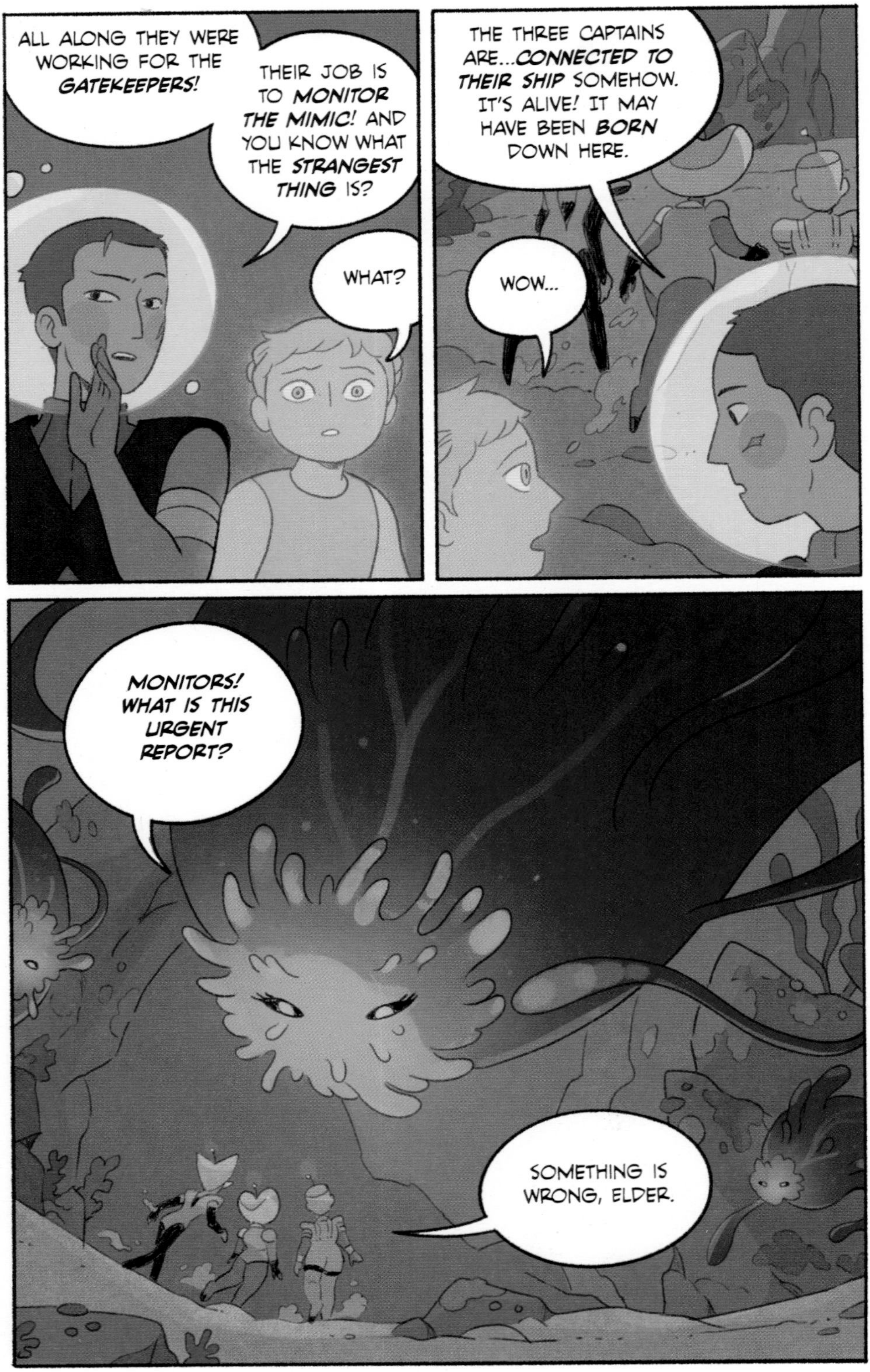
ALL ALONG THEY WERE WORKING FOR THE GATEKEEPERS!
THEIR JOB IS TO MONITOR THE MIMIC! AND YOU KNOW WHAT THE STRANGEST THING IS?
WHAT?
THE THREE CAPTAINS ARE...CONNECTED TO THEIR SHIP SOMEHOW. IT'S ALIVE! IT MAY HAVE BEEN BORN DOWN HERE.
WOW...
MONITORS! WHAT IS THIS URGENT REPORT?
SOMETHING IS WRONG, ELDER.

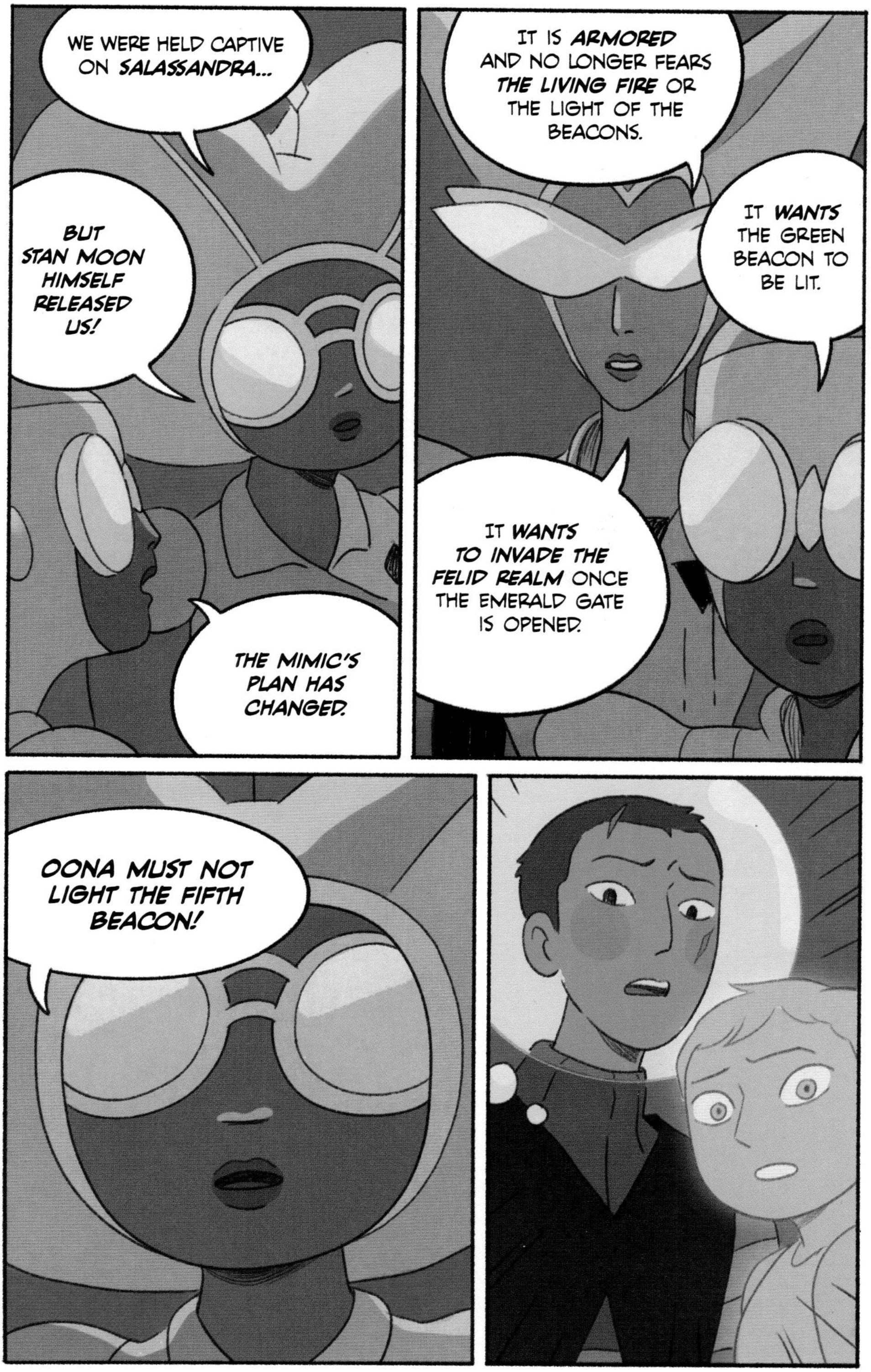
WE WERE HELD CAPTIVE ON SALASSANDRA...
BUT STAN MOON HIMSELF RELEASED US!
THE MIMIC'S PLAN HAS CHANGED.
IT IS ARMORED AND NO LONGER FEARS THE LIVING FIRE OR THE LIGHT OF THE BEACONS.
IT WANTS THE GREEN BEACON TO BE LIT.
IT WANTS TO INVADE THE FELID REALM ONCE THE EMERALD GATE IS OPENED.
OONA MUST NOT LIGHT THE FIFTH BEACON!

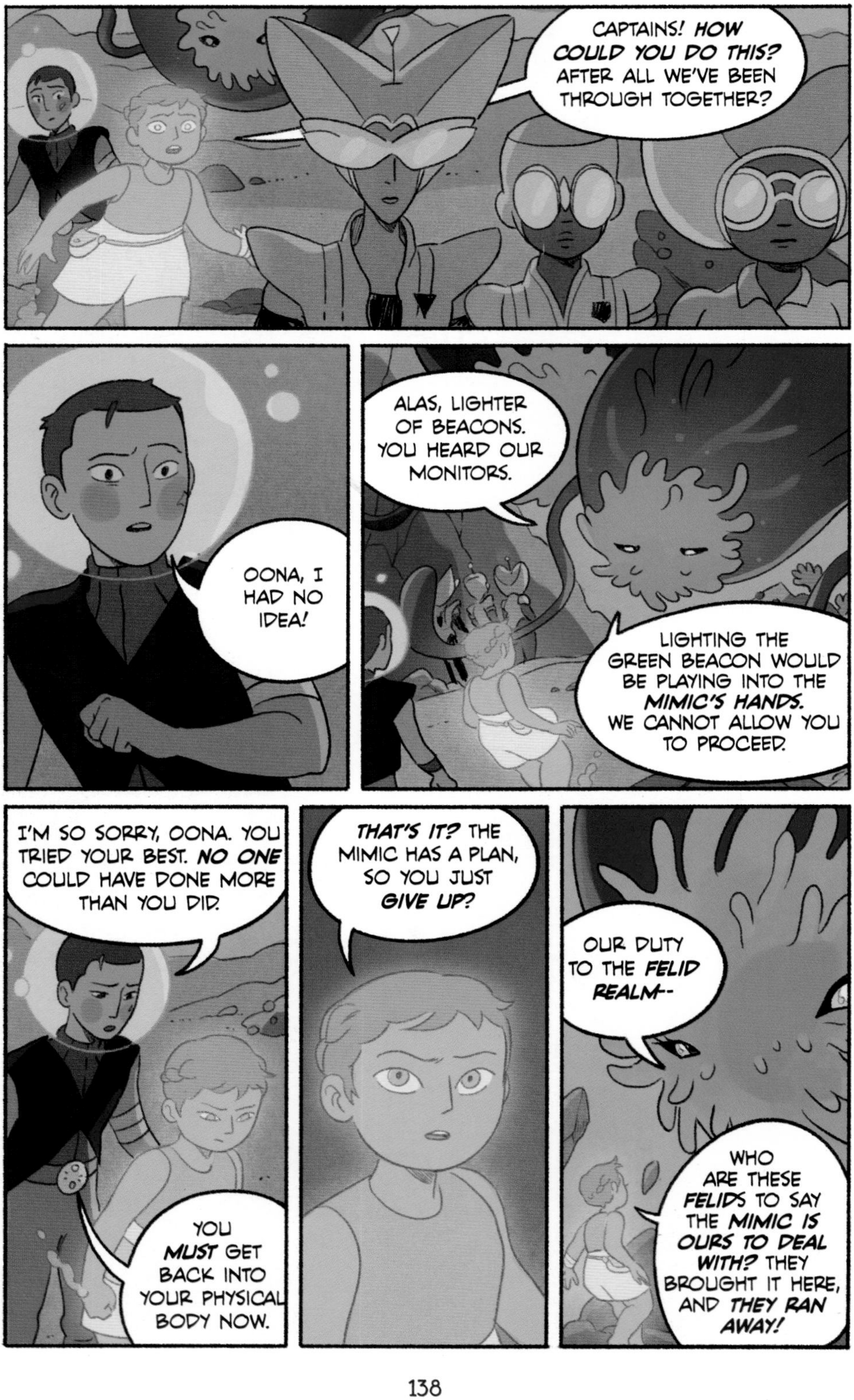
CAPTAINS! HOW COULD YOU DO THIS? AFTER ALL WE'VE BEEN THROUGH TOGETHER?
OONA, I HAD NO IDEA!
ALAS, LIGHTER OF BEACONS. YOU HEARD OUR MONITORS.
LIGHTING THE GREEN BEACON WOULD BE PLAYING INTO THE MIMIC'S HANDS. WE CANNOT ALLOW YOU TO PROCEED.
I'M SO SORRY, OONA. YOU TRIED YOUR BEST. NO ONE COULD HAVE DONE MORE THAN YOU DID.
YOU MUST GET BACK INTO YOUR PHYSICAL BODY NOW.
THAT'S IT? THE MIMIC HAS A PLAN, SO YOU JUST GIVE UP?
OUR DUTY TO THE FELID REALM--
WHO ARE THESE FELIDS TO SAY THE MIMIC IS OURS TO DEAL WITH? THEY BROUGHT IT HERE, AND THEY RAN AWAY!

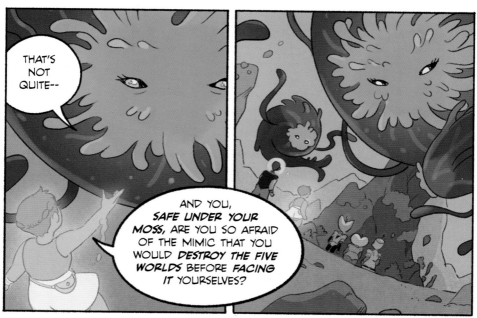

THAT'S NOT QUITE--

AND YOU, *SAFE UNDER YOUR MOSS,* ARE YOU SO AFRAID OF THE MIMIC THAT YOU WOULD *DESTROY THE FIVE WORLDS* BEFORE *FACING IT* YOURSELVES?

WHY NOT *JOIN US* AND *FIGHT THE MIMIC?*

THAT'S IMPOSSIBLE. EVEN THE GREAT *QUEEN IONA* COULD NOT DEFEAT IT.

AT EVERY STEP, IT'S BEEN IMPOSSIBLE FOR ME, AND YET *HERE I AM!*

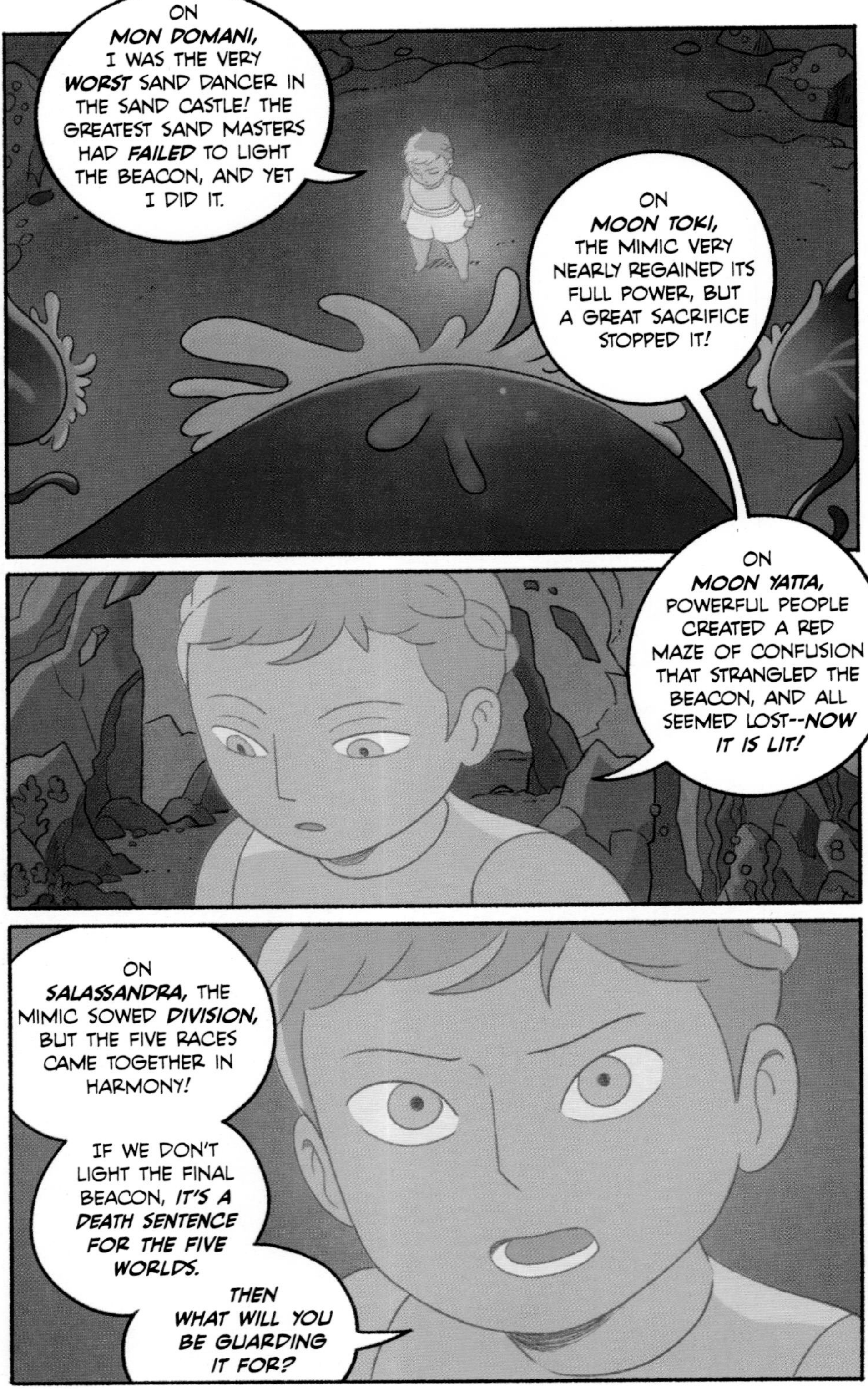
ON MON DOMANI, I WAS THE VERY WORST SAND DANCER IN THE SAND CASTLE! THE GREATEST SAND MASTERS HAD FAILED TO LIGHT THE BEACON, AND YET I DID IT.
ON MOON TOKI, THE MIMIC VERY NEARLY REGAINED ITS FULL POWER, BUT A GREAT SACRIFICE STOPPED IT!
ON MOON YATTA, POWERFUL PEOPLE CREATED A RED MAZE OF CONFUSION THAT STRANGLED THE BEACON, AND ALL SEEMED LOST--NOW IT IS LIT!
ON SALASSANDRA, THE MIMIC SOWED DIVISION, BUT THE FIVE RACES CAME TOGETHER IN HARMONY!
IF WE DON'T LIGHT THE FINAL BEACON, IT'S A DEATH SENTENCE FOR THE FIVE WORLDS.
THEN WHAT WILL YOU BE GUARDING IT FOR?

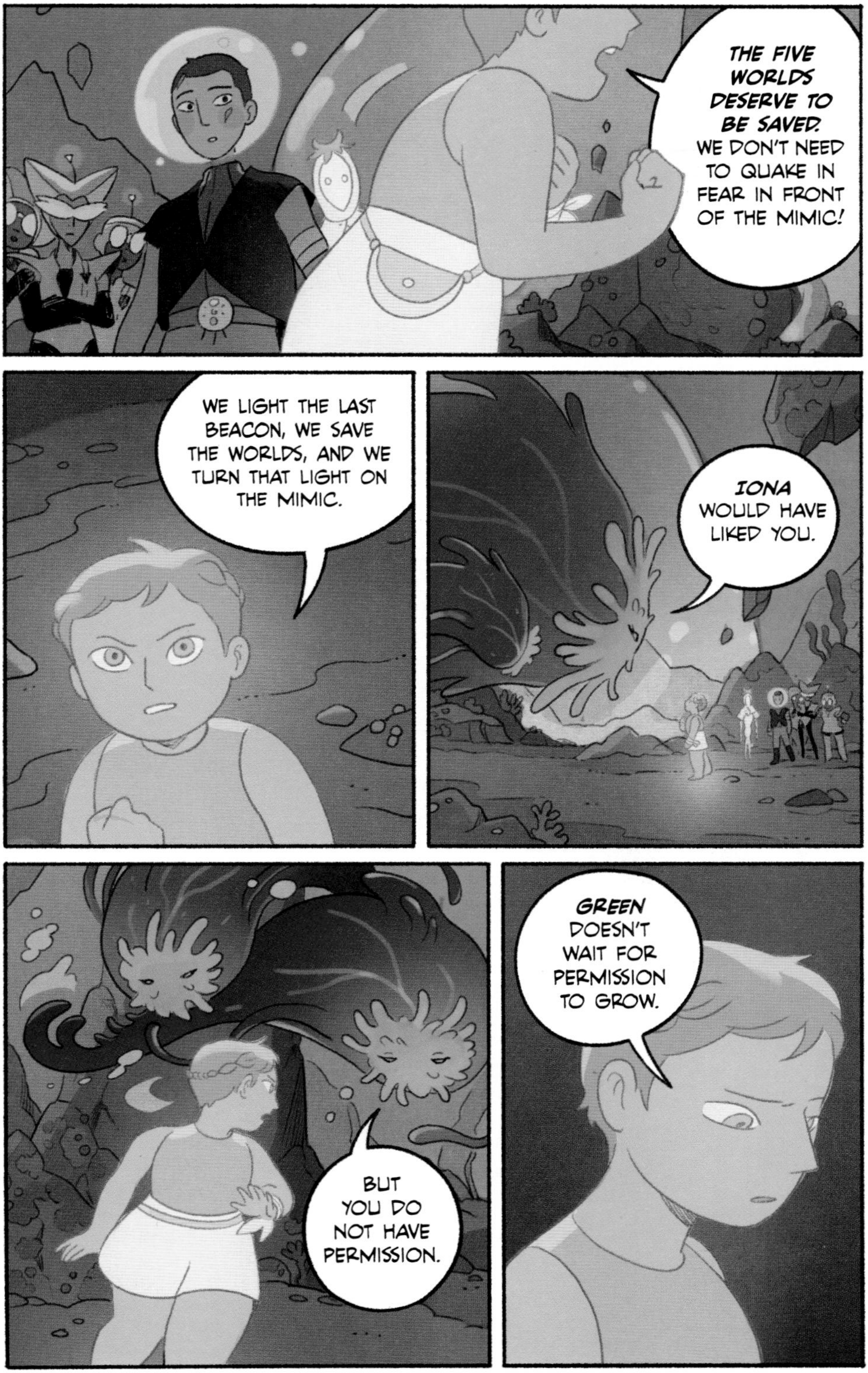
THE FIVE WORLDS DESERVE TO BE SAVED. WE DON'T NEED TO QUAKE IN FEAR IN FRONT OF THE MIMIC!
WE LIGHT THE LAST BEACON, WE SAVE THE WORLDS, AND WE TURN THAT LIGHT ON THE MIMIC.
IONA WOULD HAVE LIKED YOU.
BUT YOU DO NOT HAVE PERMISSION.
GREEN DOESN'T WAIT FOR PERMISSION TO GROW.

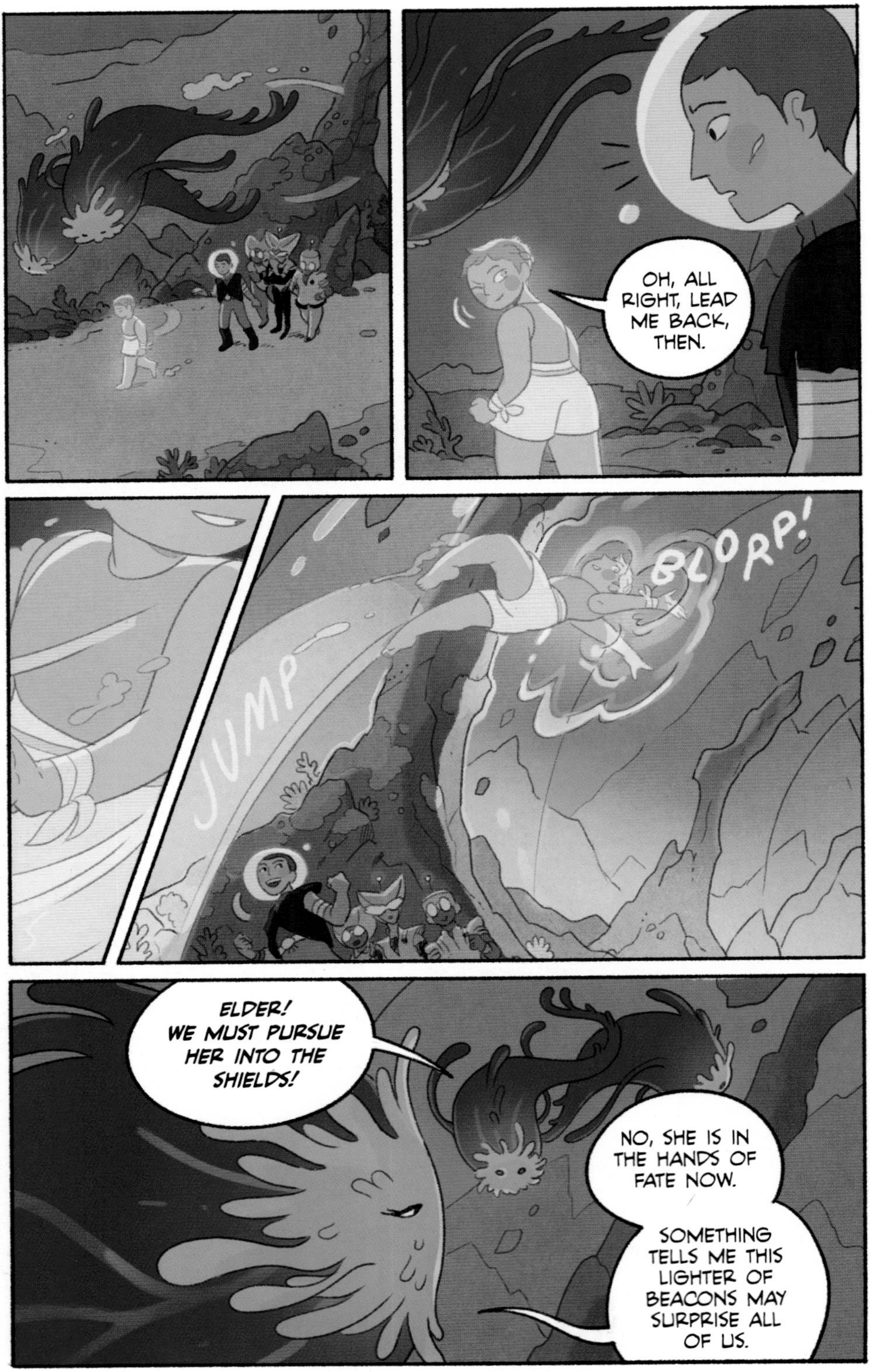

OH, ALL RIGHT, LEAD ME BACK, THEN.
JUMP
BLORP!
ELDER! WE MUST PURSUE HER INTO THE SHIELDS!
NO, SHE IS IN THE HANDS OF FATE NOW.
SOMETHING TELLS ME THIS LIGHTER OF BEACONS MAY SURPRISE ALL OF US.

CHAPTER 10

GAUNTLET OF SHIELDS

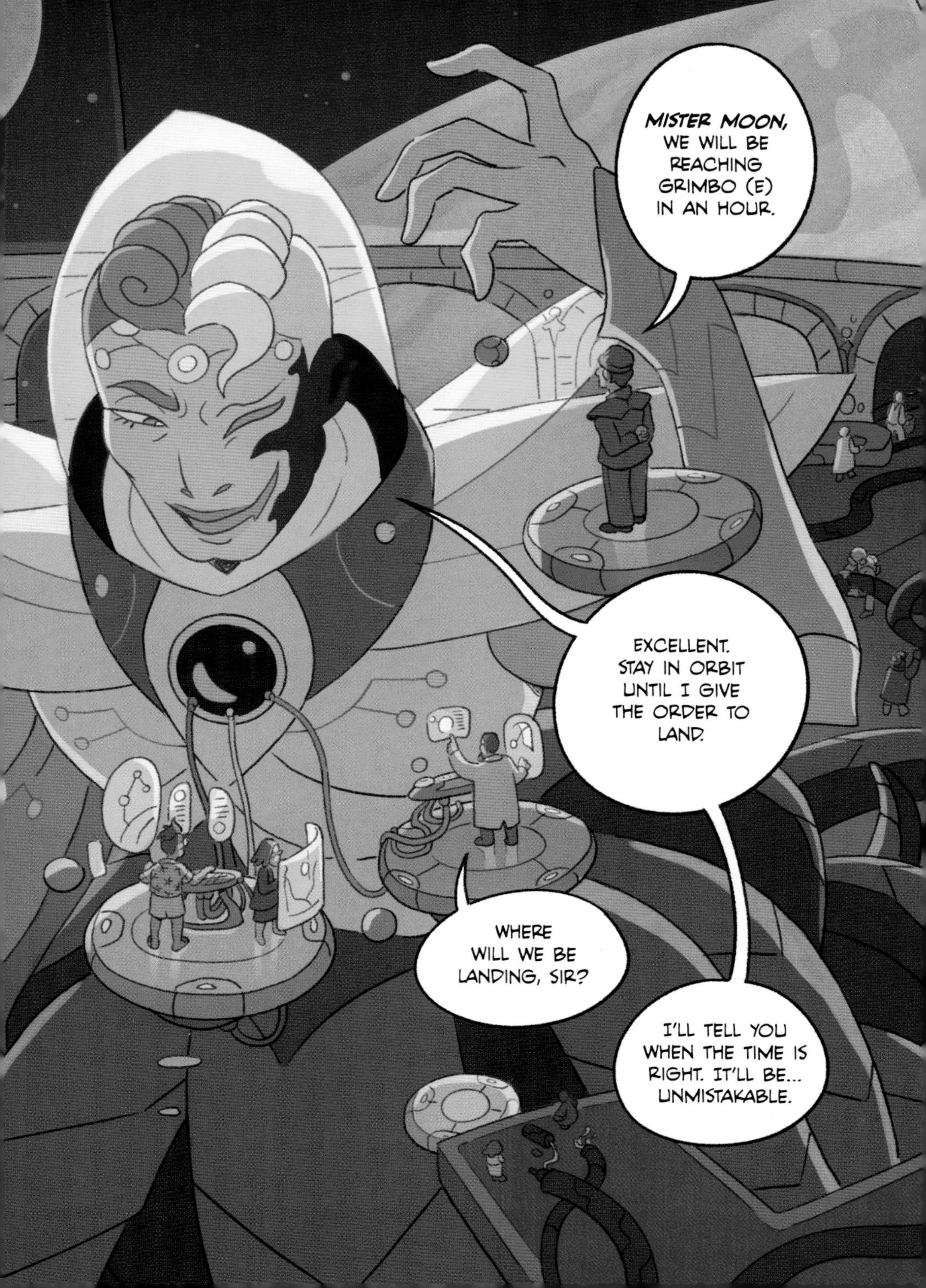
MISTER MOON, WE WILL BE REACHING GRIMBO (E) IN AN HOUR.
EXCELLENT. STAY IN ORBIT UNTIL I GIVE THE ORDER TO LAND.
WHERE WILL WE BE LANDING, SIR?
I'LL TELL YOU WHEN THE TIME IS RIGHT. IT'LL BE... UNMISTAKABLE.

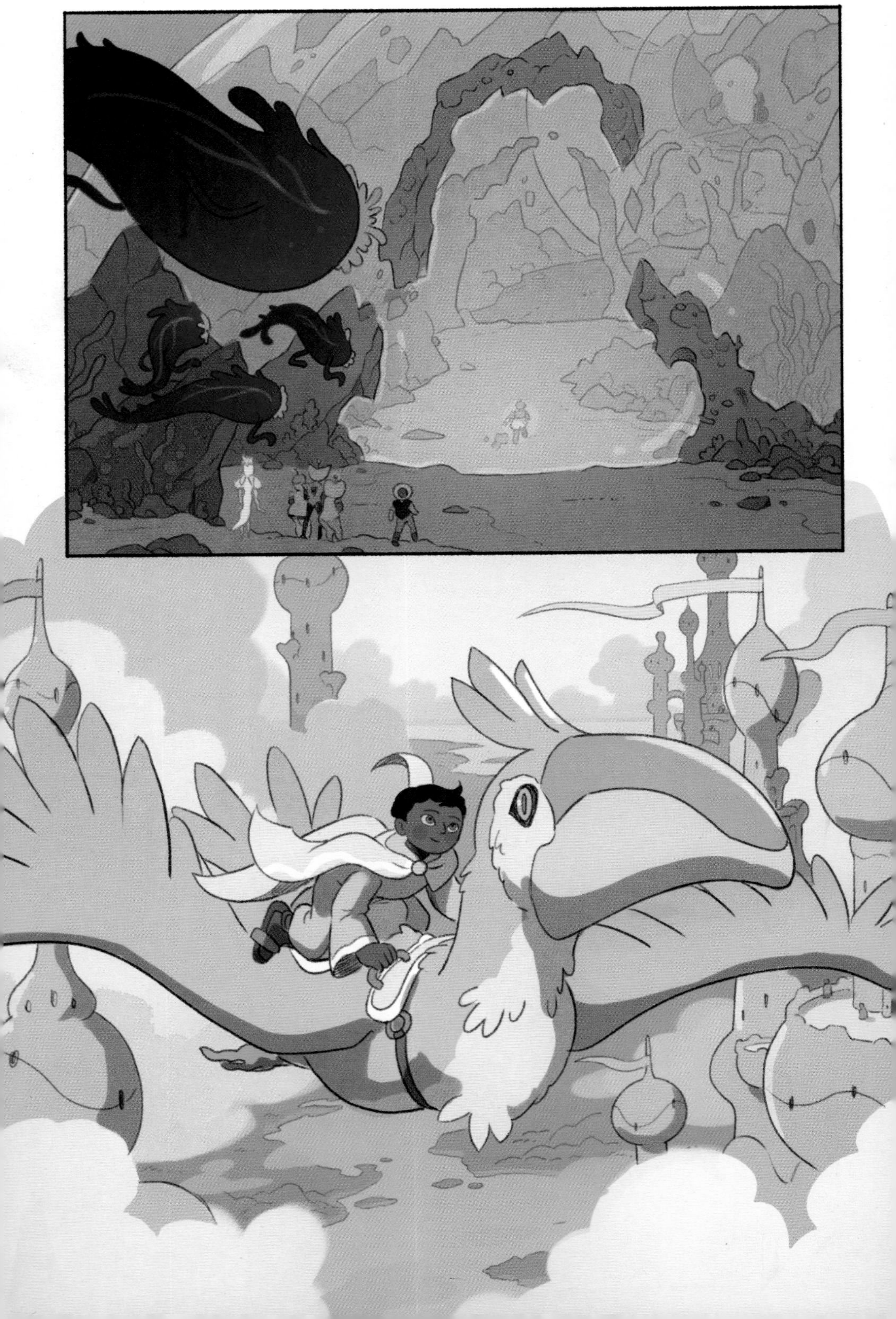

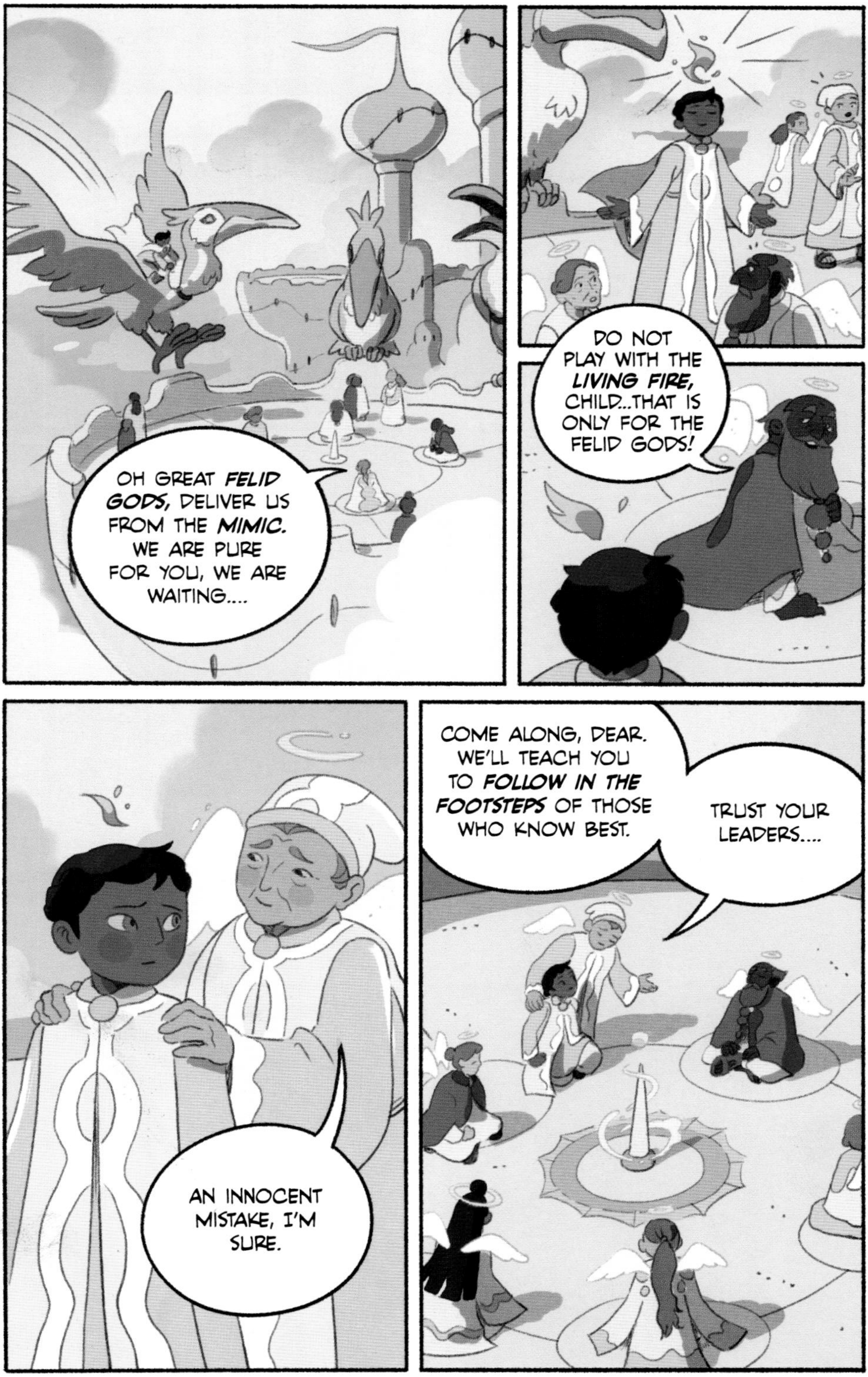
OH GREAT ***FELID GODS,*** DELIVER US FROM THE ***MIMIC.*** WE ARE PURE FOR YOU, WE ARE WAITING....
DO NOT PLAY WITH THE ***LIVING FIRE,*** CHILD...THAT IS ONLY FOR THE FELID GODS!
AN INNOCENT MISTAKE, I'M SURE.
COME ALONG, DEAR. WE'LL TEACH YOU TO ***FOLLOW IN THE FOOTSTEPS*** OF THOSE WHO KNOW BEST.
TRUST YOUR LEADERS....

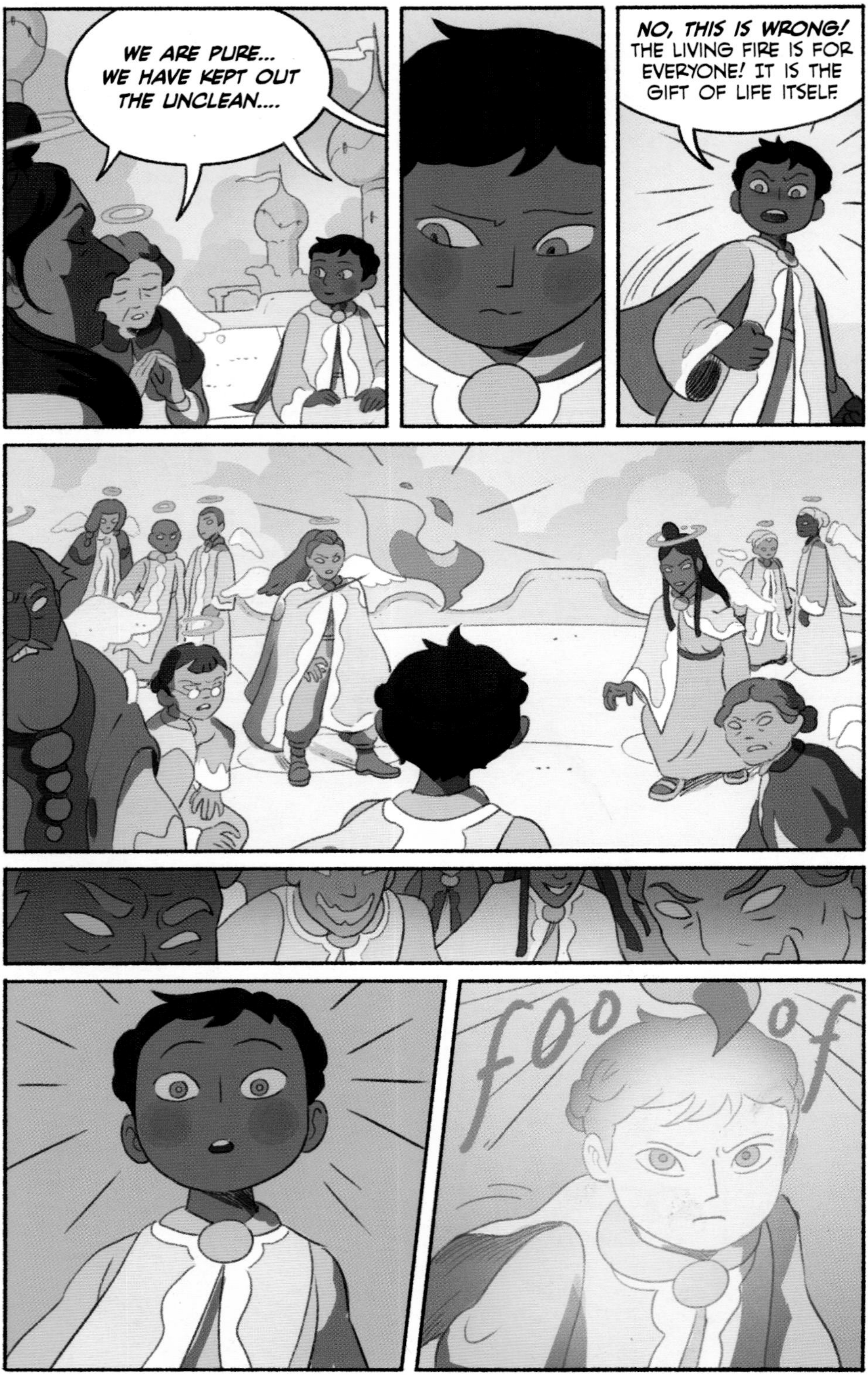
WE ARE PURE... WE HAVE KEPT OUT THE UNCLEAN....
NO, THIS IS WRONG! THE LIVING FIRE IS FOR EVERYONE! IT IS THE GIFT OF LIFE ITSELF.
fooof

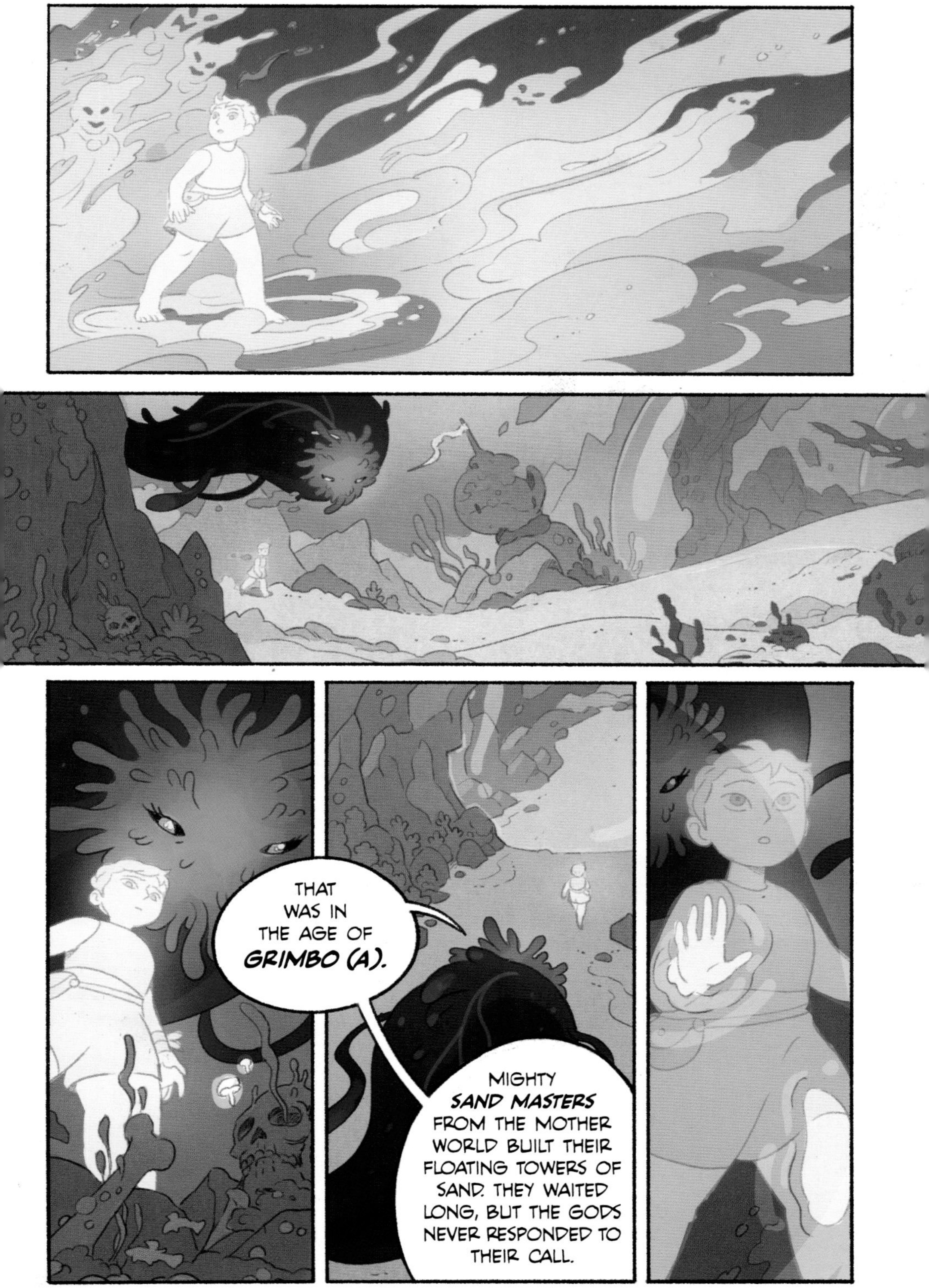

THAT WAS IN THE AGE OF GRIMBO (A).
MIGHTY SAND MASTERS FROM THE MOTHER WORLD BUILT THEIR FLOATING TOWERS OF SAND. THEY WAITED LONG, BUT THE GODS NEVER RESPONDED TO THEIR CALL.

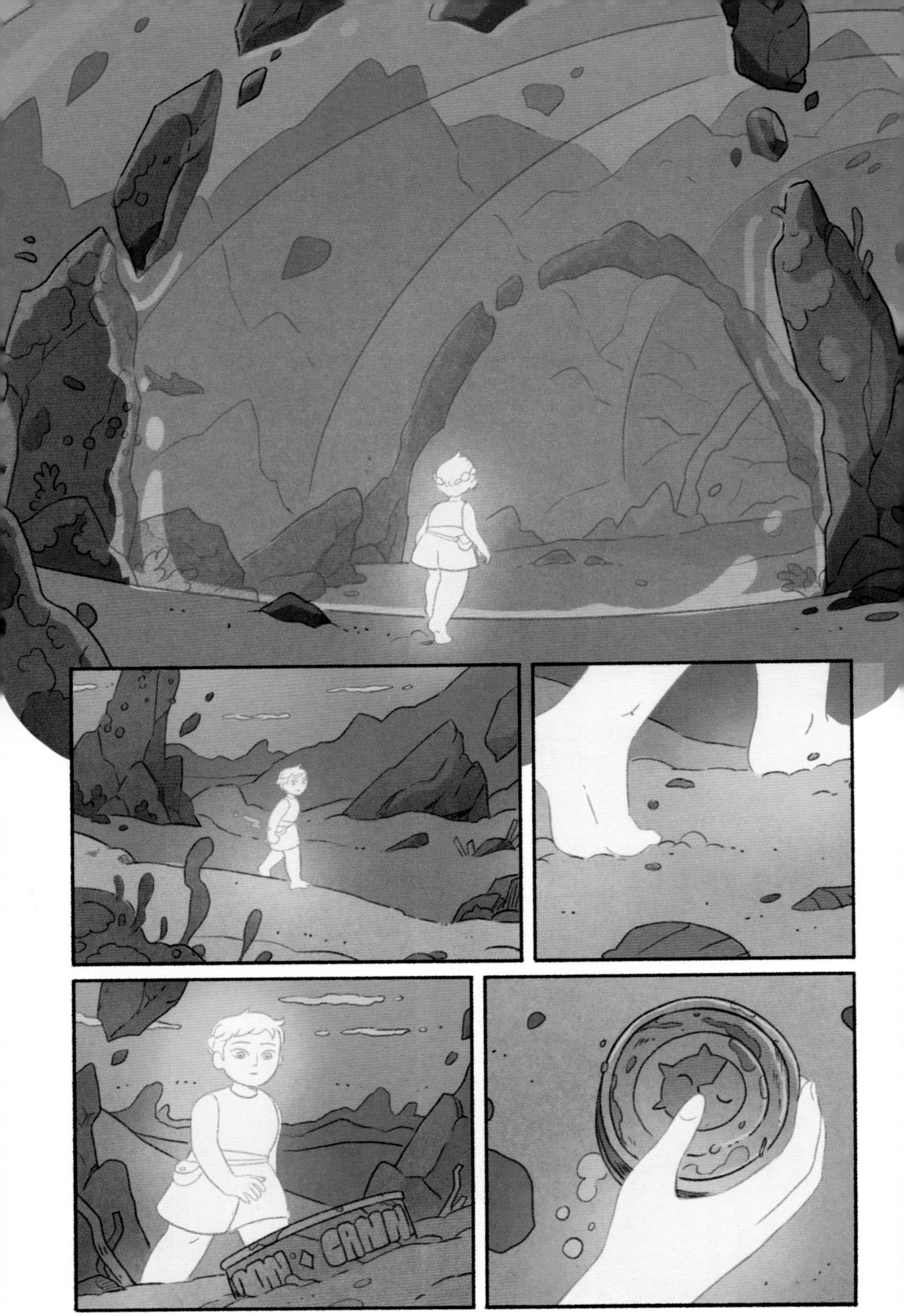
...
...
. .

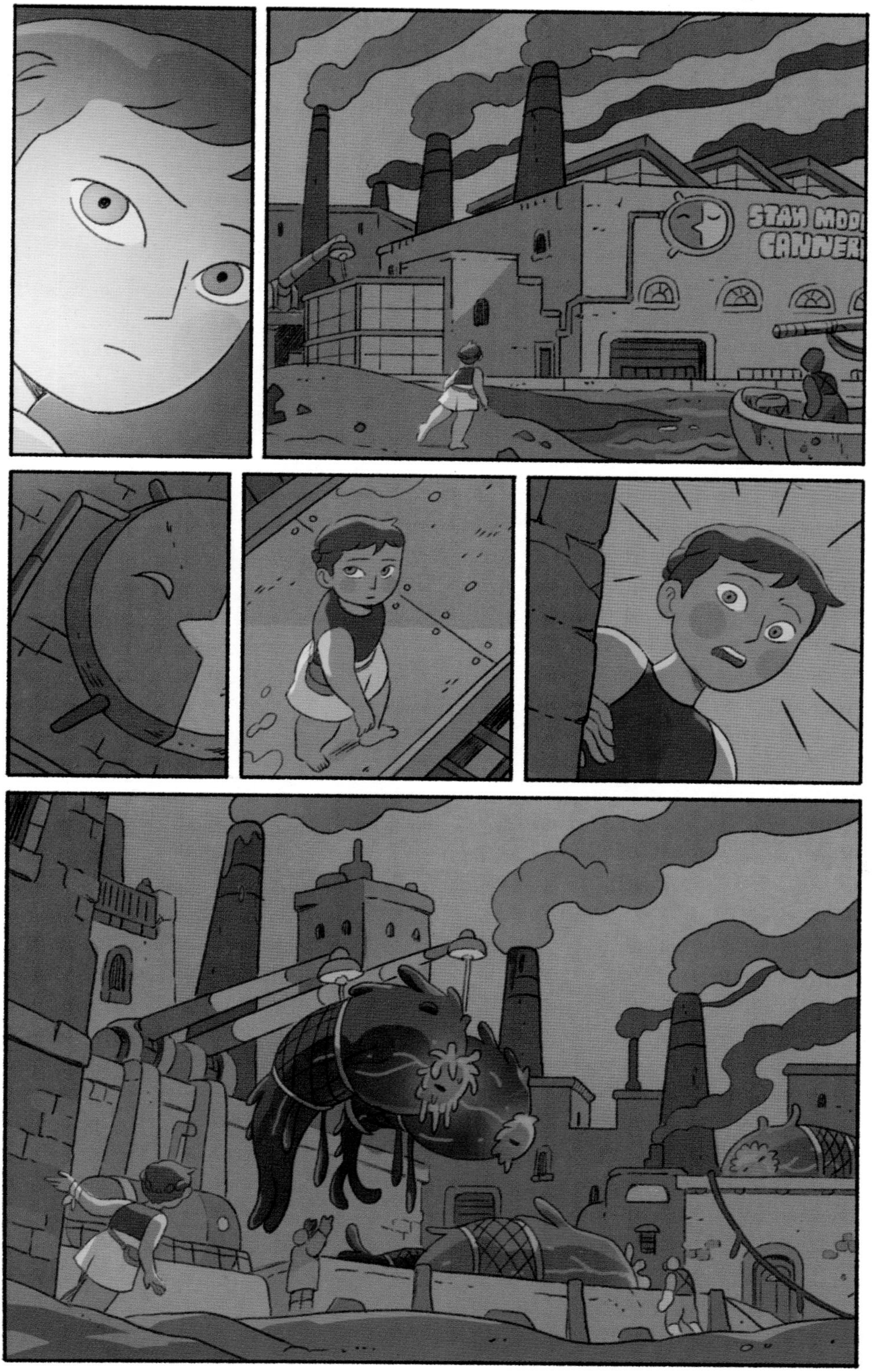
STAN MOO
CANNER

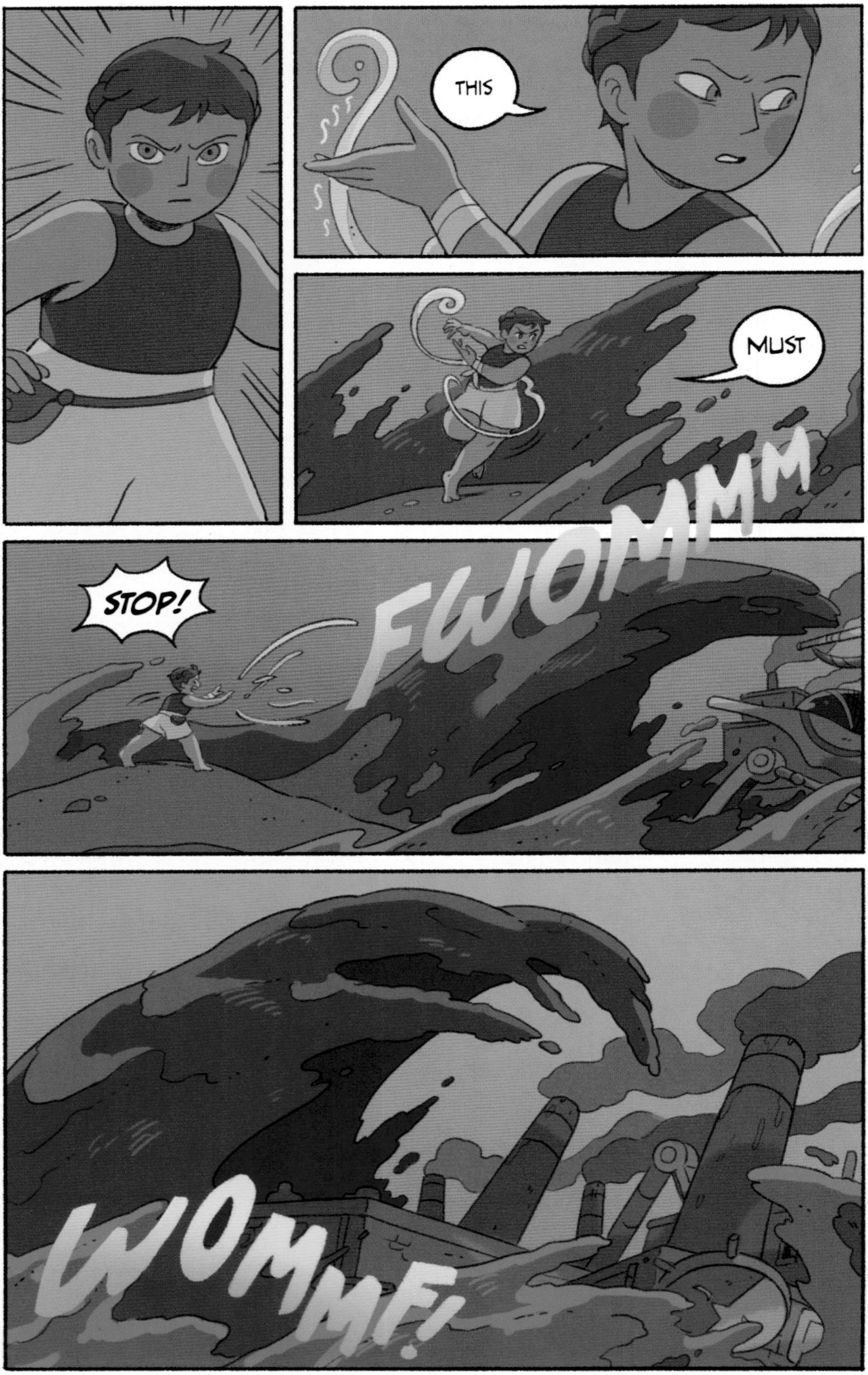
THIS
MUST
FWOMMM
STOP!
WOMMF!

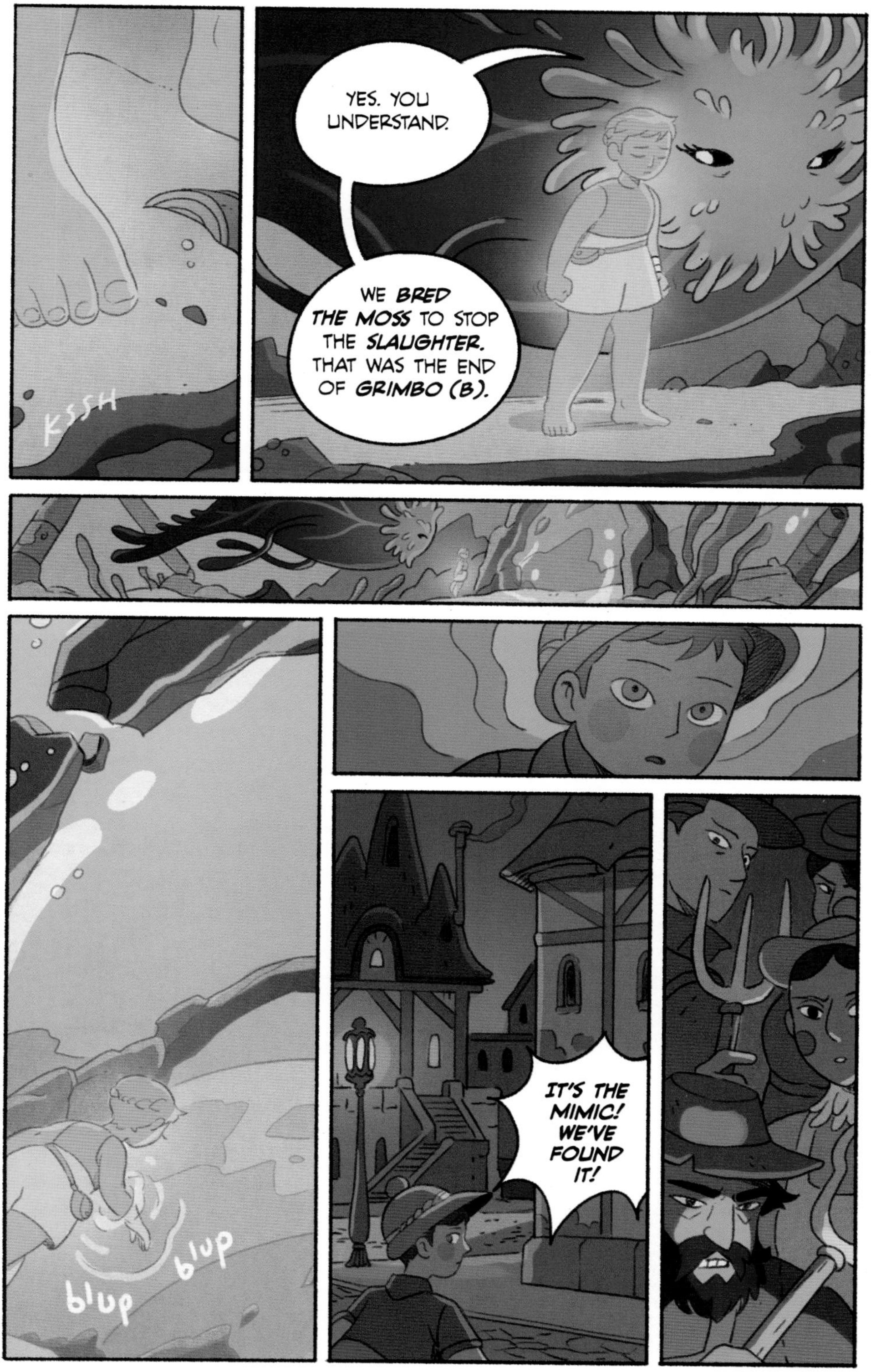
KSSH
YES. YOU UNDERSTAND.
WE BRED THE MOSS TO STOP THE SLAUGHTER. THAT WAS THE END OF GRIMBO (B).
blup
blup
IT'S THE MIMIC! WE'VE FOUND IT!

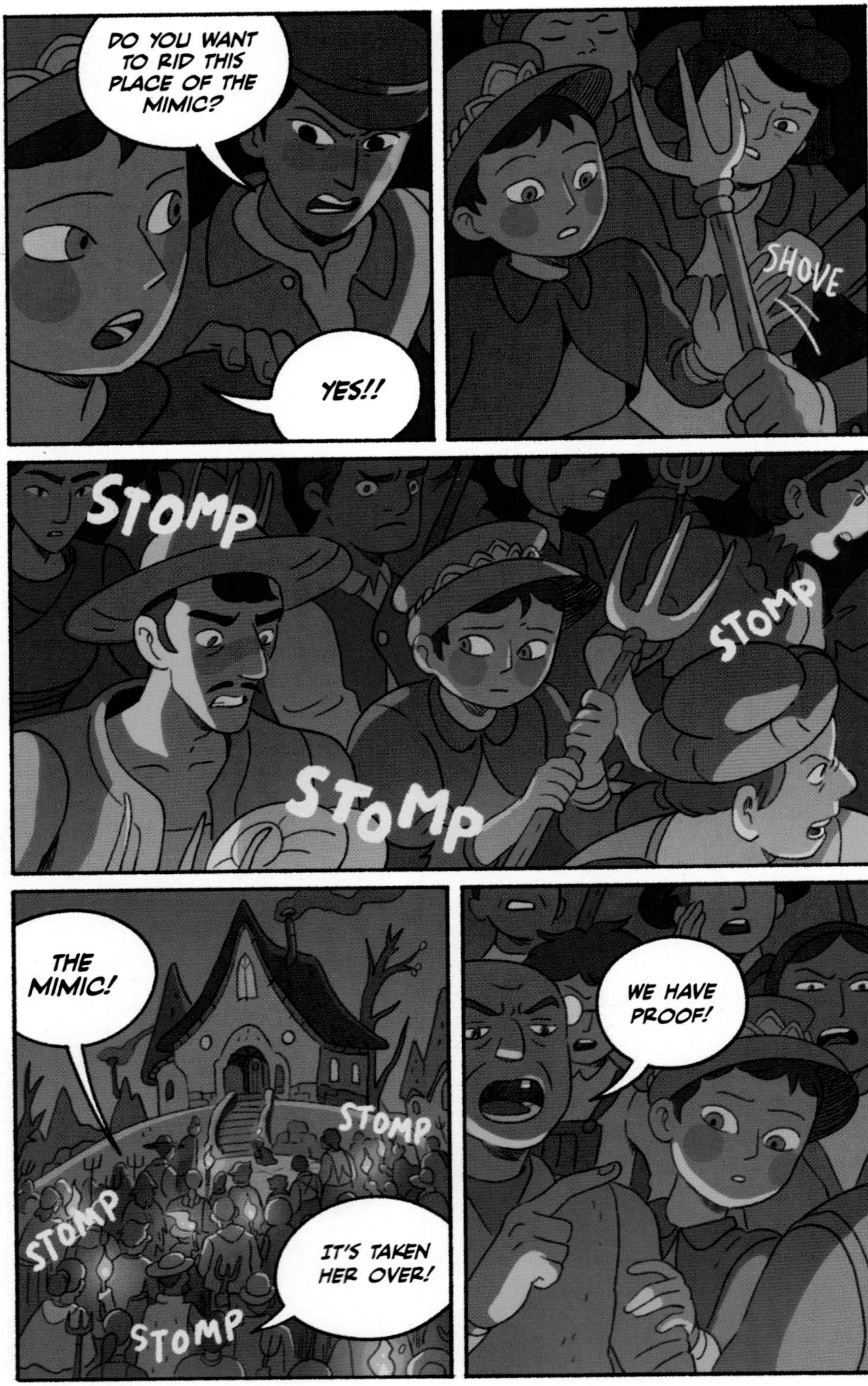
DO YOU WANT TO RID THIS PLACE OF THE MIMIC?
YES!!
SHOVE
STOMP
STOMP
STOMP
THE MIMIC!
STOMP
STOMP
IT'S TAKEN HER OVER!
STOMP
WE HAVE PROOF!

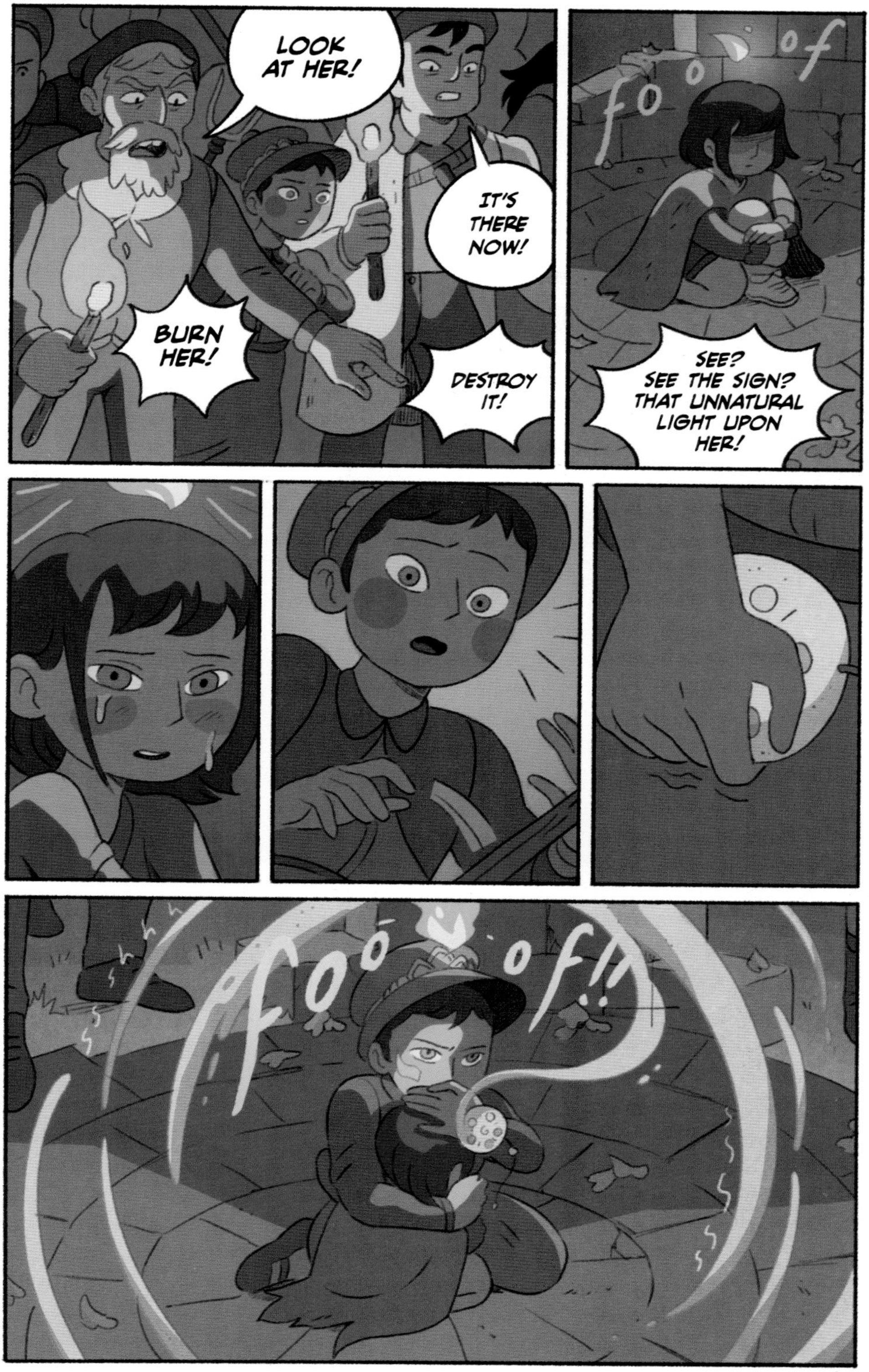
LOOK AT HER!
IT'S THERE NOW!
BURN HER!
DESTROY IT!
foo of
SEE? SEE THE SIGN? THAT UNNATURAL LIGHT UPON HER!
foo-of!!

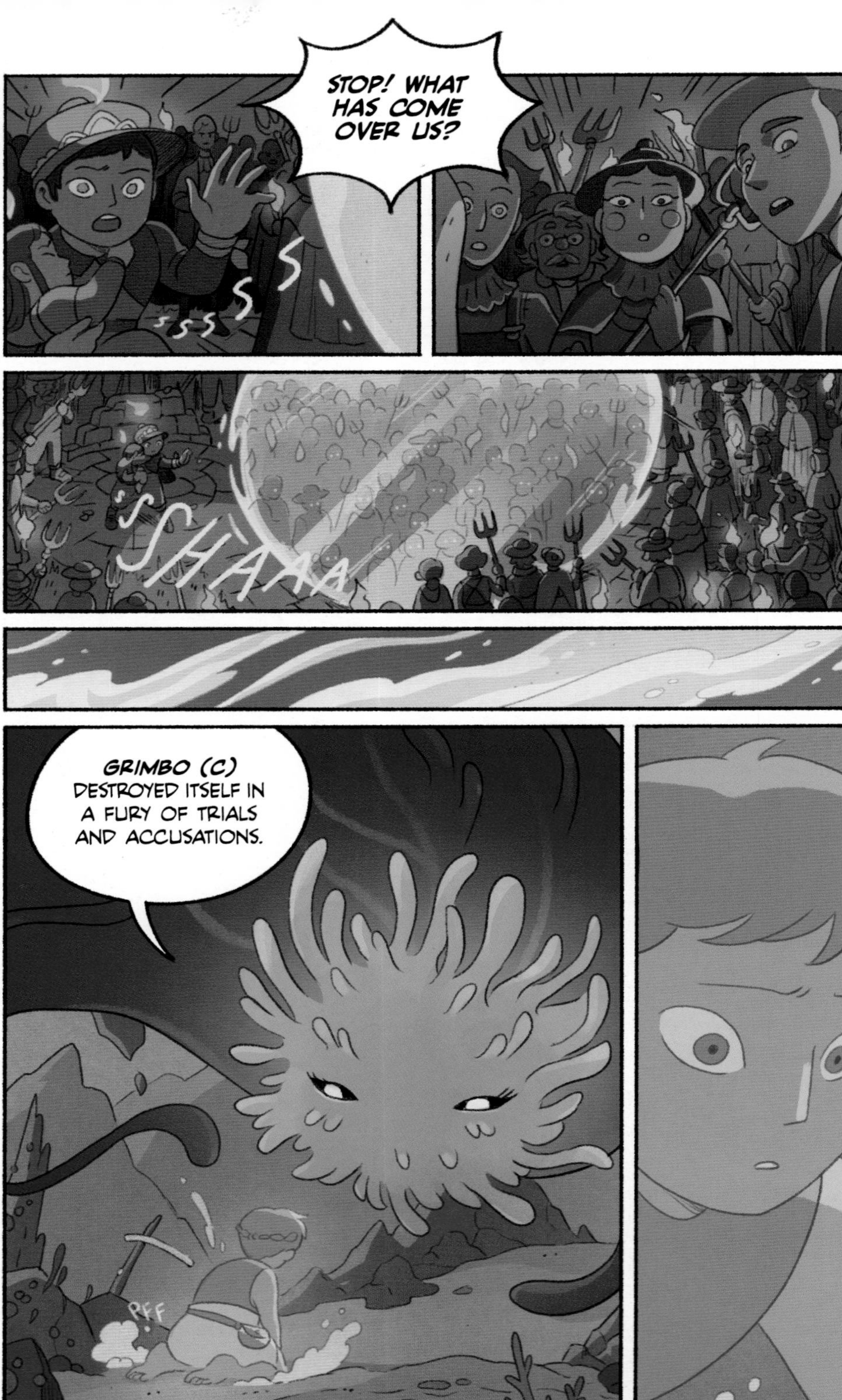
STOP! WHAT HAS COME OVER US?
SSSSS
SHAAA
GRIMBO (C) DESTROYED ITSELF IN A FURY OF TRIALS AND ACCUSATIONS.
PFF

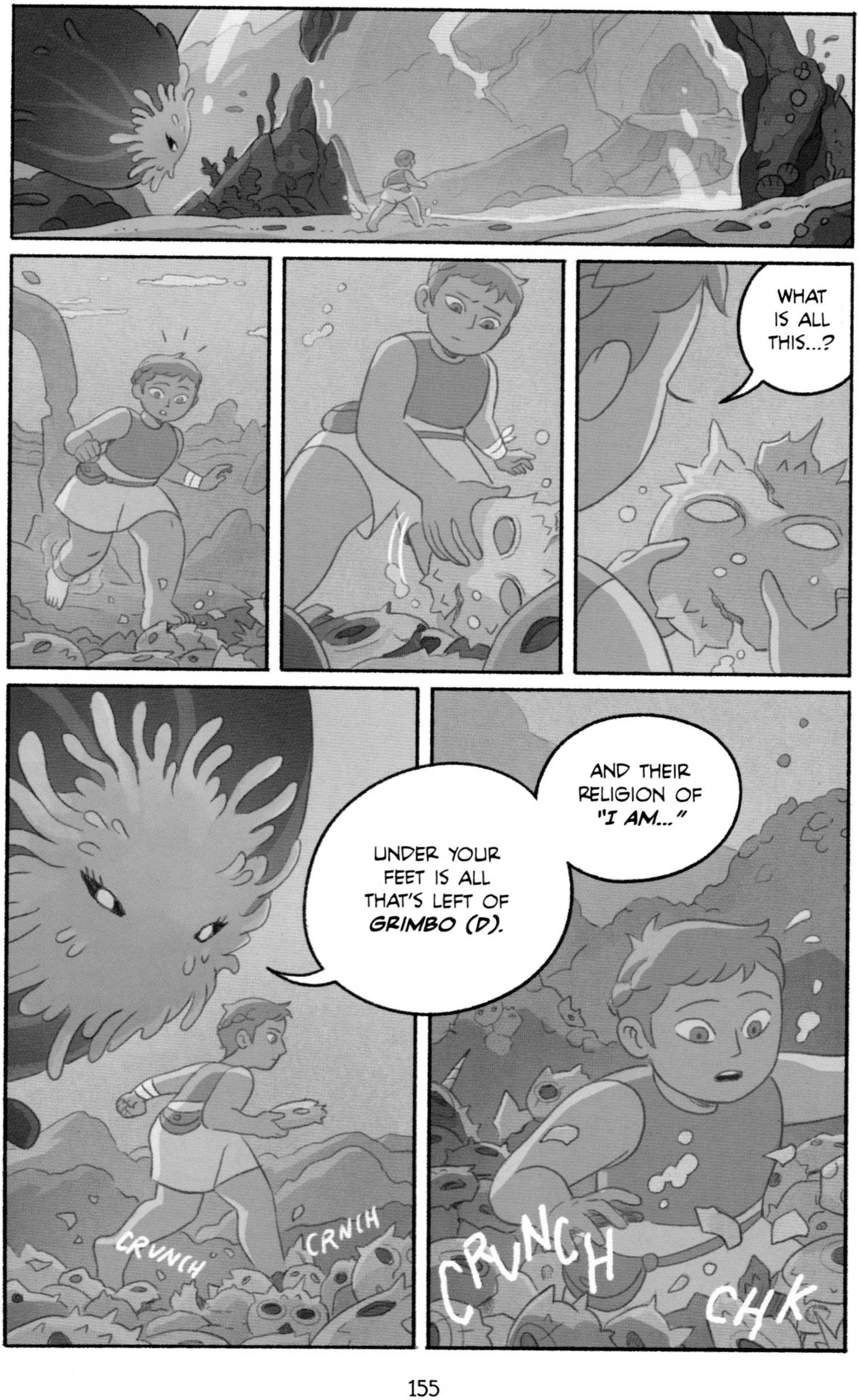
WHAT IS ALL THIS...?
UNDER YOUR FEET IS ALL THAT'S LEFT OF GRIMBO (D).
AND THEIR RELIGION OF "I AM..."
CRUNCH
CRNCH
CRUNCH
CHK

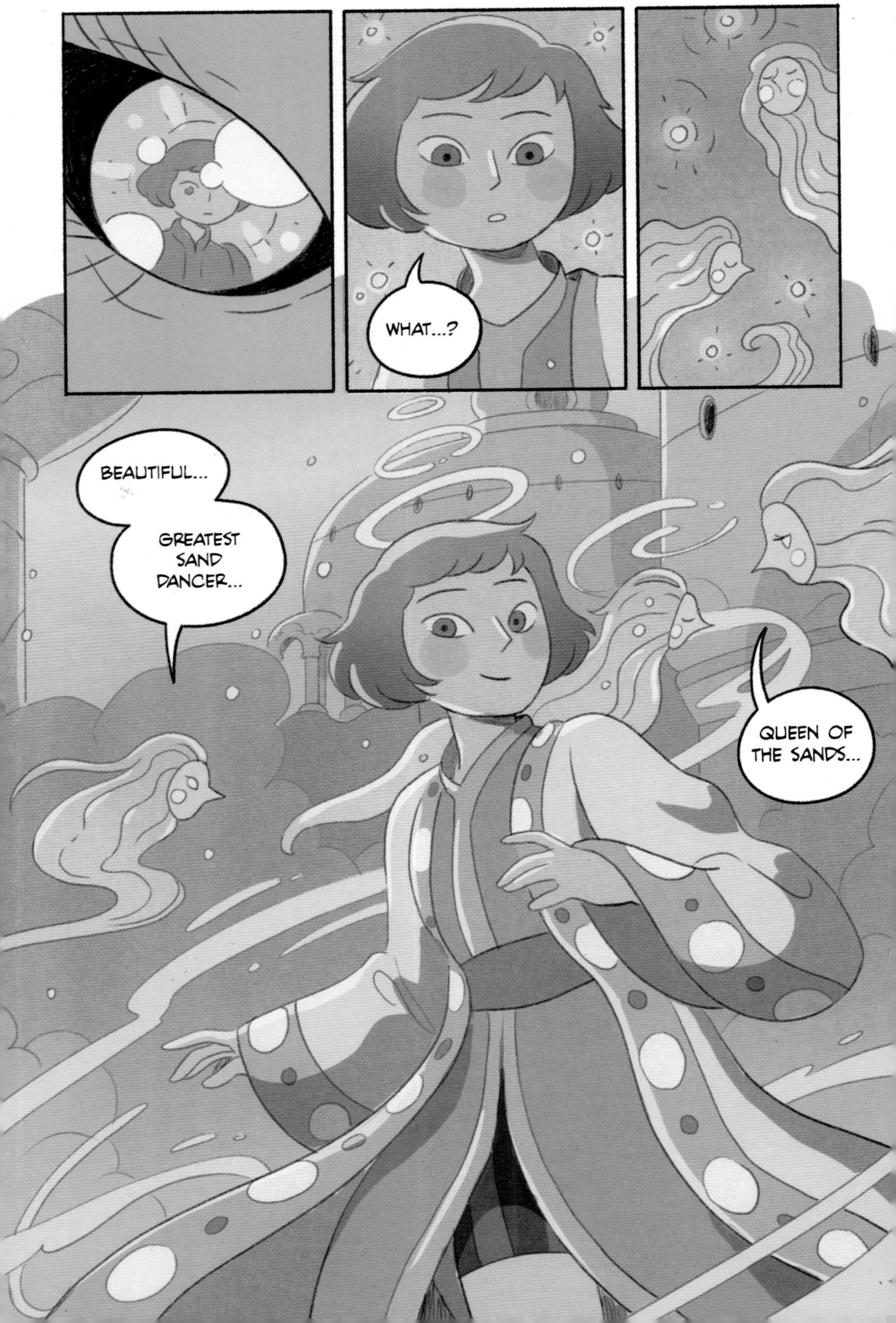
WHAT...?
BEAUTIFUL...
GREATEST SAND DANCER...
QUEEN OF THE SANDS...

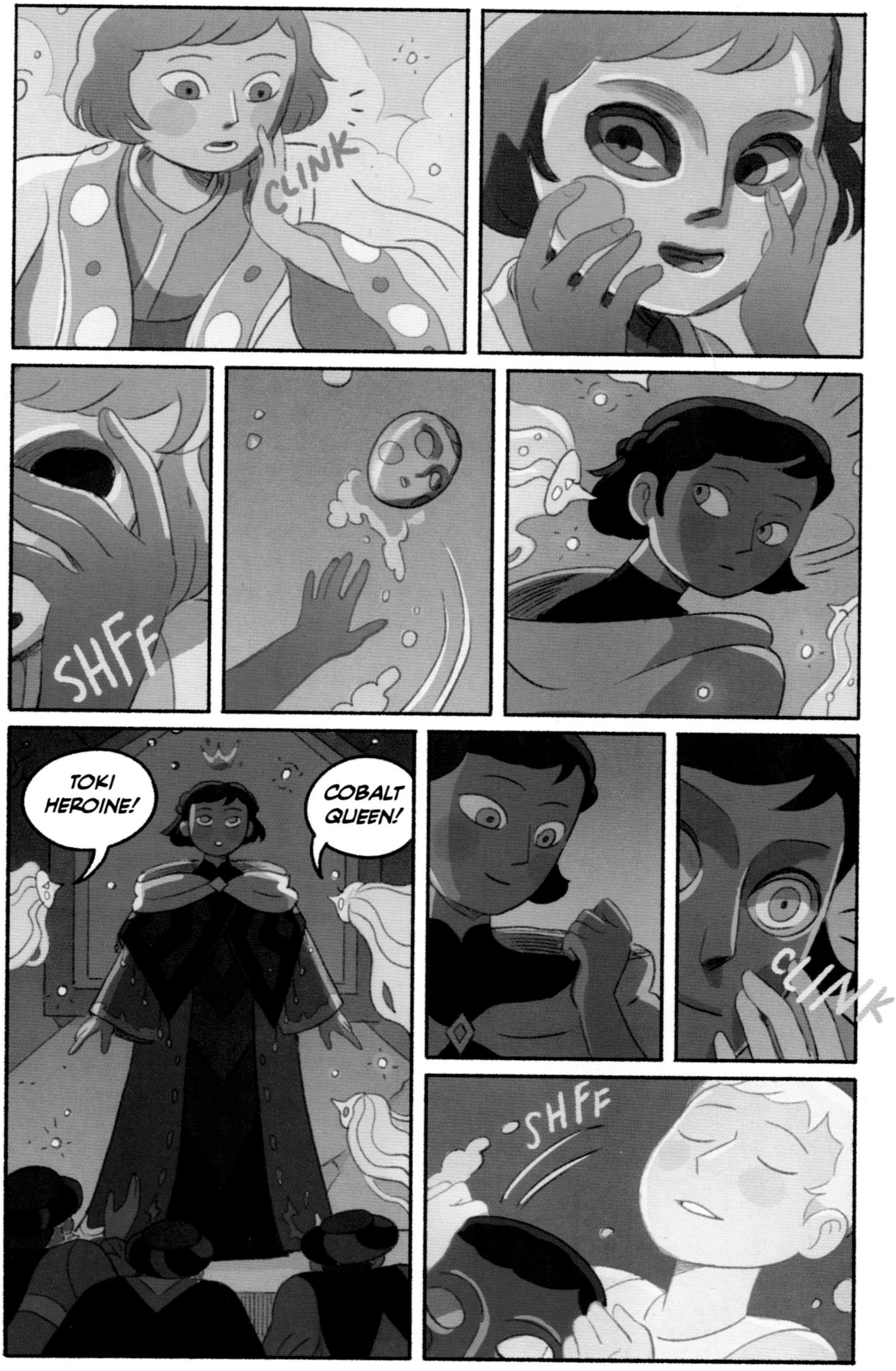
CLINK
SHFF
TOKI HEROINE!
COBALT QUEEN!
CLINK
SHFF

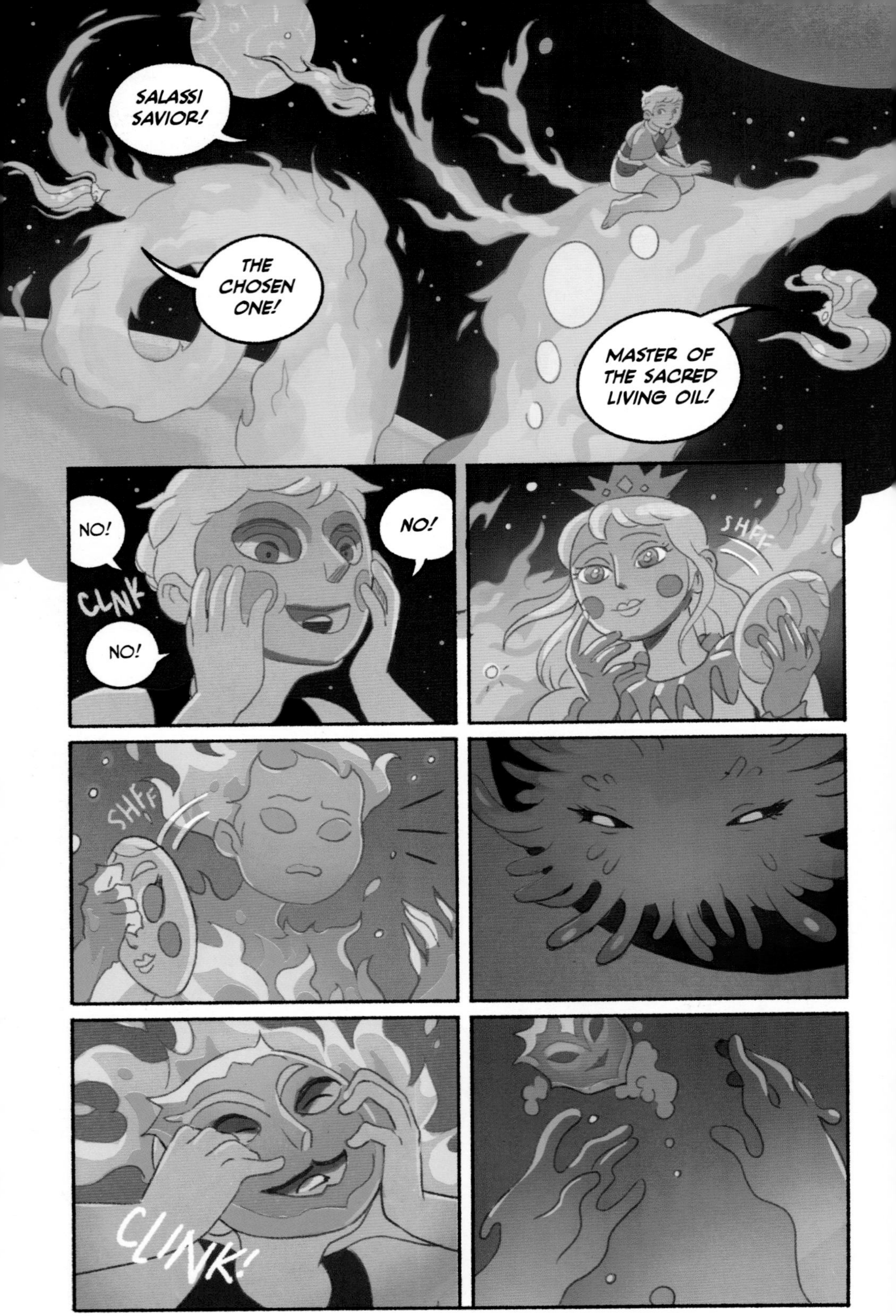
SALASSI SAVIOR!
THE CHOSEN ONE!
MASTER OF THE SACRED LIVING OIL!
NO!
NO!
CLNK
NO!
SHFF
SHFF
CLINK!

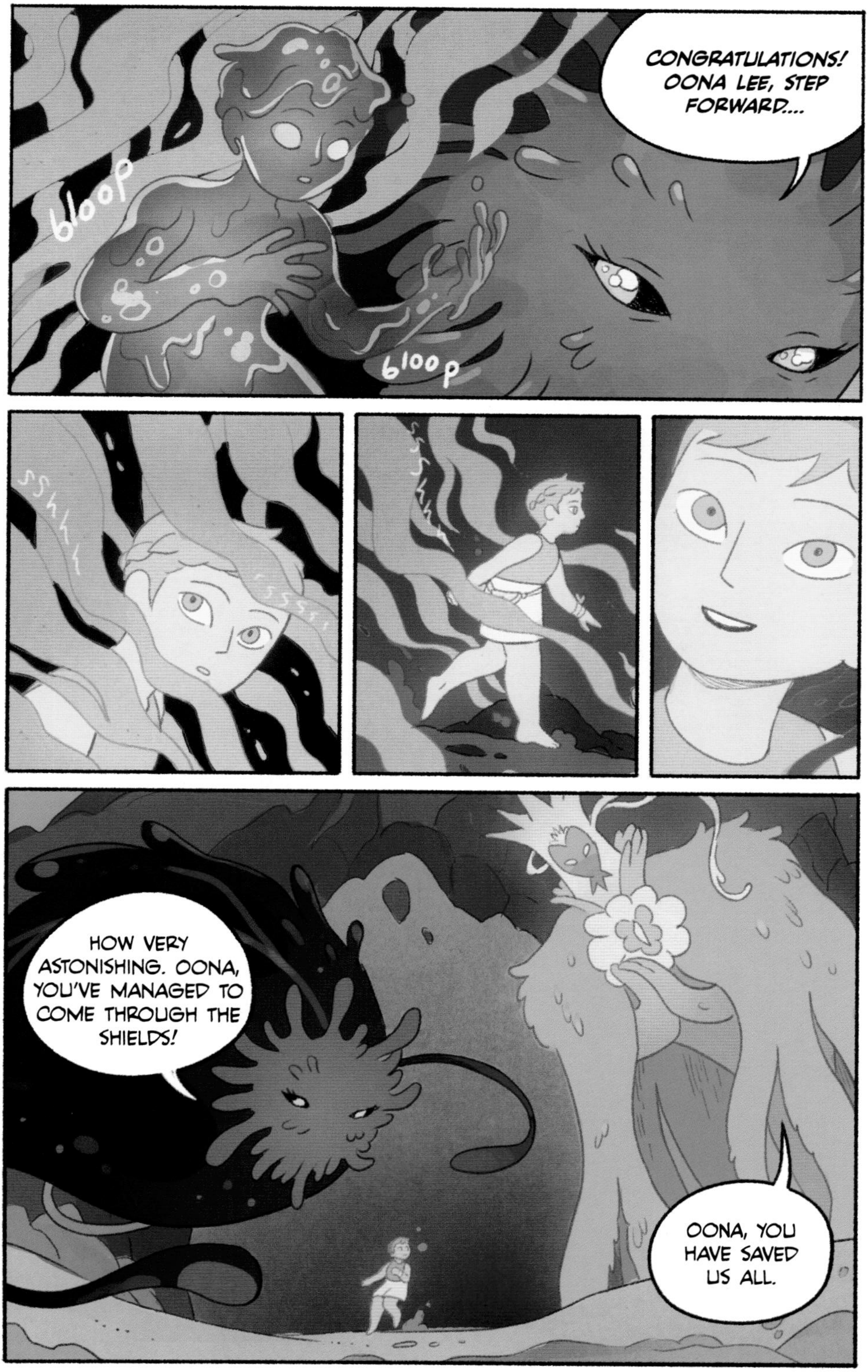
CONGRATULATIONS! OONA LEE, STEP FORWARD...
bloop
bloop
HOW VERY ASTONISHING. OONA, YOU'VE MANAGED TO COME THROUGH THE SHIELDS!
OONA, YOU HAVE SAVED US ALL.

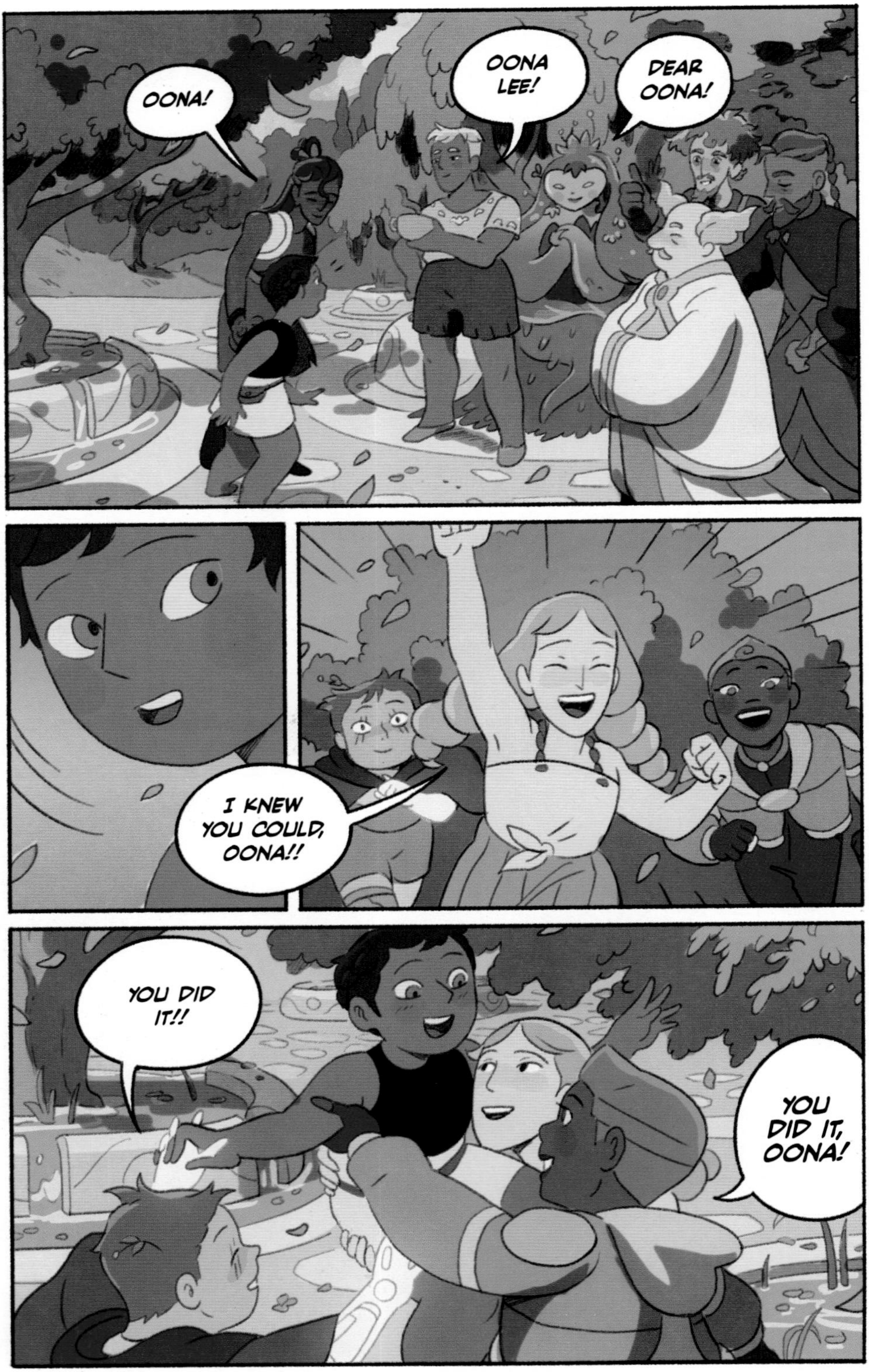
OONA!
OONA LEE!
DEAR OONA!
I KNEW YOU COULD, OONA!!
YOU DID IT!!
YOU DID IT, OONA!

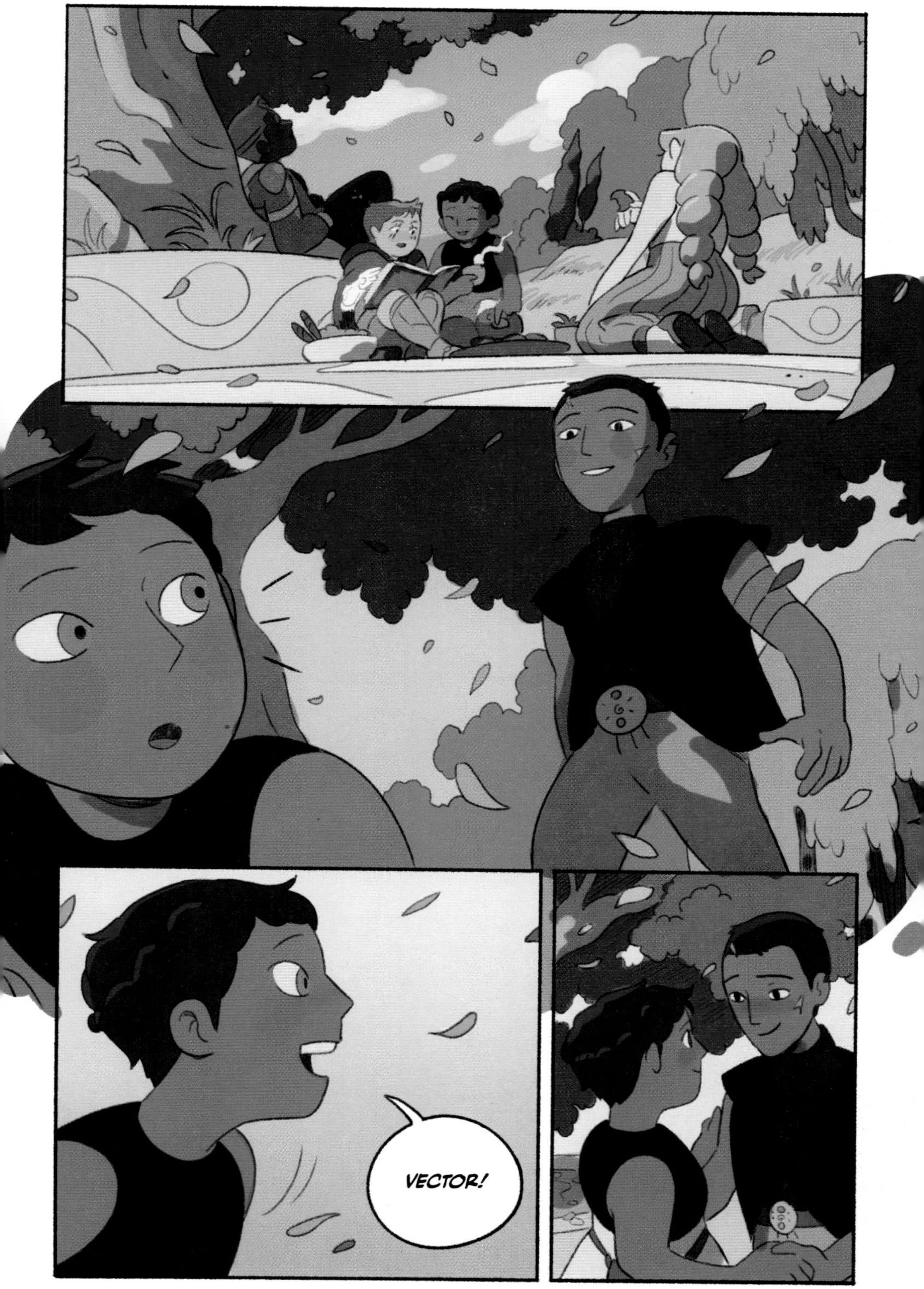
VECTOR!

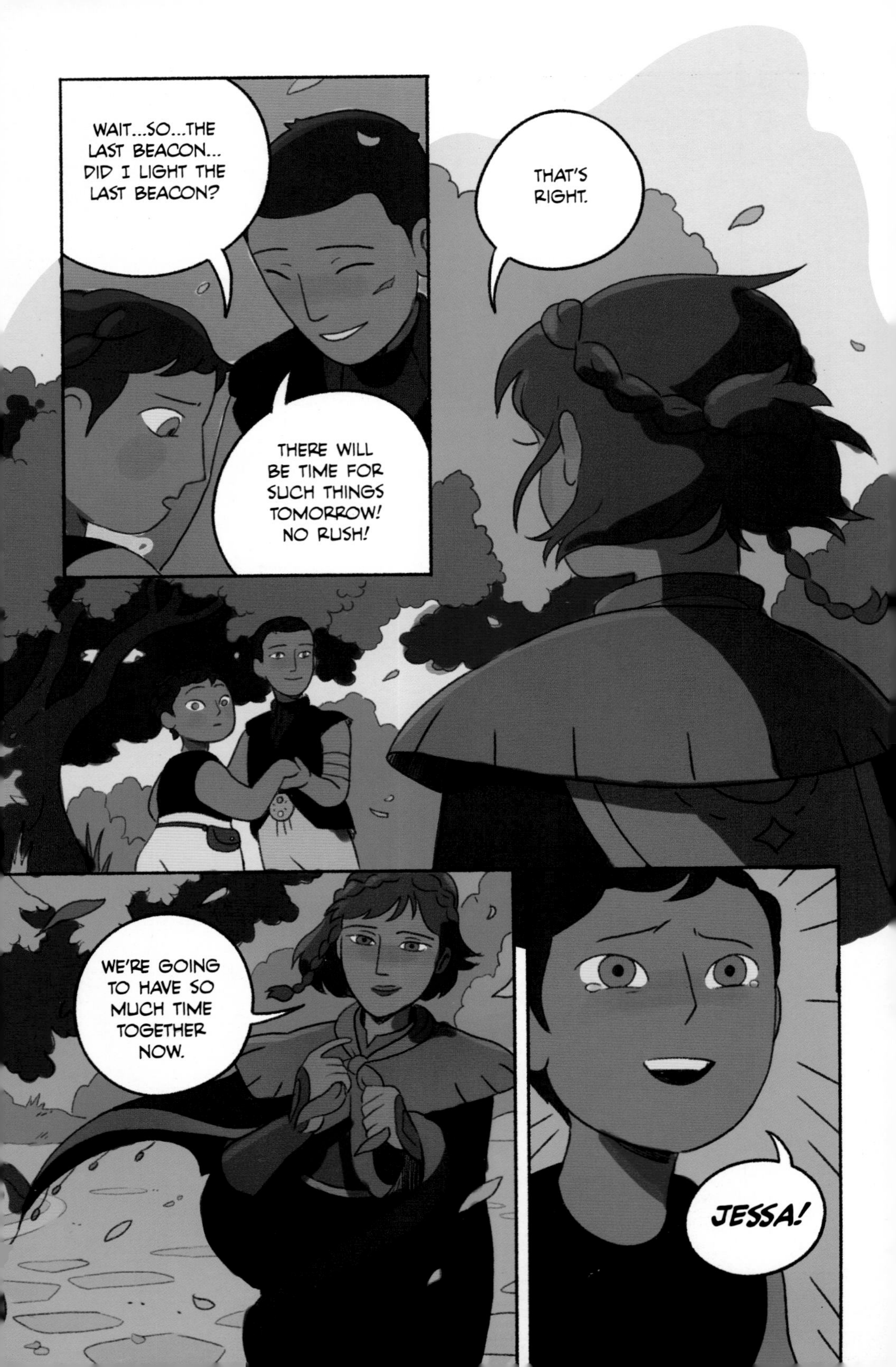
WAIT...SO...THE LAST BEACON... DID I LIGHT THE LAST BEACON?
THAT'S RIGHT.
THERE WILL BE TIME FOR SUCH THINGS TOMORROW! NO RUSH!
WE'RE GOING TO HAVE SO MUCH TIME TOGETHER NOW.
JESSA!

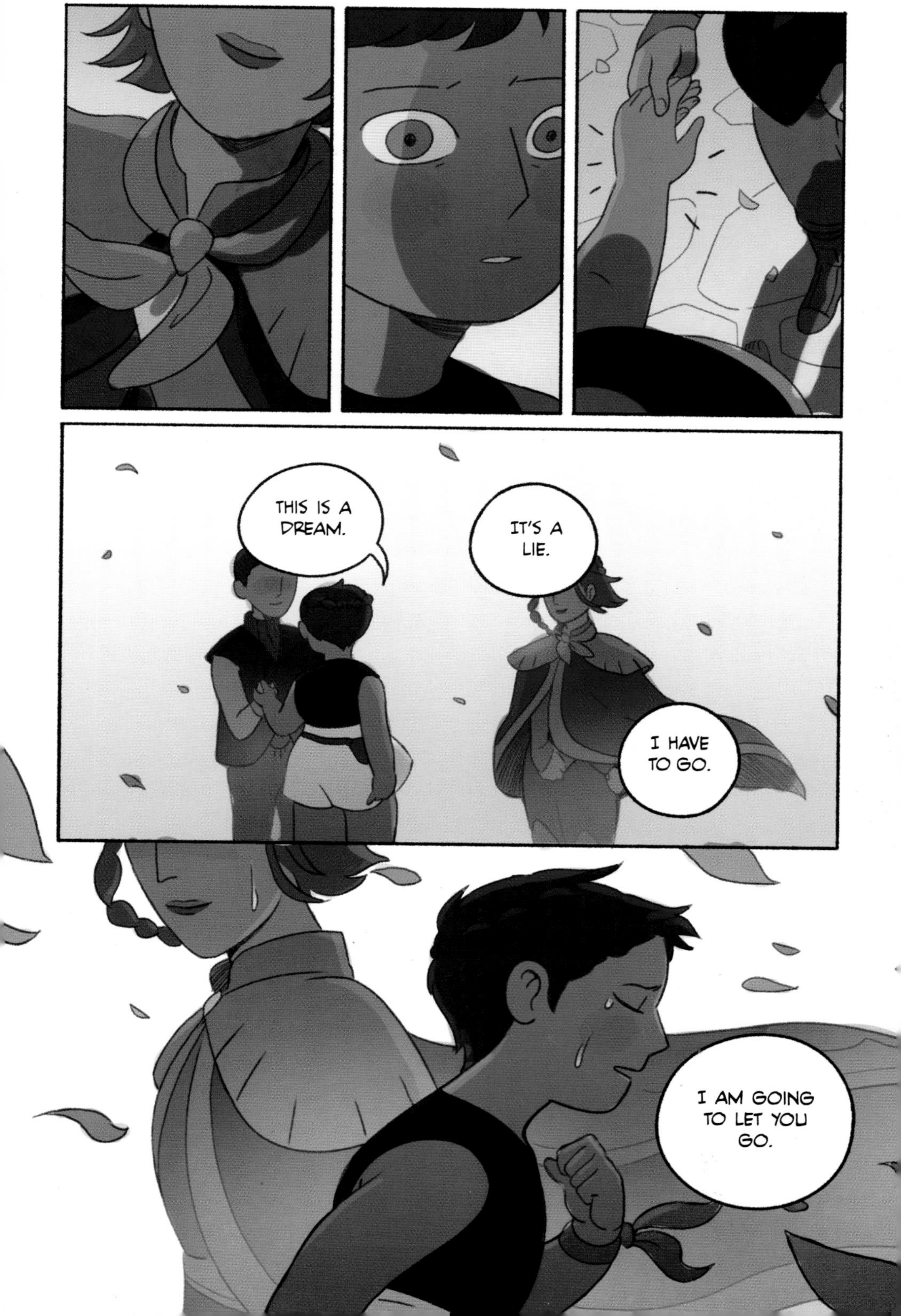
THIS IS A DREAM.
IT'S A LIE.
I HAVE TO GO.
I AM GOING TO LET YOU GO.

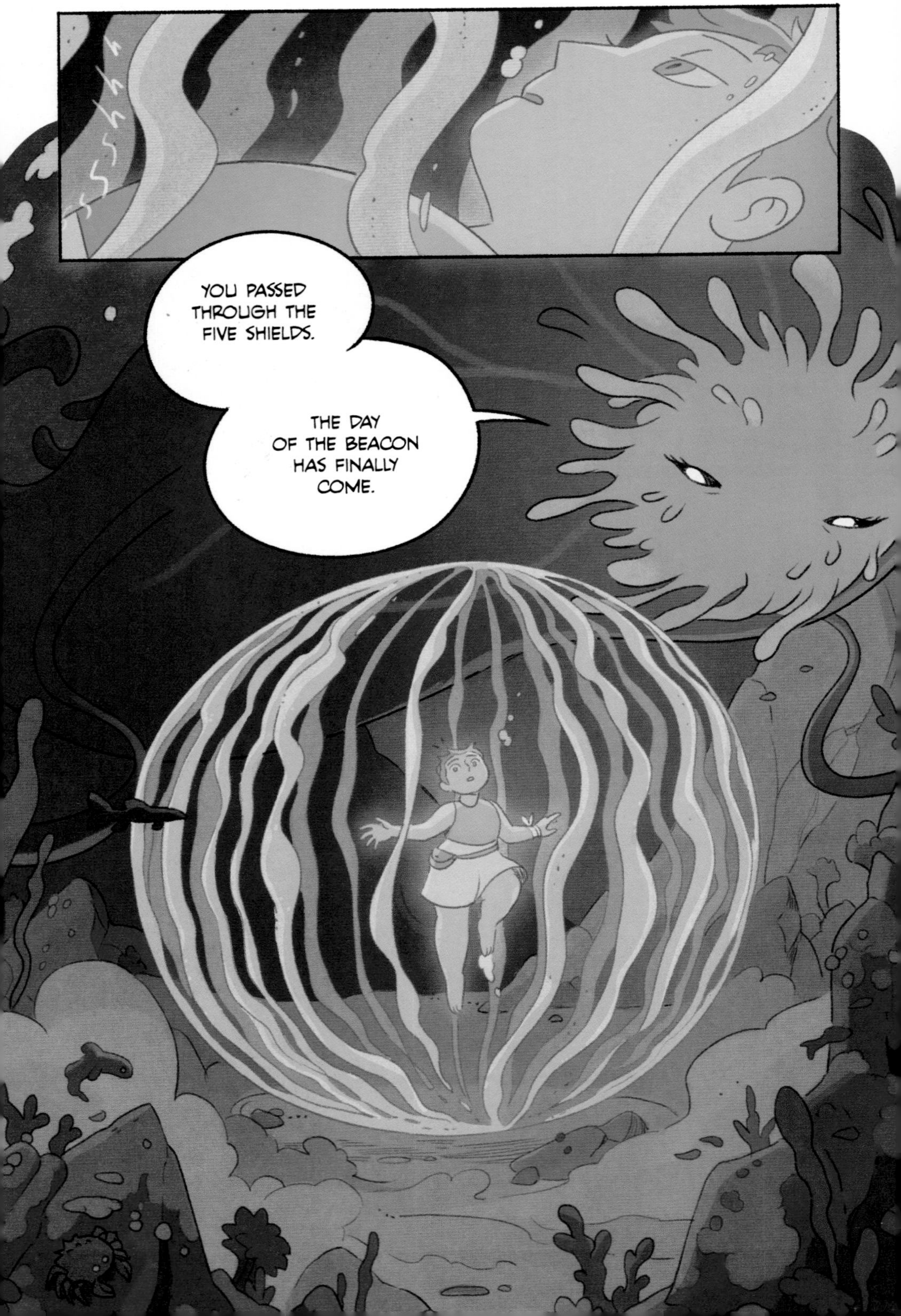

ssshhh
YOU PASSED THROUGH THE FIVE SHIELDS.
THE DAY OF THE BEACON HAS FINALLY COME.

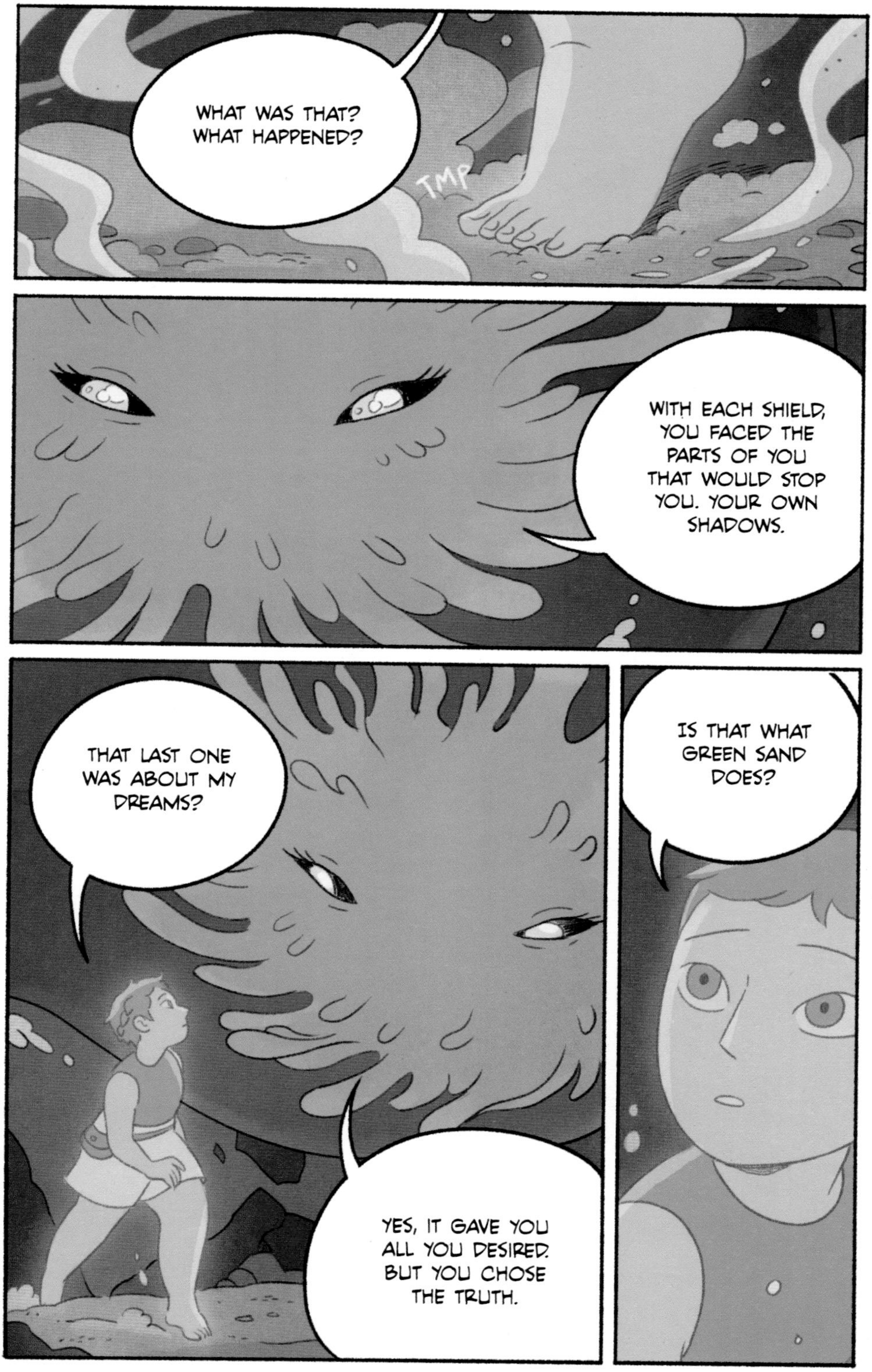
WHAT WAS THAT? WHAT HAPPENED?
TMP
WITH EACH SHIELD, YOU FACED THE PARTS OF YOU THAT WOULD STOP YOU. YOUR OWN SHADOWS.
THAT LAST ONE WAS ABOUT MY DREAMS?
YES, IT GAVE YOU ALL YOU DESIRED. BUT YOU CHOSE THE TRUTH.
IS THAT WHAT GREEN SAND DOES?

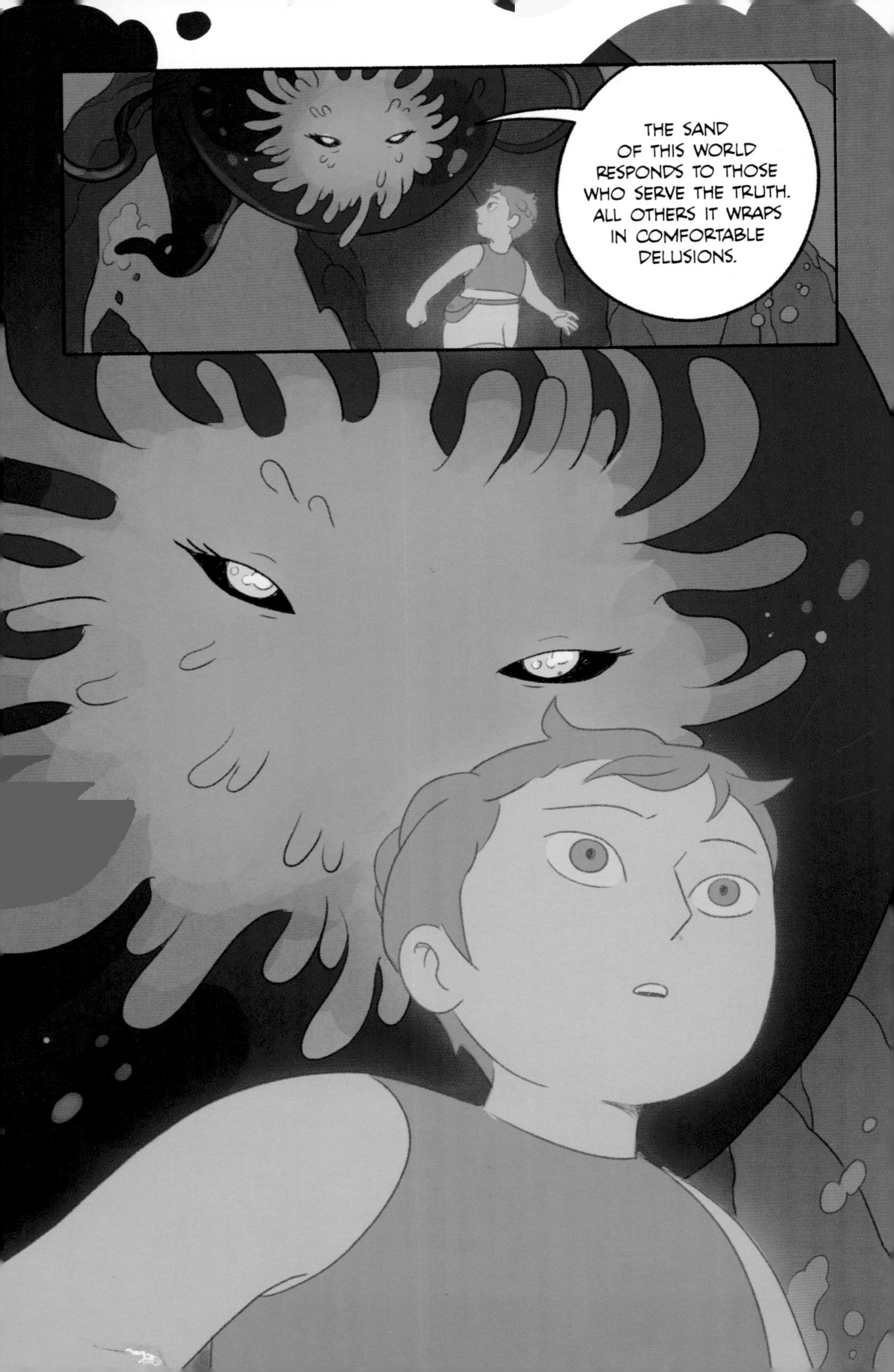
THE SAND OF THIS WORLD RESPONDS TO THOSE WHO SERVE THE TRUTH. ALL OTHERS IT WRAPS IN COMFORTABLE DELUSIONS.

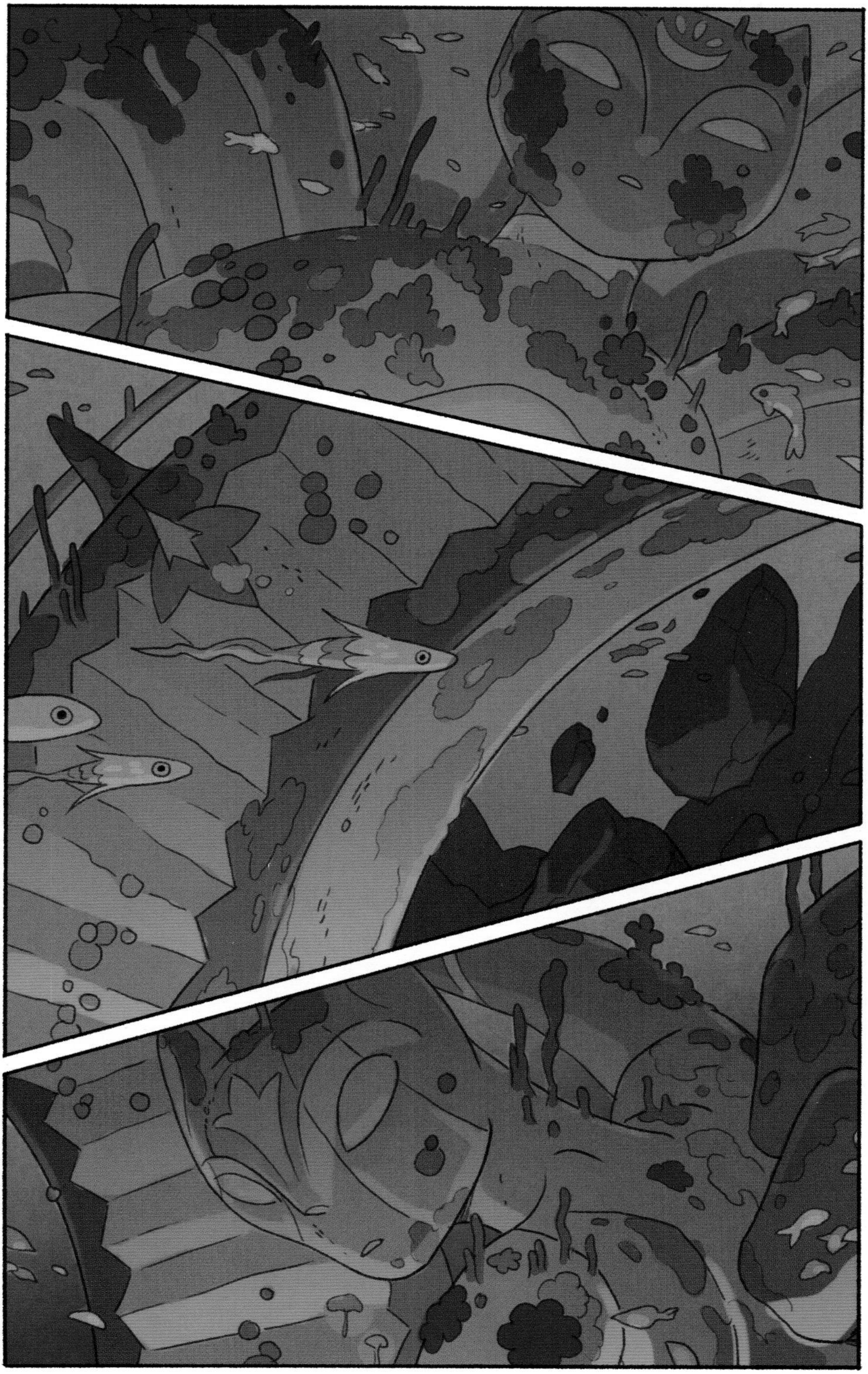

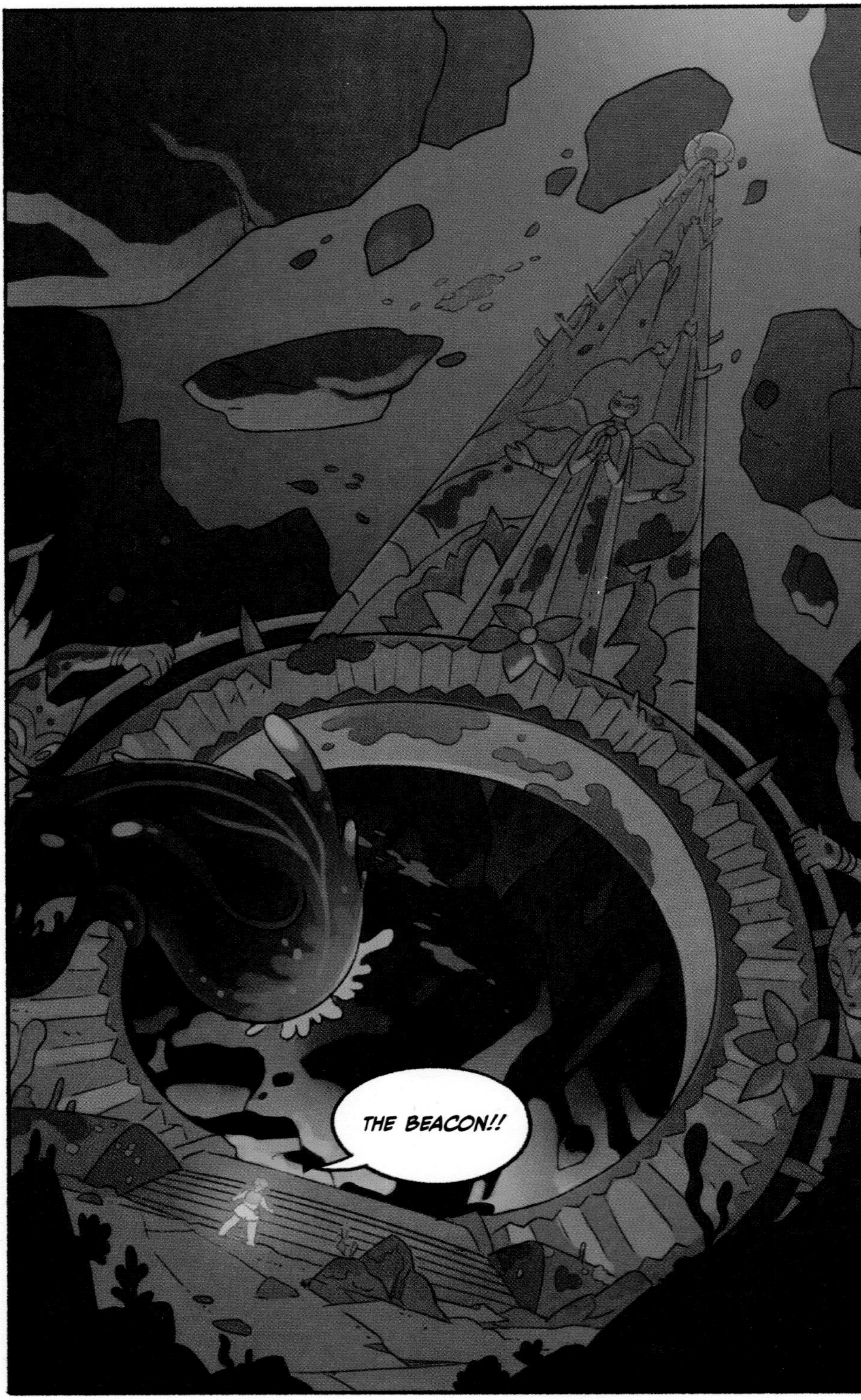
THE BEACON!!

CHAPTER 11

THE DAY OF THE BEACON

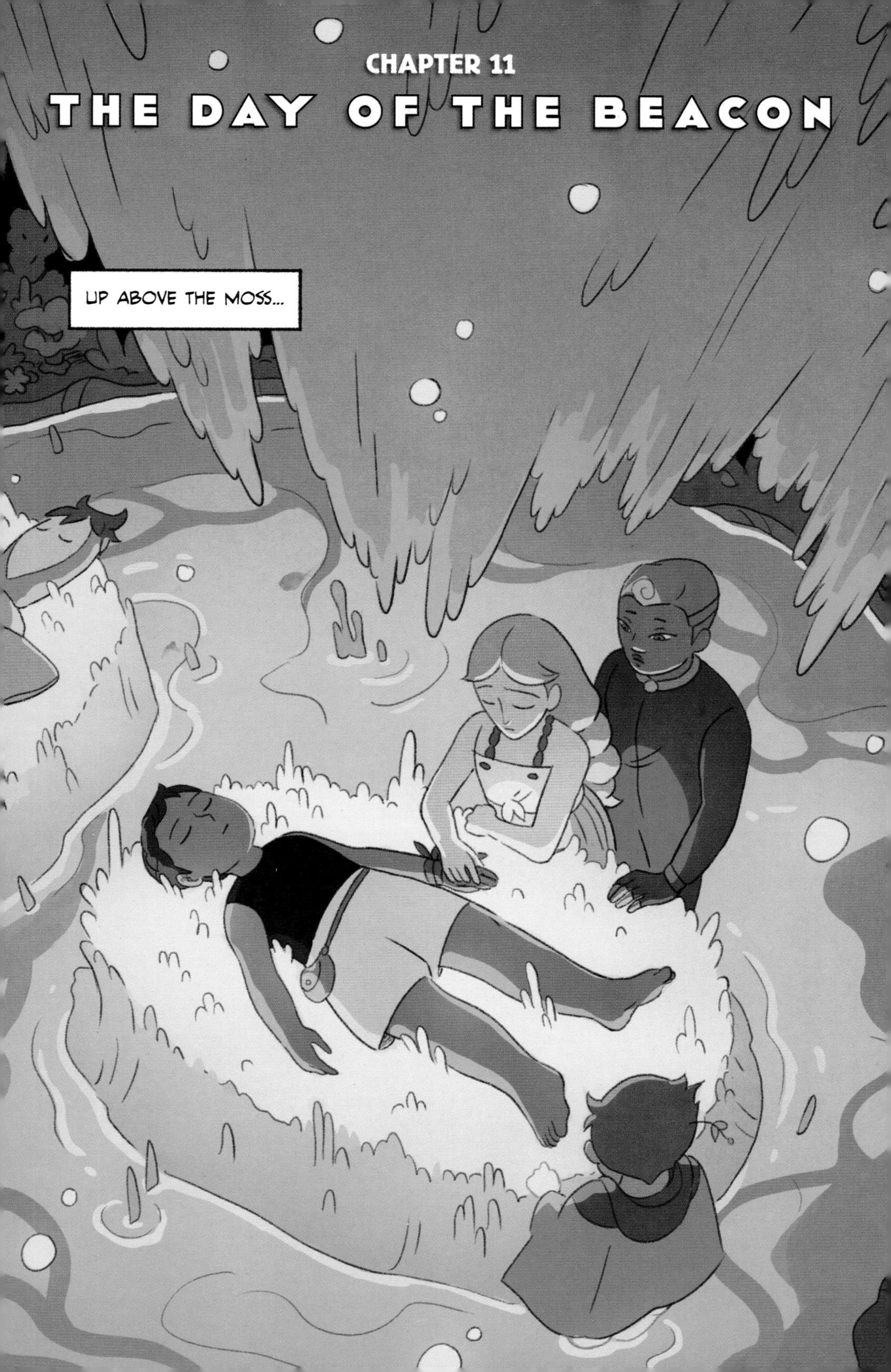
UP ABOVE THE MOSS...

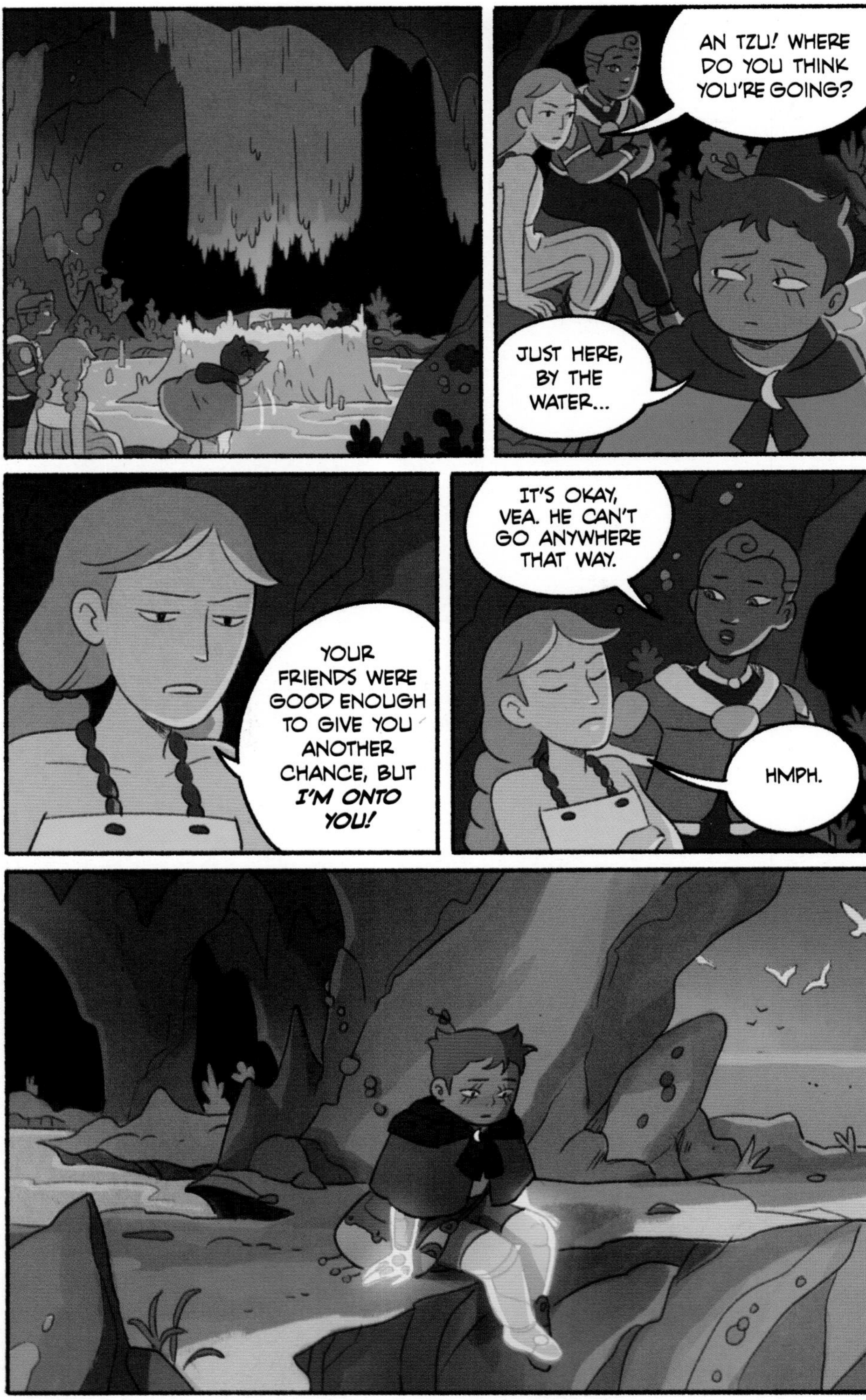
AN TZU! WHERE DO YOU THINK YOU'RE GOING?
JUST HERE, BY THE WATER...
YOUR FRIENDS WERE GOOD ENOUGH TO GIVE YOU ANOTHER CHANCE, BUT *I'M ONTO YOU!*
IT'S OKAY, VEA. HE CAN'T GO ANYWHERE THAT WAY.
HMPH.

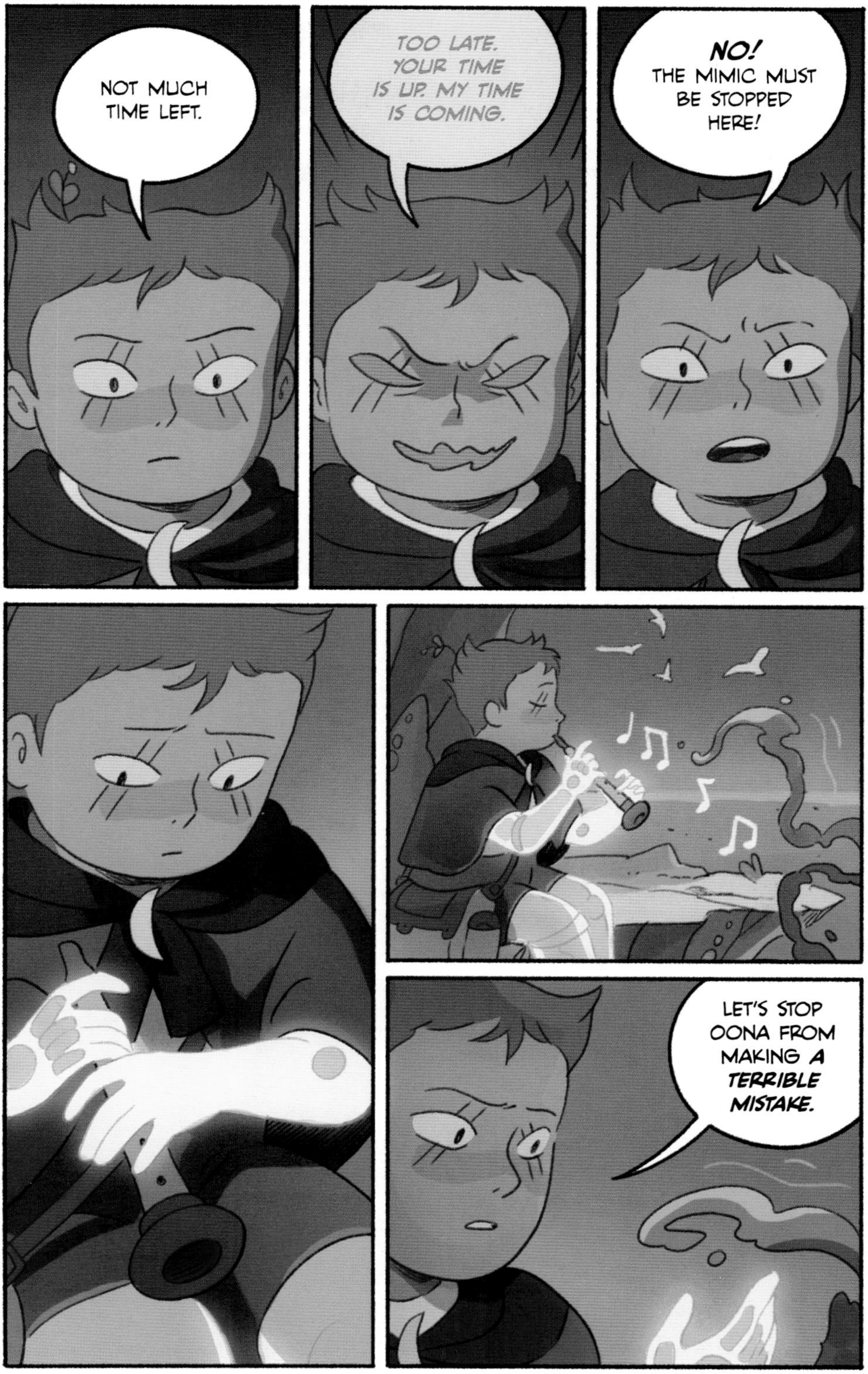
NOT MUCH TIME LEFT.
TOO LATE. YOUR TIME IS UP. MY TIME IS COMING.
NO! THE MIMIC MUST BE STOPPED HERE!
LET'S STOP OONA FROM MAKING A TERRIBLE MISTAKE.

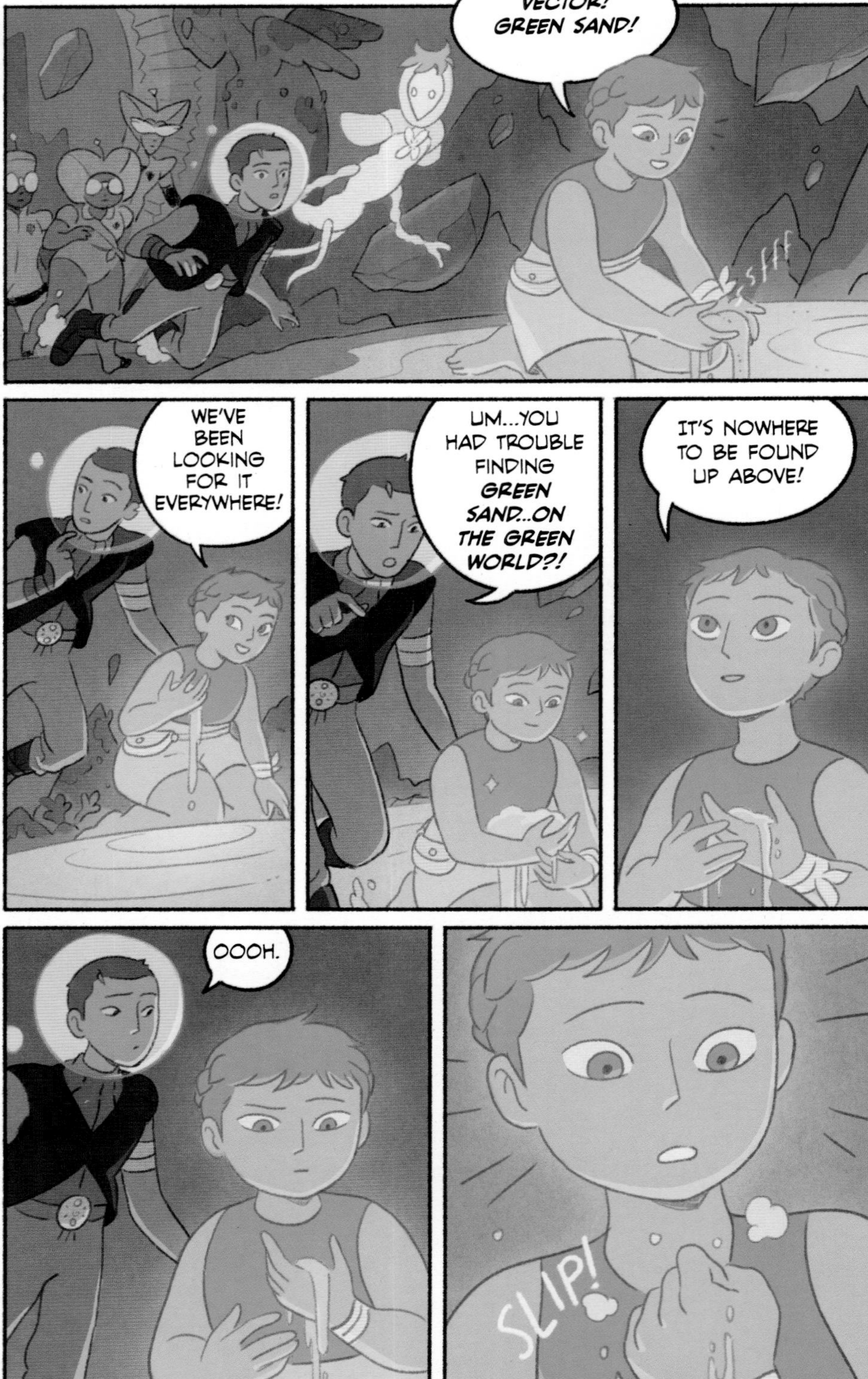
VECTOR! GREEN SAND!
SFFF
WE'VE BEEN LOOKING FOR IT EVERYWHERE!
UM...YOU HAD TROUBLE FINDING GREEN SAND...ON THE GREEN WORLD?!
IT'S NOWHERE TO BE FOUND UP ABOVE!
OOOH.
SLIP!

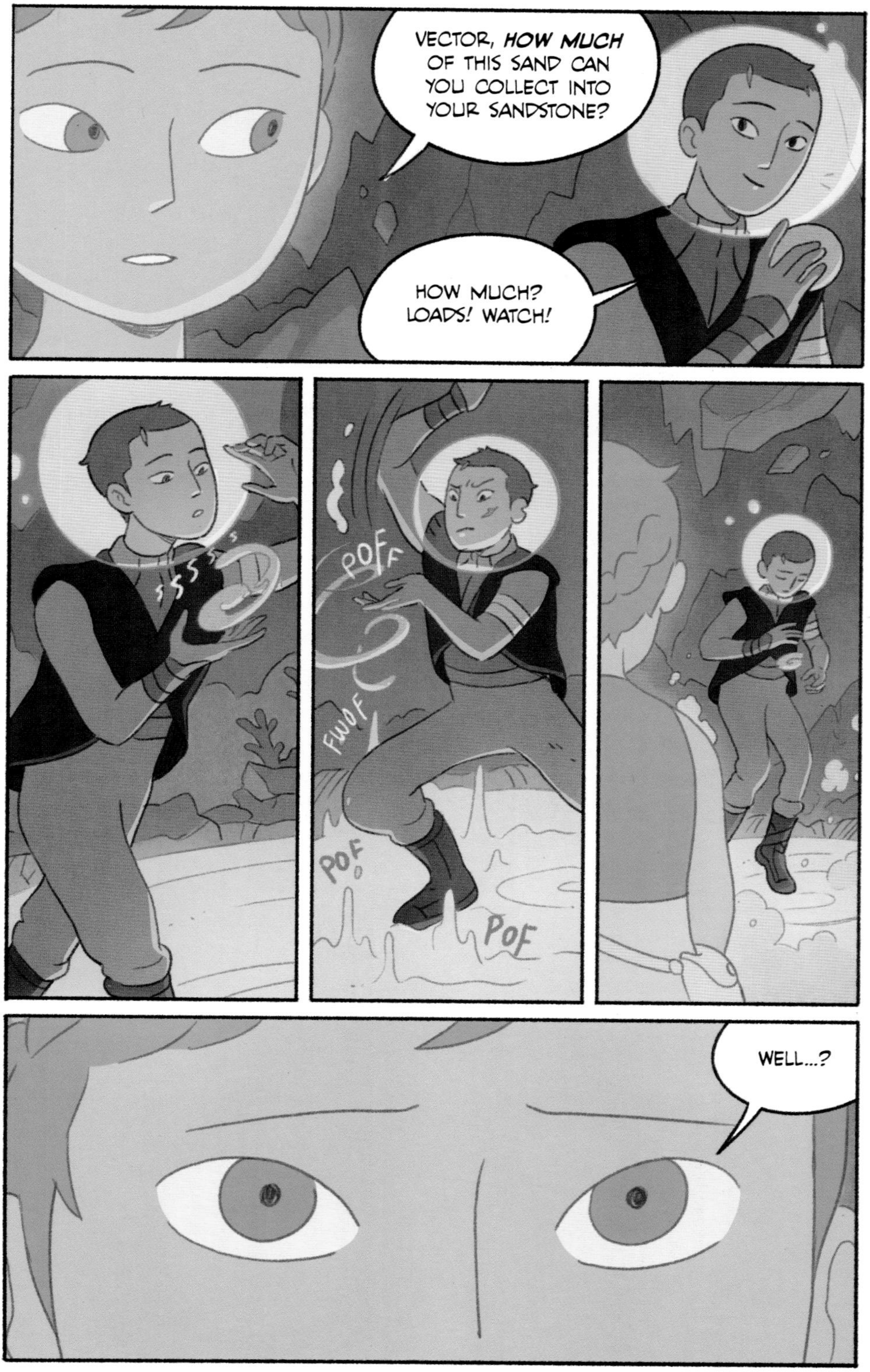
VECTOR, ***HOW MUCH*** OF THIS SAND CAN YOU COLLECT INTO YOUR SANDSTONE?
HOW MUCH? LOADS! WATCH!
SSSSS
POFF
FWOF
POF
POF
WELL...?

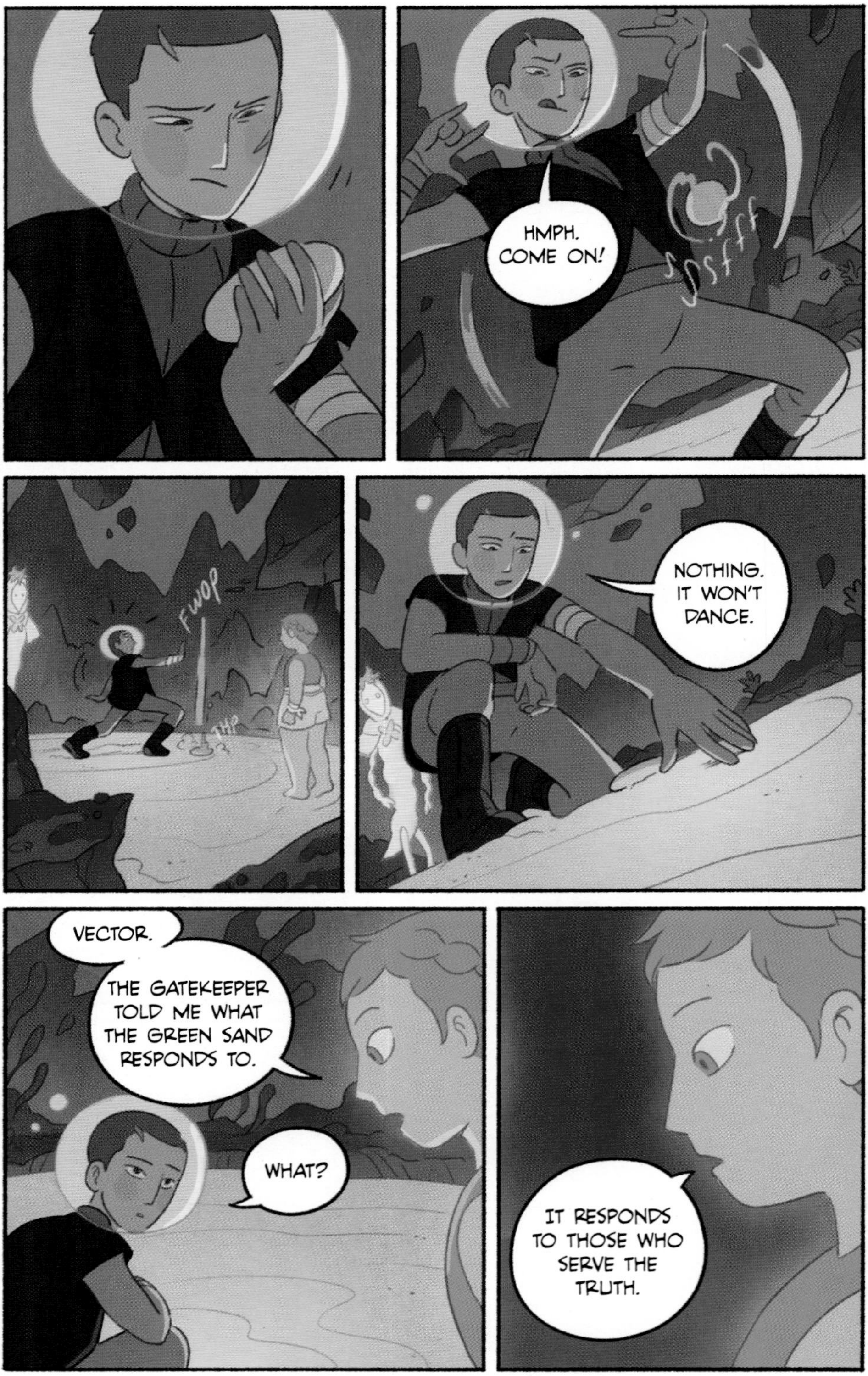
HMPH. COME ON!
SFFF
FWOP
THP
NOTHING. IT WON'T DANCE.
VECTOR.
THE GATEKEEPER TOLD ME WHAT THE GREEN SAND RESPONDS TO.
WHAT?
IT RESPONDS TO THOSE WHO SERVE THE TRUTH.

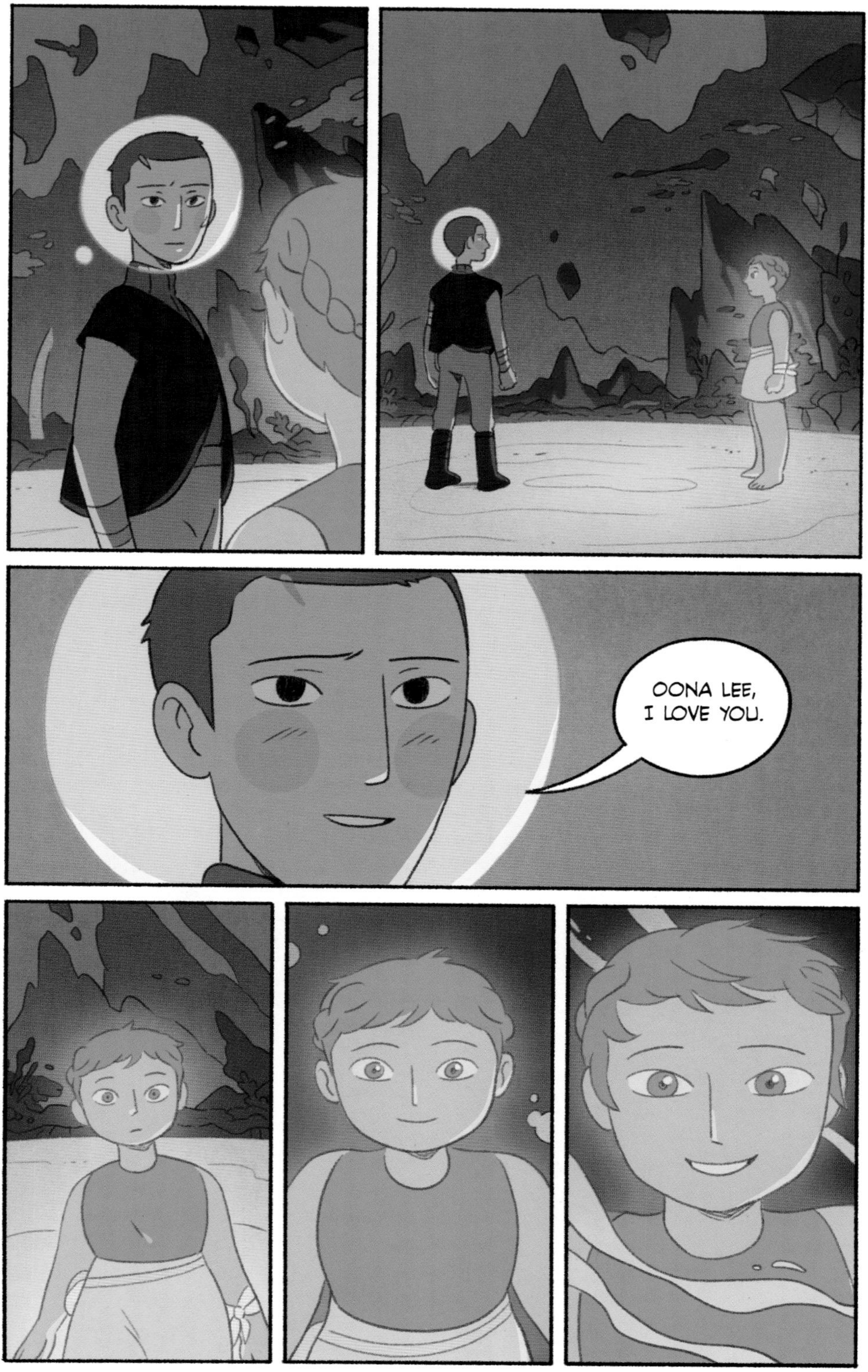
OONA LEE,
I LOVE YOU.

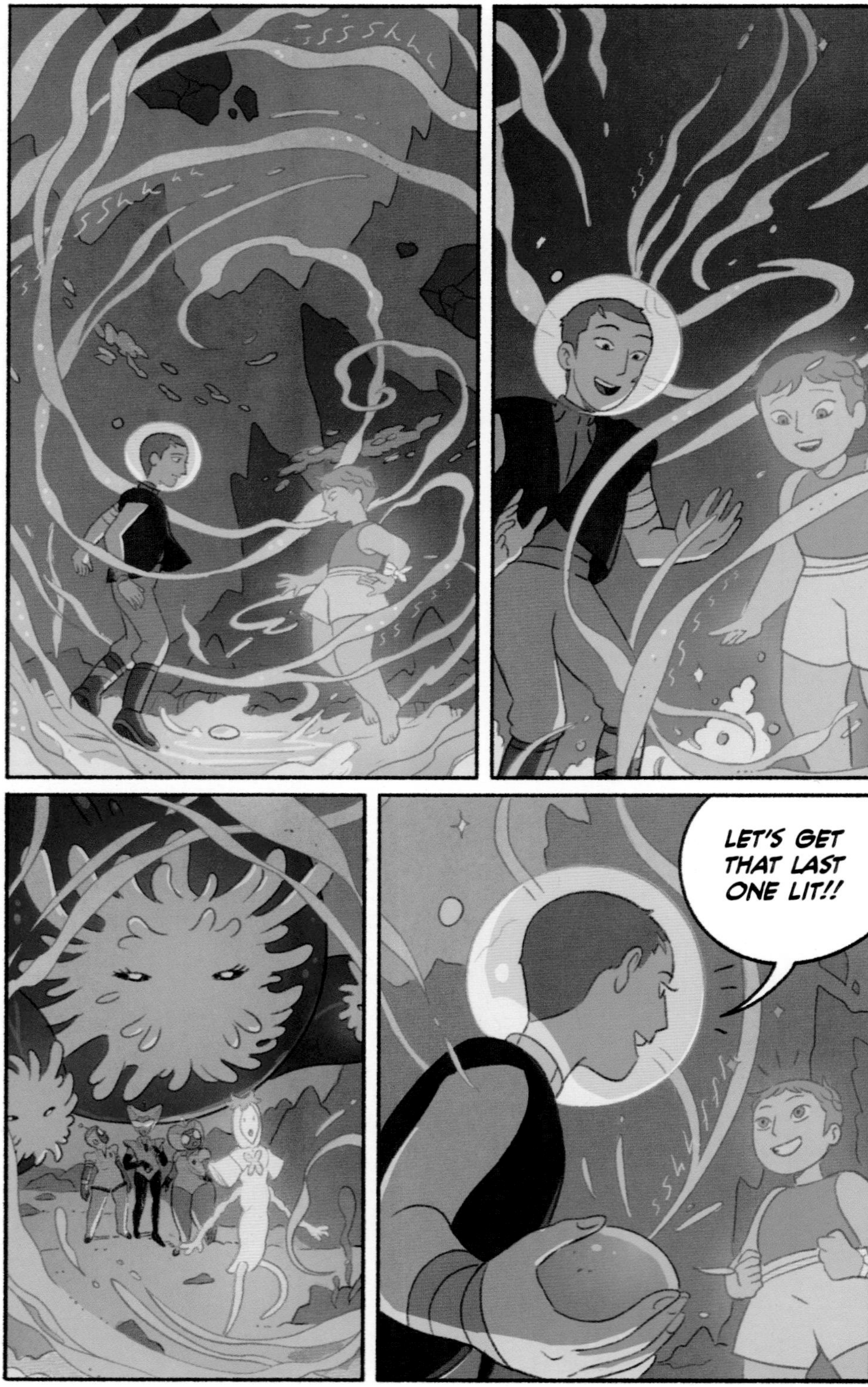
sssshhh
sshhh
LET'S GET THAT LAST ONE LIT!!

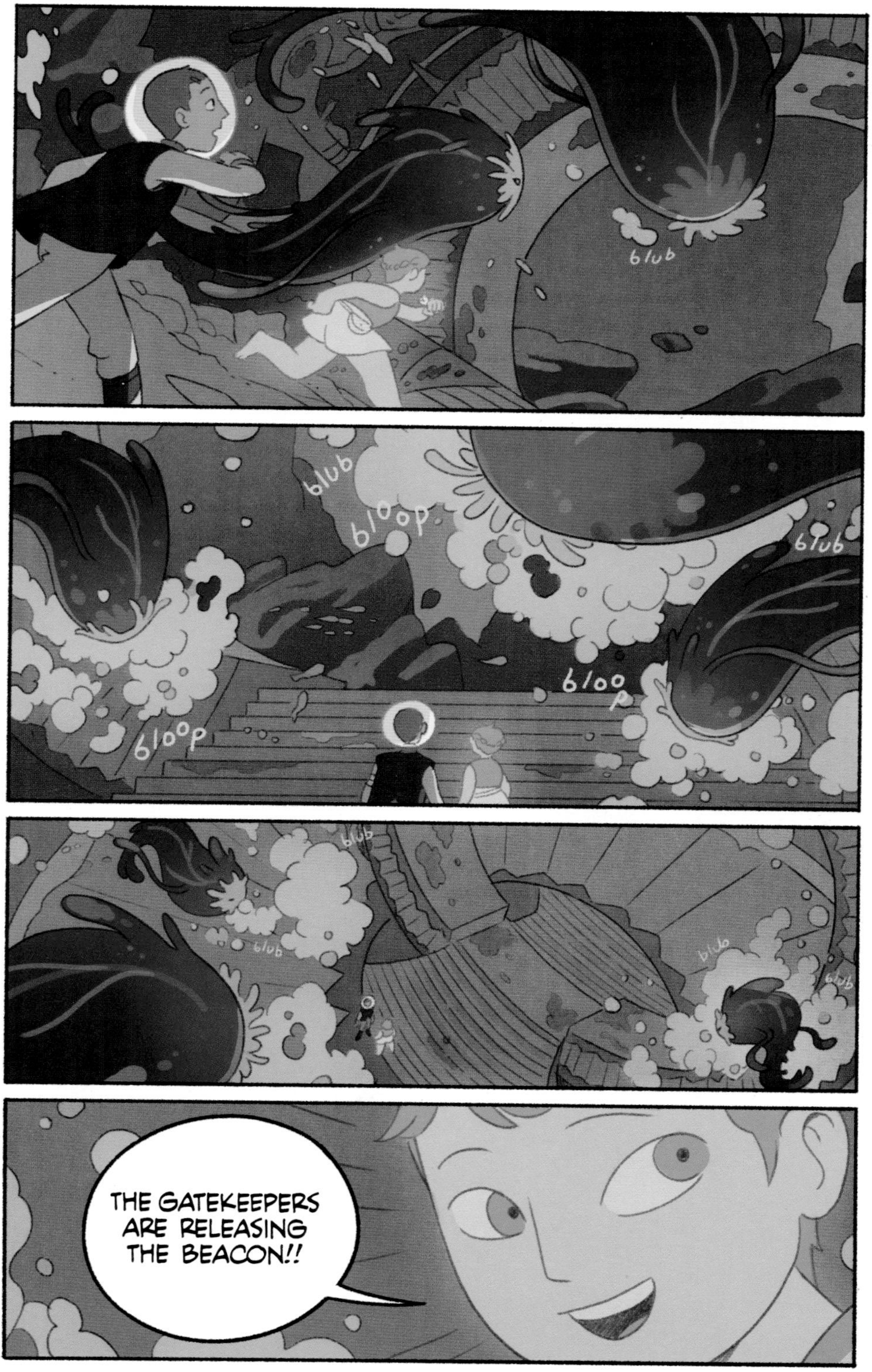
blub
blub
bloop
blub
bloop
bloop
blub
blub
blub
blub
THE GATEKEEPERS ARE RELEASING THE BEACON!!

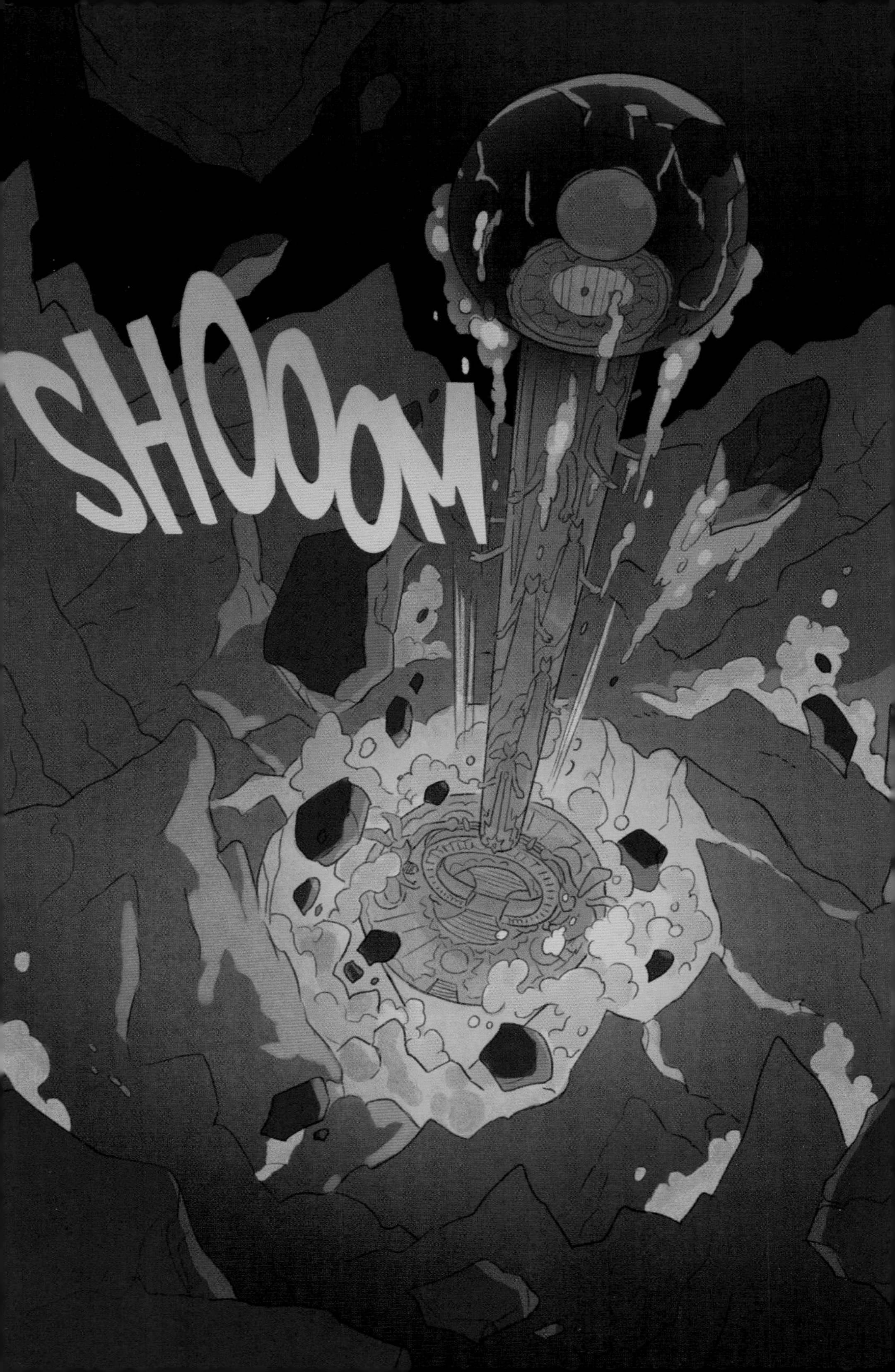
SHOOOM

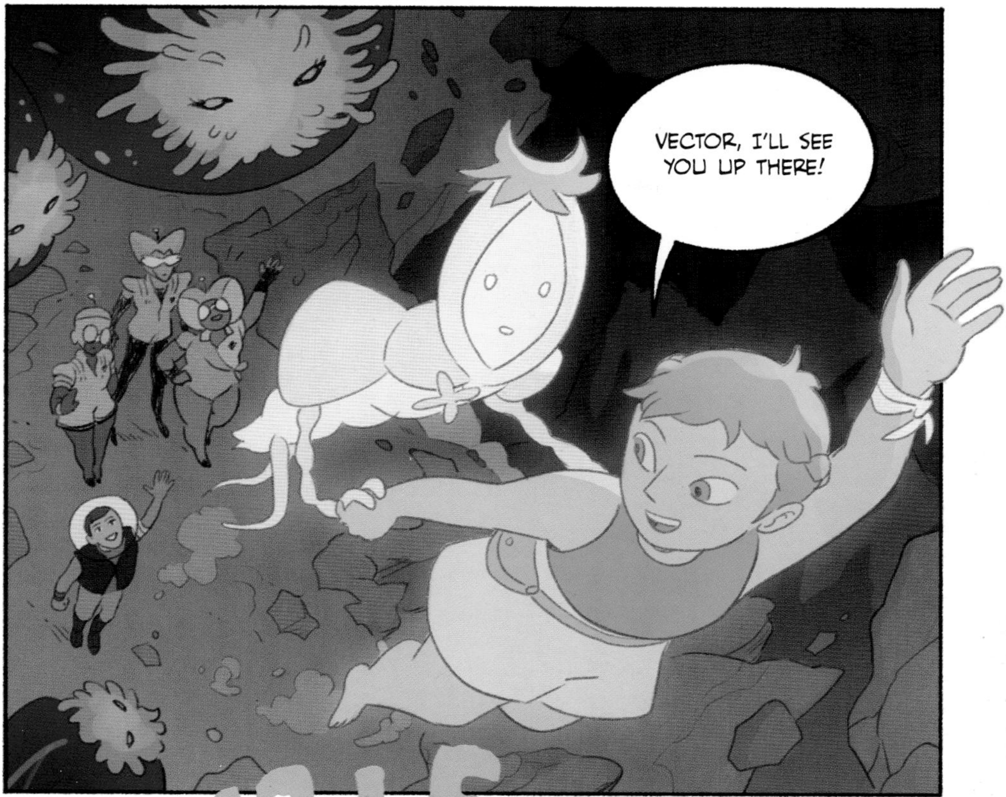
VECTOR, I'LL SEE YOU UP THERE!

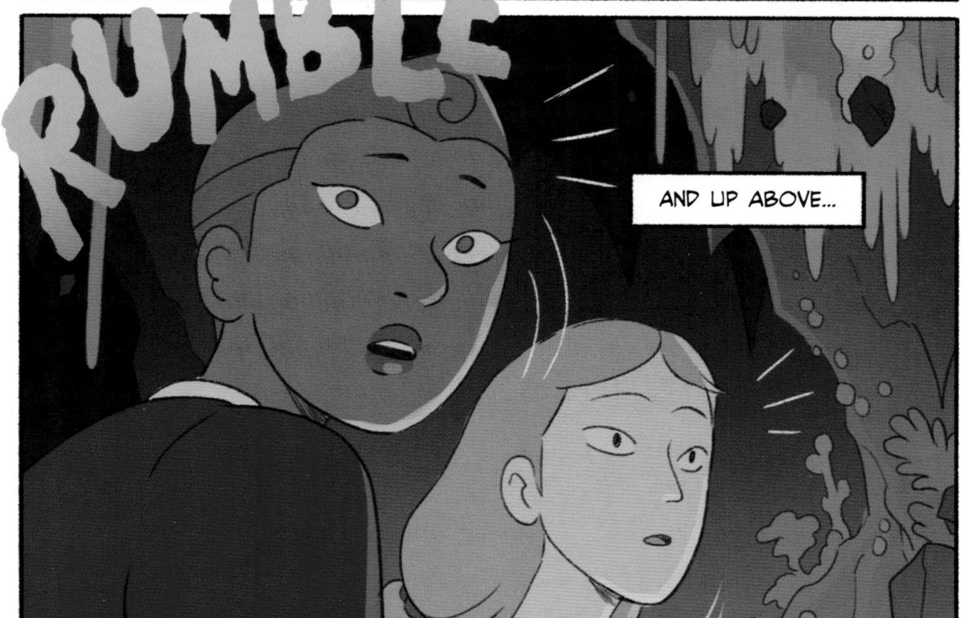
RUMBLE
AND UP ABOVE...

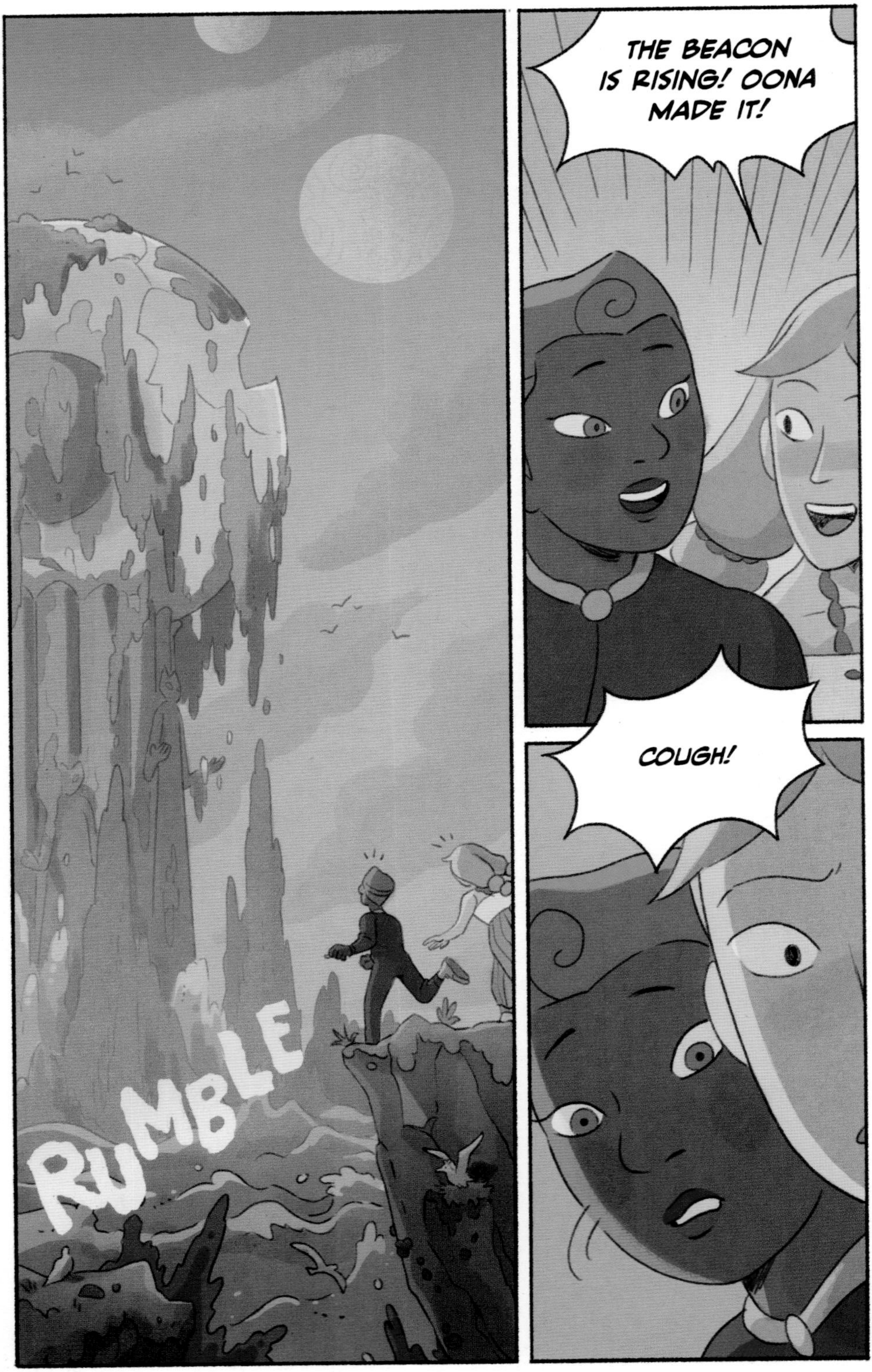
RUMBLE
THE BEACON IS RISING! OONA MADE IT!
COUGH!

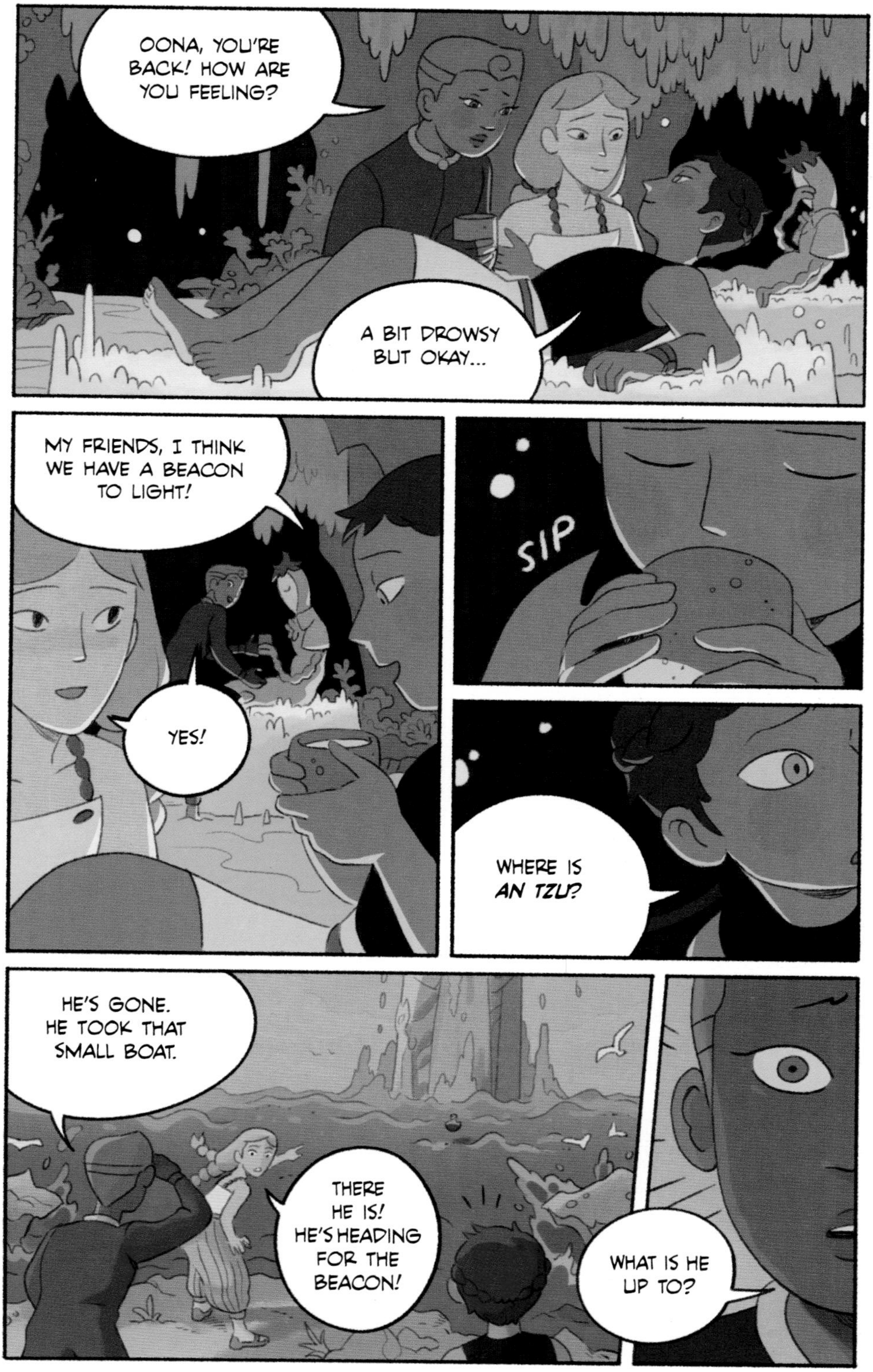

OONA, YOU'RE BACK! HOW ARE YOU FEELING?
A BIT DROWSY BUT OKAY...
MY FRIENDS, I THINK WE HAVE A BEACON TO LIGHT!
YES!
SIP
WHERE IS *AN TZU?*
HE'S GONE. HE TOOK THAT SMALL BOAT.
THERE HE IS! HE'S HEADING FOR THE BEACON!
WHAT IS HE UP TO?

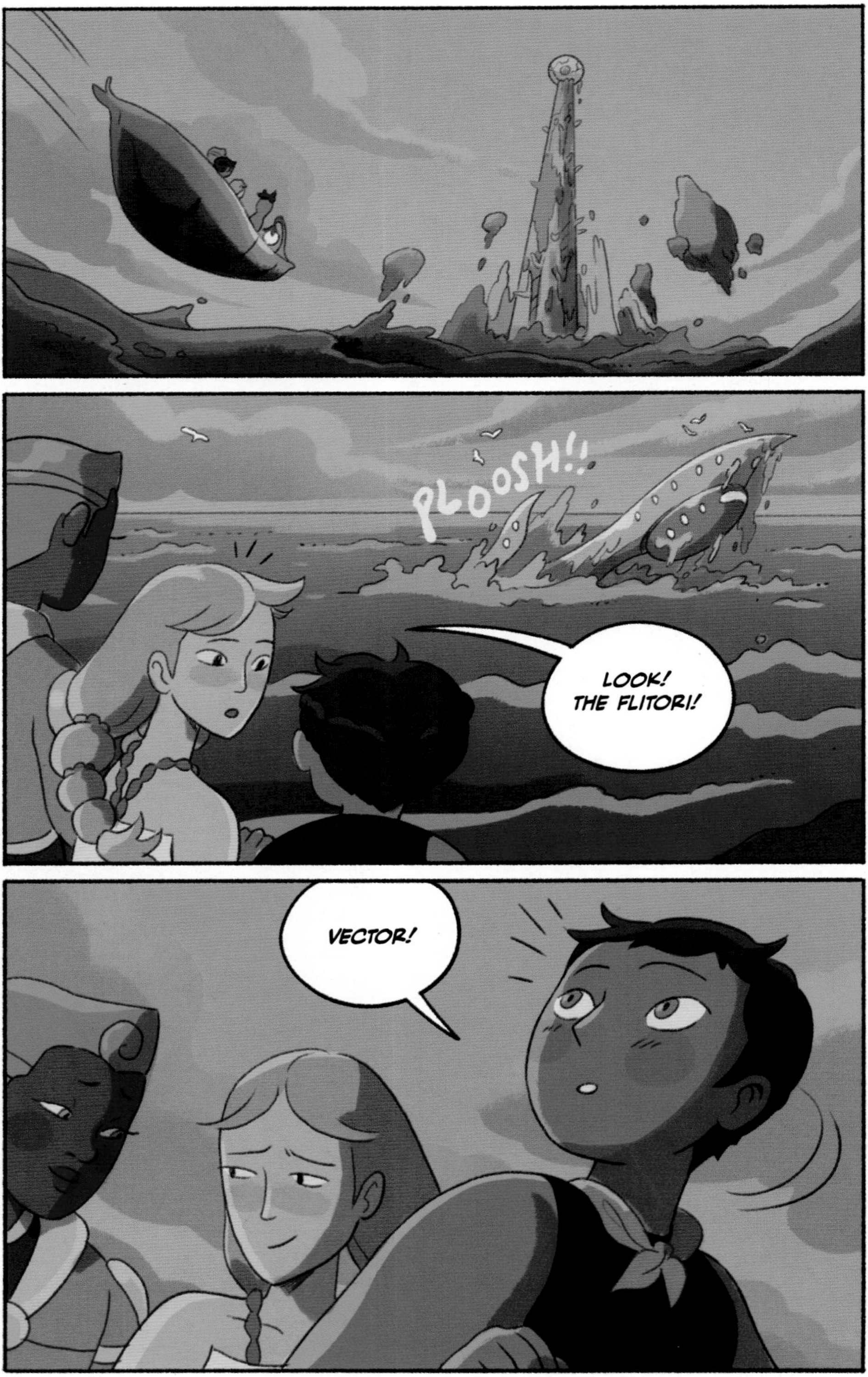
PLOOSH!!
LOOK! THE FLITORI!
VECTOR!

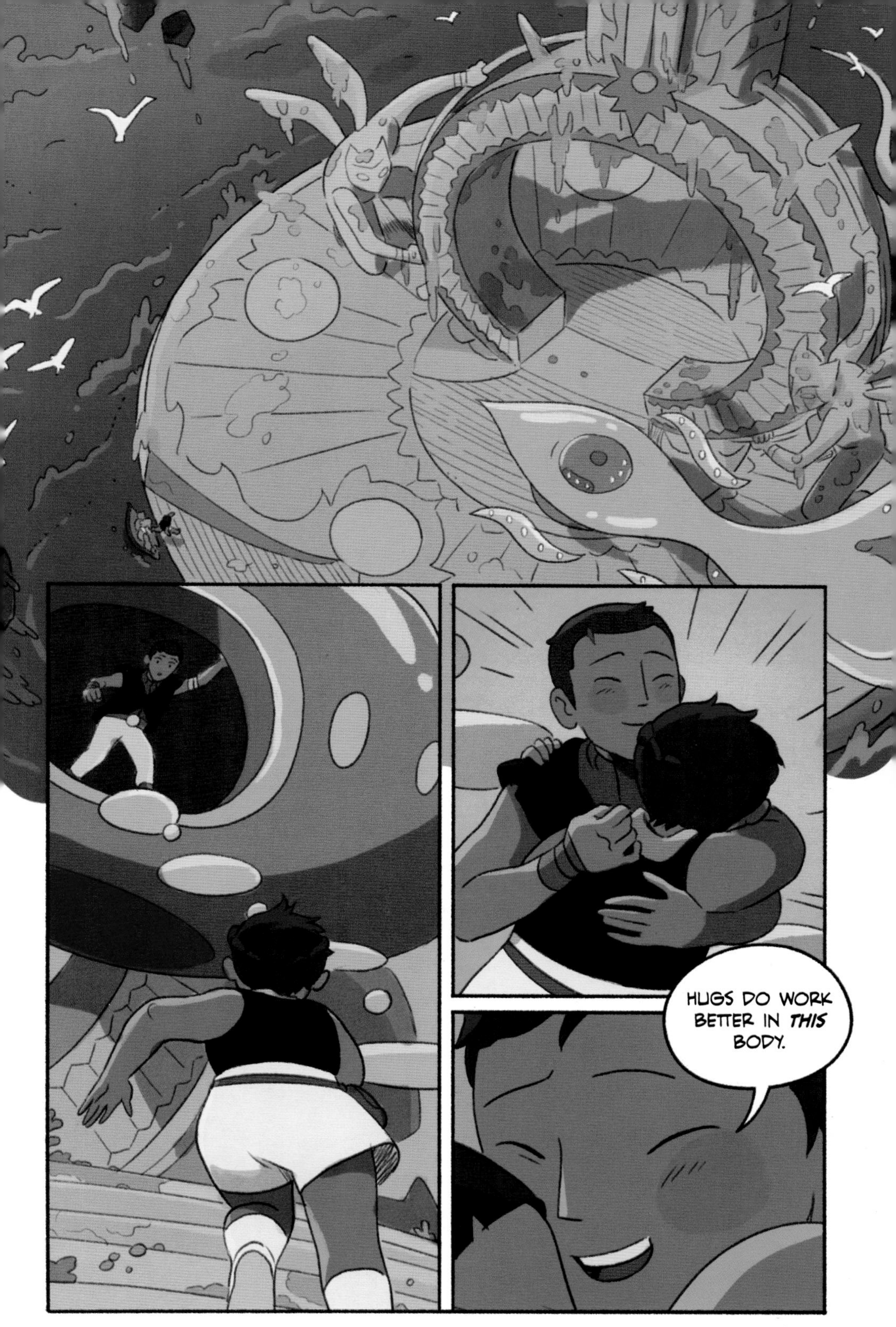
HUGS DO WORK BETTER IN *THIS* BODY.

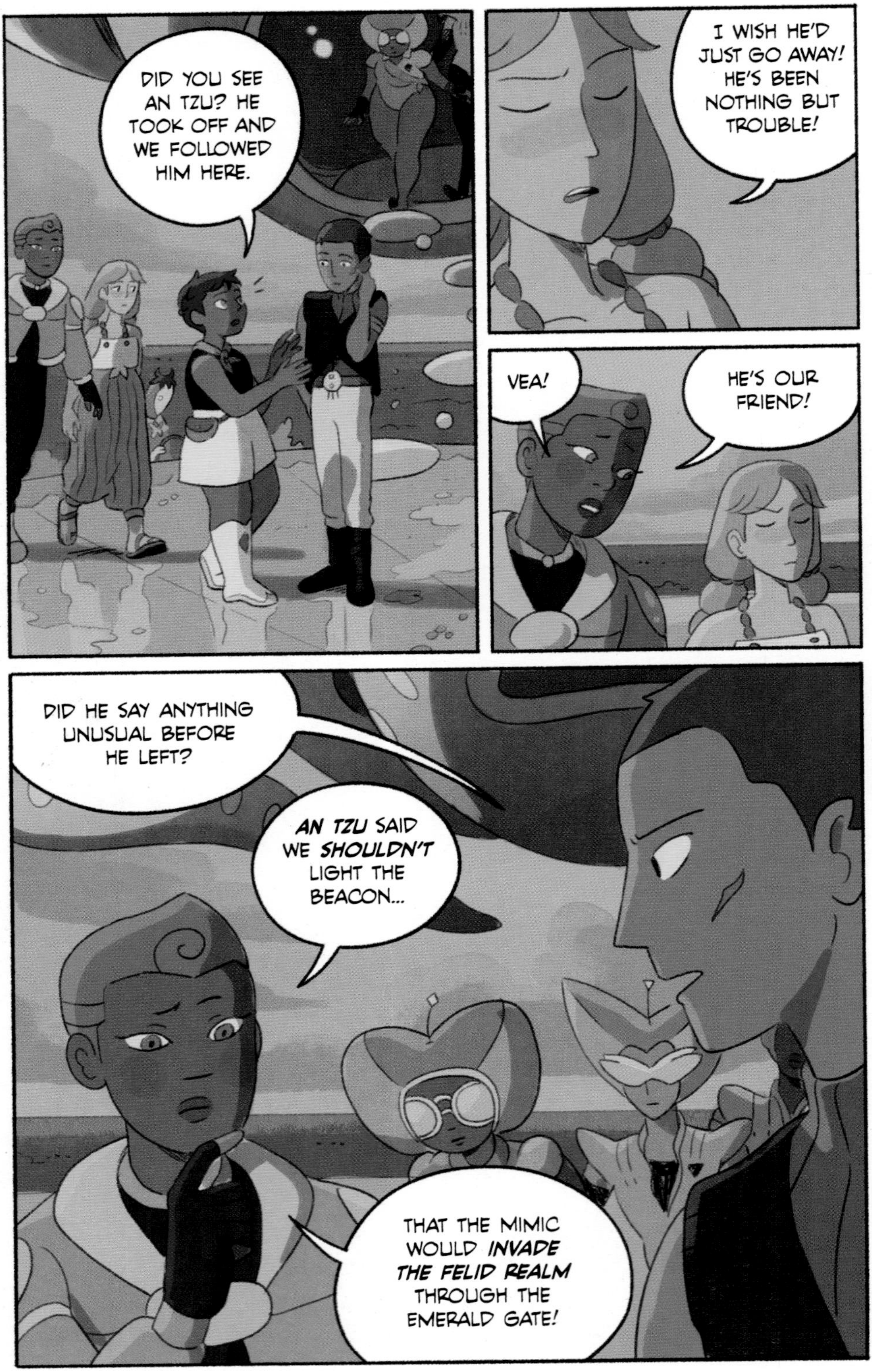
DID YOU SEE AN TZU? HE TOOK OFF AND WE FOLLOWED HIM HERE.
I WISH HE'D JUST GO AWAY! HE'S BEEN NOTHING BUT TROUBLE!
VEA!
HE'S OUR FRIEND!
DID HE SAY ANYTHING UNUSUAL BEFORE HE LEFT?
AN TZU SAID WE SHOULDN'T LIGHT THE BEACON...
THAT THE MIMIC WOULD INVADE THE FELID REALM THROUGH THE EMERALD GATE!

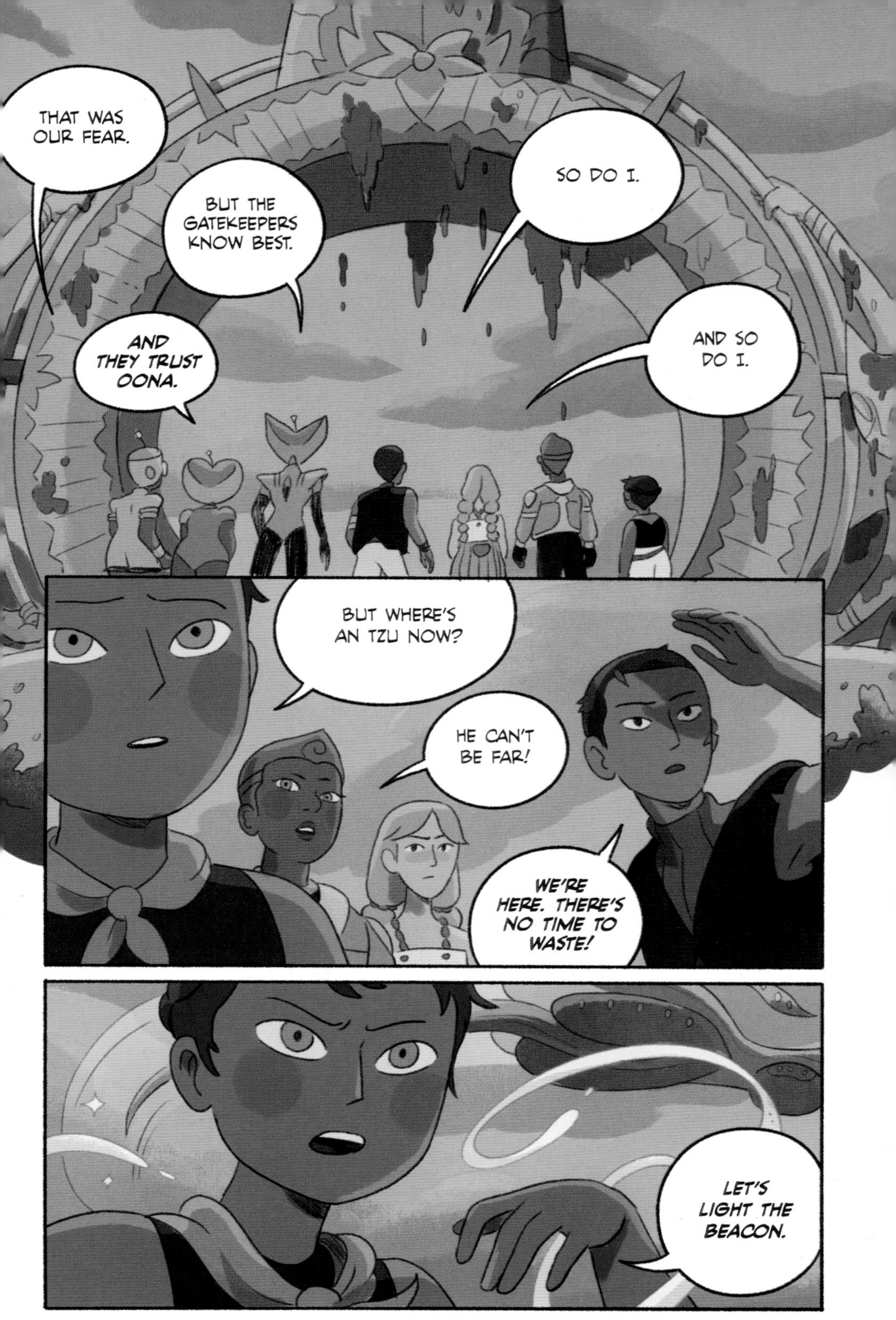
THAT WAS OUR FEAR.
BUT THE GATEKEEPERS KNOW BEST.
SO DO I.
AND THEY TRUST OONA.
AND SO DO I.
BUT WHERE'S AN TZU NOW?
HE CAN'T BE FAR!
WE'RE HERE. THERE'S NO TIME TO WASTE!
LET'S LIGHT THE BEACON.

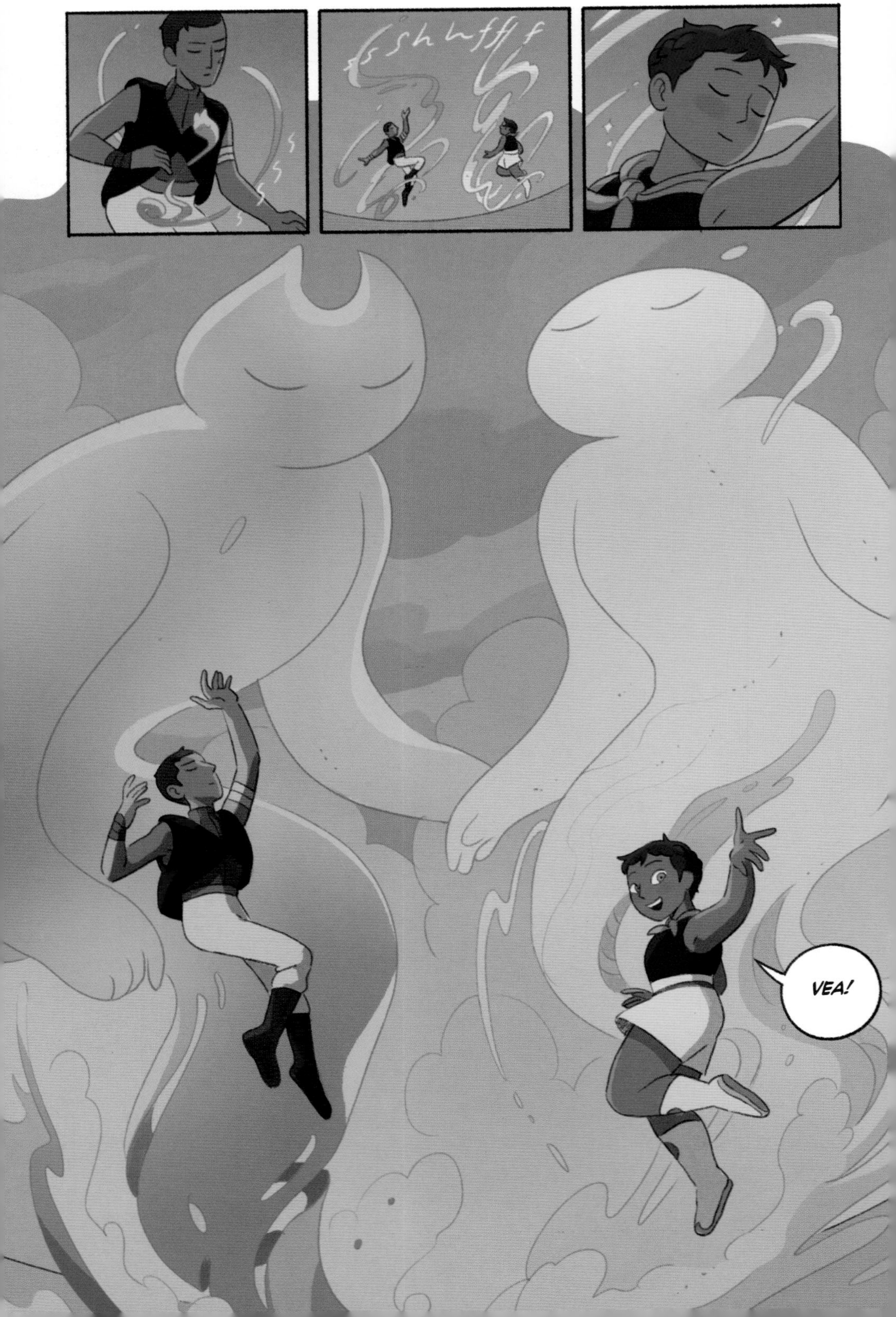
sshufff
VEA!

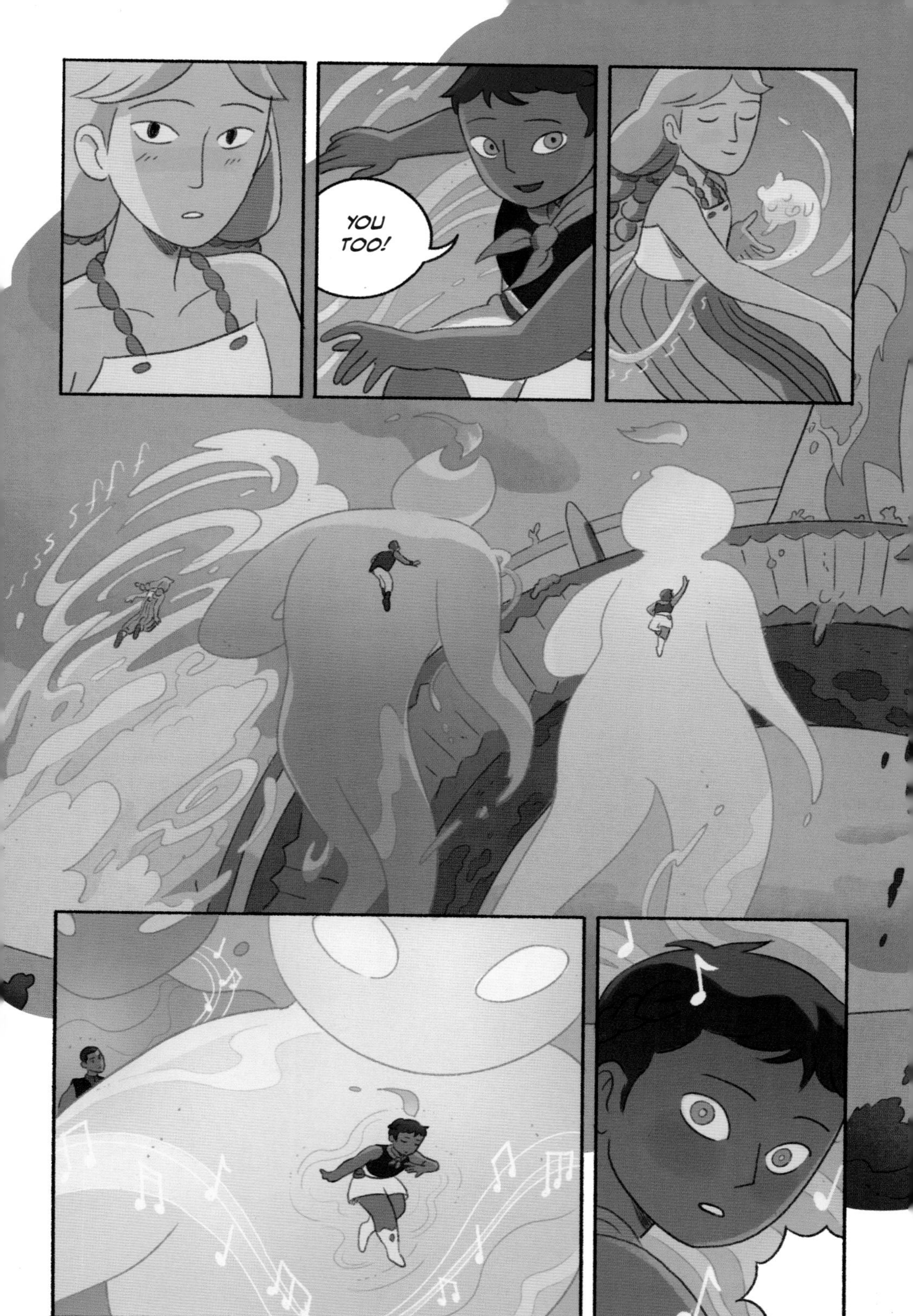
YOU TOO!

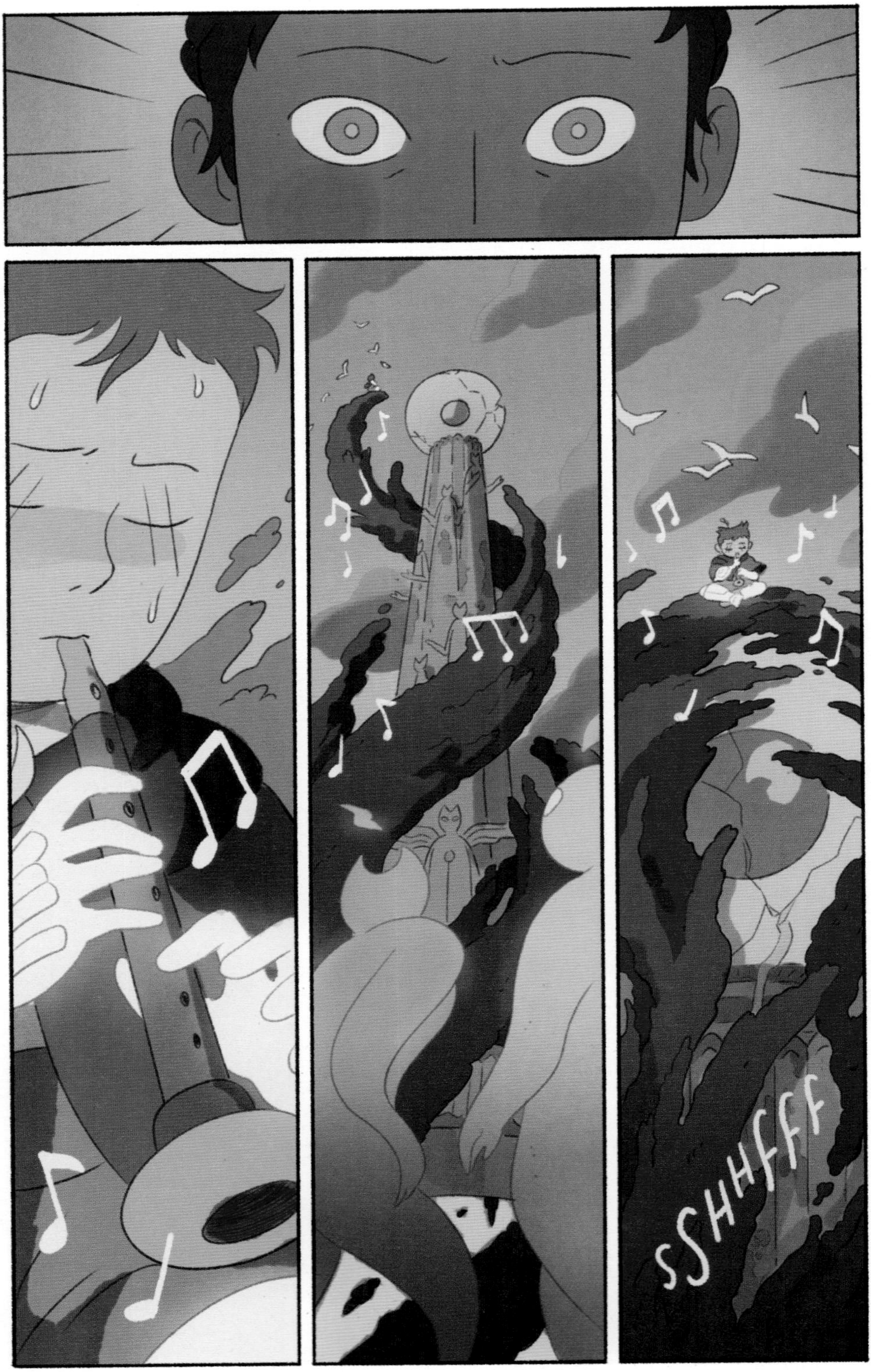
SSHFFF

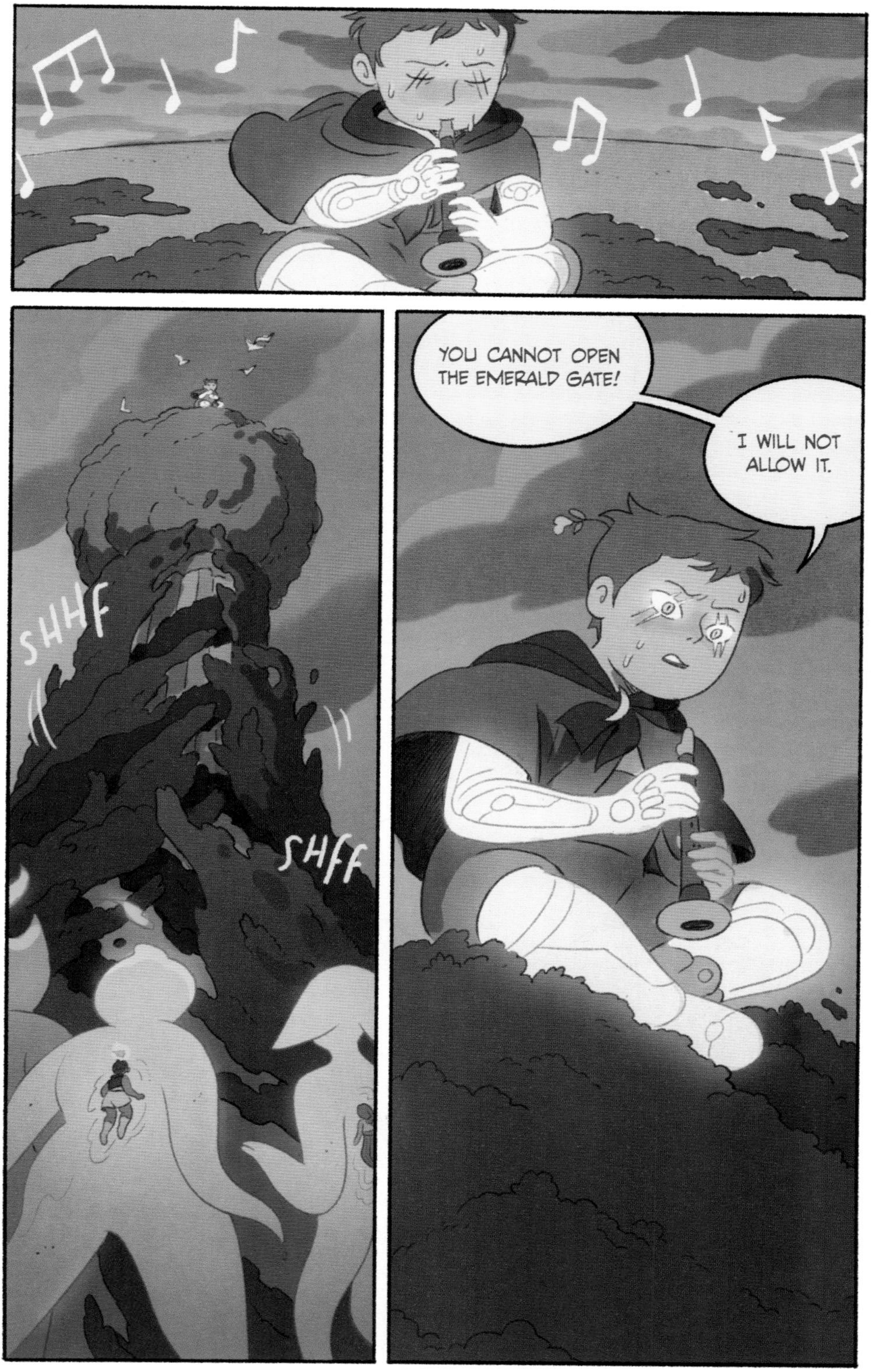
SHHF
SHFF
YOU CANNOT OPEN THE EMERALD GATE!
I WILL NOT ALLOW IT.

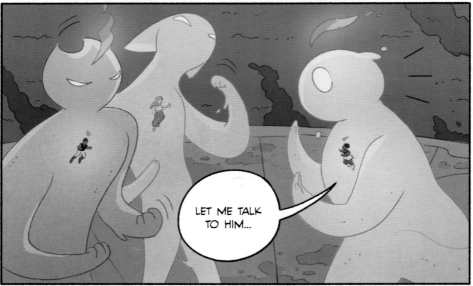

LET ME TALK TO HIM...

AN TZU, MY GOOD FRIEND...

NO, OONA.

AN TZU IS NO MORE. I AM PRINCE NEKO.

SSSHH

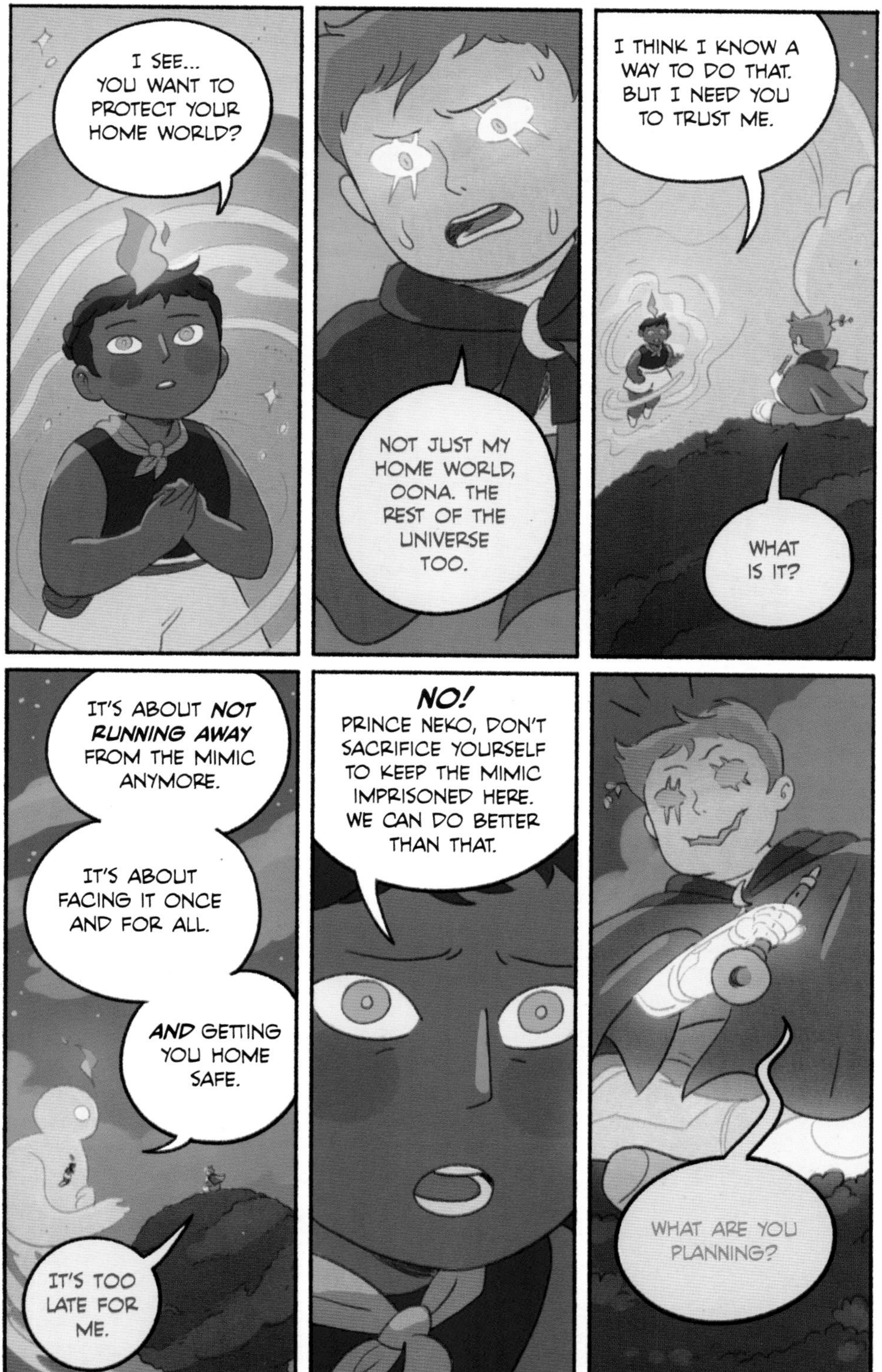
I SEE... YOU WANT TO PROTECT YOUR HOME WORLD?
NOT JUST MY HOME WORLD, OONA. THE REST OF THE UNIVERSE TOO.
I THINK I KNOW A WAY TO DO THAT. BUT I NEED YOU TO TRUST ME.
WHAT IS IT?
IT'S ABOUT NOT RUNNING AWAY FROM THE MIMIC ANYMORE.
IT'S ABOUT FACING IT ONCE AND FOR ALL.
AND GETTING YOU HOME SAFE.
IT'S TOO LATE FOR ME.
NO!
PRINCE NEKO, DON'T SACRIFICE YOURSELF TO KEEP THE MIMIC IMPRISONED HERE. WE CAN DO BETTER THAN THAT.
WHAT ARE YOU PLANNING?

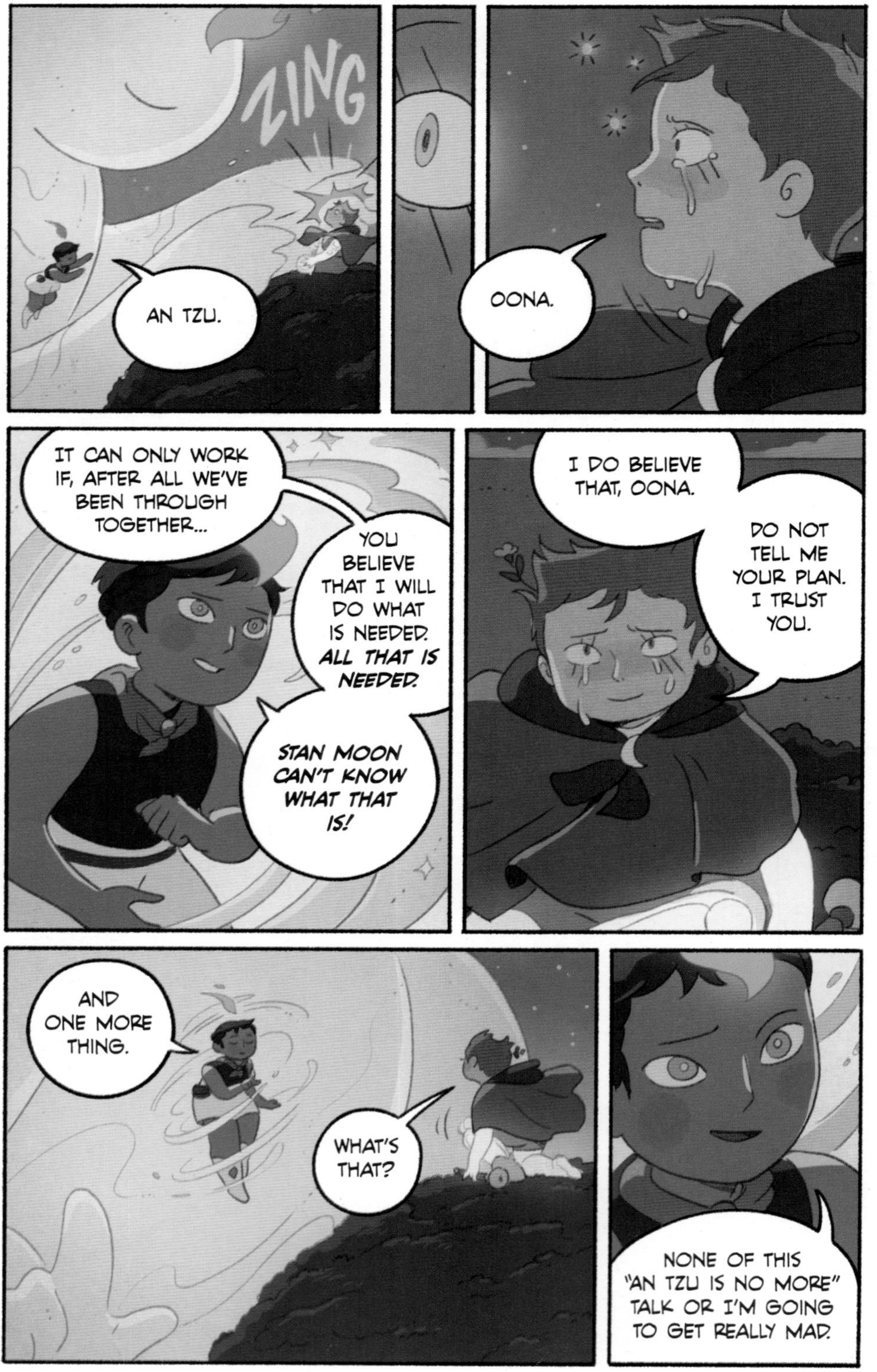
ZING
AN TZU.
OONA.
IT CAN ONLY WORK IF, AFTER ALL WE'VE BEEN THROUGH TOGETHER...
YOU BELIEVE THAT I WILL DO WHAT IS NEEDED. ALL THAT IS NEEDED.
STAN MOON CAN'T KNOW WHAT THAT IS!
I DO BELIEVE THAT, OONA.
DO NOT TELL ME YOUR PLAN. I TRUST YOU.
AND ONE MORE THING.
WHAT'S THAT?
NONE OF THIS "AN TZU IS NO MORE" TALK OR I'M GOING TO GET REALLY MAD.

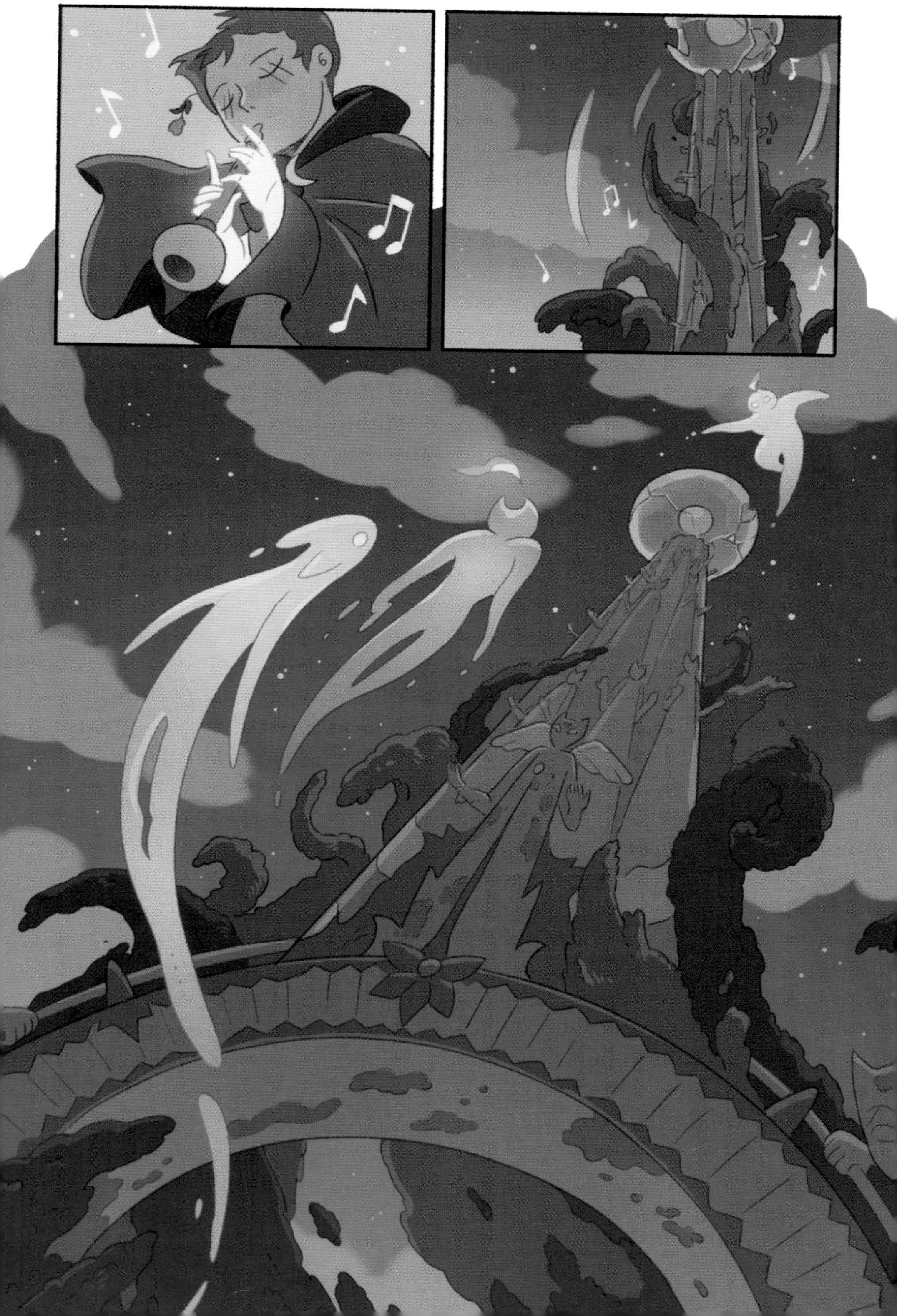

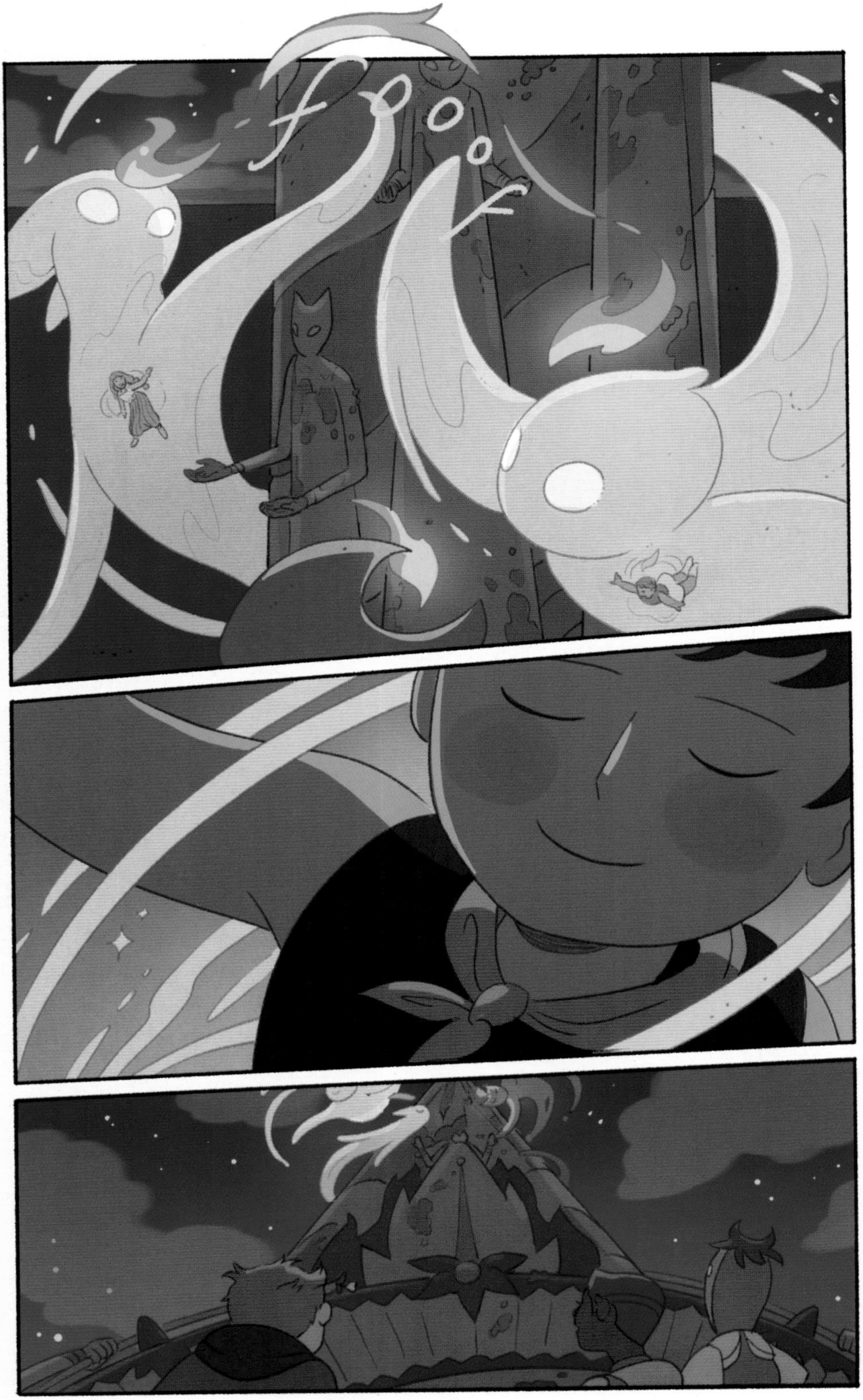
fpoof

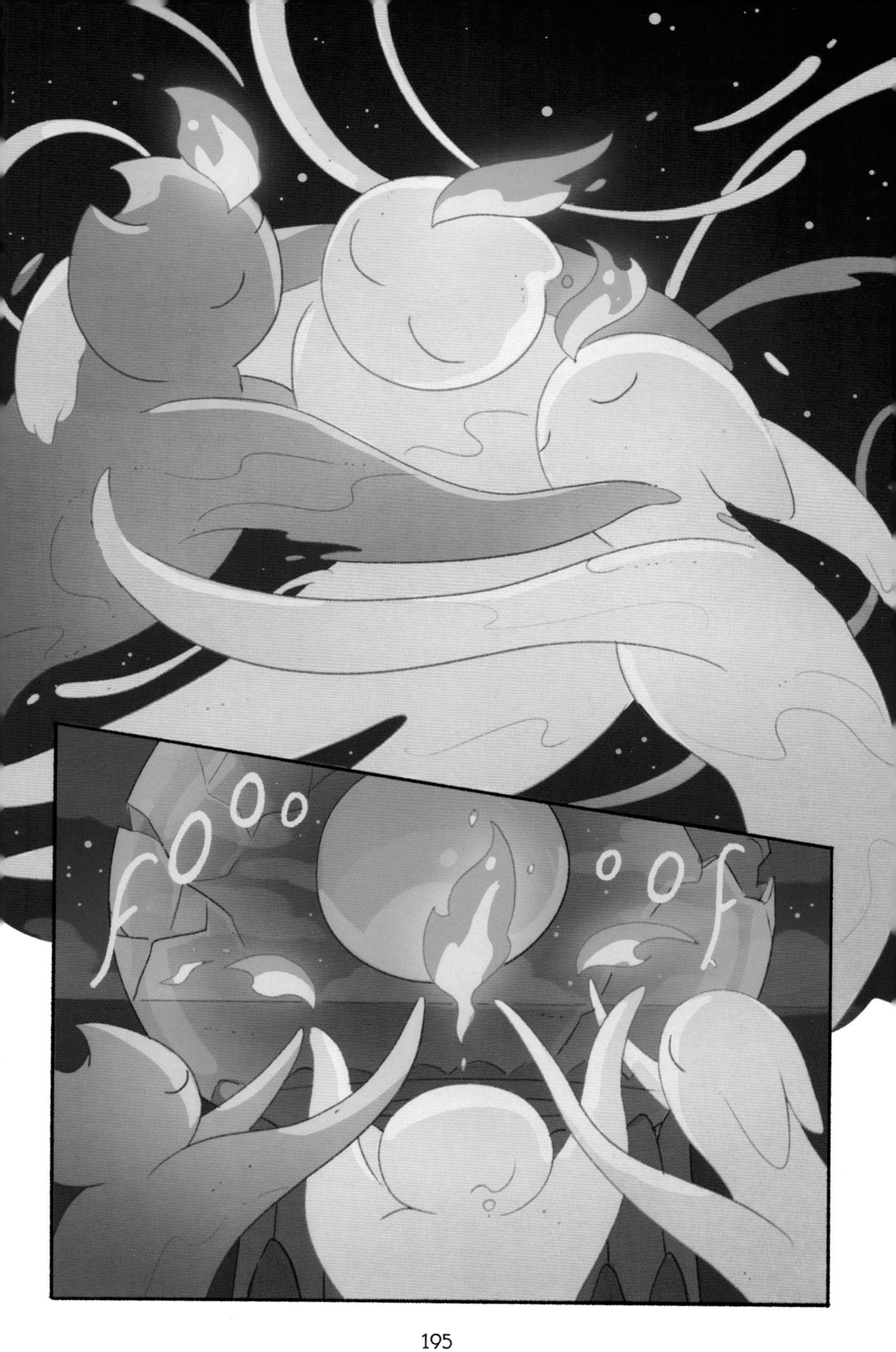
FOOO
OOF

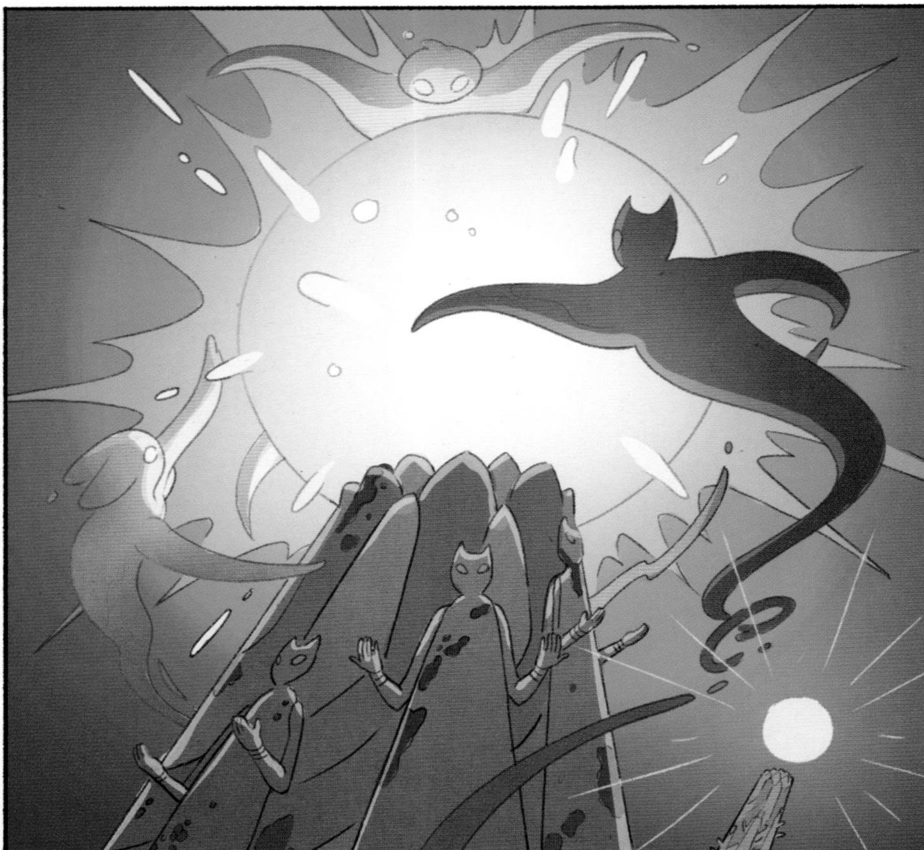

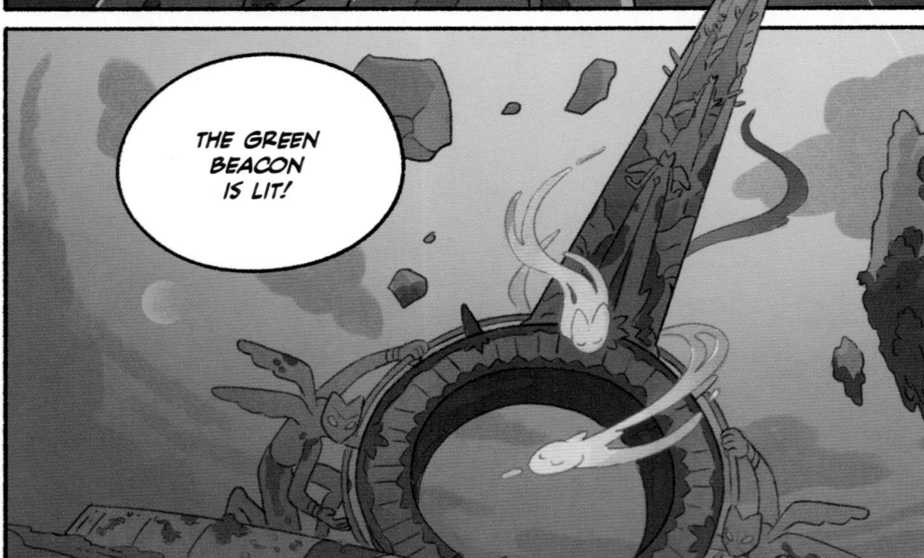
THE GREEN BEACON IS LIT!

CHAPTER 12
SUN DOMANI

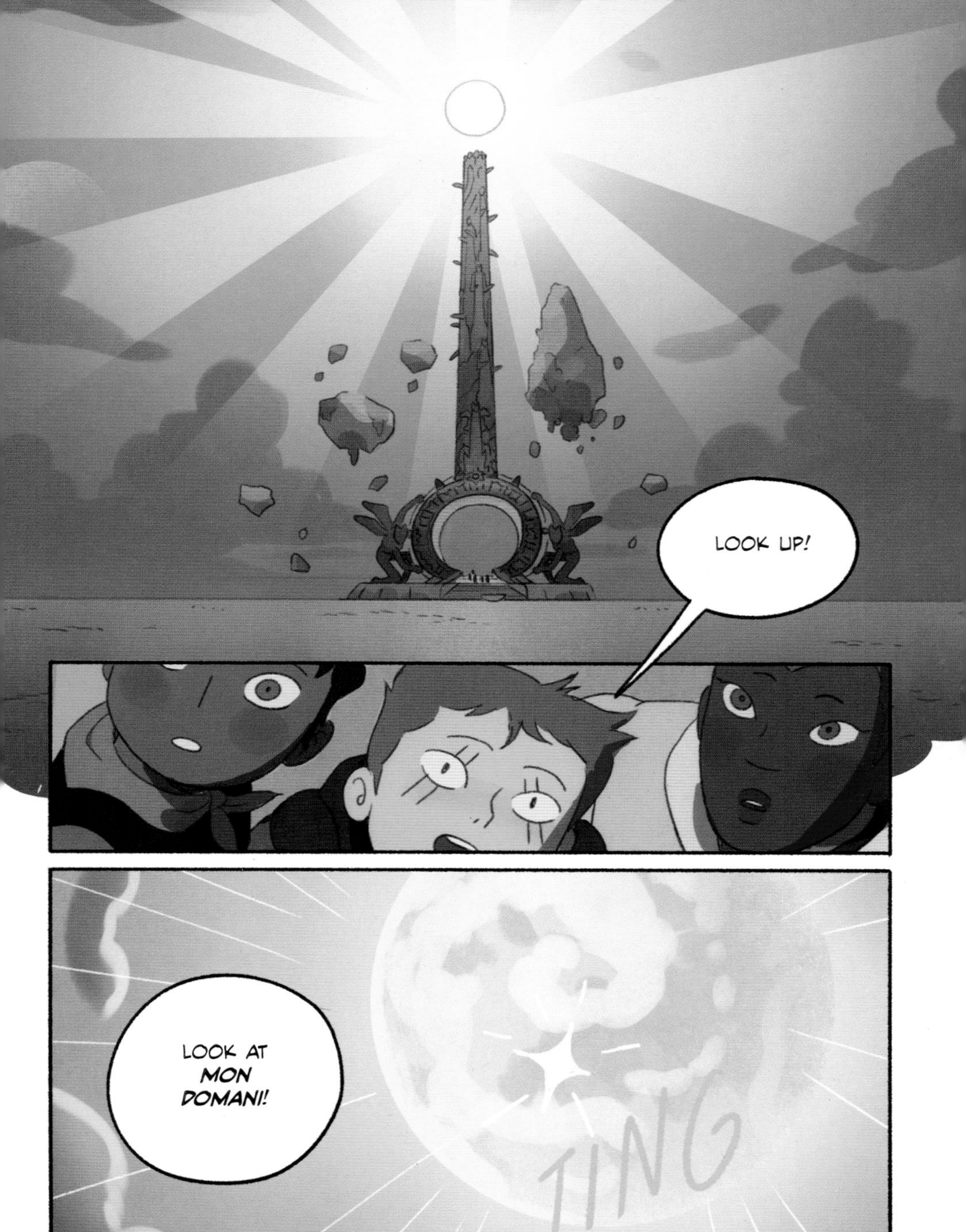
LOOK UP!
LOOK AT MON DOMANI!
TING

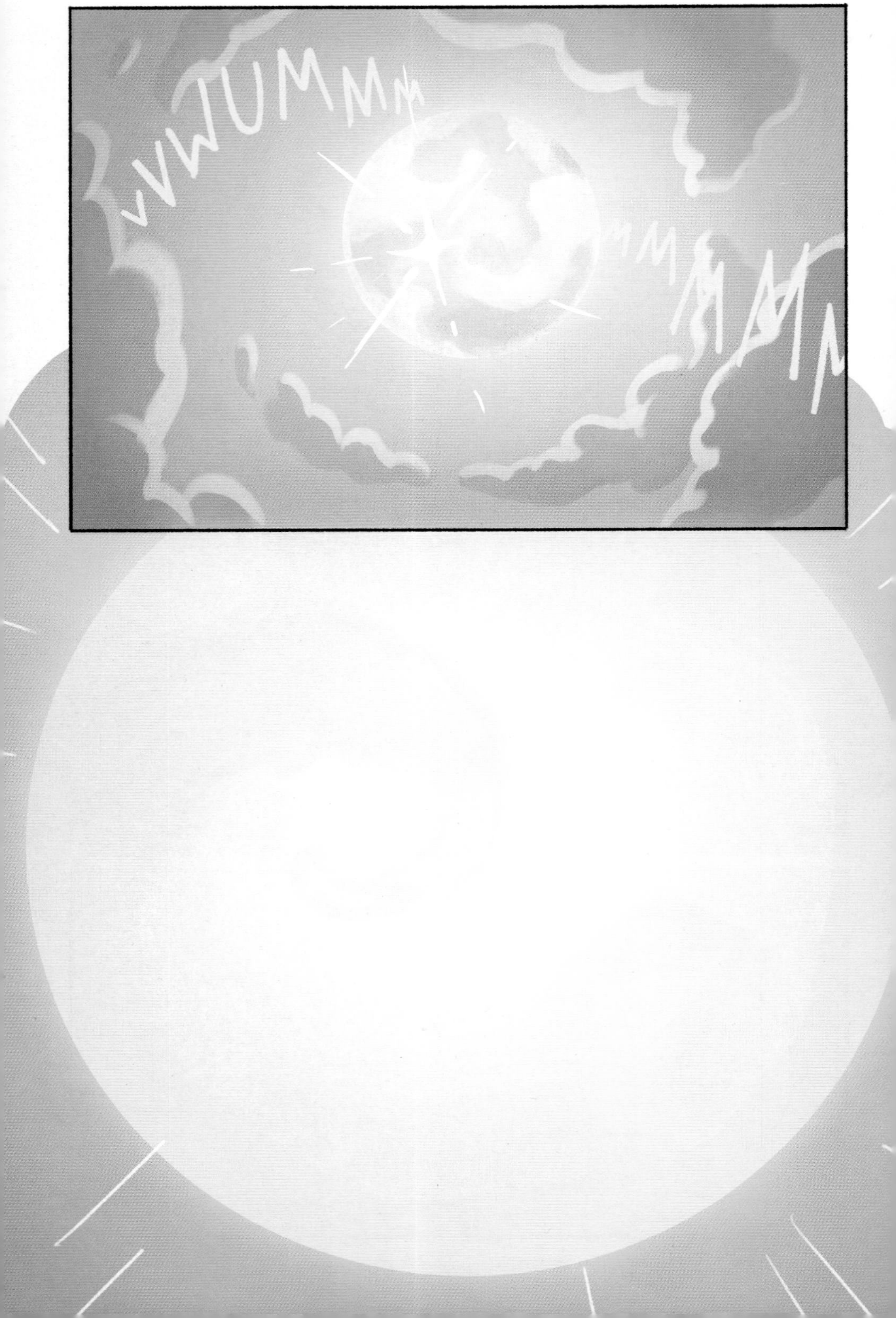
VVWUMMM
MMMMMM

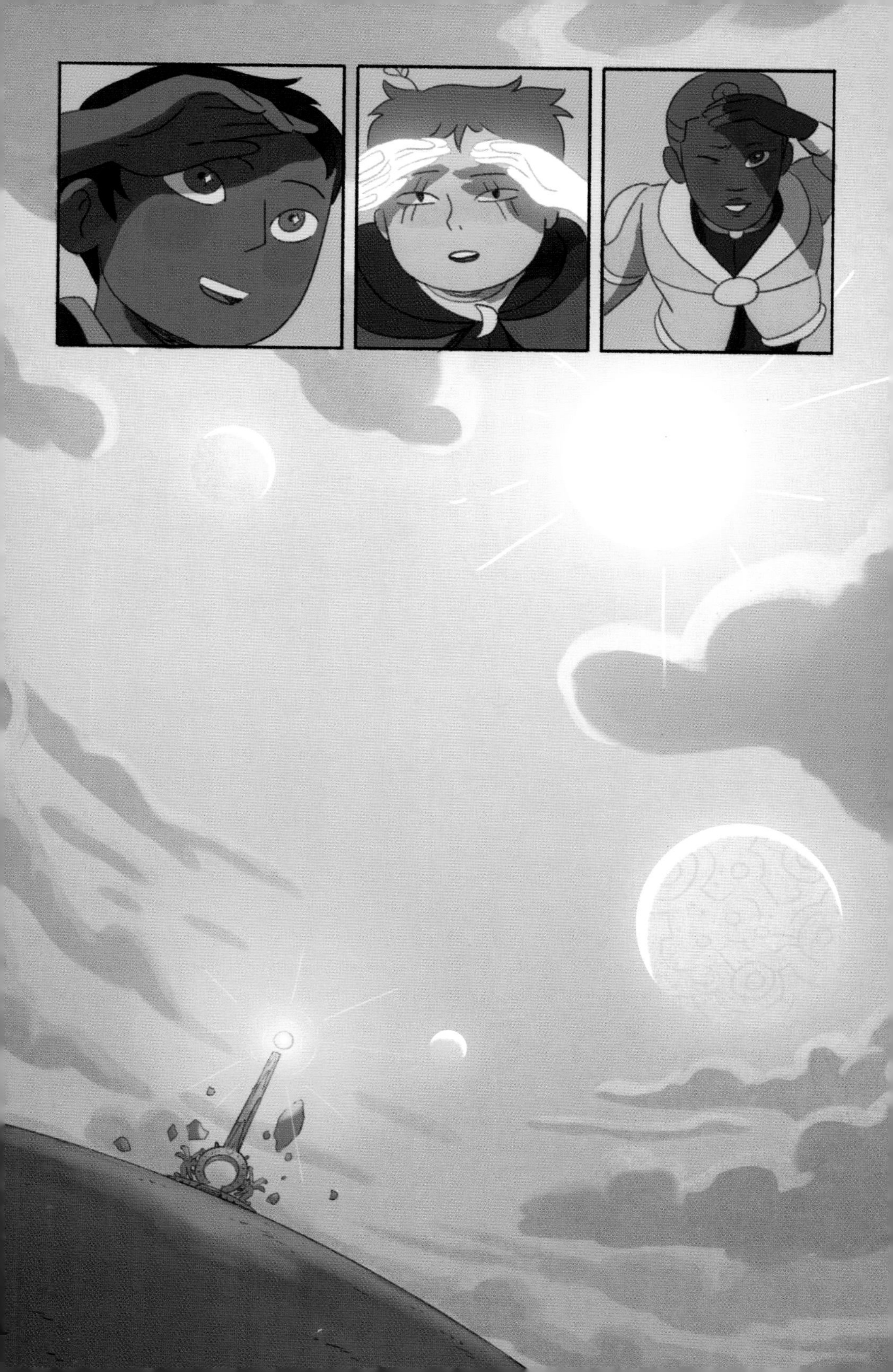

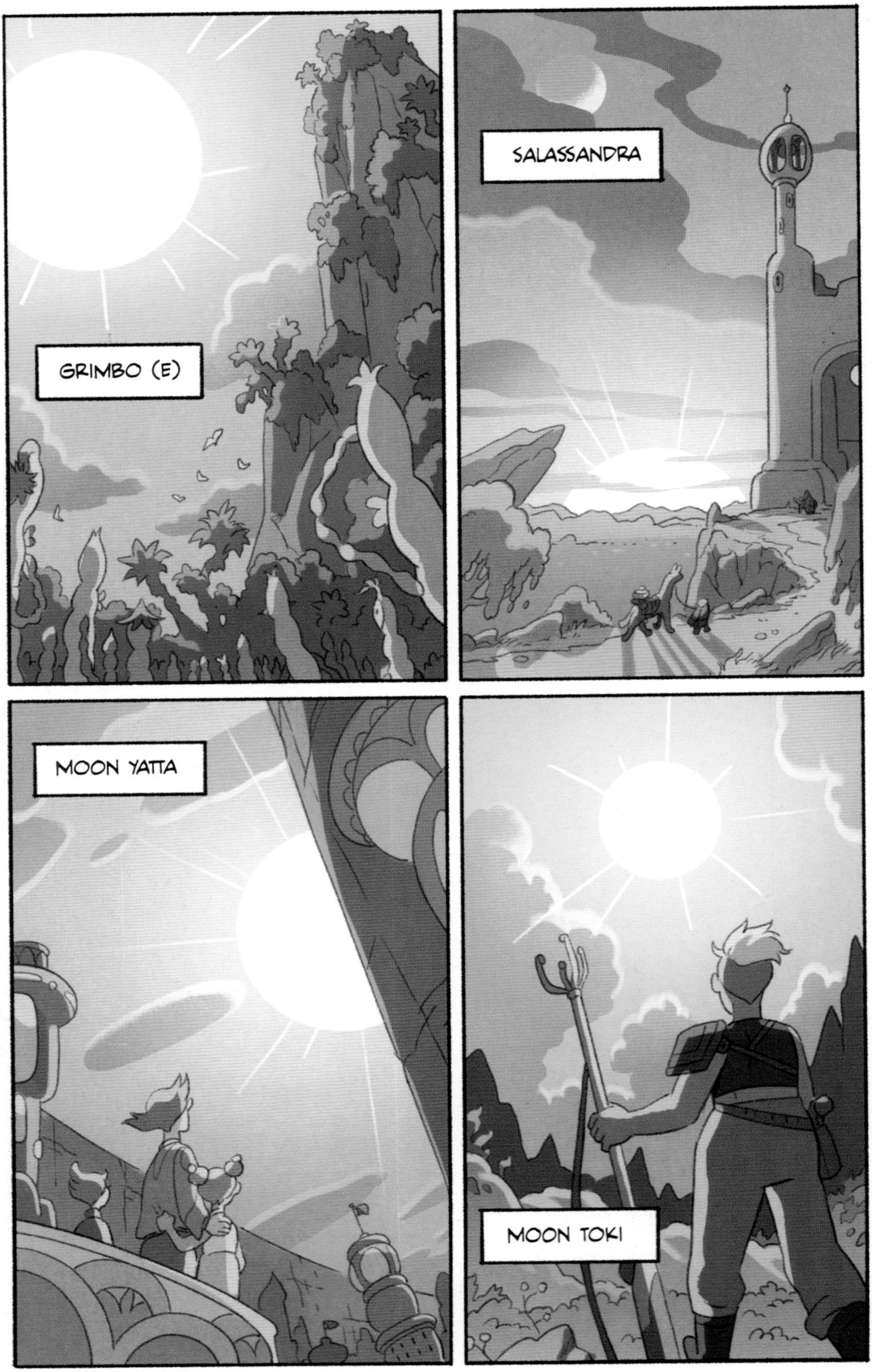
GRIMBO (E)
SALASSANDRA
MOON YATTA
MOON TOKI

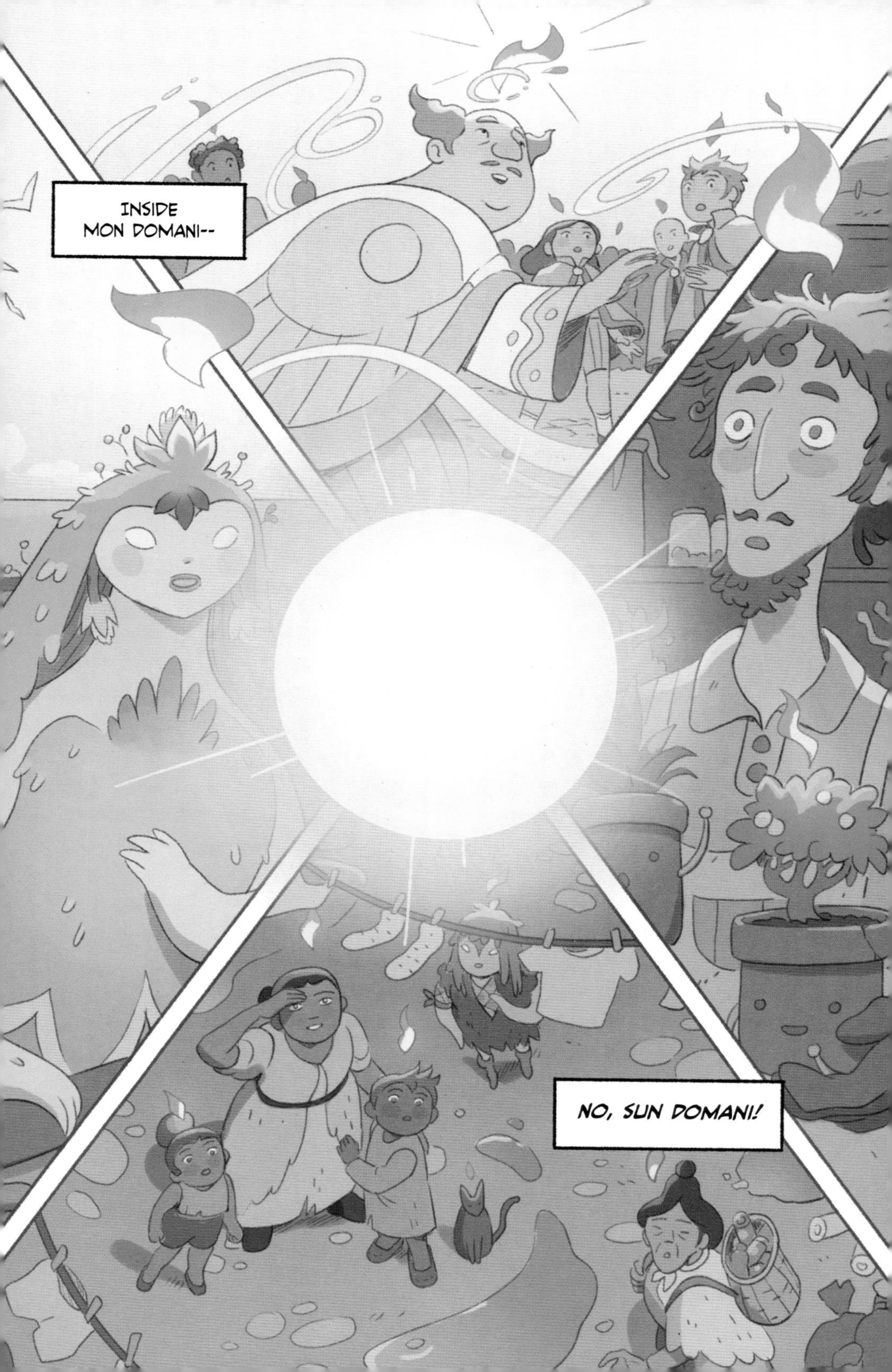
INSIDE
MON DOMANI--
NO, SUN DOMANI!

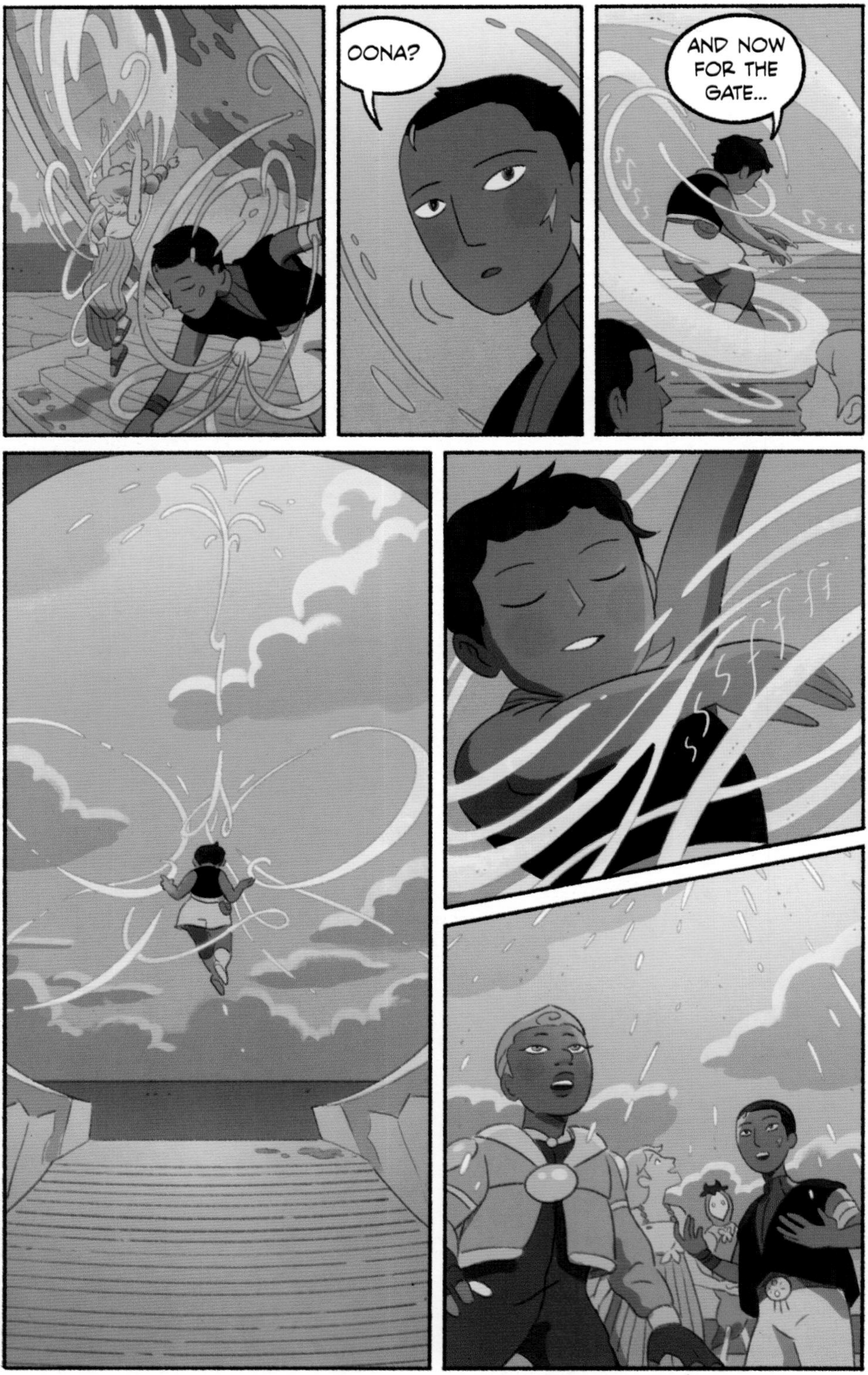
OONA?
AND NOW FOR THE GATE...

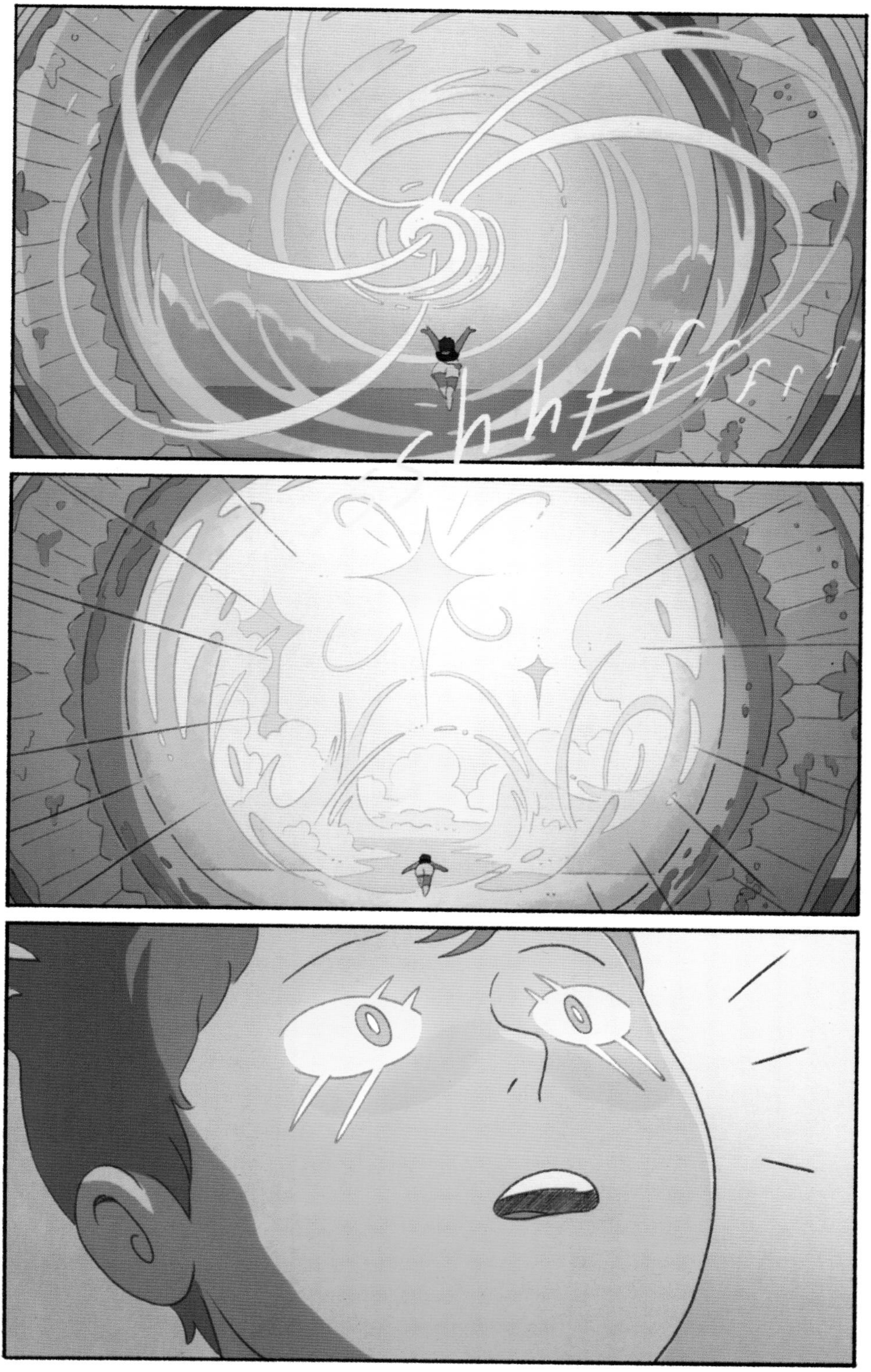
shhffffff

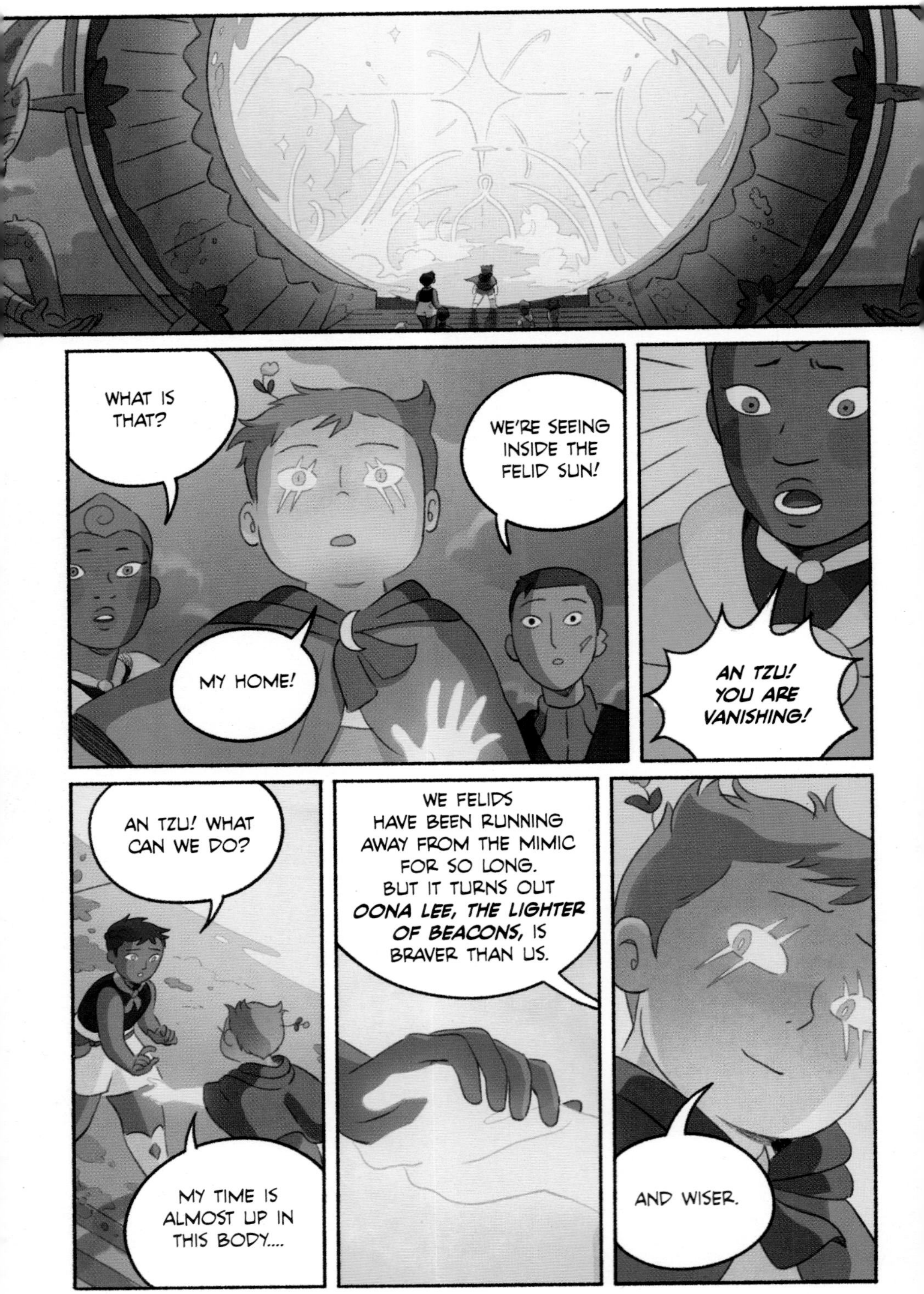
WHAT IS THAT?
WE'RE SEEING INSIDE THE FELID SUN!
MY HOME!
AN TZU! YOU ARE VANISHING!
AN TZU! WHAT CAN WE DO?
MY TIME IS ALMOST UP IN THIS BODY....
WE FELIDS HAVE BEEN RUNNING AWAY FROM THE MIMIC FOR SO LONG. BUT IT TURNS OUT OONA LEE, THE LIGHTER OF BEACONS, IS BRAVER THAN US.
AND WISER.

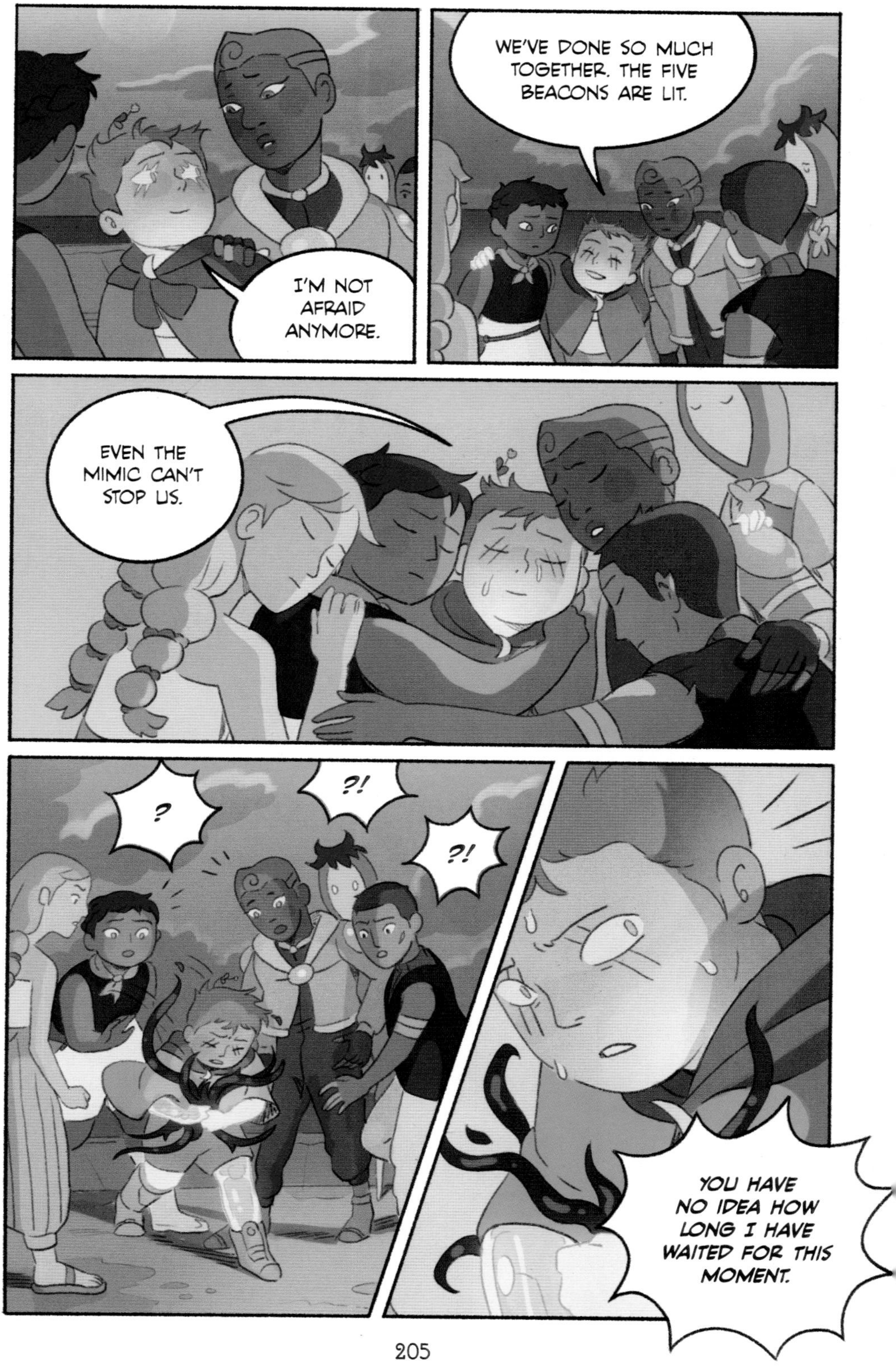
I'M NOT AFRAID ANYMORE.
WE'VE DONE SO MUCH TOGETHER. THE FIVE BEACONS ARE LIT.
EVEN THE MIMIC CAN'T STOP US.
?
?!
?!
YOU HAVE NO IDEA HOW LONG I HAVE WAITED FOR THIS MOMENT.

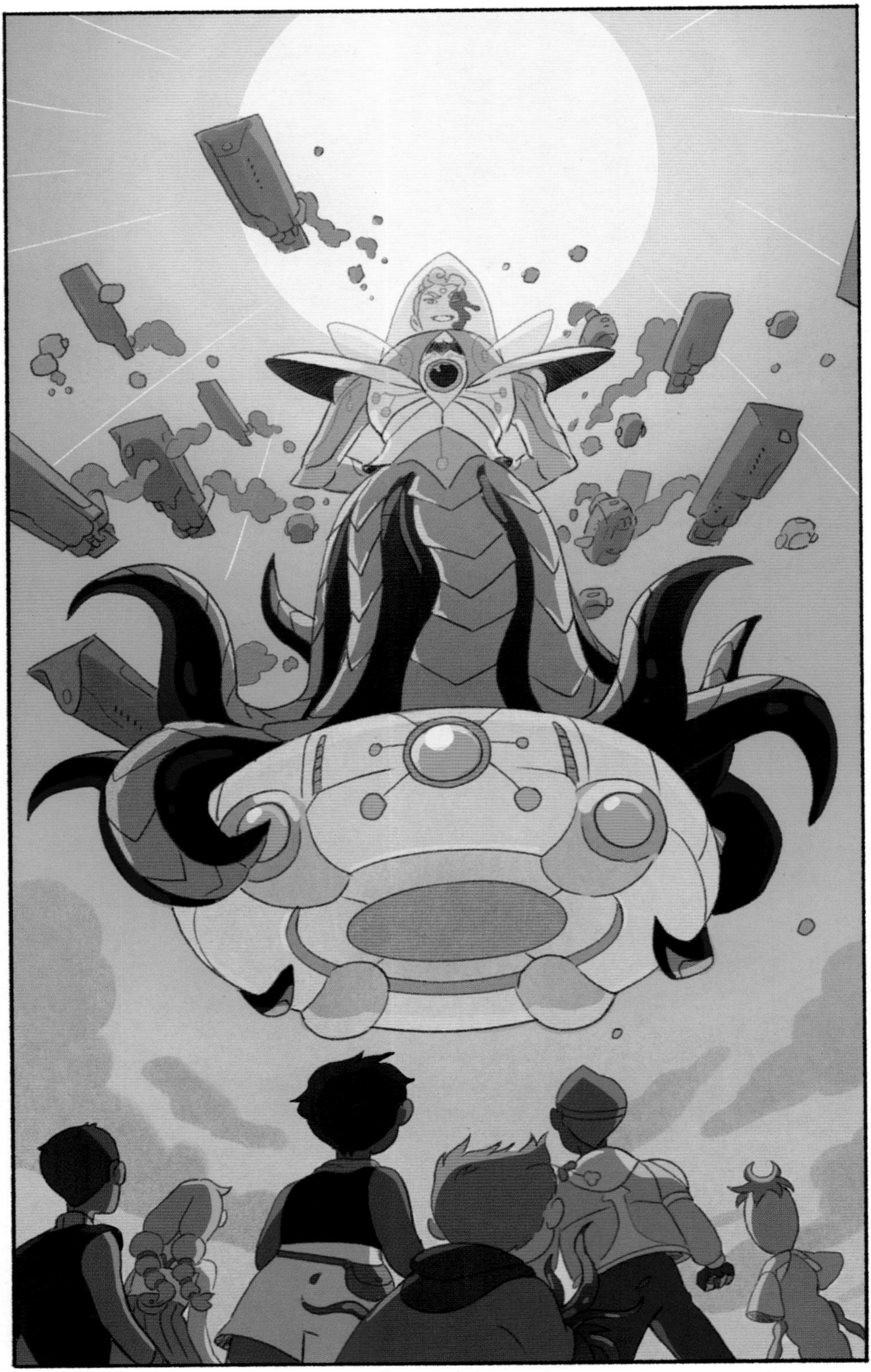

CHAPTER 13
THE EMERALD GATE

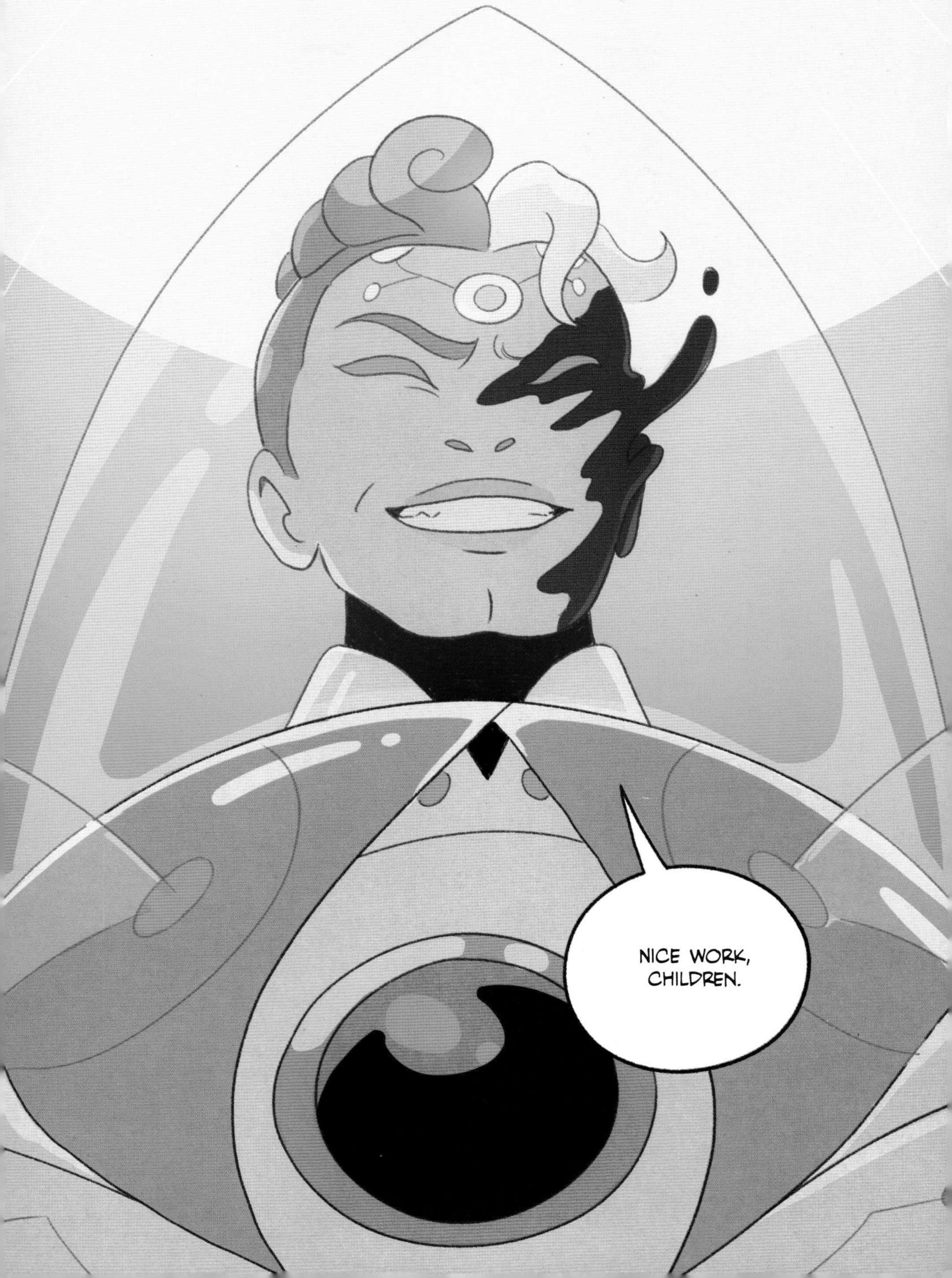
NICE WORK, CHILDREN.

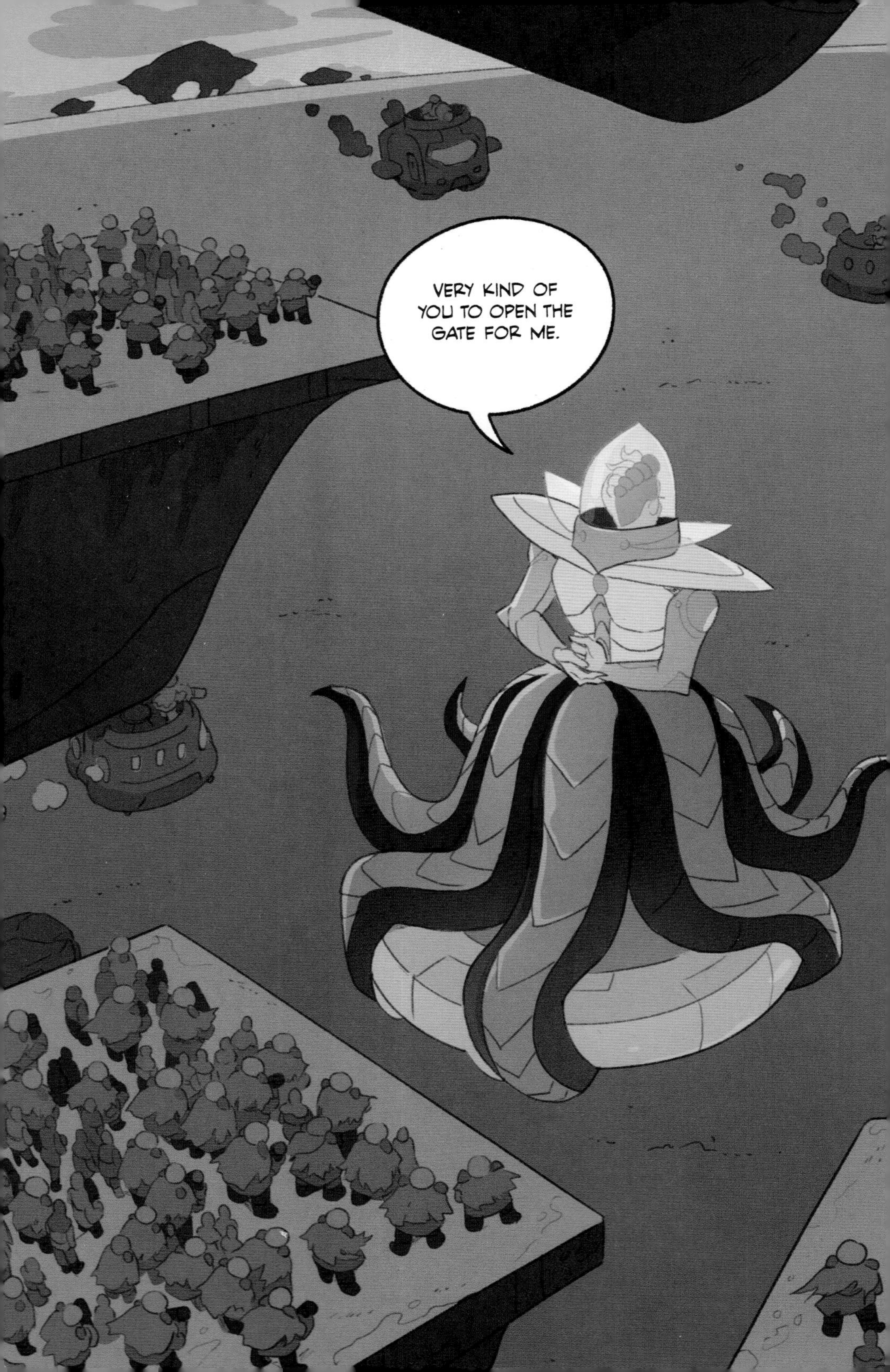
VERY KIND OF YOU TO OPEN THE GATE FOR ME.

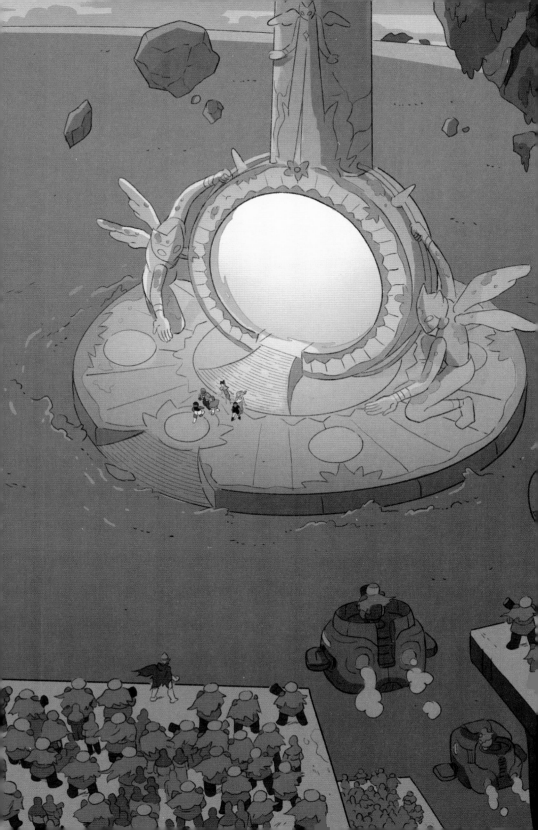

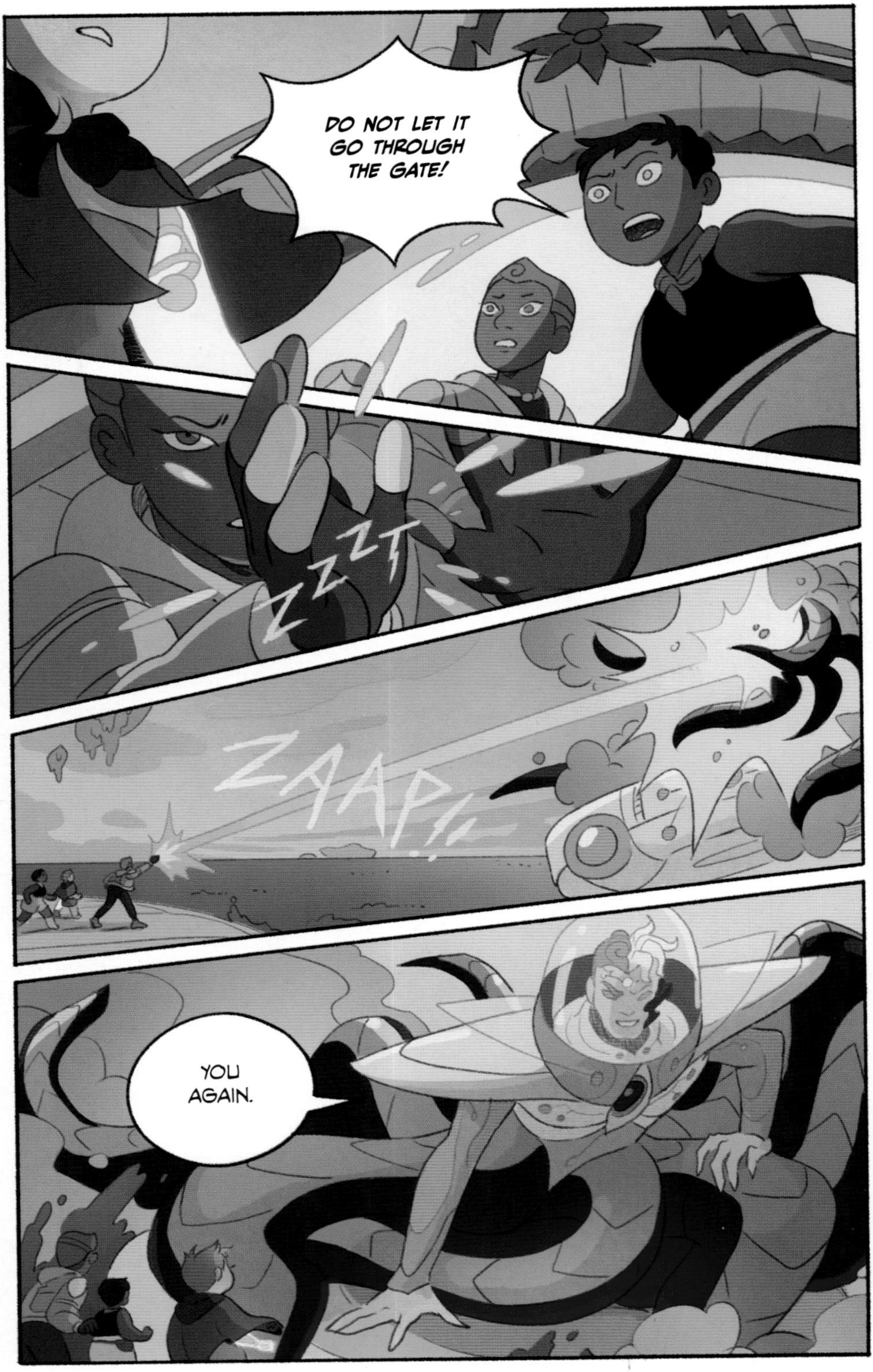
DO NOT LET IT GO THROUGH THE GATE!
ZZZT
ZAAP!!
YOU AGAIN.

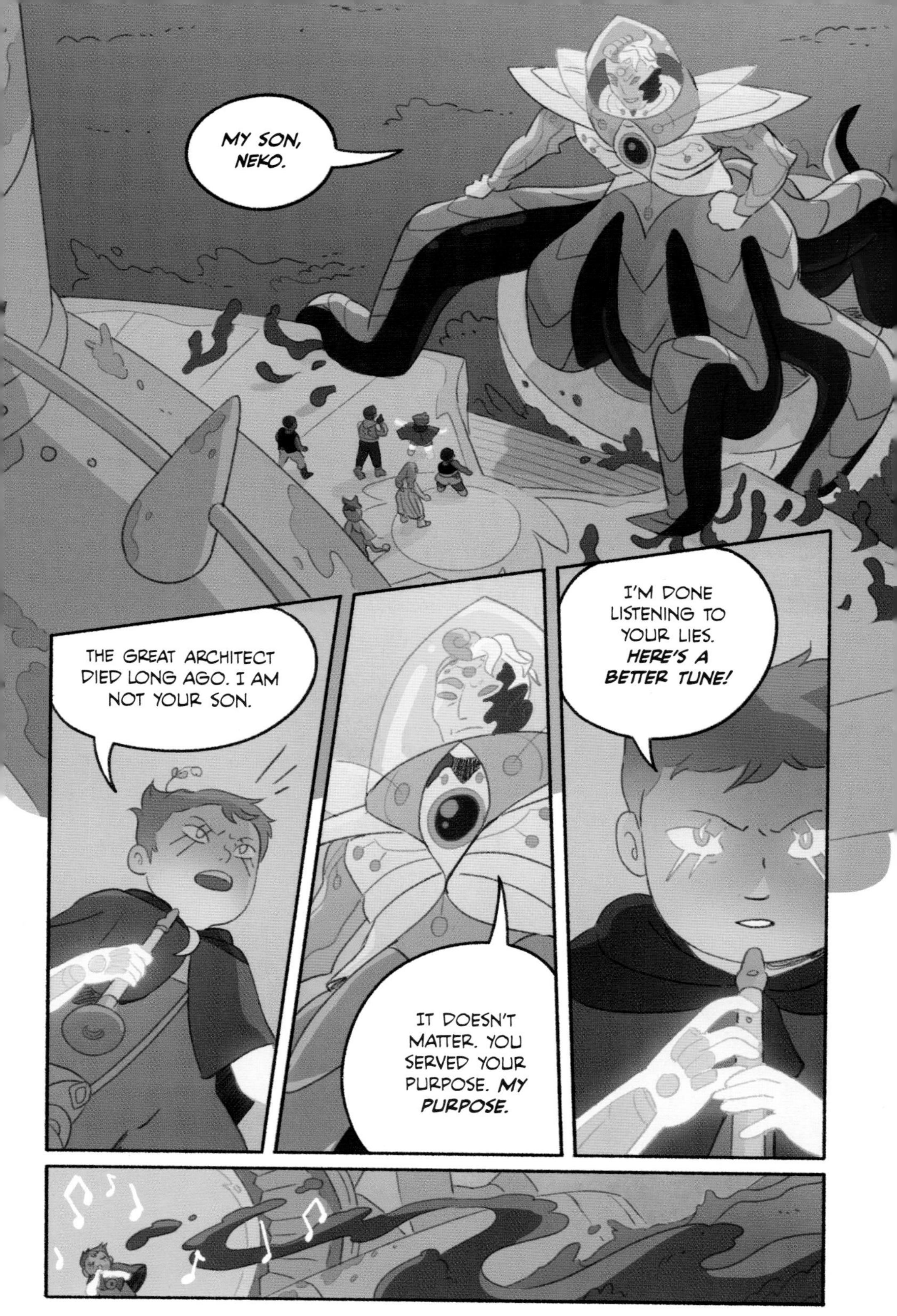
MY SON, NEKO.
THE GREAT ARCHITECT DIED LONG AGO. I AM NOT YOUR SON.
IT DOESN'T MATTER. YOU SERVED YOUR PURPOSE. *MY PURPOSE.*
I'M DONE LISTENING TO YOUR LIES. ***HERE'S A BETTER TUNE!***

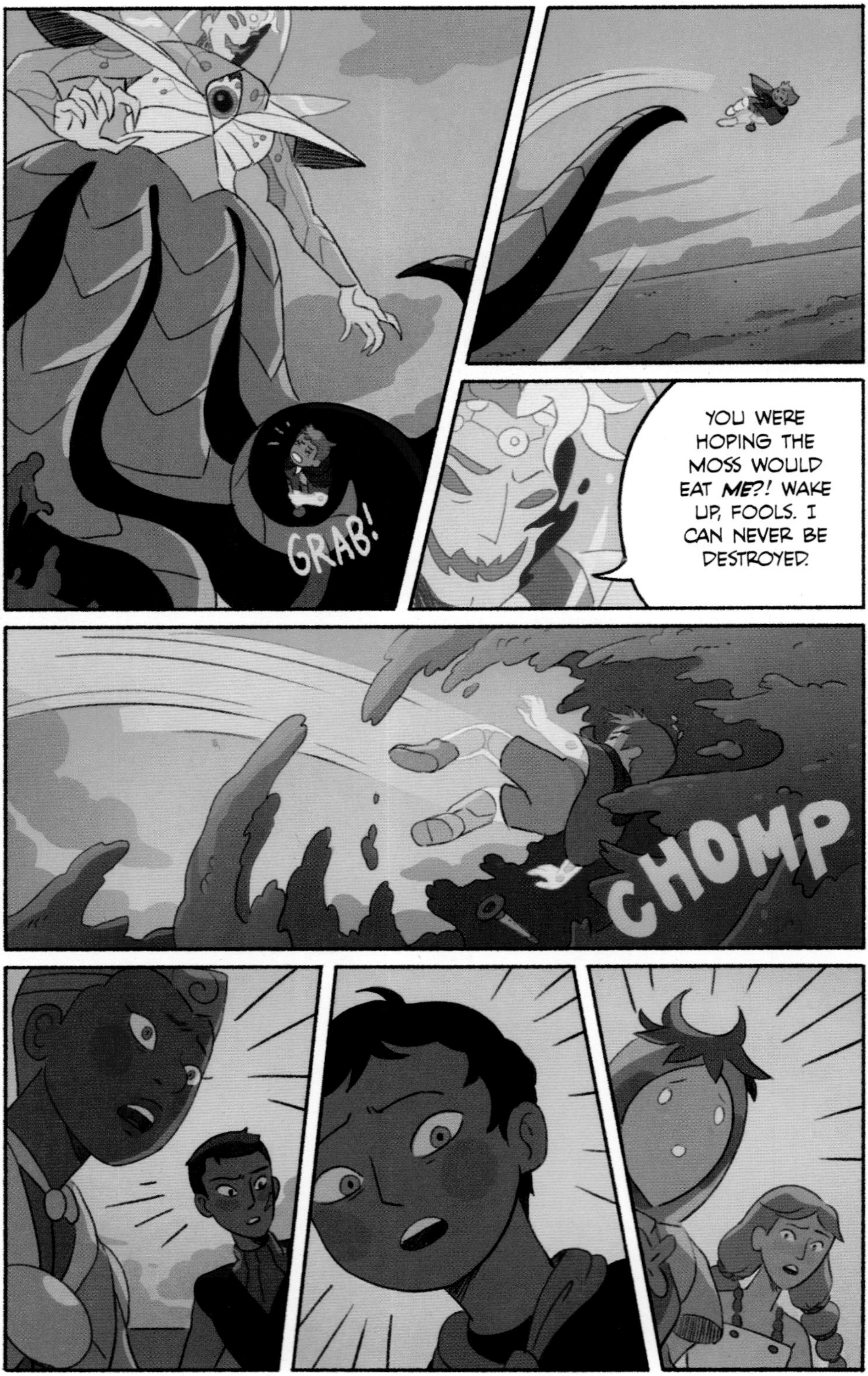
GRAB!
YOU WERE HOPING THE MOSS WOULD EAT *ME?!* WAKE UP, FOOLS. I CAN NEVER BE DESTROYED.
CHOMP

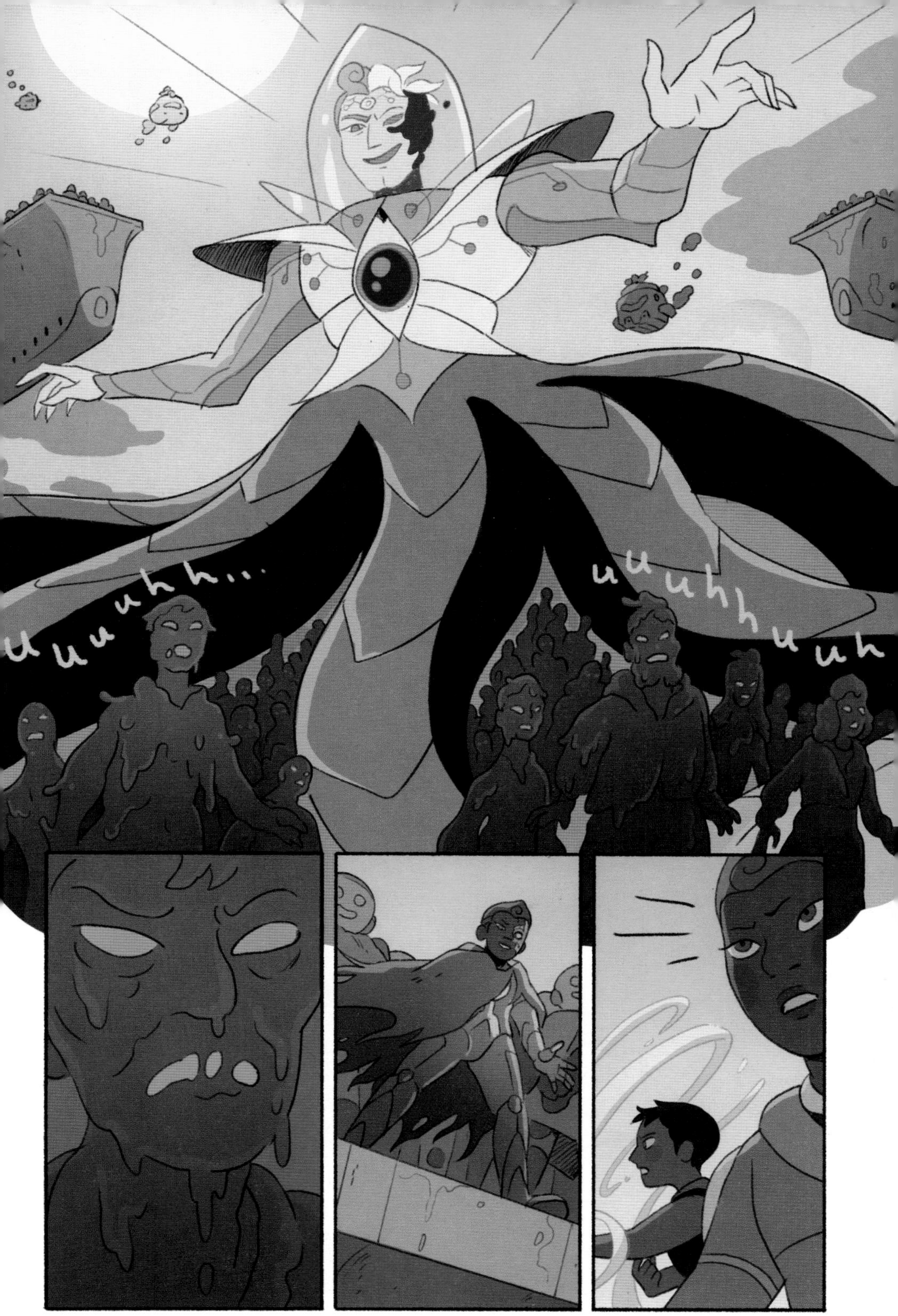
Uuuuhh...
uuuhhhuuuh

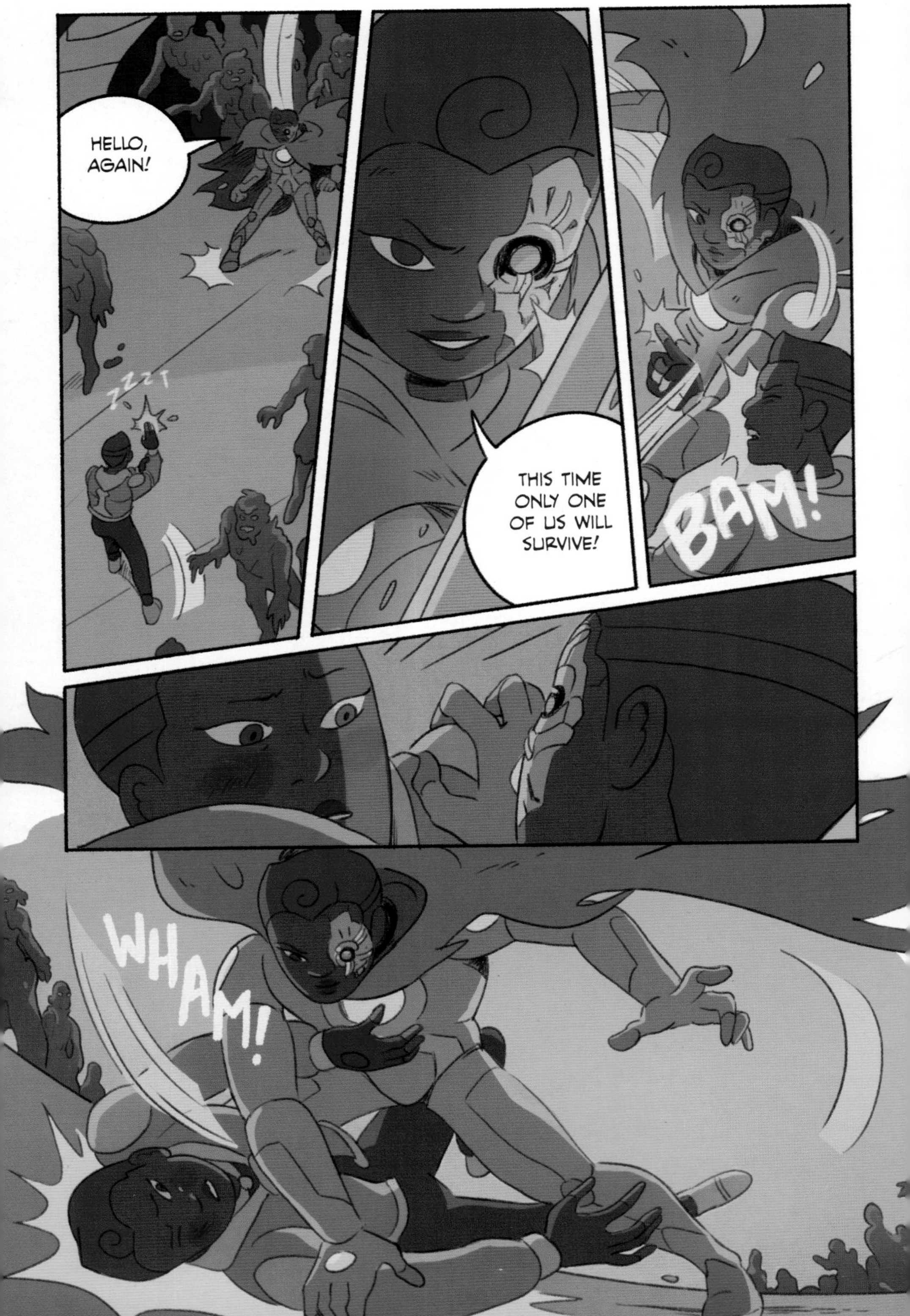
HELLO, AGAIN!
ZZZT
THIS TIME ONLY ONE OF US WILL SURVIVE!
BAM!
WHAM!

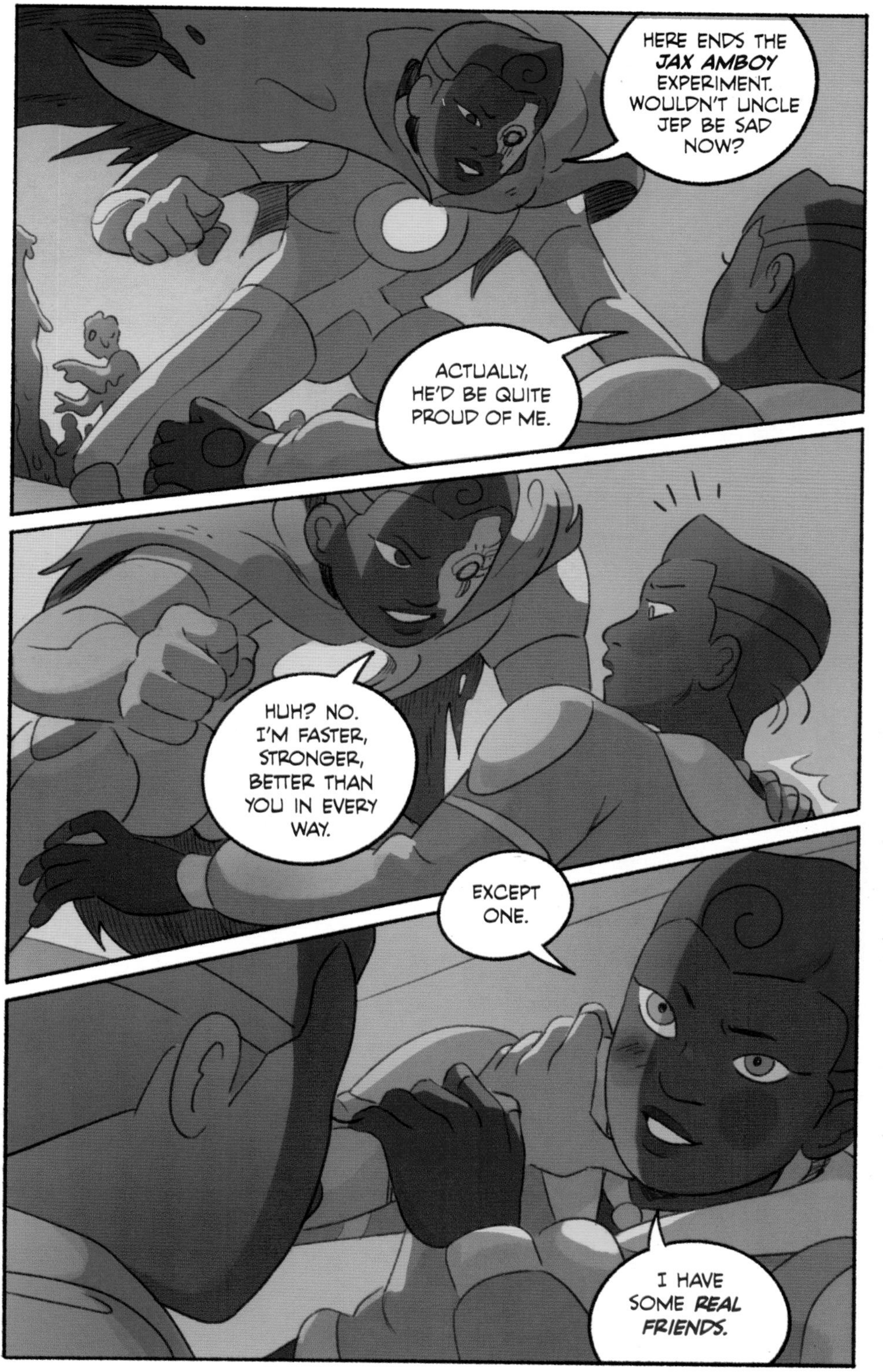
HERE ENDS THE *JAX AMBOY* EXPERIMENT. WOULDN'T UNCLE JEP BE SAD NOW?
ACTUALLY, HE'D BE QUITE PROUD OF ME.
HUH? NO. I'M FASTER, STRONGER, BETTER THAN YOU IN EVERY WAY.
EXCEPT ONE.
I HAVE SOME *REAL FRIENDS.*

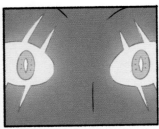

SHHWOOOf

CHOMP

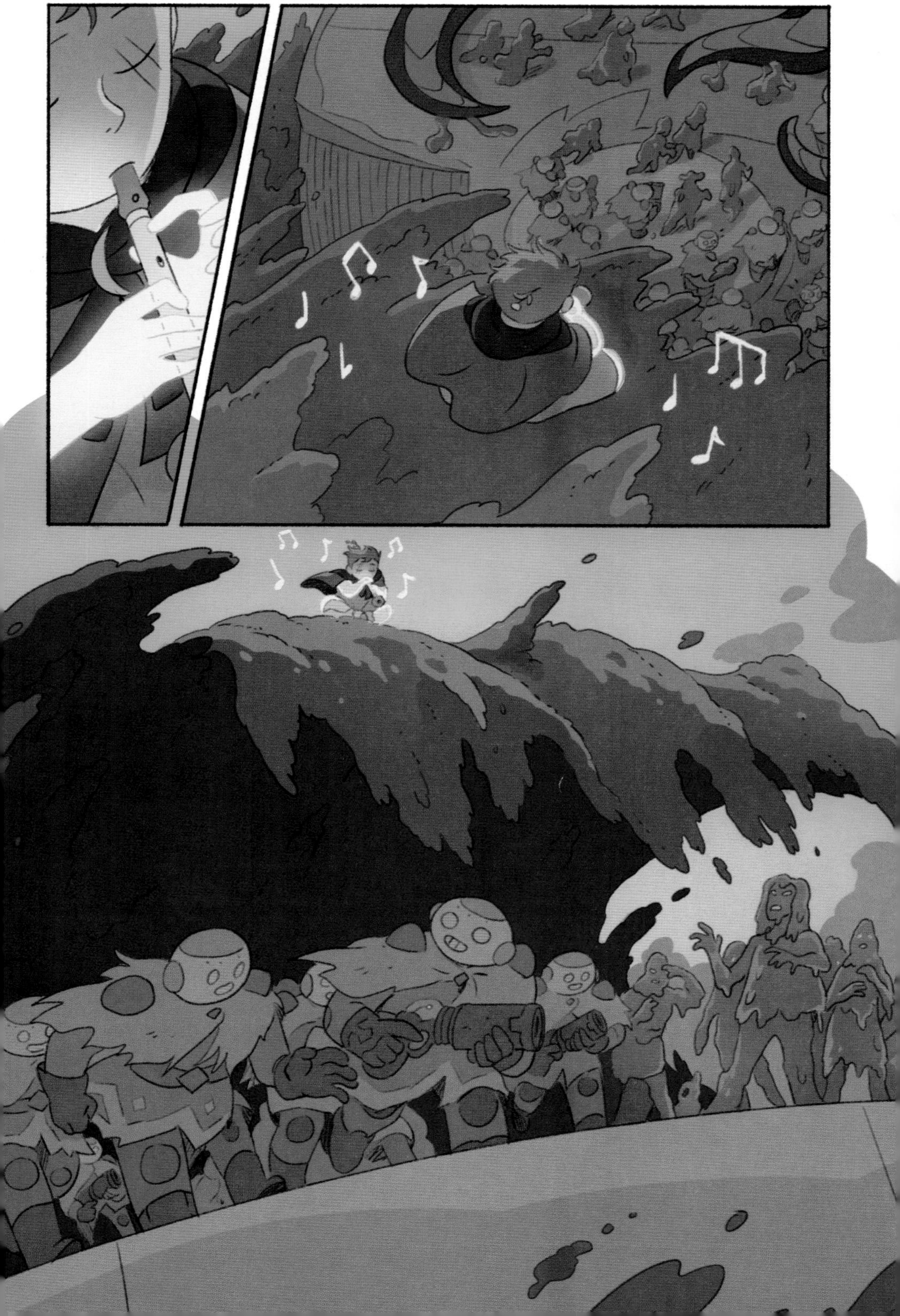

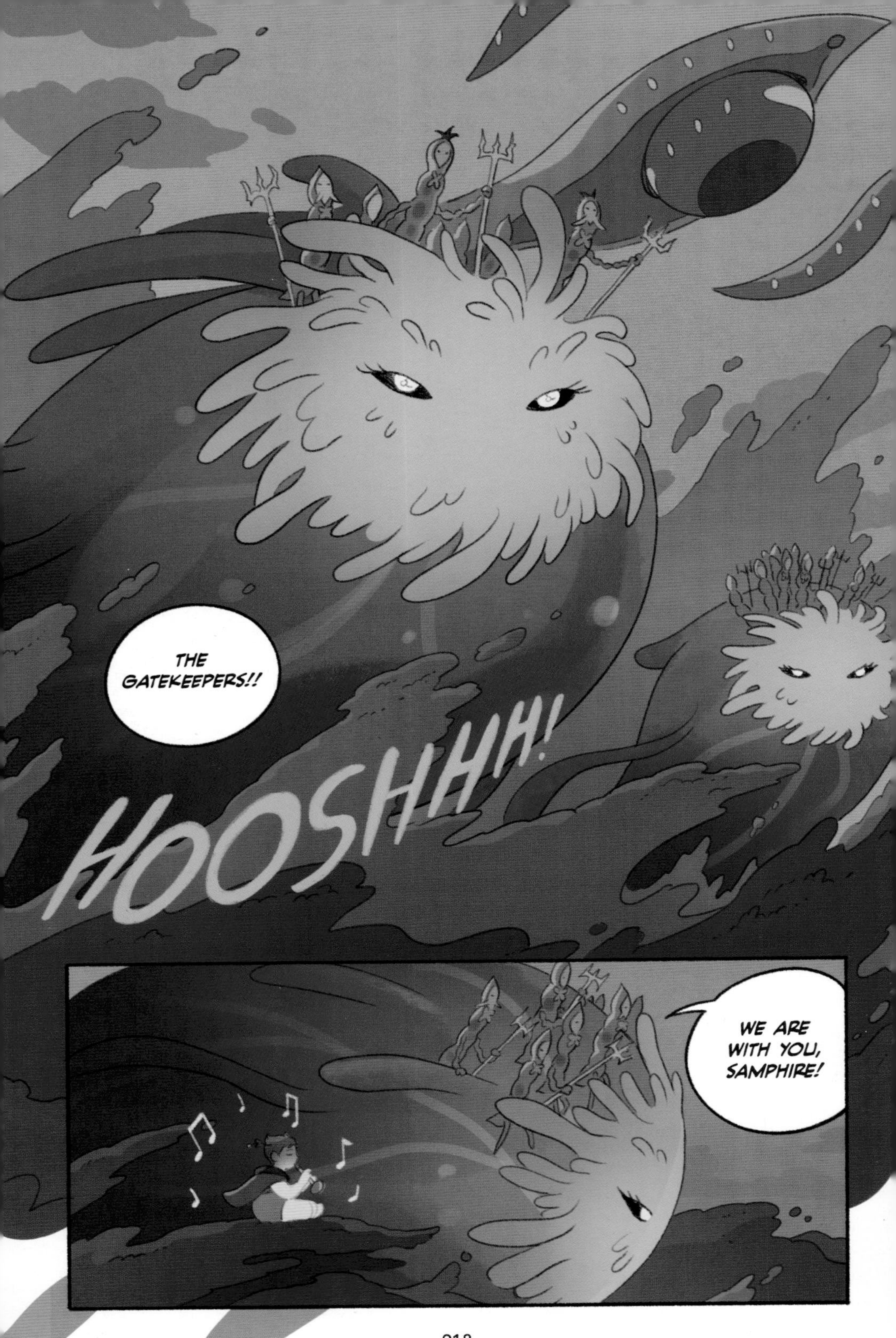
THE GATEKEEPERS!!
HOOSHHH!
WE ARE WITH YOU, SAMPHIRE!

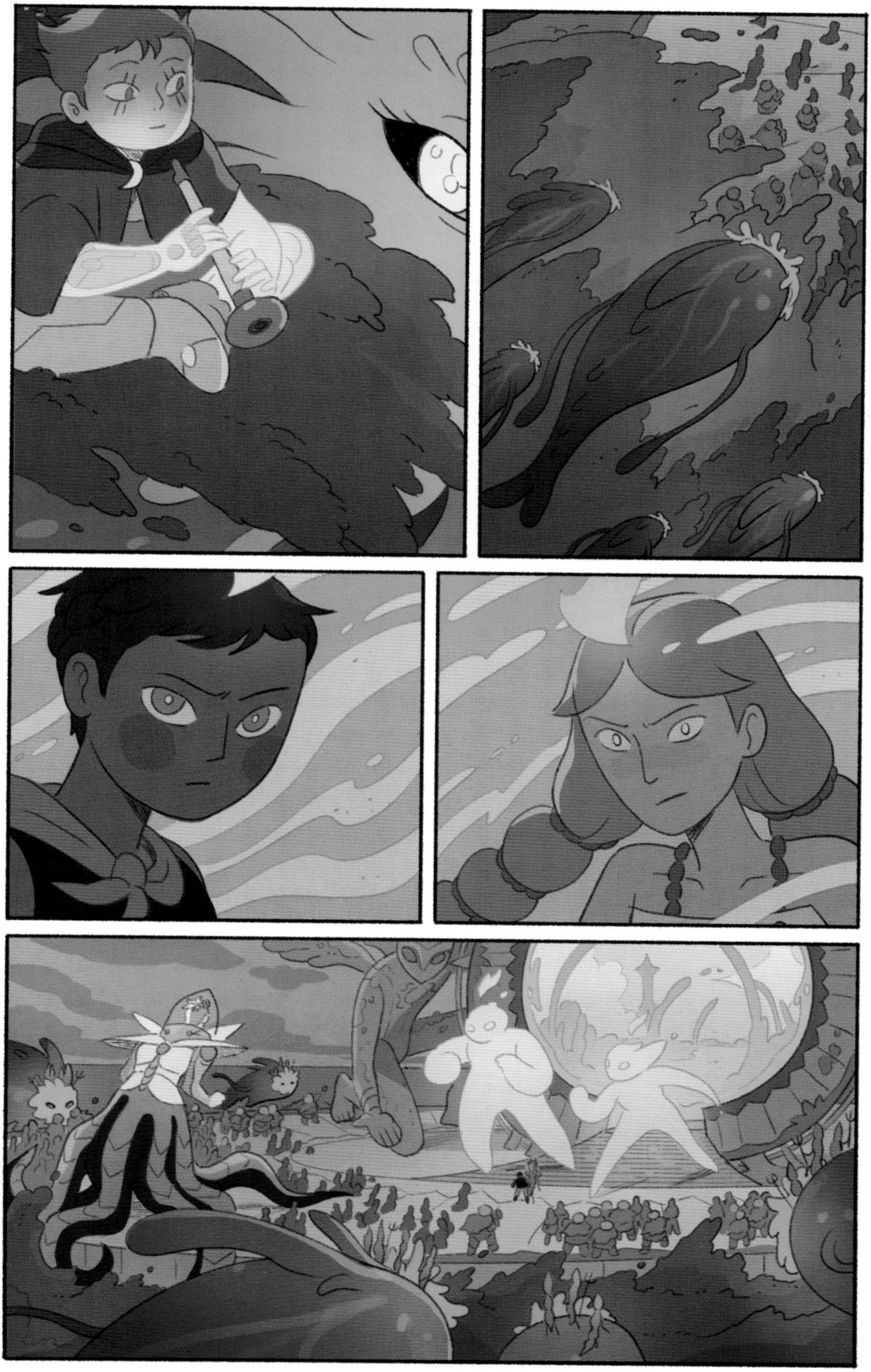

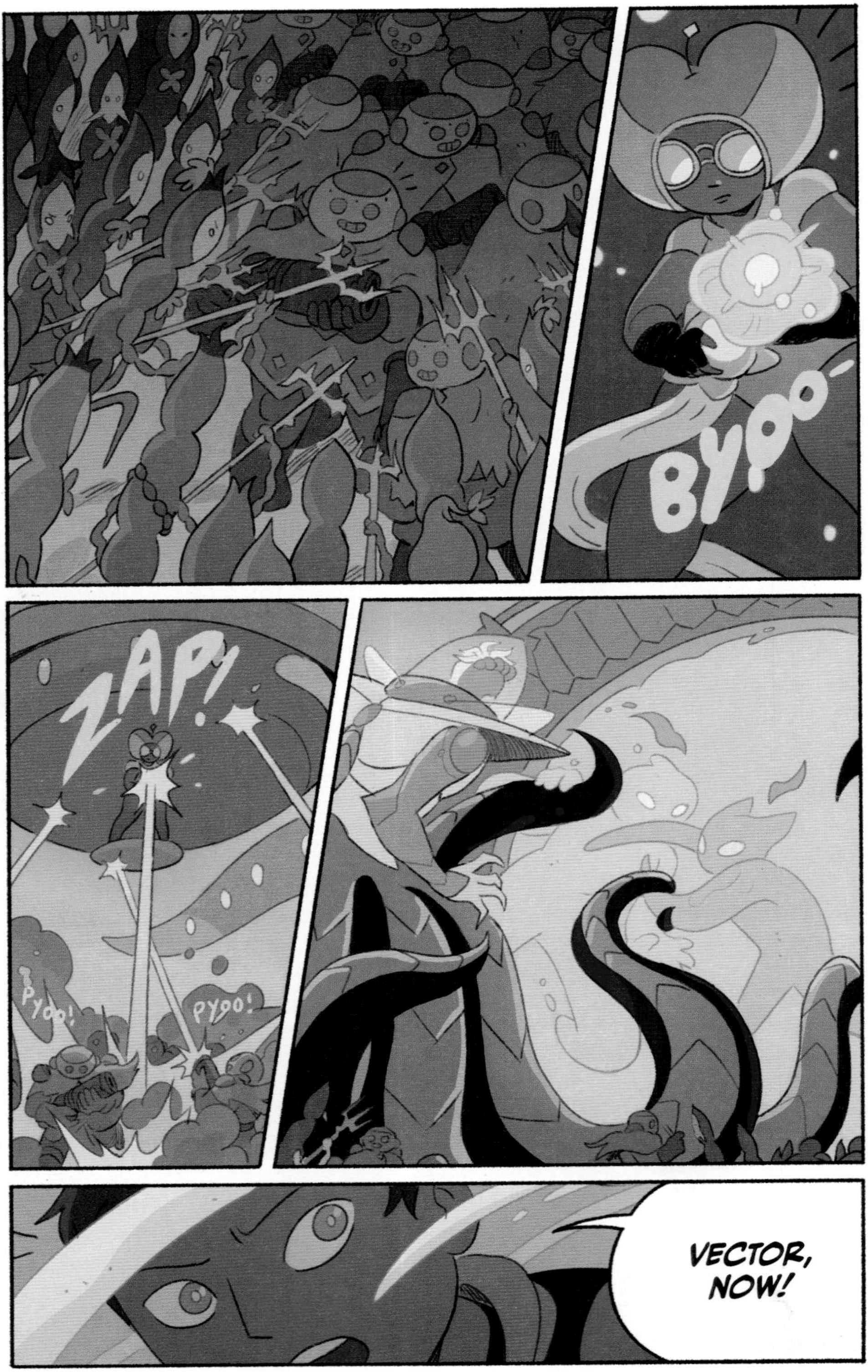
BYOO-
ZAP!
PYOO!
PYOO!
VECTOR, NOW!

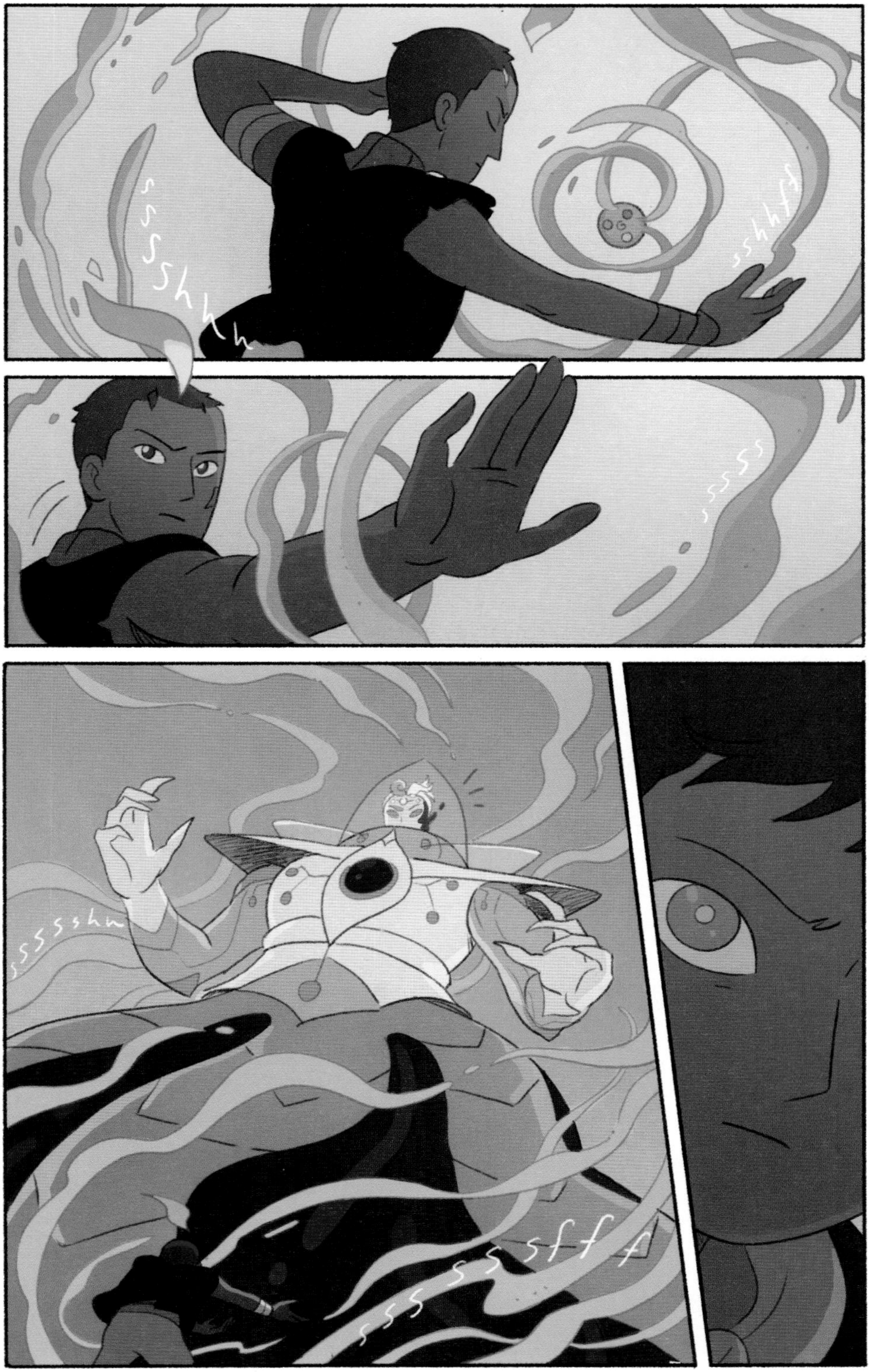
sssShhhh
sshhff
ssss
sssssshh
ssssssfff

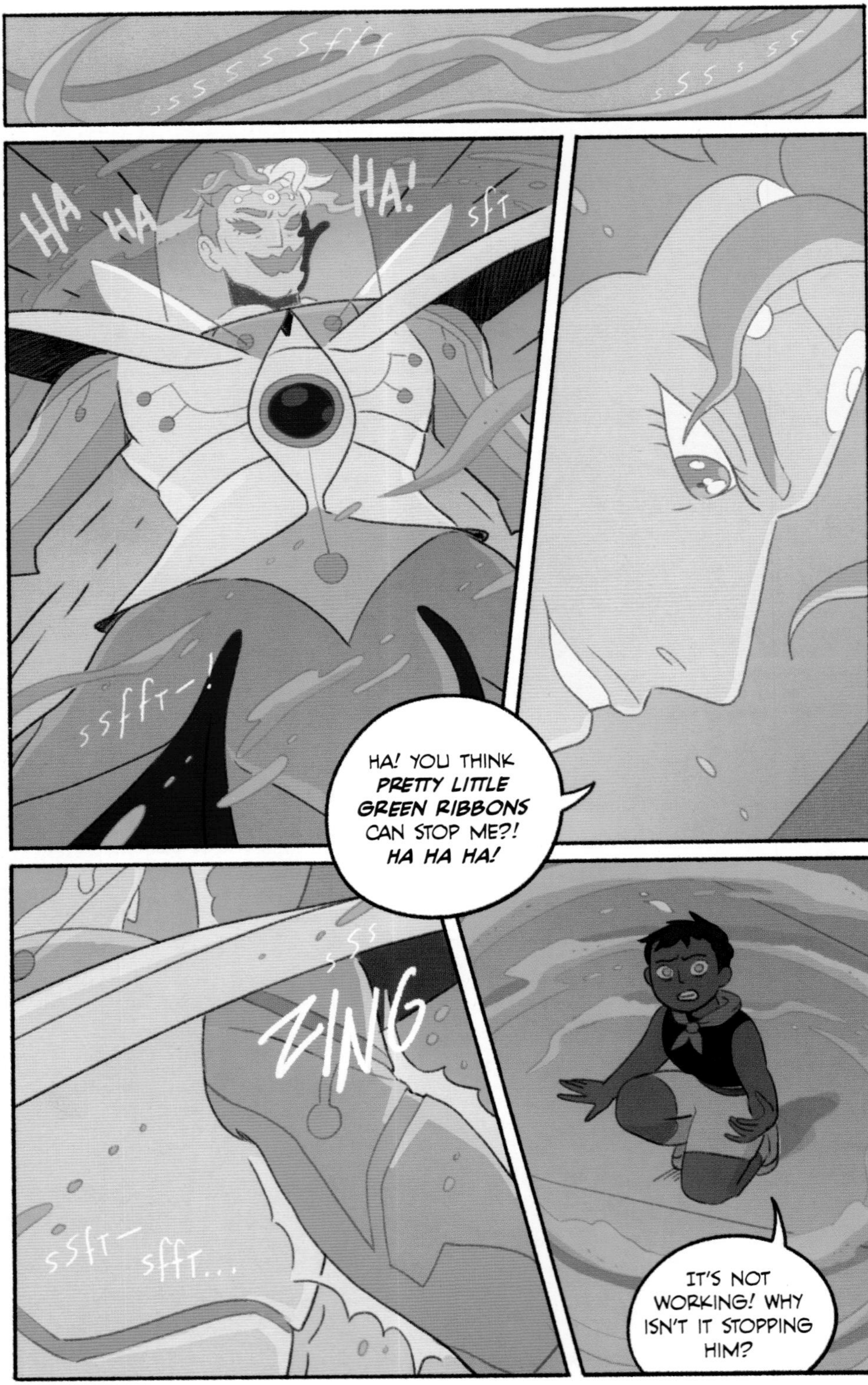
sssssfft
sssss
HA HA HA!
sft
ssfft—!
HA! YOU THINK PRETTY LITTLE GREEN RIBBONS CAN STOP ME?! HA HA HA!
sss
ZING
ssft— sfft...
IT'S NOT WORKING! WHY ISN'T IT STOPPING HIM?

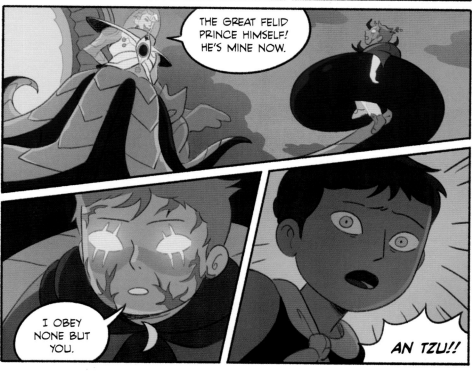

THE GREAT FELID PRINCE HIMSELF! HE'S MINE NOW.

I OBEY NONE BUT YOU.

AN TZU!!

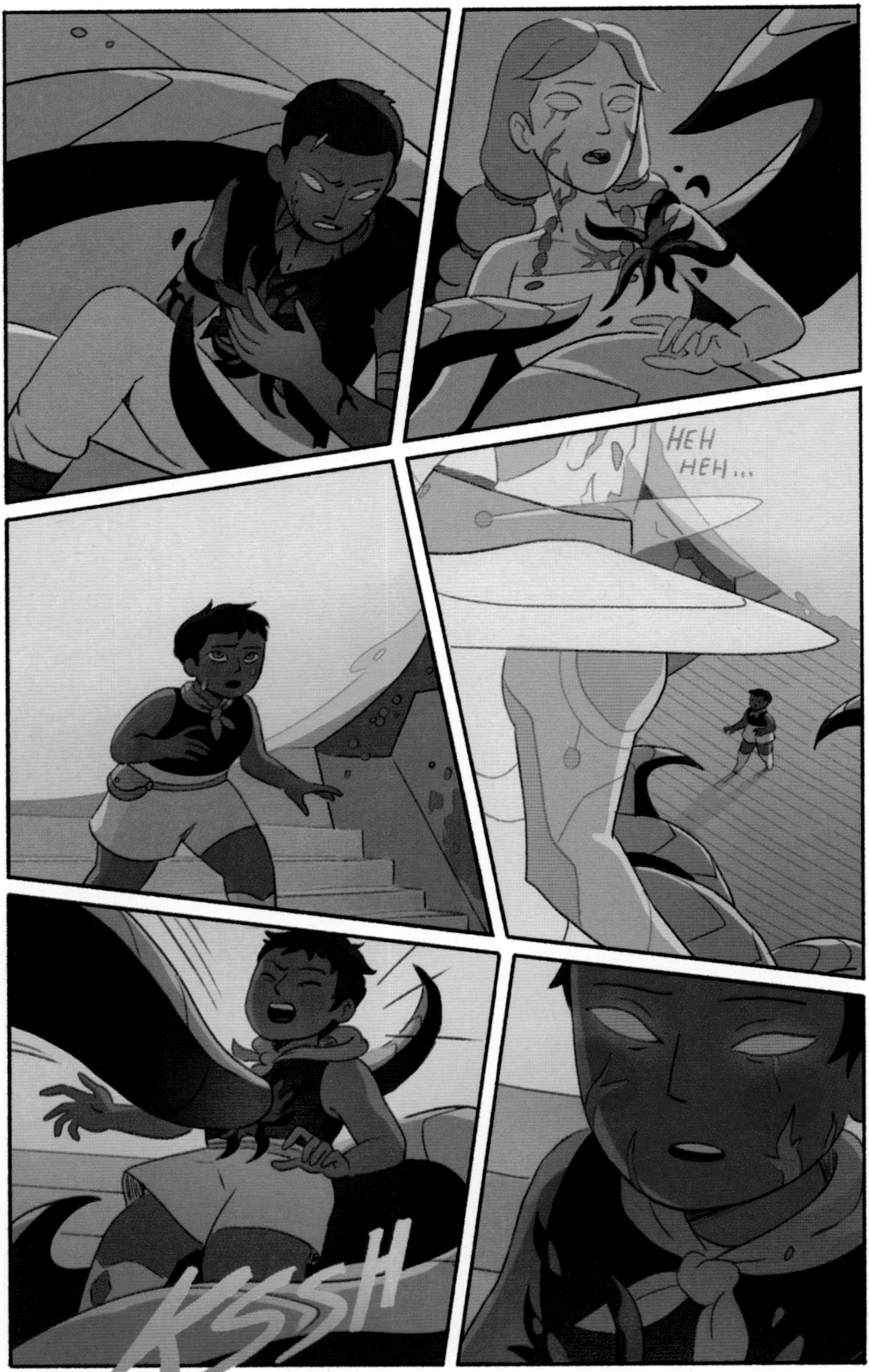
HEH
HEH...
KSSH

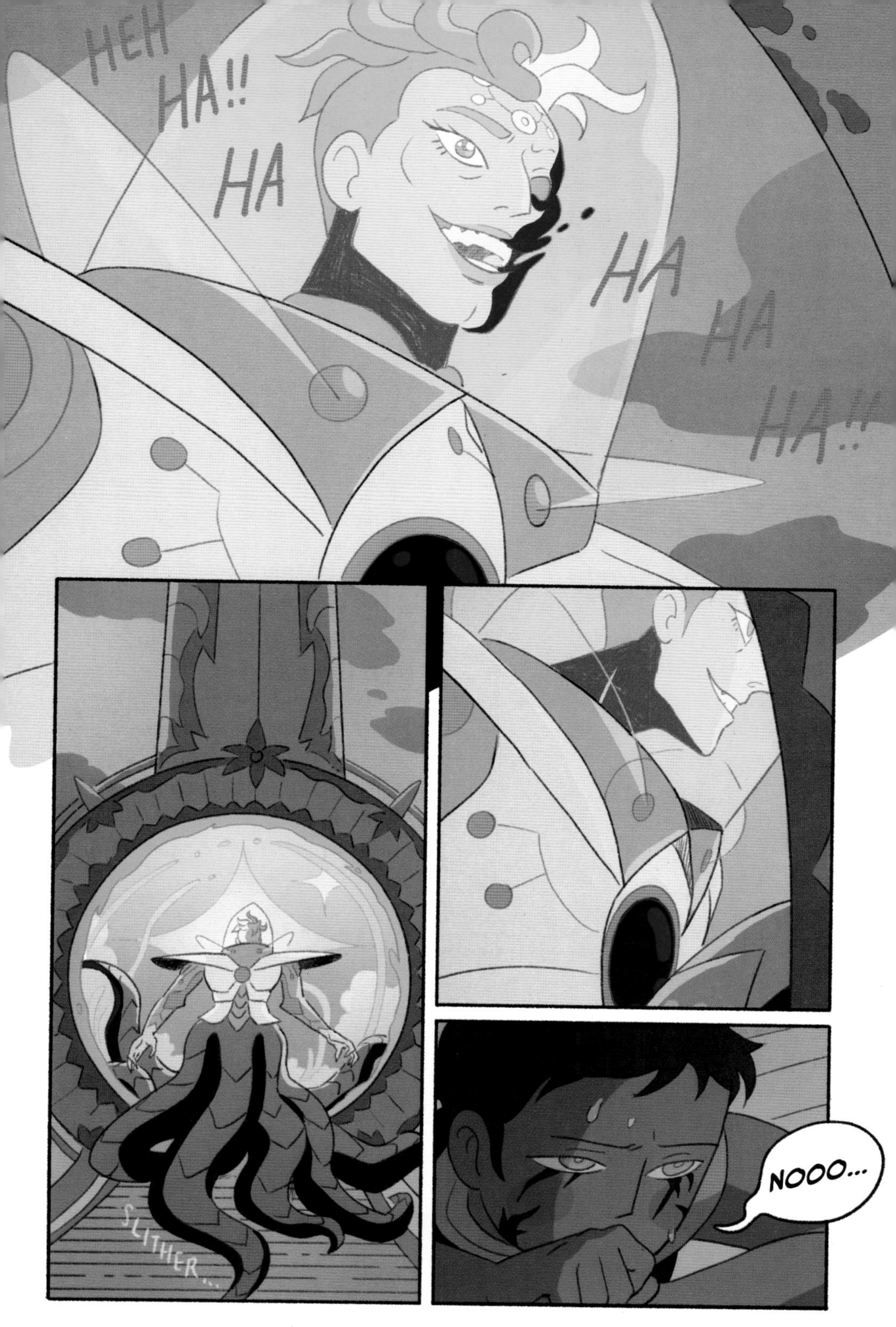
HEH
HA!!
HA
HA
HA
HA!!
SLITHER...
NOOO...

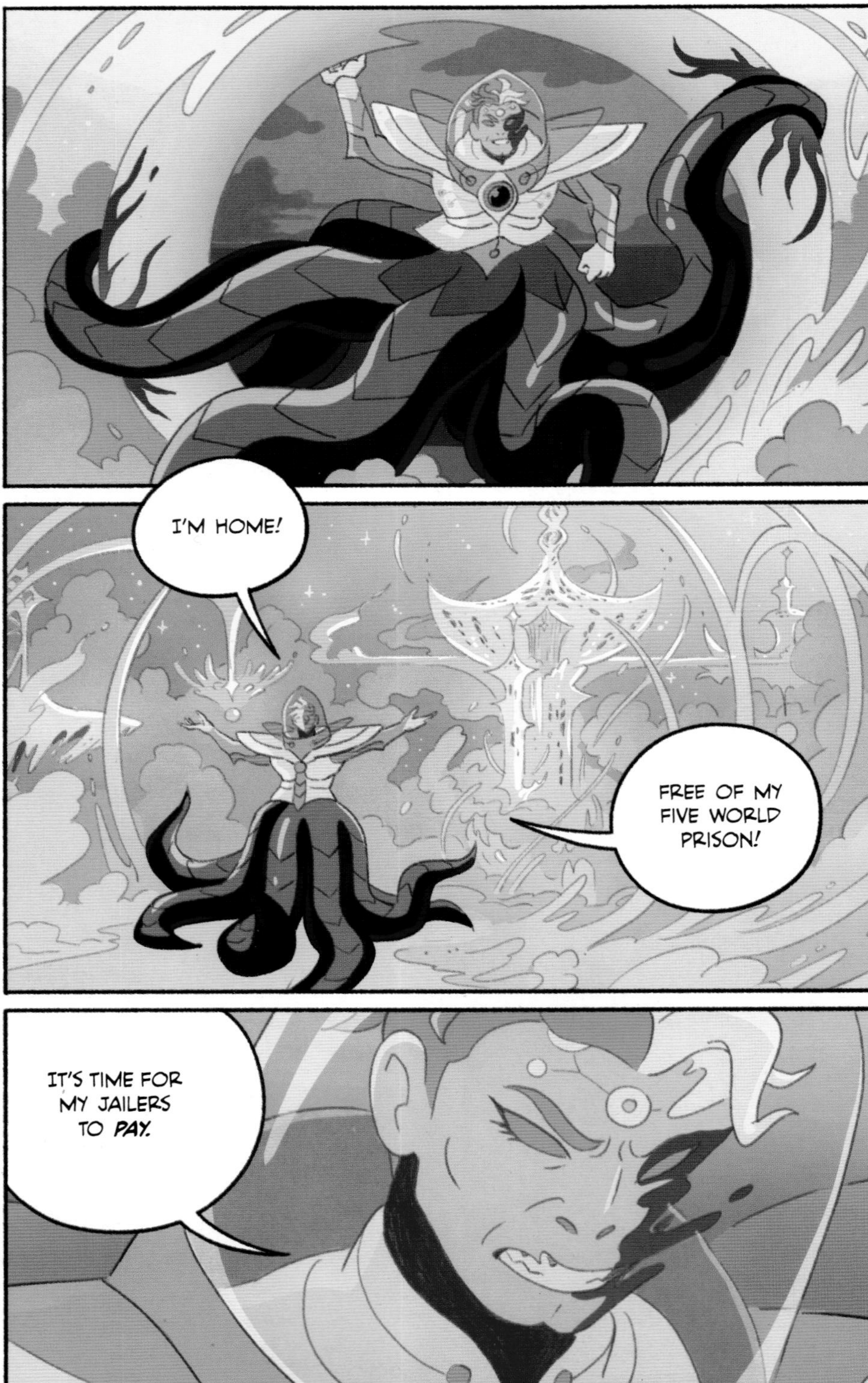
I'M HOME!
FREE OF MY FIVE WORLD PRISON!
IT'S TIME FOR MY JAILERS TO *PAY.*

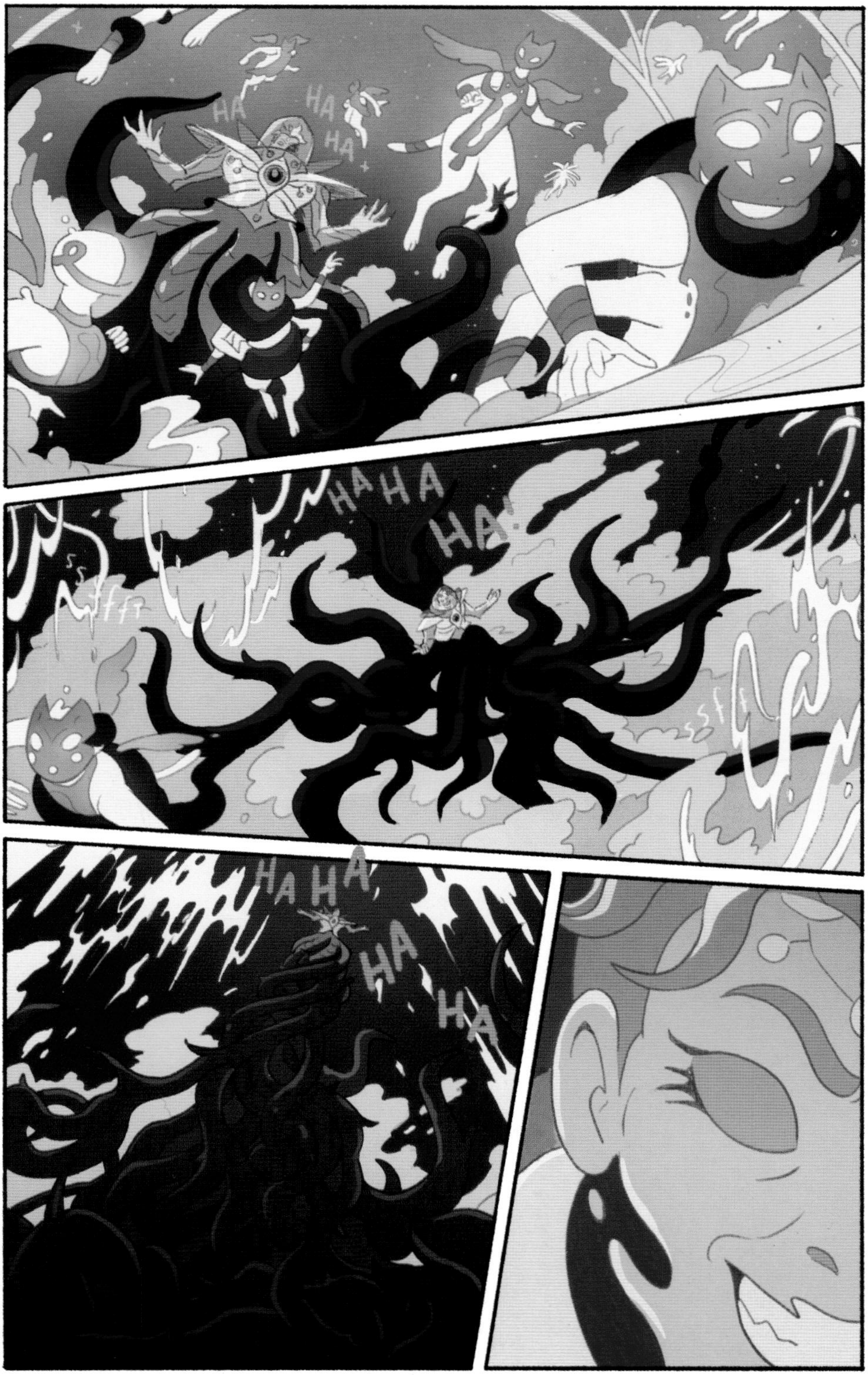
HA
HA
HA
HAHA
HA!
sfff
ssff
HA HA,
HA
HA

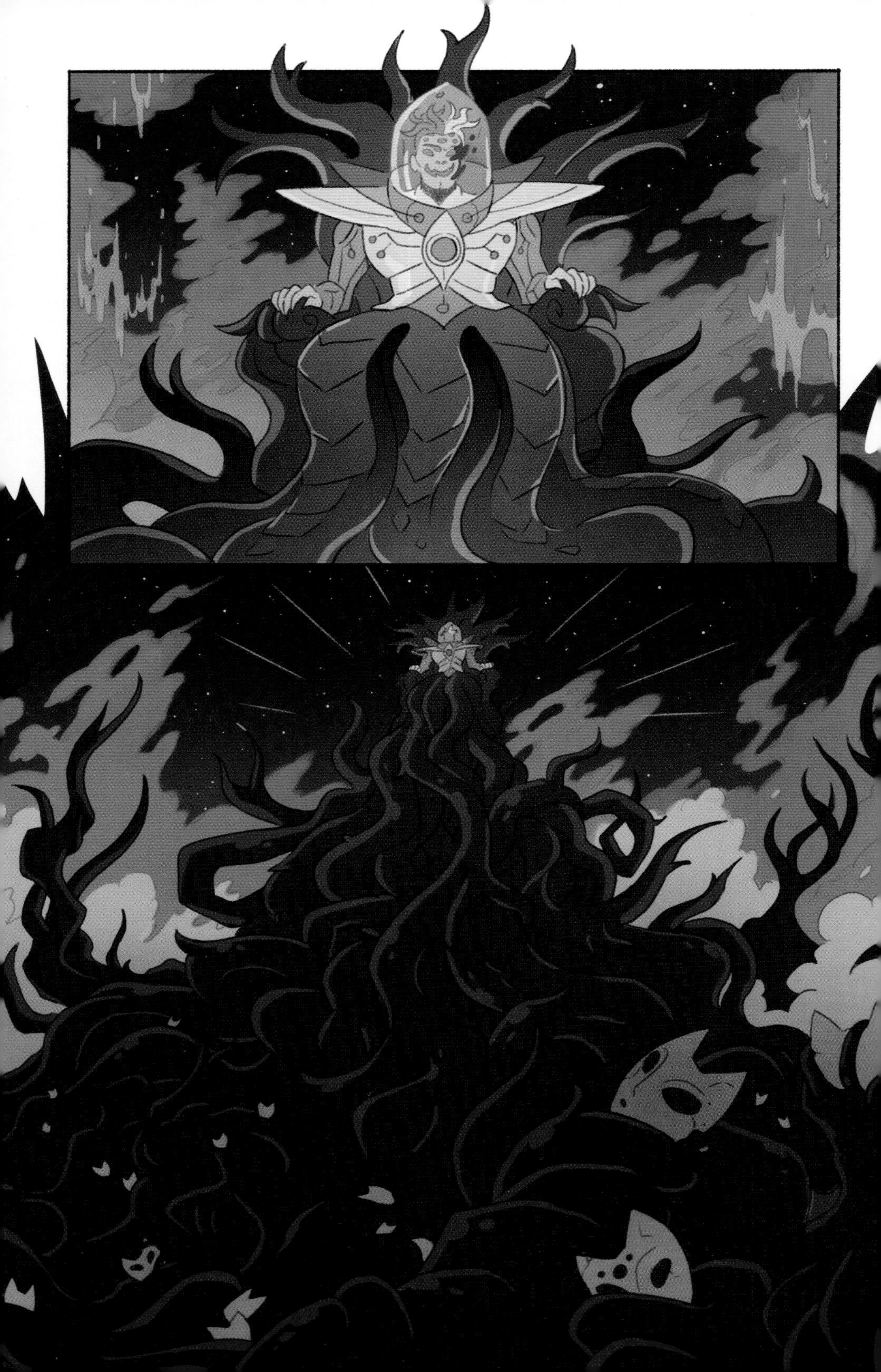

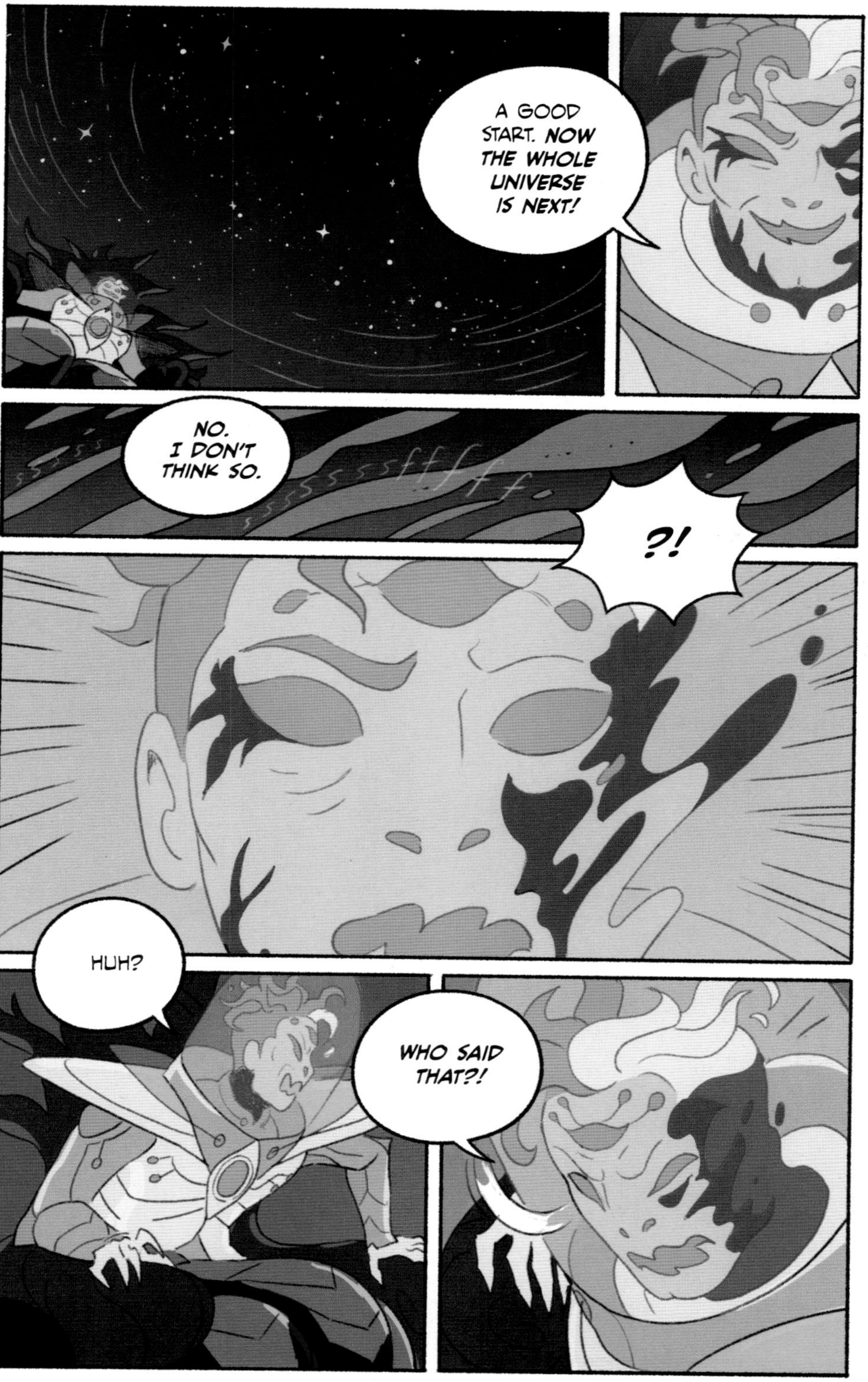
A GOOD START. NOW THE WHOLE UNIVERSE IS NEXT!
NO. I DON'T THINK SO.
?!
HUH?
WHO SAID THAT?!

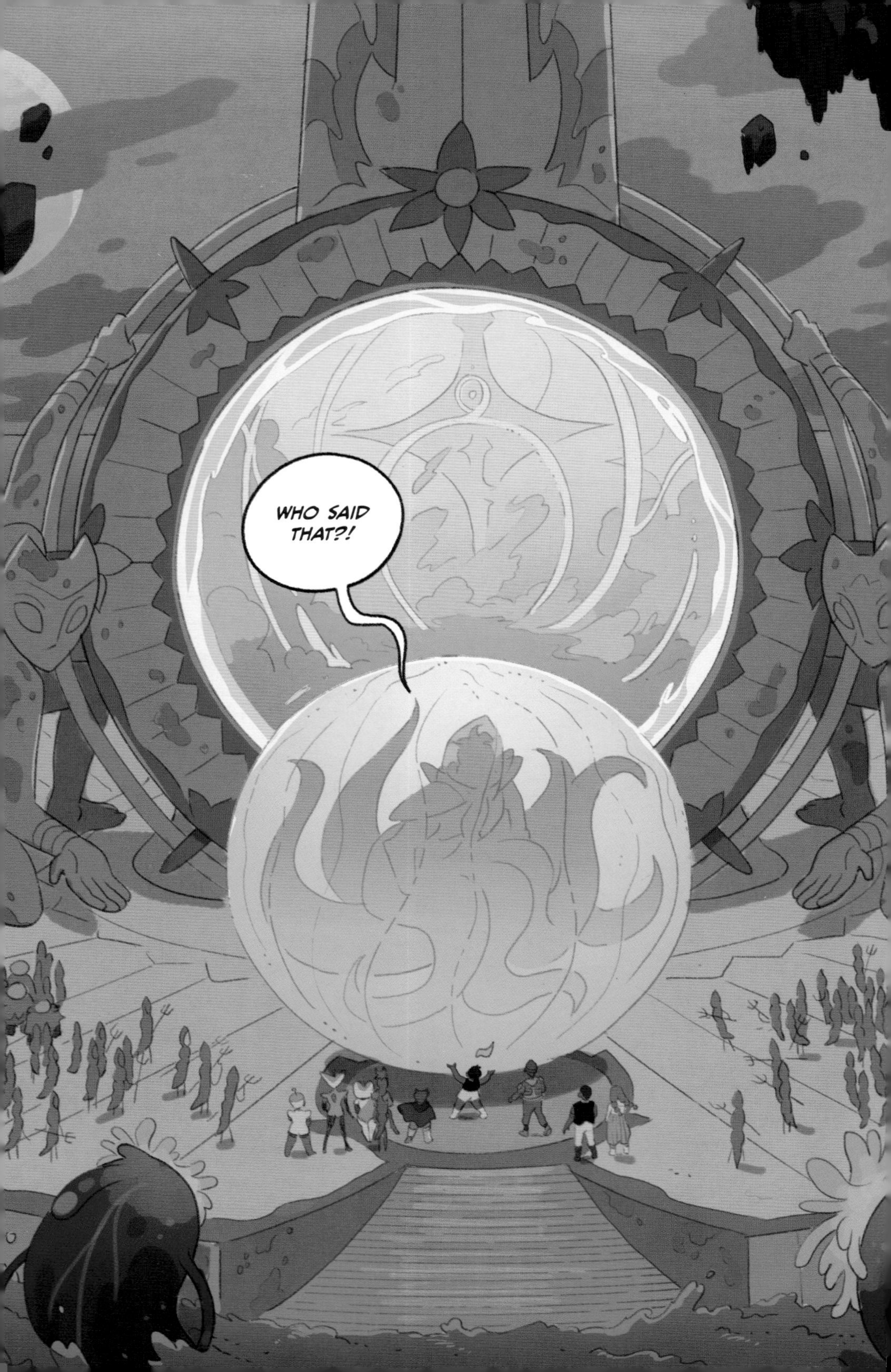
WHO SAID THAT?!

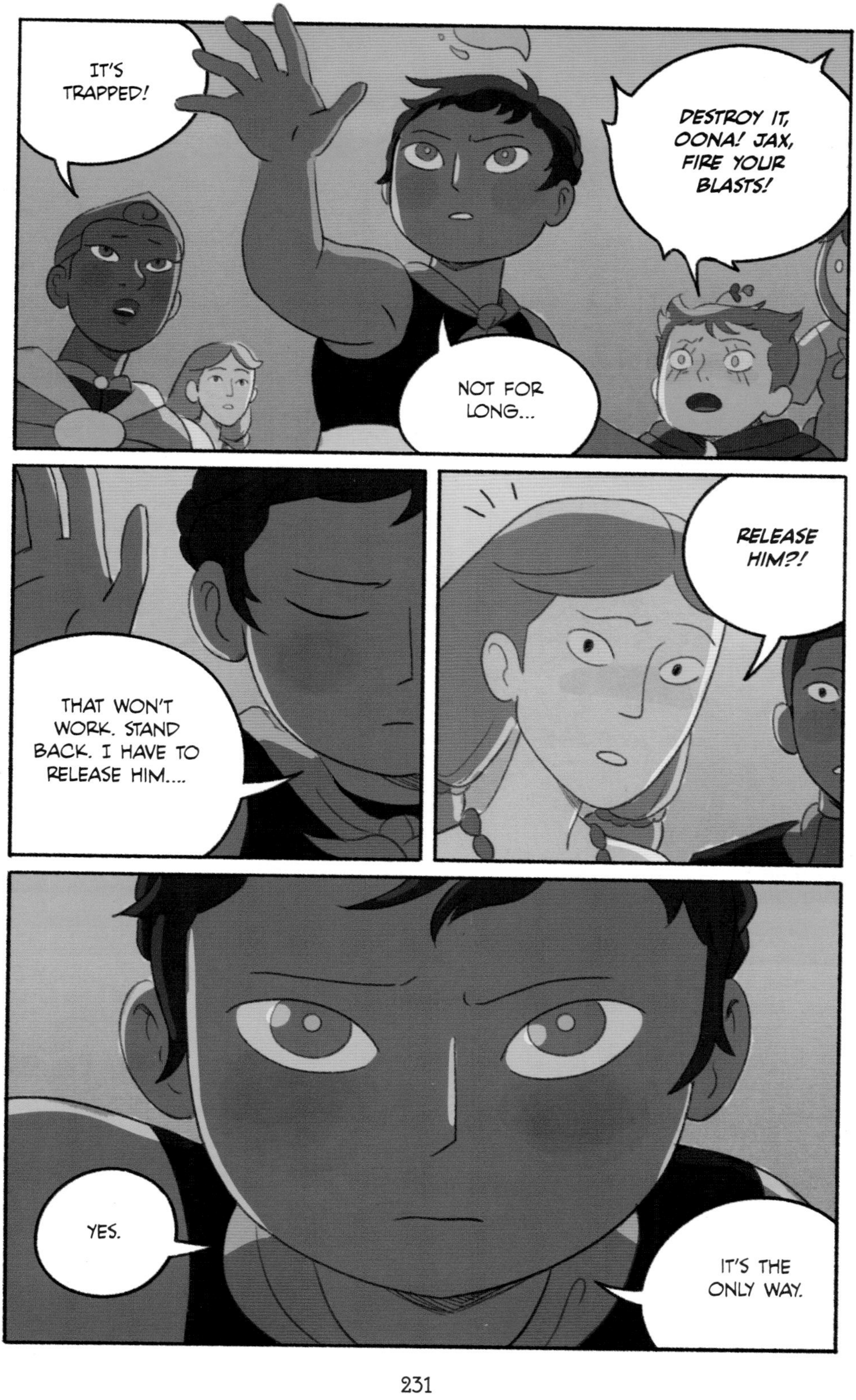
IT'S TRAPPED!
DESTROY IT, OONA! JAX, FIRE YOUR BLASTS!
NOT FOR LONG...
THAT WON'T WORK. STAND BACK. I HAVE TO RELEASE HIM....
RELEASE HIM?!
YES.
IT'S THE ONLY WAY.

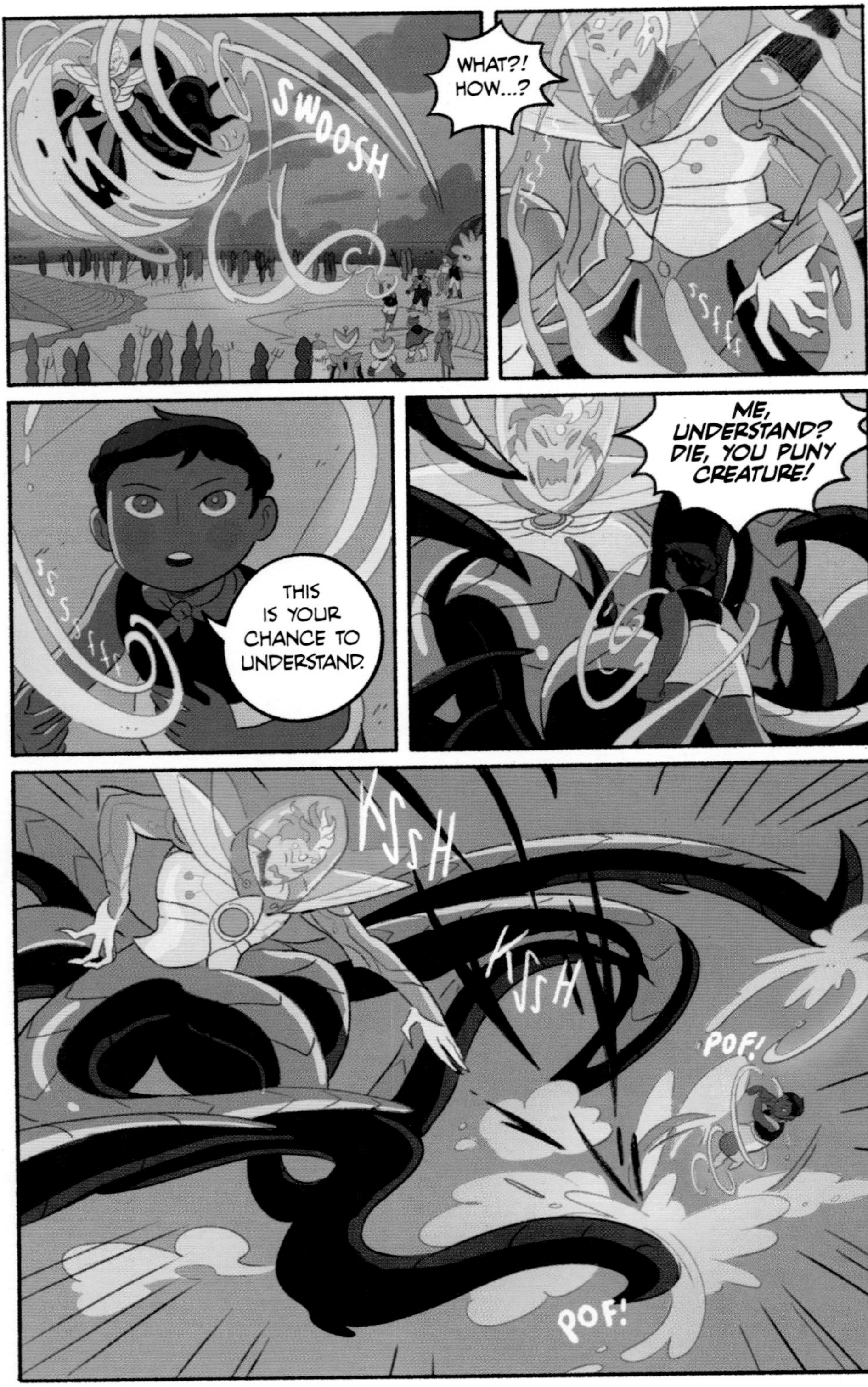
SWOOSH
WHAT?! HOW...?
sssffs
sssffs
THIS IS YOUR CHANCE TO UNDERSTAND.
ME, UNDERSTAND? DIE, YOU PUNY CREATURE!
KSSH
KSSH
POF!
POF!

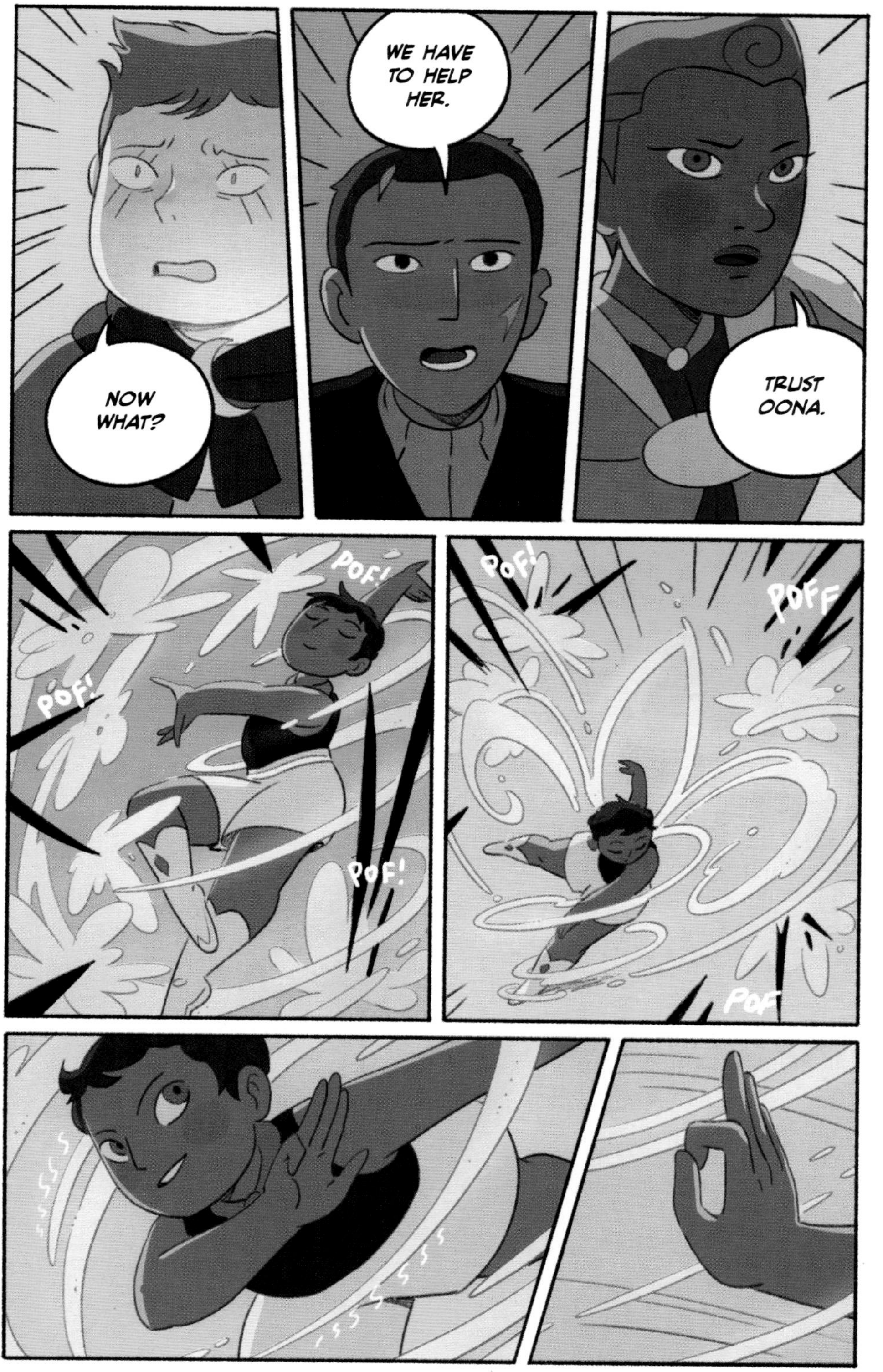
WE HAVE TO HELP HER.
NOW WHAT?
TRUST OONA.
POF!
POF!
POF!
POF!
PDFF
POF

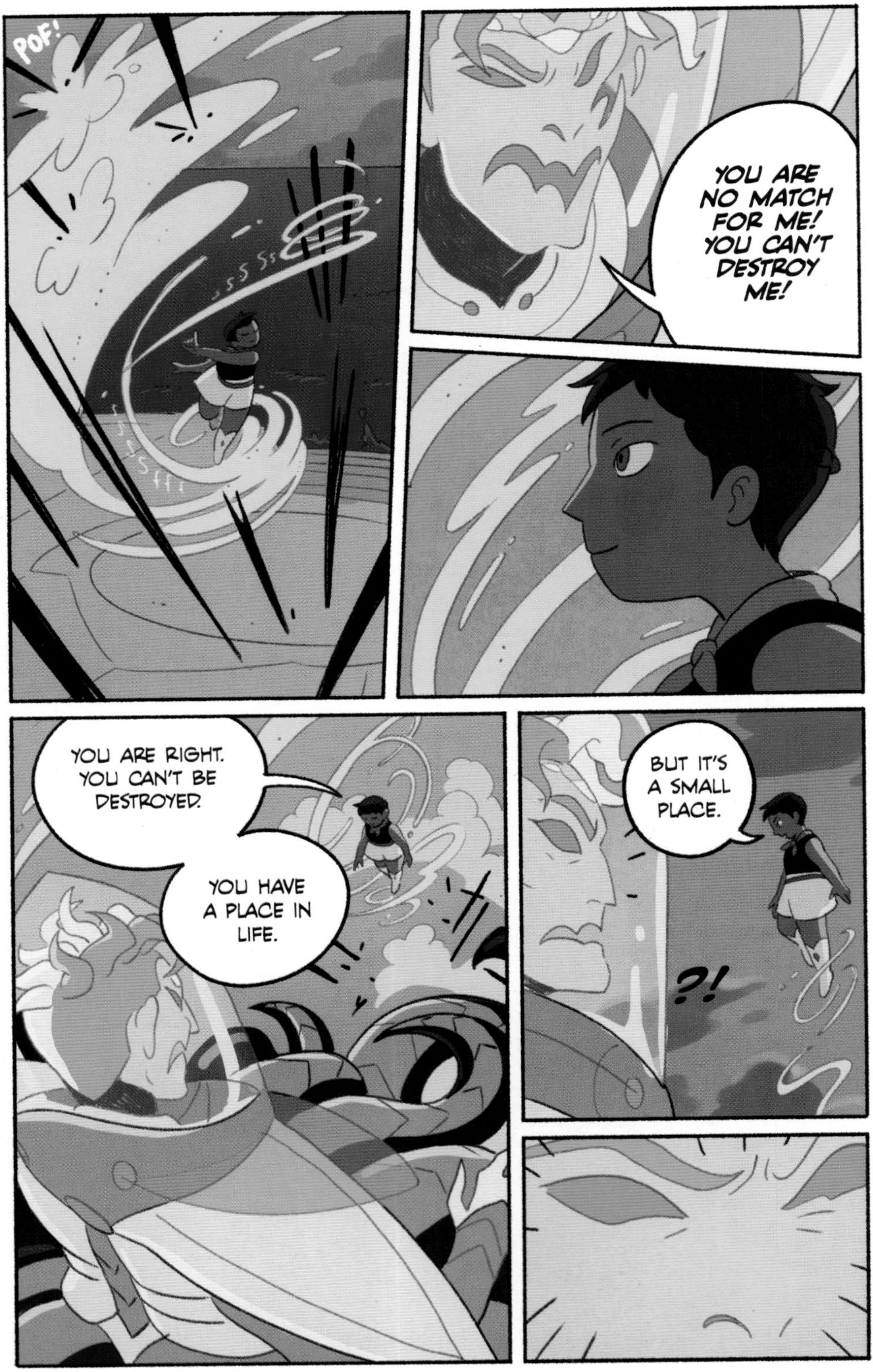
POF!
YOU ARE NO MATCH FOR ME! YOU CAN'T DESTROY ME!
YOU ARE RIGHT. YOU CAN'T BE DESTROYED.
YOU HAVE A PLACE IN LIFE.
BUT IT'S A SMALL PLACE.
?!

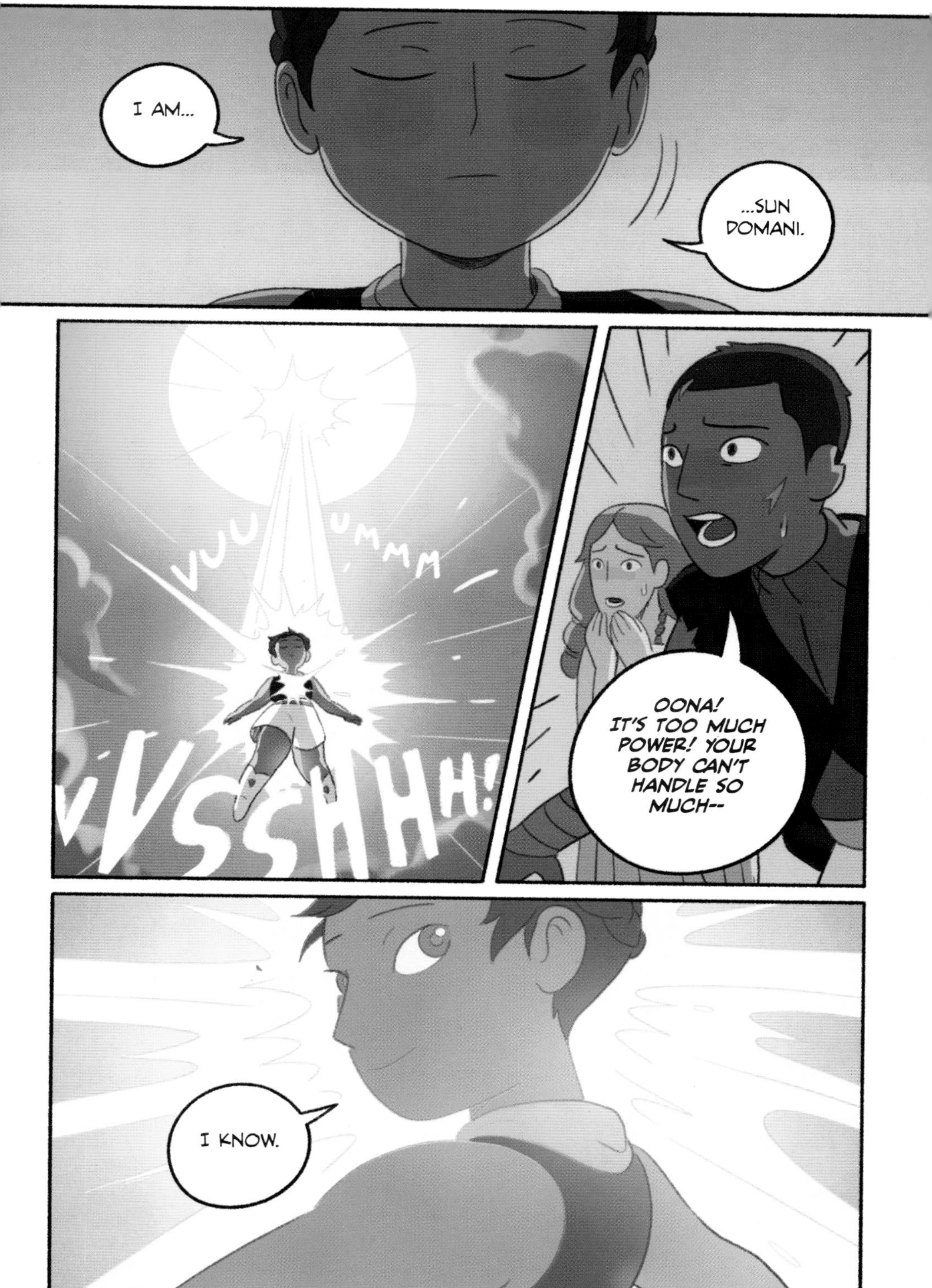

I AM...
...SUN DOMANI.
VUUUMMM
VVSSHHH!
OONA! IT'S TOO MUCH POWER! YOUR BODY CAN'T HANDLE SO MUCH--
I KNOW.

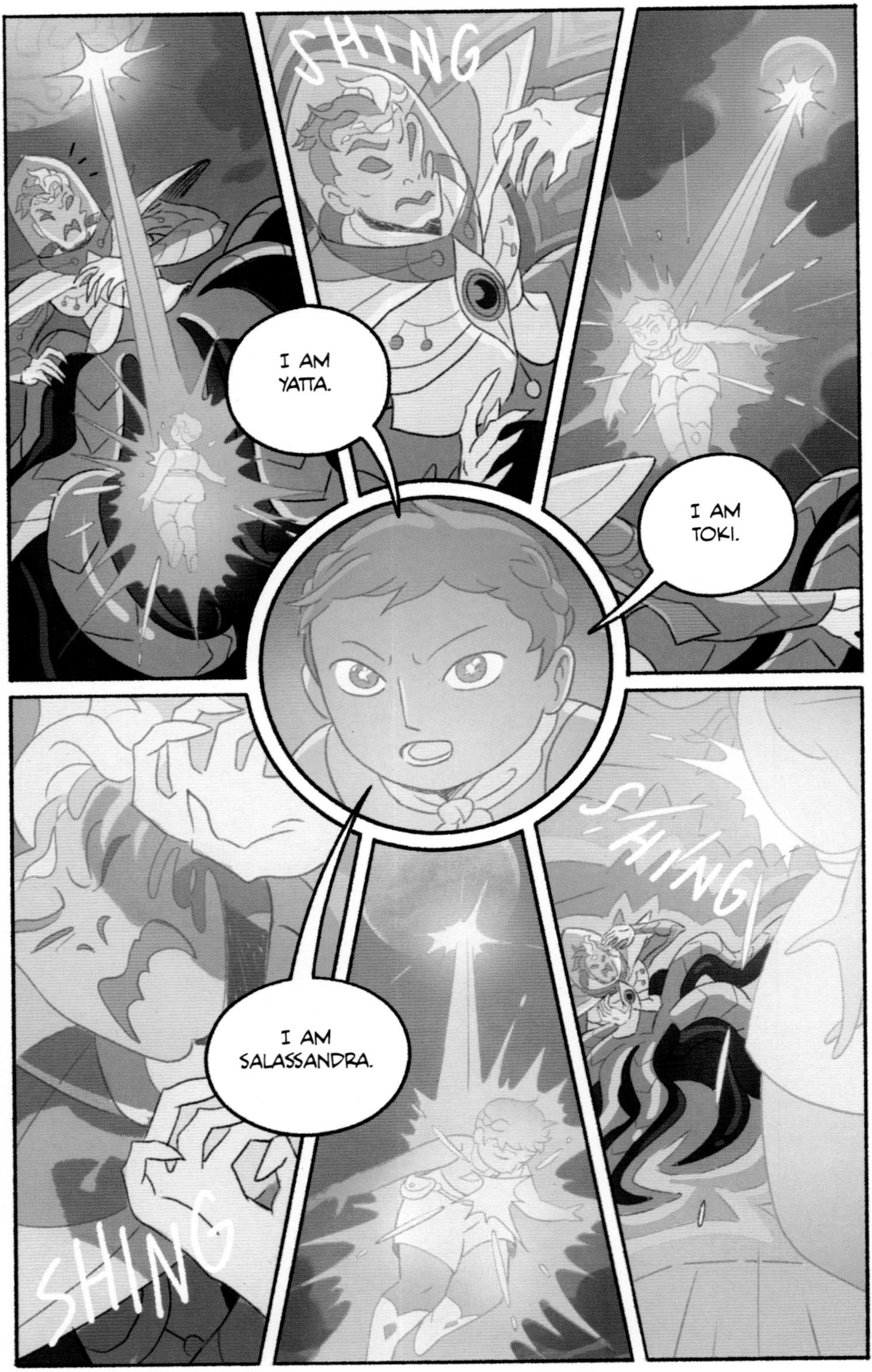
SHING
I AM YATTA.
I AM TOKI.
SHING
I AM SALASSANDRA.
SHING

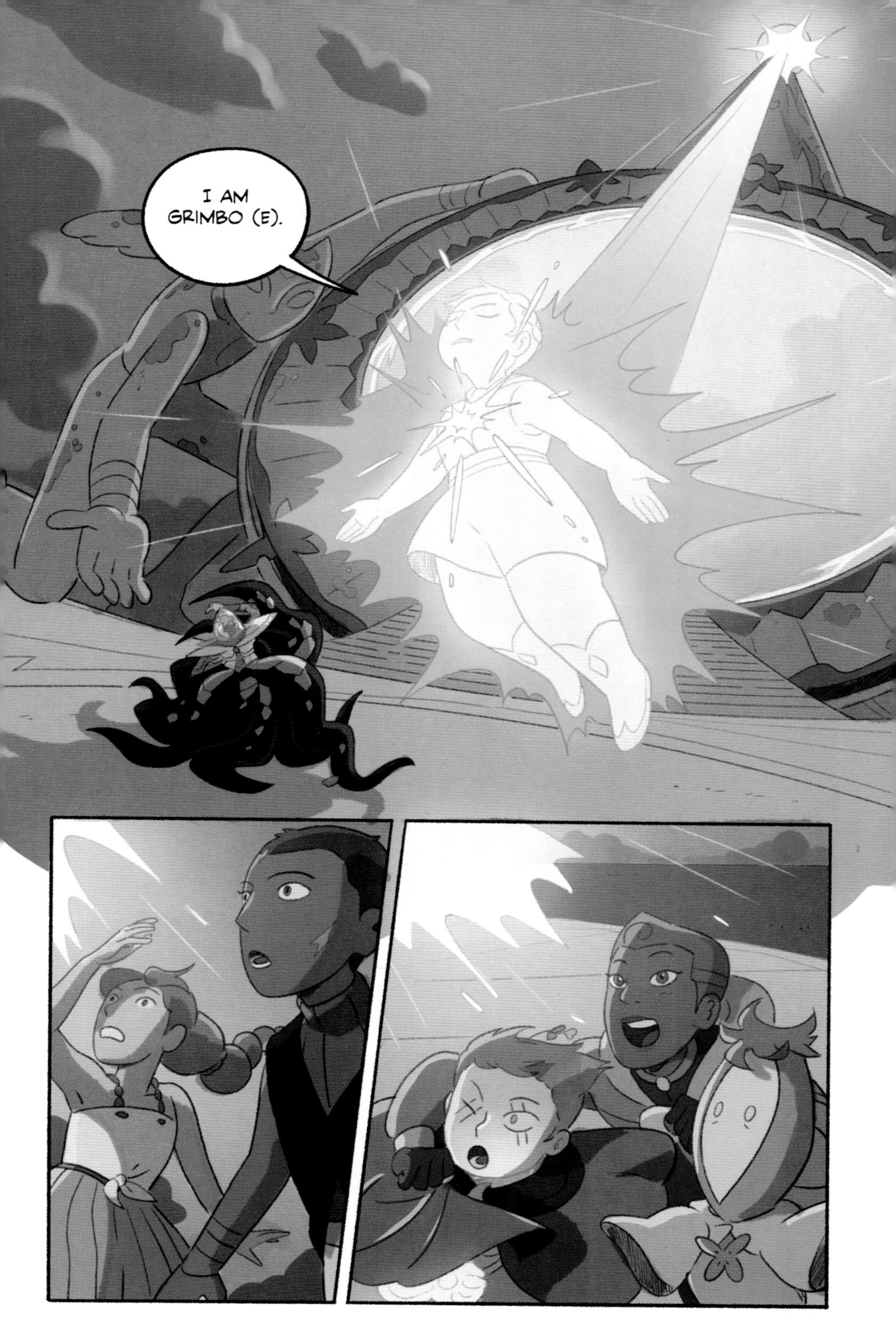
I AM GRIMBO (E).

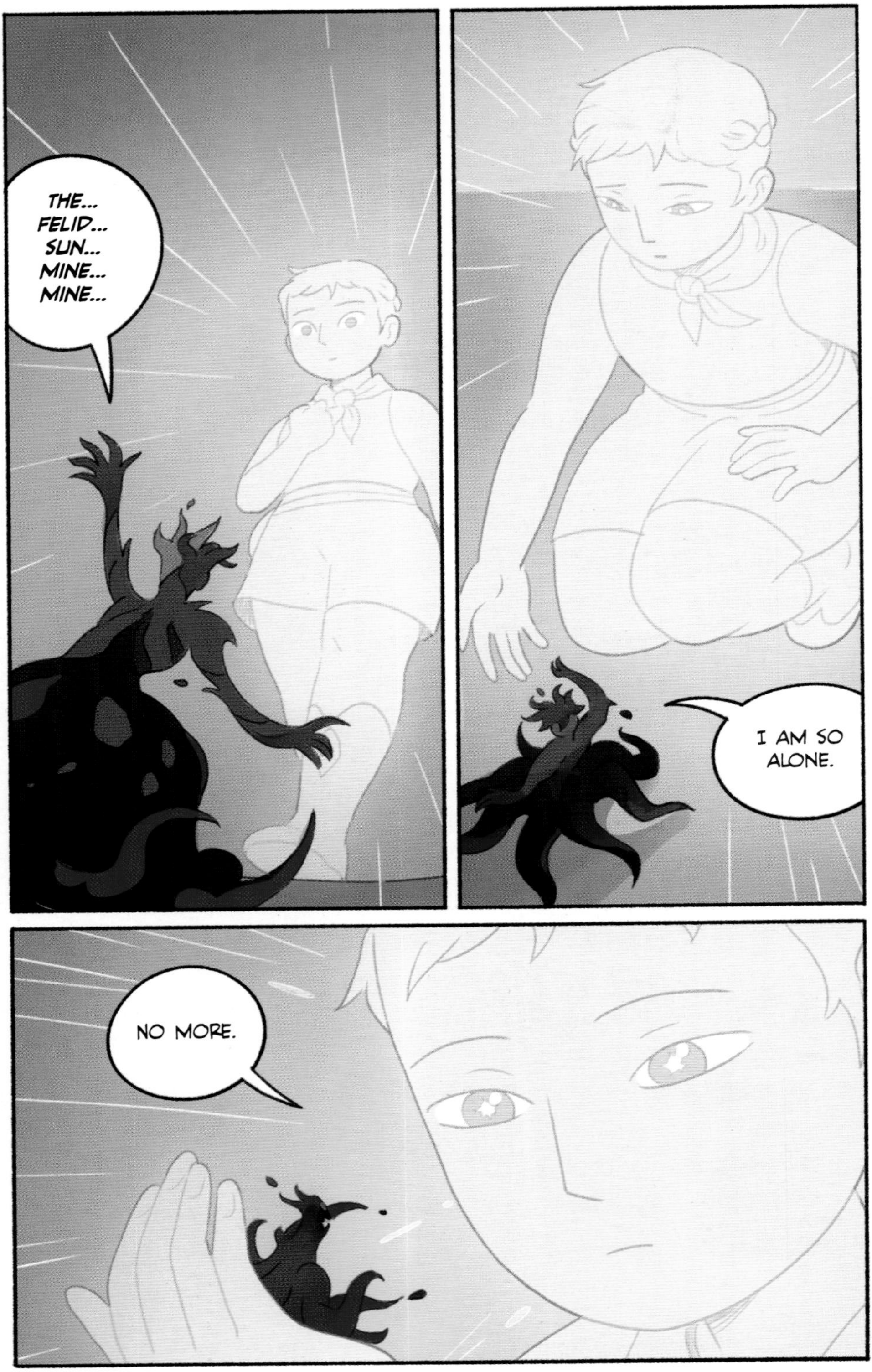
THE... FELID... SUN... MINE... MINE...
I AM SO ALONE.
NO MORE.

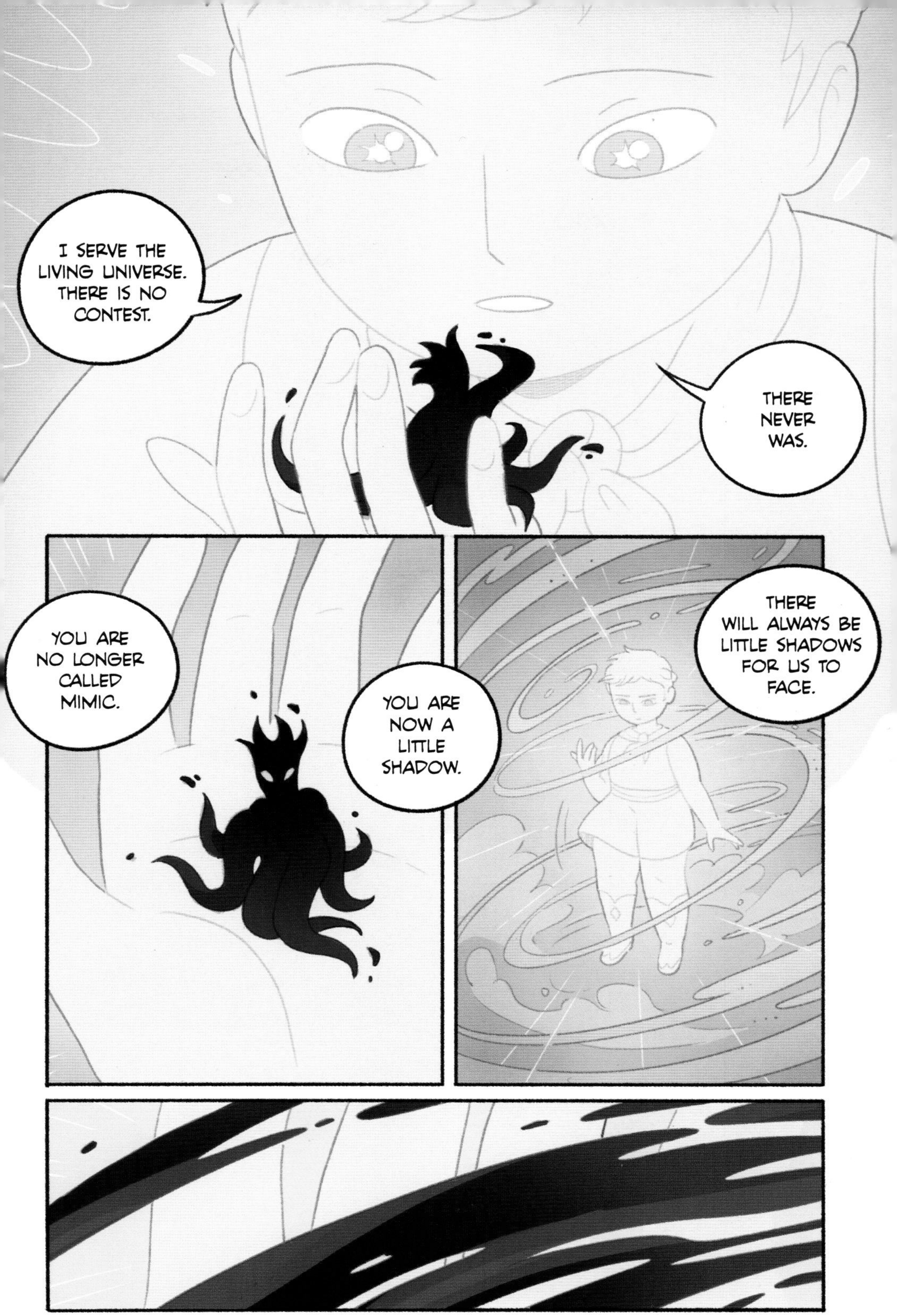
I SERVE THE LIVING UNIVERSE. THERE IS NO CONTEST.
THERE NEVER WAS.
YOU ARE NO LONGER CALLED MIMIC.
YOU ARE NOW A LITTLE SHADOW.
THERE WILL ALWAYS BE LITTLE SHADOWS FOR US TO FACE.

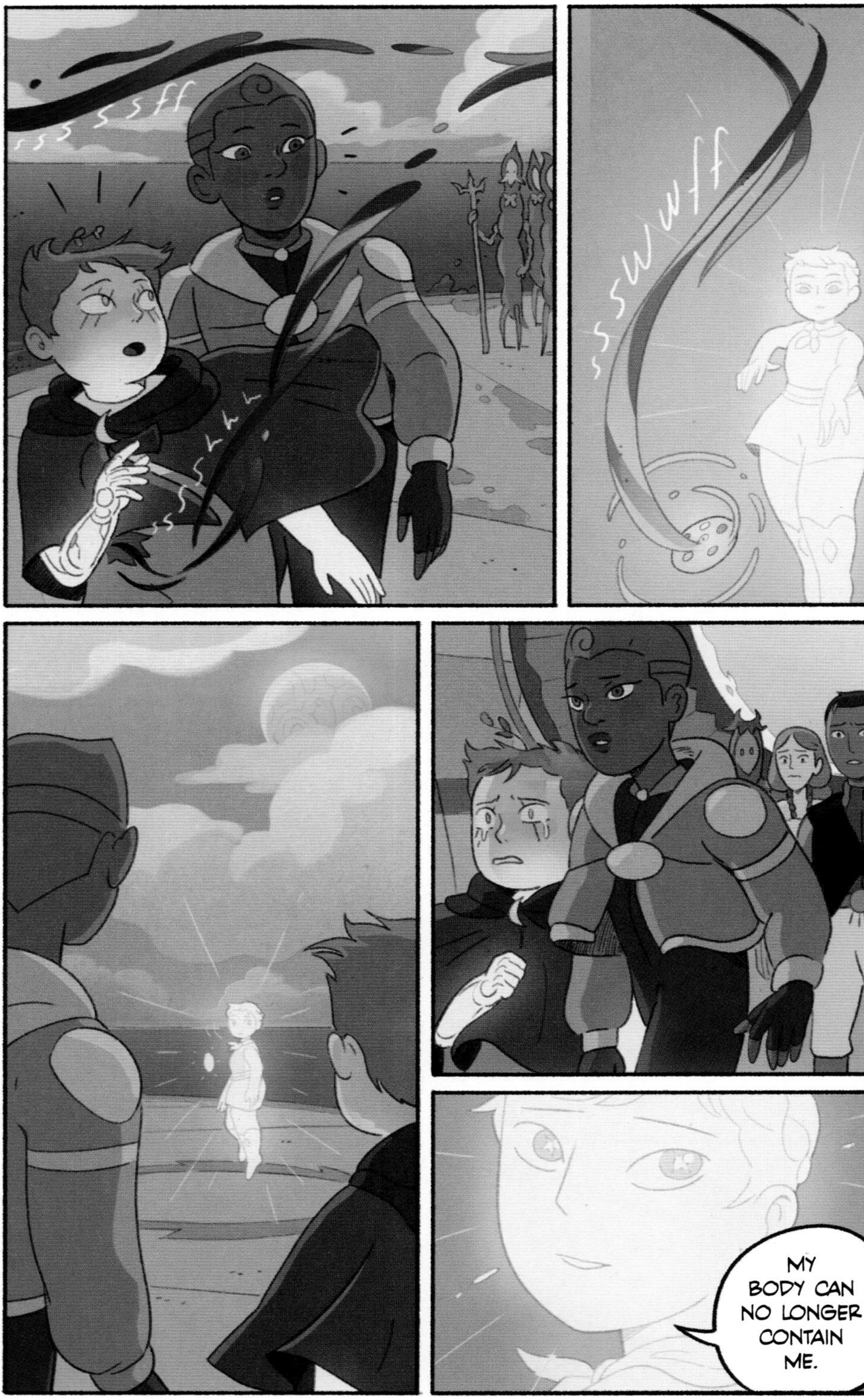
sssssff
ssswuff
MY BODY CAN NO LONGER CONTAIN ME.

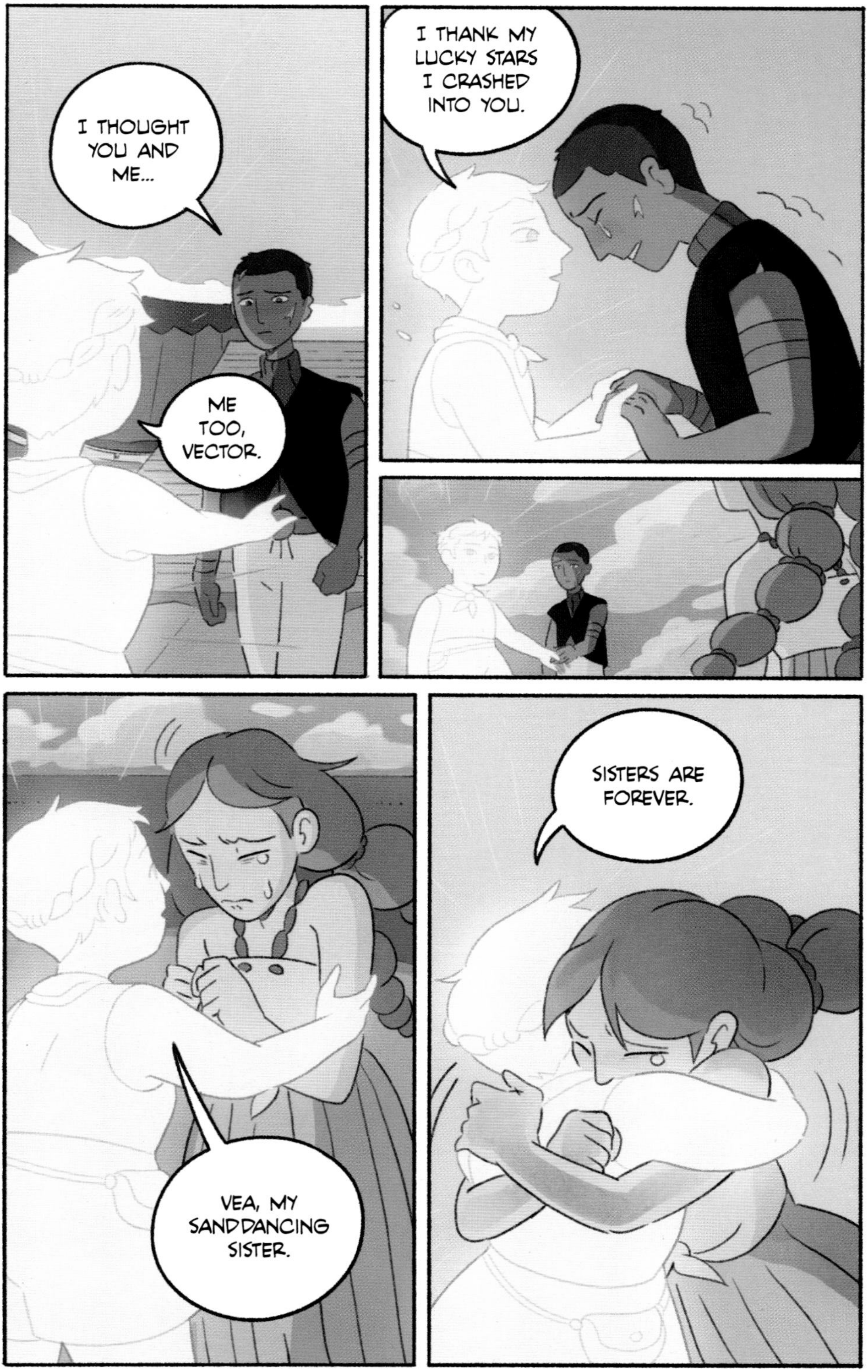
I THOUGHT YOU AND ME...
ME TOO, VECTOR.
I THANK MY LUCKY STARS I CRASHED INTO YOU.
VEA, MY SANDDANCING SISTER.
SISTERS ARE FOREVER.

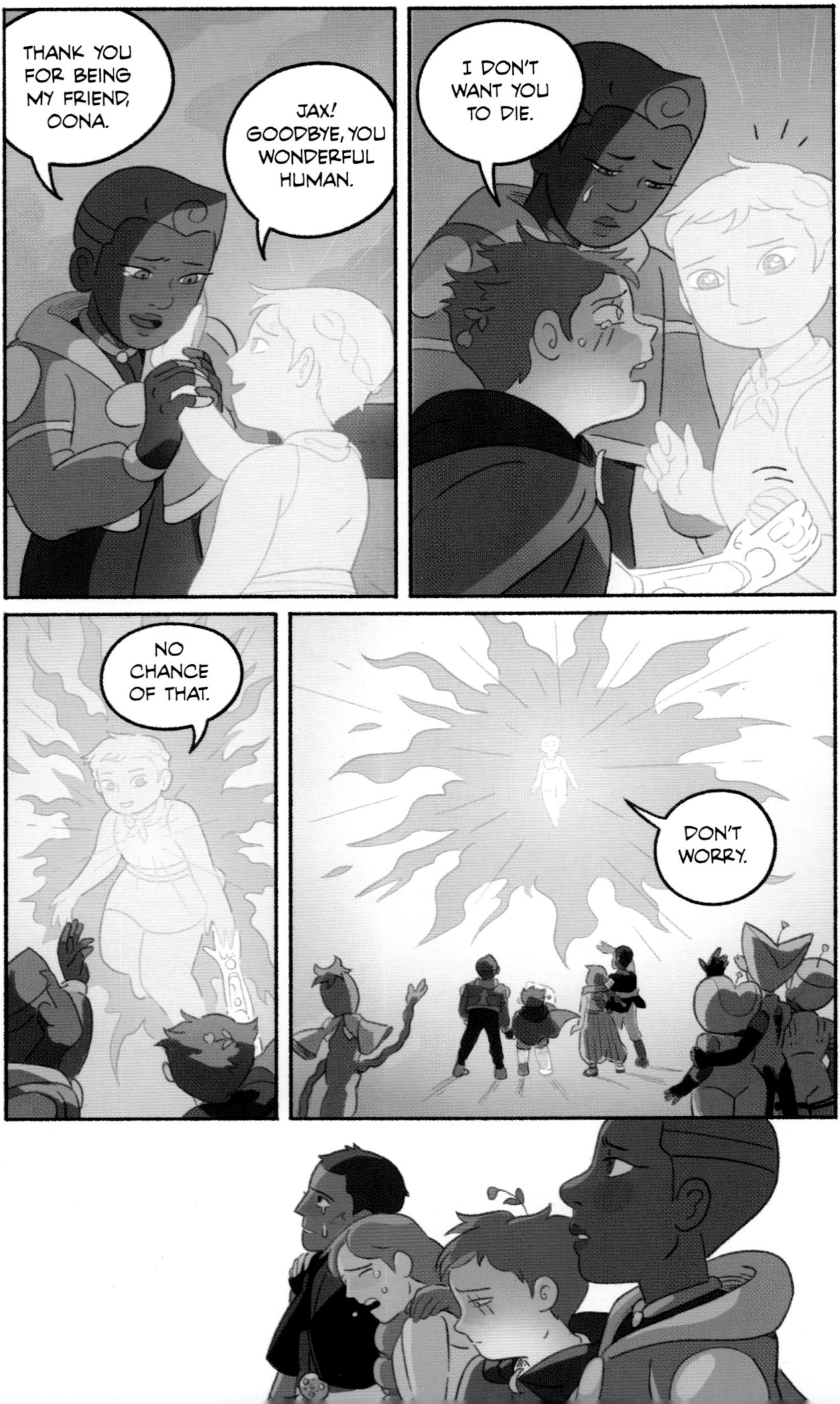
THANK YOU FOR BEING MY FRIEND, OONA.
JAX! GOODBYE, YOU WONDERFUL HUMAN.
I DON'T WANT YOU TO DIE.
NO CHANCE OF THAT.
DON'T WORRY.

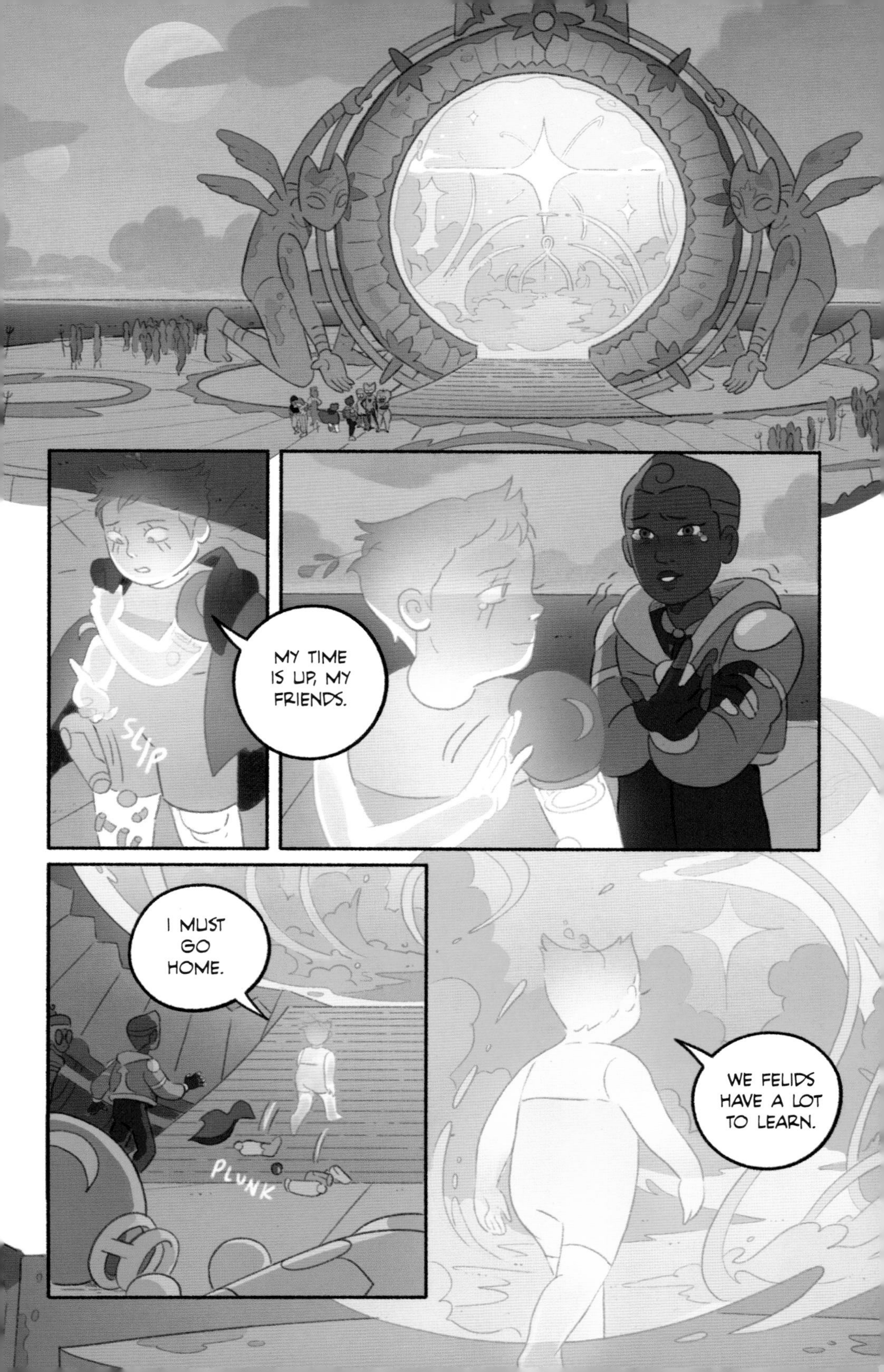
SLIP
MY TIME IS UP, MY FRIENDS.
I MUST GO HOME.
PLUNK
WE FELIDS HAVE A LOT TO LEARN.

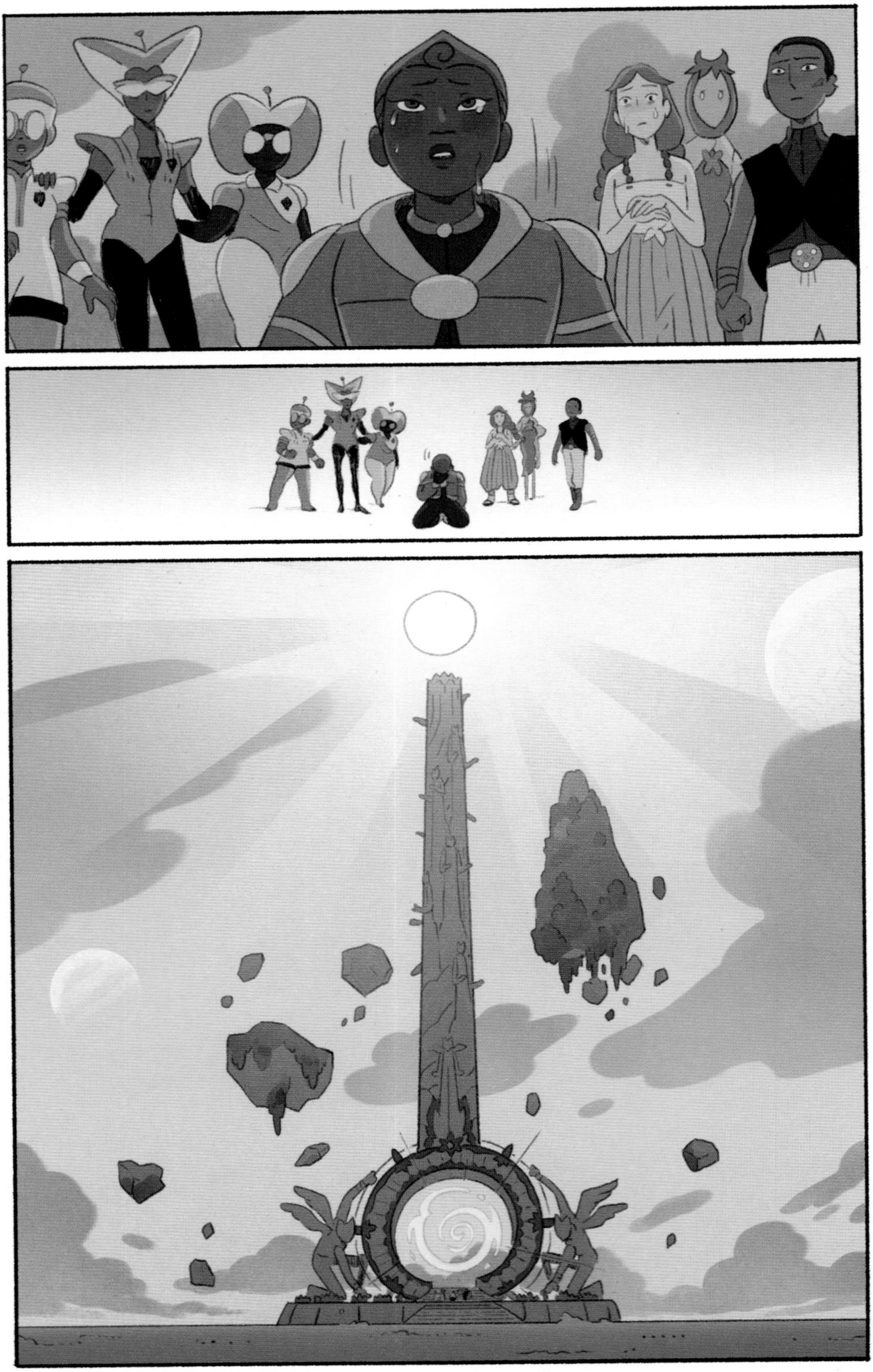

Epilogue

A NEW LIFE

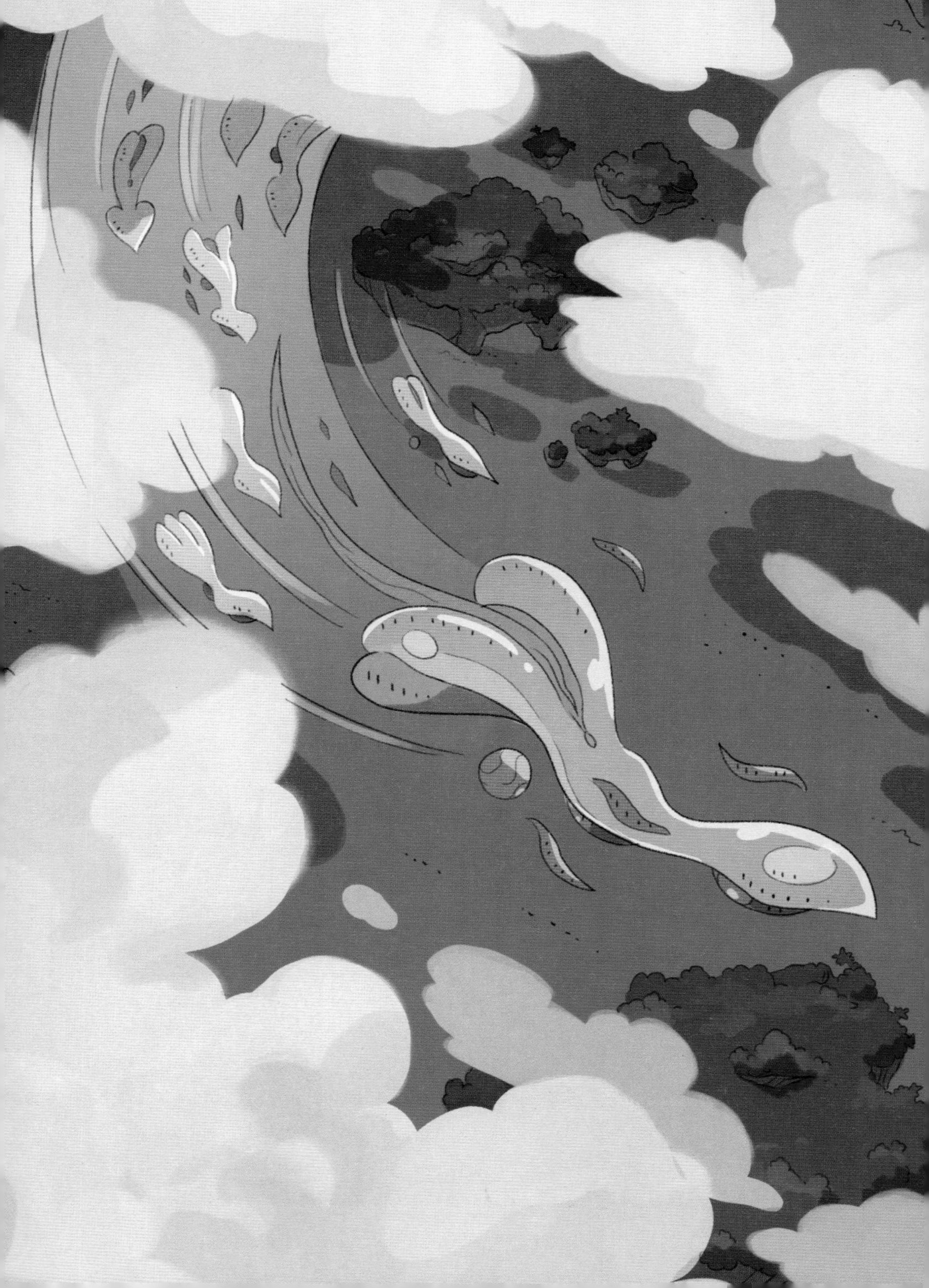

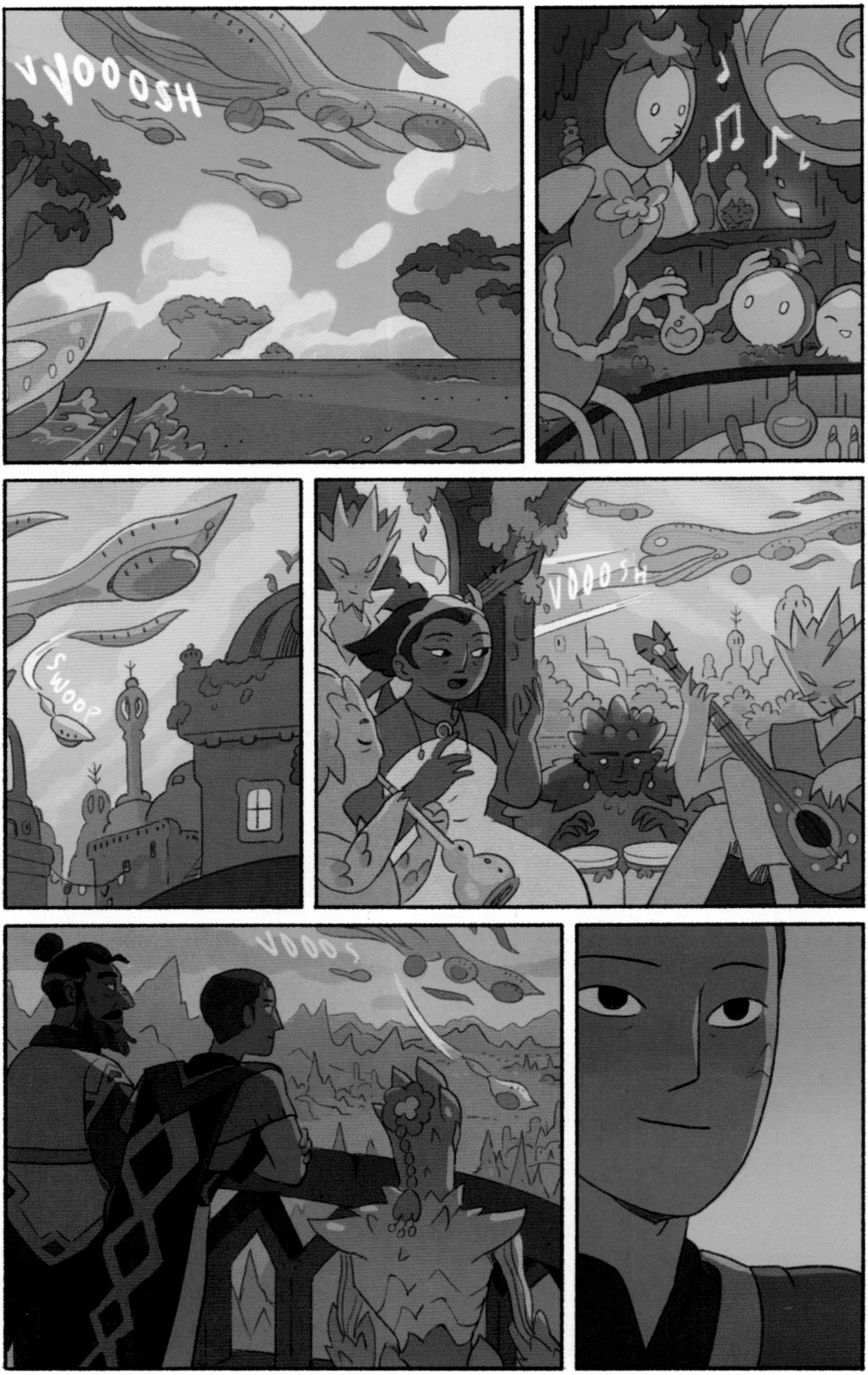
VVOOOSH
SWOOP
VOOOSH
VOOOS

VVOOSH

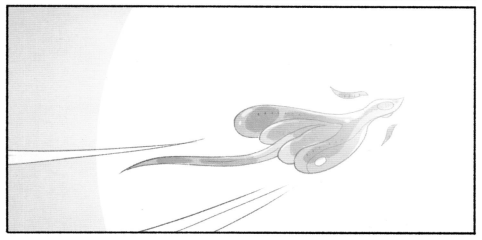

247

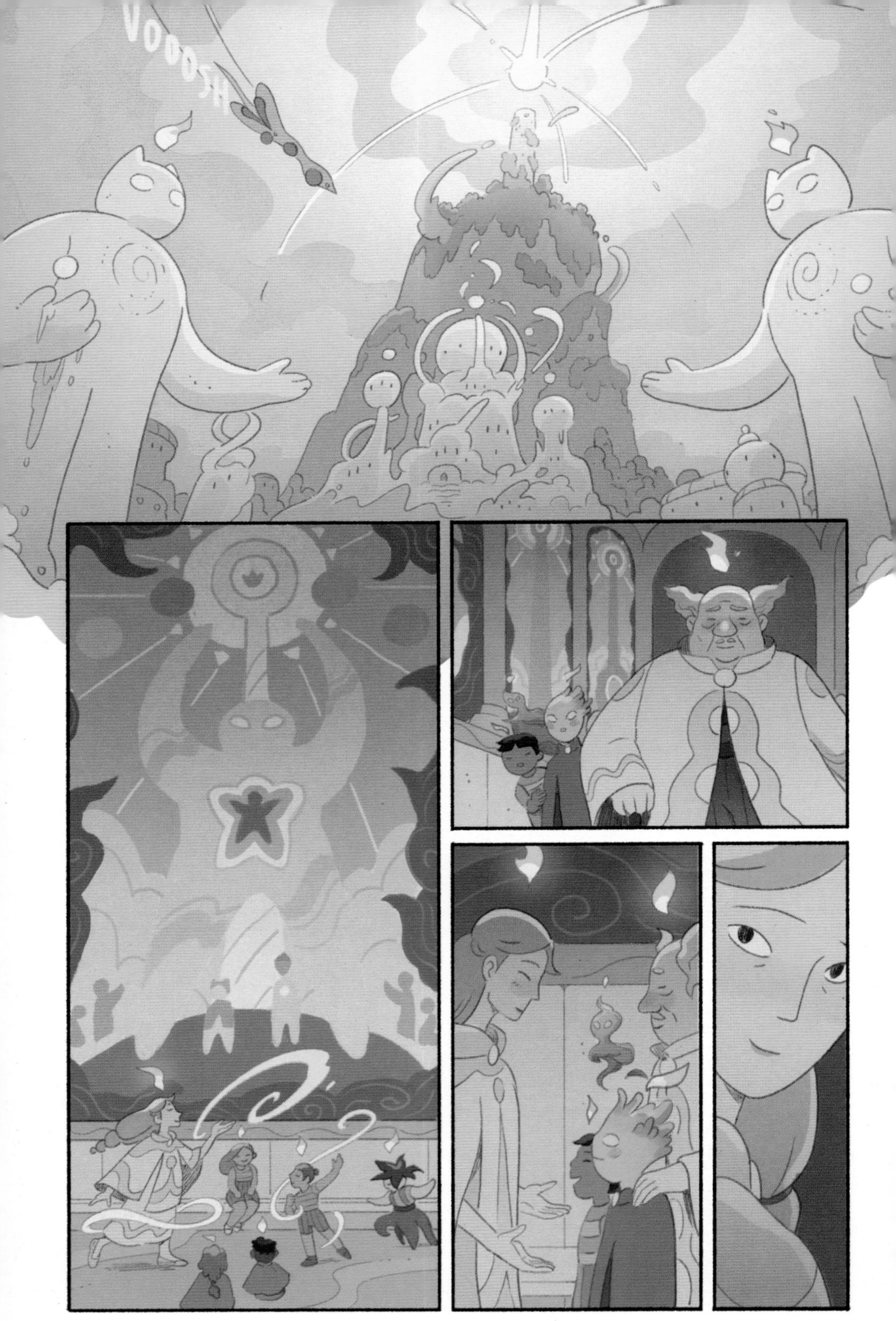
VOOOSH

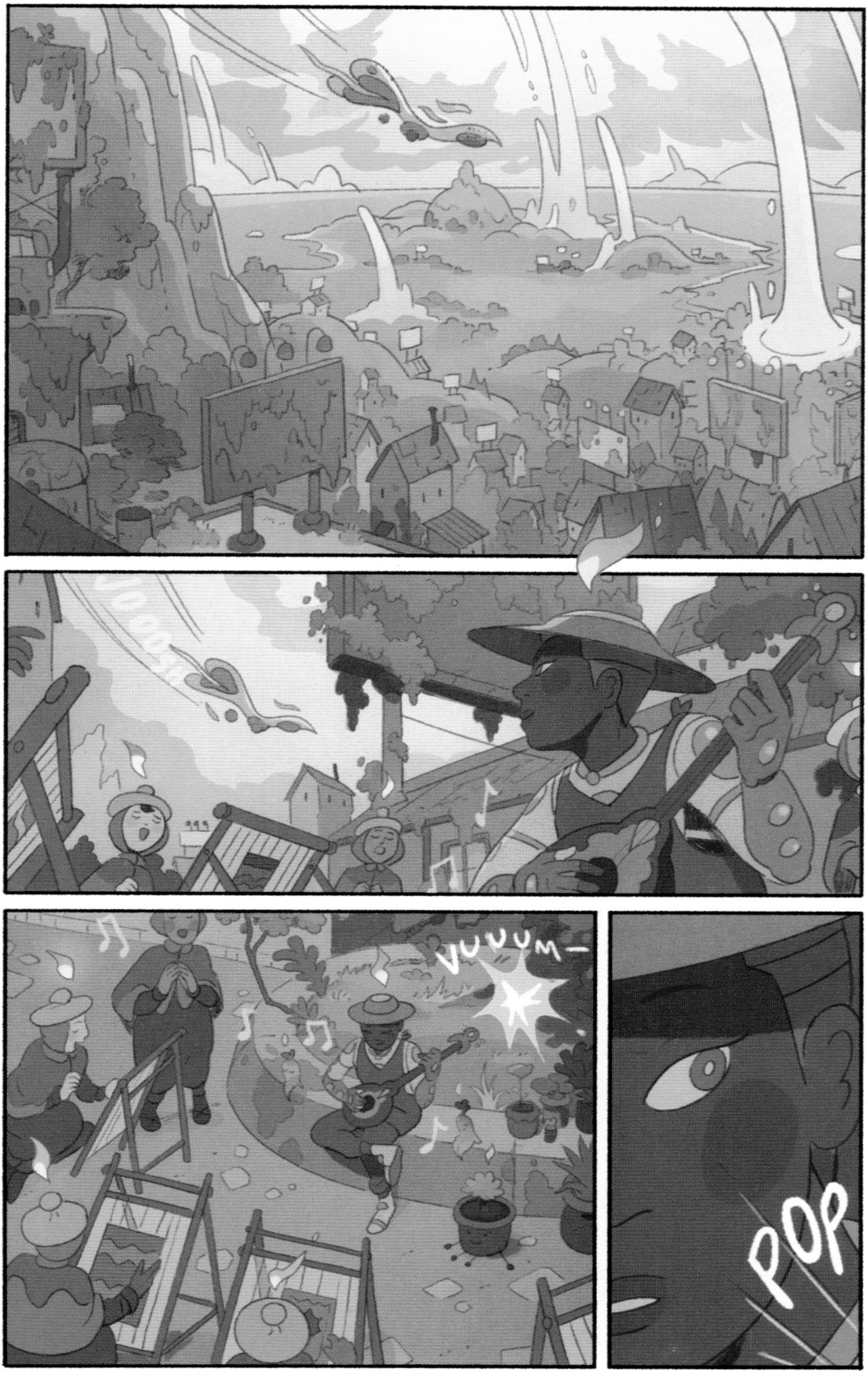
VUUUM—
POP

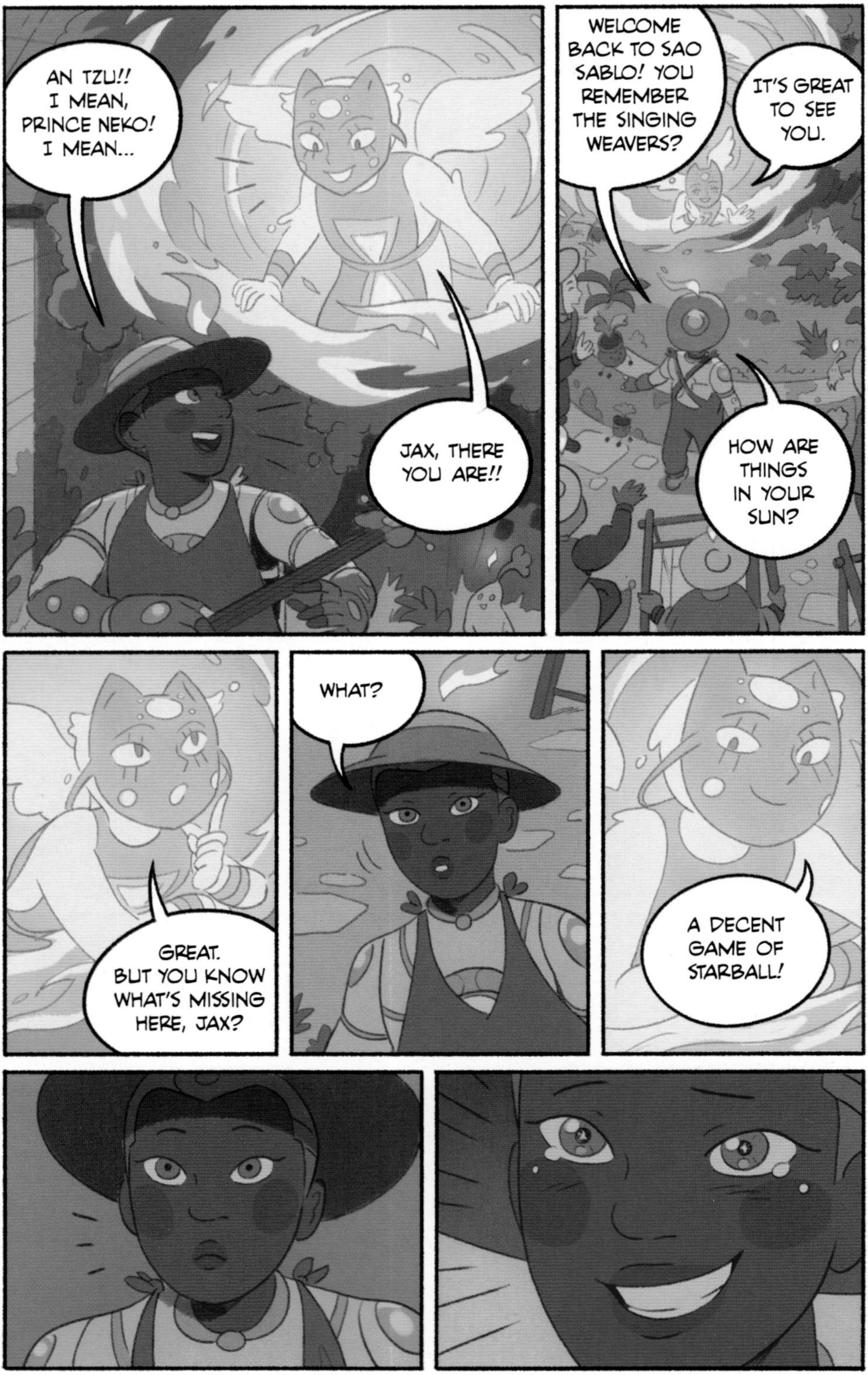
AN TZU!! I MEAN, PRINCE NEKO! I MEAN...
JAX, THERE YOU ARE!!
WELCOME BACK TO SAO SABLO! YOU REMEMBER THE SINGING WEAVERS?
IT'S GREAT TO SEE YOU.
HOW ARE THINGS IN YOUR SUN?
GREAT. BUT YOU KNOW WHAT'S MISSING HERE, JAX?
WHAT?
A DECENT GAME OF STARBALL!

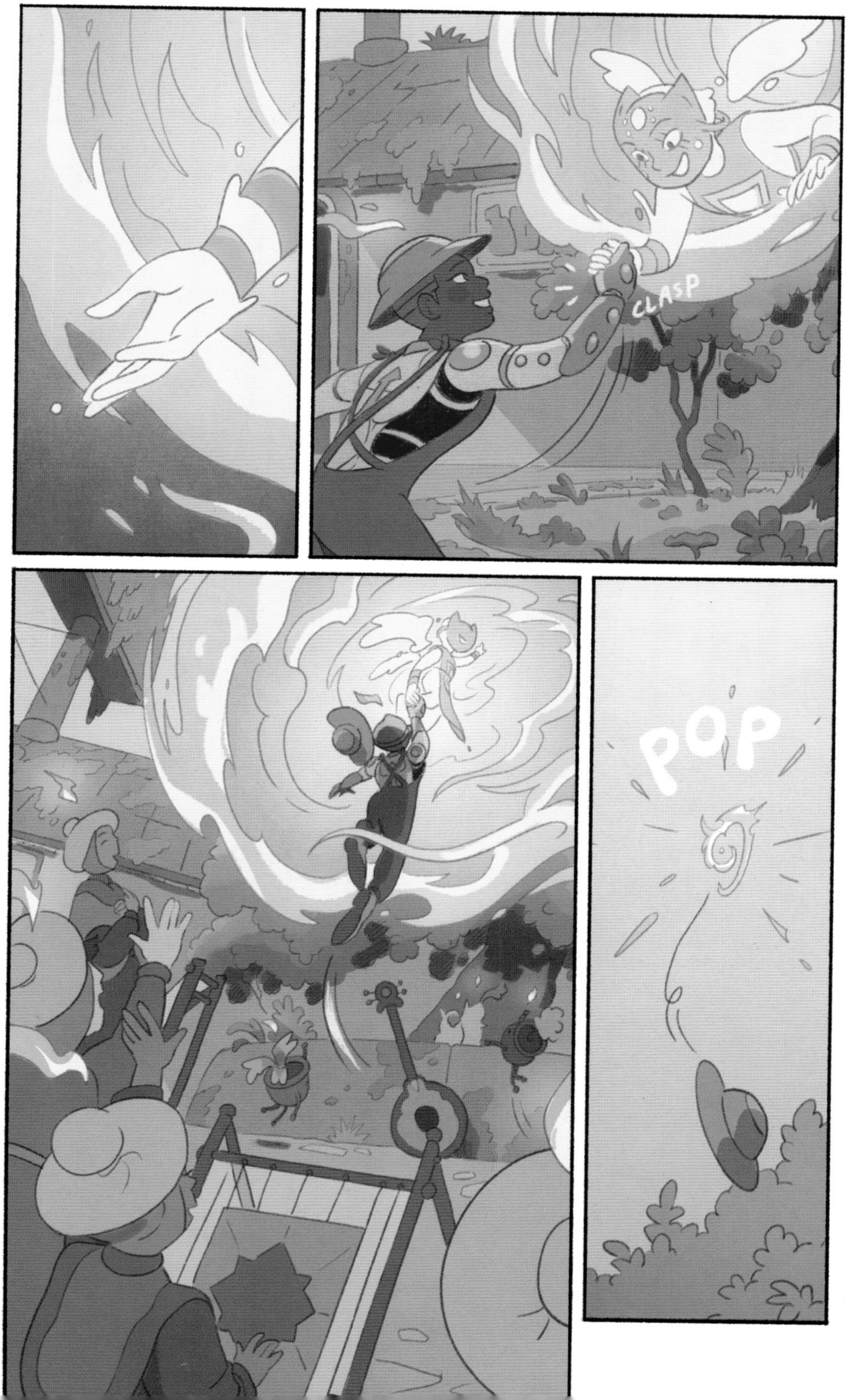
CLASP
POP

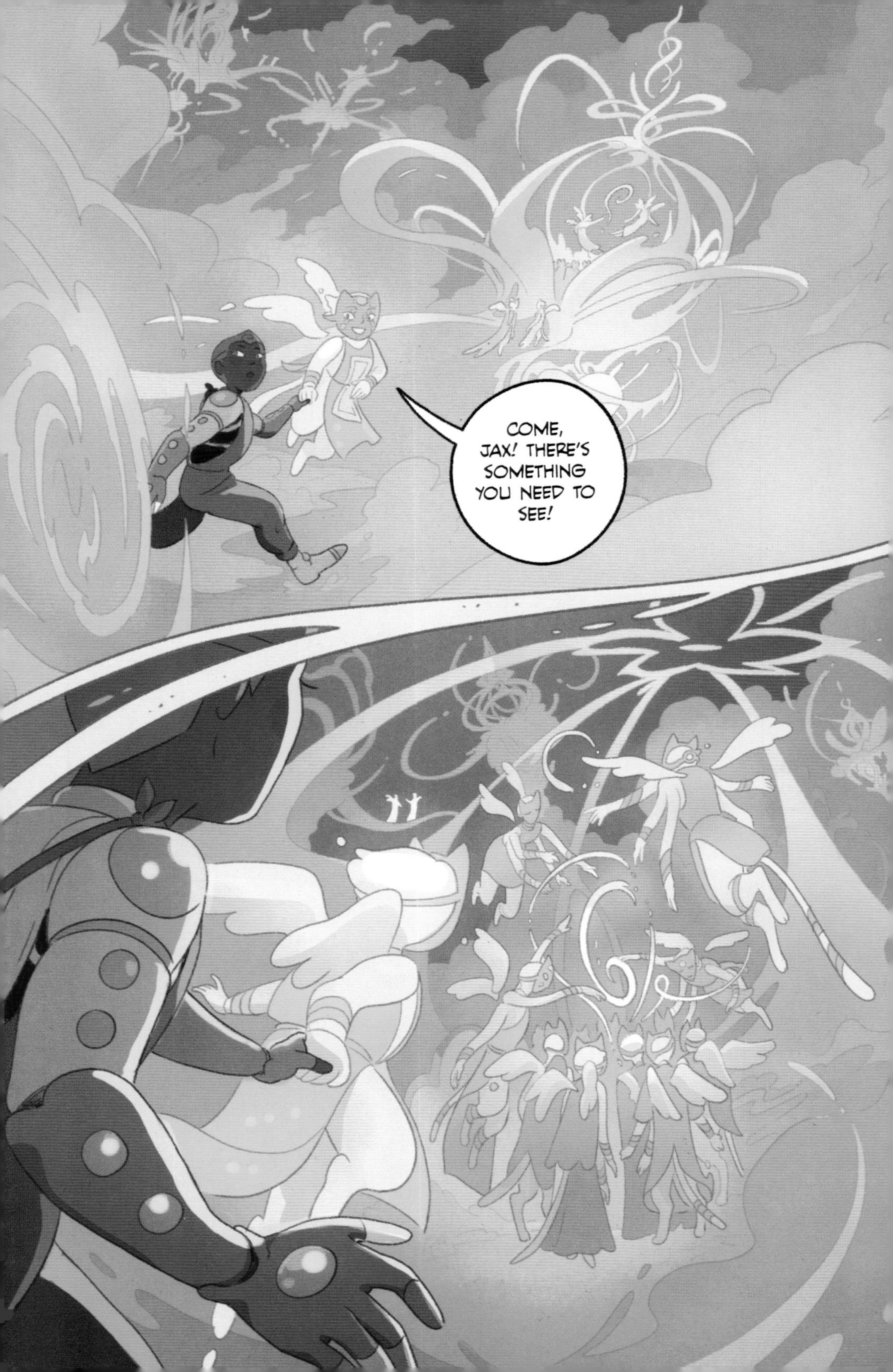
COME, JAX! THERE'S SOMETHING YOU NEED TO SEE!